Meridon

Philippa Gregory is an established writer and broadcaster for radio and television. She holds a PhD in eighteenth-century literature from the University of Edinburgh. She has been widely praised for her historical novels, including *Earthly Joys*, *Virgin Earth* and *A Respectable Trade* (which she adapted for BBC television), as well as her works of contemporary suspense. Philippa Gregory lives in the North of England with her family.

Wideacre
The Favoured Child
The Wise Woman
Mrs Hartley and the Growth Centre
Fallen Skies
A Respectable Trade
Perfectly Correct
The Little House
Earthly Joys
Virgin Earth
Zelda's Cut
Bread and Chocolate
The Other Boleyn Girl

PHILIPPA GREGORY

Meridon

HarperCollins*Publishers*

This novel is entirely a work of fiction.
The names, characters and incidents portrayed in it are
the work of the author's imagination. Any resemblance to
actual persons, living or dead, events or localities is
entirely coincidental.

HarperCollins*Publishers*
77–85 Fulham Palace Road,
Hammersmith, London W6 8JB

www.**fire**and**water**.com

This paperback edition 2002
1 3 5 7 9 8 6 4 2

First published in Great Britain by
Viking 1990

Copyright © Philippa Gregory Ltd, 1990

The Author asserts the moral right to
be identified as the author of this work

ISBN 0 00 767241 1

Set in Plantin

Printed and bound in Great Britain by
Mackays of Chatham plc, Chatham, Kent

ACKNOWLEDGEMENTS

I should like to thank Gerry Cottle and all the staff and artistes of his circus for the welcome they extended to me and my family when we stayed with them in the summer seasons in 1987 and 1988.

I owe special thanks to the Witney family: Derek, June, April and Lee-Ann who shared their family history with me, and taught me circus traditions – and (with less success) rosinback riding!

I am very grateful to Larry and Jill de Wit for their friendship, and for their unfailing patience with me both on the ground and terrifyingly high up on their trapeze.

And to Martin Lacey – the boy prince of ringmasters – whose courtesy and generosity made our visits such fun.

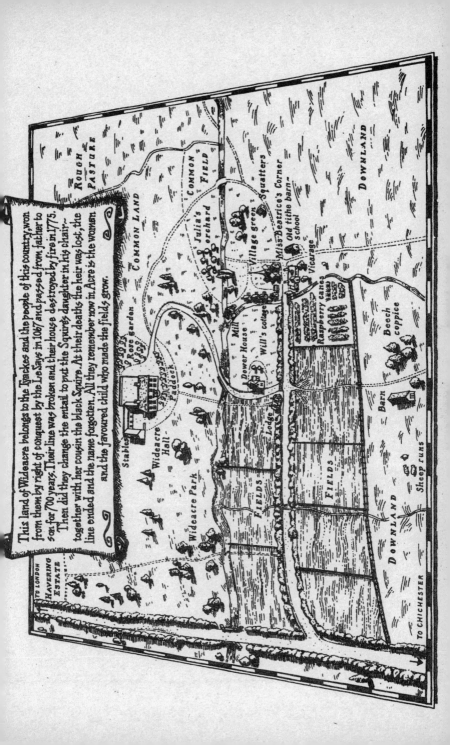

This land of Wideacre belongs to the Laceys and the people of this country, won from them by right of conquest by the Laceys in 1067 and passed from father to son for 700 years. Their line was broken and their house destroyed by fire in 1775. Then did they change the entail to put the Squire's daughter in his chair—together with her cousin the black Squire. At their deaths the heir was lost, the line ended and the name forgotten. All they remember now in Acre is the women and the favoured child who made the fields grow.

ROUGH PASTURE

COMMON LAND

COMMON FIELD

Julia's orchard

Village green

Squatters

Miss Beatrice's Corner

Old tithe barn—school

Vicarage

Rose garden

Stables

Paddock

Wideacre Hall

Wideacre Park

Mill

Dower House

Will's cottage

Lodge

Raspberry canes

Beech coppice

FIELDS

FIELDS

DOWNLAND

DOWNLAND

Barn

Sheep runs

TO LONDON

HAVERING ESTATE

TO CHICHESTER

1

'I don't belong here,' I said to myself. Before I even opened my eyes.

It was my morning ritual. To ward off the smell and the dirt and the fights and the noise of the day. To keep me in that bright green place in my mind which had no proper name; I called it 'Wide'.

'I don't belong here,' I said again. A dirty-faced fifteen-year-old girl frowsy-eyed from sleep, blinking at the hard grey light filtering through the grimy window. I looked up to the arched ceiling of the caravan, the damp sacking near my face as I lay on the top bunk; and then I glanced quickly to my left to the bunk to see if Dandy was awake.

Dandy: my black-eyed, black-haired, equally dirty-faced sister. Dandy, the lazy one, the liar, the thief.

Her eyes, dark as blackberries, twinkled at me.

'I don't belong here,' I whispered once more to the dream world of Wide which faded even as I called to it. Then I said aloud to Dandy:

'Getting up?'

'Did you dream of it – Sarah?' she asked me softly, calling me by my magic secret name. The name I knew from my dreams of Wide. The magic name I use in that magic land.

'Yes,' I said, and I turned my face away from her to the stained wall and tried not to mind that Wide was just a dream and a pretence. That the real world was here. Here where they knew nothing of Wide, had never even heard of such a place. Where, except for Dandy, they would not call me Sarah when I had once asked. They had laughed at me and gone on calling me by my real name, Meridon.

'What did you dream?' Dandy probed. She was not cruel, but she was too curious to spare me.

'I dreamed I had a father, a great big fair-headed man and he lifted me up. High, high up on to his horse. And I rode before him, down a lane away from our house and past some fields. Then up a path which went higher and higher, and through a wood and out to the very top of the fields, and he pointed his horse to look back down the way we had come, and I saw our house: a lovely square yellow house, small as a toy house on the green below us.'

'Go on,' said Dandy.

'Shut up you two,' a muffled voice growled in the half-light of the caravan. 'It's still night.'

'It ain't,' I said, instantly argumentative. My father's dark, tousled head peered around the head of his bunk and scowled at me. 'I'll strap you,' he warned me. 'Go to sleep.'

I said not another word. Dandy waited and in a few moments she said, in a whisper so soft that our da – his head buried beneath the dirty blankets – could not hear, 'What then?'

'We rode home,' I said, screwing my eyes tight to re-live the vision of the little red-headed girl and the fair man and the great horse and the cool green of the arching beech trees over the drive. 'And then he let me ride alone.'

Dandy nodded, but she was unimpressed. We had both been on and around horses since we were weaned. And I had no words to convey the delight of the great strides of the horse in the dream.

'He was telling me how to ride,' I said. My voice went quieter still, and my throat tightened. 'He loved me,' I said miserably. 'He did. I could tell by the way he spoke to me. He was my da – but he loved me.'

'And then?' said Dandy, impatient.

'I woke up,' I said. 'That was all.'

'Didn't you see the house, or your clothes or the food?' she asked disappointed.

'No,' I said. 'Not this time.'

'Oh,' she said and was silent a moment. 'I wish I could dream of it like you do,' she said longingly. ' 'Taint fair.'

A warning grunt from the bed made us lower our voices again.

'I wish I could see it,' she said.

'You will,' I promised. 'It is a real place. It is real somewhere. I know that somewhere it is a real place. And we will both be there, someday.'

'Wide,' she said. 'It's a funny name.'

'That's not the whole name,' I said cautiously. 'Not quite Wide. Maybe it's something-Wide. I never hear it clear enough. I listen and I listen but I'm never quite sure of it. But it's a real place. It is real somewhere. And it's where I belong.'

I lay on my back and looked at the stains on the sacking roof of the caravan and smelled the stink of four people sleeping close with no windows open, the acid smell of stale urine from last night's pot.

'It's real somewhere,' I said to myself. 'It has to be.'

There were three good things in my life, that dirty painful life of a gypsy child with a father who cared nothing for her, and a stepmother who cared less. There was Dandy my twin sister – as unlike me as if I were a changeling. There were the horses we trained and sold. And there was the dream of Wide.

If it had not been for Dandy I think I would have run away as soon as I was old enough to leave. I would have upped and gone, run off to one of the sleepy little villages in the New Forest in that hot summer of 1805 when I was fifteen. That was the summer I turned on Da and stood up to him for the first time ever.

We had been breaking a pony to sell as a lady's ride. I said the horse was not ready for a rider. Da swore she was. He was wrong. Anyone but an idiot could have seen that the horse was nervy and half wild. But Da had put her on the lunge rein two or three times and she had gone well enough. He wanted to put me up on her. He didn't waste his breath asking Dandy to do it. She would have smiled one of her sweet slow smiles and disappeared off for the rest of the day with a hunk of bread and rind of cheese in her pocket. She'd come back in the evening with a dead chicken tucked in her shawl so there was never a beating for Dandy.

But he ordered me up on the animal. A half-wild, half-foolish foal too young to be broke, too frightened to be ridden.

'She's not ready,' I said looking at the flaring nostrils and the rolling whites of her eyes and smelling that special acrid smell of fearful sweat.

'She'll do,' Da said. 'Get up on her.'

I looked at Da, not at the horse. Da's dark eyes were red rimmed, the stubble on his chin stained his face blue. The red kerchief at his neck showed bright against his pallor. He had been drinking last night and I guessed he felt ill. He had no patience to stand in the midday sunshine with a skittish pony on a lunge rein.

'I'll lunge her,' I offered. 'I'll train her for you.'

'You'll ride her, you cheeky dog,' he said to me harshly. 'No whelp tells me how to train a horse.'

'What's the hurry?' I asked, backing out of arm's reach. Da had to hold the horse and could not grab me.

'I got a buyer,' he said. 'A farmer at Beaulieu wants her for his daughter. But he wants her next week for her birthday or summat. So she's got to be ready for then.'

'I'll lunge her,' I offered again. 'I'll work her all day, and tomorrow or the day after I'll get up on her.'

'You get up now,' he said harshly. Then he raised his voice and yelled: 'Zima!' and my stepmother came out into the sunshine from the gloomy caravan. 'Hold 'er,' he said nodding at the horse and she jumped down from the caravan step, and went past me without a word.

'I want summat inside the wagon,' he said under his breath and I stood aside like a fool to let him go past me. But as soon as he was near he grabbed me with one hard grimy hand and twisted my arm behind my back so hard that I could hear the bone creak and I squeaked between clenched teeth for the pain.

'Get up on 'er,' he said softly in my ear; his breath foul. 'Or I'll beat you till you can't ride 'er, nor any other for a week.'

I jerked away from him: sullen, ineffective. And I scowled at my stepmother who stood, picking her teeth with her free hand and watching this scene. She had never stood between me and him in my life. She had seen him beat me until I went down on my knees and cried and cried for him to stop. The most she had ever done for me was to tell him to stop because the noise of my sobbing was disturbing her own baby. I felt that I was utterly unloved, utterly uncared for; and that was no foolish girl's fear. That was the bitter truth.

'Get up,' Da said again, and came to the horse's head.

I looked at him with a gaze as flinty as his own. 'I'll get up and she'll throw me,' I said. 'You know that, so do I. And then I'll get on her again and again and again. We'll never train her like that. If you had as much brains inside you as you have beer, you'd let me train her. Then at least we'd have a sweet-natured animal to show this farmer. The way you want to do it we'll show him a whipped idiot.'

I had never spoken to him like that before. My voice was steady but my belly quivered with fright at my daring.

He looked at me for a long hard moment.

'Get up,' he said. Nothing had changed.

I waited for one moment, in case I had a chance, or even half a chance to win my way in this. His face was flinty-hard, and I was only a young girl. I met his gaze for a moment. He could see the fight go out of me.

I checked he was holding the horse tight at the head and then I turned and gripped hold of the saddle and sprang up.

As soon as she felt the weight of me on her back she leaped like a mountain goat, stiff-legged sideways; and stood there trembling like a leaf with the shock. Then, as if she had only waited to see that it was not some terrible nightmare, she reared bolt upright to her full height, dragging the reins from Da's hands. Da, like a fool, let go – as I had known all along he would – and there was nothing then to control the animal except the halter around her neck. I clung on like a limpet, gripping the pommel of the saddle while she went like a sprinting bullock – alternately head down and hooves up bucking, and then standing high on her hind legs and clawing the air with her front hooves in an effort to be rid of me. There was nothing in the world to do but to cling on like grim death and hope that Da would be quick enough to catch the trailing reins and get the animal under control before I came off. I saw him coming towards the animal, and he was quite close. But the brute wheeled with an awkward sideways shy which nearly unseated me. I was off-balance and grabbing for the pommel of the saddle to get myself into the middle of her back again when she did one of her mighty rears and I went rolling backwards off her back to the hard ground below.

I bunched up as I fell, in an instinctive crouch, fearing the flailing hooves. I felt the air whistle as she kicked out over my head but she missed by an inch and galloped away to the other side of the field. Da, cursing aloud, went after her, running past me without even a glance in my direction to see how I fared.

I sat up. My stepmother Zima looked at me without interest.

I got wearily to my feet. I was shaken but not hurt except for the bruises on my back where I had hit the ground. Da had hold of the reins and was whipping the poor animal around the head while she reared and screamed in protest. I watched stony-faced. You'd never catch me wasting sympathy on a horse which had thrown me. Or on anything else.

'Get up,' he said without looking around for me.

I walked up behind him and looked at the horse. She was a pretty enough animal, half New Forest, half some bigger breed. Dainty, with a bright bay-coloured coat which glowed in the sunlight. Her mane and tail were black, coarse and knotted now, but I would wash her before the buyer came. I saw that Da had whipped her near the eye and a piece of the delicate eyelid was bleeding slightly.

'You fool,' I said in cold disgust. 'Now you've hurt her, and it'll show when the buyer comes.'

'Don't you call me a fool, my girl,' he said rounding on me, the whip still in his hands. 'Another word out of you and you get a beating you won't forget. I've had enough from you for one day. Now get up on that horse and stay on this time.'

I looked at him with the blank insolence which I knew drove him into mindless temper with me. I pushed the tangled mass of my copper-coloured hair away from my face and stared at him with my green eyes as inscrutable as a cat. I saw his hand tighten on the whip and I smiled at him, delighting in my power; even if it lasted for no more than this morning.

'And who'd ride her then?' I taunted. 'I don't see you getting up on an unbroke horse. And Zima couldn't get on a donkey with a ladder against its side. There's no one who can ride her but me. And I don't choose to this morning. I'll do it this afternoon.'

With that, I turned on my heel and walked away from him, swaying my hips in as close an imitation of my stepmother's languorous slink as I could manage. Done by a skinny fifteen year old in a skirt which barely covered her calves it was far from sensual. But it spoke volumes of defiance to my da who let out a great bellow of rage and dropped the horse's reins and came after me.

He spun me around and shook me until my hair fell over my face and I could hardly see his red angry face.

'You'll do as I order or I'll throw you out!' he said in utter rage. 'You'll do as I order or I'll beat you as soon as the horse is sold. You'd better remember that I am as ready to beat you tomorrow night as I am today. I have a long memory for you.'

I shook my head to get the hair out of my eyes, and to clear my mind. I was only fifteen and I could not hold on to courage against Da when he started bullying me. My shoulders slumped and my face lost its arrogance. I knew he would remember this defiance if I did not surrender now. I knew that he would beat me – not only when the horse was sold, but again every time he remembered it.

'All right,' I said sullenly. 'All right. I'll ride her.'

Together we cornered her in the edge of the field and this time he held tighter on to the reins when I was on her back. I stayed on a little longer but again and again she threw me. By the time Dandy was home with a vague secretive smile and a rabbit stolen from someone else's snare dangling from her hand, I was in my bunk covered with bruises, my head thudding with the pain of falling over and over again.

She brought me a plate of rabbit stew where I lay.

'Come on out,' she invited. 'He's all right, he's drinking. And he's got some beer for Zima too, so she's all right. Come on out and we can go down to the river and swim. That'll help your bruising.'

'No,' I said sullenly. 'I'm going to sleep. I don't want to come out and I don't care whether he's fair or foul. I hate him. I wish he was dead. And stupid Zima too. I'm staying here, and I'm going to sleep.'

Dandy stretched up so that she could reach me in the top bunk and nuzzled her face against my cheek. 'Hurt bad?' she asked softly.

'Bad on the outside and bad inside,' I said, my voice low. 'I wish he was dead. I'll kill him myself when I'm bigger.'

Dandy stroked my forehead with her cool dirty hand. 'And I'll help you,' she said with a ripple of laughter in her voice. 'The Ferenz family are nearby, they're going down to the river to swim. Come too, Meridon!'

I sighed. 'Not me,' I said. 'I'm too sore, and angry. Stay with me, Dandy.'

She brushed the bruise on my forehead with her lips. 'Nay,' she said sweetly. 'I'm away with the Ferenz boys. I'll be back at nightfall.'

I nodded. There was no keeping Dandy if she wanted to be out.

'Will you have to ride tomorrow?' she asked.

'Yes,' I said. 'And the next day. The farmer's coming for the horse on Sunday. She's got to be ridable by then. But I pity his daughter!'

In the half-light of the caravan I saw Dandy's white teeth gleam.

'Is it a bad horse?' she asked, a careless ripple of amusement in her voice.

'It's a pig,' I said plainly. 'I'll be able to stay on it, but the little Miss Birthday Girl will likely break her neck the first time she tries to ride.'

We chuckled spitefully.

'Don't quarrel with him tomorrow,' Dandy urged me. 'It only makes him worse. And you'll never win.'

'I know,' I said dully. 'I know I'll never win. But I can't keep quiet like you. I can't even go away like you do. I've never been able to. But as soon as I can, I'm going. As soon as I can see somewhere to go, I'm going.'

'And I'll come too,' Dandy said, repeating a long-ago promise. 'But don't make him angry tomorrow. He said he'd beat you if you do.'

'I'll try not,' I said with little hope, and handed my empty plate to her. Then I turned my face away from her, from the shady caravan and the twilit doorway. I turned my face to the curved wall at the side of my bunk and gathered the smelly pillow under my face. I shut my eyes tight and wished myself far away. Far away from the aches in my body and from the dread and fear in my mind. From my disgust at my father and my hatred of Zima. From my helpless impotent love for Dandy and my misery at my own hopeless, dirty, poverty-stricken existence.

I shut my eyes tight and thought of myself as the copper-headed daughter of the squire who owned Wide. I thought of the trees reflected in the waters of the trout river. I thought of the house and the roses growing so creamy and sweet in the gardens outside the house. As I drifted into sleep I willed myself to see the dining room with the fire flickering in the hearth and the pointy flames of the candles reflected in the great mahogany table, and the servants in livery bringing in dish after dish of food. My eternally hungry body ached at the thought of all those rich creamy dishes. But as I fell asleep, I was smiling.

The next day he was not bad from the drink so he was quicker to the horse's head, and held her tighter. I stayed on for longer, and for at least two falls I landed on my feet, sliding off her to first one side and then the other, and avoiding that horrid nerve-jolting slump on to hard ground.

He nodded at me when we stopped for our dinner – the remains of the rabbit stew watered down as soup, and a hunk of old bread.

'Will you be able to stay on her for long enough tomorrow?'

'Yes,' I said confidently. 'Will we be moving off the next day?'

'That same night!' Da said carelessly. 'I know that horse will never make a lady's ride. She's vicious.'

I held my peace. I knew well enough that she had been a good horse when we first had her. If she had been carefully and lovingly trained Da would have made a good sale to a Quality home. But he was only ever chasing a quick profit. He had seen a man who wanted a quiet ride for his little girl's birthday, and next thing he was breaking from scratch a two-year-old wild pony. It was coarse stupidity – and it was that doltish chasing after tiny profits which angered me the most.

'She's not trained to side-saddle,' was all I said.

'No,' said Da. 'But if you wash your face and get Zima to plait your hair you can go astride and still look like a novice girl. If he sees you on her – and you mind not to come off – he'll buy her.'

I nodded, and pulled a handful of grass to wipe out my bowl. I had sucked and spat out a scrap of gristle, and I tossed it to the scrawny lurcher tied under the wagon. He snapped at it and took it with him back into the shadow. The hot midday sun made red rings when I closed my eyelids and lay back on the mown grass to feel the heat.

'Where d'we go next?' I asked idly.

'Salisbury,' Da said without hesitation. 'Lot of money to be made there. I'll buy a couple of ponies on the way. There's a fair in early September as well – that idle Zima and Dandy can do some work for once in their lives.'

'No one poaches as well as Dandy,' I said instantly.

'She'll get herself hanged,' he said without gratitude and without concern. 'She thinks all she has to do is to roll her black eyes at the keeper and he'll take her home and give her sweet-meats. She won't always get away with that as she gets older. He'll have her, and if she refuses he'll take her to the Justices.'

I sat up, instantly alert. 'They'd send her to prison?' I demanded.

Da laughed harshly. 'They'd send us all to prison; aye, and to Australey if they could catch us. The gentry is against you, my girl. Every one of them, however fair-spoken, however kind-seeming. I've been the wrong side of the park walls all my life. I've seen them come and seen them go – and never a fair chance for travellers.'

I nodded. It was an old theme for Da. He was most pitiful

when he was in his cups on this topic. He was a tinker: a no-good pedlar-cum-thief when he had met my ma. She had been pure Romany, travelling with her family. But her man was dead, and she had us twin babies to provide for. She believed him when he boasted of a grand future and married him, against the advice of her own family, and without their blessing. He could have joined the family, and travelled with them. But Da had big ideas. He was going to be a great horse-dealer. He was going to buy an inn. He was going to run a livery stables, to train as a master-brewer. One feckless scheme after another until they were travellers in the poorest wagon she had ever called home. And then she was pregnant with another child.

I remember her dimly: pale and fat, and too weary to play with us. She sickened, she had a long and lonely labour. Then she died, crying to Da to bury her in the way of her people, the Rom way with her goods burned the night of her death. He did not know how, he did not care. He burned a few token scraps of clothing and sold the rest. He gave Dandy a comb of hers, and he gave me an old dirty piece of string with two gold clasps at each end. He told me they had once held rose-coloured pearls.

Where she got them Da had never known. She had brought them to him as her dowry and he had sold each one until there was nothing left but the string. One gold latch was engraved with the word I had been told was 'John'. The other was inscribed 'Celia'. He would have sold the gold clasps if he had dared. Instead he gave them to me with an odd little grimace.

'You have the right,' he said. 'She always said it was for you, and not for Dandy. I'll sell the gold clasp for you, and you can keep the string.'

I remember my dirty hand had closed tight over it.

'I want it,' I had said.

'I'll split the money with you,' he had said winningly.' Sixty: forty?'

'No,' I said.

'That's enough to buy a sugar bun,' he said as if to clinch the deal. My stomach rumbled but I held firm.

'No,' I said. 'Who are John and Celia?'

He had shrugged, shifty. 'I don't know,' he had said. 'Maybe folks your ma knew. You have a right to the necklace. She always told me to be sure to give it to you. Now I've done that. A promise made to the dead has to be kept. She told me to give it to you and to bid you keep it safe, and to show it when anyone came seeking you. When anyone asked who you were.'

'Who am I?' I had demanded instantly.

'A damned nuisance,' he said; his good temper gone with his chance to trick the gold clasp from me. 'One of a pair of brats that I'm saddled with till I can be rid of you both.'

It would not be long now, I thought, sucking on a grass stem for the sweet green taste of it. It would not be long now until he would be able to be rid of us. That conversation had happened a long time ago, but Da had never changed his mind about us. He never acknowledged how much meat Dandy provided for the pot. He never realized that his horses would have been half-wild if I had not had the knack of riding them. Not he. The selfishness which made it easy for him to take on a woman with two small babies at the breast and no way to keep her save a cartload of foolish dreams, now made it easy for him to plan to sell us to the highest bidder. Whatever the terms.

I knew Dandy would end up whoring. Her black brazen eyes twinkled too readily. If we had been with a gypsy family, travelling with kin, there would be an early betrothal and early childbirth for Dandy, and a man to keep her steady. But here there was no one. There was only Da who cared nothing for what she might do. And Zima who laughed lazily and said that Dandy would be street-walking by the time she was sixteen. Only I heard that feckless prophecy with a shudder. And only I swore that it should not happen. I would keep Dandy safe from it.

Not that she feared it. Dandy was vain and affectionate. She thought it would mean fine clothes and dancing and attention from men. She could not wait to be fully grown and she used to insist I inspect the conical shapes of her breasts every time we swam or changed our clothes and tell her if they were not growing exceedingly lovely? Dandy looked at life with lazy laughing eyes and could not believe that things would not go well for her. But I had seen the whores at Southampton, and at Portsmouth. And I had seen the sores on their mouths and the blank looks in their eyes. I would rather Dandy had been a pickpocket all her days – as she was now – than a whore. I would rather Dandy be anything than a whore.

'It's just because you hate being touched,' she said idly to me when the wagon was on the road towards Salisbury for the fair. She was lying on her side in the bunk combing her hair which tumbled like a black shiny waterfall over the side of the bunk. 'You're as nervy as one of your wild ponies. I'm the only one you ever let near you, and you won't even let me plait your hair.'

'I don't like it,' I said inadequately. 'I can't stand Da pulling me on to his knee when he's drunk. Or the way Zima's baby sucks at my neck or at my face. It gives me the shivers. I just like having space around me. I hate being crowded.'

She nodded. 'I'm like a cat,' she said idly. 'I love being stroked. I don't even mind Da when he's gentle. He gave me a halfpenny last night.'

I gave a little muffled grunt of irritation. 'He never gave me a thing,' I complained. 'And he'd never have sold that horse on his own. The farmer only bought it because he saw me ride it. And if it hadn't been for me Da would never have trained it.'

'Better hope the farmer's daughter is a good rider,' Dandy said with a chuckle in her voice. 'Will she throw her?'

'Bound to,' I said indifferently. 'If the man hadn't been an idiot he'd have seen that I was only keeping her steady by luck, and the fact that she was bone-weary.'

'Well it's put him in good humour,' Dandy said. We could hear Da muttering the names of cards to himself over and over, practising palming cards and dealing cards as the caravan jolted on the muddy road. Zima was sitting up front beside him. She had left her baby asleep on Dandy's bunk, anchored by Dandy's foot pressing lightly on her fat belly.

'Maybe he'll give us a penny for fairings,' I said without much hope.

Dandy gleamed. 'I'll get you a penny,' she promised. 'I'll get us sixpence and we'll run off all night and buy sweetmeats and see the booths.'

I smiled at the prospect and then rolled over to face the rocking caravan wall. I was still bruised from my falls and as weary as a drunken trooper from the day and night training of the pony. And I had that strange, detached feeling which I often felt when I was going to dream of Wide. We would be a day and a half on the road, and unless Da made me drive the horse there was nothing I had to do. There were hours of journeying, and nothing to do. Dandy might as well comb her hair over and over. And I might as well sleep and doze and daydream of Wide. The caravan would go rocking, rocking, rocking down the muddy lanes and byways and then on the harder high road to Salisbury. And there was nothing to do except look out of the back window at the road narrowing away behind us. Or lie on the bunk and chat to Dandy. Between dinner and nightfall Da would not stop, the jolting creaking caravan would roll onwards. There was nothing for me to do except to wish I was at Wide; and to wonder how I would ever get myself – and Dandy – safely away from Da.

2

It was a long, wearisome drive, all the way down the lanes to Salisbury, up the Avon valley with the damp lush fields on either side where brown-backed cows stood knee-high in wet grasses, through Fordingbridge, where the little children were out from dame-school and ran after us and hooted and threw stones.

'Come 'ere,' Da said, shuffling a pack of greasy cards as he sat on the driving bench. 'Come 'ere and watch this.' And he hitched the ambling horse's reins over the worn post at the front of the wagon and shuffled the cards before me, cut them, shuffled them again. 'Did yer see it?' he would demand. 'Could yer tell?'

Sometimes I saw the quick secretive movement of his fingers, hidden by the broad palm of his hand, scanning the pack for tell-tale markings. Sometimes not.

He was not a very good cheat. It's a difficult art, best done with clean hands and dry cards. Da's sticky little pack did not shuffle well. Often as we ambled down the rutted road I said, 'That's a false shuffle,' or 'I can see the crimped card, Da.'

He scowled at that and said: 'You've got eyes like a damn buzzard, Merry. Do it yourself if you're so clever,' and flicked the pack over to me with an irritable riffle of the cards.

I gathered them up, his hand and mine, and pulled the high cards and the picture cards into my right hand. With a little 'tssk' I brushed an imaginary insect of the driver's bench with the picture cards in a fan in my hand to put a bend in them, 'abridge', so that when I re-assembled the pack I could feel the arch even when the pack was all together. I vaguely looked out over the passing fields while I shuffled the deck, pulling the picture cards and the high cards into my left hand and stacking them on top alternately with stock cards so I could deal a picture card to myself and a low card to Da.

'Saw it!' Da said with mean satisfaction. 'Saw you make a bridge, brushing the bench.'

'Doesn't count,' I said, argumentatively. 'If you were a pigeon for plucking you'd not know that trick. It's only if you see me stack the deck that it counts. Did you see me stack it? And the false shuffle?'

'No,' he said, an unwilling concession. 'But that's still a penny you owe me for spotting the bridge. Gimme the cards back.'

I handed them over and he slid them through and through his calloused hands. 'No point teaching a girl anyway,' he grumbled. 'Girls never earn money standing up, only way to make money out of a girl is to get her on her back for her living. Girls are a damned waste.'

I left him to his complaints and went back inside the lumbering wagon where Dandy lay on her bunk combing her black hair and Zima dozed on her bed, the babby sucking and snortling at her breast. I looked away. I went to my own bunk and stretched out my head towards the little window at the back and watched the ribbon of the road spinning away behind us as we followed the twists and turns of the river all the way northward to Salisbury.

Da knew Salisbury well – this was the city where his ale-house business had failed and he had bought the wagon and gone back on the road again. He drove steadily through the crowded streets and Dandy and I stuck our heads out of the back window and pulled faces at errand boys and looked at the bustle and noise of the city. The fair was on the outside of town and Da guided the horse to a field where the wagons were spaced apart as strangers would put them, and there were some good horses cropping the short grass. I looked them over as I led our horse, Jess, from the shafts.

'Good animals,' I said to Da. His glance around was sharp.

'Aye,' he said. 'And a good price we should get for ours.'

I said nothing. Tied on the back of the wagon was a hunter so old and broken-winded that you could hear its roaring breaths from the driving seat, and another of Da's young ponies, too small to be ridden by anyone heavier than me, and too wild to be managed by any normal child.

'The hunter will go to a flash young fool,' he predicted confidently. 'And that young 'un should go as a young lady's ride.'

'He's a bit wild,' I said carefully.

'He'll sell on his colour,' Da said certainly, and I could not disagree. He was a wonderful pale grey, a grey almost silver with a sheen like satin on his coat. I had washed him this morning, and been thoroughly wetted and kicked for my pains, but he looked as bright as a unicorn.

'He's pretty,' I conceded. 'Da, if he sells – can Dandy and me go to the fair and buy her some ribbons, and some stockings?'

Da grunted, but he was not angry. The prospect of the fair and big profits had made him as sweet as he could be – which, God knew, was sour enough.

'Maybe,' he said. 'Maybe I'll give you some pennies for fairings.' He slid the tack off Jess's back and tossed it carelessly up on the step of the caravan. Jess jumped at the noise and stepped quickly sideways, her heavy hoof scraping my bare leg. I swore and rubbed the graze. Da paid no attention to either of us.

'Only if these horses sell,' he said. 'So you'd better start working the young one right away. You can lunge him before your dinner, and then work him all the day. I want you on his back by nightfall. If you can stay on, you can gad off to the fair. Not otherwise.'

The look I gave him was black enough. But I dared do nothing more. I pulled Jess's halter on and staked her out where she would graze near the caravan and went, surly, to the new grey pony tied on the back of the wagon. 'I hate you,' I said under my breath. The caravan tipped as Da went inside. 'You are mean and a bully and a lazy fool. I hate you and I wish you were dead.'

I took the long whip and the long reins and got behind the grey pony and gently, patiently, tried to teach it two months' training in one day so that Dandy and me could go to the fair with a penny in our pockets.

I was so deep in the sullens that I hardly noticed a man watching me from one of the other caravans. He was seated on the front step of his wagon, a pipe in his hand, tobacco smoke curling upwards in the still hot air above his head. I was concentrating on getting the grey pony to go in a circle around me. I stood in the centre, keeping the whip low, sometimes touching him to keep him going on, mostly calling to him to keep his speed going steady. Sometimes he went well, round and around me, and then suddenly he would kick out and rear and try to make a bolt for it, dragging me for shuddering strides across the grass until I dug my heels in and pulled him to a standstill and started the whole long process of making him walk in a steady circle again.

I was vaguely aware of being watched. But my attention was all on the little pony – as pretty as a picture and keen-witted. And as unwilling to work in the hot morning sunshine as I was. As angry and resentful as me.

Only when Da had got down from the caravan, pulled on his hat and headed off in the direction of the fair did I stop the pony and let him dip his head down and graze. I slumped down then myself for a break and laid aside the whip and spoke gently to him while he was eating. His ears – which had been back on his head in ill humour ever since we had started – flickered forward at the sound of my voice, and I knew the worst of it was over until I had to give him the shock of my weight on his back.

I stretched out and shut my eyes. Dandy was away to the fair to see what work she and Zima might do. Da was touting for a customer for his old hunter. Zima was clattering pots in the caravan, and her baby was crying with little hope of being attended. I was as solitary as I was ever able to be. I sighed and listened to a lark singing up in the sky above me, and the cropping sound of the pony grazing close to my head.

'Hey! Littl'un!' It was a low call from the man on the step of the caravan. I sat up cautiously and shaded my eyes to see him. It was a fine wagon, much bigger than ours and brightly painted.

Down the side in swirly red and gold letters it said words I could not read; with a great swirly 'E' which I guessed signified horses for there was a wonderful painted horse rearing up before a lady dressed as fine as a queen twirling a whip under its hooves.

The man's shirt was white, nearly clean. His face was shaved and plump. He was smiling at me, friendly. I was instantly suspicious.

'That's thirsty work,' he said kindly. 'Would you like a mug of small beer?'

'What for?' I asked.

'You're working well, I enjoyed watching you,' he said. He got to his feet and went inside his wagon, his fair head brushing the top of the doorway. He came out with two small pewter mugs of ale, and stepped down carefully from the step, his eyes on the mugs. He came towards me with one outstretched. I got to my feet and eyed him, but I did not put out my hand for the drink though I was parched and longing for the taste of the cool beer on my tongue and throat.

'What d'you want?' I asked, my eyes on the mug.

'Maybe I want to buy the horse,' he said. 'Go on, take it. I won't bite.'

That brought my eyes to his face. 'I'm not afraid of you,' I said defiantly. I looked down longingly at the drink again. 'I've no money to buy it,' I said.

'It's for free!' he said impatiently. 'Take it, you silly wench.'

'Thank you,' I said gruffly and took it from his hand. The liquid was malty on my tongue and went down my throat in a delicious cool stream. I gulped three times and then paused, to make it last the longer.

'Are you in the horse business?' he asked.

'You'd best ask my da,' I said.

He smiled at my caution and sat down on the grass at my feet. After a little hesitation, I sat too.

'That's my wagon,' he said pointing to the caravan. 'See that on the side? Robert Gower? That's me. Robert Gower's Amazing Equestrian Show! That's me and my business. All sorts I do.

Dancing ponies, fortune-telling ponies, acrobatic horses, trick-riding, cavalry charges. And the story of Richard the Lionheart and Saladin, in costume, and with two stallions.'

I gaped at him. 'How many horses have you got?' I asked.

'Five,' he said. 'And the stallion.'

'I thought you said two stallions,' I queried.

'It looks like two,' he said, unabashed. 'Richard the Lionheart rides the grey stallion. Then we black him up and he is Saladin's mighty ebony steed. I black-up too, to be Saladin. So what?'

'Nothing!' I said hastily. 'Are these your horses?'

'Aye,' he said gesturing at the ponies I had noticed earlier. 'These four ponies, and the skewbald which pulls the wagon and works as a rosinback. My boy's riding the stallion around the town, crying-up the show. We're giving a show in the next-door field. Two performances at three and seven. Today and Every Day. By Public Demand. For the Duration.'

I said nothing. Many of the words I did not understand. But I recognized the ring of the showground barker.

'You like horses,' he said.

'Yes,' I said. 'My da buys them, or trades them. We both train them. We often sell children's ponies. So I trains them.'

'When will this one be ready?' Robert Gower nodded to the grey pony.

'Da wants to sell him this week,' I said. 'He'll be half-broke by then.'

He pursed his lips and whistled soundlessly. 'That's fast work,' he said. 'You must take a lot of tumbles. Or is it your da who rides them?'

'It's me!' I said indignantly. 'I'll lunge him all today and I'll get on him tonight.'

He nodded and said nothing. I finished the ale and looked at the bottom of the mug. It had gone too quick and I had been distracted from savouring it by talk. I was sorry now.

'I'd like to see your da,' he said getting to his feet. 'Be back for his dinner, will he?'

'Yes,' I said. I scrambled to my feet and picked up the whip. 'I'll tell him you want to see him. Shall he come over to your wagon?'

'Yes,' he said. 'And when you've finished your work you can see my horse show. Admittance Only One Penny. But you may come Complimentary.'

'I don't have a penny,' I said, understanding only that.

'You can come free,' he said. 'Either show.'

'Thank you,' I said awkwardly. 'Sir.'

He nodded as gracious as a lord and went back to his bright wagon. I looked again at the picture on the side. The lady with the whip and the rearing white horse was dressed as fine as a queen. I wondered who she was and if she was perhaps his wife. It would be a fine life to dress as a lady and train horses in a ring before people who paid all that money just to see you. It would be as good as being born Quality. It would be nearly as good as Wide.

'Hey you!' he called again, his head stuck out of his caravan door. 'D'you know how to crack that whip, as well as flick it?'

'Yes,' I said. I ought to be able to. I had practised ever since I was able to stand. My da could crack a whip so loud it could scare the birds out of the trees. When I had asked him to teach me he had thrown an old rag down on the ground at my bare feet.

'Hit that,' he had said; and that was as much help as he was ready to give. Days I had stood flicking the whip towards the target until I had gradually strengthened my little-girl wrists to aim the whip accurately at the cloth, and now I could crack it high in the air or crack it low. Dandy had once taken a stalk in her mouth and I had taken the seed head off it for a dare. Only once. The next time we tried it I had missed and flicked her in the eye. I would never do it after that. She had screamed with the pain and her eye had swollen up and been black with a bruise for a week. I had been terrified that I had blinded her. Dandy forgot it as soon as her eye healed and wanted me to crack a whip and knock feathers off her hat and straws out of her mouth for pennies on street corners; but I would not.

'Crack it, then,' said Robert Gower.

'No,' I said. 'It would scare the pony and he's done nothing wrong. I'll crack it for you when I've turned him out.'

He nodded at that and a little puff of surprised smoke came from his pipe like a cottage chimney.

'Good lass,' he said. 'What's your name?'

'Meridon,' I said.

'Gypsy blood?' he asked.

'My mother was Rom,' I said defensively.

He nodded again and gave me a wink from one of his blue eyes. Then his round fair head ducked back in under the doorway and the caravan door slammed and I was left with the young pony who had to be schooled enough for me to ride him that evening if Dandy and I wanted to go to the fair with a penny each.

I made it by the skin of my teeth. Da's rule was that I had to get on the horse's back without him kicking out or running off – and apart from a quiver of fright the grey stood still enough. And then I had to get off again without mishap. By working him all day until we were both weary I had him so accustomed to my nearness that he only threw me once while I was training him to stand while I mounted. He didn't run off far, which I thought a very good sign. I did not work at all at teaching him to walk forwards or stop. They were not the conditions Da had set for a visit to the fair so I cared nothing for them. All he could do by the end of the day was stand still for the twenty seconds while I mounted, smiled with assumed confidence at Da, and dismounted.

Da grudgingly felt in his pocket and gave a penny to Dandy and a penny to me.

'I've been talking business with that man Gower,' he said grandly. 'As a favour to me he says you can both go to his show. I'm going into town to see a man about buying a horse. Be in the wagon when I come back or there'll be trouble.'

Dandy shot me a warning look to bid me hold my tongue, and said sweetly: 'Yes, Da.' We both knew that when he came back he would be so blind drunk that he would not be able to tell if we were there or not. Nor remember in the morning.

Then we fled to the corner of the field where the gate was

held half-open by Robert Gower, resplendent in a red jacket and white breeches with black riding boots. A steady stream of people had been going by us all afternoon, paying their pennies to Robert Gower and taking their ease on the grassy slopes waiting for the show to start. Dandy and I were the last to arrive.

'He's Quality!' Dandy gasped, as we dashed across the field. 'Look at his boots.'

'And he got dressed in that caravan!' I said amazed, having never seen anything come out of our caravan brighter than the slatternly glitter of Zima's best dress over a soiled petticoat grey with inadequate washing.

'Ah!' said Robert Gower. 'Meridon and . . . ?'

'My sister, Dandy,' I said.

Robert Gower nodded grandly at us both. 'Please take a seat,' he said opening the gate a little wider to allow us inside. 'Anywhere on the grass but not in front of the benches which is reserved for the Quality and for the Churchmen. By Special Request,' he added.

Dandy gave him her sweetest smile and spread her ragged skirt out and swept him a curtsey. 'Thank you, sir,' she said and sailed past him with her head in the air and her glossy black hair in thick sausage ringlets all down her back.

The field was on a slight slope, levelling off at the bottom, and the audience were seated on the grass on the slope looking down. In front of them were two small benches, empty except for a fat man and his wife who looked like well-to-do farmers but not proper Quality at all. We had come in at the bottom of the hill and had to walk past a large screen painted with strange-looking trees and a violet and red sunset and yellow earth. It was hinged with wings on either side so that it presented a back-cloth to the audience and went some way to hiding the ponies who were tethered behind it. As we walked by, a youth of about seventeen dressed very fine in white breeches and a red silk shirt glanced out from behind the screen and stared at us both. I know I looked furtive, expecting a challenge, but he said nothing and looked us over as if free seats made us his especial property. I looked at Dandy. Her eyes had widened and she was looking straight at him, her face was flushed, her smile confident. She looked at him as boldly as if she were his equal.

'Hello,' she said.

'Are you Meridon?' he said surprised.

I was about to say: 'No. I am Meridon and this is my sister.' But Dandy was ahead of me.

'Oh no,' she said. 'My name is Dandy. Who are you?'

'Jack,' he said. 'Jack Gower.'

Unnoticed, standing behind my beautiful sister, I could stare at him. He was not fair like his father but dark-haired. His eyes were dark too. In his shimmering shirt and his white breeches he looked like a lord in a travelling play – dazzling. The confident smile on his face as he looked down at Dandy, whose pale face was upturned to him like a flower on a slim stem, showed that he knew it. I looked at that smile and thought him the most handsome youth I had ever seen in my whole life. And for some reason, I could not say why, I shuddered as if someone had just dripped cold water on my scalp, and the nape of my neck felt cold.

'I'll see you after the show,' he said. The tone of his voice made it sound as if it might be a threat or a promise.

Dandy's eyes gleamed. 'You might,' she said, as natural a coquette as ever flirted with a handsome youth. 'I have other things to do than hang around a wagon.'

'Oh?' he asked. 'What things?'

'Meridon and I are going to the fair,' she said. 'And we've money to spend, and all.'

For the first time he looked at me. 'So you're Meridon,' he said carelessly. 'My da says you can train little ponies. Could you manage a horse like this?'

He gestured behind the screen and I peered around it. Tied to a stake on the ground was a beautiful grey stallion, standing quiet and docile, but his dark eye rolled towards me as he saw me.

'Oh, yes,' I said with longing. 'I could look after him all right.'

Jack gave me a little smile as warm and understanding as his da.

'Would you like to ride him after the show?' he invited. 'Or do you have better things to do, like your sister?'

Dandy's fingers nipped my arm but for once I ignored her. 'I'd love to ride him,' I said hastily. 'I'd rather ride him than go to any fair, any day.'

He nodded at that. 'Da said you were horse-mad,' he said. 'Wait till after the show and you can go up on him.'

He glanced towards the gate and nodded as his father waved.

'Take your seats,' Robert Gower called in his loud announcing voice. 'Take your seats for the greatest show in England and Europe!'

Jack winked at Dandy and ducked behind the screen as his father shut the gate and came to the centre of the flat grass. Dandy and I scurried to the hill and sat down in expectant silence.

I sat through the show in a daze. I had never seen horses with such training. They had four small ponies – Welsh mountain or New Forest, I thought – who started the show with a dancing act. There was a barrel organ playing and the boy Jack Gower stood in the middle of the ring with a fine purple coat over his red shirt and a long whip. As he cracked it and moved from the centre to the side the little ponies wheeled and trotted individually, turning on their hind legs, reversing the order, all with their heads up and the plumes on their heads jogging and their bells ringing ringing ringing like out-of-season sleighbells.

People cheered as he finished with a flourish with all four ponies bending down in a horse curtsey, and he swept off his purple tricorne hat and bowed to the crowd. But he exchanged a look with Dandy as if to say that it was all for her, and I felt her swell with pride.

The stallion was next in the ring, with a mane like white sea foam tumbling down over his arched neck. Robert Gower came in with him and made him rear and stamp his hooves to order. He picked out flags of any colour – you could call out a colour and he would bring you the one you ordered. He danced on the spot and he could count up numbers up to ten by pawing the ground. He could add up, too, quicker than I could. He was a brilliant horse and so beautiful!

They cheered when he was gone too and then it was the time for the cavalry charge with the barrel organ playing marching music and Robert Gower telling about the glorious battle of Blenheim. The little pony came thundering into the ring with its harness stuck full of bright coloured flags and above them all the red cross of St George. Robert Gower explained that this symbolized the Duke of Marlborough 'and the Flower of the English Cavalry'.

The other three ponies came in flying the French flag and while the audience sang the old song 'The Roast Beef of Old England', the four ponies charged at each other, their little hooves pounding the earth and churning it up into mud. It was a wonderful show and at the end the little French ponies lay down and died and the victorious English pony galloped around in a victory circle and then reared in the middle of the ring.

The drink-sellers came around then, with a tray of drinks, and there were pie-men and muffin-sellers too. Dandy and I had only our pennies and we were saving them for later. Besides, we were used to going hungry.

Next was a new horse, a great skewbald with a rolling eye and a broad back. Robert Gower stood in the centre of the ring, cracking his whip and making the horse canter round in a great steady rolling stride. Then with a sudden rush and a vault Jack came into the ring stripped down to his red shirt and his white breeches and Dandy's hand slid into mine and she gripped me tight. As the horse thundered round and around, Jack leaped up on to her back and stood balanced, holding one strap and nothing else, one arm outflung for applause. He somersaulted off and then jumped on again and, while the horse cantered round, he swung himself off one side, and then another, and then, perilously, clambered all the way around the animal's neck. He vaulted and faced backwards. He spun around and faced forwards. Then he finished the act, sweating and panting, with a ride around the ring, standing on the horse's rump absolutely straight, his arms outstretched for balance, holding nothing to keep him steady, and a great jump to land on his feet beside his father.

Dandy and I leaped to our feet to cheer. I had never seen such riding. Dandy's eyes were shining and we were both hoarse from shouting.

'Isn't he wonderful?' she asked me.

'And the horse!' I said.

That was the high point of the show for me. But Robert Gower as Richard the Lionheart going off to war with all the little ponies and the stallion was enough to bring Dandy close to tears. Then there was a tableau of Saladin on a great black horse which I could not have recognized as the same stallion. Then Richard the Lionheart did a triumphant parade with a wonderful golden rug thrown over the horse's back. Only his black legs showing underneath would have given the game away if you were looking.

'Wonderful,' sighed Dandy at the end.

I nodded. It was actually too much for me to speak.

We kept our seats. I don't think my knees would have supported me if we had stood. I found I was staring at the muddy patch at the bottom of the hill and seeing again the flash of thundering legs and hearing in my ears the ringing of the pony bells.

All at once my breaking and training of children's ponies seemed as dull and as dreary as an ordinary woman's housework. I had never known horses could do such things. I had never thought of them as show animals in this way at all. And the money to be made from it! I was canny enough, even in my starstruck daze, to know that six hard-working horses would cost dear, and that Robert and Jack's shining cleanliness did not come cheap. But as Robert closed the gate behind the last customer he came towards us swinging a money bag which chinked as if it were full of pennies. He carried it as if it were heavy.

'Enjoy yourselves?' he asked.

Dandy gleamed at him. 'It was wonderful,' she said, without a word of exaggeration. 'It was the most wonderful thing I have ever seen.'

He nodded and raised an eyebrow at me.

'Can the stallion really count?' I asked. 'How did you teach him his numbers? Can he read as well?'

An absorbed look crossed Robert Gower's face. 'I never thought of him reading,' he said thoughtfully. 'You could do a trick with him taking messages perhaps . . .' Then he recollected us. 'You'd like a ride, I hear.'

I nodded. For the first time in a thieving, cheating, bawling life I felt shy. 'If he wouldn't mind . . .' I said.

'He's just a horse,' Robert Gower said, and put two fingers in his mouth and whistled. The stallion, still dyed black, came out from behind the screen with just a halter on, obedient as a dog.

He walked towards Robert who gestured to me to stand beside the horse. Then he stepped back and looked at me with a measuring eye.

'How old are you?' he asked abruptly.

'Fifteen, I think,' I said. I could feel the horse's gentle nose touching my shoulder, and his lips bumping against my neck.

'Going to grow much?' Robert asked. 'Your ma now, is she tall? Your pa is fairly short.'

'He's not my da,' I said. 'Though I call him that. My real da is dead and my ma too. I don't know whether they were tall or not. I'm not growing as fast as Dandy, though we're the same age.'

Robert Gower hummed to himself and said, 'Good,' under his breath. I looked to see if Dandy was impatient to go but she was looking past me at the screen. Looking for Jack.

'Up you get then,' he said pleasantly. 'Up you go.'

I took the rope of the halter and turned towards the stallion. The great wall of his flank went up and up, well above my head. My head was as high as the start of his great arching neck. He was the biggest horse I had ever seen.

I could vault on Jess our carthorse by yelling, 'Hike!' to her and taking her at a run. But she was smaller than this giant, and I did not feel fit to shout an order to him and rush at him.

I turned to Robert Gower. 'I don't know how,' I said.

'Tell him to bow,' he said, not moving forwards. He was

standing as far back as if he was in the audience. And he was looking at me as if he were seeing something else.

'Bow,' I said uncertainly to the horse. 'Bow.'

The ears flickered forwards in reply but he did not move.

'He's called Snow,' Robert Gower said. 'And he's a horse like any other. Make him do as he's told. Don't be shy with him.'

'Snow,' I said a little more strongly. 'Bow!'

A black eye rolled towards me, and I knew, without being able to say why, that he was being naughty like any ordinary horse. Whether he could count better than me or no, he was just being plain awkward. Without thinking twice I slapped him on the shoulder with the tail end of the halter and said, in a voice which left no doubt in his mind:

'You heard me! Bow, Snow!'

At once he put one forefoot behind the other and lowered right down. I still had to give a little spring to get up on his back, and then I called, 'Up!' and he was up on four feet again.

Robert Gower sat on the grass. 'Take him around the ring,' he said.

One touch of my heels did it, and the great animal moved forwards in such a smooth walk that it was as if we were gliding. I sat a little firmer and he took it as an order to trot. The great wide back was a steady seat and I jogged a little but hardly slid. I glanced at Robert Gower. He was tending to his pipe. 'Go on,' he said. 'Canter.'

I sat firmer and squeezed – the lightest of touches and the jarring pace of the trot melted into a canter which blew the hair off my shoulders and brought a delighted smile to my face. Jack came out from behind the screen and smiled at me as I thundered past him. Snow jinked a little at the movement but I stayed on his back as solid as a rock.

'Pull him up!' Robert Gower suddenly yelled, and I hauled on the rope, anxious that I had done something wrong. 'Hold tight!' he shouted. 'Up Snow!'

The neck came up and nearly hit me in the face as Snow reared. I could feel myself sliding back and I clung on to the handfuls of mane for dear life as he pawed the air, and then dropped down again.

'Down you come,' Robert Gower ordered and I slid down from the horse's back instantly.

'Give her the whip,' he said to Jack, and Jack stepped forward, a smock thrown over his showtime glory, with a long whip in his hand.

'Stand in front of the horse, as close as you can, nice loud crack on the ground. Shout him "Up!" and then a crack in the air. Like the painting on my wagon,' Robert ordered.

I flicked the whip lightly on the ground to get the feel. Then I looked at Snow and cracked it as loud as I could. 'Up!' I yelled. He was as tall as a tower above me. Up and up he went and his great black hooves were way above my head. I cracked the whip above my head, and even that long thong seemed to come nowhere near him.

'Down!' Robert shouted and the horse dropped down in front of me. I stroked his nose. The black came off on my hand and I saw that my hands and face and my skirt were filthy.

'I should have given you a smock,' Robert Gower said by way of apology. 'Never mind.' He took a great silver watch from his pocket and flicked it open. 'We're getting behind time,' he said. 'Would you give Jack a hand to get the horses ready for the second show?'

'Oh yes,' I said at once.

Robert Gower glanced at Dandy. 'D'you like horses?' he asked. 'D'you like to work with them?'

Dandy smiled at him. 'No,' she said. 'I do other work. Horses is too dirty.'

He nodded at that, and flicked her a penny from his pocket. 'You're a deal too pretty to get dirty,' he said. 'That's your pay for waiting for your sister. You can go and wait by the gate and watch that no one sneaks in before I'm there to take the money.'

Dandy caught the penny one-handed with practised skill. 'All right,' she said agreeably.

So Dandy sat on the gate while I helped Jack wash Snow and brush and tack-up the little ponies in their bells and their plumes, and water and feed them with a little oats. Jack worked steadily but shot a glance now and then at Dandy as she sat on the gate with the evening sun all yellow and gold behind her, singing and plaiting her black hair.

3

We did not cross the muddy lane to the fairground until late that night after we had seen the whole show through again, and I had stayed behind to clean the horses and feed them for the night. I knew Dandy would not mind waiting, she sat placidly on the gate and watched Jack and me work.

'I have tuppence to spend,' I said exultantly as I came towards her, wiping my dirty hands on my equally dirty skirt.

She smiled sweetly at that. 'I have three shillings,' she said. 'I'll give you one.'

'Dandy!' I exclaimed. 'Whose pocket?'

'The fat old gentleman,' she said. 'He gave me a halfpenny to fetch him a drink after he had missed the drink-seller. When I brought it back to him I was close enough to get my hand in his breeches pocket.'

'Would he know you again?' I asked worried.

'Oh yes,' she said. Dandy had known she was beautiful from childhood. 'But I daresay he won't think it was me. Anyway, let's spend the money!'

We stayed out until it was all gone and our pockets were crammed with fairings. Dandy would have picked another pocket or two in the crush but there were gangs of thieves working the fair and they would have spotted her, even if no one else had. She might talk her way out of trouble with an ageing gentleman, but if one of the leaders of the gangs of thieves caught her we would both have to turn out our pockets and give them everything we had – and get a beating into the bargain, too.

It was dark when we crossed the lane back to the field and our caravan and there were no lights showing at Gower's wagon. I checked on our horses before I went in. The old hunter was lying down to sleep, I could only hope he would be able to get up in the morning. If he did not, Da would go wild. He was counting on a sale to pay for a horse he wanted to buy from one of the fairground showmen. And a dead horse is little profit, even when the butchers call it beef.

We were all asleep when the caravan lurched and he fell in the doorway. Zima did not stir. She was lying on her back, snoring like a trooper, all tumbled into bed in her finery. I had seen a new gilt necklace around her neck and guessed that she had not been wasting her time while Da was out drinking. The caravan rocked like a ship in a storm at sea when Da blundered in and then bounced like a jogging horse when he tried to mount Zima, drunk as he was. I heard Dandy snigger under her blanket as we heard him curse and blame the ale, but I could not laugh. I turned my face to the familiar stained wall and thought of a sandstone-yellow house amid a tall well-timbered park and a stallion as white as sea spray trotting down the drive towards me as I stood on the terrace in a riding habit as green as grass with a clean linen petticoat.

Da paid for his drinking in the morning, but Zima paid for it worst. He saw the gilt necklace and wanted the money she had been paid. She swore she had only had one man, and only been paid a shilling but he did not believe her and set to beating her with her shoe. Dandy and I made haste to get under the wheels of the wagon and well out of harm's way. Dandy stopped to snatch up the baby and lug her to safety with us, and got a back-handed clout for her pains. She was soft-hearted about the little wretch, she was always afraid that Zima would throw it at Da in a rage.

We were under the wagon with the swearing and breaking crockery loud above us when I saw Robert Gower come out on to his step with a mug of tea in his hand and his pipe in his mouth.

He nodded good morning to us as if he was deaf to the thuds and screams from our wagon, and sat in the sunshine puffing on his pipe. Jack came out to sit beside his father, but we both stayed in our refuge. If Da was still angry he couldn't reach us under the wagon unless he poked us out with the butt of the whip, and we were gambling he wouldn't bend over with the beer still thudding in his head. It was getting quieter above, though Zima had started sobbing noisily, and then she stopped. Dandy and I sat tight until we were sure the storm was over, but Robert Gower walked towards our wagon and called out, 'Joe Cox?' when he was three paces from the shafts.

Da came out, we felt the caravan rock above our heads and I pictured him, rubbing frowsty eyes and squinting at the sunlight.

'You again,' he said blankly. 'I thought you didn't want my fine hunter.' He hawked and spat over the side of the wagon. 'D'you want to buy that pretty little pony of ours? He'd look nicely in your show. Or the hunter's still for sale.'

The fine hunter was still lying down and looked less and less likely to get up. Da did not see it, he was watching Robert Gower's face.

'I'm interested in the pony if you can get it broken by the end of the week,' Robert Gower said. 'I've been watching your lass train it. I doubt she can do it.'

Da spat again. 'She's an idle whelp,' he said dismissively. 'Her and her good-for-nothing sister. No kin of mine, and I'm saddled with them.' He raised his voice. 'And my wife's a whore and a thief!' he said louder. 'And she's foisted another damned girl brat on me.'

Robert Gower nodded. His white shirt billowed at the sleeves in the clean morning air. 'Too many mouths to feed,' he said sympathetically. 'No man can keep a family of five and make the profits a man needs.'

Da sat down heavily on the step of the wagon. 'And that's the truth,' he said. 'Two useless girls, one useless whore, and one useless baby.'

'Why not send them out to work?' Robert suggested. 'Girls can always make a living somehow.'

'Soon as I can,' Da promised. 'I've never been fixed anywhere long enough to get them jobs, and I swore to their dead ma that I wouldn't throw them out of her wagon. But soon as I can get them fixed . . . out they go.'

'I'd take the littl'un,' Robert Gower offered nonchalantly. 'What's she called? Merry something? She can work with my horses. She's useless with anything bigger than a pony so she'd be little help to me. But I'd take her off your hands for you.'

Da's bare cracked feet appeared at the wheels at our heads as we crouched beneath the wagon. He slid off the step and went towards the shining topboots of Robert Gower. 'You'd take Meridon?' he said incredulously. 'Take her to work for you?'

'I might,' Gower said. 'If the terms were right with the pony.'

There was a silence. 'No,' Da said, his voice suddenly soft. 'I couldn't spare her. I promised her ma, you see. I couldn't just let her go unless I knew she was going to a good place with ready wages.'

'Suit yourself,' Robert Gower said and I saw his shiny black boots walk away. They went for three strides before Da's dirty feet pattered after.

'If you gave me her wages in advance, gave them to me, I'd consider it,' he said. 'I'd talk it over with her. She's a bright girl, very sensible. Brilliant with horses you see. All of mine she trains for me. She's gypsy you see, she can whisper a horse out of a field. I'd be lost without her. She'll get that pony broken and ridable within a week. You see if she doesn't. Perfect for your line of work, she is.'

'Girls are ten a penny,' Robert Gower said. 'She'd cost me money in the first year or so. I'd do better taking a proper apprentice with a fee paid to me by his parents. If you'd been willing to give me a good price for the pony I'd have taken whatever-her-name-is off your hands for you. I've a big wagon, and I'm looking for a helper. But there's a lot of bright lads who would suit me better.'

'It's a good pony though,' Da said suddenly. 'I'd want a good price for it.'

'Like what?' Robert Gower said.

'Two pounds,' Da said looking for a profit four times what he had paid for the animal.

'A guinea,' Robert Gower said at once.

'One pound twelve shillings and Meridon,' Da said. I could hear the urgency in his voice.

'Done!' Robert Gower said quickly and I knew Da had sold the pony too cheap. Then I gasped as I realized that he had sold me cheap too and, whether Da was hung-over or no, I should be in on this deal.

I squirmed out from under the wagon and popped up at Da's side as he spat into his palm to shake on the deal.

'And Dandy,' I said urgently, grabbing his arm but looking at Robert Gower. 'Dandy and I go together.'

Robert Gower looked at Da. 'She's idle,' he said simply. 'You said so yourself.'

'She can cook,' Da said desperately. 'You want someone to keep your wagon nice. She's a good girl for things like that.'

Robert Gower glanced at his perfect linen and at Da's torn shirt and said nothing.

'I don't need two girls,' he said firmly. 'I'm not paying that money for a cheap little pony and two girls to clutter up the wagon.'

'I won't come on my own,' I said and my eyes were blazing green. 'Dandy and I go together.'

'You'll do as you're told!' Da exclaimed in a rage. He made a grab for me but I ducked away and got behind Robert Gower.

'Dandy's useful,' I said urgently. 'She catches rabbits, and she can cook well. She can make wooden flowers and withy baskets. She can do card tricks and dance. She's very very pretty, you could have her in the show. She could take the money at the gate. She only steals from strangers!'

'Won't you come on your own to be with my horses?' Robert Gower said temptingly.

'Not without Dandy,' I said. My voice quavered as I saw my chance of getting away from Da and Zima and the filthy wagon and the miserable life fading fast. 'I can't go without Dandy! She's the only person in the whole world that I love! If I didn't have her, I wouldn't love anyone! And what would become of me if I didn't love anyone at all?'

Robert Gower looked at Da. 'A guinea,' he said. 'A guinea for the pony and I'll do you a favour and take both little sluts off your hands.'

Da sighed with relief. 'Done,' he said and spat in his palm and they shook on the deal. 'They can come to your wagon at once,' he said. 'I'm moving on today.'

I watched him shamble back to the wagon. He was not moving on today. He was running away before Robert Gower changed his mind on the deal. He would celebrate getting a guinea for a pony and cheating Robert Gower – a warm man – out of an eleven shilling profit. But I had a feeling that Robert Gower had planned from the start to pay a guinea for the pony and for me. And maybe he knew from the start that he would have to take Dandy too.

I went back to the wagon. Dandy wriggled out, pulling the baby behind her.

'I want to take the babby,' she said.

'No Dandy,' I said, as if I were very much older than her and very much wiser. 'We've pushed our luck enough.'

We were on our best behaviour for the rest of that week at the Salisbury fair. Dandy went out to the Common outside the town and brought back a meat dinner every day.

'Where are you getting it from?' I demanded in an urgent whisper as she spooned out a rabbit stew thick and chunky with meat.

'There's a kind gentleman in a big house on the Bath road,' she said with quiet satisfaction.

I put the bowls out on the table and dropped the horn-handled spoons with a clatter.

'What d'you have to do for it?' I asked anxiously.

'Nothing,' she said. She shot me a sly smile through a tumbling wave of black hair. 'I just have to sit on his knee and cry and say, "Oh! Please don't Daddy," like that. Then he gives me a penny and sends me out through the kitchen and they give me a rabbit. He says I can have a pheasant tomorrow.'

I looked at her with unease. 'All right,' I said unhappily. 'But if he promises you a rib of beef or a leg of lamb or a proper joint you're not to go back again. Could you run away if you had to?'

'Oh yes,' she said airily. 'We sit near the window and it's always open. I could be out in minutes.'

I nodded, only slightly relieved. I had to trust Dandy with these weird frightening forays of hers into the adult world. She had never been caught. She had never been punished. Whether she was picking pockets or dancing to please elderly gentlemen with skirts held out high; she always came home with a handful of coins and no trouble. She was as idle as a well-fed cat around the caravan. But if she sensed trouble or danger she could slip through a man's hands and be gone like quicksilver.

'Call them,' she said, nodding towards the doorway.

I went out to the step and called: 'Robert! Jack! Dinner!'

We were on first-name terms now, intimate with the unavoidable closeness of caravan-dwellers. Jack and Dandy sometimes exchanged a secret dark smile, but nothing more. Robert had seen how they were together the very first evening we had spent in the caravan and had pulled off his boots and started blacking them, looking at Dandy under his blond bushy eyebrows.

'Look here, Dandy,' he had said, pointing the brush at her. 'I'll be straight with you, and you can be straight with me. I took you on because I thought you'd do nicely in the show. I have some ideas which I'll break open to you later. Not now. Now's not the time. But I can tell you you could have a pretty costume and dance to music and every eye in the place would be on you. And every girl in the place would envy you.'

He paused, and satisfied with the effect of this appeal to her vanity went on: 'I'll tell you what I want for my son,' he said. 'He's my heir and he'll have the show when I'm gone. Before then I'll find him a good hard-working girl in the shows business like us. A girl with a good dowry to bring with her, and best of all an Act and a Name of her own. A Marriage of Talents,' he said softly to himself.

He broke off again, and then recollected where he was and went on. 'That's the best I can do for the both of you,' he said fairly. 'Where you weds or beds is your own affair, but you'll not lack offers if you keeps clean and stays with my show. But if I catch you mooning over my lad, or if he puts his hand up your skirt, you just remember that I'll put you out of this wagon on the high road wherever we are. However you feel. And I won't look back. And my lad Jack won't look back either. He knows which side his bread is buttered, and he might have you once or twice, but he'll never wed you. Not in a thousand years.'

Dandy blinked.

'See?' Robert said with finality.

Dandy glanced at Jack to see if he had anything to say in her defence. He was resolutely buffing the white of his topboots. His head bent low over his work. You would have thought him deaf. I looked at the dark nape of his neck and knew he was afraid of his father. And that his father had spoken the truth when he said that Jack would never go against him. Not in a thousand years.

'What about Meridon?' Dandy said surly. 'You don't warn her off your precious son.'

Robert shot a quick look at me and then smiled. 'She's not a whore-in-the-making,' he said. 'All Meridon wants from Jack and me is a chance to ride our horses.'

I nodded. That much was true.

'D'you see?' Robert asked again. 'I'd not have taken you into my wagon if I'd known you and Jack were smelling of April and May. But I can put you out here and you'd still have a chance of finding your da again. He won't have got far – not with that damned old carthorse of his pulling that wagon! You'd best go if you're hot for Jack. I won't have it. And it won't happen without my letting.'

Dandy looked once more at the back of Jack's head. He had started on the other boot. The first one was radiantly white. I thought he had probably never worked so hard on it before.

'All right,' she said. 'You can keep your precious son. I didn't want him so much anyway. Plenty of other young men in the world.'

Robert beamed at her, he loved getting his own way. 'Good girl!' he said approvingly. 'Now we can all live together with a bit of comfort. I'll take that as your word, and you'll hear no more about it from me.

'And I'll tell you something, pretty-face. If you keep those looks when you are a woman grown, there's no telling how high you might aim. But don't go giving it away, girl. With looks like yours you could even think about a gentry marriage!'

That was consolation enough for Dandy and she went up into her bunk early that night to comb her hair and plait it carefully. And she did not exchange another languorous smile with Jack. Not for all the time we were in Salisbury.

It was a fine summer, that hot sunny summer of 1805. I changed from the dreary unhappy girl I had been in my da's wagon to a working groom with pride in my work. My skirt grew bedraggled and my shoes wore out. It seemed only natural to borrow Jack's smock and then, as he outgrew them, his second-best breeches and his old shirt. By the end of the summer I dressed all the time as a lad and felt a delight in how I could move and my freedom from the looks of passing men. I was absorbed by the speed of the travel, by the way we went from one town to another overnight. Never staying longer than three days at any site, always moving on. Everywhere we went it was the same show. The dancing ponies, the clever stallion, the cavalry charge, Jack's bareback ride, and the story of Richard the Lionheart and Saladin.

But every night it was somehow a little bit different. The horses would go through their paces differently every time. For a while one of the little ponies was sick and went slower than the others and spoiled the dancing. Then Jack ricked his ankle unloading the wagon and had trouble with his vaults on to the horse, so all of that act was changed until he was strong again. Little changes – but they absorbed me.

It was soon my business to care for the horses from the time Jack and Robert had changed into their costumes. I had been steadily doing more and more from the first night when I had stayed behind for the sheer joy of stroking the velvety noses and smoothing the hot sides. But now it was my job. Dandy worked in the caravan. She bought the groceries and poached what food we needed. She kept the caravan as clean as Robert Gower thought fit – which was a lifetime away from Zima's rank sluttery. Then she came to the field and kept the gate while Robert did the barking for the show.

All the while we were learning the business. All the time we were getting to love the contrast between the hard life of the travelling and the magic of the costume and the disguise. And all the time we were growing addicted to the sound of delighted applause, and to the sense of power from being the centre of attention, making magic before scores and sometimes hundreds of people.

While we were learning, Robert was planning. Every time we were anywhere near another show he would go and see it. Even if it meant missing one of our own performances he would put on his best jacket – a tweed one, not his working red coat – take the big grey stallion, and ride for as much as twenty miles to see another show. But it was not horse shows which drew him. I realized that when Jack came back from crying up the show around Keynsham with a bill in his hand, and said with confidence:

'This'll interest you, Da.'

It was not a bill for a horse show but a brightly coloured picture of man swinging upside down from a bar which had been hung high in the ceiling. He looked half-naked, in a costume like a second skin and spangled. He had great broad mustachios and was beaming down as if he had no fear at all.

'Why, you're white as a sheet,' Robert said looking at me. 'What's the matter, Meridon?'

'Nothing,' I said instantly. But I could feel the blood draining from my head and I knew that I might faint at any moment.

I squeezed past Robert and that terrifying picture and stumbled to the caravan step and sat gulping in the fresh air of a warm August evening.

'Be all right to work, will you?' Robert called from inside the wagon.

'Yes, yes ...' I assented weakly. 'I just felt faint for a moment.'

He left me in silence to look at the staked-out horses and the sun low in the sky behind a bank of pale butter-coloured clouds.

'Not started your bleeding have you?' he asked, standing in the doorway with rough sympathy.

'It's not that!' I exclaimed, stung.

'Well, it's hardly an insult . . .' he excused himself. 'What's the matter then?'

'It was that picture, the hand-bill . . .' I said. I could hardly explain my terror even to myself. 'What was the man doing? He looked so high!'

Robert drew the hand-bill out of his pocket. 'He calls himself a trapeze artiste,' he said. 'It's a new act. I'm going into Bristol to see it. I'd like to know how it's done. See . . .' he pushed the hand-bill towards me but I turned my head away.

'I hate it!' I said childishly. 'I can't bear to see it!'

'Are you afraid of being up high?' Robert asked. He was scowling as if my answer mattered.

'Yes,' I said shortly. In all my dare-devil boyish childhood it had been the only thing which made me ill with fear. Only on birds' nesting expeditions was I never the leader of a game. I always insisted on staying on the ground while other travellers' children climbed trees. Only once, when I was about ten years old, I had forced myself up a tree for a dare, and then frozen, terrified, on a low branch, quite unable to move. It had been Dandy, of all people, who had climbed up with placid confidence to fetch me. And Dandy who had been able to give me the courage to scramble down. I pushed away the memory of the swaying branch and the delighted cruel upturned faces below me. 'Yes,' I said. 'I am afraid of being up high. It makes me ill just thinking about it.'

Robert said: 'Damn,' under his breath and jumped down from the caravan step to pull on his boots. 'Horses ready for the show?' he asked absently. The little puffs of smoke from his pipe came out quickly, as they did when he was thinking hard and biting on the stem.

'Yes,' I said. 'Not tacked-up yet, of course.'

'Aye,' he said. He stood up and stamped his feet down into the boots and then tapped his pipe out on the wheel of the caravan and put it carefully by the driving seat.

'What about Dandy?' he said abruptly. 'I suppose she won't climb. I suppose she's no good up high too?'

'Dandy's all right,' I said. 'Were you thinking of something for the show? You'd have to ask her, but she used to climb trees well when we were little.'

'I'm just thinking aloud,' he said, snubbing my curiosity. 'Just thinking.'

But as he went towards the show field I heard him muttering under his breath. 'Amazing Aerial Act. An Angel Without Wings. The Amazing Mamselle Dandy.'

He visited the trapeze act at Bristol; but he came back late and said nothing about it in the morning. Only Jack was allowed to ask over breakfast: 'Any good?' Dandy and I were eating our bread and bacon on the sun-drenched step of the caravan, so only Jack heard more than a mumbled reply. But I had heard enough to guess that Robert's promise to Dandy of being in the centre of the ring might come true.

She welcomed it when I told her what he had said. Already our work for the show had been expanded. When Jack went crying-up the show into new towns and villages he often took Dandy riding on the crupper behind him. I had seen Robert frown the first time he saw the white horse and his son with Dandy looking so pretty, riding behind him with her arms around his waist. But he was thinking of business and not love.

'You should have a proper riding habit,' he said. 'A proper riding habit and be up on your own. It'd look grand. Robert Gower's Amazing Equestrian Show with Lady Dandy in the Ring,' he said.

He gave Dandy five shillings for a bolt of real velvet and she made herself a riding habit in two evenings, working under the lantern until her eyes were bleary from the strain. When Jack next cried-up the show, he took her up behind him with her beautiful blue riding habit sweeping down Snow's shining side. Dandy's smile under her blue tricorne hat was heart-stoppingly lovely. In the next village we had the best gate we had ever taken.

'The public like lasses,' Robert announced at supper that night. 'I want you riding in the ring, Meridon. And Dandy you're to cry-up the show with Jack every day. Stay in your costume to take at the gate.'

'What shall I wear?' I asked. Robert looked at me critically. I had wearied of brushing my thick mass of copper hair every day and had started cutting out the tangles and the hayseeds. Dandy had exclaimed at the ragged edges I had left and had trimmed it in a bob, like a country lad. The natural curl had made it into a mop of red-gold ringlets, which tumbled about my head like an unruly halo. I had gained no weight over the summer of good living with the Gowers though I had grown taller. I was as lanky and as awkward as a young colt while Dandy had the poise and the warm curves of a young woman.

'I'm damned if I know,' Robert said chuckling. 'I'd put you in a pierrot suit for half a crown. You look like a little waif, mophead. If you're going to grow as bonny as your sister, you'd better make haste!'

'What about dressing her as a lad?' Jack said suddenly. He was wiping out his bowl with a hunk of bread, but he paused with sticky fingers and smiled his confident smile at me. 'No offence, Meridon. But she could wear a silk shirt and tight white breeches and boots. You look at her when she's in those old trews of mine, Da, she looks unladylike . . . but it would work in the ring. And she could do a rosinback act with me.' Jack pushed his bowl to one side. 'Hey!' he said excitedly. 'D'you remember that act we saw when someone came out of the crowd? The show outside Salisbury one time? We could do something like that and I could come out from the back, pretending to be a drunk, you know, and come up on the horse and knock Meridon off.'

'More falls,' I said glumly. 'I had enough of them when I was breaking horses for Da.'

'Pretend falls,' Jack said, his eyes warm on me. 'And they wouldn't hurt. And then she could get up on the big horse, and do a bit of bareback work.'

Robert looked at me speculatively.

'Bareback work in the breeches,' he said. 'The riding and clowning in a riding habit. That'd look better dressed as a girl. Two acts and only half a costume change.' He nodded. 'Would you like to do that, Meridon?' he asked. 'I'd pay you.'

'How much?' I said instantly.

'Ha'penny a show, penny a night,' he said.

'Penny a show,' I said at once.

'Penny a day whether we have a show or not,' he offered, and I stuck my grimy hand across the table and we closed the deal.

My training started the next day. I had seen Jack vaulting on and off the big skewbald horse, and I had ridden her often enough. But I had never tried to stand up on her. Robert set her cantering around the field and Jack and I rode astride together, me sitting before him. Then he got to his feet and tried to help me up. The pace, which seemed as smooth and as easy as a rocking chair when I had been seated on her back, was suddenly as jolting as a cart over cobbles. With a helpless wail I went off first one side, and then the other. And one time, earning myself a handful of curses and a cuff on the ear from Jack, I knocked him off the back of the horse as I went.

Robert called the practice to a halt when I had managed to get up and stand for a few seconds. 'Do it again tomorrow,' he said, as mean with praise as ever. 'Not bad.'

Jack and I went down to the river together and stripped off down to our sweat-stained shirts, and waded into the water to cool our bruises and our tempers. I floated on my back in the sweet water and looked up at the blue sky. It was September and still as hot as high summer. My pale limbs in the water were as white as a drowned man. I kicked a fountain of spray upwards and then looked at my feet with the ingrained dirt around the toenails with no sense of shame. I turned on my front and dipped my face into the water and then dived right under until I could feel the cold water seeping through my curls to my scalp. That made me shudder and I surfaced again, kicking and blowing out, and shaking the wet hair out of my eyes. Jack was out already, lying on the grassy bank in his breeches, watching me.

I came out of the water and it flowed in streams down my neck. The shirt was slick and cold against me and Jack's eyes followed the little rivulets of water down over my slight breasts where the nipples stood out against the wet thin fabric, down to the crotch of my legs where the shadow of copper hair showed dark under the cloth.

'D'you not mind working as hard as a lad when you're growing into a woman?' he asked idly.

'No,' I said shortly. 'I'd rather be treated as a lad by your father and you.'

Jack smiled his hot smile. 'By my father, yes possibly. But by me? Wouldn't you like me to see you as a young woman?'

I walked steadily on the sharp stones at the river edge on my hardened feet and picked up my jerkin and pulled it on. I was still bare-arsed but Jack's knowing smile had never caused me any discomfort and I was untroubled by his sudden interest in me.

'No,' I said, 'I've seen how you are with women.'

His hand waved them away down river. 'Those!' he said dismissively. 'Those are just sluts from the villages. I would not treat you in the way I treat them. You'd be a prize worth taking, Meridon. You in your funny breeches and my cut-down shirts. I'd like to make you glad to be born a woman. I'd like you to grow your hair to please me.'

I turned and looked at him in frank surprise.

'Why?' I said.

He shrugged, half moody, half wilful. 'I don't know,' he said. 'You never look twice at me. You never have looked twice at me. All this morning you have been in my arms and you have clung to me to save yourself from falling. All this morning you have had your body pressed tight against mine and I was feeling you, aye – and wanting you! And then you strip your clothes off in front of me and get into the water as if I was nothing more than one of the horses!'

I stood up and pulled on my breeches. 'D'you remember what your da said to Dandy our first evening?' I asked. 'I do. He warned her off you. He told her and he told me that he had a good marriage in mind for you and that if she ever became your lover he'd leave her on the road. She's not looked at you since that evening, and neither have I.'

'She!' he said in the same voice as he had spoken of the village girls. 'She'd come fast enough to my whistle. I know that. But don't tell me that you don't think of me to please my da, because I don't believe it.'

'No', I said truthfully, careless of vanity. 'No, it's not the reason. I don't think of you because I have no interest in you. It's true: I don't think of you any more than I do the horses.' I considered him for a moment, and then some spark of devilry prompted me to say, absolutely straight-faced, 'Actually, I think I like Snow better.'

He stared at me incredulous for a moment, then with one graceful easy movement he jumped to his feet and walked away from me. 'Gypsy brat,' he said under his breath as he went away. I dropped back down on the bank and watched the sunshine on the ripples of the river and waited until he was well out of earshot before I laughed aloud.

He did not bear me a grudge for that insult, for the next day he held me as firmly and as fairly as he had done the day before. It was my fault that I fell more and more often, and my fault when he lost his balance and fell backwards off the horse, and fell hard too, and hit his head.

'Clumsy wench!' Robert had scolded me, and clouted me lightly on my ear which made my own head ring. 'Why don't you lean back and let Jack guide you like you were doing yesterday? He's had the practice. He's got the balance. Let him take you. Don't keep trying to pull away and stand on your own!'

Jack was holding his head in his hands but he looked up at that and he smiled at me ruefully. 'Is that what's going wrong?' he asked frankly. 'You won't lean back against me?'

I nodded. His black eyes smiled into my green ones.

'Oh forget it!' he said gently. 'Forget I ever said it. I can't go on falling off a horse all morning. Let's just do the act, shall we?'

Robert looked from one to the other of us. 'Have you two had a fight?' he demanded.

We were both silent.

He took three steps away from us and then turned and came back. His face was stony. 'Now look here, you two,' he said. 'I'll tell you this once, and it's the only time. Whatever goes on outside the ring, or even behind the screen, once you are in the ring and up on the horse you are working. I don't care if you take an axe to each other when your act is over. You can't work for me unless you take this seriously. And you are not serious unless you forget everything – everything – but your act.'

We nodded. Robert could be very impressive when he chose. 'Now have another try,' he said, and cracked the whip and called to Bluebell to canter.

Jack vaulted up and went astride her and put his hand out to catch me and pull me up before him. He held the leather strap and got to his feet, his bare toes splayed out on Bluebell's sweaty white and brown back. Then I felt his hard hand clutching in my armpit and I got up to my feet, gracelessly bow-legged, and then, while Robert shouted encouragement and abuse, I cautiously straightened my knees and leaned back towards Jack and let his body guide mine and his arm steady me. We did one whole circle without falling and then Jack let me jump down with a triumphant yell and somersaulted off himself.

'Well done!' Robert said. He was beaming at us with red-faced delight. 'Well done you both. Same time tomorrow.'

We nodded and Jack clapped my shoulder with a friendly hand as I turned away and took Bluebell by the head collar to lead her around and cool her down.

'Mamselle Meridon the Bareback Horse Dancer!' Robert said to himself very low, as he walked past the screen out of the field. 'See Her Breathtaking Leaps Through a Hoop of Blazing Fire!'

4

Dandy and I had not been raised as proper gypsy chavvies. When the weather had grown colder and the caravan was so clammy that even the clothes we slept in were damp in the morning, Da would get work as an ostler or a porter or a market lad in any of the bigger towns where people were not particular whom they employed, and the Parish officers were slow and lazy and did not move us on. We had no idea of a rhythm of seasons which took you regularly from one place to another and then returned you safe every winter to familiar fields and hills. With Da often as not we were on the run from card partners, little cheats or bad business deals, with no planned route or tradition of travelling. He never knew where he was going, other than to follow his nose for gullible card players, fools and bad horses, wherever they might be gathered together.

Travelling with Gower's Show was a different life. We never lingered in any one place because Robert had found a friend or had taken a fancy to a town. We moved fast and we moved regularly, every three days or sooner if the crowds showed any signs of slackening. We only stayed longer if we were working alongside a big fair which could pull crowds from miles and miles about. But at the end of October the season of the fairs was waning and the weather was getting colder. In the mornings I had to break the ice on the water buckets and the stallion had a blanket strapped on him at night.

'Last week this week,' Robert said when we stopped for dinner. Jack and I had been practising our bareback riding and for the first time I had stood without him holding me, though I still needed to keep a tight grip on the strap.

'Last week for what?' Dandy asked. She was slicing bread and she did not look up as she spoke.

'Last week on the road,' Robert said, as if everyone knew already. 'We'll go into winter quarters next week. Down at my house at Warminster. Then we'll really start to work.'

'Warminster?' I said blankly. 'I didn't know you had a house at Warminster.'

'Lots you don't know,' Robert said cordially through a hunk of bread and cheese. 'You don't know what you'll be doing next season yet. Nor does she,' he said indicating Dandy with a wave of bread and a wink to her. 'Lots of ideas. Lots of plans.'

'Is the barn ready?' Jack asked him.

'Aye,' Robert said with satisfaction. 'And the man is coming to teach us about the rigging and how the act is done. He says he'll stay for two months, but I've got him on a bonus to teach the two of you quicker. He says two months are enough to start someone off if they've got the knack for it.'

'For what?' I demanded, unable to contain my curiosity.

'Lots you don't know,' Robert said slyly. He took a great bite of bread and cheese. 'Gower's Amazing Aerial Show,' he said muffled. 'See the Horses and the Daring Bareback Riders! Thrill to the Dazzling Aerial Display! Laugh at the Pierrot and the Wonderhorse Dancing! See the Flying Ballerina! Gower's Flying Riding Show – All the Elements in One Great Show!'

'Elements?' I queried.

'Fire,' he said, pointing the crust of bread at me. 'That's you, jumping through a blazing hoop. Air: that's Dandy, she and Jack are going to train as a trapeze act. Earth is the horses and Water I don't know yet. But I'll think of something.'

'A trapeze act!' Dandy slumped down in her seat and I looked quickly at her. My own head was pounding in fright at the thought of her being up high and swinging from some perilous rope. But her eyes were shining. 'And I get a short costume!' she exclaimed.

'One that shows your pretty legs!' Robert confirmed, smiling at her. 'Dandy, my girl, you were born a whore!'

'With sequins,' she stipulated.

'Is it safe?' I interrupted. 'How will she ever learn to do it?'

'We've got the act from Bristol coming to stay with us. He'll teach Dandy, and Jack as well, how it's done. You'll learn too, my girl, see if we can conquer that fear of yours. An act with two girls up on the swings would be grand.'

The mouthful I had just swallowed came up from my belly into my throat again and I choked and retched and then pushed away from the table and bolted for the door. I was sick outside, vomiting the bread and cheese under the front wheel. I waited until I was steady and then I came in again, white faced, to where they were waiting, staring at me in amazement.

'Were you sick at the thought of it?' Robert demanded. He was so stunned he had forgotten to eat and was still holding his bread in mid air. 'Was that it, lass? Or are you ill?'

'I am not ill,' I said. The metalic slick in my mouth made me swallow and reach for my mug of small ale. 'I'm not ill in myself,' I said. 'But the thought of having to go up high on one of those things does make me ill. I am sick with fright.'

Jack looked at me with interest. 'Well that's an odd thing,' he said unsympathetically. 'I'd never have thought Meridon was nervy. But she's as missish as a lady.'

'Leave her be,' Dandy said calmly. 'You leave her be, Robert. I'm happy to learn how to do it. And if I am doing the Aerial Act you'll need Meridon to do the horses. She can't do both.'

'Maybe not,' Robert said half convinced. 'And if the worst comes to the worst I could always buy a poorhouse girl and have her trained.'

I gulped again, thinking of the girl straight out of the work-house in conditions worse than a prison and up a ladder to swing on a trapeze. But I nodded to Robert. I had no sympathy to waste on a stranger. I had no tenderness to spare. There was only one person in the world for me, and she was happy.

'Yes, you do that,' I said. 'You know I'd try anything with the horses. But I cannot go up a ladder.'

Robert smiled. 'You're to give it a try,' he said firmly. 'A fair try. No one will force you to go up high but you'll wait and see the swing before you make up your mind, Meridon.'

'I'll have too much to do with the horses,' I said defensively. 'I can't be a bareback rider and swing on a trapeze.'

'Jack will,' he said. 'You can too. I give you my word, Meridon; I won't force you, but you're to give it a try. That's fair.'

It was not fair, but I had reached the hard core in Robert where he would not be moved.

'All right,' I said sullenly. 'I promise I'll try, and you promise that if I can't do it, you get someone else in.'

'Good girl,' he said as though I had agreed rather than been forced into it. 'And you'll have plenty of learning with the horses. I'll have you dancing bareback, aye, and going through a hoop of fire before the next season.'

I thought that was ambitious and I glanced at Jack but he had never in his life spoken one word against his father.

'Can I learn it that quick?' I asked.

'Going to have to, lass,' Robert replied with finality. 'I'm not housing you and feeding you all winter for love of your green eyes. You're going to work for your living at Warminster as you do now. Training the horses, and learning a bareback act, and doing what the trapeze man tells you. And you, miss,' he turned sharply to Dandy. 'You will get yourself off to a wise woman in the village and have her tell you about how to avoid getting a belly on you. I'm not spending a fortune training you how to swing from a trapeze to see you up there fat with a whelp. And you keep away from the village lads, too, d'you hear? It's a respectable village, Warminster, and I go there every winter. I want no trouble with my neighbours.'

We both nodded obediently. But Dandy caught my eye and winked at me in anticipation. I smiled back at her. I had never slept under a roof but always a wagon, always in a narrow bunk within touching distance of four other people. It would make me feel like Quality to get into my own bed. It would be like being a lady. It would be like being at Wide.

I took that thought with me to bed, after I had rubbed down the horses and eaten my supper nodding over my bowl with weariness. That thought took me in my dream to Wide.

I saw it so clearly that I could draw a map of it. The pale lovely sandstone house in the new style with a round turret at one end which makes a pretty rounded parlour in the west corner. That room catches the sun in the evening and there are window seats upholstered with pink velvet where you can sit and watch the sun set over the high high green hills which surround the little valley. The house faces south, down a long winding avenue of tall beech trees which would have been old when my ma was young, even when her ma was young. At the bottom of the drive is a pair of great wrought-iron gates. They have rusted on their hinges and are left open. The family, my family, never wants them shut. For out of the drive and down the lane is the source of their wealth, or our wealth. The little village with a new-built church and a row of spanking new cottages one side of the only street; and a pretty vicarage and a cobbler and a smithy and a carter's cottage and stable yard on the other side.

These are the people of Wide. These are my people, and this is where I belong. However much I might love the travelling life with the Gowers, I knew this was my home. And in my dream of Wide I knew – knew without a shadow of doubt – that I was not a gypsy's brat. I was not Meridon Cox of Gower's Amazing Equestrian Event. I was Sarah. Sarah of Wide. And one day I would be back there.

I awoke on that thought and stared at the ceiling of the wagon. This caravan was not damp like the other and there were no strange-shaped damp patches to make boggart faces and frighten me. I squeezed my finger into the hole in my straw mattress and felt for the scrap of cloth which I had twisted and hidden there. I hooked it out and unwrapped it, leaning on one elbow to hold it to the grey light filtering in through the sprigged curtains at the window. The string was grimy and old but the clasp was still shiny. It still said 'Celia' on one side and 'John' on the other, names of people I did not know. But they must have known me. Why else should I have all that was left of Celia's necklace? And I heard a voice, not my own voice but a voice in my head, call longingly, but without hope of an answer: 'Mama.'

The next day was our last day and we gave only one performance which was ill attended. It was too cold for people to relish sitting on the damp grass for long, the horses were surly and unwilling to work, and Jack was chilled in his shirtsleeves.

'Time to move,' Robert said counting the gate money in the swinging bag. 'We'll start now and stop at suppertime. Get the loading done, you three, I'm going to the village.' He shrugged on his tweed jacket and pulled on his ordinary boots and set off down the lane. Dandy scowled at his back.

'Aye, push off when there's work to be done,' she said softly. 'Leave two girls and your son to do all the hard work.' She looked at me. 'The more money that man makes, the greedier and the lazier he becomes,' she said.

'Is he making money?' I asked. I had noticed no great change, but Dandy kept the gate and knew as well as Robert how the money bag had been growing heavier.

'Yes,' she said shortly. 'He is taking shillings and pounds every day and he pays us in pennies. Hi Jack!' she called suddenly. 'How much does your da pay you?'

Jack was folding up the costumes and putting them carefully in a great wooden chest bound with hoops which would slide under one of the bunks. The props and saddles and feed were strapped on top or slung alongside the wagon. He looked up at Dandy.

'Why d'you want to know?' he asked suspiciously.

'Just curious,' she replied. She undid the bolts which held the screen together and unhitched one of the panels. 'He's doing all right, isn't he, your da?' she said. 'Doing all right for money. And this new show he's planning for next season. That'll be a big earner, won't it?'

Jack slid a sideways glance at her, his eyes crinkled. 'So what, Miss Dandy?' he asked.

'Well what d'you get?' she asked reasonably. 'Me and Meridon get pennies a week – depending what we do. If I knew how much you got, I'd know how much I ought to ask for the flying act.'

Jack straightened up. 'You think you're worth as much as me?' he said derisively. 'All you've got is a pretty face and nice legs. I work with the horses, I paint the screen, I plan the acts, I cry it up, I'm a bareback rider with a full riding act.'

Dandy stood her ground. 'I'm worth three-quarters what you

are,' she said stubbornly. 'I never said I should have as much. But I should get at least three-quarters what you earn if I'm on the trapeze.'

Jack gave a triumphant shout of laughter and swung the heavy box up on to his shoulder. 'Done!' he said. 'And may you never make a better deal! Done, you silly tart! Because he pays me nothing! And you've just bargained your way into three quarters of nothing.'

He marched towards the wagon, laughing loudly at Dandy's mistake and swung the box down to the floor with a heavy crash. Dandy exchanged a look with me, lowered the wing of the screen gently to the grass and went to unbolt the other side.

'That's not right,' she said to him when he came back to steady the screen for her. 'That's not fair. You said yourself how much work you do for him. It's not right that he should pay you nothing. He treats us better and we are not even family.'

Jack lowered the centre section of the screen down to the ground and straightened up before he answered. Then he looked from Dandy to me as if he were wondering whether or no to tell us something.

'You don't know much, you two,' he said finally. 'You see the show and you hear about Da's plans. But you don't know much. We weren't always show people. We weren't always doing well. You see him now at his best, how he is when he has money in the sack under his bed and a string of horses behind the wagon. But when I was a little lad we were poor, deathly poor. And when he is poor he is a very hard man indeed.'

We were standing in a sheltered field in bright autumn sunshine but at Jack's words I shivered as if the frost had got down my neck, his face was as dark as if there were snow clouds across the sun.

'I'll have the show when he is too old to travel,' he said with confidence. 'Every penny he saves now goes into the show, or goes into our savings. We'll never be poor again. He'll see to that. And anything he says I should do . . . I do. And anything he says he needs . . . I get. Because it was him and one bow-backed horse that earned us food when the whole village was starving. No one else believed he could do it. Just me. So when he took the horse on the road I went with him. We didn't even have a wagon then. We just walked at the horse's head from village to village and did tricks for pennies. And he traded the horse for another, and another, and another. He is no fool, my da. I never go against him.'

Dandy said not a word. We were both spellbound by Jack's story.

'How was he a hard man?' I asked, going to the central question for me. How he would treat us, how he would treat Dandy if the tide of luck started going against us? 'Did he used to hit you? Or your mother? Did she travel with you too?'

Jack shook his head and bent down so that Dandy and I could lift the screen on to his back. He walked with it towards the wagon, dragging it behind him, and then he came back.

'He's never raised his hand to me,' he said. 'He never laid a finger on my ma. But she didn't believe in him. He left her and the three little ones in the village and went on the tramp with the horse. He'd have left me behind too but he knew I was the only one that believed he could do it. He had me trained to ride on the horse within days. I was only a littl'un and I was scared of nothing. Besides, it's a very big horseback when you're only five or six. It was easy to stay on.

'At the end of the summer we went home. He'd been sending money back when he could. And after the winter we started out again. This time there was a cart we could borrow. Ma wanted to come too, but Da was against it. But she cried and said she needed to be with him. I wanted her. And Da wanted the little ones along with him. So we all went on the road.'

Jack stopped. Then he bent for the final section of screen and loaded it in silence. Dandy and I said nothing. He came back and picked up a couple of halters and slung them towards the wagon. He turned and went for the gate as if the story was over.

We went after him.

'What happened then, Jack?' I asked. 'When you were all travelling together?'

Jack sighed and leaned on the gate, looking across the field as if he could see the wagon and the woman with the two small children and the baby at the breast. The man walking with his son at the horse's head, the horse which he had trained to dance for pennies.

'It was a grand season,' he said. 'Warm, and sunny. A good harvest and there was money about. We went from fair to fair and we did well at every one of them. Da had enough money to buy the cart and then he exchanged it for a proper wagon. Then he saw a horse he fancied and bought her. That's Bluebell that we have now. He saw she had a big enough back for me as I grew bigger. And she's steady.

'We had two horses then so we didn't work the street corners any more but we took a field and started to take money at the gate. I had an act jumping from one horse to another, and through a hoop. I was still quite small you see – I must have been about seven or eight.

'Ma was on the gate, and the little babbies sold sweets that she made to the audience. We were making good money.'

He stopped again.

'And?' Dandy prompted.

Jack shrugged. Shook the past off his shoulders with one quick movement and then a long stretch. 'Oh!' he said wearily. 'She was just a woman! Da saw Snow and wanted to buy him. Ma wanted to go back to the village with the money we'd made and settle down and Da go back to cartering.

'They argued about it – night and day. Da wanting Snow with all his heart and promising Ma that he'd make his fortune with the horse. That she'd have a cottage of her own and a comfortable wagon for travelling. That we'd move up in the world. He knew he could do it with Snow.

'Ma couldn't win the argument. She didn't understand the business anyway. So she went to a wise woman and got herself a brew from the old witch and then told Da – pleased as punch – that she was pregnant and that there would be no money for Snow. And that she would not give birth to a child on the road but that they would have to go home.' Jack smiled, but his dark brown eyes were like cold mud. 'I can remember her telling him:

"I've caught you now,"' he said. 'She got a belly on herself to trap him.'

'What did your da do?' I asked.

'He left her,' Jack said briefly. 'All this happened at Exeter, our home was outside Plymouth. I never knew if she got herself home. Or the babbies. Or what happened to the one she had in her belly. He took the money he had been saving and bought Snow and we moved the next day. He wouldn't let her in the wagon though she begged and cried and my brothers and sister cried too. He just drove away from her, and when she tried to get up on the step he just pushed her down. She followed us along the road crying and asking him to let her in, but he just drove away. She only kept up for a mile or so, she had the little ones and they couldn't walk fast. And she was carrying the babby, of course. We heard her calls getting fainter and fainter as she fell further and further behind.'

'Did you ever see her again?' I asked, appalled. This calculated cruelty was worse than any of Da's drunken rages. He would never have left Zima so, whatever she had done. He would never have pushed Dandy and me off the step of the wagon.

'Never,' Jack said indifferently. 'But don't you forget that if my da can do that to his wife of fifteen years, who bore him four children and had his fifth in her belly, he can certainly do it to you two.'

I nodded in silence. But Dandy was angry.

'That's awful!' she exclaimed. 'Your ma most likely had to go on the Parish and they'd have taken her children away from her. She was ruined! And she had done nothing wrong!'

Jack swung up into the wagon and started stowing blankets and bedding for the journey.

'He thought she'd done wrong,' he said from the dark interior. 'That's enough for me. And she was cheating, getting a belly on her like that. Women always cheat. They won't do a straight deal with any man. She got what she deserved.'

Dandy would have said more, but I touched her on the arm and drew her away from the step, around to the back of the wagon to help me hump feed.

'I can hardly believe it!' she said in a muttered undertone. 'Robert always seems so nice!'

'I can believe it,' I said. I was always more wary than Dandy. I had watched Jack's unquestioning obedience to his father; and I had wondered how that round-faced smiling man could exert such invisible discipline.

'Just remember not to cross him, Dandy,' I said earnestly. 'Especially at Warminster.'

She nodded. 'I'm not going to be left on the road like his wife,' she said. 'I'd rather die first!'

That odd shudder, which I had felt when Jack started talking about his mother, put icy fingers down my spine again. I put out my hand to Dandy. 'Don't talk like that,' I said, and my voice was faint as if it were coming from a long way away. 'I don't like it.'

Dandy made an impudent laughing face at me. 'Miss Misery!' she said cheerily. 'Where are these buckets to go?'

It was sunset before we were packed and ready to leave – the sudden red sunset of autumn. Bluebell was between the shafts, her head nodding with pretended weariness. Jack was in his working breeches and smock. He was going to ride Snow the stallion, who was too valuable to be tied for a long journey like the ponies. He offered me the ride, but I was tired and felt lazy. If Robert did not order me to drive the wagon I would lie in my bunk and doze.

'You're getting as lazy as Dandy,' Jack said to me in an intimate undertone as we tied the ponies in a string at the back of the wagon. Da's little pony had settled down with the others and went obediently into line.

'I feel idle today,' I confessed, not looking up from the halter I was knotting.

His warm hand came down over my fingers as I tied the rope, and I looked up quickly to see his face, saturnine in the twilight.

'What do you dream of in your bunk, Meridon?' he asked softly. 'When you lie in your bunk and daydream and the ceiling is rocking above you. What d'you dream of then? Do you think of a lover who will take off your clothes, strip those silly boy's breeches off you, and kiss you and tell you that you are beautiful? Don't you dream of a clean bed in a warm room and me, lying in bed beside you? Is that what you think of?'

I left my hand under his warm clasp and I met his eyes with my steady green gaze.

'No,' I said. 'I dream that I am somewhere else. That my name is not Meridon. That I do not belong here. I never dream of you at all.'

His handsome dark face turned sulky in an instant. 'That's twice you've said that,' he complained. 'No other girl has ever turned away from me, not ever.'

I nodded fairly. 'Then chase them,' I said. 'You're wasting your time with me.'

He turned on his heel and left me abruptly. But he did not go back to the lighted wagon. I nearly bumped him as I came around the wagon with a hay net to hang on the side. He had been leaning against the wagon, brooding.

'You're cold, aren't you?' he accused. 'It is not that you don't like me. I've just been thinking. Dandy smiles at the old gentlemen and they chuck her under the chin and give her a ha'penny. But you never smile, do you? And now I think of it, I've never seen you let anyone touch you except Dandy. You don't even like men to look at you, do you? You won't come out to cry-up the show with me because men might look at you and desire you, and you don't like that, do you?'

I hesitated, a denial on my lips. But then I nodded. It was true. I hated the fumblings and the giggling. The dirty hands questing inside lice-ridden clothes. The tumblings behind hedges and haycocks and emerging shame-faced. It was as if my body had a pelt missing, my skin was too sensitive for a stranger's touch.

'I don't like it,' I said honestly. 'And I've never understood how Dandy can bear it. I hate the old men who want to touch me, I hate the way they look at me.

'I don't dislike you, Jack, but I will never desire you – nor anyone, I think.' I paused, turning over in my mind what I had just said. 'I'm not even sad about it,' I said. 'I've no father to care for me, and I wouldn't know how to keep house for a lover. I'm better off as I am.'

'Cold,' he said, taunting me.

'As ice,' I confirmed, quite unruffled. Then I heaved the heavy hay net up to the hook and pushed past him and went into the wagon.

Dandy was already in her bunk, combing out her black hair and singing under her breath in a low languorous hum. I climbed up into mine, and dozed off at once, barely waking when the caravan started rocking over the field and into the lane. I just opened my eyes and saw the open doorway and the stars ahead of us and heard the noise of many unshod hooves on the hard-packed mud as we headed for winter quarters and Warminster.

We stopped one night on the road. I tumbled out of my bunk to rub down Snow and Bluebell, to walk them down to the stream and let them drink when they were cool, and then the little ponies. The little ones were nervous in the dark and shied. One of them scraped my leg and trod on my toe and I cursed in a voice still husky with sleep but I was too dozy to cuff him.

We put them out on stakes because we were camped by the lane-side and did not want them wandering. Robert himself checked that the blankets were tied safe on Snow and Bluebell to keep them warm. Then we all took our suppers of bread and milk into our bunks, saying not a word to each other. We were all tired and we were used now to saying nothing when we were hard-worked on the road. It was the best and easiest way. We ate in silence, each one alone with private thoughts. Then Robert's tin mug clanked on the wooden floor as he dropped it down from his bunk empty and said, 'G'night,' into the darkness of the wagon. Then I heard Jack's mug drop, and Dandy's.

'Sarah?' Dandy whispered into the darkness, invoking my childhood love for her by use of my secret name.

'Yes?' I replied.

'You don't think he'd ever leave us behind, do you?' she asked.

I was silent for a moment, thinking. In the wordy, bargaining part of my mind I was very sure that Robert would leave Dandy, would leave me, would leave Jack his own son, if his upward struggle from his poverty demanded it. But there was a part of my mind which gave me shivers down my spine. It had given me my dream of wide, it had taught me that my name was Sarah and reminded me constantly that I belonged at Wide with my family. And that part of my mind was heavy with some kind of warning, like the distant rumble of a summer storm.

'I don't think he'll leave us behind,' I said slowly. A noise like thunder rolled in my inner ears. 'But there is no telling what he would do,' I said. I was afraid but I could not have named my fear. 'There is no knowing, Dandy. Don't upset him, will you?'

Dandy sighed. Her fear was gone as soon as she had expressed it to me. 'I can handle him,' she said arrogantly. 'He's just a man like any other.'

I heard the slats of her bunk creak as she turned over and went to sleep. I did not sleep, even though I was tired. I lay awake, my hands behind my head, looking with unseeing eyes at the ceiling which was so near my face, pattering softly with the sound of light rain. I lay and listened to the rain on the canvas and I thought it told me in a hundred tiny voices that Dandy was wrong. She could not manage Robert like any man. Indeed she could not manage men: even while she picked their pockets they were getting her cheap. She thought she was managing them; she prided herself on her skill. But they were cheating her – enjoying watching or fingering a pretty gypsy virgin, and cheap, very cheap indeed.

I shuddered and drew the covers closer up under my chin. The rain pattered softly, whispering like a priest in a Popish confession that there was only one safety for Dandy and me and that was to get away from this life altogether. To get away from the showgrounds and the fairs. To get away from the gawping villages and the street-corner mountebanks. I wanted to be safe with Dandy, safe in a Quality life with clean sheets, and good food on the table, fine dresses and days of leisure. Horses for riding, dogs for hunting, little canaries in cages and nothing to do all day but talk and sew and read and sing.

I wanted that life for Dandy and me – to save her from the world of the showgrounds and from the life of a whore. And for me: because I did not know what I would become. I could not stay in my boy's breeches and care for horses for ever. Jack was a warning to me as much as a threat. He might desire me a little, in his vain coquettish way. But other men might desire me more. I could keep my hair cropped and green eyes down, but that would not save me. There was no one in my life who would fight to keep me safe, or who would refuse a good price for me.

There was only one place where I would be safe. There was only one place where I could take Dandy and give her the things which delighted her and yet keep her from danger – Wide.

I knew it was my home.

I knew it was my refuge.

I had no idea where it was.

I sighed like an old lady who has reached the end of her musings and found she is no further forward. One day I would find Wide; I was sure of it. One day I would be safe. One day I would be able to make Dandy safe.

I turned on my side with that thought . . . and I fell asleep.

5

I don't know what I had expected of Warminster but the little grey-stoned main street with the three or four shops and two good inns pleased me. It looked like a place where nothing very much had ever happened or would happen. I looked around the broad main street and imagined the weekly market which would be held there: the stalls selling flour and bread and cheeses, the noise of the beasts from the sheep and cattle market. I was glad we were spending the winter here. It looked like a place where Dandy would find little scope for her talents of coaxing silver out of the pockets of old gentlemen – I was glad of that.

I leaned forwards to look about me and Robert Gower smiled at my eagerness, said proudly, 'Nearly there now,' and took a sharp left-hand turn off the cobbled main street down an unpaved mud lane. I expected a one-room upstairs, two-rooms downstairs cottage with a low roof and paper and rags stuffed in the windows, with a little patch of a kitchen garden at the front, and a field for the horses at the back.

'Gracious!' Dandy said as the wagon turned in off the track and we found ourselves in a handsome stable yard.

Robert Gower smiled. 'Surprised, little Miss Dandy?' he asked with satisfaction. 'I thought you would be! All your little nosiness into how much I earn and how much I pay never discovered that I'm a freeholder in a market town! Aye! I have a vote and all!' he said triumphantly.

He pulled the wagon up and Dandy and I got down. I went without thinking to the ponies at the back and untied them and brought them round. Robert nodded at me.

'Stabling I've got!' he said. 'Stabling for every one of them if I wanted them inside all winter eating their heads off and getting fat. They'll go out in the fields of course, but if I wanted to keep them in I could. Every single one of them. Ten loose boxes I've got here! Not bad, is it?'

'No,' I said, and I spoke the truth. It was a miracle of hard work and careful planning to bring a man from poverty to this secret affluence. And I respected him all the more that he could leave this comfort to travel in the wagon and work every day of the week for a long arduous season.

A door in the wall of the yard opened and a grey-haired woman came out dressed in her best apron with a matching white mob cap. She dipped Robert a curtsey as if he were Quality.

'Welcome home, sir!' she said. 'There's a fire in the parlour and in your bedroom when you are ready to come in. Shall I send the lad out for your bags?'

'Aye,' Robert said. 'And set tea for two in the parlour, Mrs Greaves. These two young women, Meridon and Dandy, will take their tea in the kitchen with you.'

She smiled pleasantly at me, but I frankly gaped at her. By travelling a few miles down a road Robert Gower had transformed himself into Quality. He and Jack made the transition. Dandy and I were what we always had been: Romany brats.

Jack saw the change too. He slid off Snow's back and handed the reins to me as if I were his groom. He passed Bluebell's leading rein to me as well, so that I was holding the string of ponies and the two big horses.

'Thank you, Meridon,' he said graciously. 'The lad will show you where they go,' and then he walked past me through the doorway to the house. Dandy, still on the step of the wagon, exchanged one long look with me.

'Phew,' she puffed out, and jumped down from the wagon to take the string of little ponies off me. 'Welcome to the servants' quarters, Merry!'

'Yes,' I said. 'No wonder Robert Gower didn't want Jack fancying either one of us. He must think he's half-way to being gentry!'

An odd sly look crossed Dandy's face, but she had her head down to the halter and was leading the ponies away so I could not see her properly. 'Aye,' she said over her shoulder. 'Our pretty Jack must be quite a catch for the young ladies of Warminster!'

Before I could answer her a lad came through the door to the stable yard. He was dressed well enough but cheaply in good breeches and a rough shirt and a fustian waistcoat. He took Bluebell's reins from me and patted her neck in greeting.

'I'm William,' he said by way of introduction.

'I'm Meridon Cox,' I replied. 'And this is my sister Dandy.'

His look went carefully over me, noting the slim-cut boy's riding breeches and the cut-down shirt; my tumble of copper curls and my wiry strength; and then widened when he saw Dandy, her red skirt casually hitched up to show her ankles, her green shawl setting off her mass of loosely plaited black hair.

'Do you work for Robert Gower?' he asked incredulously.

'I do the horses and Dandy does the gate,' I said.

'And are you the lasses that are going up on that swing?' he demanded of me.

My stomach churned at the thought of it. 'Maybe,' I said. 'My sister will, but I work with the horses. I just have to try it a little. I'm to be the bareback rider.'

'He's had the barn cleaned out, and the trapeze man came yesterday and put the ropes and the blocks and the pulleys up in it,' William said in a rush. 'Ever so high. And they've stretched a net like a fisherman's net underneath, to catch you if you fall. We tested it too with a couple of bales of hay to see if it's strong enough.

'The barn's filled with wood shavings from the wood mill – sacks and sacks of them. So when you're done with practising on the rigging, he can use the barn for training the horses when the weather's too bad to be outside.'

I nodded. Robert had meant it when he promised us a hard winter of work. 'And where do we sleep?' I asked. 'Where do we take our meals?'

'He's had the rooms above the stables done up for you,' William said. 'We've put two beds of straw in for you, and your own chest for your things. And your own ewer and basin. There's even a fireplace and we had the sweep in to clear it out for you. You'll eat at the kitchen table with Mrs Greaves and me.'

He showed us the way into the stables. Each door had a horse's name on it. William glanced at me and saw I was puzzling over the words, not knowing where I should take Snow.

'Can't you read?' he asked surprised. And taking the horse from me he led Snow into the best stall, furthest away from the door and from the draughts. Bluebell went in next door; and then the ponies, two to a loose box. I looked over the doors to see they all had hay and water.

'When they're cooled down they're to go out, all except Snow,' William said. 'Through that gateway, down the little path through the garden and there's a field at the bottom. You'll take them down.'

'What do you do?' I demanded, nettled at this allocation of work. 'Don't you look after them?'

William crinkled his brown eyes at me through his matted fringe.

'I does whatever I'm told,' he said, as if it were some private joke. 'Robert Gower took me out of the poorhouse. If he tells me to be a groom, I'm a groom. I was that last winter, and the one before that. But now that's your job and I do the heavy work in the house and anything else he asks me. Whatever he tells me to do, I does it. And as long as I please him, I sleep sound in a bed and I eat well. I ain't never going back into the poorhouse again.'

Dandy shot a look at me which spoke volumes. 'How much does he pay you?' she demanded.

William leaned against the stable door and scratched his head. 'He don't pay me,' he said. 'I gets my keep, same as Mrs Greaves and Jack.'

'Mrs Greaves gets no money?' I demanded, the picture of the smart respectable woman clear in my mind.

'He bought her out of the workhouse too,' William said. 'He gives her the housekeeping and she feeds well out of that. He gives her some money every quarter for her laundry bill and new aprons. But he doesn't pay her. What would she want money for?'

'For herself,' I said grimly. 'So that if she wanted to leave she could.'

William gave a slow chuckle. 'She wouldn't want to do that,' he said. 'No more than I would. Where would she go? There's only the workhouse, for there are no jobs going in the town, and no one would take a servant who had left without a character. There's plenty as tidy and neat as her in the workhouse – why should anyone take a woman off the street? Why should anyone pay wages when the workhouse is full of paupers who would work for free with their keep?' William paused and looked at Dandy and me. 'Does he pay you?' he asked.

I was about to say, 'Yes,' but then I paused. He did indeed pay me, a penny a day. But out of that princely sum I had repaid him for my shirt and my breeches, and I wanted to buy a jacket for the winter too. I had no savings from my wages. He had paid out the pennies and when I had saved them into shillings, I had paid them back. I looked at Dandy; he paid her the odd penny for minding the gate and she still picked the occasional pocket. 'Do you have any money saved, Dandy?' I asked.

'No,' she said. 'I had to repay Robert for the material for my riding habit. I still owe him a couple of shillings.'

'We're all treated the same then,' William said with doltish satisfaction. 'But you have a real pretty room of your own up the ladder.'

He pointed to a rough wooden staircase without a handrail which went up the side of the stable wall. I checked that all the horses were safely bolted in, and then Dandy and I clattered up the twelve steps to the trapdoor at the top. It lifted up and we were in the first room we had ever owned in our lives.

It was a bare clean space with two mattresses of straw with blankets in each corner, a great chest under the window, a fire of sticks laid in the little black grate, and two little windows looking out over the stable yard. The walls were finished in the rough creamy-coloured mud of the region, and the sloping ceiling which came down to the top of the windows was the underside of the thatched roof – a mesh of sticks and straw.

'How lovely!' Dandy said with delight. 'A proper room of our own.'

She went at once to the broken bit of mirror which was nailed to one of the beams running crosswise across the room and smoothed her hair back from her face. 'A looking glass of my own,' she breathed, promising herself hours of delight. Then she dropped to her knees and examined the ewer and bowl standing in lonely state on the chest. 'Real pretty,' she said with approval.

I ducked my head to look out of the window. I could see over the stable yard and across the lane to the yard and cottage on the far side. Beyond them was a glimpse of green fields and the glitter of light on a broad river.

William's brown head appeared comically though the trap-door. 'Come for your tea,' he invited. 'It's ready in the kitchen. You can bring your things up later.'

Dandy rounded on him with all the pride of a property dweller. 'Don't you know to knock when you come to a lady's bedroom!' she exclaimed, irritated.

William's round face lost its smile and his face coloured brick red with embarrassment. 'Beg pardon,' he mumbled uncomfortably, and then ducked down out of sight. 'But tea is ready,' he called stubbornly.

'We'll come,' I said and taking Dandy firmly by the arm I got her away from the mirror and the ewer and would not even let her stop to examine the great chest for the clothes we had not got.

Our first two days in Warminster were easy. All I had to do was to care for the horses, to groom them and water them, and discover the boredom of cleaning out the same stable over and over again. Travelling with horses I had never had to wash down cobblestones in my life, and I did not enjoy learning from William.

Dandy was equally surly when Mrs Greaves called her into the kitchen and offered her a plain grey skirt and a white pinny.

She clutched to her red skirt and green shawl and refused to be parted from them.

'Master's orders,' Mrs Greaves said briefly. She stole Dandy's finery while she was sulkily changing, and took them away to be washed but then did not return them. Dandy collared Robert as he was inspecting the stable the same afternoon.

'I warned you,' he said genially. 'I told you there'd be no whoring around this village. They're God-fearing people, and my neighbours. You'll cause all the stir you want at church tomorrow morning without being as bright as a Romany whore.'

'I'll not go to church!' Dandy said, genuinely shocked. 'I ain't never been!'

Robert glanced at me. 'You neither, Meridon?' he asked. I shook my head.

'Not been christened?' he asked in as much horror as if he had been anything but godless himself when we were on the road.

'Oh aye,' Dandy said with reasonable pride. 'Lots of times. Every time the preacher came round we was christened. For the penny they gives you. But we never go to church.'

Robert nodded. 'Well you'll go now,' he said. 'All my household do.' He looked at me under his bushy blond eyebrows. 'Mrs Greaves has a gown for you too, Meridon. You'll have to wear it for going in the village.'

I stared back, measuring the possibility of defiance. 'Don't try it my girl,' he advised me. His voice was gentle but there was steel behind it. 'Don't dream of it. I'm as much the master here as I am when we're in the ring. We play a part there, and we play a part here. In this village you are respectable young women. You have to wear a skirt.'

I nodded, saying nothing.

'You always did wear a dress, didn't you?' he asked. 'That first day I saw you, you were training the horse in some ragged skirt, weren't you? And you rode astride in a skirt as well, didn't you?'

'Yes,' I admitted. 'But I like boy's breeches better. They're easier to work in.'

'You can wear them for work,' he said. 'But not outside the stable yard.'

I nodded. Dandy waited till his back was turned and then she picked up her dull long grey skirt and swept him a curtsey. 'Mountebank squire,' she said; but not so loud as he could hear.

I said nothing about the dress destined for me. But that night, at supper in the kitchen, Mrs Greaves pushed a petticoat, chemise, grey dress and pinny across the wide scrubbed table. There was even a plain white cap folded stiffly on top of the pile of clothes.

'For church tomorrow,' she said.

I raised my green eyes to her pale blue ones. 'What if I don't want to go?' I asked.

Her face was like a pat of butter smoothed blank by fear and suffering. 'Better had,' she said.

I picked them up without a word.

They were strange to put on next morning. Dandy helped me with them, and spent hours herself, plaiting and replaiting her hair until it was to her satisfaction in a glossy coronet with the little white cap perched on top as far back as she dared. In absolute contrast I had pulled my cap down low, and stuffed as much of my copper mop inside as I possibly could. I regretted now my impatient hacking of my hair with the big scissors we used to trim the horses' tails. If it had been longer I could have tied it back. Cut ragged, it was a riot of curls which continually sprang out.

I straightened the cap in front of the mirror. Dandy was retying her pinny ribbon and not watching me. I stared at myself in the glass. It was a much clearer reflection than the water trough beneath a pump, I had never seen myself so well before. I saw my eyes, their shifting hazel-green colour, the set of them slanty. My pale clear skin and the fading speckle of summertime freckles. The riotous thick curly auburn hair, and the mouth which smiled, as if at some inner secret, even though my eyes were cold. Even though I had little to smile for.

'You could be pretty,' Dandy said. Her round pink face appeared beside mine. 'You could be really pretty,' she said encouragingly, 'if you weren't so odd-looking. If you smiled at the boys a bit.'

I stepped back from the little bit of mirror.

'They've got nothing I want,' I said. 'Nothing to smile for.'

Dandy licked her fingers to make them damp and twirled her fringe and the ringlets at the side of her face.

'What do you want then?' she said idly. 'What d'you want that a boy can't give you?'

'I want Wide,' I said instantly.

She turned and stared at me. 'You're going to have a silk shirt and breeches, aye and a riding habit, and you still dream of that?' she asked in amazement. 'We've got away from Da, and we can earn a penny a day, and we eat so well, and we can wear clothes as fine as Quality and everyone looks at us. Everyone! Every girl wishes she could wear velvets like me! And you still think of that old stuff?'

''Tisn't old stuff!' I said, passionate. ''Tisn't old stuff. It's a secret. You were glad enough to hear about it when there was just you and me against Da and Zima. I don't break faith just because I've got a place in service.'

'Service!' Dandy spat. 'Don't call this service. I dress as fine as Quality in my costume!'

'It's costume,' I said angrily. 'Only a silly Rom slut like you would think it was as fine as Quality, Dandy. You look at real ladies, they don't wear gilt and dyed feathers like you. The real ones dress in fine silks, cloth so good it stands stiff on its own. They don't wear ten gilt bangles, they wear one bracelet of real gold. Their clothes ain't dirty. They keep their voices quiet. They're nothing like us, nothing like us at all.'

Dandy sprang at me, quicker than I could fend her off. Her two hands were stretched into claws and she went straight for my eyes, and raked a scratch down my cheek. I was stronger than her, but she had the advantage of being heavier – and she was as angry as a scalded cat.

'I *am* as good as Quality,' she said, and pulled at my cap. It was pinned to my hair and the sharp pain as some hair came out made me shriek in pain and blindly strike back at her. I had made a fist, as instinctive as her scratching hands, and I caught her on the jaw with a satisfying thud and she reeled backwards.

'Meridon, you cow!' she bawled at me and came for me at a half run and bowled me back on to my straw mattress and sat, with her heavier weight, while I wriggled and tossed beneath her.

Then I lay still. 'Oh, what's the use?' I said wearily. She released me and stood up and went at once to the mirror to see if I had bruised her flower-white skin. I sat up and put a hand to my cheek. It stung. She had drawn blood. 'We've always seen different,' I said sadly, looking at her across the little room. 'You thought you might marry Quality from that dirty little wagon with Da and Zima. Now you think you're as good as Quality because you're a caller for a travelling show. You might be right, Dandy, it's just never seemed that wonderful to me.'

She looked at me over her shoulder, her pink mouth a perfect rosebud of discontent. 'I shall have great opportunities,' she said stubbornly, stumbling over one of Robert's words. 'I shall take my pick when I am ready. When I am Mademoiselle Dandy on the flying trapeze I will have more than enough offers. Jack himself will come to my beck then.'

I put my hand to my head and brought it down wet with blood. I unpinned my cap hoping it was still clean, but it was marked. I would have complained, but what Dandy said made me hold my peace.

'I thought you'd given up on Jack,' I said cautiously. 'You know what his da plans for him.'

Dandy primped her fringe again. 'I know you thought that,' she said smugly. 'And so does his da. And so probably does he. But now I've seen what he's worth, I think I'll have him.'

'Have to catch him first,' I said. I was deliberately guarding myself against the panic which was rising in me. Dandy was wilfully blind to the tyrannical power of Robert Gower. If she thought she could trick his son into marriage, and herself into the lady's chair in the parlour which we had not been even allowed to enter, then she was mad with her vanity. She could tempt Jack – I was sure of it. But she would not be able to trick Robert Gower. I thought of the wife he had left behind him, crying in the road behind a vanishing cart, and I felt that prickle of fear down my spine.

'Leave it be, Dandy,' I begged her. 'There'll be many chances for you. Jack Gower is only the first of them.'

She smiled at her reflection, watching the dimples in her cheeks.

'I know,' she said smugly. Then she turned to look at me, and at once her expression changed. 'Oh Merry! Little Merry! I didn't mean to hurt you so!' She made a little rush for the ewer and wetted the edge of my blanket and dabbed with the moist wool at my head and my cheek, making little apologetic noises of distress. 'I'm a cow,' she said remorsefully. 'I'm sorry, Merry.'

'S'all right,' I said. I bore her ministrations patiently, but to be patted and stroked set my teeth on edge. 'What's that noise?'

'It's Robert in the yard,' Dandy said and flew for the trapdoor down to the ladder. 'He's ready for church and Jack and Mrs Greaves and even William with him. Come on, Merry, he's waiting.'

She clattered down the stairs into the yard and I swung open the little window. I had to stoop to lean out.

'I'm not coming,' I called down.

Robert stared up at me. 'Why's that?' he asked. His voice was hard. His Warminster, landlord voice.

He squinted against the low winter sun.

'You two been having a cat-fight?' he asked Dandy, turning sharply on her.

She smiled at him, inviting him to share the jest. 'Yes,' she said. 'But we're all friends now.'

Without a change of expression, Robert struck her hard across the face, a blow that sent her reeling back. Mrs Greaves put out a hand to steady her on her feet, her face impassive.

'Your faces – aye and your hands and your legs and your arms – are your fortunes, my girls,' Robert said evenly, without raising his voice. 'If you two fight you must do it without leaving a mark on each other. If I wanted to do a show tomorrow I could not use Merry in the ring. If you get a black bruise on your chin you're no good for calling nor on the gate for a week. If you two can't put my business first I can find girls who can. Quarrelsome sluts are two a penny. I can get them out of the workhouse any day.'

'You can't get bareback riders,' Dandy said, her voice low.

Robert rounded on her. 'Aye, so I'd keep your sister,' he said meanly. 'It's you I don't need. It's you I never needed. You're here on her ticket. So go back up and wipe her face and get her down here. You two little heathens are going to church, and mind Mrs Greaves and don't shame me.'

He turned and strode out of the yard with Jack. He didn't even look to see if we followed. Mrs Greaves waited till I tumbled down the stable stairs pulling on my cap and patting my cheek with the back of my hand before leading the way out of the yard. Dandy and I exchanged one subdued glance and followed her, side by side. William fell in behind us. I felt no malice towards Dandy for the fight. I felt no anger towards Robert for the blow he had fetched her. Dandy and I had been reared in a hard school, we were both used to knocks – far heavier and less deserved than that. What I did not like was Robert's readiness to throw us off. I scowled at that as we turned out of the gate and walked to our right down the lane towards the village church.

There was a fair crowd beside the church gate and I was glad then that I had not kept my breeches. All the way up the path to the church door heads were turned and fingers pointed us out as the show girls. I saw why Robert had been so insistent that we behave like Quaker servant girls and dress like them too.

He was establishing his gentility inch by inch in his censorious little village. He was buying his way in with his charities, he was wringing respect out of them with his wealth. He dared not risk a whisper of notoriety about his household. Show girls we might be, but no one could ever accuse any of Robert Gower's people of lowering the tone.

Dandy glanced around as we walked and even risked a tiny sideways smile at a group of lads waiting by the church door. But Robert Gower looked back and she quickly switched her gaze to her new boots and was forced to walk past them without even a swing of the hips.

I kept my eyes down. I did not need a glance of admiration from any man, least of all a callow youth. Besides, I had something on my mind. I did not like the Warminster Robert Gower as I had liked the man on the steps of the wagon. He was too clearly a hard man with a goal in sight and nothing, least of all two little gypsy girls, would turn him from it. He had felt that he did not belong in the parish workhouse. He had felt that he did not belong in a dirty cottage with a failed cartering business of his own. His first horse had been a starting point. The wagon and the Warminster house were later steps on the road to gentility. He wanted to be a master of his trade – even though his trade was a travelling show. He had felt, as I did, that his life should be wider, grander. And he had made – as I was starting to hope that I might make – that great step from poverty to affluence.

But he paid for it. In all the restrictions which this narrow-minded village placed on him. So here his voice was harder, he had struck Dandy, and he had told us both that he was ready to throw us off.

I, too, wanted to step further. I understood his determination because I shared it. I wanted to take the two of us away. I wanted to step right away from the life of gilt and sweat. I wanted to sit in a pink south-facing parlour and take tea from a clean cup. I wanted to be Quality. I wanted Wide.

I watched him and Mrs Greaves closely and I kneeled when they kneeled and I stood when they stood. I turned the page of the prayer book when they did, though I could not read the words. I mouthed the prayers and I opened my mouth and bawled 'la la la' for the hymns. I followed them in every detail of behaviour so that Robert Gower could have no cause for complaint. For until I could get us safely away, Robert Gower was our raft on the sea of poverty. I would cling to him as if I adored him, until it was safe to leave him, until I had somewhere to take Dandy. Until I could see my way clear to a home for the two of us.

When we were bidden to pray I sank to my knees in the pew like some ranting Methody and buried my face in my calloused hands. While the preacher spoke of sin and contrition I had only one prayer, a passionate plea to a God I did not even believe in.

'Get me Wide,' I said. I whispered it over and over. 'Get me and Dandy safe to Wide.'

6

We kept the Sabbath, now that we were on show as Robert
Gower's young ladies. Dandy and I were allowed to walk arm in
arm slowly down the main street of the village and slowly back
again. I – who could face dancing bareback in front of hundreds
of people – would rather have walked through fire than join
Dandy in her promenade. But she begged me; she loved to see
and be seen, even with such a poor audience as the lads of
Warminster. Also, Robert Gower gave me a level look over the
top of his pipe stem, and told me he would be obliged if I stayed
at Dandy's side.

I flushed scarlet at that. Dandy's coquetry had been a joke
among the four of us in the travelling wagon. But in Warminster
there was nothing funny about behaviour which could lower the
Gowers in the eyes of their neighbours.

'It's hardly likely I'd fancy any of those peasants!' Dandy said,
tossing her head airily.

'Well, you remember it,' Robert said. 'Because if I hear so
much as a whisper about you, Miss Dandy, there will be no
training, and no short skirt, and no travelling with the show next
season. No new wagon of your own, either!'

'A new wagon?' Dandy repeated, seizing on the most material
point.

Robert Gower smiled at her suddenly sweet face.

'Aye,' he said. 'I have it in mind for you and Merry to have a
little wagon of your own. You'll need to change clothes twice
during the show and it'll be easier for you to keep your costumes
tidy. You'll maybe have a new poorhouse wench in with you as
well.'

Dandy made a face at that.

'Which horse will pull the new wagon?' I asked.

Robert nodded. 'Always horses for you, isn't it, Merry? I'll be buying a new work horse. You can come with me to help me choose it. At Salisbury horse fair the day after tomorrow.'

'Thank you,' I said guardedly.

He shot a hard look at me. 'Like the life less now we're in winter quarters?' he asked.

I nodded, saying nothing.

'It has benefits,' he said judicially. 'The real life is on the road. But only tinkers and gypsies live on the road for ever. I've got a good-sized house now, but I'm going to buy a bigger one. I want a house so big and land so big that I can live just as I please and never care what anyone thinks of me, and never lack for anything.'

He looked swiftly at me. 'That make any sense to you, Merry?' he asked. 'Or is the Rom blood too strong for you to settle anywhere?'

I paused for a moment. There was a thin thread of longing in my heart which was my need for Wide.

'I want to be Quality,' I said, my voice very low. 'I want a beautiful sandstone house which faces due south so the sun shines all day on the yellow stone, with a rose garden in front of it, and a walled fruit garden at the back, and a stable full of hunters on the west side.' I broke off and looked up at him, but he was not laughing at me. He nodded as if he understood.

'The only way I'll get my house is work, and hard trading,' he said. 'The only way you'll get to yours is marriage. You'd better make haste and get some of your sister's prettiness, Meridon. You'll never catch a squire with your hair cropped short and your chest as flat as a lad.'

I flushed scarlet from my neck to my forehead.

'Doesn't matter,' I said turning away, angry with myself for saying too much; and that to a man I should never wholly trust.

'Well, take your walk,' he called genially, to Dandy and me together. 'Because tomorrow you start work in earnest.'

I knew what Robert Gower's idea of earnest work was like, and I kept Dandy's saunter to a minimum – just up and down the wide main street – so that I could be home before dinner in time to muck out the stables and groom the horses. Ignoring Dandy's protests I insisted we leave the kitchen straight after our dinner, so that we could turn the horses out in the paddock just as it was growing dark. In the corner of the field stood the barn which Robert Gower had ordered to be ready, where Dandy's work would start tomorrow.

'Let's go and see it,' Dandy said.

We trod carefully across the uneven ground and pushed the wide door open. Our feet sank into deep wood shavings, thickly scattered all around the floor. Above our heads, almost hidden in the gloom was a wooden bar on a frail-looking pair of ropes swinging slightly in the draught like a waiting gibbet. I had never seen such a thing before, except in that hand-bill. Just standing on the floor and gazing up made me sick with fright. Dandy glanced up as if she hardly minded at all.

'How on earth will we get up there?' I asked. My voice was quavery and I had my teeth clenched to stop them chattering.

Dandy walked across and stood at the bottom of a rope-ladder which hung from a little platform at the top of an A-frame built of pale light wood.

'Up this, I suppose,' she said. She tipped her head back and looked up at it. 'D'you see, Meridon? I suppose we stand up there and jump across to the trapeze thing.'

I looked fearfully up. The trapeze was within reach, if you stretched out far and jumped wide out over the void.

'What d'we do then?' I asked miserably. 'What happens then?'

'I s'pose we swing out to Jack,' she said, walking across the floor of the barn. On the other side was a matching A-frame with an open top. 'He stands at the top and catches my feet, swings me through his legs and back up,' she said as if it were the easiest thing in the world.

'I won't do it,' I said. My voice was harsh because I was so breathless. 'I won't be able to do it at all. I don't care what I promised Robert, I didn't know it would be so high and the ropes so thin. Surely you don't want to do it either, Dandy? Because if you'd rather not, we'll tell Robert Gower we won't do it. If the worst comes to the worst we can make a living some other way. We could run away. If you don't want to do it too, he cannot make us.'

Dandy's heart-shaped face rounded into her sweetest smile. 'Oh nonsense, Merry,' she said. 'You think I'm as big a coward as you are. I don't mind it, I tell you. I'm going to make my fortune doing this. I shall be the only flying girl in the country. They'll all come to see me! Gentry, too! I shall be in all the newspapers and they'll make up ballads about me. I can't wait to start. This is everything for me, Merry!'

I held my peace. I tried to share her excitement, but as we stood in that shadowy barn and I looked up at the yawning roof and the slim swing and the slender rope I could feel my mouth fill with bile and my head grow dizzy.

I put my hands over my ears. There was a rushing noise, I could not bear to hear it. Dandy took hold of my wrists. She was shaking them. From a long way away I could hear her saying: 'Merry, are you all right? Are you all right, Merry?'

I shook my head, pulling away from her grip, fighting in a panic for my breath, waiting for the vomit to curdle up into my mouth. Then the next thing I knew was a sharp slapping on my cheek. I opened my eyes and put up my hand to ward off a blow. It was Jack. I was held in his arms, Dandy hovering beside him.

'You with us now?' he asked tersely.

I shrugged off his hold and sat up. My head still swam.

'Yes,' I said. 'I'm all right.'

'Was it just looking at the swing?' he asked glancing upward, incredulous that anyone could faint for fear at such a petty object.

I hesitated. 'Yes,' I said uncertainly. 'I suppose it was.' Jack pulled me to my feet before I could think more clearly. 'Well, don't look at it then,' he said unsympathetically, 'and don't go setting Dandy off neither. Da is set on having her up there, and you promised you'd try it.'

I nodded. Dandy's face was bright, untroubled.

'She's set on going,' I said. My voice was croaky, I coughed and spat some foul-tasting spittle. 'An' I'll keep my word and try it.'

'You won't be up there for a while,' Jack said. 'Look there, that's the practice one.'

He gestured over to the other side of the barn near the door where a swing hung so low that I could have jumped up to reach it. Someone hanging would be only ten inches from the floor, just enough to dangle.

'On that!' I exclaimed. Jack and Dandy laughed at my face. 'I could face that!' I said. Relief made me giggly and I joined in their laughing. 'Even I could swing on that,' I said.

'Well, good,' said Jack agreeably. 'It would please my da very much if you would swing on the practice swing. You need never go high unless you want to, Merry. But he's paying a big fee for the man from Bristol to come and teach us. He'd like to see him in full work for the two months.'

'I'd wager on that,' Dandy said nastily. 'But he agreed that Merry needn't learn if she was afeared. She's doing enough for the two of you falling off horses all day, as it is.'

'I don't mind swinging on that,' I said, and I meant it. 'I might even like it.'

'Getting dark,' Jack said. 'You two had best get back. We'll start work early in the morning.'

We went out into the grey twilight and Jack pulled the door shut behind us.

'What's it like sleeping in a house after being in a wagon all your lives?' he asked.

'Too quiet,' Dandy said. 'I miss you snoring, Jack.'

'It's odd,' I agreed. 'The room stays still all the time. You get used to the wagon rocking every time someone moves, I suppose. And the ceiling seems so high. In our old wagon, with Da and Zima, the roof was just above my head and I used to get a wet face when I turned over and brushed against it.'

'What's it like for you, Jack?' Dandy said insinuatingly. 'Will you miss not seeing us in our shifts in the morning? Or getting a little peep at us when we wash?'

Jack laughed but I guessed he was blushing in the darkness.

'Plenty of girls in Warminster, Dandy,' he said. 'Plenty of choice in this town.'

'As pretty as me?' she asked. Dandy could make her voice sound like a gilt-edged invitation to a party, if she had a mind to. I could feel Jack sweat as he walked between us.

'Nay,' he said honestly. 'But a darned sight less troublesome.' He turned abruptly as we walked into the stable yard. 'I'll say goodnight to the two of you here,' he said, and went through the little door in the wall to the garden and the main house.

Dandy went up the stairs before me humming, and unpinned her cap before the bit of mirror while I lit our one rush candle.

'I could have him,' she said softly. It was almost an incantation, as if she were making magic with her own lovely mirror-image. 'I could have him, though his da has warned him against me, and though he thinks to look down on me. I could call him into my hand like a little bird with a speck of bread.'

She untied her pinny and slid her gown up and over her head. The curves of her body showed clear as a ripple on a stream. Her breasts rounding and plump with pale unformed nipples. The dark shadow of curly hair between her legs and the smooth curve of her buttocks were like magical symbols in an old book of spells. 'I could have him,' she said again.

I stripped my Sunday gown off and bundled it into the chest and leaped into my bed, covers up to my chin.

'Don't even think of it,' I said.

At once the desirous tranced expression left her face, and she turned to me laughing. 'Old Mother Meridon!' she taunted. 'Always on the lookout for trouble. You've got ice between your legs, Meridon, that's your trouble. All you ever want there is a horse.'

'I know what a horse is thinking,' I said grimly. 'Pretty Jack could plan a murder and you'd never see it in his eyes. And Robert wants nothing but money. I'd rather have a horse any day.'

Dandy laughed. I heard the floorboards creak as she lay down on her mattress.

'I wonder what the trapeze artist will be like,' she said sleepily. 'I wonder how old he is, and if he's married. He looked fine on that hand-bill, d'you remember, Merry? Half-naked he was. I wonder what he'll be like.'

I smiled into the darkness. I need not fear the charms of Jack Gower nor the anger of his father if the man of the trapeze act would just flirt a little with Dandy for the two months that he was with us – and then go.

He was prompt, anyway. He walked into the yard at six o'clock on a bitterly cold November morning, a small bag in his hand. He was dressed like a working farmer, good clothes, made of good quality cloth, but plain and unfashionable. He had a greatcoat on and a plain felt hat pushed back. His impressive moustaches curled out gloriously along his cheeks and made him look braggish and good-humoured. William took one look at him and bolted into the house to tell Robert that he had arrived. Dandy and I observed him minutely from our loft window.

Robert came out at once and shook his hand like an equal. William was told to take the little bag into the house.

'He gets to sleep inside,' Dandy whispered to me.

'But where will he eat?' I replied, guessing that it was the entry to the dining room which was the significant threshold.

Jack came out at once and was introduced to the visitor.

'My son Jack,' Robert said. 'Jack, this is Signor Julio.'

'Foreign,' whispered Dandy, awed.

'Call me David,' the man said with a beaming smile. 'Signor Julio is just a working name. We thought it sounded better.'

Robert turned so quickly that he caught sight of us as we ducked back from the window.

'Come down you two,' he called.

We clattered down the stairs. Dandy pushed me before her. I was wearing my working breeches and a white cut-down shirt which once belonged to Jack. I flushed as I saw him look me over. But when I raised my eyes I saw that he was measuring my strength, as I would look at a new colt and wonder what it could do. He nodded at Robert as if he were pleased.

'This is Meridon,' Robert said. 'She's horse-mad. But if you could get her up high I'd be obliged. She's the one who doesn't fancy it, and I've given my word she won't be forced. She's scared of heights.'

'There's many like that,' David said gently. 'And sometimes they are the best in the end.' His voice had a singing lilt I'd heard only once before, from a Welsh horse-trader who sold Da the smallest toughest pony I had ever seen.

'And this is Dandy, her sister,' Robert said.

Dandy walked slowly forward, her eyes on David's face, a hint of a smile around her lips as she watched him scan her from the top of her dark head to the glide of her feet.

'They'll pay just to see you,' David said to her, very softly.

Dandy beamed up at him.

'Right,' Robert said briskly. 'Let's go to the barn. My lad said he'd set the rigging as you ordered but if there's anything amiss we can set it right at once. If it is all to your liking then the girls and Jack are ready to start the training at once.'

David nodded and Robert led the way through the stable gate into the garden and then down to the paddock at the end of the garden. David looked around him as he followed Robert and I guessed he was thinking, as I had done, that this was a man who had come very far with very little except his own hard work and brains.

Robert threw open the door of the barn with something of a flourish and the Welshman stepped inside and looked all around. His shoulders squared, his head came up. I watched him narrowly and saw him change from the new employee in the stable yard to a performer at home in his element.

'It's good,' he said nodding. 'You understood my drawings then?'

'I had them followed to the letter,' Robert said proudly. 'But the carpenter had no idea what was wanted so part of it was done by guess.' He took his pipe from his pocket and tamped down the tobacco.

'Good guesses,' David said. He went over to the rope-ladder and swung it gently. It quivered up its length like a snake. He cast his eye over the ring.

'Good and level,' he said approvingly.

He went over to the practice trapeze and his walk was not like that of an ordinary man. He was muscled so hard and he walked so tight that he looked as lean and as fit as a stable cat ready to pounce. I glanced at Dandy; she met my eyes with a wink.

David the Welshman made a little spring with his hands above his head and I saw his knuckles turn white as he gripped on the bar. For a second he hung there, motionless, and then he brought his straight legs up before him and then beat them back with a smooth fluid force which sent the swing flying forward. Three times he swung and the third time he let go and spun himself head over heels towards us, and landed smack on his feet, solid as a rock, his blue eyes gleaming, his white smile bright.

'No smoking in here,' he said pleasantly to Robert.

Robert had just got his pipe going and took it from his mouth in surprise.

'What?' he demanded.

'No smoking,' David replied. He turned to Jack and Dandy and me. 'No smoking in here, no eating, no drinking, no fooling around. Never play tricks on each other in here. Never show off on the ropes or the swings. Never bring your temper in here, never come in here courting. This place is where you are going to learn to be artistes. Think of it as a church, think of it as a royal court. But never think of it as an ordinary place. It has to be magic.'

Robert went quietly outside and knocked the hot ember out of his pipe into the wet grass. He said nothing. I remembered the time he had told Jack and me that we were never never to fight inside the ring. Now the barn was to be half sacred! I shrugged. It was Robert's money. If he wanted to build a barn where he was not allowed to smoke his pipe and pay a man to give him orders it was his affair. He saw my eyes on him and gave me a rueful smile.

Dandy and Jack were spellbound. They were awed by the idea of the practice barn becoming a special place where they would become special people.

'It is magic,' David went on, the lilt in his voice more pronounced. 'Because here you are going to become artists – people who can make beauty, like poets or painters or musicians.'

He turned abruptly to Robert. 'Is there no heating?' he asked.

Robert looked surprised. No,' he said. 'I know you had a stove on your drawing but I thought you'd all be warm enough, working in here.'

David shook his head. 'You can't keep the sinews of the body warm by working them,' he said. 'They get cold and then they strain and even snap. Then you can't work for weeks while they heal. It's a false economy not to heat the building. I won't work without a stove.'

Robert nodded. 'I was thinking of how we work with the horses,' he said. 'I always get hot enough working with them. But I'll have one put in this afternoon. Can you use the building until then?'

'We can make a start,' David said grandly. He looked at Dandy. 'Do you have some breeches like your sister?' he asked.

Dandy's face was appalled. 'I'm to wear a short skirt!' she said. 'Robert promised! I'm not to be in breeches!'

David turned to Robert, smiling. 'A short skirt?' he asked.

Robert nodded. 'In pink,' he said. 'A little ruffled skirt with shiny buttons, and a loose matching shirt at the top.'

'She'd be safer with bare arms,' David said. 'Easier to catch.'

Robert puffed on the cold stem of his pipe. 'Bare arms and a naked neck with a little stomacher top, and a skirt above her knees?' he asked. 'They'd have the Justices on me!'

David laughed. 'You'd make your fortune first!' he said. 'If the lass would do it!'

Robert pointed the stem of his pipe at Dandy. 'She'd do it stark naked given half a chance, wouldn't you Dandy?'

Dandy lowered her black eyes so that all one could see was the sweep of dark eyelashes on her pink cheek. 'I don't mind wearing a skirt and a little bodice top,' she said demurely.

'Good,' David said. 'But you must practise in breeches and a warm smock with short sleeves.'

'Go to the house, Dandy,' Robert ordered. 'Mrs Greaves will fit you with something from Jack or William. Make haste now.' He looked at Jack and me wearing our riding breeches and our stable smocks. 'These two all right?'

'Yes,' David said.

'I'll leave you to it, then,' Robert Gower said reluctantly. 'You'll remember our agreement is that they can spring to the trapeze and swing out to Jack and back to their platform inside two months.'

'I remember,' David said steadily. 'And you will remember my terms.'

'Daily payments in coin,' Robert concurred. 'If you work till eleven you can all take breakfast in the kitchen. Then an afternoon session until dinner in the kitchen at four.'

'Then they'll need to rest,' David said firmly.

Robert nodded. 'The girls can make their costumes then,' he said. 'But tomorrow I promised Merry she could come to the horse fair with me.'

David nodded and waited for Robert to go out and close the barn door behind him. Then he looked at Jack and me.

'Better get to work,' he said.

7

In my apprehensive fright of the ropes and the swings and the high vaulting roof of the barn I had been certain that David would insist we should climb right to the top on that very first morning. But he did not. Even before Dandy reappeared from the house looking sulky and beautiful in a pair of baggy home-spun breeches belonging to William and a linen shirt of Jack's, David had ordered Jack and me to trot and then sprint around the barn on five increasingly fast circuits.

Then he had us running backwards and dancing on the spot until our faces were flushed and we were all panting. Dandy's careful coronet came down and she twisted it carelessly into a bun on the nape of her neck. But the three of us were as fit as working ponies. Jack and I had been training hard every night on the bareback act and were as quick and as supple as grey-hounds. And for all that Dandy would sneak off to doze in the sun at every opportunity, she had been raised as a travelling child and to walk twenty or thirty miles in a day was no hardship to her – and to swim races at the end of it.

'You'll do,' David himself was puffing as we dropped to the wood shavings for our first rest. 'I was afraid that you would all be plump and lazy, but you are all well muscled and you've got plenty of wind.'

'When do we go up?' Dandy demanded.

'Any time you like,' he said carelessly. 'I'll check the rigging while you go to your breakfast and then you can go up and down whenever you wish. I'll show you how to drop into the net, and once you know that you can come to no harm.'

'I don't know I can,' I said. I was keeping my voice steady but the flutter of fear in my belly kept snatching my breath away.

David smiled at me, his enormous moustaches still curly on his sweaty cheeks.

'I know you are afraid,' he said reassuringly. 'I understand that. I have been afraid too. You will work at the speed you wish. You've the build for it, and the body, I should think. But this is something you can only do if your heart is in it. I'd not be party to forcing anyone up a ladder.'

'How did you come into it?' Jack asked.

David smiled. 'It's a long story,' he said lazily. 'The press-gang snatched me from my home at Newport and I was pressed on board a man-of-war – big it was, frightening for a country lad. I jumped ship as soon as I could, Portugal actually, Lisbon, and lived rough for a while. Then I joined a travelling show of contortionists. I didn't have the body for that, but they put me at the bottom of the heap and I could hold the rest of them up. Then I saw an act up high on Roman Rings and I set my heart on it.' He twirled his moustache. 'It made me,' he said simply. 'I apprenticed myself to the man I saw doing it, and he taught me. Then we used a trapeze instead of the rings which meant we could swing out and not just hang like other performers were doing. First I was the only one. But then his young son started to learn and we found he could swing out and reach for me, and I could catch him and swing him back to his trapeze. It was a good act.'

He paused. I saw his eyes narrow with grief at some memory. I felt my belly clench with fear.

'What happened?' I asked.

'The lad fell,' he said simply. 'He fell and broke his neck and died.'

Nobody said anything for a moment.

'Merry, you're green,' Jack said. 'Are you going to be sick?'

I shook my head. 'No,' I said. 'Go on, David. What did you do then?'

'I came back to this country and found a partner to help me with the rigging and to stand the other side and reach out and catch my feet as I swung over. But your father is the man with the ideas! I'd never have thought of putting lasses up high. The people will love it.'

'He'll be paying you a good sum,' Dandy said acutely. 'You're the only man in England who can swing on a trapeze. Yet you're teaching us. And you say yourself that girls will pull a crowd.'

David beamed. 'I'm getting old,' he said frankly. 'I get tired after two shows and my partner is getting slow. I've no savings, nothing at all. Robert is paying me a king's ransom to teach you three something that I'll have no use for in two seasons' time. And he'll pay me more yet – to refuse to teach other people the tricks I've taught you.' He grinned at Jack and moistened his fingers with his tongue so that he could curl the ends of his moustache. 'That's no secret,' he said. 'Your father knows it as well as I do.'

Jack nodded. 'How long do you last on the trapeze?' he asked.

'Till you're twenty-five or so,' David said consideringly. 'Depends how fit you are to start with. I've been hungry and ill most of my life. I don't expect to be working much after thirty.'

'It's a hard life,' I said looking at him. His skin was flushed pink and the wonderful moustaches were curly, ebullient. But the bags under his eyes were deep and shadowed.

'Isn't every trade hard?' he asked me; and I nodded, hearing an echo of my own half-starved worldliness.

'Now!' he said, suddenly active. 'To work.'

He set Jack to exercises, five hundred paces of running on the spot and then lying flat and pushing up and down using his arms. He gave Dandy a metal bar and ordered her to run on the spot holding it before her, and then above her head, and then push it up and down as she ran. But me he took around the waist and lifted me up so that my fingers closed around the smooth hardness of the low-slung trapeze bar.

I hung like a confused bat while he stepped back and called me to raise my legs and beat them down hard. I did so, and the swing rocked forward.

'Keep your legs together! Let the swing take you back!' he called. 'Now at the back-up, at the return of the swing stick your arse out, force your legs down together! Beat!'

Again and again he called the timing for me, and the barn faded, and Jack and Dandy's sweating faces faded, and my fear faded until there was nothing but a voice saying, 'Now!' and my irritatingly slow body taking too long to beat down with the legs so that I swung forward, arched like the prow of a boat.

I could not get my legs to go down fast enough, smoothly enough. Each time he said, 'Now!' I was conscious of being too late, too slow. I had never felt so fat and awkward and flustered in my life. Then when the swing bore me forward I could not bring up my legs high enough to give me the space to beat back. I worked till I was near tears with frustration and with a longing sense that I could do it – that I was only a few lazy muscles away from doing it right – when he said gently: 'That's enough Meridon. Have a rest now.'

I shook my head then and the swing drifted to a standstill and I found my arms were aching with fatigue. I dropped down off the swing and crumpled to sit where I landed. Dandy and Jack were watching me and David had a quizzical smile.

'You like it,' he said certainly.

I nodded ruefully. 'I feel so close to getting it right!' I said angrily. 'I just can't get to the beat at the right time.'

'I'll try,' Jack offered and picked himself up off the floor. His hands and wrists were plastered with wood shavings and he brushed them off. I moved aside and squatted on my haunches to watch him. My arms and shoulders were tingling with the strain and my hard-worked belly was quivering. My hands and legs were shaking but it was a trembly exhilaration from exhausted muscles and a singing delight in stretching my body to a new skill.

I had been angry with myself for missing the beat of it, but I was glad to see that I was better than Jack. It had irritated me for months, the way he could stand so easily on Bluebell's back while I was still dependent on his shoulder or on the strap for balance. David called the beat for him, and counted it. But Jack was nowhere near. He dropped off the trapeze red-faced and cursing under his voice. One level look from David's blue eyes hushed him but he stalked off to where a bar was set into the wall and started hauling himself up and down on it in irritable silence.

Dandy swayed forward. 'My turn?' she asked David.

'Your turn,' he said and put his big hands on her small waist to lift her up.

She was better than Jack. She had a sense of rhythm as natural as dancing and she could sway forward and back with the trapeze rather than struggling against it. Her upraised arms strained the shirt over her breasts and I watched David's eyes to see if he was looking at her. He was not. He was watching the beat of her legs as she tried to work the trapeze forward and back. I gave a little secret smile. I had nothing to fear from David. He might notice Dandy's looks, but he was not a man to go mad for her. He would not forget that he had a job of work to do here and a small fortune to make if he did it right.

We worked like that all the early morning until William came down to summon us for breakfast in the kitchen. We ate as if we were half starved, Mrs Greaves bringing tray after tray of fresh-baked rolls to the table with home-made creamy butter, ham, beef, and cheese. Jack and David drank great pints of ale while Dandy and I drank water. Even then, I could not resist snatching an apple from the bowl as I passed the Welsh dresser on our way out again.

David declared an hour's rest while he checked the rigging, and Dandy went to raid Jack's wardrobe for something more becoming while he and I went to check the ponies. After we had seen they were well, and watered them and humped a hay net down to them, the church clock was ringing the hour and we were due back in the barn.

Already there was a blacksmith working on a second-hand stove in the corner, rigging a chimney through a gap in the wall. I noted the speed with which David's demands were met; but I said nothing.

Dandy and Jack were wild to go up the shaking ladder to the platform at the top and David said that they might climb up. He showed Jack how to hold the ladder while Dandy climbed, by stepping into the bottom rung and weighting it for her, and then he held it steady while Jack went up too. I sat in the corner of the barn like an unfledged squab and peered at them through the cracks in my fingers. I did not dare move my hands from covering my face. David, courteously, paid no attention to me at all.

He showed them how to climb the ladder, toe-heel, toe-heel, all up the shaking length of it. And he laughed gently when Dandy called down that she was out of breath just from climbing the twenty-five steps.

'You must practise then!' he said. 'If you are going to be Mademoiselle Dandy, the Angel without Wings, then you must seem to soar up the ladder. Not waddle up like a pinioned duck!'

He went up the ladder behind Jack, with no one to hold it still for him, and he looked as if he were running upstairs he took it so swiftly. I peeped through my fingers at them, sickeningly high, and I caught parts of his low-voiced instructions. He was thoughtful for me, because he called down to warn me.

'Meridon, I am teaching them to fall into the net, so you will see us all falling, but we shall all be quite safe.'

I uncovered my face at that so that he could see me nod to show I understood. I even watched as he took hold of the trapeze firmly in his hands and stepped off the little platform, swinging gently out, letting its swing die down of its own accord until it was still – then he dropped from it. As he fell he turned his legs up so that he landed on his back and on his shoulders. He sprang to his feet and walked with an odd, bouncy, graceless stride to the edge of the net and vaulted down.

'Like that!' he called. 'Keep your legs up, your chin tucked on your chest and you cannot be hurt.'

Jack's distant white face nodded and he reached out a shepherd's crook and hooked the swinging trapeze and drew it towards him. I watched as he took a grip of it and then I had to shut my eyes as I saw his expression harden and knew he was nerving himself to step off the platform clinging to it.

The twang of the net told me he had landed safely, and his yell of elation up to Dandy. 'Come on, Dandy! It is fine! It is a wonderful feeling. Better than riding even! And the fall is scary, but it is so good to feel yourself safe! Come on, Dandy!'

That broke something in me. 'Don't make her! Don't make her!' I screamed and whirled up from the wood shavings on the floor of the barn. Jack had sprung down from the net and turned and fairly caught me as I launched myself at him. 'You shouldn't! You shouldn't!' I said. I was beyond myself, not knowing what I was saying. My hands were in fists and I went to thump Jack hard in the face, but he parried the blow. 'Don't make her!' I shrieked again. 'It ain't safe!'

Jack could not manage me, but David, a clear foot taller than him and much heavier, grabbed my arms and hugged me tight, pinning my arms to my sides.

'It is safe,' he said, his voice a low rumble in my ear. 'I would not let your sister come to harm. I would not let her up there if I thought her in danger. I want her to do well, and so do you. She wants to learn this trick. You must not be selfish and stop her going her way.'

'It's not safe for her,' I said. I was weeping in the hopeless effort to make him understand me. 'It's not safe for her! I know! I am a gypsy! I have the Sight! It's not safe for her!'

He turned me in his arms, turned me to face him and scanned my frantic wet face. 'What is safe for her?' he asked gently. 'This is the way she chooses now. She could choose worse.'

That made me pause. If Dandy could delight in the applause from hundreds of people and earn a fair share of the profits then she would not go running after strangers and let them put their hands up her ragged skirts for a penny. If I knew Dandy, she would learn airs and graces as soon as she became Mademoiselle Dandy. I could trust Robert Gower to keep his investment away from men who would hurt her. I could trust him not to leave her on the road once she was a trained act in her own right and any showman in the world would give his eye-teeth for her.

I gave a little sob. 'She'll fall,' I said uncertainly. 'I'm sure she will.'

His grip tightened on me. 'You can will her into falling,' he said ominously. 'If you carry on like this you will have wished her into a fall. You are frightening yourself and you are frightening her. You are robbing both of you of the confidence you need, and you are wrecking my training. And you're a fool if you do that, Meridon. You and I both know that Robert Gower won't keep her if she's idle.'

I shrugged off David's restraining arms and looked up into his face. I knew my eyes were blank with despair. 'We keep on travelling,' I said. 'But there is nowhere to go.'

His blue eyes were sympathetic. 'You're no gypsy,' he said. 'You want a home.'

I nodded, the familiar longing for Wide rising up inside me so strongly that I thought it would choke me like swallowed grief. 'I want to take Dandy somewhere safe,' I said.

He nodded. 'You keep the pennies,' he said softly. 'She'll earn well with this act when I've finished training her. You watch how Robert Gower did it. You keep the pennies and the gold and within a season or two you could buy your own home for her. Then you can take her away.'

I nodded. Dandy was still waiting on the little board, I could see it swaying in the air currents at the roof of the barn.

'She'll need to hear you,' he said. 'You'd better tell her you're all right.'

'Very well,' I said, surly. 'I'll tell her.'

Dandy's pale distant face peered at me from the side of the platform, looking down to where I stood far, far below her.

'All right, Dandy,' I called up. 'I'm all right now. I'm sorry. You jump if you want to. Or come down the ladder if that's all you want to do today. You'll never hear me try to stop you again.'

She nodded and I saw her hook the trapeze towards her.

'I've never seen you cry before,' Jack said wonderingly. He put a hand up to touch the tears on my cheek but I jerked my head away.

It didn't stop him. 'I didn't think you were girl enough for tears, Meridon,' he said. His tone was as soft as a lover.

I shot him a hard sideways look. 'She'll never hear me call her down again,' I promised. 'And you'll never see me cry again. There's only one person in the whole world I care for, Jack Gower, and that's my sister Dandy. If she wants to swing on the trapeze then she shall. She won't hear me scream. And you'll never see me cry again.'

I turned my shoulder on him and looked up to the roof of the barn. I could not see Dandy's face. I did not know what she was thinking as she stood there on that rickety little platform and looked down at us: at the fretwork of the brown rope catch-net, the white wood shaving floor, and our three pale faces staring up at her. Then she snatched the bar with a sudden decision and swooped out on it like a swallow. At precisely the centre of its return, at the very best and safest place, she let go and dropped like a stone, falling on to her back into the very plumb centre of the net.

There were hugs all around at that, but I stood aloof, even fending Dandy off when she turned to me with her face alight with her triumph.

'Back to work,' David called, and set us to exercises again.

Jack was ordered to hook his legs over the bar on the wall and practise trying to haul his body up so that it was parallel with the ground. I worked beside him, hanging from my arms and pulling myself up so that my eyes were level with the bar and then dropping down again in one fluid motion.

Dandy he lifted up to the trapeze and set her to learning the time to beat again.

Then we all took a short rest and swapped around until dinner-time.

Robert Gower came into the kitchen when we were at our dinner and took Mrs Greaves's seat at the head of the table, a large glass of port in his hand.

'Would you care for one of these, David?' he asked, gesturing to his glass.

'I'll take one tonight gladly,' David replied. 'But I never drink while I'm working. It's a rule you could set these young people, too. It makes you a little bit slow and a little bit heavy. But the worst thing it does is make you think that you are better than you are!'

Robert laughed. 'There's many that find that is its greatest advantage!' he observed.

David smiled back. 'Aye, but I'd not trust a man like that to catch me if I were working without a net beneath me,' he said.

Robert sprang on that. 'You use cushions in your other show,' he said. 'Why did you suggest we try a net here?'

David nodded. 'For your own convenience mostly,' he said. 'Cushions are fine for a show which is housed in one place. But enough cushions to make a soft landing would take a wagon to themselves. I've seen a net used in a show in France and I thought it would be the very thing for you. If they were using the rings, and just hanging, not letting go at all, you could perhaps take the risk. But swinging out and catching, you need only be a little way out, half an inch, and you're falling.'

The table wavered beneath my eyes. I took my lower lip in a firm grip between my teeth. Dandy's knee pressed against mine reassuringly.

'I've worked without cushions or nets,' David said. 'I don't mind it for myself. But the lad I was working with died when he fell without a net under him. He'd be alive today if his da hadn't been trying to draw a bigger crowd with the better spectacle.' He looked shrewdly at Robert Gower. 'It's a false economy,' he said sweetly. 'You get a massive crowd for the next three or four nights after a trapeze artist has fallen. They all come for the encore, you see. But then you're one down for the rest of the tour. And good trapeze artists don't train quick and don't come cheap. You're better off with a catch-net under them.'

'I agree,' Robert Gower said briefly. I took a deep breath and felt the room steady again.

'Ready to get back to work?' David asked the three of us. We nodded with less enthusiasm than at breakfast. I was already feeling the familiar ache of overworked muscles along my back and my arms. I was wiry and lean but not all my humping of hay bales had prepared me for the work of pulling myself up and down from a bar using my arm muscles alone.

'My belly aches as if I've got the flux,' Dandy said. I saw Robert exchange a quick smile with David. Dandy's coquetry had lasted only as long as her energy.

'That's the muscles,' David said agreeably. 'You're all loose and flabby, Dandy! By the time you're flying I shall be able to cut a loaf of bread on your belly and you'll be as hard as a board.'

Dandy flicked her hair back and shot him a look from under her black eyelashes. 'I don't think I'll be inviting you to dine off of me,' she said, her voice warm with a contradictory promise.

'Any aches, Jack?' Robert asked.

'Only all over,' Jack said with a wry smile. 'It's tomorrow I'll stiffen up, I won't want to work then.'

'Merry won't have to work tomorrow,' Dandy said enviously. 'Why're you taking her to the horse fair, Robert? Can't we all go?'

'She'll be working at the horse fair,' Robert said firmly. 'Not flitting around and chasing young men. I want her to watch the horses outside the ring for me and keep her ears open, so I know what I'm bidding for. Merry can judge horseflesh better than either of you – actually better than me,' he said honestly. 'And she's such a little slip of a thing no one will care what they say in front of her. She'll be my eyes and ears tomorrow.'

I beamed. I was only fifteen and as susceptible to flattery in some areas as anyone else.

'But mind you wear your dress and apron,' he said firmly. 'And get Dandy to pin your cap over those dratted short curls of yours. You looked like a tatterdemalion in church yesterday. I want you looking respectable.'

'Yes, Robert,' I said demurely, too proud of my status as an expert on horseflesh to resent the slight to my looks.

'And be ready to leave at seven,' he said firmly. 'We'll breakfast as we go.'

8

We went to Salisbury horse fair in some style. Robert Gower had a trim little whisky cart painted bright red with yellow wheels and for the first few miles he let me drive Bluebell, who arched her neck and trotted well, enjoying the lightness of the carriage after the weight of the wagon. Mrs Greaves had packed a substantial breakfast and Robert ate his share with relish and pointed out landmarks to me as we trotted through the little towns.

'See the colour of the earth?' he asked. 'That very pale mud?'

I nodded. There was something about the white creaminess of it which made me think of Wide. I felt as if Wide could be very near here.

'Chalk,' he said. 'Best earth for grazing and wheat in the world.'

I nodded. All around us was the great rounded back of the plain, patched with fields where the turned earth showed pale, and other great sweeps where the grass was resting.

'Wonderful country,' he said softly. 'I shall build myself a great house here one day, Meridon, you wait and see. I shall choose a site near the river for the shelter and the fishing, and I shall buy up all the land I can see in every direction.'

'What about the show?' I asked.

He shot me a smiling sideways glance and bit deep into the crusty meat roll.

'Aye,' he said. 'I'd always go with it. I'm a showman born and bred. But I'd like to have a big place behind me. I'd like to have a place so big it bore my name. Robert Gower, of Gower's Hall,' he said softly. 'Pity it can't be of Gowershire; but I suppose that's not possible.'

I stifled a giggle. 'No,' I said certainly. 'I shouldn't think it is.'

'That'll give my boy a start in life,' he said with quiet satisfaction. 'I've always thought he'd marry a girl who had her own act, maybe her own animals. But if he chose to settle with a lass with a good dowry of land he'd not find me holding out for the show.'

'All his training would have been done for nothing then,' I observed.

'Nay,' Robert contradicted me. 'You never learn a skill for nothing. He'd be the finest huntsman in the county with the training he's had on my horses. And he'll be quicker witted than all of the lords and ladies.'

'What about Dandy and me?' I asked.

Robert's smile faded. 'You'll do all right,' he said not unkindly. 'As soon as your sister sees a lad she fancies she'll give up the show, I know that. But with you keeping your eye on her and me watching the gate, she won't throw it away for nothing. If she goes into some rich man's keeping then she'll make a fortune there. If she marries then she'll be kept too. Same thing, either way.'

I said nothing but I was cold inside at the thought of Dandy as a rich man's whore.

'But you're a puzzle, little Merry,' Robert said gently. 'While you work well I'll always have a place for you with my horses. But your heart is only half in the show. You want a home but I'm damned if I can see how you'll get one without a man to buy it for you.'

I shook my head. Robert Gower's good-natured speculation about my future need for a man set my teeth on edge.

'Here,' he said. 'I'll take the reins, you have your breakfast. And for the Lord's sake pull your bonnet straight. Your curls are all blown out from under it.'

I handed him the reins and crammed the hat on my head, tying it more securely. It was an old one belonging to Mrs Greaves which she had offered me last night together with a demure brown cape. They were both too big for me and I looked like a little girl dressing up in a game to look like a farmer's wife. But the skirts were the worst. Every time I took a stride I seemed to get my legs tangled up in the yards of fabric. Dandy had hooted with laughter and warned me that I had better take little ladylike steps at the fair or I would fall flat on my face.

Robert kept the reins as we trotted into Salisbury and drove accurately to the Black Bull near the horse market. The streets were full of people and everywhere the warm smell of hot horseflesh as string after string of every sort of animal trotted down the street. The pavements were crowded with pie-sellers and the muffin men rang their bells loudly. Flower girls were selling heather and bright-berried sprigs of holly, and everywhere I looked there were match girls and boot boys, porters and urchins, people selling horses and people looking at them, and on one corner a gypsy telling fortunes.

I glanced across at her. I was always drawn to my own people, though I could remember next to nothing of our language and our laws. But I had a dim memory of my mother's dark-framed face and her smile, and her strange-tongued lullabies.

The Rom woman was selling clothes pegs and carved wood flowers and fairings out of a big withy basket at her side. Under her shawl she had a little mug and a well-wrapped bottle, and I noticed many men stop and give her a penny for a swig from the mug. She'd be selling smuggled rum or gin, I guessed. Strong spirits which respectable publicans would not touch but which would keep the cold out on a raw day such as this. She felt my eyes on her and she turned and stared frankly at me.

I would normally have drawn back to Robert Gower's side at such a challenging stare. But I did not, I took a couple of steps forward. In my pocket I had six pennies dedicated until this moment for ribbons for Dandy and sweetmeats for myself, but I stepped forward and held out one of them to her.

'Will you tell my fortune?' I asked her.

She bent her head in its dirty red headscarf over my palm.

'Give me another penny,' she started. 'I can't see clear.'

'Tell me a misty fortune for a penny, then,' I said shrewdly. But she suddenly pushed my hand away and put my penny back into it.

'I can't tell your fortune,' she said to me quickly. 'I can't tell you nothing you don't already know.'

'Why not?' I asked. 'Because I'm Romany too?'

She looked up at that and she laughed, a high old-woman's clatter. 'You're no Rom,' she said. 'You're a gorgio through and through. You're a landowner, a daughter of a line of squires and you're longing for their land all the time, aren't you?'

'What?' I exclaimed. It was as if she had peeped into my head and seen the childhood dreams which I had never told anyone except Dandy.

Her face creased with mocking laughter. 'They'll think highly of you!' she said. 'You with your gypsy sister and your dirty face and your common ways! You'll have to break your back and break your soul and break your heart if you want to become a lady and rule the land like them.'

'But will I get it?' I demanded in an urgent whisper, one look over my shoulder to see that Robert had not heard. She was pulling herself to her feet and picking her basket up, moving away from me into the crowd. I put a restraining hand on her shawl. 'Will I become a lady? Will I find my home?'

She turned, and her face which had been hard was no longer laughing but gentle. 'They'll bring you safely home to their land,' she said. 'In the end, I think they will. Your true ma, and her ma especially. It's their hunger you feel, silly little chavvy. They'll bring you safe home. And you'll belong to their land in a way they never could.'

'And Dandy?' I asked urgently. But the fringe of her shawl slipped through my fingers and was gone.

I waited for a moment, looking into the crowd. Then I saw her, bow-backed, slipping her way through to another corner of the square, spreading her cloth, arranging her basket, hunkering down on the cold stone. I looked around for Robert, afraid I had lost him in the crowd, but he was only a few yards away, talking to a red-faced man with his hat pushed far back on his forehead.

'A killer,' the man said emphatically. 'That horse is a killer. I bought him from you in good faith and he near killed me. He's untrainable.'

'No such thing as an untrainable horse,' Robert said slowly. He was talking very softly, keeping his temper well in check. 'And I sold him to you in good faith. I told you I had bought him for my son to ride in the show but that we could not manage him, nor waste the time training him. We were travelling through the town as you well knew, six months ago, and I warned you I would not be here to take him back if you misliked him. But you were confident you could handle him and you paid a paltry price for him because I warned you fair and square that he had been badly broken and handled worse before he ever came to me.'

'I can't give him away!' the red-faced man broke in, nearly dancing on the spot in his impatience. 'I brought him here today to sell as a riding horse and he put one buyer on his back in the mud and damn near broke his arm. Now they just laugh at me. You'll return me my money, Mr Gower, or I'll tell everyone that you're not to be trusted as a horse-dealer.'

That caught Robert on the raw, and I smiled grimly at the thought of him caring for his honour when he was trading in horse flesh, remembering Da's shady flittings from fair to fair.

'I'll see the animal,' Robert said levelly. 'But I make no promises. I care for my good name and for the reputation of my horses and I won't have it bandied around the market, Mr Smythies.'

Mr Smythies looked meanly at Robert. 'You'll return my money plus interest or you'll never sell a horse again within twenty miles of this town,' he said.

The two of them turned. I followed Robert through the crowd, keeping my eye on his broad back, but noticing how even in all this press of people there was a way cleared for the two of them. People fell back to make a way for Mr Smythies, he was evidently a Someone. Robert might find he had to buy the horse back, and I had the familiar irritated dread that it would be me who would have to ready the brute for the next fair and the next fool.

I was prepared to hate it on sight. I knew exactly how it would look, I had seen enough ill-treated horses in my time. Its eyes would be rimmed with white all the time, its coat forever damp with a fearful sweat. If you went to its head he would toss and sidle, an upraised hand would make it rear and scream. If you went anywhere near its tail it would lash out and if you got on its back it would try to get down and roll on you to break every bone in your body. If you fell and stayed down it would paw at you with wicked hooves.

The only way Da and I ever coped with really bad horses was to cut the inside of their leg and dribble as big a dose of Black Drop into the vein as we dared, sell the horse at once before the drug wore off, and clear out of town as fast as we could. I made a grimace of distaste at the thought of working on a wicked-tempered horse again and caught at Robert's coat-tails as he rounded a corner and went into a stable yard.

In the far corner, with his head over a loose box, was the most beautiful horse I had ever seen.

He was a deep shining grey with a mane as white as linen and eyes as black as ivy berries. He looked across the yard at me and all but whickered in pleasure to see me.

'Sea,' I said softly, as if I knew that was his name. Or as if it were somehow half of his name, the first half of a name like Sea Fret, or Sea Mist, or Sea Fern.

I sidled closer to Robert and gave his coat-tail a gentle tug. Mr Smythies was still complaining at his side but Robert's tip of the head in my direction told me that he was listening to my whisper.

'I can ride him,' I said, my voice almost inaudible above the rising crescendo of Mr Smythies' complaints.

Robert shot a quick look at me.

'Sure?' he said.

I nodded. 'I'll ride him if you'll give him to me for my very own,' I said.

I could feel Robert stiffen at the threatened loss of cash.

Mr Smythies on his other side had been joined by two friends. One of them, flushed with ale, had seen the buyer thrown from the horse and was telling a third man who had now joined them how dangerous the horse was.

'Should be shot,' he said. 'Shot like a dog. 'Sdangerous.'

I sensed Robert's rising discomfort and temper, and I nipped his arm through the thick sleeve of his jacket.

'A wager,' I said quietly. 'You'll win your money back, and more.'

Robert shook his head. 'He's a devil horse,' he said quietly. 'I sold him as a problem. You'd not stay on.'

Mr Smythies was reaching the climax of his tirade. 'I have some influence in this town,' he boomed. 'Aye, and I'm not unknown even in your village, I think. There's many who would be upset to know that you tried to trick me into buying a horse which no one could ride. A dangerous horse, that has this very day broken a man's arm. Could have broken his back!'

''Sdangerous,' his friend corroborated owlishly. 'Should be shot.'

Robert reached for his purse tied deep in his jacket pocket. I grabbed his hand.

'I can,' I hissed. 'If I come off, I'll work for you all year for nothing.'

Robert hesitated.

'Dandy too,' I offered recklessly. 'I really can.'

Robert wavered for a moment, and truly, so did I. If I lost a bet for him he would not beat me as Da would have done under those circumstances. Robert's anger would be infinitely worse. I remembered his wife weeping and left on the road as the wagon drew unhurriedly away from her and felt a bolt of sudden doubt. But then I looked again across the yard and saw the horse which could not possibly hurt me. I knew it. It was my horse. And this was the only way I could earn it.

'The horse is not so bad,' Robert Gower said, his voice as loud as Mr Smythies'. Some men walking past the alley paused and turned in to see what was happening in the little yard. 'I sold him with a warning that he had been badly broke and badly ridden before he came to me. But he was not a killer when he left me, and he is not one now.'

Mr Smythies looked ready to explode, his colour had flushed deeper, his hat pushed back even further on his head had left a strawberry stripe above his popping eyes.

'Why, my little housemaid here could get on his back,' Robert said beguilingly, drawing me forward. 'She rides a little with my show, she goes around crying it up, you know. But she's just a little lass. She could stay on him, I'd put money on it.'

'A wager!' shouted someone from the back and at once the call was taken up. Mr Smythies was torn between a beam of pride at being at the centre of attraction and confusion that Robert seemed to have clouded the issue.

Robert looked thoughtful. 'I did not mean to say that she could ride the horse here and now,' he said hesitantly. 'I was just saying the horse is not so black as he's been painted.'

'Yes you did,' Mr Smythies said, back into his stride as a bully. 'You said (and my friends here will bear witness) that you'd put money on your little housemaid staying on his back. Well, fifty pounds says she cannot get near him, Mr Robert Gower. If you can't put that up you'd better give me my money back and a handsome apology with it.'

Robert glanced around; it was beautifully done. 'All right,' he said unwillingly. 'Fifty pounds it is. But she only has to sit on him.'

'Keep her seat for three minutes by my watch,' said the drunken man, sobering suddenly at the prospect of some sport.

'And not here,' Robert said suddenly, looking at the cobbled yard. 'In the parish field in ten minutes.'

'Right!' roared Smythies. 'Anyone else want to bet on a housemaid who can stay on a horse which has thrown me? Anyone else with money burning a hole in his pocket? I'll take bets at two to one! I'll take bets at five to one!' He suddenly reached around Robert and grabbed my arm and pulled me forward. I made a half-curtsey and kept my face down. Da and I had sold several pups in this town at one time or another and I didn't want to be recognized. 'Damn it, I'll take ten to one!' Mr Smythies yelled.

'I'll put a guinea on the wench!' someone from the back shouted. 'She looks as if she'd keep her legs together! I'll risk a guinea on her!'

I stepped back in apparent confusion and tugged at Robert's

sleeve again. He bent down to me with an expression of benign concern.

'Start a book, for God's sake,' I hissed in an undertone. 'And find someone to put money on me for you.'

'No bets now,' Robert said authoritatively. 'We'll start a proper book down at the field. Come on! Who'll bring the horse?'

I watched as a stable lad ran to tack the horse up. It was a man's saddle, and a whole tanner's shop of leather to keep the poor beast from throwing his head up or pulling too hard, a martingale to keep him from bolting. Everything but a safety strap to bind the rider into the saddle. I slipped across the yard unnoticed.

'My master don't want that stuff on him,' I said pleasantly to the lad. 'He told me to tell you, just the saddle and the bridle with a simple bit. Not the rest of that stuff.'

The lad thought to argue, but I was gone before he could query the order. I followed the crowd down to the field. We picked up a good couple of dozen on the way. I saw Robert had got hold of a small weasel-faced man who was passing among the noisier famers and placing bets with them. The odds were getting better all the time. I took great care to walk in Robert's shadow in mincing steps and keep my eyes on the backs of his heels.

In the field they formed into an expectant circle. The horse was led down the path from the inn, he jinked at the leaves rustling on the ground at his feet. The little lad at his head led him at arm's length, wary of a sudden nip. The horse's ears were laid back hard and his face was bony and ugly. His eyes were white all around.

'Damn,' Robert said softly. The horse was worse than he remembered.

I looked at him as he came towards me under the blue wintry sky and I smiled as if I was warmed through at the very sight of him. I knew him. I felt as if I had known him all my life. As if he had been my horse before I was born, as if he had been my mother's horse, and her mother's too. As if he and I had ridden on Wide ever since the world had been made.

'Sea,' I said softly, and stepped into the middle of the circle to wait for him.

I had forgotten my bonnet and he shied and wheeled as the ribbons were whipped by the wind. There was a chorus of 'Look out! Mind his back legs!' as he backed suddenly and three drunk young bloods swayed backwards out of harm's way. But then I pulled my bonnet and my cap off too and felt the cold wind in my hair and on my face.

I stepped forward. Robert at my side took the reins from the stable lad and waited to help me up. There was a continual mutter of men placing bets behind me and some part of my mind knew that I was going to make Robert a small fortune this day, but the most important thing was that I was going to win Sea for my very own horse.

I went to his head; he sidled anxiously. Robert was holding the reins too tight, and he could sense the tension among all the people. Robert turned, waiting to throw me into the saddle; but I took a moment to stand absolutely still.

Sea dropped his head, Robert loosened his hard grip on the reins. Sea dropped his head towards me and put his long beautiful face towards me and snuffed powerfully at the front of my dress, at my face, and at my curly hair. Behind us there was a sudden rush of talk as the odds shortened and some people tried to recall bets which had not been recorded. I hardly heard them. I put a gentle hand up to his neck and touched him on that soft piece of warm skin behind the right ear and rubbed him as gentle as a mare her foal. He blew out, as if he had lost his fear and his anger and his remembered pain at that one touch and then I lifted my eyes to Robert and smiled at him and said, 'I'll go up now.'

He was too much of a showman to gawp at me, but his eyes were disbelieving as he nodded and clasped his hands together for my boot and threw me up, astride, into the saddle.

'Stand aside,' I said swiftly. It was as I had feared. At the touch of weight in the saddle the horse could remember nothing but the pain of breaking and the cruelty of training and the hard sharp joy of ripping back at the men who tormented him. He reared at once above Robert and only Robert's quick cowardly dive to the ground and swift roll kept him out of range of those murderous hooves.

'Catch him!' screamed one man at the stable lad.

But Robert was on his feet. 'Wait!' he ordered. 'There's a bet on.'

I had clung like a louse when that white neck soared up. When he thudded down I had waited for him to rear again but it had not happened. I stayed as still as a novice rider. My weight was so light, compared to the fat farmers who had tried to train him, he might even think he had thrown me, and all I would have to do was to sit still for three minutes. I saw the man with the watch out of the corner of my eye and I hoped to God he was sober enough to see the moving hand crossing off the minutes.

The horse was frozen. I reached a hand down to his neck and I touched his warm satiny skin. At my touch the fretwork of muscles in his neck trembled as if a human touch was a gadfly.

'Sea,' I said softly. 'Darling boy. Be still now. I am going to take you home.'

His ears went forward his head went up so that he was as trim and as proud as a statue of a horse. I touched him lightly with my heels and he moved forward in a fluid smooth stride. I checked him with a little weight on the reins and he stopped. I looked forward over his alert, forward-pointing ears and saw Robert Gower's face blank with amazement, jaw dropped. I gave him a little smile of triumph and he recollected himself and looked correctly judicious and unsurprised.

'Two and a half,' the drunk with the watch said.

They stared at me as if they would have preferred to see me on the ground at their feet with my neck broken. I glanced around and saw the hungry faces of an audience, avid for a show. Any show.

'Three,' the drunk said solemnly. 'Three minutes, definite. By my watch. Timed it myself.'

'Fixed!' bawled Mr Smythies. 'The horse was trained to let the girl ride him. Damn me, I bet she isn't even a girl but that dratted son of yours, Robert Gower! Fixed to make a fool of me and rob me of half a fortune!'

At his voice Sea went mad. He shot up on his hind legs so fast that I felt myself falling off the back and had to grab to the saddle to stay on his back and then he took two ludicrous strong strides still on his back legs, his hooves raking at the air. The men before us scattered, shouting in fright, and the noise made him worse. He plunged down, shoulder first to the ground, to throw me off, and I soared hopelessly over his head and smashed into the frosty ground with a blow which knocked the breath out of me, and my senses out of me.

When I came to, it was all over bar Mr Smythies' complaints. I sat quietly, with my head between my knees dripping blood on to my new grey gown while Robert ticked off his winnings in the book. Once a man patted my bowed head and dropped a sixpence beside me, one man bent down and whispered an obscenity. I pocketed the sixpence – I was not *that* faint – and waited for the shiny topboots to shuffle past me and away. I lifted my head and saw Robert looking at me.

The little weasel man was counting up the take in a big book. Robert's pockets were bulging. The little lad had hold of the horse again but was standing nervously waiting for someone to take him off him.

'He's mine,' I said. My voice was croaky, I hawked up some blood from the back of my throat and spat it out, wiping my face on my shawl. As I got to my feet I found that I was badly bruised. I hobbled towards him, putting my hand out for the reins.

The stable lad handed him over with open relief. 'You've got a shiner,' he said.

I nodded. A haziness around everything warned me that one eye was closing fast. I patted it gently with the corner of my pinny which had been so clean and white this morning.

'I thought it was fixed till I saw you come off like that,' he said.

I tried to smile, but it was too painful. 'It wasn't fixed,' I said. 'I've never seen the horse before.'

'What'll you do with him now?' he demanded. 'How will you keep him?'

'You'll feed him with the others, won't you Mr Gower?' I said, turning to Robert. There were still a few stragglers leaving the field. They waited for his reply. But I think he'd have treated me fairly even without witnesses.

'I said you could have him if you could stay on him,' he said. 'I'll feed him and shoe him, for you. Aye and I'll buy you tack for him as well. That do you, Meridon?'

I smiled at that and felt the bloodstained skin crack around my eye.

'Yes,' I said. Then I put one hand on Sea's neck for support, and started to hobble from the field.

9

Robert sent me back to the inn where we had left the whisky cart and I led Sea into a loose box and curled up in the corner myself on a bale of straw, too tired and too battered and bruised to care where I was; and much too shy and dirty to order myself a hot drink and my dinner in the parlour as Robert had instructed. Hours later, when the stable was getting dark and the cold winter twilight was closing the horse fair, he came clattering into the yard with two big horses and three little ponies tied reins to tail behind him.

I stumbled to my feet as groggy and weary as if I had been riding all day and peered over the stable door. Sea blew gently down my neck.

'Good God,' Robert said. 'You look like a little witch, Merry. Stick your head under the pump for the Lord's sake. I can't take you home like that.'

I put my hand up to my head and found my cap was lost and my curls all matted with dried blood. The eye which I had bruised was almost closed, and smeared all around my mouth and nose was dried blood.

'Are you badly hurt?' Robert asked as I came carefully out of the stable.

'No,' I said. 'It probably looks worse than it is.'

He shouted for a stable lad and tossed the reins of the two big horses towards him.

'Come here,' he said gruffly, and worked the pump for me as I dipped my head underneath it.

The icy water hit me like a blow and rushed into my ear and made me gasp with shock. But I felt better as soon as my face was clean. I rinsed most of the blood out of my hair as well.

Robert sent another lad running for a kitchen towel and I

rubbed my hair dry. I was shivering with the cold and I had horrid trickles of icy water running down my neck inside my gown, but at least I had woken up and felt fit enough to face the drive home.

'Or do you want me to ride?' I asked, eyeing the string of horses we had to get home somehow.

'Nay,' Robert said contentedly. 'You've done a day and a half's work today, Merry, and I'm better pleased with you than I ever have been with any living soul, and that's the truth. You won me £300 in bets, Merry, and it's a gamble I'd never have dared take if you hadn't urged me to it. I'm obliged to you. You can have your horse with my blessing, and I'll give you ten guineas for your bottom drawer as well. You're a fine lass. I wish I had a dozen of you.'

I beamed back at him, then I shivered a little because with the falling darkness a cold breeze had sprung up.

'Let's get you home,' Robert said kindly; and he sent the lad back inside to borrow a couple of blankets and wrapped me up on the seat of the whisky as if I were a favoured child instead of the hired help.

He decided against bringing all the horses home in the dark on his own. He tied only the big horses on the back of the carriage with Sea tied behind as well, and ordered stabling for the ponies overnight. Then he swung himself up beside me, clicked to Bluebell and we set off for home in the fading light.

He hummed quietly under his breath as we left the outskirts of the town and then he said abruptly to me:

'Did you do that with your da, Merry? Take a wager on your riding and then gull people out of their money?'

'Sometimes,' I said cautiously. I was not sure if he would approve. 'But, often it was too well known that I trained horses for my da and so people wouldn't bet heavily like they did today.' I shrugged. 'I looked different, too,' I said. 'Today I looked like a housemaid. With Da I always looked like a gypsy.'

Robert nodded. 'I've never made so much money in one day in my life,' he said. 'I'd give half of it away if I could do it again.'

I shook my head regretfully. 'I couldn't do it with any other horse,' I said. 'It would be a grand trick to earn money. But Sea was special. I knew he was my horse the moment I saw him. I knew he would not hurt me.'

Robert glanced at my battered face. 'You hardly came off scot-free,' he observed.

I made a little grimace. 'That was because he heard that horrid man's voice,' I said. 'It scared him all over again. But he was all right with me.'

Robert nodded and said nothing as the horse trotted between the shafts and the light from the lamps on either side of the cart dipped and flickered. It was growing darker all the time, I heard an owl hoot warningly. The moon was coming up, thin and very pale, like a rind of goat cheese.

'What about an act where we challenge all comers to ride him?' Robert said slowly, thinking aloud. 'Outside the field, before the show starts. We could call him the killer stallion and challenge people to stay on his back. Charge them say tuppence a try, with a purse if they stay on for more than a minute.' He hesitated. 'Make that five minutes,' he amended. 'Then, after we've called up a crowd and they've seen him throwing a few men, out you come in a pretty dress and ask for your turn. Jack makes up a book, you ride the horse, and we all make a little profit.'

He turned and looked at me, beaming.

I took a deep breath. 'No,' I said quietly. At once, his good-humoured smile vanished.

'Why not?' he asked. 'You'll get a cut of the profits, Merry. You did well today remember. I've not forgotten I promised you ten guineas. I'll pay up and all.'

'No,' I said steadily. 'I am sorry, Robert, but I won't do that with my horse.'

Something in my voice checked his bluster. 'Why not, Merry?' he asked. 'Wouldn't do any harm.'

'Yes it would,' I said certainly. 'I don't want him taught to be wild and vicious. I don't want him frightened any more. I want to teach him to be a good saddle horse, a hunter. I don't want him throwing every fool with tuppence who thinks he's a rider. I want him to have a soft mouth and a sweet temperament. He's my horse, and I won't have him working as a killer stallion.'

Robert was silent. Bluebell trotted, the clatter of the hooves behind us sounded loud in the darkness. Robert hummed under his breath again and said no more.

'You promised to keep him for me,' I said, calling on Robert's sense of fair trade. 'You didn't say he had to work for it.'

Robert scowled at me, and then broke into a smile. 'Oh all right, Merry!' he said gruffly. 'You're a proper horse-dealer for you haggle like a tinker. Keep your damned horse, but you're to ride him when you're calling up the act, and you're to look to training him for tricks in the ring. But he won't do anything you don't like.'

I smiled back at him, and in one of my rare gestures of affection I put my hand on his sleeve.

'Thank you, Robert,' I said.

He tucked my hand under his arm and we drove home in the darkness. My head nodded with weariness and my eyelids drooped. Some time in the journey I felt him draw my head down to rest on his shoulder, and I slept.

Dandy undressed me and put me to bed when we got home, exclaiming over my hurts, and the loss of my cap, and the bloodstains on my grey gown and white apron. Mrs Greaves brought a tray with soup and new-baked bread, a breast of chicken and some stewed apples for me to have dinner in bed. Jack came up to our room with a basketful of logs and lit the fire for me in the little grate in our room, and then he and Dandy sat on the floor and demanded to know the whole story of the horse fair, and the winning of Sea.

'He's a beautiful animal but he hardly let me near him,' Jack said. 'He went for my shoulder when I took his bridle off. You'll have your work cut out for you trying to train that one, Merry.'

Dandy wanted to know how much Robert had earned, and they both opened their eyes wide when I told them of the guinea bets which had been called all around me, and that Robert had promised me ten of my very own.

'Ten guineas!' Dandy exclaimed. 'Merry, what will you do with so much money?'

'I shall save it,' I said sagely, dipping my bread into the rich gravy around the chicken. 'I don't know what money we will need in the future, Dandy. I'm going to start saving for a house of our own.'

They both gaped at me for that ambition, and I laughed aloud though my bruised ribs made me gasp and say: 'Oh! Don't make me laugh! Please don't make me laugh! I hurts so when I laugh!'

Then I asked them to tell me what they had been doing all the day; but they both complained that it was the same as the day before, and looked like being the same for ever. They had both swung up high on the trapeze in the roof of the barn, but most of their work had been on the practice trapeze at ground level, and pulling themselves up and down on the bar.

'I'm aching all over,' Dandy complained. 'And that dratted David just makes us work and work and work.'

Jack nodded in discontented agreement.

'I'm starving too,' he said. 'Merry, we'll go over and get our dinners and come back to you after. Is there anything you need?'

'No,' I said smiling in gratitude. 'I'll lie here and watch the firelight. Thank you for making the fire, Jack.'

He leaned towards me and ruffled my hair so my curls stood on end.

'It was nothing, my little gambler,' he said. 'We'll see you in a little while.'

The two of them clattered down the stairs to the stable, I heard Dandy groan as she had to pull the trapdoor at the head of the stairs shut with her aching arms, and then their voices as they crossed the yard and went through the little gateway to the house. Then I heard the kitchen door open and close and there was silence.

Silence except for the flickering noise of the fire and the occasional rustle from Sea, safe in the stable beneath my room. I watched the shadows bob and fall on the wall beside me. I had never seen a fire light up a bedroom before, I had never lain in darkness and felt the warm glow of it on my face, and seen the bright warmth of it behind my closed eyelids. I felt enormously comfortable and at peace and safe. For once in my life I felt that I need not fear the next day, nor plan our survival in an unreliable and dangerous world. Robert Gower had said that he wished he had a dozen of me. He had said that he was better pleased with me than he had been with any living soul. I had let him hold my hand, and I had not felt that uneasy anxious prickle of distaste at his touch. I had let Jack rumple my head and I had liked the careless caress. I watched the flames of the fire which Jack had lit for me, in the room which Robert had made ready for me, and for once I felt that someone cared for me. I fell asleep then, still smiling. And when Jack and Dandy came to see how I did, they found me asleep with my arm outflung and my hand open, as if I were reaching out, unafraid. They put an extra log on the fire and crept away.

I did not dream in the night, and I slept late into the morning. Robert had ordered Dandy not to wake me, and I did not stir until breakfast time. I went to the kitchen then and confessed to Mrs Greaves that I had lost her bonnet in the course of winning the master a fortune. She already knew the story and smiled and said that it did not matter.

The dress and the apron were a more serious matter. The apron was permanently stained with blood and grass stains, the grey dress marked as well. I looked cheerfully at them both as Mrs Greaves hauled them out of the copper and tutted into the steam.

'I'll have to wear breeches all the time then,' I said.

Mrs Greaves turned to me with a little smile. 'If you knew how bonny you looked in them you'd not wear them,' she said. 'You think to dress like a lad and no man will notice you. That may have been true when you were a little lass, or even this summer; but now you'd turn heads even if you were wearing a sack tied around your middle. And in those little breeches and your white shirt you look a picture.'

I flushed scarlet, suddenly uncomfortable. Then I looked up at her. She was still smiling. 'Nothing to be afraid of, Meridon,' she said gently. 'You'll have seen some bad doings when you were a girl, but when a man loves a woman it can sometimes be very sweet. Very sweet indeed.'

She gave a little sigh and dumped the heap of wet cloth back into the copper and set it back on to boil.

'It's not all sluts in hedgerows and dancing for pennies,' she said, turning her back to me as she laid the table for breakfast. 'If a man truly loves you he can surround you with love so that you feel as if you are the most precious woman in the world. It's like forever sitting in front of a warm fire, well fed and safe.'

I said nothing. I thought of Robert Gower keeping my hand warm under his arm as he drove home. I thought of my head dropping on his shoulder as I slept. For the first time in a cold and hungry life I thought that I could understand longing for the touch of a man.

'Breakfast,' Mrs Greaves said, suddenly practical. 'Run and call the others, Merry.'

They were practising in the barn. David, Jack and Dandy; and Robert was watching them, his unlit pipe gripped between his teeth. Dandy was swinging from the practice trapeze and I could see that even in the day that I had been away she had learned to time herself to the rhythm of the swing. David was calling the beat for her but more and more often she was bringing her legs down at exactly the right moment and the swing was rising, gaining height, rather than trailing to a standstill as it had done on our first day.

They were glad enough to come back to the house for breakfast. David exclaimed over my black eye but it had opened enough for me to see clearly and I had taken enough knocks in my girlhood to rid me of vanity about a few bruises.

'When we were chavvies I don't think I ever saw Merry without a black eye,' Dandy said, spreading Mrs Greaves' home-made butter on a hunk of fresh-baked bread. 'If she didn't come off one of the horses then our da would clip her round the ear and miss. We didn't know her eyes were green-coloured until she was twelve!'

David looked at me as if he did not know whether to laugh or be sorry for me.

'It didn't matter,' I said. They were hurts from long ago, I would not let the aches and pains of my childhood cast a shadow over my life now. Not when I could feel myself opening, like a sticky bud on a chestnut tree in April.

'Will you be too sore to train today?' David asked me.

'I'll try,' I said. 'Nothing was broken, I was just bruised. I reckon I'll be all right to work.'

Robert pushed his clean plate away from him. 'If your face starts throbbing or your head aches, you stop,' he said. Dandy and Jack looked at him in surprise. Mrs Greaves, at the stove, stayed very still, her head turned away. 'I've seen some nasty after-effects of head injuries,' he said to David, who nodded. 'If she seems sleepy or in pain you're to send her in to Mrs Greaves.'

Mrs Greaves turned from the stove and wiped her hands on her working apron, her face inscrutable.

'If Meridon comes in ill you take care of her, ma'am,' he said to her. 'Put her on the sofa in the parlour where you can keep an eye on her.' She nodded. Dandy was frozen, a piece of bread half-way to her mouth.

'Meridon to come into the parlour?' Dandy demanded tactlessly.

A flicker of irritation crossed Robert's face. 'Why not?' he said suddenly. 'The only reason you two girls are housed in the stable yard is because I thought you would like your own little place, and it is easier for you to mind the horses. The two of you are welcome in the house, aye, and in the parlour too if you wish.'

I flushed scarlet at Dandy's slip, and at Jack's open-mouthed stare.

'It doesn't matter,' I said flatly. 'I'm well enough to work and I won't need to rest. In any case, I'd not want to sit in the parlour.'

Robert pushed his chair back from the table and it scraped on the stone-flagged floor. 'A lot of to-do about nothing,' he said gruffly and went out of the kitchen. David got to his feet as well.

'Half an hour's rest,' he said to the three of us. 'I'd like to see this famous horse of yours, Meridon.'

I smiled at that and led all of them, Mrs Greaves as well, out to the stable yard to see my horse, my very own horse, in daylight.

He was lovely. In daylight, in a familiar stable yard, he was even lovelier than I had remembered him. His neck was arched high, as if there were Arab blood in him. His coat was a dark grey, shading to pewter on his hind legs. His mane and tail were the purest of white and silver, down his grey face there was a pale white blaze, just discernible. And four white socks on his long legs. He whickered when he heard my step and came out of the stable with just a halter on, as gently as if he had never thrown and rolled on a rider in his life. He threw up his head and sidled when he saw the others and I called:

'Stand back, especially you Jack and David. He doesn't like men!'

'He'll suit Meridon, then,' said Dandy to Jack and he smiled and nodded.

Sea stood quiet enough then, and I held his head collar and smoothed his neck and whispered to him to be still, and not to be frightened, for no one would ever hurt him or shout at him again. I found I was whispering endearments, phrases of love, telling him how beautiful he was – quite the most beautiful horse in the world! And that he should be with me for ever and ever. That I had won him in Robert's bet, but that in truth we had found each other and that we would never part again. Then I led him back down through the path at the side of the garden to the field and turned him out with the others to graze.

'You'll be wanting time off to train him,' David said wryly, watching my rapt face as Sea stretched his long neck and trotted with proud long strides around the field.

'Robert wanted me to work the other horses anyway,' I said. 'I was never to be your full-time pupil.'

David nodded. 'And you've started your little savings fund,' he said. 'You'll be a lady yet, Meridon.'

I was about to smile and turn off the remark when I suddenly remembered the gypsy at the street corner in Salisbury, just before I saw Sea, just before the bet and the ride and the fall. She had said I would get my home, my gentry home. She said that my mother and her mother would lead me home, and that I would be more at home there than either of them. I would indeed be a lady, I would make my way into the Quality. David saw my suddenly absorbed expression and touched me on the shoulder. I did not flinch at his touch.

'Penny for your thoughts,' he said.

'I'll not rob you,' I replied at once. 'I was thinking nothing which was worth sharing.'

'Then I'll interrupt your thoughts with some work,' he said briskly and raised his voice so that the other two could hear: 'Come on you two! A race back to the barn to warm you up. One, two, three, and away!'

That day's training was the pattern for the following days of that week, and for the week after. Every day we worked, running, exercising, heaving ourselves up on the bar, pushing ourselves up from the floor using just our hands. Every day we grew stronger, able to run further, to do more of the exercises. Every day we ached a little less. I had learned the knack of swinging on the practice trapeze: I could build the swing higher and higher until it felt like flying. As the swing grew the swooping frightened feeling inside me grew, but I learned to almost enjoy that sudden down-rush with the air in my face and my muscles working to keep the swing moving, to build the speed and the momentum. Every day, though for some days I truly did not notice, David had raised the rigging on the trapeze so that it hung higher and higher from the floor until the only way to mount it was to go up the ladder at the side of the barn and swoop down with it.

Then one day, in the third week, while Dandy and Jack were practising swinging on the high trapeze in the roof of the barn, David called me off the practice trapeze.

I dropped to the ground and waited. I was scarcely out of breath at all now.

'I want you to try going up the ladder today,' he said gently. 'Not to swing if you don't want to, Meridon. I promised you I'd never force you, and I mean it. But for you to see if you have your nerve for heights now you are so confident on the practice trapeze. Besides, when you hang straight from the flying trapeze you are about the height from the catch-net as you are now from the floor. It's just as safe, Meridon. There's nothing to fear.'

I looked from his persuasive blue eyes up to the pedestal rigged at the roof of the barn, and at Dandy's casual confident swing on the trapeze. She and Jack were practising doing tricks into the net. As I watched, uncertain if I could face the ladder up to the rocking pedestal, Dandy launched herself off the pedestal on the trapeze and flung herself off it in a ball. She somersaulted once and fell into the net on to her back, and bounced up smiling.

'I'll try,' I said drawing a deep breath. 'I'll go up there at least.'

'Good girl,' David said warmly. He patted my back and called to Dandy. 'Go up the ladder behind your sister. She's going to see the view from the top.' To Jack he snapped his fingers. 'You come down,' he said. 'No point having all of you up there.'

I knew how to climb the ladder – heel to toe, heel to toe – and I knew to push up with my legs, not to try to haul myself up with my arms. The rope ladder trembled as I went up and I bit my tongue on a little gasp of fear.

I was afraid of stepping from the ladder to the pedestal board. It was such a tiny bit of wood with two raised poles to hold on to. It was only as wide as half my foot, and my bare toes curled over the edge as if I would grip like a dancing monkey on a stick. I clenched my hands around the poles on each side of the board, and saw my knuckles go white. I was bow-legged with fear and trying to balance. My stomach churned and I longed to piss in fright. There was nothing I could hold which was firm, which felt safe. I gave a little sob.

Dandy, coming up behind me on the ladder, heard me.

'Want to come down?' she asked. 'I'll guide you down.'

I was crouched on the pedestal now, shifted slightly to the right, both hands gripping the left-side pole. I looked at the jigging ladder where Dandy waited and feared it as much as the trapeze.

'I'm afraid,' I said. Fear had tightened my throat and I could hardly speak. My stomach pulsed with terror, my knees were bent like an old dame with rheumatism. I could not straighten up.

'Is it bad?' David called up from down below. I did not dare nod for fear that would shake the pedestal board. Dandy waited on the ladder.

'Do you want to climb down?' David called.

I opened my mouth to tell him that I did not dare climb. That I did not dare swing. I had lost my voice. All I could do was croak like a fear-struck frog.

'Get out of it,' Dandy said, careless of my deep terror. 'Grab hold of the trapeze and swing down and drop into the net, Meridon. It's the quickest way. Then you'll never have to come up again.'

I could not turn my head to look for her. I was clamped rigid by my fear. With one lithe movement she was up beside me on the pedestal and had unhooked the trapeze. She drew it towards me and took my arm and wrested it from its grip on the upright pole. I grabbed at the trapeze bar as if it might save me. It pulled me a little near the edge with its weight and I gasped a little in fright. It was dragging me off. I had not known that it would pull me so. I was midway between falling and clinging on. I did not have the strength to pull back, and my fist was clenched so tight I was not able to drop the trapeze and let it swing away.

With one swift, callous movement Dandy reached behind my back and snatched my left hand from the supporting pole. At once the weight of the trapeze dragged me forward and off the pedestal board into the void of space. In panic I grabbed at the trapeze with my free hand as a drowning man grabs at a twig in his despair. I clutched it and cried for help as I swooped down the lurching black valley of the swing in a blank haze of screaming terror.

It was like falling in dreams, in those dreadful nightmares when you seem to fall and fall for ever and the terror of them is so bad that you wake screaming. I swooped downwards clinging to the trapeze and then felt the drag as it swung up the hill of the other side of the swing. Then I was falling backwards, which was even worse, swinging back towards the pedestal and I was yelling in terror that I was going to hit the pedestal and knock Dandy off it.

'It's all right!' I heard her call from close behind me. 'Just swing, Merry! Like you do on the practice trapeze.'

The brown of the tarry string of the catch net leapt into vision as I swung down towards it again and then it fell away from me as I crested the swing. I hung like a brace of pheasants in a larder. But inside my limp hopeless body I was weeping with terror.

Three more times the swing rocked backwards and forwards with me a white doll tossed about underneath it. Then it slowed and slowed and finally stopped and I hung still above the catch-net.

'Drop down,' David called. 'You're safe now, Meridon. Drop down into the net. Keep your legs up as you drop and you'll land softly on your back. Just let go the bar, Meridon.'

I was frozen. My hands were locked tight on the bar. I looked down and there between my feet was the catch-net and, beneath it, the gleaming white of the wood shavings. Safety, solid ground. I willed myself to let the bar go.

It was no use. It was as if I had forgotten the skill to open my hands, to release my fingers. I was clenching the bar as if it were the only thing which would save me from tumbling head first into a precipice.

'Let go!' David called, his voice more urgent. 'Meridon! Listen to me! Just let go the bar and we'll have you down!'

I looked towards him and he saw the mute terror in my face. He went over to the A-frame where the catcher straddles, ready to swing the flyer forwards and back up to the trapeze. He climbed up Jack's ladder swiftly until he was parallel with me, his face on a level with my own. But too distant to reach me.

'Come on, girl,' he said, his voice soft and warmed with his Welsh accent. 'Just let your hands go and you'll drop gently in the net and we can all go and have a rest. You've worked hard this morning, you'll be ready for your dinner.'

I could feel the tears coming into my eyes and then running down my cheeks but I did not cry out. His voice was warmer.

'Come on, Merry,' he said sweetly. 'Just lift your legs up a little and lie back and you'll be down as snug as if you were laid in bed. You've seen Dandy do it a hundred times. Just lift your legs a little and let go.'

I opened my mouth to speak, but still no voice came. I took a deep breath and my overstrained back muscles shuddered. I gripped tighter with my fingers in fear of falling.

'I . . . can't,' I said.

'Course you can,' David said instantly. 'There's not the least difficulty in the world, little Merry. Lift your legs up towards me and shut your eyes and think of nothing. You'll be down in a second.'

I obeyed him, as I could, as well as I could. I did as I was bid. I lifted my legs so that when I dropped I would fall backwards into the catch net. I shut my eyes. I took a deep breath.

It was no good. My fingers were locked as if they were the latches on a door. I could not will them to open. I was clinging, like a baby monkey to its mother's back, in pure instinctive terror. I could not let go.

I did not let go.

Minutes I hung there while David talked to me gently, ordered me, begged me. Minutes while Dandy climbed up the ladder in his place and smiled at me and asked me to let go and come down to her. Her smile was strained, I could see the fright in her eyes and, despite myself, my grip tightened.

The tears poured down my cheeks, I was torn between my longing for this nightmare to be over and to be on safe ground again, and my absolute blank and helpless terror which had locked my grip so that I could not let go.

'Meridon, please!' Jack said from ground level. 'You're so brave, Meridon! Please do as David says!'

My clenched muscles around my chin and throat struggled to open. 'I . . . can't,' I said.

David climbed up the catcher's frame again. 'Meridon,' he said softly. 'Your grip is going to go soon and you will fall. You can't stop that. As you feel yourself going I want you to lift your legs so that your weight goes backwards. Then you will land on your back. If you fall straight down you will hurt yourself a little. I want you to land soft. When you feel your grip slipping get your legs up.'

I heard him. But I was far beyond obeying him. All I could feel was the singing continuous pain in my back and my shoulders and my arms and my chest. My bones felt as if they were being dragged from the sockets. My hands were like claws. But I could not tighten their grip. And though I was squeezing them harder and harder I could feel them begin to loosen and slip.

'No!' I wailed.

'Legs up!' yelled David. But I could not hear him in my panic. My fingernails clawed at the bar, my hands grasped at air. I fell like a dagger into the ground, feet first, into the catch net.

At once it threw me back up. It was stretched taut to catch Dandy falling softly on her back, not a feet-first dive. My legs doubled up, my knees cracked me in the face, my stomach lurched as the net threw me up and I fell, as helpless as a baby bird from a nest, down to the swinging merciless blow again. Four or five times I bounced, hopelessly out of control, until the last time when the fear and the shock were too much for me, and everything went blank.

10

When I came to, I was in bed; not in my own bed but in the pretty lime-washed room at the back of Robert Gower's fine house. When my eyelids quivered I could hear Robert's voice telling me in a muted whisper that I was safe in his house. He knew I could not open my eyes to see for myself. I was stone blind.

Robert Gower sat with me. He ordered Jack and Dandy back to work at once, as soon as they had carried me into the parlour and William had gone at a gallop for the Salisbury surgeon. Robert would not trust the Warminster barber. Dandy had sworn at him and said she would not leave my side but Robert had pushed her out of the room and said she might come and sit with me but not until she had swung on the high trapeze and done every single trick she had already learned.

I wanted to cry out that Dandy should not go up there, that it was too terrifying, too high for anyone, especially my beloved sister. But my throat was wracked with pain, the only noise I could make was a helpless rasping sob, and the hot tears squeezed out of my swollen eyes and stung as they ran down my scraped cheeks.

'It's for her good,' Robert said softly. I could tell from his voice that he was standing beside me. 'She's to go up at once or she'll brood over your fall and lose her nerve, Meridon. I'm not being cruel to her, or to you. David said the same.'

I would have nodded my head, but the very sinews of my neck felt as if they had been ripped out. I lay in silence, in my blind blackness, and I felt the sofa underneath me roll and shift as I lost consciousness again. 'And who will look after Dandy when I am dead?' I thought as the world slid away from me.

She was back beside me when the surgeon arrived, but she

was crying too hard to be of any help to him; easy, sorrowful tears while she washed the blood off my face with a cloth which stung as if it were on fire. I felt for her in my private darkness and whispered: 'Dandy, am I going to die?'

It was Robert Gower who held me gently so that the skilled man could feel all around my fiery neck. He had gentle hands, and I could feel him taking care not to hurt me. But every part of my neck and shoulders and throat, even the skin of my scalp, was searing with pain. It was Robert Gower who laid me back on the pillow and unbuttoned the shirt so that the man could feel my ribs. Each touch was like a burning brand but I did not cry out. Not from bravery! My throat was locked so tight I could make no sound.

'She's bad,' the surgeon said at last. 'Broken nose, contusion of the head, concussion, ricked neck, dislocated shoulder, cracked rib.'

'She'll be well again?' Robert asked.

'It will be nigh on a month at least,' the voice replied. 'Unless she takes a fever, or an ague from shock. But she seems tough enough, she should survive it. I can set the shoulder now.'

He leaned towards me; in my pain-filled darkness I could feel his breath on my cheek.

'I have to twist your arm so that it fits back into the socket of your shoulder, miss. It will hurt, but it will be better for you when it is done.'

I could say neither yes nor no. If I could have spoken I would have begged him to leave me alone.

'Best go out, Dandy,' Robert said. I was glad he was thinking of her.

I listened intently and I heard her footstep go to the door and the click of the latch. The surgeon took hold of my hand; my fist was clenched against the pain, and Robert took hold of my aching shoulders. They twisted hard with sudden force and the pain and the shock of it made me scream aloud until the darkness swallowed me up and everything was gone again.

Next time when I awoke I knew where I was. My eyes were still bruised tight shut but I could smell the lavender scent on the sheets, and I could feel the lightness of the room on my swollen eyelids. In the garden I could hear a solitary robin singing a rippling dancing tune. Some of the pain had gone. The shoulder felt better, as he had promised me it would. The eyes were eased with pads of something cool and wet. My head ached as if it had been pounded like a drum; but in the middle of my pain I smiled. I was alive.

I had truly thought that I was going to die. Yet here I was, under sweet-smelling linen sheets, with winter sunlight on my closed eyelids. Alive – able to care for Dandy, to keep her safe. Able to smell the clear scent of lavender. I felt my bruised face turn upwards in a little smile.

'Don't know what you've got to smile about.' Robert Gower spoke gruffly, he was sitting somewhere at my head. He had been so quiet I had thought myself in the room alone.

'I'm alive,' I said. It came out as a rasping croak, but I could at least speak.

'You are,' he said. 'You're the luckiest little kitten which ever escaped a drowning, Meridon. I thought you were dead when I saw David bringing you into the kitchen with blood everywhere and your arm hanging as if it were broken. Mrs Greaves shrieking, Dandy crying and hollering at David. David cursing himself and all of us for not listening to you! The whole thing was a damned nightmare, and now here you are looking like a wagon drove over you, and smiling as if you are happy!'

My smile stretched a little broader at that, but broke off in a wince as my neck hurt me. 'I am happy,' I said hoarsely. 'Is Dandy all right?'

Robert made a little 'tsk' noise of impatience. 'Aye,' he said. 'She's down in the kitchen eating her dinner. I said I'd sit with you while they ate.'

I said nothing, and we sat in silence for long minutes while the robin sang outside in the garden and the shadows on my eyelids grew darker.

Then I felt a gentle touch, as soft as a robin's feather on the clenched fingers of my hand.

'I am sorry, Meridon,' Robert said softly. 'I would not have had you hurt for the world. We're all sorry that you went up. You need never go up again. I'll get a poorhouse girl tomorrow to start training. You can stick with the horses.'

I shut my eyes on that thought and started the slide into sleep where my bruises would not hurt me and the smell of lavender might make me dream of Wide. I heard, as if from a long way away, Robert whisper: 'Good-night, my brave little Merry.' Then I thought I felt – but I must have been mistaken – the featherlight touch of lips on my clenched fist.

He was as good as his word and I heard from David and from Dandy that the workhouse girl started the next day. She was chosen because she had been a farm worker in wheat country – a lifetime of heaving stooks had given her hard muscles in her belly and arms. David also told me (though Dandy, notably, did not) that she looked ravishing up high on the pedestal. She had long blonde hair which she let fly free behind her. She had no fear of heights and no nerves, and though she started a whole month behind the other two she was swinging from the high trapeze and doing the simplest of tricks into the net within a few weeks.

The surgeon had ordered me to rest and I was glad to lie still. My face was awful. I had two black eyes which closed so tight that for the first three or four days I was fully stone blind. I had broken my nose when my knees cracked up into my face, and for the rest of my life it would be slightly skewed.

It was many days before I was able to walk down across the field to see them working. I passed the horses on the way and saw Sea in the far corner of the field, his coat a deep grey shimmer. Robert had promised me that no one would touch him while I was ill. He might grow a little wilder, but he would have no fresh memories of rough handling. He was fed with the other horses, and brought indoors when nights were cold. But while Robert trained them and taught them their new tricks, Sea was left out in the field.

There was a hard frost on the ground, it looked as if it might snow for Christmas. I cared little either way. Da and Zima had never celebrated Christmas in our dirty little caravan and my only memory of the festival was that it was a good time for Dandy to pick pockets while the mummers went around, and a good time for selling horses for spoilt children. Our birthday fell some time after Christmas. This year we would be sixteen. We never paid no mind to either Christmas nor our birthday – whenever it was.

'Cold,' Robert said. He was walking with me, his hand under my elbow to help me over the frozen molehills and hard tussocks of grass.

'Yes,' I said. 'Will you bring the horses in all day if it snows?'

'Nay,' he said. 'I can't afford to make them soft. The time will come when we do shows all the year round. I've already turned down work at a Goose fair outside Bath over the Christmas holidays. If you'd been well I'd have taken at least you and Jack to work the fair. I'll let it go this year, but next year we'll lay off in October, work for December and the Twelfth Night fairs, and then lay off again until Shrove Tuesday.'

He looked at the barn as if he were staring into the future.

'I'll take a complete show out on the road. The horses will open the show and do the first half, and then during the interval we'll rig up the net and the frames. When I can get a barn we'll take it and do evening shows by lamplight as well.' He looked beyond the barn, to where the afternoon sun was red on the horizon. 'There's more and more places which stay open all year round,' he said longingly. 'Where they've built a hall with the ring in the middle, aye, and a stage behind for singing and dancing. A few good years on the road, and maybe I could build my own place with the rigging up high and the ring underneath, and we would not need to travel from fair to villages – the audience would come to us.'

I nodded. 'You could do that,' I said with a little smile, looking at his rapt face. 'It might work. A big enough town, with lots of people travelling through, and wealthy people who would come again and again. It might work.'

He glanced down at me. 'You believe in me,' he said.

'Aye,' I said simply. 'I always have.'

There was a little silence then, between us.

'Now,' he said. 'You see how your sister is doing!'

He flung open the door to the barn and we went in. They were losing the light inside and were doing the last tricks of the day before stopping work. The poorhouse girl, Katie, was on the ladder. Dandy was on the pedestal. Jack was standing astride on the catcher's frame.

I felt my throat grow dry and I swallowed at the sight of Dandy looking so small and up so high.

'Right!' David called. He was on the ground below the flyers' ladder. 'Last trick of the day, and we have an audience so let's show what we can do! Dandy! Let's have that trick again.'

Dandy climbed two paces up an extra ladder above the pedestal to give herself more height and took the trapeze in both hands. Jack checked the buckles which held the thick leather belt at his waist, and rubbed his hands together, scowling and looking upwards. I hardly saw him. I was watching Dandy like a field-mouse watches a circling hawk far above him. I saw her smile. She was happy enough.

I looked back to Jack. He was watching Dandy's swing build up until she came so close that if he reached out he could tap her on the feet. He shifted a little, as if to ready himself and then he called, 'Pret!' in the way David had taught him. Dandy beat with her legs and swung a little harder, then Jack shouted, 'Hup!' and Dandy stretched her feet out towards him as far as she could.

For a moment she seemed to hang in space, quite motionless. Then Jack reached out and we heard the firm slap of his hands on her ankles. At that moment Dandy let go the trapeze and swung, head down, arms trailing, through Jack's legs, through the A-frame, while Jack bent low to swing her.

She crested the swing on the other side and Jack let her swing back underneath him just as the trapeze swung back towards them. Then, with a scowl of concentration, Jack twisted his arms and Dandy half turned so she slewed around, still travelling in the air to face the trapeze as it came towards her, reached out her hands to it and took a firm grip as Jack released her feet.

Dandy swooped upwards, clinging to her trapeze, and then back to the pedestal. Katie at the top reached out and caught her round the waist and helped her up. Dandy turned around and shrieked, 'Bravo!' to herself, Robert, and me, and we burst into spontaneous clapping.

'Well done!' Robert called up. 'That is wonderful, Dandy! Well done Jack and well done David! That's grand! Is there any more?'

Again they readied themselves. Dandy built up the swing and then put her legs back and looped them around the bar of the trapeze. Jack watched her, called, 'Pret!' to Dandy to warn her he was ready for her on the next swing. Then we heard him shout, 'Hup!' This time she had further to reach and there was almost a second when she released the safe lock of her legs on the trapeze before we heard the slap of his hands on her wrists. He swung her forwards and then back and Dandy flew from his hands, turning a languid elegant somersault before bouncing safely into the net.

I was sorry that I was such a fool with the ladder and the height that I could not be up there beside her. I should have liked to have been close to Dandy when she was swinging. I should have liked it to have been me who grabbed her around her slim waist and hauled her in. I would have liked to have helped her back on to the pedestal from the sickening drop beneath her.

'What can Katie do?' Robert called to David.

'She's not being caught yet,' David called back. 'The idea is that she does the trick and she and Jack just touch – so that they learn where each other is. She's not ready to finish the trick yet.'

Robert nodded and we watched as Katie swooped across, and Jack slapped her ankles with a sound which echoed around the frosty air and she dropped into the net, turning up her feet and falling on her back.

'Good work,' Robert said. He took David by the shoulder and led him out of the barn, pausing only to damp down the stove.

Katie climbed out of the net and smiled at me. We had already met – Dandy had brought her up to the spare bedroom to meet me when she started work for Robert – but we had hardly spoken.

'Well done!' I said. 'You are far ahead of me, and I had a month's full practice.'

'I had a good teacher,' she said with a sly little smile. I thought for a moment that she had meant David, but then I saw that she was looking towards Jack as he came down the ladder hand over hand, his legs and feet held clear to one side.

Katie pushed back her mass of yellow hair. 'You slapped me hard enough today,' she said to Jack. Her voice, heavy with the Dorset burr, had a provocative little lilt to it. 'My wrists is all red.'

She held her arms out to him, palms up so that he should see the red marks. I shot a look at Dandy. She was staring at Katie as if she had never seen her before.

'That's nothing,' David said baldly. 'Hello, Merry. Are you walking all right?'

'I'm stiff,' I confessed, 'and a bit unsteady. But I feel well enough now.'

Jack's smile was openly warm. 'I missed you,' he said frankly. 'It's good to see you in here again. What did you think of Dandy?'

He drew me towards him and put an arm around my waist to support me as we walked towards the door. I let him help me over the hard ground, as I had let his father guide me before. I did not flinch from the touch of the Gowers. Father and son, I had come to trust them. And Jack's touch on my waist was warm, I could feel the roughness of his hand through the linen shirt.

Katie popped up on his other side, took his arm.

'What did you think of the act, Meridon?' she asked. 'Isn't Jack fine? I feel so brave when I hears him calling the swing. I just jumps when he tells me!'

I hesitated. I felt as if during my illness a whole world had shifted slightly so that everything was out of frame. I looked past Jack at Dandy. She was blank-faced too.

'It was fine,' I said neutrally. 'Robert was pleased.'

'Robert!' The poorhouse girl gave a little affected scream. 'I calls him Mr Gower. I'd never dare call him Robert!' She seemed to cling a little closer to Jack. 'I really do respects your da,' she assured him.

Jack turned his head to me and gave me one of his slow provocative winks.

'So you should,' he said. 'Merry and my father are old friends. He gave her the right to call him by his given name. And Dandy. Everything is different when we're working all together on the road.'

'I can't wait!' she exclaimed. 'I can't wait to get away from this horrid little village where everyone looks at me and points at me. I can't wait to get away to do shows every night, and me and Dandy wear our pretty short skirts!'

I looked across at Dandy. It was my guess that she would be seething with temper. I was right. Her face had that curiously intense expression which came over her in one of her sudden total rages.

'Dandy,' I said quickly, before she could explode. 'Dandy, can you take me to the kitchen? I want to sit down.'

Jack stopped, went to lift me, but I put out an ungracious elbow and pushed him off.

'I'll go with Dandy,' I said.

'All right,' Katie said blithely. 'We'll check the horses together, won't we Jack?'

Jack gave me another of his rueful lazy looks and let her turn him, let her lead him away into the gathering darkness towards the stable and the hay loft.

'My oath, what a whore,' I exclaimed to Dandy under my breath.

Her black eyes were blazing. 'The damned she-dog!' she said. 'I'll scratch her eyes out if she tries anything on with Jack!'

'You can hardly be surprised,' I said. 'She's been here a good three weeks. Surely she was like this all along?'

Dandy was almost incoherent with temper. 'No! No!' she said. 'D'you think I'd have stood for it? With my Jack? Not a damned look, not so much as a whisper. All she's done is work night and day on the trapeze and learned to swing. She never so much as glanced at him!'

'Why now, then?' I asked puzzled.

Dandy scowled dreadfully towards the bright lights of the kitchen which shone over the darkening garden. 'It's you,' she said suddenly. 'It must be you. She's never done it before. She thinks he's after you. He came down the ladder all showy to please you, and he put his arm around you. He's been asking for you every day, and he went to Salisbury twice to buy you flowers and once for fruit. His da never told him wrong for wasting the time either. She must think he's courting you and she's trying to cast poison.'

I gaped. 'She's mad,' I said blankly. 'Doesn't she know what Robert would do if he thought any of us were setting lures for Jack?'

'No,' Dandy said swiftly. 'She's hardly seen Robert. He's been training the horses all day, while we've been working. He's never told her what he plans for Jack. He's hardly spoken to her.'

We stood for a moment in silence gazing at each other and then suddenly we both broke into laughter. 'Oh don't! Oh! Don't!' I said, holding my sides. 'My ribs still hurt! Don't make me laugh, Dandy!'

'Won't he be absolutely wild when he finds out!' Dandy crowed. 'Won't she catch it then! It'll be back to the poorhouse for her! Act or no act!'

I stopped laughing for a moment. 'That's a bit hard,' I said. 'It's a high price to pay for being a bit of a flirt.'

Dandy's face was stony. 'Who cares?' she demanded. 'I won't have her hanging on Jack. If Jack goes with any one of us, he goes with me. I've been ready enough to keep things cold between us because his da ordered it and you begged me; but if she is crawling all over him I'm damned if I see him taken away from me!'

'Now Dandy, it's nothing,' I said swiftly. 'It's probably as you say – that she was trying to tease me, to put me in my place. She doesn't know that none of us court Jack. That none of us work like that. I'm back sleeping in the stables tonight. I'll tell her then.'

Dandy tossed her thick black hair and looked mulish. 'I'd rather we just told Robert that she was chasing Jack and let her go back to wherever she came from,' she said unkindly. 'I don't like having her in my room. I don't like her hanging on Jack. I saw him first. He saw me. He's had eyes for me from that first day, Merry. We only did nothing to please his da. You know that.'

I thought a moment. I remembered Jack's hot eyes upon me, and how he had asked me if I dreamed of him. I thought of him watching me as I swam and being angered by my indifference.

'He's a coquette as bad as her,' I said without sympathy. 'He'd go with any girl who flattered his vanity, and he'd be challenged by any girl who kept him at a distance. I'd not be surprised to see him take up with her.'

Dandy grabbed my arm. 'I mean this, Merry,' she said rapidly. 'I've held off from him because I wanted to see how the land lay with his da, and it's been so different here. I wanted to see if there was any chance of this damned future that Robert plans for him. But I wanted him when I first saw him. And I want him still.'

I held her away from me and looked at her carefully. I knew Dandy, I had watched and loved her as close as a mother, as intently as a lover. I knew she was only speaking half the truth. The part which she would not admit was her vanity and her pride. She could not stand the thought that Jack might go into the hay loft with the pretty fair-headed pauper when he had obeyed his father and not laid a finger on Dandy for month after tempting month. Dandy had been the prettiest girl any of us had ever seen for so long, that the thought of coming second best was enough to overset her.

'Oh come on, Dandy,' I said reasonably. 'I know you fancy him. He's a nice enough young lad. Vain as a monkey, but nice enough. But you know how Robert is about him; he looks very high for him. There's no chance for anything more for you than a kiss and a romp. You could do better than that. When you're

Mamselle Dandy you'll meet better men than Jack could ever be. It's as Robert says: if you keep your head then you could marry well. That's better than a roll in the hay with a lad whose father could ruin you if he caught you.'

For a moment she looked uncertain, but then we heard the trapdoor to the upstairs room at the stables slam and Dandy's eyes blazed.

'The little whore!' she said, and she tore herself out of my grip and raced towards the stables.

I tried to run after her but my ribs still hurt, and my shoulder. I followed on behind, and by the time I reached the stables Jack was tumbling down the stairs shrugging his jacket on. He gave me one of his naughty sideways grins.

'Hey, Merry,' he said. 'Dandy's thrown me out of your room, says she wants to change into her gown for dinner. I'll see you later.'

'What were you doing in my room, Jack?' I asked him, curious for his answer.

He gave me a wink. 'Nowt serious, Merry,' he said.

'Hasn't your father warned you off Katie?' I asked curiously.

Jack's dark gaze twinkled. 'Half of Warminster has had her,' he said. 'My da wouldn't waste his breath. He knows I won't let it affect my work. He knows she won't get a belly on her. He knows it's not loving. He don't care.'

Jack beamed at me for a moment. 'Are you jealous, Merry?' he asked softly. 'Did you think I was kissing the soft hairs on the back of her neck, and licking the hollow between her shoulder blades? Did you want that for yourself?'

I stepped backwards so that he could see my face clearly in the light of the horn lantern. I knew my face was calm, my eyes clear, unmoved.

'No,' I said. 'I did not want that for myself. I will never want that. Not from you, not from any man. I wondered if you were man enough to go against your da's word or if you would stay a virgin all your life to please him. Now I understand, you'll only have your poke where he permits.'

Jack flushed brick-red with anger at that gibe.

'I don't admire your taste,' I said loftily. 'But don't forget that your da only allowed her. He said you were not to have Dandy.'

Jack threw his hands up in impatience. 'Dandy!' he said. 'She's all you ever think of!'

'Don't you think of her?' I demanded, quick as a hawk in training to a lure.

Jack shrugged. 'Not much,' he said lightly. 'I can live without her.'

'Good,' I said, and I meant it. Robert Gower was the only man in the world who would feed and house Dandy and me while I was bruised and battered and unable to work and while Dandy had no skill she could sell on her own. We were as dependent on him as if we were his pauper servants. I knew now that Dandy desired Jack and I feared she would make a set for him. The only thing which stood between us and the frozen road out of Warminster was Jack's respect for his father's wishes.

'Don't forget your da said you were not to look at her,' I insisted.

Jack shrugged his shoulders and rolled his eyes at the darkening night sky. 'Merry, you carry on like some prioress. I don't want your damned sister. I could do with a roll in the hay. Katie offered it for free. I'd do it with Katie, I wouldn't touch Dandy with a ten-foot barge pole. All right?'

'All right,' I said at last.

I hoped to God it was.

11

I expected to find Katie with her shirt ripped and her face scratched. Poorhouse brat she might be, Warminster whore she might be, but I did not think she would exceed my sister in the art of dirty fighting. But when I climbed slowly up the stairs to the loft-bedroom they were sitting side by side brushing each other's hair and giggling together.

'He put his hand down the inside of my shirt!' I heard Katie say. Dandy giggled delightedly. 'I said to him: "I don't know what you're looking for down there, Jack!"'

Dandy rocked with laughter at this sally. 'You never did!' she said. 'What did he do then?'

'He took my hand and put it down his breeches!' Katie said triumphantly.

'And?' Dandy prompted.

Katie's sharp hungry little face grew avid. 'He was hot,' she said. 'He was hard as a stallion to a mare.'

I was watching Dandy's face and I saw a shadow of absolute envy pass across it. But she laughed merrily enough.

'I'm sorry I came in and spoiled sport then!' she said lightly. 'Would you have done it with him, if I had not come in?'

'Oh aye!' Katie said at once. 'I was hot for it too!'

She and Dandy fell into each other's arms and rocked with laughter. Dandy's eyes met mine across the fair head and her dark eyes were cold as ice.

'I'm surprised he dares,' she said. 'When Merry and I joined the show his da told us plain that there was to be no courting.'

Katie's smile was world-weary. ''Tis hardly courting,' she said. 'It's just a bit of fun. You'd hardly call it courting. We're neither of us new to it. And neither of us would speak of love.

Mr Gower told me I was to mind my ways in the village. He didn't say nothing about at home.'

'But you don't care for Jack?' Dandy asked sharply.

Katie laughed lazily, put her hands to her head to pin up her tumbling blonde hair. 'I cared enough a minute ago,' she said lazily. 'I'd have cared to do it with him then. But I don't mind now. If I get needful I can sneak down to the Bush in the village. There's a couple of lads down there I know well. They'll meet me behind a hedge somewhere so Mr Gower don't know. They'll give me a penny as well.'

Dandy's smile was as warm as ice on a bucket. 'Would you refuse him then?' she asked. 'I've had my eye on him since last summer. His da said "no" and he hasn't dared. But I've had my eye on him for my very own. Would you refuse him if he comes to you again? To oblige me, Katie?'

Katie threw back her lovely head and laughed aloud. 'Nay!' she said. 'I shouldn't have the heart! And I had my hand down inside his breeches, Dandy, and he felt real fine to me. I couldn't find it in me to say "no".'

'I'd pay,' Dandy said patiently. 'I'd pay you more money than you'd ever think to earn in all your life.'

Katie sneered. 'Got your pennies saved up have you, Dandy? Saved your pennies from your horseback riding?'

'I'd pay you a guinea,' Dandy said. She heard my gasp and she avoided my eyes. 'I'd pay you a guinea if you promise not to have him. I'd pay you a guinea and I'll give it to you at Whitsun.'

'Where'd you get a guinea from?' Katie said, impressed despite herself.

'We've got it already,' Dandy said proudly. 'You know Merry's got her own horse. We're doing better than you think. We've got ten guineas between the two of us, and some shillings for spending money. You're straight out of the poorhouse, you don't understand what it's like for us with our own act. You've never seen Merry work the horses. She can earn a lot of money. We're only staying with Robert Gower this year. Next year we could go anywhere. Anyway, I've got a guinea all right. And it's yours if you keep your hands off Jack.'

'Dandy,' I said in an urgent undertone.

But it was too late. The poorhouse whore spat into her dirty palm and Dandy shook quickly, before she could change her mind. Dandy got up and went to the mirror and pulled at the string bow which was tying her hair. 'I'll know if you cheat, mind,' she said to her reflection.

Katie slumped back on her pallet. 'I won't cheat,' she said disdainfully. 'You can keep your Jack. I have lovers I don't have to buy. I wish you good luck with him.'

Dandy turned away from the mirror. I thought she would be angry at the gibe but her face was serene. 'I have to get around his father yet,' she said thoughtfully. 'Buying you off is just the start of it.'

She pulled her gown out of the clothes chest and slipped it on over her shift. She brushed out her hair and pinned it on top of her head. There was a very faint tide mark of grime at her bare neck and she rubbed at it with a damp forefinger and then put a clean white collar atop.

I sat on my bed and said nothing. Katie got to her feet and pulled on her poorhouse skirt as a replacement for her working breeches. She looked from Dandy to me and then went down the stairs to the stables below in silence.

'One guinea,' I said grimly.

Dandy turned from the mirror and put out her hands to me. 'Don't look like that, Merry,' she said. 'If I pull Jack and marry him then we won't need your little ten guineas, we'll have this house and the whole show.'

'If you so much as try then my little ten guineas is all we'll have,' I said miserably. 'Robert warned you, Dandy, and he warned Jack in front of us, and neither of you said so much as a whisper. He'll put us out, both of us. And then where will we be? All we'll have is a sixteen-hand hunter trained to nothing, you a trapeze artist without a trapeze, and me a rosinback rider without a horse.'

Dandy went to hold me but I put my hands up to fend her off. I was still too sore all over, and anyway I did not want her caresses.

'He'll never marry you, Dandy,' I said certainly. 'If you're lucky he'll have you and then forget all about it.'

Dandy smiled at me, a long slow powerful smile. Then she dived under the straw mattress of her bed and brought out a little linen bag.

'Robert sent me to the wise woman,' she said. 'I lied and told him it was double the price. She told me how to get rid of a baby if I should have one. She told me when it was safe to go with a man so I should not get with child; and . . .' Dandy opened the drawstring at the neck of the bag and showed me the few dusty leaves inside, 'she sold me this!'

'What is it?' I asked. I sat down on my bed. I was feeling deeply weary. Tired because of my bruising and aches, but sick inside at the way that some danger and trouble seemed to be growing greater every moment without me being able to stay it or turn Dandy from her course.

'It's a love potion,' she said triumphantly. 'She knew I was Rom and I would know how to use it. I shall hex him, Merry, and I shall bring him to me. I shall have him begging for me. And then he'll persuade his da to let us be wed.'

I leaned back against the wall and closed my eyes. Night had fallen outside and the room was lit only by the firelight.

'You're mad,' I said wearily. 'Robert Gower would never have you wed Jack.'

'That's where you're wrong!' Dandy said triumphantly. 'Everyone has noticed how he is about you. Mrs Greaves, David, even Jack himself. Jack said that he was as worried about your fall as if you had been his own daughter. He's softer with you than he is with any of us, even Jack. You're the key to Robert Gower, Merry! He wants you to work for him for always. He wants you to train his horses for him. He sees now that you're as good as he is, he'll soon see that the way to keep you with his show is to marry one of us into it. He knows you'd never marry so that only leaves me. Me and Jack!' she concluded.

I closed my eyes and tried to think. It was possible. Robert Gower could not have taken more care of me if I had been his own child. The surgeon's fees alone would run into pounds. It was true that I trained horses better than anyone I had ever seen. I had won him a fortune that day in Salisbury. There were other shows looking for horses and trainers. I had only Sea, but he could be made into a wonderful act if I wished. Dandy was only an apprentice, but there could not be a prettier girl flyer in the world. She was certainly the only girl flyer in the country.

But ... I stopped and opened my eyes. Dandy had tucked away her little bag of herbs inside her shift and was tying her pinny around her waist. 'You'd never persuade Robert,' I said. 'Not in a hundred years, not on your own. The only person who could turn him around would be Jack. And you will never get Jack to stand up to his da.'

Dandy's face was as clear as a May morning. 'I will,' she said confidently. 'When he's my lover he'll do anything for me.'

If I had been stronger I should have argued more. Even then, as I closed my eyes against the dizzy hazy pain of headaches and old bruises, I knew that I should sit up and make Dandy see sense. That she needed my protection more than she had ever done in her life. But I failed her. I leaned back against the wall and rested until she had pinned her cap and was ready for us to go to dinner. Even then, as the three of us walked over to the house, I should have told Katie that the promised guinea was mine and not Dandy's, and that I should not pay it. She could have Jack with my blessing.

But I was tired and ill and, I suppose, lazy. I had not the strength to go against Dandy's overpowering conviction. I did not even have the wit to keep my eyes open to see if she palmed the herbs and got them into his cup of tea at dinner. I just let her go her own way, even though there was something in the back of my mind which told me that I had let the dearest person in the world slip through my fingers and had not put out a hand to save her.

My sense of miserable foreboding stayed with me so long that Robert spoke of sending for the surgeon again.

'You've lost your smiles, Merry,' he said. We were in the stable yard and I was ready to start working Sea. I had decided to treat him as if he were unbroken – train him to a lunge rein, and take him slowly through all the stages of a young horse as if he had never been ridden before. His head nodded to me over the loose-box and I was anxious to begin, but Robert touched my arm.

'I'd send for the surgeon,' he offered. 'He'll not be working from Christmas Eve tomorrow till Twelfth Night, but if you feel ill, Merry, he'll come out for me.'

I paused and looked at Robert. His face was kindly, his eyes warm with concern.

'Robert,' I said directly. 'Would you let me be a partner in your business? The ten guineas I have – would you let me buy more horses with them and we could work them jointly? Would you let Dandy and me be joint owners with you?'

Robert stared at me blankly for a moment, as if he could not think what the words meant. Then I watched the coldness spread across his face. It started at his eyes which lost their affectionate twinkle and became as hard and stony as a man driving a bad bargain. The smile died away from his lips and his mouth set hard in a thin line. Even the lines of his profile became sharper, and under the joyful, laughing showman I saw the bones and sinews of the ruined carter who staked his livelihood on his little boy dancing on the back of one horse, and drove away from the woman who had tried to trap him with her love.

'No,' he said, and his voice was icy. 'No, Meridon. This is my show, my own show, and God knows I have worked hard enough for it and long enough for it. There will never be a share in it for anyone but Jack. It will never go out of my family. It is all the kin I now acknowledge. I'll pay you a better wage, if you're discontent. I'll pay Dandy tuppence a show whenever she works. But I'll not share it.'

For a moment his face was almost pleading, as if he were asking me to understand an obsession. He looked down at me. 'I've come so far to make it my own,' he said. 'I've done things I'll have to answer for to my Maker . . .' He broke off and I wondered if he could hear in his head the voice of the woman calling him from behind the swaying wagon. 'I can't share, Merry,' he said finally. 'It isn't in my nature.'

I waited, then put out a placatory hand to him. 'Don't be angry,' I cautioned. 'I want to ask you a question but don't rip up at me.'

His face grew even more closed. 'What?' he said.

I had a moment's intense impatience that I should have to stand in a stable yard and ask a man not to be angry with me for a question which I had not even yet voiced. Dandy's intense female need had brought me to the slavish role of trying to prepare a man for a request which I myself thought was unreasonable. Something of this must have shown in my face, for Robert suddenly grinned:

'Not like you to tread cautiously, Merry,' he said. 'Are you learning pretty pleasing girlish ways from your sister and the Warminster whore?'

I gritted my teeth and then, unwillingly, laughed. 'No,' I said. 'But it's a question you might dislike.'

'Get on with it then,' he said, weary of this fencing.

'I want a share in the show,' I said. 'If you couldn't abide strangers coming in, how would it be if Dandy and Jack were to make a match of it? I know you looked higher for him, but he and Dandy working together make a good team. They could make their fortunes. Marriage is the only way you'll keep Dandy. And where she goes, I go.'

Robert looked at me and I could see the pinched impoverished man looking out of his eyes.

'No,' he said blankly. 'No woman is irreplaceable. If Dandy gets a better offer she can go. You can go with her. There are times when I love you like a daughter, Merry, but I have loved and left a daughter before now, and never regretted it. If you can't work for me on wages then you'd best leave.' He nodded at the stable, at the barn beyond where Dandy and Jack were practising the only touring trapeze act in England. 'I'd change my plans for the season, I'd throw away all my hopes rather than see Dandy wed Jack,' he said. 'You're a pair of draggle-tailed gypsies and she's as hot as a bitch in heat. I look a good deal higher for my son, I'd see you both dead at my feet rather than have him wed either of you and bring your tainted gypsy blood into my family and into my show.'

I took a deep breath of the cold winter air and I dropped him a curtsey, as low and as slavish as Zima's broad-arsed bobs.

'Thank you, sir,' I said, as if he had tipped me a farthing. 'I quite understand now.'

I turned from him and walked towards my horse, Sea. I slid the bridle on his head and opened the door to let him out in a daze of anger and hatred. I walked past Robert – Robert who had been so kind to me and had held me when the surgeon pulled at my arm – I walked past him and I hardly saw him. There was a hot red haze around my eyes and I think if I had spat on his boots as I passed it would have come out as blood. My pulse was thundering in my head and my hand on Sea's lunging reins gripped by instinct, not care. In the back of my mind I knew it was Dandy's folly that had led me into this idiot's babble of marriage and sharing. But I knew also that the warm summer days in the wagon and the hard wintry work at Warminster had led me to see Robert's interests and ours as running in harness. Dandy's foolish lust for Jack had blinded me as well as her. She had convinced me she could have him. She had nearly convinced me she could keep him. I had needed Robert's coldness to sober me.

He had looked in my face and had spoken to me as a man of substance speaks to a servant girl. Worse. He had spoken to me as a freeholder and a citizen speaks to a dirty travelling slut. All the work I had done for him and the knocks I had taken for him had not served to alter the fact that he had bought me from Da as a job lot in with a pony and a girl they both knew was a slut. I walked away from him, and I walked away from the tiny growing hope I had felt that there might be bridges which I could build from the world of the people who belonged, who slept soft and kept clean, and mine. There were no bridges. There was an absolute division.

As I led Sea down to the paddock I longed for Wide with as much passion as if I were still in my lice-ridden bunk listening to Da humping Zima. I had not belonged there. I did not belong here. I felt as if I would belong nowhere until I could own my own land and command servants of my own. There was no middling course for me, there was no staging place. It seemed I was condemned to the very ditch of society unless I could somehow scramble my way, all alone, to the top. I had to get to the top. I had to get where I belonged. I had to go to Wide.

I stepped back from the horse and clicked to him to get going. He was new to the work or else he had forgotten the skill. I worked with him all morning though my hands were stiff and my cheeks were icy. It was only when I went into the kitchen for my breakfast that I found they had become red and chapped because I had been crying into the cold east wind for all of the time.

We hardly noticed the Christmas season. Robert was distant and cold to us all since that time in the yard. He spun a silver coin down the table to Jack at breakfast on Christmas morning and he gave Dandy and Katie and me a thrupenny piece each. Mrs Greaves had a bolt of material, William a penny, David a rather good pair of second-hand gloves.

That was it. We all went back to work, and Christmas was just another day of training horses for me and working on the trapeze for the rest of them.

The new ponies bought at Salisbury were going well with the others and Robert had taught me the moves with the stick in one hand and the whip in the other and the words to call at them. We had a pretty little act with them coming into the ring and splitting into two teams, crossing from one side to another, passing while they circled (I always lost the smallest one who would tag on to the wrong team), pirouetting on the spot, and finally taking a bow while I stood in the middle of them smiling at where the audience would be, with my back to them as if I could trust them on their own – which I absolutely could not.

I worked them every morning before breakfast, while Robert watched the trapeze practice or worked at his accounts inside the house. After we had eaten we took Bluebell and the new horse,

Morris, into the field and I practised vaulting on them, and standing. Bluebell was steady as a rock, she had learned the job with Jack all those years ago and I was probably a welcome relief – a good deal lighter even if I did tend to overshoot and go flying off the far side.

'Don't jump!' Robert would yell irritably from the centre of the ring while his pipe puffed little signals up at the cold blue sky. 'Let the horse's speed take you up. All you do is get your feet off the ground. Her canter will do the rest!'

I had mastered standing up on the horse with Jack to hold me, but with Robert keeping the horse at a steady pace I was learning to stand alone. First, hanging on like grim death to the strap, but gradually – as we trained every day, snow or shine – learning to let the strap drop and balance with my arms outstretched holding nothing, standing head up, my feet shifting and stepping on the horse's bouncing haunches.

In the later afternoon Jack would come out of the barn to work with us. Dandy and Katie would train without him, sometimes flying tricks to David who would catch them, sometimes practising by flying a trick to the right position but dropping into the net, but most of the time practising the new trick David had taught them – a cross-over – where Dandy swung out on the trapeze and was caught by Jack as Katie took off on the returning trapeze. Dandy would somersault from Jack's hands into the net as Katie was caught by him, then Katie could either try to swing back up to the pedestal board, or drop down to the net too. David, Jack and Robert all said it looked wonderful. It was to be the final trick of the show. Katie and Dandy preened themselves and looked smug once they had the timing right. I had no opinion on it at all. I simply could not watch it.

By the end of December David had all but finished his task, on time, and earned the promised bonus. He had given Robert a trained trapeze troupe: one boy catcher and two girl flyers; and that without too many mishaps. They had a routine of tricks: Dandy could swing from her bar to Jack into a leg-catch, she could do a bird's nest across when she got her feet tucked behind the trapeze bar while still holding on with her hands and then, at the last moment, stretched out her hands to be caught. She could do a pass they called the angel pass with one leg pointing to the roof and the other pointing down, when he handed her back to her own trapeze holding a hand and a foot, and she and Katie could reliably do a cross-over. Katie's best trick was the angel pass. It looked showy but actually it was one of the easiest. David had taught them all how to do somersaults and twisters, into the net. They would have to practise them on their own.

He spent the last few days working with me on the practice trapeze. As long as I did not have to climb the ladder up to the pedestal I did not feel that icy shaking fear. I could do a number of tricks, get the trapeze swinging, drop underneath it so that I was upside down, get into the bird's nest position, hang from my feet alone. Robert had it in mind to sling the trapeze under Dandy's A-frame, and to use me as a warm-up act after the interval to get the crowd ready for the real trapeze work which would go on high above my head. I had no objection except I stipulated I should wear my breeches and a shirt.

'For God's sake, Meridon!' Robert said irritably. 'You can't do a trapeze act dressed like a stable lad. You'll wear a short skirt and a stomacher top and air your bubbies like the other girls.'

'Nowt to show!' Katie whispered.

I narrowed my eyes and said nothing.

David intervened. 'It takes something of the excitement away from the aerial act,' he said judiciously. 'It detracts from the girls up high if Merry is only half-way up but dressed the same. Why don't we dress her like Jack? She can wear tight white breeches like him and a billowy shirt top. She'd look grand, and that leaves the two girl flyers half-naked as they like to be!'

Katie and Dandy simpered. Jack nodded. 'It suits us all better, Da,' he said. 'And you'll have the Justices down on you for sure if you have a lass half-naked that near ground level.'

'All right,' Robert said. 'The girls can wear blue costumes, and Jack and Meridon can have blue silk shirts. Meridon can use one of your short blue skirts when she's doing her rosinback act.'

'She should have her own, in a different colour,' said Dandy. Katie nodded. Neither of them wanted to share.

'She'd look nice in green,' Katie volunteered.

David and Robert shook their heads in unison. 'Green's unlucky in the ring,' David said.

'Share your damned skirts you lazy wenches,' Robert said. 'Or make up another one in red.'

'Down to my knees,' I said.

Robert nodded. 'That's settled then,' he said briskly. Then he turned to David. 'You've done a grand job, I'm proud of you. We'll have a dinner tonight to celebrate. Mrs Greaves is roasting a haunch of venison now.'

David did his little showman's bow, his hand on his heart. 'I'm obliged, sir,' he said formally.

Robert nodded at us. 'Finish your practice and turn out the horses and then come in, the rest of you,' he said. 'You can all take a glass of wine tonight to say farewell to your trainer. He's done you proud.'

He turned and went out of the door. I dropped from the practice trapeze and watched Jack catching as Katie came towards him, her little face grimacing with concentration.

David called them down and all three of them threw somersaults into the net, a showy confident end to a good act. I watched the wood shavings underneath my boots.

'Listen to me, you three,' David said, his voice lilting. 'I've done with you now and these are my final words to be taken seriously.' He turned to Jack. 'Watch the rigging,' he said. 'These are good frames and I've used such things myself. But the net is a new idea. I don't know when it will get old. I don't know whether it will stretch. Test it every time you get it out with a couple of hay bales into the middle, and watch it. Your lives depend on it. Don't forget.'

Jack nodded, his face grave.

'You keep the beat,' David said to him as if he were passing on a mantle of office. 'You call the trick, and if they're not ready or out of time, you keep yourself out of their way and let them swing back, away from you again. It's not your job to grab at them. Only catch the good tricks.'

Jack's dark eyes were wide. He nodded.

David turned to Dandy and Katie. 'Don't do the catcher's work for him,' he said. 'He's paid to catch. You swing to where you're supposed to be and let him earn his money. He catches you, you just stretch out to where he ought to be. If he's not there, you swing back again, or do the trick to the net and you get on your back and you fall soft.'

Katie and Dandy nodded, as earnest as apprentices.

'Trust him,' David said. His voice sent a great shudder down my spine.

'Trust him,' David said again. 'He's your catcher. You've got to fly to him as if you loved him entirely and are certain that he will be there. Trust him and give yourself over to him.'

Robert had left the door ajar and it swung open. A gust of icy wind blew in, and with it, a great white tumbling bird. A barn owl, eyes glaring and dazzled by our lanterns. It flew in, a massive wide-winged bird, entirely silently, not a whisper of its passing, its open crazed face turning right and left, seeking its way out. It flew directly over Dandy and Jack, and then wheeled around, so close to her that its passing stirred her hair. It flew between her and the lantern hung on the ceiling. Its shadow fell black over her and Dandy gave a little affected shriek and clung to Jack's arm, then the door swung open again, the bird turned and was gone. I fell back against the wall and felt the flints and mortar sharp against my fingers. I was shaken.

'My God,' Katie exclaimed. 'That was like a ghost!'

I saw David rub his hands hard against his cheeks. I saw him square his shoulders, I saw him wipe his hand across his mouth as if he were painting on his bright professional smile.

'Just a barn owl trying to get out of the cold, poor thing,' he said lightly. I think only I heard the strain in his voice. 'Snow is coming, we'd best run up to the house and get ready for dinner. It's the last decent meal I'll have for days. I'm cooking for myself tomorrow.'

He looked across at me and his bright smile faltered for a moment while we met each other's darkened gaze.

'You hungry, Merry?' he asked determinedly, willing me to

pretend that I had not seen that second of his superstitious fear. I pushed myself away from the wall to stand on my own two feet.

'Starving,' I said. My voice was thin, but the others noticed nothing. David's speech had been planned to send them out with their new act full of confidence. He wanted them to trust each other entirely, he wanted them to work without him, as well as they had done for the past two months. He had wanted to send them out with his blessing. He did not want them thrown and frightened with the easy superstition of travelling people.

We clattered around, banking in the stove, blowing out the lanterns except one to light our way back to the house across the fields. I looked for the barn owl when we were outside, but it had gone.

We all got tipsy at dinner. Robert became maudlin and blinked at the shiny surface of the table, and then insisted on singing loud and mournful ballads. David declared that all Welshmen could sing from birth without training and blasted out some convincing evidence in an incomprehensible language to prove it. Dandy danced very prettily with her skirts held high, and Katie sang a bawdy ale-house ditty. Jack and I became morosely quiet with the drink, though neither of us had more than a couple of glasses.

Robert called a halt at eleven o'clock.

'Work tomorrow, same as usual,' he said.

'I'll be gone as you're rising,' David said to the three of us. 'I'll say my farewells to you now.'

He spread his arms wide and hugged all three of us: Katie, Dandy and me. Katie he bussed and put to one side and whispered something in her ear which made her giggle and blush. Dandy he held very close for a moment and then set her on her feet.

'Keep your wits about you and push out on the beat,' he said. 'If you know a trick isn't going to work then drop into the net. And don't get lazy! And practise every day!'

He turned to me and put his arms around me. 'I wish I could

have got you up high, Merry,' he said. 'But I am sorrier than I can tell you about your fall.'

I shrugged. 'I'll have others,' I said, thinking of Sea waiting to be broken to the saddle.

He did not hug Jack. He took him by the shoulders and he looked into Jack's guileless open face. 'They're your responsibility now,' he said. 'It is your job to keep the flyers safe. Do you swear to me on your life that you will do that?'

Jack blinked, surprised at David's tone. 'Yes,' he said simply. 'I'll do the best I can.'

I felt my hands clench into fists, like they do when I'm afraid. David scanned Jack's face once and then smiled.

'Well, good luck to the three of you then,' he said. He nodded to Robert over our heads. 'You'll always have my direction,' he said. 'If you need me for new tricks or re-training I'd be glad to work with the four of them again.'

Robert rose from the table, and clasped his hand with a smile. 'I'm obliged to you,' he said. 'It's better than I'd dreamed.'

David saw us to the kitchen door. The room was cosy, the stove banked-in for the night. A dog in its basket. A cat curled in the hearth. We opened the back door and a gust of icy air blew in, a swirl of snowflakes with it. Dandy and Katie pulled their shawls over their ducked heads and dashed out down the path towards the stables. I hesitated on the doorway, careless of the blowing snow. David looked down at me, waiting.

'Does it mean anything,' I asked, 'in shows? Does it mean anything when an owl flies across the ring? When a bird flies in?'

David's smile was easy. 'Nothing at all, my fey little gypsy,' he said tenderly. 'Now run to your bed before you get cold. And try to stop tumbling off those horses of yours. If you're worried about Dandy there's little need. I've done the best I can and she knows her job.'

I nodded, longing to be convinced.

'It's all right then?' I said.

'It's all right,' he said, and he bent and gave me a gentle kiss on the forehead. I held my ground and did not pull away from his touch.

I stepped out of the back door and the wind hit me in the face and the snowflakes dazzled me. I dipped my head and ran in the direction of the stables. David had said it was all right. David had said that the bird meant nothing, its shadow falling on Dandy meant nothing. If there had been danger David would have warned me.

I tumbled up the stairs to our bedroom, shucked off my clothes in the cold room and fell into by bed. I did not want to think about anything.

12

We all missed David, but the routine of our days went on as if he had been there. Jack called the beat instead of the sweet low Welsh voice, and the three of them quarrelled and argued and settled on the way they would train and practise. Jack came out often to Robert and me in the paddock and we would practise our new acts with the horses.

Robert's seed of an idea of an act with challenging people to ride Sea had developed into a comical routine. Firstly I was to ride Bluebell around the ring, vaulting on and off and then dancing on her back. I had yet to learn to jump through the hoop but I managed a couple of flat-footed jumps and a couple of skips.

'Straighten up!' Robert yelled at me time after time as I went bow-legged with my bottom stuck out backwards trying to keep my balance.

Straightening my legs on horseback was an act of pure will, I found. It was no easier in the ungainly crouch which came natural to me. I was probably making it harder for myself. But I found it such a relief to be within grabbing distance of the skewbald mane. Then:

'Straighten up!' Robert would yell again, and I would force myself to stand tall and even to look straight ahead with my chin up instead of gazing longingly at Bluebell's broad back.

The act we planned would have me skipping and then jumping through an open hoop on Bluebell's back. Then Jack, dressed in fustian breeches and gaiters, would come out from the back of the crowd like a drunken young farmer and demand a turn. At first I was supposed to refuse and turn my head away from him, at which Jack was to take a run from the far side of the ring and vault on to my place, pushing me off the other side.

Often we cracked heads, occasionally we would bounce off each other and fall back, off our own sides. Bluebell was excellent and stood as steady as a rock, even when Jack went up and I failed to drop off and we clung to each other and howled with exhausted laughter.

Then I was supposed to try to carry on with my act while Jack vaulted on to the horse. As long as I stayed well towards the tail and out of the way we were in little danger of collision. Jack vaulted on and ended up facing the tail, then he spun himself around so that he was facing the head, but both his legs were the same side. Then he lay flat on his back, his legs and arms on either side of the cantering horse. Then he spun around like a sack of meal. In the finale he crawled all around under Bluebell's belly and then under her neck.

We practised it so often that we grew skilled and quick at it but it did not seem funny to us. We only realized how good it would be in the show when Dandy and Katie finished their practice early one day and came over to watch us, and actually collapsed on to the grass they were laughing so loud.

Robert, who had stood in the centre of the field for day after frozen day, had looked very thoughtful at that and had wandered off chewing on the stem of his pipe muttering to himself: 'Lady and the Jester, the Girl and the Tramp, the Clowns on Horseback.'

Next day he had a sign-writer up and spent a long time with him in the stable yard while I worked the team of ponies in the paddock and Jack and Dandy and Katie practised in the barn.

The horse acts had grown almost beyond recognition now that I could ride in the ring and we had two rosinbacks. I did not yet know what order Robert planned to run the show but we had the dancing pony team, Snow doing his tricks with counting numbers and flags, Jack and me doing a two-horse bareback riding act, my dancing on the back of Bluebell, and then the second part of the act when Jack came in dressed as the farmer. The little ponies could still do the Battle of Blenheim of course; and it was rather more impressive now that the flower of British cavalry outnumbered the French by four to three, and for the end of the show Robert planned some kind of historical tableau.

'Summat like Saladin, but with the three lasses,' he said to himself, chomping on his pipe as he did when he was struggling with an idea. He walked around the stable yard in a small half-circle. The pipe puffed a little cloud of triumph. 'Rape of the Sabine Women,' he said to himself.

We would be an impressive sight on the road, too. There was Snow, Robert's grey stallion; Sea, my grey stallion; Bluebell and Morris, the two rosinbacks; Lofty, the new wagon horse; and seven little ponies. Lofty was a heavy draught horse bought with Robert's profits from the Salisbury gamble to pull the new wagon which would carry the heavy flying rigging and the new screens he ordered. Bluebell and Morris would pull the two sleeping wagons. This summer William would come on the road too, for the first time. Robert might be parsimonious but even he could see that Jack and he could not set the rigging alone. We would need help with the horses at the end of two shows as well.

Then we worked. Worked and waited. It snowed hard in January and when I fell off the back of Bluebell I fell soft into drifts on either side of my track. I fell wet and cold too and Robert took pity on me and ordered me two new pairs of breeches and smocks so that I could change into dry clothes at each break. Mrs Greaves kept them warming for me on the front of her stove and I would dash into the kitchen, my teeth chattering with the cold and strip off my icy cold breeches and smock and drop them on the floor.

William came in one time, as I stripped from my snow-encrusted smock, and dropped the pallet of wood he was carrying and had a tongue-lashing from Mrs Greaves and was banned from the kitchen. But then she turned to me.

'You must cover yourself, Merry,' she said gently. 'You're not a little girl any more.'

She reached behind the dresser and pulled out a big looking glass, at least a foot square. She held it up for me to see myself, and I craned my neck trying to see all of me in the one glass. I had shot up in height, I was nearly full grown and I had fattened up at last, I was no longer wiry and scrawny. I had filled out. The curves of my body were usually hidden by my smock or by the cut-down shirts of Jack's I wore for work. Now, in my chemise I could see that my breasts had grown. I had a shadow of hair in each armpit and at my groin. My buttocks were smooth and as tightly muscled as a racehorse. My legs were long and lean, bruised like a charity schoolboy. I took a step closer to the mirror and looked at my face.

The hair I had hacked off in the summer had regrown and now fell to my shoulders in thick copper waves. The tumbling colour of it softened the hungry hard lines of my face and when I smiled the reflection which I saw was that of a stranger. My eyes seemed to have grown more green this winter, they were still set slanty as a cat, black-lashed. My nose was slightly skewed from the fall from the trapeze, my face would never be perfect. I would never have Dandy's simple rounded loveliness.

'You will be a great beauty,' Mrs Greaves said. She took the mirror gently from me and tucked it back. 'I only hope it will bring you some joy.'

'I don't want beauty,' I said, and though I was a young girl and not very wise I told her the truth. 'I don't want beauty and I don't want a man,' I said. 'All I want is a place of my own and some gold under my mattress. And Dandy safe.'

Mrs Greaves chuckled and helped me tie the strings at my cuffs. 'The only way for a lass like you to get that is to find yourself a man and hope he's a rich one,' she counselled. 'You'll like it well enough when you're older.'

I shook my head but said nothing.

'What about that sister of yours?' she asked me. 'She's set her sights on Master Jack, hasn't she? Small change she'll get there.'

I looked warily at Mrs Greaves. She worked in silence at the dinner table, she cooked in silence in the kitchen. But she saw a good deal more than anyone might expect. I knew she was not in Robert's confidence, but I feared what she might tell him.

'Who says?' I asked, cautious as a hedgerow brat.

Mrs Greaves chuckled. 'Think I'm blind, child?' she asked me. 'My tea doesn't have great lumps in the pot, yet night after night that poor lad has drunk down God knows what nonsense. Is it working for her?'

My face was guarded. 'I don't know,' I said. 'I don't know what you mean.'

I did know. And it was working. The love potion, or the boredom of the short winter days and the long winter evenings. The flattery of two pretty girls or the importance of being their catcher. Something was calling Jack over to our little room above the stable for evening after evening while his father pored over maps and over almanacs of fairs.

We would hear his step on the foot of the stair and then his low: 'Hulloa!' and Dandy would call back: 'Come up, Jack!' in a voice of lazy sweetness.

She would toss a handful of lavender seeds on the fire so it smoked with an acrid sweetness. She would kick a pair of soiled clouts under the mattress, and she would loosen the top of her bodice so that it showed the creamy curves of the tops of her breasts. Then she would wink at Katie and me and say, 'Ten minutes, mind,' in quite a different voice to the two of us.

Night after night Jack's head came through the trapdoor wearing his half-rueful, half-roguish smile.

'Hello Meridon, Dandy, Katie,' he would say. 'I brought you some apples from the store room.'

He would hand them out and we would sit and munch the icy fruit and talk about the work we had done that day. The tricks that had worked or failed and our hopes for the season ahead of us.

After about ten minutes or so Katie, who had now seen the golden guinea she was to collect at Easter, would prompt me.

'I'll help you water-up, Merry,' she would say; and the two of us would go down the stairs to check all the horses had water and hay for the night and that they were safe in the paddock. Snow and Sea were kept indoors and we would check them too. Sometimes we would idle then, in the loose-boxes, giving Dandy and Jack time to be alone together. I would half listen to Katie's chatter about lads in Warminster and one time a real gentleman from as far away as Bath, but most of the time I would lean my cheek against Sea's warm neck and wish we were far away.

All I had to do to stop this courtship in its tracks was to tell Robert. He would be angry but it would be no worse than one of his bawled tirades. I could cool Jack's ardour by just a hint of such a thing. Or I could promise Katie a further guinea if she intrigued with him behind Dandy's back. But for some reason I felt powerless. I felt as if Dandy's hex on Jack had bound us all, so that Katie and I lingered in the stables though neither of us wished the affair well. And I lied to Mrs Greaves who might have told me what to do.

'Dandy doesn't fancy Jack,' I said unconvincingly. 'We're all three of us close, through being on the road together and working together like we do. Robert's aiming higher than us for his son; and Dandy has her work.'

Mrs Greaves nodded and let it go at that. 'Dinner in twenty minutes,' she said and picked up my wet things from the floor.

I nodded and went out into the gathering darkness to the stable yard. William should have lit the fire in our little room by now and I thought I would steal some moments on my own. Half-way up the ladder I heard voices and I paused. I heard Jack's voice, and Dandy's amused ripple of laughter.

'I think you've hexed me, Dandy, with some damned gypsy brew,' he said. 'I truly do!'

'Only the magic that's in your breeches,' Dandy said softly, a smile in her voice. 'What's this then, my bonny lad, if it isn't magic?'

'Oh Dandy,' Jack sighed. 'Nay, keep your hands off, lass. I won't be teased by you. You'll make me too weak to catch you at practice tomorrow.'

'David told me to fly to you as if I loved you,' she said. 'I can do that Jack. I can fly to you as if I love you. I do love you, you know.'

'Dandy,' Jack sounded uncomfortable.

'D'you love me?' she asked earnestly.

'Dandy,' Jack said again.

'You love me when I touch you there,' she said in a soft breathy voice. 'You love me well enough when I open my bodice like this, don't you Jack? You love me well enough when I kiss you like this, don't you Jack?'

I could hear Jack's breathing suddenly grow harsher and I heard an abrupt scuffle as he broke away from her.

'Now stop this, Dandy,' he said rapidly. 'We've got to stop this. If my da finds out he'll throw us both off the show and we'll have nowhere to go and nothing to live on. He warned us both. I'm a fool to come up here and be with you on my own, and you're a devil to lead me on like this. You know I can't promise to love you. I don't promise to love you. When we started you said it was just all for fun. I can't make promises to any lass, you know that.'

There was utter silence in the little room. I crept a bit closer to the trapdoor and strained my ears to hear. I thought that Dandy would be mad with anger that he should pull away from her, but I had not realized how clever she was with him.

'All right,' she said sweetly and the laughter was back in her voice. 'All right, bonny Jack. We'll play by your rules and we won't upset your da. You make no promises to me and I'll make no promises to you.'

I heard the floorboard creak as she stood up and the whisper of her petticoat as she slid down her gown.

'Now,' she said, and her voice was full of potent female power. 'Now you tell me, and you can tell me true. Not whether you love me, bonny Jack, for we've agreed not to say that word. But tell me if you like the look of me, mother-naked.'

I heard a sound from Jack that was like a groan and then the tumbling sound of them falling together back on to a bed. I heard my sister gasp as he thrust into her and then her little whimpering cries as they sought their pleasure together. He gave a muffled shout and then a little later I heard Dandy sigh deeply as if she had finally got what she wanted.

I sat with my chin cupped in my hands on the draughty stairs and waited for them to have done so that I could get into my room. I felt neither shock, nor that second-rate desire which comes from watching or hearing. I had heard and seen my da and Zima ever since I was a baby and it meant nothing to me except the increased likelihood of more quarrels later when their appetites were slaked.

I had warned Dandy off, Jack had warned her against asking him for love. She had been hot for him since the summer day she first saw him in his red shirt and his white breeches in the field outside Salisbury fair. Now she had wooed him and had him. I did not know if that would be enough for her. I felt, in every aching bone of my chilled body, that no good would come to us of this, Jack might be as randy as a stud dog, but he was not in love. If she was counting on him to treat this romp as a betrothal she would be sorry before she was done.

I shrugged and stood up. Dandy had been likely to lose her maidenhead young, and I could have stopped it as easily as stopping the wind blowing. The affair might cool within weeks and my worry would have been for nothing. Certainly when we were working together on the road under Robert's eye there would be fewer opportunities for pleasuring. Jack had told her clearly that he would not love nor marry her, and she had taken him with that knowledge to satisfy his lust and hers. I judged they had enjoyed the private use of our room for long enough and crept down to the foot of the ladder. By the time I clattered slowly up they were huddled into their clothes and Jack was tending the fire. He nodded at my sullen face and took himself off to wash before dinner.

Dandy shot me a sideways glance. 'I've had him,' she said.

'I know,' I said. 'I was on the stairs.'

She nodded. Neither of us had ever been house-dwellers, we never minded being overheard.

'Will that be enough for you now?' I asked her. 'Have him for pleasure, as you said, and leave the rest alone.'

She pulled the bow that tied her hair and the great black wave tumbled down over her face. 'Oh surely,' she said, from underneath it, and retired to her pallet and started brushing it through.

I stared at her in silent frustration. She was putting up a wall around her thoughts as surely as if she had told me to mind my own business. We had both learned that trick. Dandy could lie with her lover, learn her skill, wash her body in front of me without embarrassment. She and I were raised in a wagon, we had no sense of private place. Our private rooms were all in our own minds and she could shut me out of her plans and imagination as surely as I could close her out of mine.

'You won't be able to have him without Robert knowing when we're on the road,' I said warningly.

Dandy swept back a wave of glossy black hair. She smiled at me, her eyes were sated. She looked as if she knew what she was doing and was well pleased.

'I'll be ready to move on by then,' she said sweetly. 'Don't fuss, Meridon, you're like an old mother hen. I know what I'm doing. I've got ten weeks.'

I turned from her and stared into the fire, the fire which Jack had tended for us. If I were a real Romany I should see in the fire what the danger was which sent shivers up my spine. If I had the Sight instead of pretending to it, and a few worthless dreams of Wide, I should know what I feared so. I turned my fears over in my mind like the mother hen she called me, turning her eggs. Robert could abandon us in his rage when he found that Dandy and Jack had lain together. I knew that did not matter now. There would be other shows which would be glad to have us. Dandy had a unique skill and I had special talent. Dandy was the only girl flyer in the country and I was the best trainer and rider I knew. We had ten guineas (nine, thanks to Dandy's desires) and a fifty-pound hunter. We would not starve. It was not the fear of being left by Robert which clutched at my heart.

Dandy might fall. But Dandy always might fall. She was skilled and Jack was a good catcher. They had been taught well and they were practising daily. Robert had sworn that they would never work without the catch-net. The height might make me sick with fear but it did not trouble Dandy. And her happiness was sound enough. I knew she was hot for Jack but it was partly lust and partly pique because he had fancied Katie. I did not believe in love. I had never seen such a thing. I had never seen a man or a woman in love. I had never seen a man or a woman do anything except please themselves. While Dandy wanted Jack I thought she would be able to have him. If his da spoiled sport when we were on the road she could make her choice to leave him go, or find ways to be with him. Either way it was Dandy's amusement. Not her life's need.

'Are you done? Old Mother Merry?' Dandy asked me mockingly. She had tied up her hair again and had a fresh kerchief tied at her neck. She had been watching me as I stared at the flames, and she had read my face aright. 'Worried all you can?' she taunted me.

'Yes,' I said. Then I put my finger on the one, last fear. 'You are sure the old woman showed you how to stop a baby,' I said. 'And told you when you are safe to lie with a man?'

Dandy chuckled, a deep rich laugh and her blackberry eyes danced. 'Oh aye,' she said. 'There's a time when you cannot make a child, and a time when you will. There's herbs which will help you do it, and herbs which will make it less likely. There's some nasty stuff which turns your guts half inside out but washes a baby out if one is started. I know how to make sure I don't get with child.' Her black eyes teased me. 'And how to get a belly on me if I wish it,' she said.

'You would not wish it,' I said stiffly.

Dandy chuckled. 'And let Katie be the only one up on the high trapeze in a pink stomacher, Meridon? You must be mad!'

13

February was freezing and cold. In early March there was a thaw but then it froze hard again. Robert made us work in all weathers and we all four grew bored and rebellious, but we kept our complaints to ourselves. We all set to costume and harness making, Mrs Greaves teaching Dandy and me to sew. We were less handy than either Jack or Katie. He had been making costumes and harness all his life and she had learned a speedy careless stitch in the poorhouse. Only Dandy and I puckered up the cheap silk with great ungainly running stitches where we should have hemmed. Time and time again Mrs Greaves made us rip it back and start at the beginning, until the fabric grew damp and grimy from handling.

'It'll wash,' she said placidly when I complained that the costumes would be spoiled before we ever wore them.

Dandy and Jack had less time to be alone but generally they would offer to water the horses last thing at night and Katie and I would give them a clear half-hour to satisfy the horses' and their own needs before we pulled shawls over our heads and ran out into the cold from the back door to the stable block.

I only asked Dandy about the progress of her love affair once; she never volunteered information. I thought it unlikely she would hold Jack for long, already he was flirting, furtive and roguish, with Katie while we sat around the kitchen table sewing. Dandy's black eyes snapped at Katie but her smile to Jack was steady and sweet. I only spoke to her once in those long cold ten weeks. It was when I was tacking up the little ponies in the new harness and Dandy was there polishing the bells and fitting them on for me.

'You can't love him,' I said positively.

She brushed back a dark wave of hair and smiled at me. 'Nay,' she said. 'I don't think any of us has a lot of faith in love.'

'Then why go on?' I asked. I was genuinely mystified.

Dandy smiled a slow smile, she was as sleek as a stroked cat these days. 'Oh chilly little Meridon, you'll never understand,' she said. 'I like it. If it was not Jack it would be another man. I like the touch of his hands and his lips and his body inside me. And the feelings are getting better and better. I like it more and more.'

'But you don't like *him* more and more,' I argued. 'You don't like him giving Katie the glad eye.'

Dandy grimaced. 'I don't,' she said. 'And if that little whore so much as smiles at him she'll feel the weight of my hand. But I want Jack still.'

'For pleasure?' I asked. One of the little ponies threw his head up because the harness was too tight. I loosened it. It was new stiff leather and my fingers were freezing. I cursed under my breath.

Dandy passed the bell over to me and watched me screw it into the socket at the crown of the headband.

'He is part of my plans,' she said grandly. Then she gave me a wink. 'I'll be wedded and mistress of this house before I'm done, Merry, I promise you.'

I flinched and the little bell rang shrilly like a warning.

'Don't count on winning Robert's consent,' I said. 'I spoke to him and he called us gypsy trash. He don't want Romany blood in his family, Dandy. Don't count on his agreement. Take Jack for pleasure if you must. But look forward too far and you'll fail.'

I moved to the next pony and Dandy handed me the bridle.

'You always worry so,' she said idly. 'Leave be, Merry. I know what I'm doing, and you know nothing about courting and how it is between a lad and a lass then. Leave be. You don't understand.'

I shrugged at that, feeling a little sour. Then I tacked-up the rest of the ponies and led them out into the boggy field to practise their paces on the melting ground.

'We're going to do a gala,' Robert announced. He had dined in his dining room with Jack, while Dandy, Katie, William, Mrs Greaves and I ate in the kitchen. Robert came through the door, port glass in one hand, pipe in the other. Jack followed him and they both seated themselves at the kitchen table. Mrs Greaves melted away, towards the stove. William went to fetch some more wood and then hovered within earshot with the woodbasket.

'I'll invite the mayor and the aldermen of Salisbury,' Robert said. 'Aye and ladies too. Local gentry, the JPs. That sort of person. We'll put on a gala show for them. Proper chairs we'll need,' he said half to himself. 'That's in the afternoon. In the morning we'll do a show for the village. Penny a time admittance. That's our first and last show here and you can count it as your coming-out. After that we're on the road and working for real.'

I looked around the table and saw my own anticipation mirrored in the other bright faces. We had all practised for so long, we had all been cooped up here for so long. For Jack and Katie it had been a long tedious winter. But for Dandy and me it had been unprecedented. We had never been under a roof for so long before. We had never been in one place for so long before. We had never slept in the same bed under the same roof for the whole season. I was impatient to move on.

'Here's the programme,' Robert said, pulling a dog-eared black-backed notebook from his jacket pocket. He flipped open the page and lit his pipe. We waited in silence.

'Opening parade,' he said. 'That's you two girls in your flying costumes with your capes on. Meridon and Jack in breeches riding Snow and Sea.' He broke off and looked at me. 'D'you agree to ride Sea into the ring, Merry? He'd look fine alongside Snow.'

I nodded and he went on.

'Followed by troop of little ponies with full tack and bells, and Morris and Bluebell bringing up the rear harnessed together.'

Jack and I nodded, thinking about the horses.

'First half is horses,' Robert said. 'There's to be no catch-net for the first half.' He glanced at me with a little smile. 'Don't look so white, you silly girl. We put it up in the interval.'

I nodded and felt my colour come back to my cheeks.

'Now,' he said. 'First act on is Meridon with the little ponies dancing. Just turns and pirouettes. Meridon, you're to wear a riding habit and jacket and a little hat with a feather.' He looked at me critically. 'You've filled out,' he said with some surprise. 'I'd not noticed, Meridon. You'll be quite pretty in the ring.'

Everyone stared at me as if I were a not very welcome cuckoo.

'You'll fit Dandy's riding habit from last summer,' Robert said. 'And you'll look quite smart in it too.'

He looked at my hair. 'No hat,' he said. 'And wear your hair loose and long. It looks nice like it is. Don't hack it about again.'

I nodded. I was getting accustomed to being dressed with as much care and as little emotion as if I were one of the ponies.

'Next: Jack's rosinback act with Bluebell,' Robert said returning to his list. 'You can wear your new blue shirt, Jack, and your breeches.'

'Not Morris as well?' I asked.

Robert shook his head. 'He's not ready,' he said. 'It takes years to get a rosinback perfect, this season he's just to get accustomed to working in front of an audience. We'll have him in the opening parade and in the historical finale. But we won't use him as a rosinback in the ring yet.'

I nodded. Robert opened his notebook again.

'Then me,' he said, 'with Snow doing tricks. Counting and picking out flags. I'll have him in his new harness and a new ostrich plume on the top. Meridon, you see to the plume and his tack.

'Then Meridon does her rosinback act in her short red skirt and white shirt and Jack comes out the back dressed in his farmer costume.' He paused. 'Make a little red waistcoat to go with the skirt, Merry.' He glanced at Mrs Greaves. 'Easy enough to make isn't it, ma'am?' She nodded.

Robert went on. 'Then Merry and Jack do the knockabout act, and last of all we'll have the Battle of Blenheim. Dandy, you and Katie make sure the ponies have flags instead of bells in their harness. I'll be in the ring for the Battle of Blenheim. Meridon, you'll be changing.'

'Into what?' I asked.

'Into your costume for the low trapeze,' Robert said. 'White breeches and blue silk shirt,' he turned another page in the book.

'Interval,' he said. 'During the interval William and Jack and I rig the trapeze frames and the catch-net. Dandy and Katie you sell drinks and sweetmeats and whatever. You'll wear your flying clothes but with your capes on top.' A little puff came from the top of his pipe. 'Capes fastened properly. No tarting around,' he said firmly. 'You can take tips but remember you are artistes, not street walkers. All tips are to be handed over to me.'

Katie and Dandy both looked offended. Robert paid them no heed at all.

'After the interval we have Mamselle Meridon on the low trapeze, doing your tricks, Merry.' I nodded. 'And then we have the trapeze act. Finale with all of us taking a bow under the catch-net.' He paused. 'That clear?' he asked.

'No historical tableau?' Jack asked.

'No rape?' I asked him with a little smile.

Robert puffed on his pipe. 'This is a Quality show,' he said sternly. 'No rapes. When we get out into the villages we'll do the Rape of the Sabine Women at the end of the first half. Dandy and Katie are the Sabine women in their flying capes, unfastened. Maybe veils on their heads. Jack and Merry are the rapists on Morris and Bluebell.'

All of us around the table nodded.

'It's to be two weeks from now,' he said. 'Shrove Tuesday. I'll want to see all the costumes and all the tack ready and laid out on the Friday.'

He looked at Mrs Greaves. 'That give you enough time, ma'am?' he asked.

She nodded. 'Can you make us some buns and some sweetmeats and some drinks on the day?' he asked. She nodded again.

'That's all then,' Robert said pleasantly. 'We'll work that Tuesday here, final practices and move out two days later.'

'Starting the tour in Lent?' Jack asked raising an eyebrow at his father.

Robert grinned. 'This tour is going to go through all high

days and holidays,' he said certainly. 'This tour will play Sundays. This tour is unlike anything anyone has ever seen before. Wherever we go we are going to draw crowds. If the ground is too wet we'll do a trapeze show. If we can hire a barn we'll do horse shows. We won't be able to pack everyone in even if we were to do shows all through the night of Good Friday!'

Jack nodded. 'Yes, Da,' he said with his usual instant obedience. 'Yes, Da.'

Robert nodded at the sewing baskets on the welsh dresser. 'Get on with your sewing then,' he said. 'You'll need to have it all done in ten days' time.'

He left the room and we all made a concerted dash to the costume boxes and set to work. Even my stitches went better knowing that I would be wearing the costume in a fortnight's time. The cloth which had seemed so intractable already had some of the special circus magic about it. We would be wearing it in the ring. It would be packed up. We would be moving on.

I had never thought to see Katie, that hard-faced girl, in the vapours. But I had forgotten that she had never worked before a crowd. She was cool as a lady-in-waiting in practice: on the high trapeze, throwing tricks to the net, reaching out to pass over to Jack. But once she knew an audience was coming she started to miss her cue and fall.

She got well jolted for a lesson, and she started to get a red sore back from the number of tumbles she took wrong into the catch-net.

'I'll never get it right,' she moaned as she bounced unwillingly over to the ladder and went up again.

I had finished with the ponies for the day and was watching them practise by the light of their lanterns, and warming my damp breeches on the back of their stove. I had not watched them much since David had gone and I expected to see Jack calling the time and telling them what tricks they should throw.

He called the time for them, as I had thought he would. And he called 'Pret' when he was ready to catch them, and 'Hup' when he wanted them to swing from the board out to him.

But to my surprise he was not the teacher or leader of the three.

It was my sister, Dandy.

'Katie's got to do the angel pass,' she called across to him. And when Katie murmured that she had done it twice already she said firmly:

'With a leg cocked like a pissing dog. You do it again Katie and stretch out this time, or you'll do it over and over.'

I craned my neck to look up at this new, authoritative Dandy. Katie did the pass and Jack took her by her leg and her foot and then tossed her up towards the trapeze. Katie snatched at it, and fell with a despairing wail to bounce harmlessly into the net.

Dandy called across to Jack.

'That was your fault Jack! She was right as she came over, but you let her go too late. She needs to get away at the crest of your swing or she can't reach out to get the trapeze.'

Jack nodded, his face dark with irritation. 'That's enough for one evening,' he said. 'We're bound to make mistakes late in the day.'

'We're not wrapping up yet,' Dandy said briskly. 'I'll try the high pass to you. We'll just touch hands to see if we're right.'

Jack nodded and readied himself in his harness, stretching out towards her.

I turned my back and heard but did not look round when he called 'Pret' and then later 'Hup', then I heard the catch-net twang and I heard Dandy say mischievously:

'You can look now, Meridon, I'm down in one piece.'

They finished their practice then; Dandy pushed her feet into her clogs and came over to me by the stove.

'How come you decide the tricks?' I asked. 'I thought Jack would.'

Dandy shrugged. 'He couldn't see what Katie was doing wrong. I do the tricks, Jack just catches, it's easy for me to see what's amiss.' She shrugged her shoulders impatiently. 'He's damned idle, Meridon. If he was calling the tricks we'd be finished by noon every day.'

I nodded, and Katie and Jack joined us and we said no more.

Katie's nerves got no better as the date of the performance approached. When she laid out her costume for Robert's inspection on the Friday evening her hands were shaking so much that the sequins rattled. Robert was surprisingly sympathetic.

'You'll do,' he said kindly to her. 'Just do it as it was in practice.' He looked at Jack. 'Is she reliable in practice?'

Dandy answered, not Jack. 'She's a bit lazy,' she said. 'But she can do it when she works at it. She'll work at it in front of an audience. I should think she'd be better then, than she is in practice.'

Robert nodded. 'Good,' he said. He turned to me. 'Nervous, little Merry?' he asked.

I shook my head. 'No,' I said. 'All I have to do is to let Jack knock me off Bluebell, and God knows I've done that enough times.'

Robert smiled. 'Aye,' he said, 'I'm happy.'

He had reason. The takings added up to pounds for the gala performance and the pennies of the village people at their show made the sack of money as heavy as a couple of saddles.

The ponies behaved well, even the three bought at Salisbury who had never been in front of an audience before. Bluebell was as steady as she always was, Morris threw his head up at the noise and the cheers, but I had harnessed them so tight to Bluebell he virtually had to breathe in time with her. People laughed till they cried at the act Jack and I did when he pretended to be a drunk farmer. It had never gone better, and at the end when we cantered around the ring with me standing high and Jack going around under Bluebell's neck the Quality audience got up from their benches and cheered as loud as common folk.

Dandy and Katie were well tipped during the break, but I saw Dandy walk with her head as high as a queen. She kept her eyes open for any likely young bucks, but her mind was on her trapeze act and Robert had no grounds for complaint when she came back with an empty tray and a purse which chinked with pennies.

They cheered my trapeze tricks as if they were something prodigiously skilful and brave. I suppose to people who had never seen such a thing before, the top of the swing when I was above their heads, seemed very high. It did not frighten me, even when I swung back and could see their faces below me. I knew if I hung straight that my toes were only a foot above the ground. I felt safe enough.

The queasy churn of fear in my belly was for Dandy's flying act. I was such a fool I could not even stay in the barn to watch her. I went out the back to where we had tethered the ponies and I put my arm around Sea's warm neck and listened to the sounds and guessed what they were doing.

There was the rustle of anticipation as Jack did handstands and chin-ups on his frame, and then a murmur of approval as Dandy and Katie posed at the top of their frame. Then I heard the gasp as either Dandy or Katie gripped the trapeze and swooped down off the pedestal. I flexed my arms around Sea when I heard that. And then there was a great 'ooh!' from the audience and a burst of clapping as one of them reached out from the trapeze to Jack's hands. Then there was another gasp as he swung her out, made that little twist, and passed her up to the swinging overhead bar. A great roar of applause told me that she was safe on the pedestal again.

Four times I tightened my grip on Sea's neck, sweating even in the frosty air, listening for the gasp as Dandy came off the board, the 'ooh!' as she swung, the ripple of applause as she was caught and then the uproar when she was safely back on the board or somersaulting down into the net. Sea shifted uneasily. I was squeezing him so tight, and he could smell my fear. Then I heard a great scream from the audience and my stomach churned bile. Dandy had finished her act by dropping from her bar so she was utterly free in the air, into Jack's hands and then somersaulted down into the net. There was a roar of applause and another shriek as Katie and then Jack tumbled downwards and bounced safely up to their feet. Then there was a roar of applause as people called for the act again and shouted, 'Bravo!' and then I heard the chink of coins as people tossed money into the ring.

Robert Gower called out into the darkness from the barn door.

'Meridon! It's over! Come in and see your sister! Come and take your bow!'

They were cheering and cheering as if they would never stop. I heard a volley of curses as a bench was tipped up and crashed down on someone's toes.

Robert called for me more urgently and then went in to take his bow.

They had their finale without me that night. I was out at the back in the field retching helplessly into the frosty grass. Even as I took care to vomit away from my clean white breeches I could have laughed at myself for my stupid girlish nerves. But my laugh would have been bitter.

Two days later, as Robert had planned, we moved out. We started early, we had packed the night before. All the new gear was stowed in the fresh-painted wagons. There was the repainted picture of Snow rearing before the lady on the side of Robert's wagon. But he had ordered the sign-writer to paint her riding habit blue and her hair bright copper. She looked like me, so I had my portrait on the side of the wagon with 'Robert Gower's Amazing Aerial and Equestrian Show' written in red curly letters all around. On the back of the wagon was a picture of the little ponies, and on the other long side there was a picture of me and Jack in matching blue shirts and white breeches standing side by side up high on the back of Bluebell and Morris – both looking more noble and a good deal wilder than usual. At the top of the right-hand corner was another picture of me in my short skirt jumping through a hoop of fire – a trick which existed nowhere but in Robert's imagination at the moment. And there it said, in blue paint, 'Mamselle Meridon the horseback dancer!'

Katie and Dandy had looked rather askance at all the rippling copper hair and long bare legs until they had seen the wagon with the flying rig. In gold letters it said 'Robert Gower's Amazing Aerial Show' and it had a wonderful painting of Katie with her blonde hair streaming out behind soaring up to where a trapeze was painted in the top right corner. 'Mamselle Katie!' it said, the 'e' a little squashed for space.

The other side of the wagon I could not bear to look at. It was a picture of Dandy and I looked at it only once. She was supposed to be flying from the top left-hand corner down to the net. But because the sign-writer had been cramped for space it looked as if she were falling; falling down with her black hair rippling and a smile on her face. It said 'Mamselle Dandy! The only girl flyer in the world!' in scarlet. Dandy liked the picture because it showed her with long long legs and an enormously inflated chest. Also because Katie was put out that Dandy was called the 'only' flyer.

'You do more than swing out and grab for him, and I'll change the writing,' Robert said firmly. I did not smile as Dandy did. I knew Robert was thinking that flyers fall often and hurt themselves often. There would be many a show in this long season when he would have only one girl flyer, and he was taking no chances.

The rig wagon was to be pulled by Lofty and driven by William. Bluebell pulled the wagon for us girls and we would take it in turns to drive. Even Katie could drive Bluebell. The horse was as steady on the road as she was cantering around the ring. Morris would pull the men's sleeping wagon and the ponies would be split up and tied on in teams. Snow and Sea would be ridden in the mornings but tied on in the afternoons.

'Have to take the chance,' Robert said. 'You and Jack won't always want to be riding. You'll maybe need to rest on the road sometimes. And Sea is steady enough now.'

I found I was sorry to say goodbye to Mrs Greaves. She was the first woman I had ever known who had spoken to me kindly, and on our last evening I lingered in her kitchen as if it had become some sort of refuge for me. Jack and Dandy had gone on ahead. Katie was throwing the last bits of rope and string into a bucket in the stable yard. I said a gruff farewell to Mrs Greaves and she turned from the slate sink and held out her arms to me.

I stepped back. I still had my old dislike of being pulled about, and she saw the gesture and the warmth went from her face.

'God bless you, Merry,' she said, and I was ashamed of my prickly coldness.

'I am sorry,' I said awkwardly, and I stepped forward and offered her my forehead for her kiss.

She put her hands on my shoulders, gently, as I would handle a touchy young foal.

'Keep safe, dear,' she said softly. 'If you are ever in trouble and I can serve you, you should send for me.'

I stepped back and looked in her face. 'How can I keep Dandy safe?' I asked her, demanding an answer as if she should know everything, just because she was a woman old enough to be my mother who had put out her arms to me.

Her pale eyes fell before my urgent gaze.

'You cannot,' she said.

14

We only travelled a short way, that first day. I think Robert had planned the route to see how the journey went, to test the pace of the horses. We went north from Warminster, a little chalk-white lane still sticky with winter wet which skirted the great slope of Warminster Down on our right. We went slowly through the village of Westbury, and past the mill where the miller's wife sold us some fresh-baked bread rolls which we ate as we rode. Robert had a hand-drawn map on his knee and ignored the sign-post to Trowbridge. Katie and Dandy looked longingly down the road as we went past but Robert's wagon led the way into a bank of trees ahead called Castle Wood. Jack and I were riding and we left the lane and the swaying wagons and rode ahead. Sea and Snow were well matched but we did not race, we cantered side by side under the fretwork of bare branches. Deeper in the wood to my left, a robin was singing.

When the horses were sweating and blowing we pulled them up and walked slowly, waiting for the wagons to catch us up. Robert's wagon was in the lead and I trotted back to him.

'We'll stay at Melksham tonight,' he said. He was back in his element on the driving box of the wagon, his pipe sending little contented puffs upwards to the wintry white sky. 'You can ride on ahead and pick somewhere for us to pull in. Make sure there's firewood near, we'll need a good fire tonight.'

'Cold?' I challenged him.

He grinned and hunched his coat up around his shoulders. 'It's not midsummer,' he conceded.

'You're well served,' I said unsympathetically. 'No one I know sets out in the middle of winter.'

'Go ahead you hedge-bit,' he said unperturbed. 'And get the fire going before I pull in.'

Jack and I rode on and pulled in at the left of the road where there was some common ground and a little brake of woods with plenty of kindling. Jack hobbled the horses and rubbed them down while I went into the woods to fetch sticks for the fire. We had it lit and burning by the time the first wagon turned in.

William was handy at lining up his wagon, but Dandy had to take over from Katie who could only drive in a straight line. Then while we were taking the horses out of the shafts and feeding and watering them, Dandy strolled quietly off deeper into the wood. Katie watched her go with a scowl and muttered in Robert's hearing that Dandy was skipping off without doing any work. Robert glanced at me as he was setting up the trivet for the pot and I told Katie to wait and see where Dandy had gone. Sure enough, she came back within the hour with three plump brown trout with a string through their gills swinging from her hand.

'Tickled 'em,' she said to Robert's glance of inquiry. 'I know this stream, I've been here with Da and Zima. The keeper's old and the squire don't care about fish, he only cares about his game. I'd never touch a pheasant in these woods, not if it dropped dead at my feet I wouldn't.'

She gutted the fish and washed them. There was a little bacon in our stores and she fried that and then tossed them into the smoking fat. They sizzled and grew brown. Katie and I took the bread from the crock and unpacked the plates and the knives, and by the time Robert, William and Jack had come from hobbling the ponies the meal was ready.

'Damn,' Robert said suddenly. 'Forgot the salt again.' He smiled at us all, impartially. 'There's always something,' he said. 'I can't think how many years I've been on the road and yet there's always something you forget. I made a list this time as well and Mrs Greaves packed every darned thing on it. And then I forget the salt!'

'We'll buy some,' Dandy said. 'I could go into Melksham this afternoon and get some. We'll need some more bread too, and bacon.'

Robert nodded his approval. 'One of you girls go too,' he said.

'Or William. I don't want any one of you girls wandering around on your own. The show's got to seem classy. You little whores have got to be chaperoned like young ladies.'

Katie and Dandy giggled, I smiled. There was no malice in Robert. He was miles away from the town where respectability was his ambition. He was once more the man who had sat in the sun and watched me work the little pony. Who had praised me for a job well done and then bought me in a job-lot from my cruel and doltish stepfather. He could call me a little whore if he chose. We were none of us any better than we needed to be when we were working on the road. We were a team again, we belonged together.

The next day set the pattern for the rest of the days of the tour. We got up at dawn, around five or six o'clock, and gave the horses water. Sea, Snow and the carriage horses got some oats as well; Robert said the ponies were as fat as butter and should make do with the grass in the fields and waysides. He liked early rising. He was always the first to wake, and it was his knock on the side of our wagon which waked Dandy and me. When we tumbled out into the sharp morning air Robert would be stripped to the waist shaving in cold water and when he finished he would ask one of us to tip the bucket over his head and shoulders. He would burst out of the icy deluge puffing and blowing, ruddy with health.

Dandy would get the kettle on the fire and William and I would fetch dry crisp kindling for a quick blaze. We always carried some dry wood slung under the wagons for wet days. Jack never emerged until he heard the clink of the tin cups then he would come out, frowsy-eyed with his blanket huddled around his bare shoulders for his cup of tea – the last in the pot and as strong as it could be.

'My God you're an idle whelp,' Robert would say; and Jack would smile apologetically and dip his face into the wide mug.

Katie was the worst of all. She would stay in her bunk until the last possible moment and not the hiss of the boiling kettle nor the smell of frying bacon was enough to get her out. Not until we were starting to pack up to leave and Robert was hammering on the side of the wagon and threatening to fetch her out would she come. She was a sight in the mornings! Her eyes red-rimmed and puffy, her hair in a straggly plait. Robert was at his most dour when he saw Dandy and Katie before they had combed their hair and washed their faces, and he often glanced over to Jack, convinced that his son could not desire such girls having seen them at their sleep-dazed worst.

But Robert was blind. He missed all the clues. It was some snobbery in him which made him oblivious to what was happening every day on the road. Dandy and Jack collecting kindling, Dandy and Jack fetching water from the stream, Dandy and Jack dropping behind and then running, flushed and sweaty to catch up with the wagons. Robert was looking for something else, he was watching for signs of tenderness, for Jack seeking one of us out. He did not know that Jack was well past the courtship time when he had halloed up the stairs and watched Dandy in the firelight. Now he needed her to slake his thirst, but between the repetitive cycle of lust and sating they did not seek each other out.

They were not companions. Dandy would always seek my company for choice. On the road once more we fell back into the casual companionship of our childhood. When I drove she sat beside me, leaning back against my shoulder. When she drove I would deal imaginary hands of cards on the driving seat, stacking hands with all hearts, dealing off the bottom, dealing off the top, dealing out of the middle.

'Did ye see that, Dandy?' I would ask her over and over. Her eyes were sharp enough but I often fooled her.

When she went poaching she would bring me back a little trophy – a blue feather shed by a jay, a single early white violet. When I rode Sea and she was driving I would sometimes rein him in to go alongside the wagon, glancing at her from time to time, watching her lazy absorption in her private dreams.

'What are you thinking of, Dandy?' I asked her once and she smiled at me her sweet feckless smile.

'Same as you,' she said, nodding at the thick muddy road and the leaden wintry sky. 'Of a warm hearth and a good meal which has been caught and cooked by someone else.'

When we settled for the night and Katie was out of the way, rolled up tight in blankets in her bunk, Dandy would hand me her comb without speaking and I would comb and braid her hair as I had done since we were the smallest of chavvies. Then sometimes, if I was not feeling prickly and untouchable, I would let her tackle the tangles in mine, comb it smooth and plait it for the night.

Then I would kiss her good-night as she lay in her bunk. Her skin smelled musky: the smell of female sweat and warmth, hay and cheap perfume. The beloved familiar smell of my sister.

She and Jack were not friends. When Jack wanted company, wanted to walk alongside someone on the road, wanted someone beside him on the driving seat, he would crane his neck around the side of his wagon and whistle, 'Hey! Merry!'

When he rode Snow I was often riding Sea and we sometimes left the road for a canter across the fields or a gallop to the top of a hill. If I was walking behind the wagons he would fall into step beside me and we would chat – idly, easily. He would tell me about the villages and towns he had worked, I would tell him about breaking horses, cheating gulls and sharping cards. He learned to leave me alone when I shook my head and strayed away from the line of wagons. He learned to keep his hands out of my wind-blown curls and his arm from around my shoulders.

'Don't pull me about,' I said irritably, one evening when we were watering the horses down by a stream and he had put a careless hand around my waist.

He took his hand away. 'I barely touched you!' he complained. 'And I wasn't pulling, I was ...' he searched for a word. 'Patting. Like I would a horse.'

I giggled. 'Well, don't pat me then,' I said. 'I'm not a pony.'

He grinned back at me and kept his hands to himself as I had bid him. Friendly-like.

He was a healthy young animal at the pitch of fitness, hot for a mate. He would have flirted with me if I had given him the smallest of welcomes. He eyed Katie when he thought no one was watching. And Dandy and he strayed off the road together to kiss and hump every day or so. Purely for lust, I think he did not even like her.

For Dandy he was the first man she had ever had, and she revelled in the pleasure he gave her. Jack was no virgin, but with Dandy he had discovered a passionate partner whose desire matched his own. They were never in love, but they were addicted. That spring, as we headed east into the sunrise every morning, they sought and found each other, regular as a water-wheel turning over, every other day. Between times they were merely civil.

Katie watched them with her knowledgeable smile. She thought Jack would tire of Dandy, and she was right. She gave him not a word of encouragement nor a smile – she had her mind on my gold guinea. But I was sure that once the debt had been paid the bargain would be off and she would flirt and tease Jack until he took her, in preference to Dandy. What would happen then I could not imagine. But I did turn it over and over in my mind, worrying whether Dandy would fly out at her, or whether she would disdain to struggle.

'Mother Merry!' Dandy said laughing as she saw my downcast face.

Least happy of us all was William. He did not complain but his round face grew moonlike and his eyes were sad. Robert asked him at the end of the second week what was troubling him and he confessed that he did not like travelling. He felt as if we ought to arrive somewhere; not just go on and on. Dandy and I stared at him in utter incomprehension but Katie nodded as if she understood.

'I 'specs he's never been out of Warminster in all his life until now,' she said. 'Is that right, William?'

He nodded mournfully.

Robert tossed his enamel plate on the grass and leaned back, picking his teeth with a grass stem.

'Well, if you dislike it so much I daresay I can send you home,' he offered. 'There's work enough for you there, lord knows. Mrs Greaves would have had to take on a lad to do the garden and the vegetables alone.'

William's face lit up as if someone had placed a candle behind a round Chinese lantern.

Robert tapped his teeth with his thumbnail. 'I'll have to find a lad to come in your place,' he said thoughtfully. 'One that's handy with horses and knows how to travel.'

He said nothing more but when we stopped outside Winchester he put on his best brown coat and went into town on Snow. He came back with a skinny young lad in poorhouse homespun breeches behind him. I recognized a gypsy as soon as I saw him.

'His whole family've been gaoled,' Robert said by way of introduction. 'His da'll likely hang. His ma'll be transported. And his grandparents will be in gaol for seven years apiece. They couldn't prove he'd been in on it, so they just put him in the poorhouse.'

'In on what?' I asked eyeing the black-eyed vagrant askance.

'Thieving with violence,' Robert said. He swung the lad down from Snow's high back, and slid off himself.

'It wasn't as it sounds,' the lad said and Dandy and I smiled as we heard the gentle burr of the Rom accent. 'My grandma was telling a fortune. A lady gave her a shilling to tell her if her own true love was faithful. My gran has the Sight and she looked into the lady's palm and told her "no".' He sighed. 'The lady tried to take the shilling back and she was rough with my gran. The old man went to help her and the lady's footman hit him. My da went in, and so did my ma. The lady's coachman whipped us all and yelled for the watch. They took us all up for thieving with violence because a lady couldn't believe that her man preferred another woman.'

Robert shook his head. Katie and Dandy cooed in dismay and concern. I looked at the lad hard-eyed. I had nothing against him and what he said might well be true. I cared nothing one way or another. It was a world full of big thieves and little thieves. Little thieves like his family unquestionably were – for a shilling for a fortune is a gull and a thievery. And big thieves – for the lady and her lord would be the thieving sort who say that the land is theirs, and put up fences; or that the animals and birds which fly and run freely are theirs, and put in man-traps. I had no sympathy for him or his raggle-taggle kin. But I was glad he had joined us. He could do the poaching instead of Dandy, and if anyone hung to put meat in Robert Gower's stewpot it would not be my sister.

I cared only for her. I had no love to waste on any other living human being. Dandy and Sea were all I loved in the whole world. One selfish young girl and a horse. It was not very much for one person to love, I thought, watching the tear roll down the lad's face for the father who would hang and the mother who would go far, far away, and the grandparents who would undoubtedly die in gaol. But the years in the wagon with Da and Zima had somehow shrunk my heart so that there was no room in it for more than one young woman and one horse.

'Can you handle horses?' I asked him.

His face brightened. 'Yes,' he said. 'I love horses. My da used to travel around training them in winter.'

I looked at Robert wryly. 'So you have another rider if you need one,' I said. The boy was slighter than Jack and wiry; a perfect body for a bareback rider.

Robert beamed back at me in satisfaction. 'Aye,' he said. He chinked a purse of coins in his pocket. 'And they paid me to take him on,' he said. He turned to William. 'So you can go home,' he said. 'We'll send you off first thing in the morning. I'll show you the direction and give you coppers for your meals on the road. You can walk and take lifts. It shouldn't take you long.'

William's simple face glowed like a delighted child. 'Thank you, Mr Gower,' he said, heartfelt. 'Thank you very much.'

'Thank you very much indeed,' I thought to myself in silence, looking at William's boots which I thought would not last the distance home and the roads he would have to walk waiting for a passing wagon or cart. But I said nothing. William was not my concern either.

'The lad can sleep in with you girls tonight,' Robert said. 'Tomorrow he'll come into William's bunk with us.'

'Not till he's washed he won't,' I said firmly. 'He'll have fleas and lice. I won't have him sleeping in our wagon until he's stripped down and washed and gone over his clothes.'

Robert nodded. 'You're very nice all of a sudden, Merry,' he said mildly. 'I remember when I first saw you, you were all over flea-bites then; aye and lice.'

I nodded. 'Yes,' I said. 'That was the last time. I like to be clean now, and I'll stay that way. William can take the lad down to the river and make sure he washes clean.'

The lad clutched at the neck of his shirt as if he were afraid I was going to dip him in boiling oil as a cleansing method. I could not help but chuckle.

'Don't look like that, lad. What's your name?'

'Rea,' he said sulkily. 'What's yours?'

'I'm Meridon, and this is my sister Dandy,' I said. 'We're Rom too; and we survived washing. Go now and get clean. And if you see a rabbit or a hare on the way home you can bring it back with you.'

Robert could judge people like he could judge horseflesh. Within days he had Rea setting the rigging as well as William ever did; and before the show he had him practising standing on horseback, and vaulting on and off. He was little, but he was wiry, and he would get up early in the morning and work all the day long without ever seeming to get tired. He was excellent with the ponies and even Sea, who still hated most men, would allow his touch. I was glad, for working with the horses and my little act on the trapeze at every show was tiring.

We kept the show much the same as that first time when the Quality had come from as far away as Salisbury and stood to cheer and showered the flying act with coins.

When we had a barn we would do the show indoors. It meant a smaller audience but Robert charged twopence a head at the gate and people paid willingly, aye, and came back for the second performance and paid all over again. Very few people had even heard of a trapeze act. No one had ever seen girl flyers. We were as much a novelty as if we had two heads apiece.

If Robert could not hire a barn we would work in a field, with the A-frames for Jack and the girls fixed deep into the wet ground and a mesh of rigging pegging it down to hold it still. It was cold working on the outside but people huddled together and cheered and did not seem to mind. I was mortally tired at the end of a day with two shows, and it was worse when we worked in the open air because I was chilled by the end of the show as well. Preparing the ponies and showing them, changing their harness, and then my two rosinback acts were hard work. I could hand the horses over to Rea for the second half but my trapeze act strained my tired muscles, and always I stiffened in a frenzy of tension while Dandy was working up high. Then I had to force a smile on my face for the historical tableau at the end when Jack and I rode Snow and Sea around the ring at a fast canter and snatched Dandy and Katie up behind us to represent the rape of the Sabine women. The crowd loved that. Katie and Dandy wore their indecent trapeze costumes with a veil over their faces and screamed like banshees. Jack and I wore our breeches and blue shirts with little fez hats. We tried it one time with burnt cork smeared on our faces and it went even better.

We did three shows a day if we were in a barn. Robert would hire lanterns and we would work until the light was going. He would sometimes hire benches and do a gala show for invited local gentry if we were in an area of big houses. Katie and Dandy would be on their mettle then, catching the eye of the local squire.

I used to peep through the door of the barn to see the clothes, to smell the clean perfume smell that came off from them. The clothes were so smooth, the cloth so silky. The colours of the women's dresses were so pale and so regular – the dyes seemed never to have run streaky. Their collars were always white, and if it got hot in the barn they brought out exquisite painted fans and wafted them gently at their necks where you could not see a line where they had stopped washing.

I used to watch them and long to be one of them. It was a dream as foolish as Dandy's thought of taking the fancy of one of the young squires. But it was part of my old dream of Wide, and I longed for clean sheets and a quiet room. The tick of a well-oiled clock and flowers in a vase. The smell of beeswax and the view from the window of other people bent-backed working on my land.

The dream of Wide which had slipped away from me in Warminster came back to me now we were on the road again. Every day as we went eastward into Hampshire and then towards Sussex it grew stronger. I used to close my eyes every night and know that I would see on my eyelids a high horizon of green hills, a lane white with chalky mud, a straggle of cottages down one main lane. A vicarage opposite a church, a shoulder of bracken-strewn brown common reaching up behind the cottages and a blue sky overarching it all.

I would dream that I was a girl just like myself, with a tumble of copper hair and green eyes and a great passion for things she could scarcely hope to have. Once I dreamed of her lying with a dark-haired lad and I woke aching with a desire which I had never felt in real life. Once I awoke with a shriek for I dreamed that she had ordered her father's death and had held the great wooden door open and stared stony-faced as they carried him past her on a hurdle with his head stove in. Dandy had shaken me awake and asked me what was wrong and then hugged me and shielded me from Katie when I told her I had dreamed of Wide, and something awful. That I must stop her, the girl who was me. That I must run to her and warn her against the death of her father.

Dandy had rocked me and held me in her arms as if I were a baby and told me that Wide was a place we had none of us seen, nor heard of. That the girl was not me. That I was Meridon, Meridon the gypsy, the horse-trainer, the showgirl. And then I cried again and would not tell her why. But it was because the gulf between me and the girl in the dream was unbridgeable.

I had another dream too. Not one which woke me screaming, but one which made me long with a great loneliness for the mother that Dandy and I had lost so young. I had somehow got her muddled in my mind with the story Jack had told us of the loss of his mother – of her calling and calling as the wagon went away from her down the road. I certainly knew that my mother had not run after any wagon. She was too ill, poor woman, to run after anything. The memories I had of her were of her lying in the bunk with her mass of black hair, Dandy's thick black hair, spread out on the pillow all around her, saying to Da in an anxious, fretting voice, 'You will burn everything when I die, won't you? Everything. All my dresses and all my goods? It is the way of my people. I need to know you will burn everything.'

He had promised yes. But she had known, and he had known, and even little Dandy and I had known that he would not complete the ceremonies and bury her as a Romany woman should be treated. He took her body off on a handcart and tossed it in the open hole which served as a pauper's grave. Then he sold her clothes, he did not burn them as he promised. He burned a few rags in an awkward shame-faced way, just things he could not sell. And he tried to tell Dandy and me, who were watching him wide-eyed, that he was keeping his promise to our dead mother. He was a liar through and through. The only promise he kept was to give me my string and gold clasps. And he would have had that off me if he could.

But it was not that death that I remembered. That was not the mother I grieved for in my dream. I dreamed of a thunderstorm, high overhead, a night when no one who could close shutters would venture out. But out in the wind and the rain was a woman. The rain was sluicing down on her head, her feet were cut in many places from the sharp flints in the chalk soil and she limped like a beggar come new to the trade. The pain in her feet was very bad. But she was crying not for that pain but because she had a baby under her arm and she was taking it to the river to throw it away like an in-bred whelp which should be drowned. But the little baby was so warm beneath her arm, hidden from the storm by her cape. And she loved it so dearly she did not know how she could let it go, into the cold water, away into the flood. As she stumbled and sobbed she could feel it nuzzling gently into her armpit, trustingly.

Then the dream melted as dreams will and suddenly there was a wagon, like the one I live in now, like all the wagons I have lived in all my life. And a woman leaning down from the seat by the driver and reaching out for the baby, and taking the baby without a word.

And then – and this is the moment where I suppose the

dreams become muddled with Robert G ~ver's wife calling after him on the road – then the wagon moved off and the woman was left behind. In one part of her heart she was glad that the child was sent away, off the land, away from her home. And in another part she longed for her child with such a passion that she could not stop herself from running, running on her bleeding feet after the rocking wagon, and calling out, though the wind ripped her words away: 'Her name is Sarah! Sarah . . .'

She called some more, but the wind whipped her words away and the woman on the box did not turn her head. And I awoke, in the early, cold grey light, with tears pouring down my cheeks as if I was grieving for a mother who had loved me and given me away; sent me away because there was no safe place for me in my home.

15

The dreams kept waking me at night, and even when I slept I woke weary. Robert looked at me askance around the stem of his pipe and asked if I were sickening. I said, 'No,' but I felt tired to my very bones.

I was sleeping poorly, and we were in counties where they watched for their game and we were eating sparingly. Bread, cheese and bacon; but no rich gamey stews. I was working hard. Harder than I had ever worked for my da. At least my da had taken the odd day, sometimes days at a time, when he had done no work at all, disappearing to drink and gamble, and coming home reeling and worthless. With Robert we worked in a steady rhythm of work and moving, and there was nothing else.

Katie kept going, working and practice, doing her act. But she was ready to drop after the last show of an evening. Especially if we were working in a barn and she was doing three shows a day. She would roll into her bunk as soon as she had stripped her costume off. I often saw the two of them, her and Dandy, sleeping naked under the blankets, with their fine flyers' cloaks spread out over their bunks, when they had been too weary to fold them and put them in the chest. Dandy was exhausted. She had to order the two of them into the rigging for extra practice when the tricks went badly, she had to watch the act, not just as a performer but as a trainer too. And she had to work and work at her own skill. Long after Katie and Jack had dropped down, cursing with weariness into the nets, Dandy would be up there throwing somersaults to an empty trapeze, falling into the net, and going heel-toe, heel-toe, up the ladder to go through the trick again.

I would be working the horses, or fetching them hay and water for the night, and I would go into the barn when I heard the twang of the catch-net and ask Dandy to leave her practice and come to bed. Sometimes I brought her a cup of mulled ale and she would drop from the net and drink it, sitting on one of the benches.

'Shouldn't eat nor drink in the ring,' she said to me once, her face wreathed in steam from the hot ale.

'Shouldn't swear either, and all of us do,' I replied unrepentant. 'Now you go to bed, Dandy. We've another three shows to do tomorrow, you'll be tired out.'

She yawned and stretched herself. 'I will,' she said. 'You coming?'

I shook my head, though I ached for sleep. 'I've got to clean the harness,' I said. 'It's getting too dirty. I'll not be long.'

She went without a backward glance, and when I came to the wagon two hours later she and Katie were fast asleep; Dandy on her back, her hair a rumpled black mass on the pillow.

I crept into my own bunk and gathered the blankets around my shoulders in their comforting warmth. But as soon as I shut my eyes I started dreaming again. I would dream I was the redheaded girl and the land was turning against me. I would watch the fields grow ripe and yet know an absolute fear of loss clutch cold at me. I would dream I was the woman who had been out in the storm and I would ache for the loss of the baby whose name was Sarah. Then I would hear her anguished call, and sometimes I would sit bolt upright in my bed, cracking my forehead on the roof of the wagon, as if I were trying to answer her.

In the morning I would be heavy-eyed and pasty-faced. But still there would be the horses to train and the ponies to work. The hay and the water to take around, the tack to be checked, and every single one of the twelve animals to wash and groom.

Rea helped. But Robert was training him for rosinback riding and he was tired and bruised from his falls. Jack helped. But he was training on the trapeze and helping Rea learn to stand. Most of the work fell to me. I could not ask Katie for help; she was afraid of Snow and Sea and would only groom the little ponies. I would not ask Dandy. I always wanted her to rest.

Our quietest time was around noon. We ate early, and Katie and Dandy did most of the cooking. Robert ordered Jack and Rea to clear up the plates and wash them. Sometimes we would pile back into our bunks and sleep the early afternoon hours away. Sometimes, as it grew warmer, we would find our way to the nearest river or lake – going three-up on Morris or Bluebell – and spend an hour splashing in the cool water. One time, when we were playing in a field outside a little fishing village called Selsey in west Sussex, we all five of us went down to the sea: Jack and Rea on Snow, Dandy, Katie and me on Sea. We rode them along the pebbles of the beach down to the hard sand at the water's edge and then urged them in. Sea jinked and fretted at the little waves and Katie cried to be let off. Dandy and I let her go and Dandy held tight around my waist while I urged Sea into the water. The waves came up to his knees and I still pressed him on until he made a little leap deeper into the sea and he was swimming with great heaving magical lunges. Dandy and I clung to his mane, swam beside him, letting his great heaving movement tug us through the water, buffeted by the waves. Jack and Rea were shouting with delight, trying to stay on Snow, and Katie lost her fear and played at the water's edge. We five became children again for that little time, playing as we had never been allowed to play in our overworked childhoods. But then Jack looked at the sun and nodded at me.

'Time to head back,' he said. The others wanted to stay for longer under the warm sun, by the washing sea, but Jack and I carried our way against them.

'I've got to get these two clean,' I said ruefully, looking at Sea's coat which was matted with salt and his mane which was drying in tangles.

'I'll help,' Dandy promised lightly. 'I'll help and then we can all stay longer!'

'No,' I said, and Jack nodded his agreement with me.

'Come on,' he said, vaulting up on to Snow. 'Time to get back.'

Katie rode home between Jack and Rea. Dandy and I came along behind, slowly, on Sea.

It was only mid-April, but warm as Maytime. The sun was hot on our heads.

'You named him well when you called him Sea,' Dandy said sleepily. 'Why did you call him that, Merry?'

She was riding before me and I felt happy and easy with her in my arms.

'Because of Wide,' I said. 'I felt that I had seen him before at Wide and that he had a name there like Sea – something. I don't know what. So I called him Sea.'

'Oh, Wide!' she said lazily. 'D'you still think of it, Merry? I thought it only gave you nightmares now.'

'I do,' I said. The old longing was still calling me. 'I think I always will,' I said.

Dandy leaned back against me and dozed, and when I kissed her hair, softly not to wake her, I tasted salt from the sea.

She stirred and glanced back over her shoulder at me, her dark eyes smiling. 'I've got him at last,' she confided.

'Who?' I asked. I was stupid with my usual weariness and with the dizzy dancing feeling behind my eyes from being out in the bright sunlight and watching the sparkle on the waves. I was aching all over from my swimming and I knew I would be stiff tomorrow. I was dozing like Dandy had been. I did not think what she was saying.

'Got who?' I asked.

Dandy nodded her tousled head towards the other horse which was ahead of us. Just a little way ahead, turning into the gate where the wagons were pitched and the little ponies hobbled.

'Jack,' she said. Her voice was a purr of satisfaction. 'I've got him so that he won't escape me, and the show will be half ours as I promised.'

'Dandy, what have you done?' I exclaimed, struggling to wake and understand what she was saying; but Sea followed Snow into the field and Robert Gower was tumbling out of his wagon, his face flushed and his eyes bright.

'Where the hell have you been!' Robert exclaimed. 'Meridon Cox, you're going to have to work like a sugar-island slave to get these horses ready for tonight! And tonight of all nights! Don't you bodge it, m'girl. Either the first or the second show there's a man coming specially to see us! I had a letter after you'd all gone jauntering off! If it'd come before you left I'd have kept you back.'

'What man?' Dandy asked.

Robert beamed at her. 'Never you mind, little Miss Nosey,' he said. 'Just you remember that he's coming to either the first or the second show. He could make my fortune too if he likes what he sees.' He nodded at all of us. 'If he makes me an offer for the show you'll all see the benefit of it,' he said. 'A London season! A proper-built ring. Quality audience. Two shows a day but never out of doors! No more travelling! No end to what we could do!'

He broke off and looked around at us. 'My God, you look like a camp of gypsies!' he said irritably. 'Meridon! Get to work on those horses! Rea! Help her! Jack! Check the rigging and then come and see what Merry needs doing.'

He rounded on Katie and Dandy. 'You two are supposed to be flying angels! Belles of the ball!' he said angrily. 'You look like a pair of sluttish hedge-hoppers! Get under the tap both of you, and wash and braid your hair. Check your costumes! I want you to look absolutely your best.'

He took Dandy by the arm and led her away and I knew he was telling her to get hold of me after I had finished work on the horses and make sure my hair was brushed through. I smiled ruefully. Robert always wanted everything. Perfect horses and a pretty little Miss to present them too.

The girls rushed off for water and their combs. I got hold of a couple of heavy iron buckets and set about washing Sea while Rea dealt with Snow. Then there was Morris and Bluebell to wash and brush down. Morris had been rolling in the mud and lush grass and it took me nearly an hour to get the green grass-stains off his legs and haunches where his patches were white.

Then Jack came over and rolled up his sleeves and helped me with the little ponies. Every one of them had to be washed and brushed. Every one of them had to have their rumps wetted and combed criss-cross so that they looked sparkling under the lanterns of the barn. Every one of them had to have harness and bridle and keeper-reins on, every one of them had to have hay and water, and each one had to have his little brass bell checked and quickly rubbed and laid carefully to one side, ready to put on the moment before they went in.

Dandy came up while Jack and I were finishing grooming the last two and getting ready to tack-up.

'You're to leave it,' she said abruptly. 'Both of you. Robert says to leave Rea to finish and the two of you get ready.'

I straightened up and looked at her.

She was so lovely I could hardly believe that she and I were sisters. She had braided her hair into four little flying plaits which fell each side of her face twisted with gilt and green ribbons. The rest of her black hair she had brushed loose and it cascaded over her shoulders and down her back. She had rouged her lips and her cheeks and had put a bit of cork-black around her eyes. She looked like some Arab princess. She looked strange and lovely.

'Oh Dandy!' I said. 'You are so beautiful!'

She smiled. The sweet beguiling smile of her childhood.

'Am I?' she said with innocent total vanity. 'Am I beautiful, Jack?'

He dropped the bell he was polishing and put out his arms to her.

'Yes,' he said, in the only tender tone I had ever heard him use towards her. 'Yes, you are lovely.'

Dandy floated towards him with a sigh, but then she suddenly saw the dirt on his hands and stepped back, fending him off. 'Don't touch me, you're filthy!' she exclaimed. 'Anyway, there's no time! Robert says I'm to help you dress, Meridon, and wash your hair. Go to the pump and I'll bring the comb and a towel. Jack, you get washed too. You're hands are black and they're already waiting outside in the lane. Your da's on the gate already.'

I ran to do her bidding, but out of the corner of my eye I caught sight of a brief resentful look which went across Jack's face. He did not like taking orders from Dandy. He had not liked it on the trapeze swings, he liked it even less on the ground. And least of all did he like it when he had just, for the first time ever, held open his arms to her, openly, in broad daylight. He turned away, as sulky as a spoilt child, and went to his wagon. I watched the slouch of his back and thought how that little gesture of desire from him was curdling to resentment. I don't think Dandy noticed him at all.

The water from the pump was icy and it made me cold all through. I shivered in my wet shift as Dandy combed my hair and pulled roughly at the tangles.

'If you combed it every day it wouldn't tangle like this!' she said crossly as I flinched and complained. 'Now I'm going to plait it like mine!'

'Oh leave be, do, Dandy!' I begged. 'It will take you ages, and I hate being fussed about.'

'Robert wanted all us girls with the same hair,' she said. 'Katie's wearing blue and gold ribbons in her plaits, me with green and gold, and you'll have red. Now kneel down,' she said inexorably. 'It will only take longer if you fidget, Merry!'

I knelt. The grass under my knees around the pump was soaked and made me cold. My wet hair hanging down my back dripped chilly droplets down my spine. The sun had lost its heat and I was shivering from the cold by the time Dandy had finished.

'What were you going to tell me when we came into the field?' I asked her. 'What were you going to tell me about Jack?'

The odd secretive look came over her face again. 'Not now,' she said. 'I'll tell you after the show, when we're not in such a rush.'

'All right,' I said, unwilling to wait. 'But it's nothing bad is it, Dandy?'

She smiled at me, the warm complacent smile of a woman who knows she has everything. 'Nothing bad,' she said. 'And if this man likes the flying act then that makes it better and better.'

I would have pressed her for more, but Rea came running to tell us that Robert had opened the gate and had a full house already. Dandy and Katie must go quick and start selling drinks and sweetmeats.

'And the man from London's here,' he said.

'How d'you know?' Dandy demanded, pausing in her flight. 'What does he look like?'

'Great driving coat,' Rea said, very much awed. 'Enormous buttons, huge capes, high high hat. And very shiny boots.'

Dandy nodded. 'I'm gone,' she said and picked up her short skirts and dashed to our wagon for her cape.

'You look nice, Merry,' Rea said awkwardly. I knew I did not. Dandy and Katie had chosen colours to suit themselves. Neither of them had thought how I would look with red ribbons in my copper hair. The colours screamed at each other. Dandy had scraped my curls roughly into plaits, and tied them too tight, so that the skin on my scalp and forehead was sore. I was scowling with the discomfort.

'I know I don't,' I said unhelpfully. 'But it doesn't matter.'

Rea grinned sympathetically. 'Shall I take them out for you again?' he offered.

I shook my sore head. 'I don't dare!' I said. 'Anyway, I've got to get ready.'

I ran off to my wagon and Rea went back to watch the gate and collect the pennies of latecomers.

As soon as I was dressed in my blue riding habit I went back out to the horses with my working smock pulled over the top.

This was rich farming country, good flat land with a dark fertile soil. The barns here were huge, big enough for all of the horses to be inside at the same time. As soon as he had seen the extra space in the corn-rich counties Robert had put the little ponies in the opening parade and we had trained them to go two by two behind Snow ridden by Jack. I came behind all of them on Sea. Then Dandy and Katie came riding in dressed in their flying capes, both sitting sideways bareback on Morris. Bluebell brought up the rear with his steady reliable canter and two billowing flags set in either side of his harness. It was a good start to the show but it meant that all the horses had to be ready at once.

Jack was already behind the barn with the ponies, screwing the bells into the ponies' headbands. Rea was trying to put a plume into Sea's headband, who was tossing his head and shying away from the bright feather although he had seen it a hundred times before. Rea was cursing him in a soft gentle voice, careful not to frighten him more.

'I'll do that,' I said. 'You put the coats on Bluebell and Morris.'

Each of the rosinbacks now had a little cape in the bright pink of the girls' flying capes. They should have been in the box for the horses' special tack, with the plumes and the bells.

'They're not here!' exclaimed Rea.

We had a few moments of whispered rage. Jack blamed me, but I could clearly remember folding them and putting them away the night before. Rea swore they had been there a moment ago and Jack cursed him and said he must have lifted them out and laid them down somewhere. Rea denied it, and I told Jack to stop trying to swing the blame to one of us and help look. In the midst of all the confusion and anger Dandy came swaying up as lovely as an angel with her pink cape floating behind her, and the horses' capes over her arm. She had taken them to brush them clean. Jack cursed her roundly for not telling us, and Dandy smiled back at him as if nothing could touch her, as if she cared nothing for his anger or for his likes and dislikes. I felt that same coldness I had felt when the water had run down my back while she was washing my hair. I shuddered.

Robert opened the big double barn door and put his head out to see us. Behind him I could hear the clatter of many people crowded into the small space.

'Everyone ready?' Robert asked. He was red with suppressed excitement, but trying to be calm. 'Good audience tonight. Full up. And the man from London is here to see the show.'

He had himself well under control, but I could see that his hand on his whip was shaking. 'This could be the making of us,' he said softly. 'I cannot tell you how important it is you work your best tonight.' His voice was almost imploring. He looked around. 'Horses ready, Meridon?'

'Yes, Robert,' I said, and I smiled at him. He might have worked me until I was weary through to my very bones with tiredness, but he was a man with one goal in view and I could not help but smile with pleasure to see him coming steadily and surely towards it.

'Well, better start then!' he said. He stepped back into the barn and I could imagine him striding into the very centre of the floor. We had scattered fresh woodshavings down that morning and Robert's boots would look as black and shiny as Quality against the whiteness. We had put down hay bales to mark out a ring for the horses and all the little children would be sitting on the other side of them, their faces wide-eyed, looking over the top. Behind them would be the double row of benches reserved for the Quality and for those willing to pay thruppence a seat. Behind them was a row of straw bales for the twopenny spectators, and behind them, and standing in the doorway, and scarcely able to see at all, were the people who could afford nothing more than a penny but who clapped the horses longest and loudest for they knew – as the front benches did not – how long and hard you have to work with a horse to make him mind a whisper.

'My Lords, Ladies, Gentlemen; and Honoured Guest!' Robert bawled. An immediate hush descended on the barn. It was so quiet I could hear Jack tapping his thumbnail against his teeth.

'Stop that Jack, it's irritating,' Dandy said softly.

'We are proud to present, tonight, and for three nights only, Robert Gower's Amazing Equestrian and Aerial Show!'

That was our cue. Rea threw his slight weight against the big double doors and thrust them open. Jack wiped the scowl off his face and rode into the ring, head up, smiling. Snow picked up his feet and pranced when he heard them gasp at the size and the beauty of him and tossed his head so that the new ostrich plume waved.

I nodded at Rea who was holding the keeper-reins of the front pony and he sent them in behind, their bells jingling. There was an instant 'aaahhh!' from the little children which spread to the adults; as if none of them had ever whipped a horse to death in their lives. I slid a finger under Sea's girth to check it was tight enough and glanced behind me to see that Dandy was all right. She was up on Morris's back already and she smiled at me, her satisfied secretive smile.

'Go on, Merry!' Rea said urgently, and I dragged my eyes away from Dandy's smooth inscrutable face and rode into the ring and smiled at the ripple of applause that greeted me. I was not won to vanity by that. They were clapping because I was slim and dainty and because the horse was tall and moved with his head up as proud as a hunter. The lithe slimness of my body gave me a claim to be a beauty in the ring, and the blue riding habit did the rest. Besides, as Robert had taught me, they had paid their money to see beautiful women and fine horses and they would try to see nothing else. I smiled and got another round of applause.

Any vanity I had nurtured would have been put to flight by Dandy and Katie's entrance. The audience cheered and stamped their feet at the very sight of the girl flyers on the back of the big horse. Katie and Dandy nodded their heads as gracious as a pair of queens. We all did two rounds of the ring before Jack led the way out.

Rea caught the ponies as they came out and turned them around for me to take in. Jack took Sea from me, and led him and Snow to their hitching posts. Dandy was responsible for Morris and Bluebell who knew well enough to go to their place and stand still. Robert had stayed in the ring as we had circled around and bowed to the roar of applause as we went out. He waited a few seconds to give me time to tumble off Sea and stand at the head of the ponies behind the closed barn door. Then when the crowd was hushed again, after the excitement of the opening parade, he cracked his whip and with much flowery introduction presented Mamselle Meridon and the Dancing Ponies!

The act went well. The ponies had been getting better every day since we had been on the road, they were getting their exercise just by moving from one village to another. They had slimmed down too, and they looked better than when I had learned to train them in Robert's field at Warminster. They watched me carefully enough and I made sure that I made my cues clear to them. Step forward, whips up: stop. Turn around whips held out sideways meant circle round the ring. Whips twirled meant pirouette. We finished the act with them all backing slowly towards the barn door and then kneeling down to take a bow. I stood before them and smiled at the crowd, looking for the man from London.

He was not hard to spot. He sat in the front row smoking a large cigar with a fat glowing ember held perilously close to the bale of straw before him. He was smiling at me, and he put the cigar between his teeth to slide his gloves off his large hands and clap hard: three times. I dipped an awkward little bow – I could never learn Dandy's graceful sweep of a curtsey – and then I had the ponies circle the ring once more before sending them out and taking another bow before going out myself.

Rea caught the ponies as they came out and took them to their hitching posts. I pulled my smock on over my riding habit as soon as I was out of the ring, and went to help Jack with Bluebell and Morris.

'She's gone to get some more drinks and buns,' Rea said seeing my glance around for Dandy. I nodded. I pulled back the barn door for Jack as he strolled into the ring when his father announced him. Then Rea heaved back the double door and I gave Bluebell and Morris a hearty slap each on the rump and sent them in for Jack's bareback riding act.

'Did you need her?' Rea asked. 'I could run and fetch her. You don't need me here.'

'No,' I said absently. 'It's nothing.'

'She has a shadow tonight,' Rea said suddenly.

I jerked up my head to look at him. His eyes were hazy, vague. He saw my stare and he met my eyes and smiled at me. 'Don't look so scared Meridon! It's what my grandma used to say. When she was dukerin – fortune-telling! I just thought that Dandy looked as if she had a shadow.'

'Is that bad luck?' I demanded. 'Would it be bad luck for her to do the trapeze tonight?'

'It would be bad luck for anyone trying to stop her!' he said fairly. 'No. I don't have the Sight, Meridon. And neither did my grandma, really. I don't know what made me say it.'

'Well, keep your mouth shut till you do know,' I said sharply. 'And get ready to catch the horses. Jack's finishing.'

I heard the roar of applause that greeted the end of Jack's act and Rea hauled the barn doors open and caught Bluebell and Morris as they cantered steadily out. Jack ran after them, his face shiny with sweat, his eyes sparkling.

'He likes me! He clapped me!' he said. 'Da is really pleased!'

'Good,' I said dryly, thinking of the measured three claps.

'Three claps he gave me!' Jack said as if it were a bouquet of flowers flung at his feet.

'All three!' I said sarcastically. Then I turned to get Snow, as I heard Robert inside the barn shout:

'The amazing, the mind-reading, the magical counting horse!'

Snow went in and I went back to my wagon, pulling off my working smock as I went. Dandy was unpacking food into trays in the men's wagon and I stripped off my riding habit without anyone to help me with the buttons at the back. I shook out the little red skirt and put it on. The red waistcoat was smart – close-fitting. Mrs Greaves had trimmed it with a little left-over gold braid. It matched the gilt and red flying ribbons in my hair – even if my copper curls clashed appallingly. I tugged my working smock atop the lot and then pushed my bare feet into a pair of clogs and trotted back to the barn for I heard the applause at the end of Robert's act with Snow.

Bluebell was ready for my rosinback act, with a warm blanket over her so she did not cool after her work with Jack, and fresh rosin on his broad rump.

I kicked off my clogs and Rea gave me a leg-up so I was sitting astride. I got to my feet as we heard Robert starting his patter, and stood balancing carefully on Bluebell's back: 'The graceful, the charming, the brilliant Mamselle Meridon!'

There was a burst of applause from inside the barn, I took Bluebell's strap to steady me and nodded at Rea and he pulled back the door. I went in upright, standing high on Bluebell's back, the top of my head just clearing the barn door, and there was an 'oooohhh!' from the audience as Bluebell thundered into the ring and Robert cracked the whip. I tossed my head and my hair streamed out behind me. I kept my balance, and I did not come off, but I was tired and not ready to work my best, not even for the man from London. Three times we circled the ring, as I got my balance steady and let Bluebell establish her stride. Then Rea came darting out from a crack in the doors with a little gilt stick. He stood at the side of the ring and held it out at shoulder level as Bluebell went cantering around. He dipped it down for me to jump it, and I watched it carefully and then bobbed over, landing solidly and surely on Bluebell's broad back.

Robert kept Bluebell's pace going with a flick of his whip at her heels for another circle of the ring while the people cheered that trick, and then Rea reached up to me and handed me a gilt rope and I skipped a few skips with it. It was a trick I still hated – I had to swing the rope myself and the movement of my arms put me off balance. Robert in the middle of the ring shouted, 'Hurrah!' at each skip but gave me a very hard look when he saw how low I was skipping. I remembered the Honoured Guest again, and skipped higher.

Robert's whip cracked and Bluebell threw up her head and went a little faster. I kept my bright show smile on my face but the look I shot Robert was pure green anger. He knew how hard I found it to stay steady when Bluebell went faster, but he also knew that it made the trick look far more exciting. Rea disappeared through the barn door and Robert talked-up the finale of my act:

'And now, honoured guest, ladies and gentlemen, Mamselle Meridon will perform for you her most daring and dangerous trick – a leap through a paper hoop! As performed before Countless Crowned Heads in Europe and Further Abroad!'

Everyone said 'oooh!' and I took half a dozen nervous little steps on Bluebell's back and prayed Robert would send her no faster.

Rea jumped up on one of the hay bales at the ring's edge and raised the hoop high above his head in readiness. At the next circuit he brought it down. Bluebell had seen it a thousand times and kept steady, fast and steady. I jumped into the paper centre, there was a second's blindness and then my feet were solidly down on Bluebell's rolling rump and the barn was filled with cheering.

People jumped to their feet and flung flowers and even a few coins, and I somersaulted off Bluebell's back into the centre of the ring and took a bow with Robert holding my hand and sweeping his tall top hat down in a bow to me. Then he put his hands on my waist and I went up on to Bluebell's back again to take another bow. Just as the cheers quietened there was a drunken yelling of, 'Hurrah! wonderful!' and Jack came weaving through the crowd.

I was watching the man from London and he gave a start at the interruption and looked to Robert to see what he would do to stop the drunkard ruining the show. Other people shouted, 'Sit down!' and one person tried to stop Jack but he slid past them and was into the ring and at the horse's side before anyone could catch him. I saw the London man look anxiously at Robert and I smiled inwardly thinking that he was not as clever as he thought, that we could catch him with this trick to amuse the children. They were wide-eyed as ever; and their parents too were utterly silent, waiting to see what would happen to this man who dared to break into the most exciting show which had ever come to their village.

Jack took four steps back and made a little run at Bluebell and vaulted on her, facing her tail. He looked owlishly at my feet, and then up to my face. People started laughing as they saw the point of the joke and one by one the little children's faces lit up as Jack spun himself around and ended up lying across the horse forwards, and then on his back. Robert clicked to Bluebell and she moved to the ring edge and started her reliable canter.

All I had to do was to keep my face straight and my feet on her back and my head up. Jack did the rest and there were gales of laughter as he scrambled from one side to another. We finished the act with him clinging around under her neck as we cantered around the ring. I glanced at the man from London.

All his elegant town poise had gone. His cigar was out, he was rolling on his seat with laughter and there were actual tears from laughing on his cheeks. Robert and I exchanged one triumphant beam and Bluebell left the ring to a standing ovation and the welcome chink chink of people throwing their coppers into the ring and cheering me and Jack until they were hoarse.

16

The ponies went past us in a ripple of coloured flags as Jack and I slid wearily from Bluebell's back. Dandy and Katie were back with a tray of buns and toffee, and a big pitcher of lemonade. Dandy nodded her head at the noise.

'They liked your act, then,' she said coolly.

Jack was triumphant. 'They threw money and cheered!' he said. 'And the man from London was laughing and laughing. Whatever he thinks of the flying act, me and Meridon are made! It'll be London for us!'

Dandy looked at him from under her eyelashes. 'I reckon it'll be London for all of us,' she said. 'I'll go with you, Jack.'

'They cheered so loud!' Jack said, not heeding her. 'I've never known it go so well.'

'You were the funniest you've ever been,' I said, giving credit where it was due. 'You really looked like a drunken farmhand. When you came out from the back everyone thought you were a stranger. Even the man from London did. I saw him look at Robert and wonder what he was going to do.'

Jack nodded. 'I saw his face when I first vaulted up,' he said. 'I nearly laughed myself. He looked as if he could not believe what he had let himself in for.'

I laughed. 'But who exactly is he, Jack? Your da didn't say.'

Jack glanced behind him but Robert was still in the ring doing the Battle of Blenheim with the ponies. We heard the audience take the tune from him and then they started singing 'The Roast Beef of Old England!' with the rounded drawl of Sussex in their voices.

'He runs a show he calls a circus in London,' Jack said in an undertone. Dandy and Katie were out of earshot, preening at the barn doors, ready to go in with their trays. 'Da says he's looking for acts that he can put on inside. He's got a special-built building with a great ring and an entrance and an exit, and he charges people a shilling to go in!'

'For one show?' I asked.

Jack nodded. 'Aye. And the money he is offering for an act is amazing! David knew him and told him about us. He's come all this way to see us. My da is right, Merry; if he likes us, then our fortunes are made. He hires by the season and he buys an act he likes in gold for the season. We could make enough in one year to live on for the rest of our lives if we wanted!'

I thought at once of Wide. Dandy might have forgotten it, but I had spoken the truth when I said I never would. My dreams might be frightening, but they were clearer and clearer. The land of Wide could not be far from here, I knew it. I felt it every day. Every time we moved I wondered if the next day would bring me to a place which I had looked for all my life, as if someone might say: 'Oh, this is Wide-fell, or Wide-moor, or Wide-land.' I knew it was close. The landscape was like this one. The trees were the same, and the lightness of the sky. If Wide was near here and could be bought . . . I broke off my thoughts and turned to Jack.

'How are you and Dandy?' I asked.

Jack glanced at her back at the barn door. 'All right,' he said briefly. Then he shot me an imploring look. 'Don't ask me now, Meridon. Damn me, you do pick your times! My da'll come out in a second and there's a man from London in the front row! We're as we always were. Hot as a pair of stray dogs, and a deadly secret. She has seldom a civil word for me, and I hate her as much as I want her. Now hush, Meridon. Ask Dandy. Don't ask me. I try to not even think about it!'

Rea pulled back the doors and the ponies came out in a rush. Jack caught the two first through the door, and I grabbed the next. Rea got hold of two as they trotted past him, and the smallest followed on behind. We took them to their hitching posts and I left Rea to feed them and take their tack off them while I went to my wagon to change. Jack ran past me to his wagon to get into costume for his flying act.

I was back first. I wore a shimmery blue shirt and a pair of thin white breeches, a scaled-down copy of Jack's flying costume. I was not nervous of the low practise trapeze; and besides my job was only to whet the appetite of the audience for the main trapeze act. But my feet were icy in my clogs as I trudged back to the barn door. And I ached as if I had fallen and been kicked hard in the belly. Dandy and Katie's elation at their record sales, and the smile the man from London had given them when he had said, 'No thank you,' went over my head. I hardly heard them. I had a deep dark feeling, as if I were a bucket going slowly down a deep well. The others' voices came as an echo from far away.

'You all right, Merry?' Jack said as he joined us. 'You look sickly.'

I looked around for him. My vision was slightly blurred and his face kept coming and going.

'I feel ill,' I said. I thought for a second and then recognised that cold feeling in my belly. 'I feel frightened,' I said.

Jack's hand came on my shoulder and I held still and let him touch me.

'Not that little practice trapeze!' Katie said scornfully. 'You can't be scared of that!'

I looked for her in the fog that was gathering around me. 'No,' I said uncertainly. 'I'm not scared of that.'

I was looking for Dandy. I could not see her. Robert came out and called for Jack to come and help finish rigging the catch-net with him and Rea.

I said: 'Dandy!' in sudden fright and then her beloved face was before me and she was saying kindly:

'What's the matter, Merry? You're as white as if you've seen a boggart. It should be me that's sickly!'

I could hear a distant rushing in my ears as if there was a waterfall far away pouring down a cliff. Something seemed to be coming towards us as fast as the tumbling water.

'Why?' I asked urgently. 'Why should it be you who is sickly?'

Dandy threw back her head and laughed. 'I wanted to tell you later,' she said.

She paused and I heard Robert say from the ring inside the barn:

'And now, Ladies and Gentlemen, Honoured Guest, Welcome Visitors All, We Commence the Second Half of our Nationally-Famous Show with Robert Gower's Amazing Aerial Display. First with Mamselle Meridon on the trapeze!'

'You're on!' Katie said urgently, holding open the door for me.

Through the gap I could see Rea and Jack checking the stakes which held the catch-net taut. Jack had his back to me, but I could see Rea's face furrowed with concentration. I had a moment of relief from worry. I knew Rea would make sure the catch-net was safe.

I could hear the clapping, the noise an audience makes when they are excited, waiting. They were waiting for me in the barn, but my feet would somehow not go forward. Jack was coming out past me.

'Go on Meridon!' he said softly. 'You're on.' He went on past me to check the set of his shirt in a little mirror Dandy had nailed up near the lantern.

I turned back to Dandy. 'I won't go until you tell me!' I said. It was as if I were seeking for a light at the top of the deep well.

She gave me a little push in the back and her face was alight with triumph and laughter.

'Go on, Merry!' she said. 'You're stubborn as a mule! I'll tell you it all later.' Then as my feet made no movement, she gave me another little push and said, 'Go on! It's as I said it would be! I've caught Jack and I'm going to tell his da. I'm breeding his child so there'll be a grandson Gower to inherit all this! And I'll be his ma. I told you I'd win all this, and I have done! I've caught him now and he'll not get away. I'll tell him after the show.'

I spun around and caught her hands but Katie tore me away from her and pushed me through the barn door. I saw Jack wheel around from the mirror. I saw his stunned face, blank with incomprehension at what he had overheard. Rea had one of the doors and was pulling it shut behind me. I knew that Jack had heard. I knew he had caught Dandy's exultant tone, I knew he had heard the words. He had turned in time to see her smile as she said: 'I've caught him now, and he'll not get away.'

I stood helplessly before the audience as if I had forgotten what I was there for. I looked behind me. The barn door had stuck on some roughness on the ground and Jack had come forward to help Rea shut it, obedient as ever to the orders of his father who said that it must always be kept closed during acts.

I walked over to the low trapeze slung underneath the girls' frame and kicked off my clogs and held my arms above my head. Robert lifted me up and I hung for a moment as if I had forgotten what to do. Then I started working the trapeze and it seemed to go backwards and forwards like the clapper of a bell tolling inside my head.

I could make no sense of what Dandy had said to me. I was too weary and overworked to make any sense of it at all. And the show had its own inexorable rhythm. I saw the man in the front row look at me and I smiled my shallow unreal smile and turned and hooked my knees through the trapeze bar and hung upside down. There was a little ripple of clapping. I swung my head up and leaned outwards, gripping the trapeze with my hands behind my back, and held the bird's nest pose. They clapped me again, more warmly. The trapeze seemed to go tick . . . tock . . . tick . . . tock in my head as I worked it to pick up speed.

I felt as if a long way away there was the red-haired woman in the big house waiting for her destiny to come to her. And that here I was, a ticking clock, waiting for mine to come to me. I raised myself up and over the trapeze in the pose that David called the kip, with the bar of the trapeze against my hips and my head up and smiling. My red ribbons blew across my eyes but I did not even blink. I was in a deep spiralling haze and I could not think nor see.

I leaped down from the trapeze with a cheating half-somersault and landed on my feet. They clapped me very loudly, someone cheered from the back. I looked around for Dandy.

'And now!' Robert yelled as the applause died down. 'We Present. The Daredevil, the Amazing . . . Jack Gower!' Jack came in and took a bow. I saw he was white as his breeches, his eyes dazed. He looked as if his life was about to collapse around him. He shot one bewildered look at me as I stood, my upraised hand gesturing towards him as David had taught us. His face was as puzzled and as scared as a lost child.

I tried to smile at him, he should be thinking of nothing but the task of catching the girls as they swung out towards him; but I found I could not. My lips were drawn back over drying gums in a blank parody of a smile. I was baring my teeth at the audience, not smiling. Jack looked at me as if I could help him. He looked at me as if he would ask me what he should do. He looked at me as if he was puzzled, disbelieving what he had heard.

My face was expressionless. I hardly even saw him. We were far, far away from each other. Somewhere deep down inside us we both knew that after the show there would be the end of this life. An end to the comfort and the friendship, the quiet early mornings and the hard-working days. The sense of belonging, all of us, one to all the others. There would be a row which would mean the end of this life. All the long months of training, and this afternoon's triumph, would count for nothing.

Robert Gower would not be caught by a slut like Dandy. Dandy would never let go. Jack would be trapped between their two conflicting wills. And I would have to take her away, pregnant, idle, incapable of earning money. She and me, a horse and a small purse of guineas. Jack gestured towards me with his hand, directing the applause towards me, and his face was white and imploring. He took his bow as if all the thief-takers in London were after him and started to climb his ladder slowly.

Robert watched him for a second, puzzled. Then he called: 'And Performing. For Your Entertainment. Flying at incredible height and speed, the Only girl flyers in the World! The Angels Without Wings: Mamselle Katie –' Katie strode into the ring, smirked all round especially towards the man from London, and started climbing the ladder. 'And Mamselle Dandy.'

She walked in without a glance to me. I was standing before the trapeze at the foot of her ladder, like a scarecrow in a field, my hand outflung, gesturing towards the middle of the ring where my sister took her bow with her green ribbons flying and her smile bright with the triumph at the trap she had sprung. I went to hold the foot of her ladder and her brilliant smile and her laughing eyes went past me as she climbed up.

'Old misery!' she whispered. 'I planned this all along! You'll see.'

I put my weight on the ladder to hold it steady for her and I waited until I could feel she had stepped from the ladder to the pedestal. I did not look up. I never looked up. I left the ring with my head up and my bright meaningless smile stuck on my face, and my eyes down, and I pulled the door shut behind me and leaned my forehead against the hard wooden planks and listened, as I always listened. So that I should hear the gasp of the crowd when one of them was stretching across to Jack, and then the roar when they were back on the pedestal. So that I should know that Dandy was safe.

I was so bone-weary I nearly dozed, standing upright, keeping my vigil for my sister with my face pressed against the rough wood plank. I heard the excited applause as they watched Jack on his pedestal vault up into a handstand, and the sudden rush of clapping when he swung right over to be standing upright again. Then there was the rustle of delicious apprehension as they watched Jack strap himself into his belt, and shuffle his feet on the blocks. They saw him rub his hands together – as he always did – and then reach purposefully out.

That would make them look to the right, where the girls were, and then I heard the great 'oooh' as Katie took hold of the trapeze and stepped out into space. She always went across first, I knew. I heard the audience hold their breath and Jack's, 'Pret!' was as clear as if I were in the front row. I pressed my palms flat against the door. The sense of sinking into the darkness was so strong that I could scarcely keep from slumping against the door and letting it wash over me. I felt someone beside me, and glanced quickly to one side. It was Rea.

'You all right?' he asked.

Inside the barn Jack yelled, 'Hup!' and there was a muted scream from the crowd as Katie swung her legs forward. I heard the smack as Jack caught her ankles and then the cry from the crowd as he swung her towards the back wall, and then twisted her around so she turned and caught the swinging bar, and then their burst of cheering when she reached the pedestal and turned and held up her hand and smiled.

I nodded at Rea's worried face. He seemed to be wavering, the whole world around me seemed to be melting and undulating.

'You're sweating and shivering,' he said. 'And you look awful white. Are you ill, Meridon?'

I heard the crowd rustle as Dandy and Katie changed places on the pedestal board and Dandy took the trapeze in her hands. I heard the little gasp as Dandy made her characteristic confident little leap downwards, and I heard Jack wait as she built-up her swing. Then I heard him call, 'Pret!' and I knew it would be Dandy he was watching now, Dandy he was reaching out for. Dandy with her legs hooked over the trapeze bar so that she could reach out for him with her hands. That little extra distance which made the trick that little extra bit more difficult. She would be stretching towards him now with her green ribbons flying away from her face and that triumphant dazzling smile on her face which Jack would unerringly recognize as Dandy's delight that she had gulled him and trapped him, and defeated him and his father.

'You going to faint?' Rea asked urgently. 'Can you hear me, Meridon?'

Jack yelled, 'Hup!' and I heard something in his voice which I had never heard before.

The sinking feeling in my head snapped, the planks of the door became suddenly clear. I scrabbled against them in sudden urgency.

'Let me in!' I shouted.

The door gave way before me, I looked up; for the first time, I looked up. I saw their hands touch, I saw Jack's safe hard grip, then I saw him swing her, with the speed of her swing and all his own whipcord strength, he swung her out, and flung her towards the high flint and mortar wall at the back of the barn. And as she flew towards it, her hands uselessly plucking at air, she screamed a long terrified scream which I heard, and recognized at once, as if I had been waiting to hear it for months. Then there was an awful thump as she smashed head-first into the wall and dropped like a nestling to the ground, and an echo of the scream from everyone in the crowd and a hundred voices shouting.

I went in like a bolting horse. They were all on their feet, all crowding round, mobbing her on the ground by the back wall. I went through the crowd like a weasel through a henhouse. I felt someone brush me and I knocked them off their feet with my shoulders as I ran through them. I could see the edge of Dandy's pink skirt and her pale bare leg twisted around.

Behind me Robert was yelling. 'Get back! Get away! Give the lass air! Is there a surgeon here? Or a barber? Anyone?'

I pushed a little child to one side and heard him fall and whimper and then I was at her side.

Everything was very slow and quiet then.

I put my hand to the tumbled mass of black hair and the green and gilt ribbons and I gathered her up to me. Her shoulders were still warm and sweaty, but her head lolled back, her neck was broken. The top of her head was a mess of blood, but it was not pumping out. Her eyes stared unseeingly at the wall behind her, they were rolled back in her head so the whites showed. Her face was frozen in a grimace of terror, the scream still caught in her throat.

I laid her down, gently back down on the ground and pulled the short skirt down over her bare legs. She was lying all twisted, her head and shoulders one way, her legs and hips the other, so her back was broken as well as her neck. There was a dribble of blood at the corner of her gaping mouth but that was all. She looked like a precious china doll smashed by a feckless child.

She was dead, of course. She was the deadest thing I had ever seen. Dandy, my beloved, scheming, brilliant sister, was far far away – if she was anywhere at all.

I looked up. Jack was struggling to undo his belt, I guessed his hands were shaking so much that he could not hold the buckle. He looked down at me from the catcher frame and he met my gaze. His mouth was half open as if he was appalled at what he had done. As if he could not believe what he had done. I nodded slowly to him, my eyes blank. It was unbelievable, but none the less he had done it.

I stood up.

The crowd all around me had fallen back. I saw their bright faces and their mouths moving but I could not hear anything.

Rea was beside me. I turned to him and my voice was steady.

'You'll see she's buried aright,' I said. 'In the manner of our people.'

He nodded, his face yellow with shock.

'Her clothes burned, her plate smashed, her goods buried with her,' I said.

He nodded.

'Not the wagon,' I said. 'The wagon is Robert's. But all the things she wore, and her bedding, and her blankets.'

He nodded.

'And her comb,' I said. 'Her ribbons. Her little pillow.'

I turned away from the crumpled body, and Rea standing beside it.

I went two steps and Robert held out his arms to me. I ignored him as if I had never loved him, nor anyone in all my life. I turned back to Rea.

'No one but you may touch her,' I said. But then I was uncertain. 'Is that right Rea? Is that the way of our people? I don't know how it is done.'

Rea's lips were trembling. 'It shall be done in our way,' he said.

I nodded and I walked under the catcher frame, where Jack's hands were shaking so hard he could not undo his belt. I did not look up again. I walked past Robert and felt his hand brush my shoulder and I shrugged it off without looking at him. I went through the barn door where I had stood like a fool when Dandy went laughing to her death, and I went out to where the horses were tethered.

I heaved the saddle on to Sea's back, and he dipped his head for the bridle. I could see the shine on the metal girth buckles and the bit, but I could not hear them chink when they rattled. I tightened the girth and led him across the grass to our wagon.

Her bedding still smelled of her. A warm smell like cornflowers, like hay. The wagon was scattered with her clothes, her ribbons, her hairpins, a mess of powder and an empty bottle of perfume.

I stripped off my trapeze costume and I pulled the ribbons out of my hair. It tumbled down in a sweep of copper curls and I pushed it back. I pulled on my shirt and my working smock and my riding breeches. I had a pair of old boots of Jack's and I pulled them on without a shiver. I reached under my mattress and pulled out my purse of ten guineas. I laid one on Katie's pillow. She had kept her part of the bargain and left Dandy a free hand with Jack. She had earned her coin. I slipped the purse inside my breeches and tied the string to my belt. Then I reached into the hole in my mattress and took out the string with the two gold clasps. I fastened it around my neck and tucked it under my shirt, and I shrugged myself into an old worsted jacket which once had belonged to Robert and was warm and bulky. There was a flat cap stuffed in the pocket; I piled my hair into it and pulled it on my head.

Katie was at the door of the wagon.

'Robert sent me,' she said breathless. 'He says you're to go to his wagon and lie down until he can come to you. He's getting the crowd out of the barn.' She hesitated. 'Rea's watching over Dandy,' she said. 'He's covered her up with her cape.'

She gave a little frightened sob and put out her hands to me for comfort.

I looked at her curiously. I couldn't for the life of me see what she had to cry about.

I went past her, careful that she should not touch me, and stood for a moment on the step of the wagon. Sea raised his head at the sight of me and I unhitched his reins.

'What are you doing?' Katie said anxiously. 'Robert said you were to . . .'

She tailed off into silence as I jumped up into the saddle.

'Meridon . . .' she said.

I looked at her and my face was like a frozen stone.

'Where are you going?' she asked.

I turned Sea's head and rode towards the edge of the field. People made way for me, their faces alight with interest, watching me avidly, recognizing me even out of costume. They had enjoyed a fine show tonight. The best we had ever done. Certainly the most exciting. It is not every day you see a girl flung across a barn into a flint wall. They should have paid extra.

They parted either side of me as I rode towards the gate. Sea paused, looked down the road. South was towards the beach where we had ridden together that morning and I had tasted the salt on her hair when I had kissed her. I turned Sea's head north and his unshod feet sounded soft on the mud of the lane. To our left the sun was sinking in a haze of pale saffron and apple-blossom clouds. Sea walked quietly, I rode him on a loose rein.

I did not sob. I did not even weep inwardly. I rode carefully past the people walking back to their homes and talking in high excited voices about the accident and what they had seen! and her face! and that awful scream! I rode past them in silence and I kept Sea headed north until we were through the little village and heading for the road towards London. Still heading north, with Sea's hooves making little squelchy noises in the ruts but quiet on the dried mud. North while the sun went lower and lower in the sky and the evening birds started to trill in the hedges which bordered the darkening lane. North, and I did not sob, or rage. I scarcely took breath.

17

I reached the road which plies along the line of the coast as it was growing dusky with the early grey twilight of spring. Sea turned to the right and I let him go where he would. It meant we were travelling east and I was glad of it for the sunset was now behind me. I did not want to ride into the setting sun, the colour of it hurt my eyes and made them sting as if I were going to cry. I knew I was not going to cry. I knew I would never cry again. The little isolated corner of affection which had been my love for Dandy had gone as swiftly and completely as she had gone. I did not expect to love anyone, ever again. I did not wish it.

A stage-coach went past us going in the opposite direction towards Chichester and the guard on the back blew his horn merrily as he saw me. I turned the collar of the jacket up against the cooler evening air. It was not cold, but I was icy inside. The jacket could not warm me. I saw my hands were trembling slightly on the reins and I looked at them carefully until they were steady. To our left, low on the horizon, a single pinprick of light shone very white and clear in the evening sky. I stared at it, and it seemed to stare back at me.

It mattered very little which way I took. It suited my whim to turn Sea's head towards the star which looked as icy and as cold as I felt inside. As it grew darker I saw that the lane was climbing, up to the crest of a hill. There was a sweet light singing all around us. Sea walked softly, his head up, snuffing at the air as if the chalk grass smelled good to him. It was quiet and dusky and he was unafraid, though his ears raked our surroundings for sounds of danger. I gave a solitary little chuckle at the thought of fear. Fear of living, fear of falling, fear of dying.

All gone.

I had achieved a state of absolute confidence. At last I had nothing left to lose, and the little girl who had looked at the ceiling above her bunk and known herself to have only one good thing in her life was now a woman with nothing. I felt gutted of love, of life, of tenderness. I felt clear and simple. I was as clean and cold as a freezing stream or like a chalk rock face with a sheen of ice on it.

The road was heavily wooded; under the trees the blackness of the evening was thick and blinding. Sea walked as if he were balancing on eggshells, his ears went forward and back, his head turned so that he could look everywhere. I slumped in the saddle as if I were a squire who had been hunting all day. I was bone weary. I even dozed as we went quietly up that lane; Sea's hooves made no sound on the pine needles and the mud. I only wakened when we came out from under the trees at the crest of the hill and found we were in the light of the rising half-moon.

I rubbed my eyes. We had climbed to a great rolling sweep of hills which had risen softly up from the coast. Now we were clear of the dark pine and budding beech trees the grass was short and sweet, cropped by sheep. Three or four of them scuttered out of our way as we came out of the wood. Little lambs scampering behind, butting at their mothers in their nervousness.

I looked back. Behind me the moonlit sea glowed like silver. The little islands of mud showed black in the darkness like a model of a landscape, not the real thing. I could see the fist of the land around the village of Selsey as it stuck out into the sea, and further to the west were other sludgy promontories of land, little points where we had halted in our slow progress to this damned county where Dandy had gone up to fly once too often, and I had been too slow and too great a fool to stop her. Sea turned his grey head to look down the road we had climbed and blew out through his nostrils as if he were impressed at the distance we had already travelled. I did not know where he thought he was going. I did not know where I thought I was going. I had not the energy or the ability to think of it. Due north seemed a good enough direction, and this lane was pleasant riding and the countryside quiet. I clicked softly to him and he turned his head and walked on.

We went along the crest of the hill in a beautiful clear sweep and then the track started to drop down towards the valley on the other side. It looped and turned in hairpin bends in an effort to make the track easier for coach horses. I thought one might get a light coach up the hill in summer, but nothing too heavy. Nothing in winter at all. I guessed the road would be a quagmire of pale chalky mud by then. Something in the idea of that colour of pale chalky mud made my mind stop still, and made me think where I had seen thick creamy mud before. But it was gone before I had time to catch at it.

Sea walked faster as we started down the steeper slopes, then he tossed his head a bit and tried a few paces of a trot, his back legs slipping and sliding. I steadied him with a touch on the reins. I could not be troubled to tighten the reins and rise for a trot. I could not be bothered with his change of pace. He slackened off when he felt my unwillingness and walked steadily in the moonlight again.

I thought it must be between seven and eight of the clock, but I could not be sure. It did not matter. If I was anxious to see the time there would be a village church with a steeple and a clock soon enough, even on this deserted road. I was not hungry. I was exhausted with fatigue but I did not crave sleep. It did not matter to me if this night was just begun, or half done, or if it never ended at all. I slouched in the saddle and let Sea make his own way carefully down the hill, under the shadows of trees again, the reins loose on his neck.

We came to a village at the foot of the hill. A pretty little place with a stream running alongside a bigger broader lane, and several of the cottages had little bridges over the water so that the householders could walk dry-shod to the road even when the stream was in flood. There were candles set at some of the windows to light the way home for weary men who had been out working late in the fields. I wondered idly what farm workers found to do at this time of year, perhaps ploughing? or planting? I did not know, I had never needed to know. I thought then, as Sea stepped like a ghost of a horse through the evening village, that there was precious little I did know about ordinary life;

about life for people who did not dress up and dance on horse-back. I thought then that I would have served Dandy a good deal better if I had worked on my skill at training horses for farmers and gentry rather than letting us be bound on the wheel of the show season. And now broken by that wheel, too.

The road went uphill out of the village and Sea brightened his pace and I let him trot uphill. If it had been light I guessed there would have been a great sweep of country on our left. I could smell the fresh greenness of it, and the hint of meadow flowers closing their little faces for the night. On our right was the high shoulder of the hill. The hill of the South Downs, I thought. I considered for a moment where I was.

I could see a map in my mind's eye now. I was heading north from Selsey, I had skirted the town of Chichester, and this road must surely be the London road. That accounted for the firmness of the going, and the wideness of the track which was broad enough for two passing carriages for much of the way. That reminded me to keep a careful look-out ahead of me for toll cottages. I did not want to waste my money paying for use of the road when a little ride cross-country would save me a penny. I watched out too for coaches before or behind me. I did not want to speak to anyone, I did not even want them to look on my face. I had a silly belief that my face was so set and so stony that anyone looking into my eyes would cry for me. That they would see at once that I was a dead person looking out of a live face. That there was no one behind my eyes and my mouth and my face at all. I practised a smile into the darkness and found that my lips could curve and my face rise with no difficulty and with no difference to the weight of ice inside me. I even tried a little laugh, alone into the darkness of the fields on the far side of the village. It sounded eerie, and Sea's ears went back flat and he increased his pace.

I checked him. I was so tired I did not think I could bear the jolting of his trot, and I felt as if I would never canter again. I could hardly remember the girl who used to vault on to the back of a cantering horse and dance with a hoop and a skipping rope. She seemed like a hopeful little child to me now, and I wondered idly why they had worked her so hard. Her and her poor little sister . . . I broke off my thoughts. It was odd. I was speaking and feeling as if I were an old woman. An old woman tired and ready for death.

The girl who had played in the sea this morning was a lifetime away from me now. I thought that I was more like the woman who had seen the wagon go away from her in that awful dream of the storm, and known that she would never see her baby again. The woman who had called after the wagon, 'Her name is Sarah . . .' I felt like that woman now. I felt like any woman feels when she has lost the love and the saviour of her life. Old. Sick at heart. Ready for her own death.

I sighed and Sea took it as a signal and broke once more into a trot which brought us over the top of the hill and down to the village which lay at its foot on the spring line.

It was getting later and the lights were doused in this hamlet. Sea went by in silence, not one man saw us pass. Only a little child looking from an upstairs window at the moon saw me go by. He raised his hand like a salute and his eyes sought mine, and he smiled a friendly, open little smile. I neither smiled nor waved. I hardly saw him, and I felt nothing when I saw his mouth turn down in disappointment that the stranger on the horse had not acknowledged him. I did not care. He would be worse disappointed than that before tomorrow was out. And I did not wish to be kindly to little children. No one had ever had a kind word for me when I was his age. No one had a kind word thereafter. Except she was kind to me. In her own light way, she had loved me. But that was little comfort now.

Quite the contrary.

It was a scattered little village this one. A public house with a lantern in the window the last building along the road, a little fir tree nailed above the door. I thought idly that perhaps I should stop and go in and eat and take a drink. I thought wearily of a bed and a warm fire. But Sea kept on walking and I did not care very much that I was cold and tired and hungry. Indeed I did not care at all. Sea's head pointed due north and he scanned the road ahead of us with his shifting ears. I wondered idly what he heard.

What I could hear, what sung in my ears so that I shook my head irritably, was a high singing noise. Too high for human voices, too sweet for a squeaking hinge. It had started as soon as I had got into the saddle this afternoon, at Selsey. And it was calling me louder and clearer all along the road. I stuck my finger in one ear and then the other. I could not block it out and I could not clear it. I shrugged. It was all one with the clamminess of my skin and the cold inside my belly. The way my hands trembled when I did not remember to watch them and keep them steady. A singing in the air made little difference either way.

Sea broke into a trot again and I sat down in the saddle and let him go what speed he wished. I was far away in my thoughts. I was thinking of a summer years and years ago when she and I had been little grimy urchins and we had gone scrumping for apples in a high-walled orchard. I had been quite unable to face the thought of climbing up the wall or jumping down the other side and in the end had squeezed through a fence which had ripped half of my ragged dress off me. She had laughed at my scratched face. 'I don't mind being high,' she had said.

I wished now that I had made her fear heights as I do, that I had somehow insisted that she always stay on ground level. That I had turned Robert against the idea of the trapeze as soon as he mentioned it. That I been warned by the barn owl. That I had remembered in time that the one unlucky colour in shows is always green.

Sea suddenly wheeled sharply to the right and nearly threw me off sideways. I clutched at his neck and stared around me. For some reason, clear only to his horse's brain, he had turned off the main track and was heading down a little lane scarcely wider than a hay wagon. I stopped and thought to turn his head back towards the main road. But he was stubborn and I was too weary to be able to bend him to my will. Besides, it mattered so little.

I listened. I could hear the ripple of a river ahead of us in the darkness and I thought that perhaps he was thirsty and it was the noise of the clear water which was drawing him away from the road and down this little cart track. I let him go where he would, obeying my training which said that the horses must be fed and the horses must be watered. Whether you are hungry or thirsty or no. Whether you have forgotten what it feels like to want water or food. Still the horses have to be fed and watered.

He went easily down the dark slope towards the ford where I could hear the river rippling. The singing in my head was louder, clearer. It was almost as if it were coming from the river. The night-time air blew gently down the valley and set the trees sighing with the smell of new grass. There were tall pale flowers at the riverside and they glowed in the moonlight. Sea went out into mid-river and bent his proud head and drank. The endearing sound of the sweet water sucked in by his soft lips echoed loud around the little valley. I sat still on his back and felt the cool night air caress my cheeks, as soft a touch as a lover's hand. An owl called softly to its mate one side of the river then the other, and as I sat there in silence, in the silvery moonlight, a nightingale began to sing a few clear notes which rippled like the river and were as clear as the singing in my head.

The trees stood back a little from the river and the banks were grassy with great clumps of primroses and sweet-scented violets. There were silver birches in a clump near a boggy patch of ground and their stiff catkins pointed spiky at the silvery sky. Sea blew out softly and when he raised his head from drinking it was so quiet that I could hear the water drip from his chin. Down river, the banks overhung the deep curves of water and there were dark standing pools where I thought one would find trout and maybe even salmon. Sea raised his head again, then lumbered awkwardly on the sandy river bed to the far side of the bank. I thought we should really turn back to the main road, but I was too desolate to think clearly about inns and stabling and a bed for the night. I let him have his head and he went smoothly and steadily on down the little track as confident as if he were going home, home to a warm stable for the night.

I did not even check him when he turned sharply to the left, though it was obviously a private drive. I could not find it in me to care. We went past a little lodge cottage and past the high wrought-iron gates. The cottage windows were dark and the drive was soft mud. We made no noise. We rode past like a pair of ghosts, a ghost horse and a ghost rider, and I let Sea go where he wished. It was not just that I was so weary that I was dreamy with tiredness, but I also felt as if I were in the grip of one of my dreams of Wide. As if all the dreams had been leading me steadily here, till I had nothing left of my real life at all, no ties, no loves, no past, no future. All there was for me was Sea's bobbing head and the rutted drive, the woods and the smell of violets on the night air. Sea walked carefully up the drive and his ears flickered forward as the dark bulk of a building showed itself against the lighter sky.

It was a little square house, facing the drive, overshadowed by the trees. There were no lights showing at any of its windows, all the shutters were bolted as if it were deserted. I looked at it curiously. I felt as if the front door should have been open for me. I felt as if I should have been expected.

I thought Sea might check and go around to the stable block but he walked past it, as steadily as if he had some destination in mind. As assured as if we belonged somewhere, instead of wandering around in circles under a pale springtime sky. His ears went forward as we went under the shadow of a great spreading chestnut tree and I smelled the flowers as fat and thick as candelabra on the tree as he broke into a trot.

We rounded the bend of the drive and I pushed the cap back on my head a little, and leaned forward. After all these years of dreaming and hoping, of waiting and being afraid to hope, I thought I knew where I was at last. I thought I had come home. I thought this was Wide.

The drive was right, the drive where the man I called Papa had taken the little girl up on the horse and taught her how to ride. The trees were right, the smell of the air was right, and the creamy mud beneath Sea's hooves was right. The horse was right as well. There had been other beautiful grey hunters here before. I knew it, without knowing how I knew. Sea's stride lengthened and his ears were forward.

There was a great chestnut tree on the corner of the drive and

I recognized it, I had seen it in my dreams for years. I knew the drive would bend around to the left, and as Sea drew level and we went around the corner I knew what I would see, and I *did* see it.

The rose garden was on my left, the bushes pruned down low and the rose-beds intersected by little paths all leading to a white trellised summerhouse, a smooth-cropped paddock behind it, and behind that a dark wall of trees which were the parkland.

On my right was the wall of the terrace. It ran around the front of the house bordered by a low parapet with a balustrade and stone plant pots with bushy heads of flowers, dark against the darkness. In the middle of the terrace was a short flight of shallow steps leading to the front door of the house. I checked Sea then; he was on his way around the house to where I knew, and he seemed to know, there was stabling and straw on the floor and hay in the manger; but I stopped him so that I could look and look at the house.

It was a lovely house, with a smooth rounded tower at one side, overlooking the rose garden and the terrace. Set in the middle of the façade was a double front door made of some plain pale wood, with a brass knocker and a large round ring door-handle. It was as if it spoke to me with easy words of invitation, as if to say that this was my house which I had been travelling towards all the weary journeys of my life.

There were no lights in the house, it looked deserted, but in measureless confidence I slid from Sea's back and went stiffly up the steps and to the front door.

Out the back, from the kitchen quarters, I heard a dog bark, insistently, anxiously. I turned around on the doorstep and looked outwards over the terrace. I looked once more at the rose garden and beyond it the paddock, and beyond that the darker shadow of the woods, and high above it all the high rolling profile of the Downs which encircle and guard my home.

I breathed in the smell of the night air, the sweet clean smell of the wind which blows from the sea, over the clean grass of the Downs. Then I turned and put my small hand in the wide ring of the door, twisted the handle around, and leaned against the door so it slowly swung inwards and I stepped into the hall.

The floor was wood, with dark-coloured rugs scattered on top of the polished planks. There were four doors leading off the hall and a great sweep of stairs coming down into the hall. There was a newel-post at the foot of the stairs, intricately carved. There was a smell of dried rose petals and lavender. I knew the house. I knew the hall. It was as if I had known it all my life, as if I had known it for ever.

The dog from the kitchen at the back was barking louder and louder. Soon he would wake the household and I should be in trouble if I was found trespassing, my old boots on the new rugs. But I did not care. I did not care what became of me; not tonight, not ever again. There was a great bowl of china raised on wooden legs and I went over to it curiously. It was filled with dried rose petals and lavender seeds, sprigs of herbs, and it smelled sweet. I took up a handful and sniffed at it, careless that it spilled on the floor. It did not matter. I could not feel that anything mattered at all. Then I heard a noise outside on the terrace and the stone steps, and there was a shadow blocking the moonlight in the doorway, and a kind voice said softly:

'What d'you think you're doing?'

I turned and saw a working man in the doorway, blocking the moonlight, his face half in shadow. A rugged, ordinary face, tanned with weather, smile-lines etched in white around the eyes. Brown eyes, broad mouth, a shock of brown hair, ordinary homespun clothes. A yeoman farmer, not Quality.

'What are you doing here?' I replied, as if it were my own house and he a trespasser.

He did not challenge my right to ask.

'I was watching in the woods,' he said politely. 'There've been some poachers, out from Petersfield I think. Using gin traps. I hate gin traps. I was waiting to catch them and see them off when I saw you riding down the drive. Why are you here?'

I shrugged, a helpless weary little gesture. 'I'm looking for Wide,' I said, too tired to think of a better story. Too sick at heart to construct a clever lie. 'I'm looking for Wide, I belong there,' I said.

'This is Wideacre,' he replied. 'Wideacre estate, and this is Wideacre Hall. Is this the place you are looking for?'

My knees buckled a little under me, and I would have fallen but he was at my side in one swift step, and he caught me and carried me out to the night air and dumped me gently on the terrace step and loosened my shirt at the throat. The gleam of the gold clasp on the string caught his eye and he touched it gently with one stubby forefinger.

'What's that?' he said.

I unfastened it and drew it out. 'It was a necklace of rose pearls,' I said. 'But all the pearls were sold. My ma left it to me when she died, I was to show it when they came looking for me.' I paused. 'No one ever came looking for me,' I said desolately. 'So I kept it.'

He turned it over in his hands and held it close so that he could read the inscription. 'John and Celia,' he said. He spoke the names like an incantation. As if he had known what the inscription would say before he looked at it in the moonlight, as if he knew that was what he would see in the old worn gold. 'Who are they?'

'I don't know,' I said. 'Maybe my ma knew, but she never told me. Nor my da. I was to keep it and show it when they came looking for me. But no one ever came.'

'What's your name?' he asked. His gaze under the ragged fringe of hair was acute.

I was about to say 'Meridon', but then I paused. I did not want to be Meridon any more. Mamselle Meridon the bareback rider, Mamselle Meridon on that damned killer trapeze. I did not want the news of Gower's Amazing Show to reach me here, I wanted to leave that life far behind me as if it had never been. As if there had been no Meridon, and no Dandy. As if Meridon were as dead as Dandy. As if neither of them had ever been.

'My name is Sarah,' I said. I cast about in my mind for a surname. 'Sarah Lacey.'

18

The next few days were a blur, like a dream you cannot remember on waking. I remember that the man who hated gin traps picked me up in his arms, and that I was so tired and so weary that I did not object to his touch but was a little comforted by it, like a hurt animal. He took me inside the house and there were two other people there, a man and a woman, and there were a great many quick questions and answers over my head as it rested on his shoulder. The homespun tickled my cheek and felt warm and smelled reassuring, like hay. He carried me upstairs and the woman put me to bed, taking away my clothes and bringing me a nightgown of the finest lawn I had ever seen in my life with exquisite white thread embroidery on the cuffs and hem and around the neck. I was too tired to object that I was a vagrant and a gypsy brat and that a corner of the stables would have suited me well. I tumbled into the great bed and slept without dreams.

I was ill then for two days. The man who hated gin traps brought a doctor from Chichester and he asked me how I felt, and why I would not eat. He asked me where I had come from and I feigned forgetfulness and told them I could remember nothing except my name and that I was looking for Wide. He left a draught of some foul medicine, which I took the precaution of throwing out of the window whenever it was brought to me, and advised that I should be left to rest.

The man who hated gin traps told me that Sea was safe in the stables and eating well. 'A fine horse,' he said, as if that might encourage me to tell of how I got him, how a dirty-faced, stunned gypsy brat came to be riding a first-class hunter.

'Yes,' I said, and I turned my face away from his piercing eyes and closed my eyelids as if I would sleep.

I did sleep. I slept and woke to the sunlight on the ceiling of the bedroom and the windows half open and the smell of early roses and the noise of pigeons cooing. I dozed again and when I woke the woman brought me some broth and a glass of port wine and some fruit. I ate the soup but left the rest and slept again. In all of those days I saw nothing but the light on the ceiling of the bed chamber and ate nothing but soup.

Then one morning I woke and did not feel lazy and tired. I stretched, a great cat-like stretch with my toes pointing down to the very foot of the bed and my arms outflung, and then I threw back the fine linen sheets and went over to the window and pushed it open.

It had rained in the night and the sunlight was glinting on the wet leaves and flowers of the rose garden and mist was steaming off the paddock. Immediately below me the paving stones of the terrace were dark yellow where they were damp, paler where they were drying. Beyond the terrace was the gravel of the drive where Sea and I had ridden that first night, beyond that the rose garden with pretty shaped flower-beds and small paths running between them. A delicate little summerhouse of white painted wood stood to my left; as I watched, a swallow swooped in through the open doorway, beak full of mud, nest-building.

Beyond the rose garden was a smooth green paddock with Sea, very confident, cropping the grass with his tail raised, a stream of silver behind him. He looked well, perhaps even a little plumper for his stay in a good stable with fine hay and spring grass to eat. Behind the paddock was a dark mass of trees in fresh new foliage, copper beeches red as rose-shoots, oak trees with leaves so fresh and green they were lime coloured, and sweet green beeches with branches like layers of draper's silk. And beyond the woods, ringing the valley like a guardian wall, were the high clear slopes of the Downs, striped with white chalk at the dry stream beds, soft with green and lumpy with coppices on the lower slopes. The sky above them was a clear promising blue, rippled with cloud. For the first time in my life I looked at the horizon and knew that I was home. I had arrived at Wide, at last.

There was a clatter of horse's hooves and I looked along the drive and saw the man who hated gin traps riding up towards the house, sitting easily on an ungainly cob. A working horse, a farmer's horse, able to pull a cart or a plough or work as a hunter on high days and holidays. He scanned the windows and pulled up the horse as he saw me.

'Good morning,' he said pleasantly, and doffed his cap. In the morning sunlight his hair showed gleams of bronze, his face young, smiling. I guessed he was about twenty-four; but a serious young man appears older. For a moment I thought of Jack, who would have been a child at forty as long as he was under his father's thumb; but then I pushed the thought away from me. Jack was gone. Robert Gower was gone. Meridon and her sister were gone. I could remember nothing.

'Good morning,' I said. I leaned out of the window to see his horse better. He sat well, as if he spent much of his day in the saddle. 'A good working horse,' I observed.

'Nothing like your beauty,' he replied. 'But he does well enough for me. Are you feeling better? Are you well enough to dress and come downstairs?'

'Yes,' I said. 'I am quite better. But that woman took my clothes.'

'That's Becky Miles,' he said. 'She took them and washed them and ironed them. They'll be in the chest in your bedroom. I'll send her up to you.'

He turned his horse and rode past the front door round to the back of the house to the stables. I shut the window and opened the chest for my clothes.

There was warm water in a jug with a bowl beside it in exquisite cream china with little flowers painted on the outside, and a posy at the bottom of the jug. I splashed a little water on my face and dried myself reluctantly on a linen towel. It was so fine I didn't like to dirty it.

I dressed and felt the luxury of ironed linen and clean breeches. There was a minute darn on the collar of Jack's old shirt where I had torn it weeks ago. I shrugged on the old jacket as well – not that I would need the warmth, but because I felt awkward and vulnerable in this rich and beautiful house in my shirtsleeves. My breasts showed very clear against the thin cotton of the shirt; I pulled the jacket over to hide them.

There was a comb, a silver-backed hairbrush, a small bottle of perfume and some ribbons laid out before a mirror of the purest glass I had ever seen on the dressing-table and I stopped in front of it to brush my hair. It was full of tangles as always, and the riot of copper curls sprang out from the ribbon bow I tried to tie around them. I gave up the struggle after the third time and just swept it back from my face and left it loose. The man who hated gin traps did not look as if he were a connoisseur of female fashions. He looked like a simple working man, and one who could be trusted to deal with a person fairly, however they looked. But the house, this rich and lovely house, made me feel awkward in my boy's clothes with my red hair all tumbled down my back. It was a fine house, I somehow wanted to be fine to suit it. I didn't look right there, in darned linen and someone else's boots.

There was a tap at my door and I went to open it. The woman he called Becky Miles stood outside. She smiled at me. She was taller than me, a large-built woman running to plumpness, her fair hair starting to turn grey at the temples, a little sober cap on her head, a dark dress and a white apron.

'Hello,' she said kindly. 'Good to see you up. Will sent me up to bring you down to the parlour when you're ready.'

'I'm ready,' I said.

She walked ahead of me, talking over her shoulder as she went towards the shallow curving staircase and down the stairs to the hall.

'I'm Becky Miles,' she said. 'Mr Fortescue put us in here, me and Sam, to work as housekeeper and caretaker. If there's anything you want, you just ring the bell and I'll come.'

I nodded. There was too much to take in. I wanted to ask why they should wait on me, and who was Mr Fortescue but she led me across the shadowy hall, her heels clicking on the polished wooden floor, silent on the bright rugs, and opened a door at the front of the house and gestured that I was to go in.

'I'll bring you some coffee,' she said, and shut the door behind her.

The room was a parlour, the walls lined with a silk so pale as to be almost cream, but pink in the darker corners. The window-seat, scattered with cushions of a deep rose colour, ran around the inside of the tower at the corner of the room and overlooked the terrace, the rose garden and the drive in its circular sweep. The carpet, set square on the polished floorboards in the main part of the room, was cream with a pattern of pink roses at the border. The half-circular turret part of the room had its own circular rug in deep cherry. There was a harpsichord on the wall beside the fireplace, and a number of occasional tables standing beside comfortable rose-cushioned chairs. In the middle of all this pinkness was the man who hated gin traps, with his brown cap clutched in his big hands.

We smiled at each other in mutual understanding of each other's discomfort.

'It's a lady's room really,' he said. 'It's the parlour.'

'A bit pink,' I said.

'Aye,' he said. 'It'ud suit some.'

He paused and looked at me, as awkward as himself in my hand-me-down boots and my plain riding breeches and my too-big jacket.

'We could go into the dining room,' he suggested.

I nodded and he led the way across the hall and through handsome double doors into a dining room dominated by a massive mahogany table which would seat, I thought, sixteen people. On one side was a huge sideboard gleaming with silver, on another a table set with chafing dishes. The man who hated gin traps pulled out a chair for me at the head of the table and sat by my side.

'Now,' he said. 'We'll wait the main business until Mr Fortescue comes and I'm pledged to tell you nothing till he arrives. He's the trustee for this estate. He came down from his London offices when I sent word that you had come here. He'll be in to take coffee with us in a moment.'

'Who is he?' I asked. I was nervous, but the man who hated

gin traps gestured to me to sit in one of the high-backed chairs
and I gained confidence from his ease.

'He's the trustee of the estate,' he said. 'The executor of the
will. He's a straight man. You can trust him.'

I nodded. I thought, 'I can trust you too,' but I sat down in
silence, and put my hands together on the polished table as if we
were about to start some business.

The door opened and Miss Miles came in carrying a tray with
a silver coffee pot, some biscuits and three cups. Behind her
came a tall man dressed like Quality, but he held the door for
her. He made much of helping her with the tray and setting the
biscuits on the table and the cups before the three of us but I
knew that he had taken in my appearance in his first quick
glance as he came into the room, and that he was scanning me
under his dark eyelashes still.

He was about the age of Robert Gower, with clothes cut so
soberly and so well that I had never seen their like. He had an
air of such authority that I thought he must have been born
wealthy. His face was lined and severe, as if he were sad. I
thought that he was being polite to Becky Miles to cover his
searching survey of me but also because he was always polite to
her, to all servants.

He set the things to his satisfaction and then he gave an
assumed and unconvincing little start of surprise. 'I'm not introducing myself,' he said to me. 'I am James Fortescue.'

He held out his hand and looked at me inquiringly. The man
who hated gin traps said nothing, so into the little silence I
volunteered my own introduction.

'I'm Sarah,' I said.

The hand that clasped mine tightened a little, and his sharp gaze
narrowed. 'Have you used that name all your life?' he asked me.

I hesitated for a moment. I thought, with my quick tinker's
brain, about stringing some lie together; but nothing came.

'No,' I said. 'I had a dream, like a belief that it was my real
name. But the people I lived with called me by something else.'

He nodded, let my hand go and gestured for me to sit down.
In the silence that followed the man who hated gin traps pulled

the tray towards himself and carefully poured three cups of coffee. When he handed one to James Fortescue I could see that the gentleman's hands were trembling.

He took a sip of coffee and then looked at me over the rim of the cup. 'I think I would have known her anywhere,' he said softly, almost to himself.

'You need to be sure,' the man who hated gin traps said in a level voice. 'For your own sake, for all our sakes.'

I turned and looked at him. 'What are you talking about?' I asked. There was an edge of irritation in my voice and the man heard it. He gave me a slow reassuring smile.

'You'll know at once,' he said. He nodded to James Fortescue, 'He'll tell you in a moment.'

Mr Fortescue put down his cup and took some papers and a pen and ink-pot out of a little case beside him.

'I have to ask you some questions,' he said.

Ask he did! He asked me everything about my life from my earliest memories until the time when I rode up the drive to Wideacre Hall. After two or three slips I dropped the pretence that I could not remember and told him all he wanted to know: all that I could remember of my ma, what her family name had been, where her gypsy family travelled and where they stayed. Then I shook my head.

'She died when we were just little babbies,' I said. 'I can hardly remember her at all.'

Then he asked me everything I could remember of my early life. I told him about Da, and the travelling around. The grand projects and the few jobs. I glided over the bad horses and the cheating at cards. And I found, although I tried to say her name once or twice, that I could not say it at all. Even to think of her was like scratching at an unhealed scar on my heart.

I did not want them to know about Gower's Show and Mamselle Meridon, so I told him only that I had been apprenticed to a man who trained horses, that I had chosen to leave him, and found myself here. I came to a standstill and trailed into silence. James Fortescue looked at me over the top of his coffee cup as if he were waiting for more.

'There are things I do not want to talk about,' I said stubbornly. 'Nothing criminal. But private.'

He nodded at that, and then asked to see my string and clasps and asked me once more where I had got it. He looked at it carefully through a special little glass he took from his pocket, and then finally he handed it back to me.

'Do you have none of your baby clothes?' he asked. 'Did you never see them?'

I screwed my eyes up with an effort to remember. 'I saw them,' I said hesitantly. 'We shared them, of course. I saw a white lace shawl, very fine, trimmed in lace. Someone must have given it to us.' The memory of the white lace shawl slipped away from me as if it had disappeared into darkness. 'Everything was sold after Ma died,' I said again.

Mr Fortescue nodded, consideringly. Then he said, very softly. 'You say "us". Who was the child who shared your childhood?'

My chair scraped as I suddenly pushed it back. My hands on the table had started their trembling again. I looked at them carefully until they were still. Then the man who hated gin traps leaned over and put his large calloused hand over mine.

'You don't need to say,' he said softly.

I took a deep shuddering breath. 'I won't say more than this,' I said. 'We were raised together, we were sisters. She never dreamed of Wide as I did. We were twin sisters, but we looked different.'

'And where is your sister, your twin sister, now?' Mr Fortescue asked.

I heard a low cry like an animal in pain and I hunched up over the pain which was like hunger-cramps in my belly. I felt a thud of pain on my forehead, over my eyes, and I heard a low thumping sound. Then another, and then another, and then someone grabbed my shoulders and I realized I had been banging my head on that dark shiny table. The man who hated gin traps pulled me around and held my shoulders tight until I stopped shaking and that distant moaning noise stopped.

'That's enough,' he said over my head to James Fortescue. 'We've got enough. It's her. She can't bear to tell us more now.'

I heard footsteps cross the room and the clink of a decanter on a glass. 'Drink this,' Mr Fortescue said, and I knocked back half a glass of cognac as if I were my da.

It hit me in the cold sad part of my belly and spread a warmth all through me. I rubbed my face with my hands, my cheeks were dry and warm. I had shed no tears, I felt as if I would never cry again. My forehead was sore. I felt a flicker of fear that I had been hurting myself so. But then the cold dullness was all around me and I did not care what they thought of me. I did not care what I did.

'I'm all right now,' I said. The man who hated gin traps still had his hands on my shoulders. I shrugged him off. 'I'm all right now,' I said again, irritably.

There was a silence in the dark room. Outside in the stable yard someone was whistling.

'I have enough,' Mr Fortescue said. 'I had enough as soon as I saw her. I won't vex you with more questions, Sarah. I shall tell you why I needed to ask you them.'

I nodded. I was still trembling from that welling-up of pain, but I took the cup of coffee for its warmth. There was a knack to balancing it on the little plate which was under the cup. I watched it carefully until I had it safe up to my mouth, and then I blew on it cautiously and supped it. It was a strange taste, but hot and sweet and strong. I thought about the taste of it, I watched the little plate under the cup, I curled my toes up hard inside my boots until I could get the picture of her, and my pain at losing her, out of my mind.

Then I looked up and listened to Mr Fortescue.

'I believe that you are the daughter of Julia and Richard Lacey, and the only heir to this estate,' he said simply. 'Your mother was in fever after your birth and she gave you away to the gypsies. Your father was killed by an escaped criminal who came back here seeking his revenge. Your mother died shortly after.' He was silent for a moment. When he spoke again his voice was even. 'She wrote to me before her death,' he said. 'She had no close relations and she entrusted to me the task of trying to find her daughter and to care for the estate until the child was of age.'

He looked at me. 'I am sorry I failed you so badly, Miss Lacey,' he said. 'I did indeed try, for all these years I have had men looking for you. We traced the gypsy family and then much later your foster mother; but then the trail went cold. I never knew of the man you call your stepfather.'

I nodded, but I said nothing. If they had found the two of us before some of the beatings I had taken. If they had only found us before Da sold us to Robert Gower. Or if they had found us just yesterday, when we were a day's ride away and she had been playing in the sea and her hair had tasted of salt when I kissed her.

I shrugged off the pain and took a deep breath. In a few moments the picture of her would be out of my mind and I would be able to hear Mr Fortescue's voice again.

'I've done better with the estate, I think,' he said. 'We restored it to the profit-sharing scheme started by your mother, and we have expanded. It is now quite famous as a village corporation – an experiment in communal planning and communal land-use. Will Tyacke here acts as foreman and keeps in touch with me in my offices in London or Bristol. I only supervise. All of the decisions are made here, by the people themselves.'

'Is it a wealthy estate?' I asked bluntly.

Mr Fortescue looked down at a little case he had by his chair. 'Run as a corporation it does not make a profit,' he said. 'It pays you an annual share of some £10,000. If you were to withdraw an economic rent you would earn some £40,000. I have the figures here for you to see.'

He went to pick them up but I checked him.

'I . . . I cannot read,' I said awkwardly.

He nodded as if there were no reason to think that anyone could. 'Of course,' he said gently. 'Then we can go over them together another time. But you may believe me that you have a good estate, run as a corporation, with the people who live here sharing in the wealth. It is showing substantial and steady profits.'

I thought of the nine guineas I had in my little purse and the work I had done to earn them. I thought of her dancing with her skirts up for pennies, and of Da selling us in a job lot with a young pony. I thought of Jack, so fearful of his father's ambition that he killed to keep his favour, to inherit the show. And I thought of myself, flint-hearted and hungry . . . and wealthy beyond anything I could ever have dreamed.

I blinked. 'It is mine?' I asked.

Mr Fortescue nodded. 'You are the heir to the whole of the Wideacre estate,' he said. 'All the debts on the land are paid, you own it entire. Your mother wanted it gifted to the village, I have a letter she wrote to me in which she makes clear that is her intention. She died before she could write it into her will. She wanted you to have the Hall as your home. The Hall, the gardens and parkland. We have set up a trust so that you could sign your rights to the land over to the village as soon as you wish. But while you are a minor,' he looked at my confused face, 'until you are twenty-one or married, then you may draw an allowance from me, and I shall act as your guardian and run the estate as I think fit. When you are twenty-one or married it is yours.'

I rose slowly from the table and went to look out over the cobbled yard. There was a man there mucking out a stable, I watched him fork over the soiled straw.

'That man works for me,' I said slowly.

Mr Fortescue, in the room behind me cleared his throat and said, 'Yes.'

'And Becky Miles,' I said.

'And Mistress Miles,' he repeated. 'Indeed,' he said, 'if the village were run in the usual way with the workers hired by the quarter and paid wages instead of our profit-sharing scheme you would have something like a hundred people working for you.'

I leaned my head against the coldness of the thick glass and thought what this sudden wealth, what this sudden power meant. I need never go hungry, I need never go cold, I need never work in the wind or the rain or the cold. I need never work again at all. I would have a meal on the table, set before me by someone else, a servant, my servant, more than once a day, four times a day! I had won through to what I had always wanted, to what I had always thought was impossible. I had not had to whore, I had not had to trap someone into marriage as Robert Gower had foretold. I had inherited as easily and as naturally as if I were one of the Quality.

I stopped myself there. I *was* one of the Quality. I was born Sarah Lacey with a silver spoon in my mouth and I was now where I belonged. Where I had an absolute right to be. And this house, this huge beautiful house was all mine, staffed with servants who were mine to command. No one would ever make me do their bidding again. I held that thought in my mind for a long moment. And I thought what it meant for me now.

'It's too late,' I said desolately.

'What?'

'It's too late,' I said again.

I turned back to the room; they were both watching me, puzzled, uneasy. I looked at Mr Fortescue.

'It's too late for me, damn you for a fool!' I exploded. 'I wanted it for me, oh! yes, of course I did! I was hungry, I was beaten! I was tired all the time from working too hard and not enough food! But I wanted it for her! I wanted to give it to her! I wanted to bring her here and make her safe!'

I could hear my voice rising into a scream. 'And all the time you have been sitting here, you fat merchant, sitting here on my land while I was out there, beaten and cold, and she was out there too and I could not keep her safe!'

'Sarah . . .' The man who hated gin traps was up from the table, coming towards me, his hand held out, like you would try to calm a frightened horse.

'No!' I screamed as loud as I could and dodged past him towards the door.

'Where were you three nights ago?' I shouted at James Fortescue. 'I was a day's ride down the road! You weren't looking for me then! You weren't doing all you could then! I was there alone, not knowing what to do to keep her safe! And she . . . and she . . . and she . . .'

I turned to the door and scrabbled at the panels in an agony of haste to get out of the room. I found the door handle and tore it open and ran up the stairs to the room they had given me, my own room in my own house, while she lay cold and still in the ground and all her little things burned and scattered.

I flung myself into a corner of the bedroom and sobbed, deep aching hopeless dry sobs which seemed to tear me apart.

And when my throat was so sore that I was hoarse with sobbing, so that no more sound would come, the pain had not eased at all. It was still there, unslaked, as hot and hard and heartbroken as ever.

There was a knock at the door and James Fortescue opened it softly and came into the room.

He squatted down on the floor beside me, careless of creasing his fine breeches and coat, and he did not offer to touch me, nor did he say easy foolish words of comfort. He looked quickly at my red eyes which were still dry after nigh on an hour of weeping, and then he looked down at the carpet underneath his fine shoes.

'You are right to blame me,' he said softly. 'I have failed you, and I have failed the woman I love. I know the grief you are feeling because I also loved a woman and I did not keep her safe.'

I looked up a little.

'It was your mother,' he said. 'Her name was Julia Lacey and she was the bravest, funniest, most beautiful girl I ever met.' He paused for a moment, and then nodded. 'Yes,' he said. 'Those were the things that I loved most about her. She was very brave, and she used to tease me all the time and make me laugh, and she was very very lovely.'

He took a little breath. 'You are very like her,' he said. 'Though she was fair and your hair is copper. Her eyes were set aslant like yours, and her face was shaped like a flower, like yours is; and her hair curled like yours does.'

He paused for a moment. 'She was forced into marrying her cousin, your father, and he destroyed the plans she had made with the village,' he said. 'She wanted to send you away, off the land, so that you would be safe. And she wanted to end the line of the squires here so that people could make their own lives in their own ways.'

'I've dreamed it,' I offered. He turned quickly to look at me, as we squatted side by side on my bedroom floor, a foolish sight if there had been anyone there to see.

'Dreamed?' he asked.

'Aye,' I said. 'I used to dream of Wide, of here. And often I dreamed I was a woman going out in the rain to drown her baby. Then she saw the gypsies and gave them the baby instead. She called after the wagon as it went away,' I said. 'She called after the baby. She said, "Her name is Sarah".'

James Fortescue rubbed his eyes with the back of his hand.

'I posted advertisements in all the local papers, I employed men to search for you,' he said. 'And I have gone on doing that, Sarah. Every year I changed the advertisements to show your right age and appealed for anyone who knew you to contact me. I offered a reward as well.'

I shrugged. 'It's too late now,' I said bitterly.

He got to his feet slowly, as if he were very weary.

'It is *not* too late,' he said. 'You are young and you are the heir to a fine estate. There is a fine future ahead of you and I will find ways to make up to you for the pains and sadnesses of your childhood, I promise it.'

I nodded, too sick at heart to argue with him.

'You are home now,' he said warmly. 'Home on Wideacre; and I will love you like the father you never had, and you will be happy here in time.'

I looked at him and my face was as hard as every street-fighting hungry little wretch which has ever had to beg for food and duck a blow.

'You're not my father,' I said. 'He sounds like a real bad 'un. You're not my mother either. I *had* a woman I called Ma; and now you tell me I don't have her either. I had a sister too . . .' My voice was going, I swallowed hard on a dry throat. 'I had a sister and now you tell me I never even had her. You're no kin to me, and I don't want your love. It's too late for me.'

He waited for a moment longer, but when I said nothing more he gently touched the top of my head, as you would carefully pat a sick dog. Then he went out of the room and left me alone.

19

I had thought it would be awkward speaking to James Fortescue again but I had not understood Quality manners. It seemed that if you were Quality, someone could rage and shriek at you and you could be deaf to their anger and their sorrow. Quality manners mean you only hear what suits you. Becky Miles called me to come down to drink a dish of tea with Mr Fortescue in the afternoon and he was in the parlour waiting for me, as if I had never sworn at him and screamed at him and blamed him for failing me.

Becky poured the tea for us both and handed me a cup. I kept a wary eye on James Fortescue and saw that he did not hold the plate under the cup and drink like that. He held them separately, one hand on each. I did not dare take a plate with a little cake on it as well. I did not think I could balance them all.

When he had finished, and Becky had cleared away he asked me to come with him to the dining room.

He had spread out a map on the dining-room table.

'I can't read,' I said again.

He nodded. 'I know that, Sarah,' he said. 'I can explain this to you. It's a map of Wideacre, of the Wideacre estate.'

I stepped a little closer and saw it was a picture of land, like you would see if you were a buzzard, circling high above it.

'Look,' he said. 'Wideacre is like a little bowl with the Downs on the south and west, and the Common to the north.' His hand went a great sweep around the map and I saw the land was coloured green and brown.

'Here we run a mixed farm,' he said. 'Much more fruit and vegetables than our neighbours because we have a skilled work-force who see the benefits of good profits. But we also farm sheep for their wool and meat, and a dairy herd.'

I nodded.

'We grow our own fodder for the animals,' he said. 'As well as a lot of wheat which we sell locally and in the London market for bread.'

I nodded again.

'It's a most lovely country,' he said, warmth creeping into his voice. 'Here is Wideacre Hall, set in the middle of the parkland, d'you see Sarah? At the back of it is the Common: that's free of fields for people to use for their own animals' grazing, and for walking and gathering firewood or brushwood, taking small game and putting out hives. It's bracken and gorse, some small pine trees, and in the valleys some beeches and oak trees and little streams.

'Over here,' he brushed the area south of the house, at the front, 'here is the ornamental garden you see from the front window, a little rose garden, and a paddock. Then there is the woodland which stretches along the drive and right up to the road. There are some fields new planted here; but we've mostly kept it as a wood. This is your property, your mother wanted the parkland kept with the Hall. She played here when she was a little girl, by the side of the Fenny which runs through these woods, in the little pools and streams. She learned to tickle for trout, and she learned to swim with one of the village girls. In spring the woods are full of wild daffodils and bluebells. In summer there are little glades which are thick with purple and white violets.

'Your boundary to the west is the Havering land.' He pointed to a dotted line drawn on the map. 'This map doesn't show Havering Hall. It's empty most of the year, the Havering family lives in London. They are distant kin to you,' he said, 'but they are only here in summer.'

'Is this the village?' I asked, pointing to a mess of little squares on the map on the right-hand side.

'Yes,' James Fortescue said. 'If you come out of Wideacre Hall drive and turn right you go along the lane to the Chichester road, see? But if you go out of the drive and turn left you go down to Acre village.

'Most of it is along the main street. The church is here,' he pointed. 'It was struck by lightning and has a new spire. The cottages on this side of the street were damaged in the same storm and some of them are new. But those on the other side of the street are older. In need of repair, too. Opposite the church is the vicarage – you'll find the vicar, Dr Reed, does not wholly approve of the way Acre runs itself! And there are cottages down these lanes towards the common land. Then there are squatter houses, where people have come to make their homes but have not properly built yet.'

I nodded. I knew about squatters' rights. It was one of the reasons the parish wardens always moved Da on. They were always in a terror that he would claim that he had been there long enough to be a member of the parish and claim parish relief.

'Don't you move them on?' I asked shrewdly.

James shook his head. 'No,' he said. 'We give them a chance to work and they can either take a wage – not a very big one – or take a share in the profits of the estate. If they plan to stay then they join the corporation. We don't have so many people that we cannot afford to take them on.'

'And where does that man live?' I asked. 'The manager?'

'That's Will Tyacke,' James said. 'He comes from a very old family. They have been here longer than the Laceys. His cousin was the first manager here after your mother died. But he had an accident and Will came over from another estate and took over. He lives in the manager's cottage,' he pointed to one of the little squares on the map set a little back from the main street. The blue wriggling line which indicated the River Fenny went past the back of the cottage through a small paddock.

'And south of the road and south of the village are fields,' James said. 'Some of them are resting, we leave them to grass every third year. Some of them are fruit fields – it's very sunny there. Most of them are wheat fields. This is a famous estate for high wheat production,' he paused for a moment. 'There were battles about that in the past,' he said. 'In the old days, before it was a corporation. There was a riot, and arson when the Laceys

were sending wheat out of the country but starving their workforce. But that changed when we started sharing the crop, and
sharing the profits. We have fields as high up the hill as the
horses can pull the plough. Above that the land is only good for
sheep to graze. It's very high land – up there on the Downs –
covered with short sweet grass, and in springtime there are
thousands of little flowers and orchids. There are great flocks of
butterflies up there: tiny blue and yellow ones. The larks sing
very loudly, and there are curlews.' He broke off.

'You love it here,' I said. 'Why don't you live here?'

He shook his head. 'I was going to marry your mother and
build a house here with her,' he said. 'Once she was gone, I
could not have lived here alone.' He was silent for a moment.

'I visit often,' he said. 'Will Tyacke knows more about farming
than I will ever learn, but I like to come down to keep an eye on
things.'

I nodded, looking at my land, spread out over James's map
like a patchwork of rich fabrics.

'You will need to learn the land,' he said quietly. 'Now you
are here, you will need to know your way around, and the crops
that are planted, and the people who live and work here.'

I stared down at the map. It was as if it were my future laid out
here, not just fields.

'I suppose I will,' I said.

'Perhaps you would like to ride out, look round it,' James
suggested. 'Will Tyacke said he would come this afternoon and
take you out for a ride if you would like that. He is the best man
to show you the land, and he knows everyone.'

I looked up at James and he could see the emptiness in my
face. 'All right,' I said. 'I'll go.'

'And Sarah . . .' he said as I was at the door.

I turned. 'Yes?'

'You have wanted to be here, and now you are here,' he said
gently. 'Let yourself enjoy the things here which are good. I
won't say forget the past because that would be folly and it
would deny your previous life and the people you have loved.
But open yourself up to Wideacre, Sarah. It is only you who are

247

hurt when you see this place as something which has come too late for you.'

I paused for a moment. He was right. The hurt inside, the coldness inside would not go away, would not be healed by more grief and more disappointment. But I was stubborn. And I was angry.

'Is that all?' I asked.

'Yes,' he said, resigned.

I waited in my room until I saw the brown cob trot up the drive but when I got down to the stable yard Will was in one of the loose boxes, trying to get a bridle on Sea.

'I told Sam not to worry him,' he said pleasantly over the half-stable door. 'He was having some difficulty with him and the horse was getting distressed. He looked frightened. Has he been ill-treated?'

'Yes,' I said. 'He don't usually like men.'

Will smiled. 'I don't usually like hunters,' he said. 'We'll both make an exception.'

He tightened the girth and led him out. 'We've a lady's saddle somewhere,' he offered. 'Sam can hunt it out for you if you prefer side-saddle.'

I shook my head and took Sea from him. 'Nay,' I said. 'I wear my breeches so that I can ride astride. I only ever wore the habit . . .' I broke off and cursed myself inwardly. 'I don't have a habit.' I said. 'I s'pose I'll have to get one and ride side-saddle all the time.'

Will nodded, and held Sea's head while I swung into the saddle.

'I thought I'd take you up to the Downs,' he said. 'So you can get a hawk's-eye view of the estate. It's a good day. We'll be able to see clear across Selsey to the Island looking south.'

I flinched inside at the mention of Selsey, but kept my face impassive. Will mounted his horse and led the way down the gravel of the drive, past the terrace with the rose garden on our right and out into the rutted stony lane.

The track was so old it seemed to have sunk into the soil and become part of the earth itself. The stones in the ruts were wet and shiny, yellow in colour and the little drainage ditches either side of the road were pale and yellow too, speckled with the black of peat.

'Sandy soil,' Will said, following the direction of my look. 'Wonderful for farming in the valley.'

We were shaded from the spring sunshine by a network of branches over our heads. The new leaves were showing like a green mist and the hedgerows and the woods looked as if a light grey-green scarf of gauze had been tossed over the black bones of their branches. Sea pricked his ears forward at the clip-clop noise of the hooves on the wet stones.

On our right were great old trees, growing thick right up to the very margin of the drainage ditch and the road. High grey-trunked beeches and the broad knobbly trunks of oaks. On the first bend the massive chestnut tree swooped its branches low over the track, the leaves spreading like fingers in their tiny greenness, bursting out of shells of buds as brown and sticky as toffee. Deeper in the woods, on little hummocks, there were tall pine trees and the scent of their rising sap made the spring air sweet, like a premonition of summer warmth. The birds were singing in the higher branches, as near to the sun as they could get, and in the depths below the trees was a rug of old leaves and bright spots of primroses and white violets.

'These trees are all parkland,' Will said gesturing with his whip. 'Ornamental. They belong to the grounds of the Hall, we only fell the timber for clearing. But there's game in them. Rabbits and pheasants, hares, deer. Ever since the estate was made into a worker's corporation we've had no game laws here. The people from Acre hunt as they wish for the pot. We don't allow hunting for sale. A few poachers come over from Petersfield or Chichester and we keep an eye out for them. We take it in turns to watch for them if it gets out of hand. But generally we're left well alone.'

I nodded. I had a passing sense of belonging, as sweet as cold water after a day's thirst. My mother – the woman who had called after the cart – had come here often. I could feel it. And her mother, too.

We rode in silence, I was looking around at the woodland on one side of the road and the tidy fields on the other.

'This is the Dower House,' Will volunteered. 'Your family lived here until the Hall was rebuilt. It was your ma's childhood home.'

I nodded and looked at it.

It was deserted but well secured. The double door at the front was shut tight, all the windows barred with shutters. The front garden was tidy, a flood of golden crocus under the front windows.

'No one lives there now?' I asked.

'No,' Will said. He gave me a rueful little smile. 'The way the estate is run does not attract the gentry,' he said. 'We've not been able to get a tenant for it for some time.'

I nodded. I did not understand what he meant yet, but I was not ready on this ride to ask questions. I wanted to take the measure of this place, of these people. To see what this place was in reality that I had been dreaming of for so long.

'It's a good estate,' he said tentatively. 'Productive.'

I glanced at him sideways. He was watching the stony drive between his horse's ears.

'It's not what I was bred to,' I said frankly. 'I don't know anything about it.'

'Not too late to learn,' he said gently. I guessed he was thinking of my scream at James Fortescue that I had come to Wideacre too late. 'If you were the son of the house, a Lacey, you'd be coming home from school at your age, ready to learn about the land,' he said.

'If I was coming home from school I'd have had a gentry childhood and I'd know how to read and write,' I said.

'Not the schools I'm thinking of!' Will said smiling. 'Real Quality schools teach lads to be as ignorant as peasants!' He shot a little smile at me as we rounded a curve of the drive and came within sight of the little box of the gatehouse and the great iron gates which stood permanently open with white flowering bindweed entwined up the hinges. Will nodded to the left.

'That's one of our new crops,' he said. 'Strawberries. We're harrowing now, to make the soil nice and soft. We'll be planting later. I reckon we'll sell in Chichester. There's a growing market for soft fruit. Wideacre strawberries could be famous.'

I glanced over the hedge. Two great shire horses were pulling a harrow, a little lad walking behind them, yelling instructions, the earth turning sweetly under the tines.

'We planted it when the land was handed over to the people,' he said. 'It's a crop which needs a lot of careful work. Weeding, and especially picking and packing. A casual paid workforce could waste more than they earned. But when people know they are working for themselves, they take more pride.'

I nodded. I was trying to get used to the strangeness of it all. I was wondering if it were not really a dream. I might wake up at any moment to the rocking caravan roof and the bitter hard life of my childhood; and look over and see her . . .

I shook my head to clear my thoughts and saw that Will had pulled his horse up at the end of the drive. The door of the lodge house opened and a woman with a babby in her arms came down the garden path and dipped me a low curtsey when she reached her garden gate.

'Good day, Miss Sarah,' she said.

For a moment I did not smile. I did not reply. She had called me Miss Sarah. Miss. Not the only other handle to my name I had ever had – Mamselle Meridon the bareback rider – but Miss Sarah. As though I were gentry born and bred. As though it were natural to her to call me thus, and natural to me to respond to it.

I nodded my head awkwardly at her.

'This is Mrs Hodgett,' Will Tyacke said. 'She is a Midhurst woman who married the gate-keeper. The Hodgetts have always kept this gate.'

I nodded again. 'Good day,' I said. I found I could smile my show smile, and I pinned it on my face. Then Will clicked to his horse, and Sea fell into pace beside it as we turned left down the drive to head towards the village of Acre.

'Your village,' he said half in jest. 'In the old days, when Beatrice and Squire Harry ran the land, they owned outright every one of the cottages in the village, aye, and even the church and the parson's house as well.' He paused. 'I suppose you still do,' he said, surprised. 'We've been without a squire for so long that we've forgot how the deeds run. Of course it would still be your village outright. The cottagers have not paid rent for years. Not since Squire Richard – your papa – was killed. Mr Fortescue excused all rents and fees so that we could launch the land-sharing scheme. All he withdraws for the Lacey estate is your share of the profits. We call the village Acre, you know,' he said. 'It's a Saxon name, like mine. My family were here in this village long before the Le Says came over with the Conqueror and fought for it and won it from us.'

'The who?' I asked. I had never heard of the Le Says. Nor of the conqueror. I had a vague idea that it might be Bonnie Prince Charlie.

Will looked at me in some surprise. 'The Le Says were your family,' he said. 'They were French. Their name was changed later to Lacey.'

'Oh,' I said. Changing names was nothing new to me. Every-one in my world always changed their names when they were running from debts or from thief-takers.

'They came with the Normans. When William the Conqueror invaded England,' Will said.

I kept my face blank and nodded. I was ashamed of knowing nothing.

'They fought for the land?' I asked.

'Oh aye,' Will said. 'I can even show you where. It's called Battle Field and the ploughboys still turn up human bones and bits of armour. Three days they fought – the village against the Le Says – and the battle only ended when everyone was dead.'

'Then where d'you come from?' I asked quickly.

Will smiled. 'Everyone was dead except one man from my family,' he said. There was a twinkle in his brown eyes but his face was serious as if he were telling me the truth. 'He was especially saved to found a dynasty of Tyackes. Saved from the field of battle because of his great skill.'

'In fighting?' I asked.

'In running away!' Will said and chuckled. 'It's old history, Sarah, nobody really knows. Anyway, the Laceys won the land from the people and they have kept it for themselves. Up until now. But the Tyackes have always lived here. And now it is my home.'

I could hear the love and pride in his voice and we halted the horses so that I could see the place properly.

It was a broad street, clean enough, with a few chickens scratching in the dust of the road. A line of cottages on the north side of the road had gardens bobbing with the fat green buds of daffodils and studded with primroses and dark purple crocuses. In one of them a young woman was sitting peeling potatoes in a bowl on her lap, a little child toddling towards her with a scrap of leaf in her hand, her face bright with discovery.

The church stood at the end of the row. An old building with a spire of newer stone. Re-built, as James had said. On the other side of the road the cottages had yards on to the lane. There was a carter's yard with a wagon being mended inside, a cobbler's house facing the street with the cobbler cross-legged at his window, head bowed. A smithy, and a great shire horse tied outside waiting. A thatcher's yard with piles of wood left to season and stooks of reeds under a thatch of straw to keep them dry. It looked what it was, a humming prosperous little village of some thirty houses.

'Most of the people are out working,' Will said. 'I thought you'd rather take a glance at it now before everyone wants to meet you.'

I looked down the street. The cobbler was watching us, but when he saw me look his way he waved a hand and bent his head to his last again as if he did not want to seem prying. The woman in the front garden raised her head and smiled but did not leave off her work.

'I told them you'd come down and meet them all after church on Sunday,' Will said. 'I thought you'd want some time to look about you and gather your wits before you speak to everyone.'

I nodded. The place made me angry, though I wouldn't show it. The place was so solid. It seemed as if these people had been here, planted deep as trees for years. And I had been blowing like a burr looking for somewhere to catch on to, somewhere to root.

'How many people?' I asked.

'With the small farmers who own their own fields and pay rent, and the squatters who live on the Common and claim squatters' rights; it comes to about three hundred,' he said watching my face with a little smile. 'But you'll rarely see them all together. Only a few of them come to church now they don't have to. You'll just walk up the aisle of the church to the Lacey pew so that everyone can get a good look at you, and when you come out I'll make you known to the people you want to meet. The vicar will most likely invite you to Sunday dinner, so he'll tell you about the village as well.'

I nodded. Five new acquaintances would have terrified me, but walking up the aisle of a church and being stared at was just a performance like bareback riding. I thought if I had the right costume and a little training I could act it.

Will saw the hardness in my face. 'You need not do it, you know,' he said gently. 'If you have friends elsewhere that you would rather be with, or a life you would rather lead, you can just go away again. Mr Fortescue can arrange to send you your money. You need not live here if you do not wish it. The estate has run well in your absence, nothing need change unless you want to be here.'

I looked down so that he should not see the flame of anger in my face at his suggestion that I might go elsewhere. I had nowhere else to go. I had longed for this place for all of my life. If I could not belong here then I was lost indeed. I no longer had her; if I lost Wide I would be a vagrant indeed.

'Which is your house?' I asked.

He gestured at a lane which ran down to the right.

'That's mine,' he said. 'Set back off the main street, overlooking the watermeadow and the river. I came to live there with my aunt when my cousin Ted was hurt in a ploughing accident, three years ago. She needed help with him. When he died I stayed on. That's how I come to be in charge here though I'm young for the job. Ted was foreman for the village, and they decided I could take over early. The Tyackes have always been an important family in the village. They've a stone in the church wall which is the oldest in the church.'

I nooded. I could see the chimney and the stone-tiled roof. It looked like the best cottage in the village. Only the vicarage was bigger.

'Where were you before?' I asked.

Will smiled. 'Not far,' he said. 'Just down the road on the Goodwood estate. I was working in the bailiff's office there, so I was used to farming and keeping the books too.'

'Married?' I asked.

Will flushed a little. 'Nay,' he said awkwardly. 'I'm not court-ing either. I had a lass but she wouldn't stay in the village. She wanted to go into service and me go with her. I'm handy with horses and she wanted me to try for a job as coachman with the Haverings. I wouldn't leave Acre. I'd not leave Acre for any lass, however bonny. So she went without me. That was last summer. I've had no one serious since then.

'We go this way up to the Downs,' he said, and turned his horse away from the church up a little track which climbed the hill.

The horses went shoulder to shoulder up the track, but I loosened the rein and let Sea increase his speed and go ahead of Will so that I could ride alone without him watching my face. The singing noise which I had heard in my head from the very first time I had come to this land, through the dark and the cold, lit only by the moon, was now louder. I was riding up the track which I had seen so many times in my dreams. We were clear of the planted fields and the tall quiet beech trees were crowding close around us. The horses' hooves were silent on the damp earth and on the leafmould. Sea's ears pointed forward at the bright circle of light where the trees ended and we would come out . . . out to what?

I knew how it would be and yet I was suddenly afraid that it would not be as I thought it should. That so much else in this place was so different from my dream. Instead of finding a warm house and a father and being a copper-headed beloved daughter I was a gypsy who had come in out of the darkness, a stranger, an intruder. James Fortescue might say he loved me for my mother's sake, or because it was his duty, or because he felt guilty that he had failed to find me – but those things meant nothing. In my world none of those things would make a man lift his hand to brush away a fly.

Will Tyacke might take an afternoon to show me around the estate and make me welcome – but I could see that this private little world had run perfectly well without me for sixteen years. They were used to having no one at the Hall. They preferred it that way. I was not a welcome heir, finding her way home at last. I was an unwanted orphan. My so-called guardian and the foreman of my village had done well enough without me all this time.

If the land was not right, I thought, I should go away. Not as they hoped, not a ladylike organized departure, telling people that I did not like the country, that I preferred to live in a little town. If the land was not right I should run off tonight. I would hack my hair into a bob, I would steal the silver and the pretty miniature portraits on the small tables in the parlour, and anything else light enough to carry in my pockets. I should ride until I found a hiring fair and hire myself out as a groom to a good stud farm where I could work with young horses. I was fit for nothing. I did not know the ways of the Rom – and besides, as the old woman in Salisbury had seen, I was no Rom. I was not one of those special people.

I could not go back to work with a show. I would never work again in a ring. I could not have smelled the woodshavings and the horse sweat without freezing with horror. And I did not belong here. Not in the Hall with this difficult mannered life, not in those rooms where you could scream at someone and then they would pour you tea, not in this mad village with these peculiar people who let squatters settle and paid them wages, and who paid a pension to people too old to work

If the land was wrong I would go away and try and find somewhere that I could be myself. Another place.

Another place to search for again.

Sea put his head down and cantered towards the circle of light at the head of the track and we scrambled up the last slope. Will had stayed behind, letting me ride alone. The light dazzled me, the sudden piercing sound of a lark singing up high was as sharp in my ears as the swelling singing which had come to me on this land. The spring grass was a bright mouth-watering green, the sky a pale pale blue streamered with white slight clouds. Sea breathed deep and blew out. I turned his head towards the valley and looked over Wideacre.

I could just see the house. Its pale sandstone yellow colour was like good butter, a little pat among the green of the park. I could see the round turret of the parlour and the wedge of the terrace in front of it. The heads of the trees were thick, like a sheep's winter fleece, the pines standing out dark against the light spring green.

At the foot of the hill I could see the village. My village. The village my mama had known. I saw it through my eyes, I saw it through her eyes. I saw it as I had dreamed it for one longing dream after another. I knew that it was my home. I had been coming towards it all of my life, for all of my life. I had loved it and missed it and needed it, and now I was coming into the very heart of it.

I breathed in a deep gasp of the wind which was blowing softly across the top of the Downs. I wanted to belong here. I wanted this place. Even though I knew it was too late for me, I longed for it as a man might long for a woman who left him long, long, ago.

Will's horse came up behind me and he pulled it up. 'That's our land, beyond the village: that's Wideacre Common land up as far as you can see north,' he said, pointing with his whip. 'To the west that is the Havering estate. These Downs are Wideacre estate too, twenty miles going north, ten miles to the west. Then it's Havering land again. All of this valley is Wideacre land.'

I breathed in the smell of it, you could almost taste the chalk in the soil. The grass was fine as hair and short-cropped, studded with flowers and in the hollows there were great clumps of violets and the pale yellow of primroses.

'Gets thick with cowslips later on,' Will said, following my gaze. 'We come up and pick them to make cowslip wine. We come up here on Mayday morning too. You'd like that. We come up and watch the sun rise.'

I nodded my head, not speaking. I had a distant memory of a dream of standing looking towards Acre and seeing the sun come up pale and pink on a May morning.

'It is as I always thought it would be,' I said speaking half to myself. 'I have dreamed and dreamed of this place ever since I can remember. I have wanted to be here all my life.'

Will brought his horse closer alongside Sea and put his calloused hand over mine as I held the reins. I flinched at the touch and Sea stepped to one side.

'It will not be as you thought it,' he said gently. 'It could not be. Nothing ever is. And while you have been dreaming of us, things have been changing here, we have been working towards a dream of our own. We are trying to do something here which is both an example and a model to the rest of the country. And it is part of a long tradition. A forgotten tradition which people try to ignore. Ever since there have been landlords there have been ordinary men and women claiming the right to run the land in their own way, of earning their own bread, of living together as a community. It may seem strange to you now, Sarah, but I think we can be the family you don't have.'

I shook my head. 'I've got no family,' I said coldly. 'I dreamed of a landscape. I didn't dream of you, or of James Fortescue. All the family I had are dead, and now you two tell me they weren't even kin. And my real kin . . . well they're dead too. I've got no one, and I need no one. It was the land I dreamed of; and it's the land I want.'

Will shrugged his shoulders; and did not try to touch me again. He pulled his horse over to one side and let me admire the view on my own.

'Would you like a gallop over the Downs and then round by the Common to your home?' he asked, his voice carefully polite. 'Or do you want to see more of the village?'

'Common land and home,' I said. I glanced at the sun. 'What time do they eat dinner?'

'At six,' he said coldly. 'But they'll wait till you are home before they serve dinner.'

I looked aghast. 'That would be awful,' I exclaimed.

The black look was wiped off his face in a second. Will laughed aloud. 'If you think so,' he said chuckling. 'I'll get you home in plenty of time. Could your horse do with a gallop?'

'Oh yes,' I said. Sea had been fretting ever since his hooves had been on the soft turf.

'This way then!' said Will and his brown cob sprang forward, suprisingly quickly for a horse that size. Sea was after him in a moment, and we chased them along the level track which arrowed, straight as a die, along the top of the Downs. We drew level in a few minutes and I heard Will laugh as we forged past them, Sea put his ears forward at the thunder of the hooves and then slackened his speed so that the brown cob inched forward again. They raced side by side, changing the leads as if they were enjoying themselves until Will called 'Hulloa! Woah!' and we slowed them down and they dropped into a canter and then we pulled them up.

'We'll go down this little track,' Will said, and led the way down a track which was sticky with white creamy mud. Sea blew out and followed the cob as it skidded and slipped. The ground levelled off at the bottom and the mud gave way to white sand.

'This is the Common,' Will said.

It was a different kind of landscape entirely, but as familiar to me and as beloved as the Downland and parkland of my home. It was wild countryside, there were no hedges or fields or any sign of farming. As I listened I could hear the faint tinkle of a cow-bell or goat-bell. The busy village of Acre and the well-tended fields, away to the south, seemed miles away.

The hills were covered in heather, the fresh growth showing as a pale mist around the dead white flowers and grey of the old plants. All around us young fronds of ferns were growing leggy and short, necks curled up towards the sky. Over to my right there was a little coppice of silver birches, their trunks pale as paper.

'Some of this has been enclosed, it is wonderful growing soil,'

Will said. 'But most of it has been left as it always has been. A bit of a wilderness.'

He turned his horse's head and Sea fell in beside the cob. The path was very wide, pure white sand, with a covering of black soil at the edges.

'We keep this open for a firebreak,' Will said.

'It catches fire?' I asked, bemused.

'Sometimes in a very hot summer, but also we burn off the old heather and bracken so that it stays fit for grazing,' he explained. 'Even in the old days, when the Laceys ruled the land as they wished, it was always a right for the people of Acre to graze their own beasts up here. Cows mostly, but some people keep goats or sheep. Quite a few pigs, too.'

I nodded.

'We'll just go and look at the orchard, and then cut across the Common for home,' he said. 'Have I lost you yet?'

I screwed up my face to think. 'No,' I said. 'The Downs curve around the village and we came down that path so that we were north of the village. I reckon it's that way . . .' I gestured with my left hand.

Will nodded. 'You've a good sense of direction,' he said. 'But you would have that with the travelling you must have done.'

He waited in case I should tell him something about my travelling but I said nothing and he trotted on ahead of me along the firebreak, across a marshy little stream, where Sea jinked and shied, and then in a long easy canter along a path and into a wood of tall beech trees and the occasional pine. Ahead of us was the river and I followed Will on the brown cob when he turned to the left and rode along its banks. The water was deep, dark brown in the curves and bends by the banks, but sparkling and bright in the shallows. We came out on to a cart track and then Will pulled his horse up and said, 'There.'

Ahead of us was a high and lovely fold of hills, capped by silver birches and the ungainly growing heads of baby ferns. Over to our left the hills ran down to the river, brown with last year's bracken but lightened with the new growth. The old heather showed as dull pewter and old silver. Before us, in a huge sprawl of a field, were straight well-planted rows of apple trees, the leaves green with soft silvery undersides as the wind rolled through them.

'Your ma planted this,' Will said and his voice was filled with wonder. 'Before you were born. Your ma Julia planted it, and my cousin Ted Tyacke was here when she did it. He said it took them all day to plant it and when they had finished they were so tired they could hardly walk home.'

I nodded. For a moment I forgot my sadness and my anger as I looked at the great fertile sweep of the land and saw how the strong branches bobbed as the wind played through them.

Will's voice was warm. 'Ted told me that none of them had ever planted apple trees before, it was a new idea. To set the estate back on its feet after the fire and everything going bad. He said that it was one of the first things Julia ever did on her own. She worked all day on her own down here and she counted out all the trees and got them set in straight rows.'

I looked again at the orchard. I thought I could even tell that they had planted from left to right, the first two rows were a bit wobbly, as if they had been learning how to keep to the line. After that they were straighter. I thought of my mother, a young woman little older than me, trying to set the land right.

'He said she was up and down each row twenty times,' Will said, a laugh in the back of his voice. 'And at the end of it, all the trees were in and she looked around and there was one left on the cart! They laughed until they cried and she swore that she would give the sapling to the village to keep so the children could have apples off it.' He paused. 'She planted it on the green,' he said. 'The tree is getting old now, but the apples are very sweet.'

I felt a rush of tenderness for the mother I had never known, for the other Tyacke who had worked with her and laughed when she ended with one tree too many, for all the people she knew who worked with her to set this land on its feet again so that it could grow rich and fertile.

'Thank you,' I said, and for that moment I was simply grateful that he had taken the time and the trouble to bring me down here, to show me the orchard, and to explain to me what the land had meant to my mother. How she had been when she had been a young girl with the rights and duties of a squire. How she had been when she had loved and owned the land.

Will nodded and clicked to his horse so that we rode on beside the river, past the orchard. 'She wanted to end the line of the Laceys,' he said gently. 'She told them that in the village one day. When her husband Squire Richard was bringing in day labourers and paying only the poor-rate wages. She said there should be no more squires.'

I felt myself stiffen, and the cold hardness which had been around me all my life came back to me.

'Then she should have drowned me in the river as she planned, and not given me away,' I said. 'She should have had the courage to do the thing properly, or not at all. She gave me away and I was lost for all those years. So now I do not understand the land, and the village is used to having no squire.'

Will looked very attentively at the path ahead of us, at the stream moving so sweetly and easily across the land.

'We could become accustomed,' he said. 'We will both have to change a little. We will become accustomed to having a Lacey in the Hall again. You will learn how to be Quality. Perhaps this is the best way. For she did not end the squires, but here you are, a squire who knows what it is to be poor. It is different for you, because you were not bred to it. You've seen both sides. You've not been trained in Quality ways, you've not learned to look away when you see beggars. Your heart is not hard in the way they learn.'

He kept his eyes straight ahead so that he was not looking at my clothes, hand-me-downs, of a cheaper quality than his own. There was a hole in one of the boots. 'You know what it is like for poor people,' he said discreetly. 'You would not make their lives hard for them if you could choose.'

I thought about that as I rode. And I knew it was not so. Nothing in my life had taught me tenderness or charity. Nothing had taught me to share, to think of others. I had only ever shared with one person. I had only ever had a thought for one person. Will's belief that my knowing the underside of a cruel and greedy world would make me gentle could not have been more wrong.

We rode without speaking, listening to the river which flowed clattering on stones and whirlpooling around twigs beside us. In the distance I could hear the regular slap slap and creak of a mill wheel. Then we rounded a little bend and I saw it on the opposite side of the river, a handsome plain square building in the familiar yellow stone.

'That's the new mill,' Will said with satisfaction. 'The Green family run it as their own business. They grind Wideacre corn for free but they also take in corn from the other farmers and charge them a fee for grinding.'

'Who owns it?' I asked.

Will looked surprised. 'I suppose you do,' he said. 'Your mother got it running again, but it was built by the Laceys. The Green family came as tenants, long ago. But they've paid no rent since the corporation was established.'

I nodded. I looked at the trim little building and at the bright white and purple violets in the windowboxes. I looked at the pretty curtains in the windows, and the mill wheel turning around. On the roof there were white doves cooing. I thought of the times I had gone hungry, and she had been hungry too. I thought of the times we had been cold, and how very often Da had beaten me. I thought of her sitting on gentlemen's laps for a penny, and me being thrown from horse after horse for ha'pence. And I thought that all the time, for all of that time, these people had been living here in comfort and plenty, beside this quiet river.

Will set his horse to a trot and then we went alongside the strawberry field I had seen in the morning. The lad had nearly finished the harrowing and he waved to us as we rode by. There was a little track between two fields and it brought us out on the driveway towards the Hall.

'You've never been poor have you?' I said shrewdly. 'You've always worked, wherever you said it was – Goodwood – and here. But you've never gone short.'

The horses walked shoulder to shoulder up the drive. The birds still sang in the treetops but I could not hear them. The sweet singing noise had gone from my head, too. 'You'd never have such hopes of me if you had been poor, hard poor. You would know then that the only lesson anyone learns from poverty is to take as much as you can now, for fear that there will be nothing for you later. And don't share with anyone, for certainly they'll never share with you.'

Will kept his eyes on the lane before his cob. He never turned his head.

'In all my life I only ever shared with one person,' I said, my voice very low. 'I only ever gave anything to one person. And now she is gone. I shall never share nor give to anyone else.'

I thought for a moment. 'And except for her,' I said consideringly, 'no one ever gave me a damned thing. Every penny I saw I worked for. Every crust I ate I earned. I don't think I'm the squire you hoped for, Will Tyacke. I don't think I'm capable of gentry charity. I've been poor myself, and I hate being poor, and I don't care for poor dirty people. If I'm rich now, I'll stay that way. I don't ever want to be poor again.'

20

Mr Fortescue was waiting for us in the stable yard. He asked Will to stay for dinner but Will said he had to go. He waited while I slid down from the saddle and then nodded to Mr Fortescue and to me.

'I'll come back this evening,' he said. 'When I finish work at dark.'

Then he gave me a friendly smile which also seemed somehow forgiving. Then he rode away.

'I had better wash,' I said. I put a hand to my cheek and felt the grime from the dust of the road.

'Becky Miles has put some clothes in your room,' Mr Fortescue offered, his voice carefully neutral. 'They belonged to your mother, but she thinks they would fit you if you cared to try them.'

I could tell he was trying hard to pass no comment on my eccentricity of boys' clothes. I looked down at the shabby breeches and jacket and I laughed.

'It's all right, Mr Fortescue,' I said. 'I know I cannot dress like a stable lad for the rest of my life. I was wanting to ask you about clothes. I also need to ask you about all sorts of other things which I will have to learn.'

Mr Fortescue brightened. 'I only hope I can help you,' he said. 'We'll talk over dinner.'

I nodded and went indoors and up to my room.

For the thousandth time that day I had a pang of pain and anger that she could not be with me, when I saw what was laid out on the bed.

It was the finest riding habit of plum velvet, edged with silky violet ribbon in a great double border. There was a matching tricorne hat to go with it, and dark leather boots with silky tassels and even cream-coloured stockings with plum clocks on the side.

I thought of how she would have flown at them and how ravishing she would have looked in them and I had to lean back against the panels of the door and take a deep breath to ease the sudden pain which thudded, as hard as a blow into my belly, at the thought that she would never see them. That in all her beauty-seeking life she had never known anything better than rags and trumpery.

So there was little delight for me in the thick smooth feel of the cloth, nor the fineness of the linen shirt and stock that went underneath. But when I had slipped on the skirt and gone to the mirror in the smart little boots I could smile with some pleasure at my reflection.

It was a half-mirror so I could not see the hem of the gown nor the boots without dragging over a chair and standing high on it to admire them. Then I slowly got down and saw how my linen shirt looked white against the neat purple waistband of the skirt, and how I looked somehow taller and older and quite strange and unlike myself. I stared at my face. The hazy green eyes looked back, the lines of my cheek, of my throat above the tumble of lace as clear as a drawn line.

My hair was still hopeless. I made a few half-hearted passes at it with the silver-backed brush but the soft bristles slid over the curls and the tangles and hardly straightened them at all. It remained an obstinate tumble of copper curls half-way down my back, and only the memory of the ragged mess of a bob stopped me from ringing for Becky Miles to bring me some scissors and hacking it all off again.

I turned from the glass and went down to dinner, feeling already stronger and more confident in boots which clicked on the floorboards of the hall and did not clump.

Mr Fortescue was waiting for me in the dining room and when he saw me his jaw dropped and he gaped like a country child at mummers.

'Good God!' he said.

Becky Miles who was setting a soup tureen on the table swung around and nearly dropped it in her surprise.

'Miss Sarah!' she said. 'You look beautiful!'

I felt myself flush as vain and as silly as a market-day slut.

'Thank you,' I said steadily and took my seat at the head of the table.

Mr Fortescue sat at my right-hand side and Becky Miles loaded the rest of the expanse of mahogany with as many dishes as she could, to conceal the fact that there were just the two of us, camped out at one end of the table.

'Did you enjoy your ride?' Mr Fortescue asked politely as he started to eat his soup.

I watched him. He did not bend over his bowl and spoon directly from bowl to mouth with as little distance as possible. Nor had he crumbled his bread up into hearty bits to float in the soup as I had already done. I flushed again, this time with annoyance. He had kept his bread on his plate and every now and then broke off a little piece and buttered it. I tried to sit straighter but it seemed to put me a long way off from the table. I was sure my hand would shake as I was lifting the soup to my lips and then I would drop soup on my new dress. I remembered the small cloth and spread it on my lap. It all seemed designed to make it harder to eat. But if this was the way it had to be done I thought I could pick it up in time.

'Yes, it was a nice ride,' I agreed inattentively. When Mr Fortescue finished his soup he did not wipe around his bowl with a piece of bread. He left the bowl dirty, he left nigh on a whole spoonful spread around the bottom. I followed his example though I watched the wasted soup longingly as Becky Miles took the bowl away.

She set a great silver salver with a rib of beef on it before Mr Fortescue and he started carving into wafer-thin slices which he laid in a fan on a plate for me and Becky Miles walked around the table and placed it before me. The smell of the roast beef, dark on the outside and pinky in the middle, made me lean forward and sniff, water rushing into my mouth. Becky Miles brought me roast potatoes, crunchy and brown, new potatoes glazed with butter, tiny young carrots and new peas and half a dozen things which looked like green miniature bulrushes.

'Do you like asparagus, Sarah?' Mr Fortescue said, pointing at them.

'I don't know,' I said honestly. 'I've never had them before.'

'Try one or two then,' he recommended. 'We grow them on the Home Farm here under glass. Will Tyacke has it in mind to put some more glass houses up and grow more of it.'

I nodded and Becky Miles put two of the green slivers on my plate.

She held out a great sauce boat of deep red shiny gravy and poured it thickly over the meat.

I was so hungry I could have grabbed my knife and cut up the bigger bits at once and shovelled the rest into my mouth with the spoon. But I forced myself to wait and watch Mr Fortescue.

He took an age, while I sat there and my nostrils flared at the scent of the food and I ached to begin. First he was served with all the vegetables, then Becky Miles brought wine for him and water and wine for me. I would rather have had small beer, but I did not feel able to say so. Then finally, after he had made a little pile of salt at the edge of his plate he picked up his knife and his fork, at once, in both hands and cut and prodded, and managed to talk at the same time without showing what he was chewing.

It was beyond me. I ate as daintily as I could but when I was trying to cut the meat some gravy slopped over the side of my plate and stained the tablecloth. And the asparagus dripped butter into my lap so the napkin was soiled. If I had not been so starving hungry I should have lost my appetite at the discomfort of sitting opposite such a neat feeder as Mr Fortescue. But I had been hungry once, and he had not, and I was sure that the difference between us went deeper than manners. He could see food as something he could leave or take, as he pleased, with the knowledge that there were other meals if he wished for them. I ate as if I might never see food again, and I thought I should never learn to treat meal times lightly.

After the meat there was apple pie and a creamy kind of dish which Becky Miles served in a glass. After that came some cheeses and biscuits and port for Mr Fortescue and a glass of sweet yellowy ratafia for me. I thought of Robert Gower offering David a glass of port after dinner, that time. It seemed like another lifetime. It seemed as if they were years away from me.

'Now Sarah,' Mr Fortescue said gently as Becky Miles cleared away everything but a bowl of fruit on the table and the two decanters. 'If this were a proper household you would withdraw to the parlour and leave me to my port and my cigar. But since it is just the two of us will you sit with me?'

'Yes,' I said.

He seemed to be waiting. He gave me a little smile. 'And may I smoke?' he asked. 'I know it is a disgusting habit, but . . .'

I looked at him in utter incredulity. 'Why d'you ask me?' I demanded.

'Because you're a lady,' he said. 'A gentleman cannot smoke in a lady's presence without her specific permission.'

I was still blank. 'Whyever not?' I asked. 'What's it to do with her?'

Mr Fortescue could not seem to explain. 'I suppose it is about showing respect,' he offered.

We looked at each other in mutual incomprehension.

'I'm never going to understand this,' I said miserably. 'I'll need to have someone to teach me.'

Mr Fortescue brought out a little silver pair of scissors and snipped at the end of his cigar, then he lit it, and blew out thoughtfully, watching the smoke curling off the glowing ember.

'I've had some thoughts on that,' he offered. 'There's something I can suggest. What you are going to need is the education of a country lady.' He stopped and smiled. 'Nothing very sophisticated! Your mother was brought up here with only the teaching of her mother. She never saw a city bigger than Chichester until she went to Bath. She never went to London at all.'

He glanced at me. I kept my face still.

'I spoke with my sister Marianne, as soon as I heard you had come home. Marianne was a special friend of your mother's and she suggested to me that as soon as you are settled here you will need a companion. Fortunately she knows someone who might do. It is a lady who used to be a governess. She's a friendly lady, the widow of a naval officer and the daughter of a country squire herself so she would understand the life you are going to lead. She'd be prepared to come here and to teach you the things you need to know. To read, and to write. How to run a house and how to engage servants. What your duties are in the house and what church and charitable works you should do.'

He paused, waiting for a response from me. 'It's not all dull,' he said encouragingly. 'She'll teach you how to dance and how to play the piano and sing and paint. She'll teach you how to ride side-saddle, and you can go hunting. She'll chaperone you into country society and advise you about the people who you can visit and those you should not meet.'

Still I said nothing. Mr Fortescue poured himself another glass of port. I knew he was uncomfortable with my silence. He could not judge for himself what it meant.

'Sarah,' he said gently. 'If you mislike any of these plans you need only say. All I want to do is the best for you. I am your guardian until your marriage or until you are twenty-one but I know you are no ordinary young lady. You have special needs and special abilities. Please tell me what you would like, and I will try and provide it for you.'

'I am not sure yet,' I said. And I spoke the truth although certainty was gathering around me all the time. 'I've been angry since I came here, but neither you nor that Will Tyacke pay me any mind at all.'

James Fortescue smiled at me through the cigar smoke.

'I don't know enough about this life to be able to say what I want,' I said. 'It's clear you don't plan that I should run the estate like my mother did. I saw her apple orchard today and Will told me that she supervised the planting of it herself.'

'No,' Mr Fortescue said definitely. 'I don't want you working directly on the land. It would be contrary to your mother's wishes and quite contrary to the way the estate is now run. For the past sixteen years, ever since your birth and your mama's death, the estate has been developed by the people who work here, for themselves.

'There is no place now for a squire of the old sort to run the land. The time when a Lacey squire was needed to keep the village together has long gone. It is run now as a joint venture by the labourers themselves and that is what your mother wished for it. She specifically told me that she did not want her daughter to be another Lacey squire. She wanted you to have the house and the gardens and the parkland – and you will see for yourself that is a handsome legacy – but she wanted the farming land, the Common land and the Downs to be owned legally and entirely by the village.'

I nodded. That was what I had thought he would say.

'So the life you think I should live is mostly idle?' I asked. I was careful to keep my voice neutral so that he could not shape his answer to please me.

'As you wish,' he said agreeably. 'My sister Marianne works long hours and gets much pleasure out of a charitable school she set up all on her own for the education of young orphans or children abandoned by their parents. Her husband is an alderman of London and she saw much poverty and hardship. She works longer hours than I do! Yet she is unpaid. She leads a most worthwhile life. There are many good causes you could work for here, Sarah.'

I kept my lashes lowered over the gleam in my green eyes. I knew what his sister Marianne was like. When I was little we used to pick the pockets of her sort most successfully. One of us would sit on a lady's silken lap and cry and say our da beat her, and one of us would take a sharp little knife and cut the strings which tied her purse to her belt and run off with the booty. We were caught only once and when we burst into floods of tears the lady made us promise never never to do it again or Baby Jesus would not be able to save us from hell. We promised readily and she gave us a shilling out of her recovered purse. A simpleton.

'Or you could pursue interests of your own,' Mr Fortescue went on. 'If you found you had a talent for music or singing or painting you could work at that. Or if that horse of yours is anything to go by, you could find a good manager and have him set up a stud of horses.'

I nodded. 'And there are people who could teach me everything I need to know?' I asked. 'Music teachers and dance
teachers and manners teachers? I could learn everything?'

He smiled as if I was being engagingly eager. 'Yes,' he said.
'Mrs Redwold could teach you everything you need to know. She
could teach you to be a young country lady.'

'How long?' I asked.

'I beg your pardon?' he said.

'How long?' I asked. 'How long would it take for me to learn
everything about being a young lady.'

He smiled at that as if the question were funny. 'I think one
learns good manners all one's life,' he said. 'But I should think
you would be comfortable in good society within a year.'

A year! I thought to myself. It had taken me less than that to
learn to be a bareback rider with my own act. It had taken her
two months to learn tricks on the trapeze. Either gentry skills
were very difficult – or else they were full of nonsense and
idiocy, like eating things while sitting so far away that you were
certain to drop them.

I said nothing and Mr Fortescue leaned forward and poured
me another glass of ratafia.

'It's a lot to take in,' he said gently. 'And you must be tired,
this is your first day up after your illness. Would you like to go
to your bedroom now? Or sit in the parlour?'

I nodded. I was learning some of the gentry rules already. He
did not mean he thought I was tired, he meant he did not want
to talk to me any more. I felt a bad taste in my mouth and I went
to spit but caught myself in time. 'I am tired,' I said. 'I think I
shall go to my room. Good-night, Mr Fortescue.'

He got to his feet as I went towards the door and he went past
me and opened it for me. I hesitated, thinking he meant to go
out too but then I realized he had opened it for me for politeness'
sake. He took my right hand and raised it to his lips and kissed
it. Without thinking what I was doing I whipped it away and
put it behind my back.

'I beg your pardon!' he said, surprised. 'I just meant to say
good-night.'

I flushed scarlet with embarrassment. 'I am sorry,' I said gruffly. 'I don't like people touching me, I never have.'

He nodded as if he understood; but I wagered he didn't.

'Good-night, Sarah,' he said. 'Please ring the bell if there is anything you want. Shall I ask Becky Miles to bring you up a cup of tea later?'

'Yes please,' I said. Having a cup of tea in bed would be comfortingly like eating dinner in my bunk, in the old days when it was too cold to eat out of doors, or when we were so tired we took our dinners into our bunks with us and dropped the tin plates down on the floor when we had done.

I had never thought then that I would look back on those times with any of this lonely longing I had now.

'And you may call me James if you wish,' he said. 'Uncle James, if you prefer.'

'I have no family,' I said dully. 'I won't pretend to an uncle I don't have. I'll call you James.'

He made a little bow with a smile but he took care not to take my hand again.

'James,' I said as I turned to leave, 'how often do you come down to the estate?'

He looked surprised. 'Once a quarter,' he said. 'I come down to meet with Will and I make up the books for the quarter.'

I nodded. 'How do you know he is not cheating you?' I asked bluntly.

He looked deeply shocked. 'Sarah!' he exclaimed, as if it were wrong to even think such a thing. But then he recollected himself and he gave me a rueful smile.

'I am sorry,' he said. 'This evening you look so like a demure young lady it is hard to remember that you have been brought up in a quite different world. I know he is not cheating me because he brings me bills of sale for all his purchases for the estate and we agree what the main expenses are to be each quarter before he buys them. I know he is not cheating me because I see the wage bills of the estate. I know he is not cheating me because the village is on a profit-sharing system with the estate and he sees that we all get good profits and thus a

good share. And finally, but most important to me, I know he is
not cheating me because, although he is so young, he is an honest
man. I trusted his cousin and I trust him.'

I nodded. The trust based on bills of sale and agreed expendi-
ture I understood but ignored. I don't believe I had ever seen a
straight reckoning in all my life. Bills of sale meant nothing.
Same for the wages bill. The trust based on Will Tyacke as an
honest man was worth a good deal. It also told me something
that I needed to know about how the estate was run.

'Does the corn mill pay rent?' I asked.

James Fortescue's look of surprise that I was thinking of such
a thing turned into a smile. 'Now Sarah,' he remonstrated. 'You
need not puzzle your head with such detail. The corn mill has
paid no rent since the setting up of the Acre corporation. The
corn mill was obviously a separate business and is run in the
same way as the blacksmith's forge or the cartering business.
They charge special rates, or no rates to Acre people and they
make their profits with outside customers. They take a share in
the profits of the village when they work as labourers, otherwise
they are independent. When the village was getting back to work
Will's cousin Ted Tyacke and I decided that the mill should pay
no rent so that it could work for free for Acre. Things have
stayed that way.'

I nodded. 'I see,' I said quietly, then I half concealed a
pretended yawn. 'Oh! I'm tired,' I said. 'I'll go to bed.'

'Sleep well,' he said gently. 'If you are interested in business
you can have your first lesson on how to read the estate books in
the morning. But you will need a night's rest for that. Sleep
well, Sarah.'

I smiled at him, a smile I had learned long ago from her when
she was trying to be charming, an endearing childlike sleepy
smile. Then I went slowly towards the staircase.

I had heard enough for one night. James Fortescue might be
an astute man of business in Bristol and London – though I
frankly doubted that – but in the country here he could have
been cheated every day for sixteen years. He trusted entirely in
one man who acted as clerk, manager and foreman. Will Tyacke

decided what was to be spent and what was to be declared as profit. Will Tyacke decided what share individuals in the village could claim from the common fund. Will Tyacke decided on my share of the profits. And Will Tyacke was Acre born and bred and had no wish to see the Laceys taking a fortune from the village, or even claiming their own again.

My fingers touched the carved newel-post at the foot of the stairs and I heard a cool voice in my head which said, 'This is mine.'

It was mine. The newel-post, the shadowy sweet-smelling hall, the land outside stretching up to the slopes of the Downs and the Downs themselves stretching up to the horizon. It was mine and I had not come all this way home to learn to be a pretty parlour Miss in that sickly pink room. I had come here to claim my rights and to keep my land, and to carve out an inheritance of my own whatever it cost me, whatever it cost others.

I was not the milk-and-water pauper they thought me. I was a rogue's stepdaughter and a gypsy's foster child. We had been thieves and vagrants all our lives, for every day of our lives. My own horse I had won in a bet, the only money I had ever earned had been for trick riding and card sharping. I was not one of these soft Sussex people. I was not even like their paupers. I was no grateful village maid, I was a baby abandoned by its mother, raised by a gypsy, sold by a stepfather and wise in every gull and cheat that can be learned on the road. I would learn to read the estate books so that I would know how much this fancy profit-sharing scheme had cost, and who were the rogues who were cheating me. I would take my place in the Hall as a working squire, not as the idle milksop they hoped I would be. I had not come home to sit on a sofa and take tea. I had come through heartbreak and loneliness and despair for something more than that.

I walked lightly up the stairs and sat for a while on the window-seat in my bedroom looking out over the sunlit garden, watching the pale clouds gather away to my right and turn palest pink as the sun sank towards them. 'This is mine,' I said to myself, as cold as if it were mid-winter. 'This is mine.'

21

I woke at dawn, circus-hours, gypsy-hours: and I said into the grey pale light of the room, 'Dandy? are you awake?' and then I heard my voice groan as if I were mortally injured as I remembered that she would not answer me, that I would never hear her voice again.

The pain in my heart was so intense that I doubled up, lying in bed as if I had the hunger-cramps. 'Oh Dandy,' I said.

Saying her name made it worse, infinitely worse. I threw back the covers and got out of bed as if I were fleeing from my love for her, and from my loss. I had sworn I would not cry again as long as I lived, and the ache in my belly was too great for tears. My grief was like a sickly growth inside me. I believed that I could die of it.

I went to the window; it would be a fine day today. Before me was the prospect of another day of gentle lessons from Mr Fortescue, and a sedate ride with Will. Both of them watching me, both of them seeking to control me so that I would not threaten this cosy little life they had made here in this warm green hollow of the hills. Both of them wanting me to be the squire my mama had promised I should be – the one to hand back the land to the people. I grimaced like the ugly little vagrant I was. They would be lucky, they would be damnably lucky if I did not turn this place upside down in a year. You do not send a baby out into the world with a dying foster mother and a drunken stepfather and expect her to come home a benefactoress to the poor. I had seen greedy rich people and wondered at them. But I never questioned hunger.

Robert Gower was hungry for land and for wealth because he had felt the coldness of poverty. I was a friendless orphan with nothing left to me but my land. It was hardly likely I would give it away because the mother I had never known had once thought it a good idea.

It was early, perhaps about five of the clock. They kept Quality hours in this household, not even the servants rose till six. I went to the chest for my clothes and put on my old breeches and my shirt and swept my tangled red hair under Robert's dirty old cap. I took my boots in my hand, and in my stockinged feet I crept out of my room and down the stairs and across the floor to the front door. I had expected there to be a heavy bolt and chains but as on the day I arrived, the door handle yielded to my touch. They did not lock their doors on Wideacre. I shrugged; that was their business, not mine. But I thought of the rugs and the paintings on the walls and the silver on the sideboard and thought they should be grateful that some friends of Da had never got to hear of it.

Out on the terrace I paused and pulled on my boots. The air was as sweet as white wine, clear and clean as water. The sky was brightening fast, the sun was coming up. It was going to be a hot day. If I had been travelling today we would have started now, or even earlier, and gone as far as we could before noon. Then we would have found a shady atchin-tan to camp and hobbled the horses and cooked some food. Then she and I would have idled off into the woods, looking for a river to swim or paddle, looking for game or for fruit or for a pond to fish. Always restless, always idle, we would not get home until the sun started to cool and then we would cook and eat again, and maybe – if we had a fair to go to, or a meeting ahead of us – we would travel on again in the long cooling afternoon and evening until the sun had quite gone and the darkness was getting thicker.

But there was no travelling for me today. I had found the place I had been seeking all my life. I was at my home. My travelling days, when the road had been a grey ribbon unfolding before me, and there was always another fair ahead, another new horse to train, were ended before my girlhood was over. I had arrived at a place I could call my own, a place which would be mine in a way those two raggle-headed little girls had never owned anything. Odd, that morning, that it should have given me so little joy.

I went around the house towards the stables. The tack room was unlocked too and Sea's saddle and bridle were cleaned and hung up. I reached up and pulled down the saddle and held it before me, over my arm, and slung the bridle over my shoulder. I put my hand down to keep the bit still so that it did not chink and wake anyone. I could not have borne to speak civilly to anyone that morning.

That was odd, too. I don't think ever in my life before had I pined to be alone, and I had always slept four to a caravan, and sometimes five. But when you live close you learn to leave each other alone. In this great house with all these rooms we seemed to live in each other's pockets. Dining together, talking and talking and talking, and everyone always wanting to know if there was anything I wanted. If there was anything I wanted to have, if there was anything I wanted to do.

I walked through the rose garden, the buds of roses splitting pink as the petals warmed in the early sunshine, and I opened the gate at the end of the garden. Sea's head jerked up as he noticed me, and he trotted towards me, his ears forward. He dipped his proud lovely head for the reins as I passed them over his neck and stood rock-still as I adjusted his bridle and then put his saddle on. For old time's sake I could have vaulted on him, but the heaviness in my heart seemed to have got down to my boots, and I took him to the mounting block near the steps of the terrace as if I were an old woman; tired, and longing for my death.

Sea was as bright as the morning sky, his ears swivelling in all directions, his nostrils flared, snuffing in the scents of the morning as the sun burned off the dew. He had forgotten how to walk, his slowest pace was a bouncy stride as near to a trot as he thought I would allow. I held him to it while we were on the noisy stones in front of the house, but once we were on the tamped-down mud of the drive itself I let him break into a trot, and then into a fast edgy canter.

At the end of the drive I checked him. I did not want to go

into Acre. Working people rise early whatever their jobs, and I knew that farming people would wake with the light just as I did. I did not want them to see me, I was weary of being on show. And I was sick of being told things. Taught and cajoled and persuaded as if I were an infant in dame school. If one more person told me how well Wideacre was being run – as if I should be pleased that they were throwing my inheritance away every hour of the day – I should tell them what I truly thought of their sharing scheme nonsense. And I had pledged myself to hold my tongue until I really knew what this new world, this Quality world, was like.

I turned Sea instead towards the London road, the way we had come all those nights ago, fleeing from what now seemed like another world. The way we had come slowly, slowly, in the darkness up an unfamiliar road, drawn as if by a magnet to the only place in the world where we would be safe. Where they had prepared a homecoming for me – only by the time I got there, I was not the girl they had wanted. It struck me then, as Sea stepped lightly down the road, that I was as bitter a disappointment to them, too. They had been waiting all these years for a new squire set in the mould of my real mother: caring for the people, wanting to set them free from the burden of working all their lives for another man's fields. Instead they had found on their doorstep a hard-faced boyish vagrant who could not even stand the touch of a hand on her arm, and who had been taught to care for no one but herself.

I shrugged. I could not help their dreams. I had my own dream of Wide, and it had not been a place where I had stared suspiciously at gentlemen and wondered if they were cheating me. My dream of Wide had been a place where the land was smiling and where I recognized my home. We had all been foolish dreamers. We all deserved disappointment.

I clicked to Sea and he threw his head up and broke into his smooth easy canter. We soon came to the London road and I checked him, wondering whether to turn north towards London or south towards the sea. While I considered a man came into sight, leading a horse.

I looked at the horse first. It was a bay gelding, prime bred. Arab stock in it somewhere, I thought. A beautiful arched-necked wide-eyed proud animal. It was dead lame, the nearside foreleg was so tender the animal could hardly place it down; and I looked with surprise at the man who was leading it. A man who could choose and buy a near-perfect animal and then work it so ill that it could be injured so badly.

I caught my breath as soon as I looked at him. I had seen drawings of angels, drawings that people had done long ago in great churches in faraway countries, and he was as beautiful as any drawing I had ever seen. He was bareheaded and his hair was as curly as a statue of Cupid. He was watching the road beneath his well-shined riding boots and his perfect mouth was downturned in an endearing pout. The cast of his face, the bones, the nose, were drawn as fine as if he were a clean line on paper. But just now all the lines were downturned, the eyes with the curving line of the light brown brows, the mouth, the gaze which was down to the ground. He had not even heard Sea, he did not see me until he was nearly upon me.

'Morning, sir,' I said confidently. I was sure he would not have heard of me, he did not look like a young man who would be familiar with the likes of Will Tyacke. I had the old cap pulled low over my revealing mass of red hair, I had my coat jacket turned up. I knew I would pass as a lad and for some reason, I wanted to see his face upturned towards me as I sat on my horse, high above him.

He jumped at the sound of my voice, and his feet weaved in the white chalk dust. I guessed then that he had been drunk some time ago and was not yet sober. He had hazy blue eyes and I saw him screw them up as he tried to focus on me.

'Good morning,' he said blearily. 'Damme, I suppose it is morning?' He giggled slightly and his feet took two more unbidden converging steps. 'Listen here, fellow,' he said pleasantly. 'Where the devil am I? D'you know? Am I far from Havering Hall, eh?'

'I'm a stranger to these parts myself,' I said. 'This is the lane which leads to the village of Acre on the estate of Wideacre.

Havering Hall is somewhere near here, but I am not certain of its direction.'

He put a hand on his horse's neck to steady himself.

'This is Acre lane?' he said delightedly. 'By all that's wonderful – I believe I've won!'

His beaming smile was so delighted that I found I was smiling too.

'D'you know,' he said owlishly. 'I bet Tommy Harrap three hundred pounds that I could get home before he could get home. And he's not here now!'

'Is this his home?' I asked, bewildered.

'No!' the young man said impatiently. 'Petworth! Petworth. We were both in the Brighton Belle Tavern. He took the bet. Because he had further to go than I, I let him go first. But now I've won! Three hundred pounds!'

'How d'you know he isn't home?' I asked. I knew this was drunken folly of the first order, but I could not help smiling into that laughing careless face.

He looked suddenly serious.

'Parson!' he said. 'You're quite right, lad. That was part of the wager. I have to get the parson to witness what time it was when I got home. Good thinking, lad! Here's a shilling.'

He dived into the deep pocket of his jacket and fumbled around while I waited.

'Gone,' he said sepulchrally. 'Gone. *I* know I didn't spend it. *You* know I didn't spend it. But it's gone all the same.'

I nodded.

'I'll write you an IOU,' he said, suddenly brightening. 'I'll pay it when I get next quarter's allowance.' He paused. 'No I won't,' he corrected himself. 'I've had that and spent it already. I'll pay you out of the quarter after that.' He paused and leaned against his horse's high shoulder. 'It gets very confusing,' he said in bafflement. 'I think I'm into the twentieth century already.'

I laughed aloud at that, an irresistible giggle which made him look up at me, very ready to take offence.

'Sniggering, are you?' he demanded.

I shook my head, straight-faced.

'Because if you are, you can feel the flat of my sword,' he threatened. He fumbled among the wide skirts of his coat and failed to find his sword.

'In hock,' he said to me and nodded confidentially. 'Like everything else.'

'Who are you?' I asked, wondering if I should take him to Havering Hall or send him on his way.

He drew himself up to his slight height and made me a flourishing bow.

'I'm Peregrine Havering,' he said. 'Heir to the Havering estate and great name. I'm Lord Peregrine Havering if you really want to know. Three sheets to the wind, and not a feather to fly with.'

'Shall I escort you home, my lord?' I asked politely, a half-smile on my face.

He looked up at me and something in the childlike blue eyes made me happy to be of service to him, drunkard and wastrel though he might well be.

'I should like to buy your horse,' he said with immense dignity. 'Or at any rate, I shall swop you for it. You may have mine. I will have yours.'

I did not even glance at the bay.

'No, my lord,' I said politely. 'I am accustomed to this horse and I would do badly with any other. But if you would deign to come up behind me, we can ride to Havering Hall and lead your horse.'

'Right,' he said with the sudden decisiveness of the very drunk. 'Right you are, young lad.'

He stopped then and looked up at me. 'Who are you anyway?' he asked. 'You're not one of our people are you? One of our stable lads or something?'

'No my lord,' I said. 'I'm from Wideacre. I am new there.'

He nodded, well satisfied with my half-truth; and I let it go at that. He was too drunk to understand anything but the most simple of explanations, and anyway, I wanted to take him home. I was sure that he was quite incapable of finding his way without me. I knew that he had no money, but if he carried on roaming around the highways in this state someone would rob him of his fine linen and lace. For some reason, which I did not pause to consider, I did not mind him riding Sea behind me with his hands on my waist. His touch did not make me shrink away. He mounted behind me gracefully and his hands on my waist were warm and steady. Sea did not mind the extra load but stepped out in an extended walk. The fine bay hunter limped alongside.

'I am not sure of the direction, my lord,' I said.

'I'll tell you,' he said confidently. Then the next minute I felt the weight of his head as he slumped forwards and leaned against me. Fast asleep.

Havering Hall has two entrances, though I did not know it then. The main one is on the London road which Lord Peregrine had already trotted blithely past; but there is another way, a little bridleway which leads to the hall off the Acre lane. I should have missed it, and ended up taking Lord Peregrine to breakfast at Wideacre if I had not met Will Tyacke riding towards us, going to Midhurst to see if he could beg or borrow a spare harrow. He stared in surprise when he saw the double load on Sea, and then recognized me with Lord Peregrine at my back.

'Sarah!' he said. 'What are you doing here? And with Lord Peregrine too!'

I shot him a level look. 'He's drunk,' I said briefly. 'He'd never get home on his own. What would you have had me do? Leave him where he dropped in the road?'

Will hesitated. 'As you wish, Sarah,' he said politely. It was obvious that he thought that *would* have been a reasonable, even a desirable thing to do. 'Where are you taking him?'

'To Havering Hall,' I said. 'But he went off before he could tell me the way. Can I find it alone, is it near here?'

Will nodded, stiff with disapproval. 'It's a track which runs off to your left, just before the ford,' he said. 'If you follow the track you will come out at the hall. His mother, the Dowager Lady Clara, is at home. But they keep town hours there, Sarah. They'll all be still asleep. The only people awake will be servants.'

'They'll do,' I said. 'They can put him to bed and stable his horse. Have you seen how lame it is?'

'I saw at once,' Will said. 'Looks as if it lost a shoe and he rode it like that for miles. It's to be hoped the sole of the hoof isn't damaged. Can that grey of yours carry the weight of two?' Will asked. 'I can take him up behind me if you wish me to take him home.'

I was about to answer when the words stuck in my throat as I remembered riding home from the sea with her up before me and her hair blowing in my face as we cantered on the soft grass at the verges of the road. I could remember the smell of her, and the taste of salt on her hair, and the warm afternoon breeze blowing in my face. When Sea had last ridden with two on his back.

Instinctively I tightened his grip around my waist, as if I were holding her safely on behind me. 'The horse can manage two, he's done it before,' I said gruffly, and I touched his sides to make him start.

'I'll come to Wideacre Hall later, when I've run this errand,' Will called after me as I rode away. 'I'll ride with you this afternoon.'

I nodded. I did not want to speak. The thought of that afternoon had set the pain working again in my belly as if I had swallowed some burning poison. Without thinking I leaned back a little for the comfort of Lord Peregrine's nodding head on my shoulder, as if he could comfort me with his drunken feckless warmth.

Will was right, Havering Hall was easily found. The track to it was more overgrown than the drive to Wideacre, few people used it. Carriage folk took the main drive off the London road, only logging carts and poachers came this way. The track was deeply rutted and I took Sea slowly and steadily. The bay alongside us stumbled once or twice, bone weary. Lord Peregrine was foolish to neglect such a good horse, I thought. I shrugged. I had known minor gentry at fairs and shows. They seldom cared for their possessions, even for the things they loved. This dazzling idler was of better breeding than any I had ever seen. I did not doubt he would be even more careless.

A pheasant suddenly exploded out of the bushes on our right and Sea shied sideways in alarm. The bird shot away through the trees scolding, and I put a hand backwards to steady Lord Peregrine. He had moved with the horse as if he were born to the saddle, even in his sleep. I heard his lazy chuckle and I felt myself smile as if he had told me some jest.

'I was dreaming,' he said as delighted as a child. 'I was dreaming I was home in my bed. Where the devil are we?'

'I'm taking you home, sir,' I said politely. 'I think you dozed off.'

'Oh yes, I remember,' he said with quiet satisfaction. 'Good lad. I'll give you a shilling. That's two I owe you. Don't forget.'

I smiled. 'I won't,' I said.

'When we get there, if it's early morning . . .' he broke off. 'Is it early morning?' he asked.

'Yes,' I said. 'About six I should think.'

'Still?' he said interestedly. 'When we get there, you shall come round to the kitchen with me and we can have breakfast together. You'll like the kitchen at my house.' He paused. 'Because I am a lord,' he said confidently, 'I can eat anything I like!'

'Gracious,' I said.

'I haven't always been a lord,' he said thoughtfully. 'When Papa was alive and George was alive I was only a second son. That was a dead bore. But then George died of the typhus fever and Papa was drowned on his way to the Americas. So then there was just Mama and me and the girls. That made me a lord and since then I have always done whatever I wanted.'

I nodded, but said nothing.

'What about you?' he asked, demanding some information in return.

I shrugged. 'I think we are some sort of cousin,' I offered. 'I'm not a stable lad, I'm Sarah Lacey of Wideacre Hall. I've come home. I was just wearing these clothes because I haven't got my new ones yet.'

'You're a girl?' he asked.

I nodded. He leaned to one side and tapped me on the shoulder so I turned my head so that he could see my face.

'Stop,' he commanded. 'Get down.'

I shrugged and checked Sea and we both dismounted. He put his hand up to my hat and I let him take it and pull it from my head. My hair tumbled down in a shower of red and bronze and I laughed at the amazement on his face as he saw me properly for the first time.

'Then you can't come to the kitchen,' was all he said. 'You'll have to come into the parlour. And I thought we could have been friends.'

The disappointment on his face was so great that I could have laughed.

'I'll put my cap back on and come to the kitchen,' I offered. 'No one need ever know I'm Sarah. Or you could go into the larder and bring some food out. I am hungry.'

He brightened at once. 'I'll do that!' he said. 'You wait here. I won't be long. It won't take a moment. Go down that way –' he waved to where I could hear the sound of water, the river where Sea had stopped the first night, 'go and find us somewhere nice to sit and I'll bring back a picnic!'

He took the reins of his horse from me and set off down the path, the dappled bars of sunlight shifting over them as they walked, making his hair gleam like gold and then brass.

22

I found a patch of sunlight where the old beech leaves were warm and dry and smelled nutty. I took Sea to the river bank and he leaned over and drank some sweet water and then I hitched him to a nearby tree. I sat and watched the flow of the river over the sandy yellow stones, and once or twice I saw the mottled brown shadow of a trout moving slowly upstream.

Lord Peregrine was so long that I thought he had forgotten, or taken his horse into a stable and fallen asleep on the hay bale. But then I heard footsteps and a voice calling, 'Halloo! Halloo!' like an unseasonal huntsman and I jumped to my feet and called, 'Over here!'

He came crashing through woods, ducking beneath the low branches, carrying a large wickerwork picnic-box.

'Look what I've got!' he said proudly. 'It's later than we thought, about seven o'clock. Most of the kitchenmaids were up and they made me this. Our housekeeper was there as well and Mama asked to be wakened early this morning for she's going to Chichester today. They told Mama I had met you and you're to come and see her when we've had our breakfast and she's dressed.'

'I can't,' I said, suddenly fearful of another person who would watch me like Will and James Fortescue watched me. My sense of holiday from those two drained away from me at the thought of having to face Lord Peregrine's mother.

He grinned. 'Oh you'll be all right, don't worry,' he said bracingly. 'She's got her eye on you all right. You could walk in there stark naked and she would tell you how pretty you were looking. We've all been waiting to see what would happen to the estate. My papa had a mind to buy it years ago, but your guardians or whatever would never sell. As soon as I said in the kitchen that I had met you, old Mrs Bluett our housekeeper was up the front stairs like a whirlwind to tell Mama that the mystery heiress had come home.'

He lifted the lid of the picnic box and suddenly checked. 'I say, it isn't all a hum is it?' he asked. 'You weren't making a fool of me? You really are her?'

I nodded. 'I am,' I said. 'It's not a game I would play if I had a free choice, I am her.'

'That's all right then,' he said, uninterested in anything else. 'Here, have some chicken.'

He heaved the picnic basket between us and laid aside the napery and the silverware, the fine china with the crest on it and chose instead to eat with his fingers. I hesitated for a moment, unable to believe that Lord Peregrine himself could eat like a gypsy brat; and then weak with relief and hunger I tore a drumstick off the perfectly roasted chicken and settled down into the leaves to eat the first meal I had enjoyed since coming to Wideacre.

We were like children, Lord Peregrine and I in the equal uncritical sunshine. We were like children of the childhood I should have had. I was only sixteen, I guessed he was little older; and we sat in the warmth of the early day and ate greedily and messily until there was nothing left but chicken bones sucked clean and a handful of crumbs. I leaned over the stream and drank deeply of the sweet chalk-clean water until the bones of my face ached with its icy touch. I dipped my face right in and washed in the coldness. I came up with dripping bedraggled hair and Lord Peregrine carelessly tossed a fine linen napkin to me and I wiped myself dry.

'There should have been wine,' he said, lying on his back and looking up at the sky. In the tops of the trees a cuckoo was calling and wood-pigeons cooed. 'Or champagne would have been nice.' He put both hands behind his head, his profile a line as clear as a statue against the darkness of the wood behind him, the wind lifting his fair curls off his forehead. 'They keep trying to stop me drinking,' he said sulkily. 'They even suggested I had come home inebriated!'

'You were drunk as a lord,' I said plainly, watching the droop of his lazy eyelids.

They flashed open at that but the blue eyes were merry. 'I say, that's rather good!' he said with a chuckle. 'And yes, I was! But what else is a chap supposed to do? Anyone would think it was a household of Methodists the way my sisters go on. Mama is all right most of the time. But even she scolds a bit. And now I'm down from Oxford it'll be even worse.'

'Down?' I asked, not understanding him.

'Thrown out,' he explained. He grinned at me, his white teeth even and straight. 'I never did any work – not that they cared for that – but I kicked up a few larks as well. I think it was the hole in the dean's punt which finished me off!'

I stretched out beside him, lying on my belly so I could watch his quick, fluid face.

'Candlewax!' he said. 'I made a hole and then filled it with candlewax. It took ages to do, and a good deal of planning. It went perfectly as well! It didn't sink till he was well out in the river. It was a wonderful sight,' he sighed, a smile haunting his mouth. 'Everyone knew it was me, of course. He never could take a joke.'

'What will you do now then?' I asked.

Lord Peregrine frowned a little. 'Where are we?' he asked vaguely. 'Not July yet is it?'

'No,' I said. 'Nearly May.'

His face cleared at once. 'Oh well then,' he said. 'London for the end of the season if Mama will give me some money that will take me till June. Then I'll be here and Brighton for the summer, as well as going to some house parties. I go to Scotland for the shooting in August, every year, and then to Leicestershire for the fox-hunting. That sort of thing.'

I nodded. I had not known that the Quality had a seasonal movement as clear as that of travelling folk. It was only the respectable middling sort, from the yeoman farmers like Will Tyacke up to city folk like James Fortescue, who stayed in the same place and could tell you what they were doing year in, year out with no changes for any seasons.

'It sounds fun,' I said cautiously.

Lord Peregrine closed his smiling eyes. 'It is,' he said with deep satisfaction. 'If there were more money in my pockets I should think myself in heaven. And if I don't have to go back to university in September I shall be in heaven indeed.'

He stretched out and dozed and I rested on one elbow and watched his face. The trees sighed over our heads, the river babbled softly. We were so still that a kingfisher came out of its hole a little further upstream and darted away, a fat little dart of turquoise, past us. Then he stirred and sat up and yawned.

'Come and meet my mama then,' he said. He got to his feet and put a hand out to me and pulled me up. I went unwillingly and unhitched Sea.

'I had better go home and change and come back in my riding habit,' I said. 'And I should tell Mr Fortescue where I am.'

Lord Peregrine laughed. 'Don't you dare!' he said. 'She's delighted to catch you before anyone has a chance to warn you off. She and Mr Fortescue have been daggers drawn for years. She doesn't like the way he runs Acre, she thinks he keeps wages up and wheat prices down. She'll love you just as you are, and if it upsets Mr Fortescue – all the better!'

I led Sea out through the wood and Lord Peregrine came behind swinging the basket.

'Does she really dislike him, Lord Peregrine?' I asked. A seed of an idea was in my mind. If Lady Havering knew anything about wages and wheat prices she might be the very person I needed to give me an outsider's view of what was talking place on my land.

'Call me Perry,' he said negligently. 'They were on good terms at first, she approached him about buying the Wideacre estate. Papa was alive then and there was some money around, we would have mortgaged it of course, and rented it out. Probably built some houses on the farmland, or planted more wheat. Your Mr Fortescue read her a lecture on profiteering and refused outright to sell. They didn't like that much of course. But then when the whole estate went over to this Levellers' republic both Mama and Papa thought that Mr Fortescue was simply insane! Playing ducks and drakes with your money, too!'

I nodded. 'Did she ever tackle him with it?' I asked.

'Oh yes! He told her,' Perry's eyes sparkled. 'He told her that there were more important things than an extra percentage on investment! He told her that there were more important things in life than a quick return on capital!' He laughed aloud, a joyous innocent laugh. 'My papa had died by then and my mama would say that there was nothing more important than money. Especially if you don't have enough of it!'

I nodded and said nothing. I liked the sound of her ladyship more and more.

'Does she run this estate or do you?' I asked.

Lord Peregrine looked at me as if I had suggested an impossibility.

'Well I can't yet,' he said. 'Not while I'm at university. My mama does it all with her bailiff. When I'm married and take over I shall run it then, I suppose. Or I'll keep the bailiff on and he'll do it all.'

'So she does it now?' I confirmed.

'She does it,' he said. 'Until I marry or come of age.' He broke off and looked at the trees consideringly. 'It's a plaguey long time to wait,' he complained. 'I'm only seventeen now and I never get enough money. I shall owe the place a thousand times over by the time I get hold of the full income.'

The track we were following took us to the side of the house and Lord Peregrine led the way around the back of a tall-walled garden. 'Formal garden,' he said nodding at one section. 'Kitchen garden,' he said where the pale greying stone turned to soft red brick. He opened a little gateway into a cobbled stable yard and showed me the loose-box where I could leave Sea. I went in with him and took off his saddle and bridle. Lord Peregrine watched me over the half-door, not offering to help.

'Why are you dressed like that?' he asked, as if it had just occurred to him.

I glanced up. The sunlight behind him was glinting on his fair hair so that it gave him a halo around his perfect face. The world of the show and the travelling life and the noise and the hardship was unspeakably distant.

'I was working before I came here,' I said briefly. 'These were my working clothes. I haven't any new ones yet.'

He nodded and opened the stable door. He leaned towards me confidentially. I could smell the warm hint of brandy on his breath, he had taken a drink in the house while they were packing the picnic.

'It's awfully improper,' he said owlishly. 'Thought you should know. I don't mind. Mama won't mind, because it's you. But there's no point in setting other people's backs up for nothing. Much the best thing to wear girls' clothes.'

I nodded, 'I will,' I said as serious as he.

'Now,' he said. 'Mama.'

He took me in through the stable door across a marble floor patterned with black and white tiles where my boots sounded common and loud and where Lord Peregrine's footsteps weaved noticeably from the direct path. He led me up a shallow graceful flight of stone steps. I had a confused impression of another floor and a huge arched window making the whole place coldly bright. Then up another flight of stairs, dark noisy wooden ones this time and along a gallery lined with pictures of forbidding ladies and gentlemen who looked down on Lord Peregrine as he tacked from side to side, narrowly missing the occasional armchair and table. Then we went along a carpeted corridor and he tapped on a large double door set in the middle of the wall.

'Enter,' said a voice, and Lord Peregrine made a funny face at me, and we went in.

The Dowager Lady Clara was sitting up in a massive four-poster bed, holding a delicate scarlet cup in one hand, swathed in impressive folds of pale blue silk. Her hair was hidden by a blue silken cap, very grand and high with many bows; her face was smooth and pink and smiling, her eyes were as sharp as gimlets.

'Here she is,' Lord Peregrine announced. His mother shot one cool look at him and Lord Peregrine swung into a deep bow. 'Mama, may I present Miss Sarah Lacey of Wideacre Hall? Miss Lacey this is my mama, the Dowager Lady Clara Havering.'

I made a little bow, as if I were in the ring. A curtsey did not suit breeches, and anyway I was too awkward to move.

Lady Havering reached out her hand, heavy with large-stoned rings.

'You may kiss me, my dear,' she said. Her voice was low-pitched and strong. 'I think I must be your aunt. Certainly your nearest relation. Welcome home at last.'

I stepped forward awkwardly and brushed my lips against her cheek. She smelled heavenly, of flowers. I had never smelled such perfume before. Her cheek was cool and dry under my reluctant lips and she let my hand go at once, before I had time to feel uncomfortable.

'Peregrine, you may go,' she said. 'Tell someone to bring a fresh pot of chocolate and two cups. You should go and bathe and change your linen. Miss Lacey will stay here with me, send someone over to Wideacre Hall to tell them where she is.' She turned her face to me. 'Will you keep us company for the day, Sarah?'

I flushed. 'I cannot,' I said stumbling. 'I thank you, I should like to, but I cannot. Mr Fortescue will expect me home and there are business affairs to attend to . . .'

'Well thank the Lord you are able to attend to them yourself at last!' she said waspishly. 'And thank the Lord there are any business affairs left on that estate!' She smiled at me again. 'Very well, not today. But within the week you must come to us for the day.' She gave a rich deep chuckle. 'I should think you would be glad to escape from that awful Bristol merchant, won't you, my dear?'

She turned to Lord Peregrine. 'Go then, dear,' she said sweetly. 'You may come back when you have changed.'

Lord Peregrine smiled at me and wavered out through the double door. I turned back to his mother with some trepidation. She was openly staring at me.

'Tell me then,' she said invitingly. 'Where in the world did you spring from? And where have you been all this while?'

I hesitated. Meridon of Gower's Equestrian Show was dead and gone. I would never bring her back.

'I was given away to gypsies,' I said evasively. 'I had to work for my living. I was travelling with them.'

She nodded. 'Poor?' she said. It was hardly a question.

'Very,' I replied.

She nodded. 'But now you are poor no longer,' she said. 'Now you are one of the Quality, and wealthy. How do you think you will like it?'

I looked away from her towards her bedroom window. The Hall faced west and I could see some of the Downs away to the left. 'I shall accustom myself,' I said steadily.

She laughed, a rich deep throaty chuckle at that. 'Any dependants?' she asked and at my shake of the head she pursued her theme: 'No cousins? Nor aunts? Foster brothers and sisters? No sweethearts? No friends? No young husband? No secret babies?'

'No one,' I said.

She looked at me narrowly, looking past my young face, past my old tired eyes, past my clothes, into my heart. 'Are you a virgin?' she asked.

I flushed scarlet. 'Yes,' I said awkwardly, and when she said nothing but merely raised her beautifully curved eyebrows in surprise, I said: 'I don't like being touched.'

She nodded as if she understood. 'And the people who brought you up?' she asked. 'Those that you have been living with, you've ditched them all?'

I met her bright look without wavering. 'All of them,' I said.

There was a tap on the door and a dark-gowned maid came in with a silver tray and a pot of chocolate. Lady Havering threw back the bedcovers and rose from her bed and swished over to take her seat at the window. She gestured me into the seat before her so that I faced her and the clear light.

'What will you do?' she asked. 'You're rather alone. Unless you have taken a fancy to the little Bristol trader.'

'I haven't,' I said. I felt a moment's discomfort at my disloyalty. But then I remembered the quiet house and the noise of my drinking soup and my heart hardened. 'I don't know what to do. Mr Fortescue talks of teachers of elocution and dancing, and tells me I should have a lady companion.' I grimaced. 'Then there's the land,' I said. 'I need to know what's being done on it and yet there is no one to ask but Mr Fortescue and Will Tyacke.'

Lady Havering poured the chocolate and then sat back and looked at me again. 'Do you disapprove of his guardianship of your land?' she asked, her voice very neutral.

'Yes I do,' I said firmly. 'It is being run for the gain of the working people, that means the Hall makes a loss every time we sow and reap. The village is doing well out of it, but the estate gets a share of what it ought to have entire.'

Lady Havering nodded grimly. 'I've not seen the estate books,' she said. 'But I have eyes in my head and I have seen them undersell me in the Midhurst market for season after season until the price of food has been forced down and held down. It's revolutionary! It destroys the value of property.'

I nodded.

'How old are you?' she asked.

'Sixteen or thereabouts,' I said.

She nodded and tapped her teeth with her long fingernail. 'Five years until you can run the estate for yourself,' she said softly. 'A long time to have to endure Mr Fortescue's amateur farming.'

'A long time to live with a lady companion,' I said with feeling. 'Life with a lady companion in that house, with Mr Fortescue coming to stay.'

Lady Havering nodded, as if she had come to some decision. 'Not to be borne,' she said briskly. 'Drink your chocolate up, child, and I will come with you to see Mr Fortescue. I'll take you under my wing, you need not fear the lady companion. I've launched one daughter successfully into the world and I can certainly do it again with you. And you won't shock me. Your lady companion would probably pop off with spasms within a week!'

I obediently raised my cup but I did not drink, I looked at her over the rim.

'What do you mean, "take me under your wing"?' I asked.

She gave me one of her rare sweet smiles. 'I will look after you,' she said pleasantly. 'You can come and stay here and I will teach you the things you need to know to be a lady in society. When the Season starts again I will bring you out, introduce you to the people you need to know. I will choose your dresses for you and teach you how to dance, how to eat, how to behave. You are my cousin, you have no family but me. It is fitting.'

I did not stop to think that Lady Havering did not look like a woman who was burdened with a sense of duty. I put my cup down with a clatter.

'Would you do that for me?' I demanded. 'For me?'

'Yes,' she said. 'I will.'

I said nothing for a moment and she was silent too. Then I spoke, and the delight had gone from my voice.

'What for?' I said shrewdly. 'What d'you get out of this?'

She poured herself a fresh cup and she chuckled. 'Very good, Sarah,' she said. 'Yes, I do "get something out of this". Firstly, I irritate your precious Mr Fortescue which will be a great delight to me. Secondly, while I am chaperoning you I shall charge my dress bills to your estate which can very well afford them, whereas I cannot. Thirdly, by doing this I am making it more likely that you are not infected with Wideacre Jacobinism which is something I cannot afford to have on my doorstep. The more Mr Fortescue leaves you well alone, the sooner you can get the estate back into order.'

'You would teach me to read the accounts and understand what is going on?' I asked.

'Yes,' she said. 'You can hire my manager yourself and use him to check this madness on Wideacre. You can stop it going any further by refusing to hand over the land to the village as they want. And as soon as you are of age you can turn it into the profitable place it by rights should be.'

I spat in my palm and reached it out to her across the little table. 'Done,' I said.

The pleasant smile on her face never flickered. She spat in her own and shook hands. 'Done,' she repeated. Then her face changed and she turned my hand over, palm up, so that she could see the deep hard lines and the callouses and rope burns.

'Gracious me,' she said. 'Turning you into a young lady will be no sinecure. We will start with your hands! Whatever have you been doing to get them into this state? I doubt we'll ever get them soft.'

I looked at my palms for a moment. The bulge at the thumb and at the base of the fingers was as tough as old leather. I thought of the reins I had held and the ropes I had pulled and the trapeze bar.

'I was working,' I said, taciturn.

She nodded. 'You needn't tell me,' she said. 'As long as no one from your past comes pestering me, then it is none of my affair and it can stay that way. But tell me one thing: Is there anyone who would recognize you or follow you?'

'No,' I said. Robert Gower would let me go. Jack would run a mile rather than face me.

'Did you commit any crimes?' she asked bluntly.

I reviewed the poaching and the gambling, the horse-breaking and the little cheats. I looked up and her eyes were on me.

'Nothing spectacular,' I said.

She threw back her head and laughed at that and the bows on her cap bobbed.

'Very well,' she said. 'Nothing spectacular. I shall ask no more. Have you told Mr Fortescue all this?'

I shrugged. 'A little,' I said. 'Enough to prove to him who I am. Nothing more.'

She nodded as if she were pleased. 'Good,' she said. 'As your duenna I shall make rules for your behaviour. The first is that you will wear gloves all the time, and the other is even more important.'

I waited.

'You'll speak of your past to no one,' she said bluntly. 'What you have told me you will tell no one else. When you move in society we shall say merely that you were living quietly in the country with humble people before you were found by the trustees. Your background will be obscure but deeply respectable. Have you got that?'

I nodded. 'Obscure but deeply respectable,' I said turning the words over in my mouth. 'Yes, I've got that.'

She shot a sideways smile at me. 'Good,' she said.

There was a tap at the door and she turned her head and called: 'Enter!'

Lord Peregrine put his head tentatively around the door. 'It's me, Mama,' he said.

'Excellent, you can come in,' she said briskly.

Bathed and dressed he was radiantly beautiful, as lovely as a girl. He was wearing a dark blue riding coat with pale tight breeches and high patent-leather hessian boots. His blond hair was tightly curled and still wet from his bath. His eyes were a limpid blue and only the violet shadows under them showed that he had missed a night's sleep. His mother looked at him coolly.

'You'll do,' she said.

Lord Peregrine flashed an engaging smile at her. 'Why, thank you, Mama!' he said as if at a great compliment and then he stood quite still, as if he were awaiting orders.

He soon had them. He was to escort me back to Wideacre Hall and to take his mama's card to announce that she would visit Mr Fortescue that afternoon. He was to await a reply but to stay no longer than twenty minutes, and he was to drink nothing but tea or coffee.

'I don't know what sort of table you think he keeps there, Mama,' Lord Peregrine said pleasantly. 'But he doesn't look to me like the sort of chap who offers you champagne at ten in the morning.'

She smiled grimly. 'I don't doubt it,' she said. 'And then you'll come straight home.'

'Yes, Mama,' he said, his smile unblemished.

I took it that I was dismissed and I rose to leave. Lady Clara shot a quick measuring glance at me.

'Properly dressed, you would be beautiful,' she said. 'I'll have the Chichester dressmaker come out tomorrow. You will come to me then and be fitted for new clothes.'

I nodded. 'Thank you, Lady Clara,' I said politely.

She held out her hand to me and raised her cheek for a kiss and then I managed to get myself past the delicate little table and over the pale-coloured rugs without accident. I don't think I breathed easy until the door was shut behind us, and Lord Peregrine was leading the way back down the gallery.

'Taking you in hand, is she?' he asked.

'Aye,' I said.

He nodded, and paused at the top of the wooden staircase to look at me. 'Well that's good,' he said encouragingly. 'She'll get you a girl's dress. I was thinking about it while I was having my bath and I couldn't think where to get one. I'm glad about that.'

I chuckled. 'I'm glad too,' I said.

'And you'll be coming here again!' he said. 'That's grand. I was afraid it was going to be awfully slow until I went to London, but you and I can ride together and I can show you around.'

'Thank you,' I said.

'No trouble at all,' he said cordially and then he took my arm and we strolled across the marble hall as if we were young brothers, as if I had been born and bred in such a place, as if we were best friends.

23

Peregrine escorted me home riding a showy hunter from his mama's stables. Mr Fortescue came out on the terrace when he saw us riding up the drive and I saw by his face that he was not pleased to see me with Perry.

He invited him inside and offered him a dish of tea. Perry rolled his eyes at me and graciously accepted. He sat in the parlour with one eye on the clock, delivered his mama's message – word-perfect – and then left as the clock ticked precisely to the twenty minutes.

Mr Fortescue looked gravely at me.

'You have attracted the attention of Lady Clara,' he said. 'She isn't the woman I would have chosen to be your adviser.'

I looked back at him, my face as insolent as when I used to face my da.

'I daresay,' I said. 'But then you wanted me locked up here with some country widow for five years.'

James half gasped and shook his head. He strode over to the window and jerked back the curtain to look out. I wondered why he did not yell at me, then I remembered Quality manners. He was waiting until he could speak to me civilly.

I thought him a fool.

'You are trying to misunderstand me,' he said in a soft voice when he turned back to the room again. 'I do not want to lock you up here, I do not want to dictate how you should live. You may have the friends you please. But I would not be doing my duty if I did not tell you that Lady Clara has a reputation in the wider world for being a spendthrift, a gambler and a woman of the world. Her son, Lord Perry, is still at university but even so he has the reputation of gambling and heavy drinking.'

I looked at James and my face was hard. 'You are saying they are not well-behaved people,' I said blankly.

James nodded. 'I am sorry to speak ill of them and I would not gossip. But you do not know the world they move in and I have to tell you they are not suitable company for a young lady.'

I smiled. 'Then they'll do well for me,' I said. 'There's a lot I've not told you, Mr Fortescue, for I see no need for you to know. But hear now that my father was a drunkard and a gambler, that I made my living by horse-breaking and bad trading and by stacking the card decks for him. I am not the young lady you want me to be, and I'll never learn to be. I'm too old and too wild and too hard to be made into that mould now. The Haverings will do well enough for me.'

He was about to answer when Becky tapped at the door and asked if I was riding with Will Tyacke, for he was waiting for me in the yard.

I nodded at James and it was me who ended the little scrap this time. I went out into the yard feeling elated with my victory. I had gone some way to even a score that was running between us; between him who was trying to make me the child I should have been if he had found me and brought me here in time – and the real hard-hearted vagrant I was.

Will was in the yard, high on his horse. He smiled to see me.

'You got Lord Perry home safe then, I see,' he said.

'Aye,' I said. I didn't choose to tell him any more.

'He's a pleasant enough youngster,' Will said, invitingly.

'Aye,' I said. I swung up into the saddle, and bent my head to tighten the girth.

The horses moved off, Will was waiting for me to say more.

'Bit wild,' he offered.

'Aye,' I said. I had the girth to my liking and I leaned forward and flicked Sea's mane all over to the right side of his neck.

'Still, there's many a young woman who finds him handsome,' Will said judicially.

'Aye,' I assented.

'Some of the lasses don't see him drunk, don't see that he's a lad who cares for no one but himself,' Will said pompously.

I nodded.

'Then they think he's a fine young gentleman, they're mad for a smile from him.'

'Oh aye,' I said by way of variation.

Will surrendered. 'Do *you* like him, Sarah?' he asked.

I checked Sea and looked straight at him. His face was serious, I knew that this question mattered very much to him. He wanted an honest answer.

'Nowt to do with you,' I said blankly and shut my mouth on my silence.

We rode without speaking down the drive to the lane, and then turned left to the village. I was looking around me as we went, at the greening hedge on either side of the lane and the rustle where birds were feeding their young in hidden nests. Will was scowling at the road between his horse's ears.

'I thought I'd take you to see the village schoolmaster today,' he said as we came within sight of the first cottages. 'He was away the other day when we were riding through. We're rather proud of our school.'

He led the way down the village street. The cobbler was at his last again in the little window. He waved at me and I waved back. The carter shouted 'G'day' from his wagon where he was hammering a loose board. I smiled my bright meaningless show smile and he beamed back at me – glad of false coin.

Will rode past the church and past the track up to the Downs to a long square barn which stood parallel with the lane. From inside I could hear the hum of children chanting a song or a poem or some rhyme.

Will whistled, a long sharp sound and after a few minutes the door at the side opened and a young man came out, blinking in the bright sunlight after the shade of the classroom.

He was dressed very oddly! He was all in green. Baggy green breeches tucked into sound leather boots, and a baggy green jerkin with a wide leather belt. His straight black hair was cropped short and parted in the middle in a way which made his face look broad and strong and ugly but somehow nice at the same time.

'This is Michael Fry,' Will said. 'Michael, this is Sarah Lacey.'

'Hello, sister,' the man said. 'I do not call you by any title because I call no one by any title. I believe that we were all created equal and I show the same respect to you as I do to anyone else. You may call me Michael or you may call me brother.'

Sixteen years on the road had prepared me for all sorts of people. I had met men like Michael before.

'Hello Michael,' I said. 'Are you the teacher here?'

He smiled and his dark face suddenly lightened. 'I am the teacher of the young citizens,' he said. 'And in the evenings I read and talk with their parents. We study together to prepare ourselves for our work here, and our plans to expand this community so that it is an example for the rest of the country and a mission to them!'

'Oh,' I said.

'Michael came to us three years ago from a community in Wales,' Will said. There was laughter in the back of his voice, but it was not directed at Michael. 'He has served the corporation very greatly in his advice to us, and by working with the children.'

Michael smiled at Will. 'They are the future,' he said. 'They must be prepared for it.'

Will nodded. 'This was set up as a school by your mother's mother,' he said. 'When they started setting the place to rights and handing over to the workers. Before that it was a tithe barn.' He looked at the height and length of it. 'It makes you realize how costly are the benefits of a spiritual life,' he said wryly.

'I don't understand,' I said.

Michael flashed a smile up at me. 'This was a barn where they stored the share of the crop they had to give to the church and to the vicar,' he said. 'We still have a vicar but he is supported by a small fee from the estate. We do not allow him to take his share of wealth when he has neither ploughed nor sown.'

I nodded. 'He'll like that,' I said.

Michael choked on a little crow of laughter and Will grinned at me.

'Yes,' he said. 'He does.'

'Anyway, now it is a school in this end of it, and the other half is lodging for Michael and for the children whose parents are dead or run away. We have three at the moment.'

I nodded. I knew enough about village life to know this was unheard of. Orphans and pauper children should be taken to the local poorhouse where they dragged out a miserable childhood and were sold to employers as soon as possible. Rea and Katie had agreed that the poorhouse was worse than anything. 'They hit me all the time,' Rea had once told me, surprised at violence which was not done in anger but as routine. 'Every morning before breakfast. For being a Rom.'

'And in the middle section,' Will went on, 'is where the old people work who are no longer fit for outside work. They spin together, they mind the babbies when the mothers are away in the fields, they do some carving, they make up herbs. And we pay them a little for their work and sell the goods for the Wideacre corporation.'

An idea struck him. 'You were brought up gypsy, weren't you, Sarah? Could you show them how to carve those wooden flowers and dye them the pretty colours? We could sell them at Midhurst fair.'

I chuckled. 'The only skills I learned were thieving and gambling,' I said. 'You don't want me teaching a load of old women how to sharpen cards.'

Will laughed as well. 'Nay,' he said. 'I don't want you sharing those skills.'

'And here,' Michael said, gesturing to the open doorway, 'this is my model school. When I came here there was a dame-school, it taught the children to be servants, to be farm-hands. Only a few learned to read, hardly any to write. They taught the girls to be house-servants and the boys to be ploughboys.

'I changed that!' he exclaimed. 'They learn the same lessons with me: boys and girls. I will not have them taught differently. They all know how to steer a plough, they all know how to shoe a horse, they all know how to cook a meal for a family of four. Everyone should know these things and then the stamp of servitude and the idleness of the rich would be at an end!'

'Oh,' I said again.

Will was openly smiling at my bemused face.

'But I also teach them skills which they would learn nowhere else,' Michael said. 'Here they learn to read, so that all the knowledge of the world is open to them. They learn to write, so that they can speak with one another even when they are apart. And I teach them the study of geography so they know where they are, and history, so they understand how it is that they are poor but the victors of the struggle are rich. And I teach them French so that they can talk with their brothers and sisters in the glorious republic of France.'

'Oh,' I said again. I closed my mouth because my jaw was gaping.

Will laughed aloud. 'You will frighten Sarah with your Jacobinism,' he said cheerfully. 'She will think you want to cut off her head at least.'

Michael looked quickly upwards, and smiled. He had an endearing crooked smile, one of his front teeth was quite gone. I saw now that he was younger than I had thought. And his face was not ugly at all but somehow crumpled. His clothes were not as odd as they had first appeared. I had thought he was in costume, but I now understood that his clothes must mean something. That everything must mean something.

'I do not want to guillotine my sister,' he said simply. 'How could I? She has been a poor girl and lived a simple life as we do. I am glad to welcome you to your home, sister. I hope you will find much worthy labour to undertake here.'

My mouth twisted a little wryly at the thought of my 'simple life' which had been all deceit and costume and magic and cheating; and as for worthy labour – I did not think I had done a day of what this man would consider worthy, or even honest, labour since I was born. But I did not want to explain this to him.

'You cannot be glad I have come home,' I said baldly.

He smiled at me again, that sweet smile which had so much confidence in it.

'Of course,' he said. 'There would have been a squire come to this village sooner or later, I am very glad it is you. You have lived among poor good people, you will have seen their sufferings. You will help us here to lead a better life. I do welcome you, sister.'

I stared at him suspiciously. Either he was an utter rogue or else a simpleton. It was not possible that he could be glad I had come home.

He turned to Will. 'Would you like to come in, brother?' he asked. 'The young citizens would like to see their new sister.'

Will glanced at me. 'No,' he said, guessing rightly that I did not want to meet the children before I had time to think about their extraordinary teacher in this odd village. 'Sarah is looking around today. She needs to get her bearings before she meets any more of us. Take them her greetings.'

Michael nodded. 'Fraternal greetings,' he said.

Will chuckled. 'Aye,' he said. 'Take them her fraternal greetings and tell them she will see them later, tomorrow or the next day.'

Michael smiled at us both, and went back towards the school. We waited until we had seen the school door close and heard the rhythm of the rhyme break up into many high voices all asking questions, and then we turned our horses back towards the way we had come and past the church towards the Common.

'He's a great find,' Will said. 'You may think him odd at first but he has done more to help this village than anyone else. He has had experience of half a dozen corporations and communes and experimental farms and everything else. He was over in France in the early days of the republic. He is a member of every legal society you can think of – and a good deal more which would be called illegal, I imagine. We're lucky to have him with us. It took a deal of persuading.'

'You asked him here?' I asked in surprise. I had thought him an idiot who had come here because he could not find work elsewhere.

'I nearly had to go on my knees, only that would have been old-fashioned servility,' Will said. 'He is a dedicated and brilliant teacher with a commitment to a new world. Even after all the work he has put in here I do not think we can be sure of keeping him for ever. There are other communities who would badly like him, and I think in his heart he would rather be in the Americas than anywhere else. This country offers nothing for a man of his talents, they persecute him when they should see how urgently he is trying to make the lives of working people better.'

'Is he safe?' I asked. I had a dim awareness of people in France and a king toppled from his throne and a riot.

Will smiled. 'He is a man of peace,' he said. 'I never met his like. He will not even eat meat because an animal will have met its death for his pleasure. When I think of him, and I think of the vicar!' He broke off and sighed.

'Now!' he said. 'I'll guarantee to win a race against that racehorse of yours on this going!'

I looked down at the path under the horses' hooves. It was deep sand, dusty on top and thick. Very heavy going. A horse would have to have strong legs and sound wind to gallop far and fast on that.

'A wager?' I asked.

Will laughed. 'Aye,' he said. 'I bet you a side-saddle (for I've found it already but it'll have to be repaired for you) against,' he paused – 'now, what do I want?'

His eyes twinkled at me. I found I was smiling back.

'*I* don't know,' I said. 'I don't know what you want.'

His eyes were suddenly a little darker. 'If you were an ordinary girl,' he said, suddenly serious. 'I'd ride a race against you for a kiss. *That's* what I want from you!'

There was a silence between us for a moment which was no longer playful, and I was not smiling.

I was about to say: 'But I am not an ordinary girl ...' when Will interrupted me before I could speak.

'But since you're not an ordinary girl,' he said. 'I don't want a kiss from you at all. I'll ask instead that you let me read you a pamphlet on corporations and corporation farming.'

I choked on a laugh. Will was a rogue and a cheat – I suddenly thought how Dandy would have loved him and the familiar pain thudded into my belly.

'What's the matter?' he asked quickly as he saw my face fall. 'What's the matter, Sarah? It's only a jest.'

'It's not that,' I said. I struggled to find my show smile which can go on my face and hide everything, meaning nothing. 'It's nothing. A little pain in my belly.'

His face was very gentle. He went to put a hand out to me but then he checked himself as he remembered that I did not like to be touched.

'Well enough to ride?' he asked.

'Oh aye,' I said, reining Sea in. 'It'll pass. And the bet's on!'

He said, 'One two three and away!' and I gave Sea his head.

The race track was a wide white sand firebreak which wound for miles across the Common. I was in the lead as we broke out of the trees but the horses were neck and neck as we forged up towards a steady slope.

Sea was panting, he hated heavy going, but the cob had a steady rolling stride which ate up the ground. As the hill got steeper the cob went ahead by a nose, and then by a little more.

I raised myself up in the saddle and bawled at Sea, over the noise of the creaking leather and the thudding hooves and the flying sand, and he put his head down and went that extra bit faster. I guided him to the side of the path where the greening heather was a better foothold and his strong white legs reached forward, he put his heart into his speed and we forged ahead with a yell of triumph.

'You win!' Will shouted as the hill levelled out, and I pulled Sea up. He was panting, his flanks dark with sweat. 'You win!' Will said again. 'And I'll pay up, though riding on the edge of the firebreak is cheating.'

I beamed at him. 'I always cheat,' I said. 'Especially if the stakes are high.'

Will nodded. 'I should have known. What's your game, Sarah? The bones?'

I shook my head. 'Cards,' I said.

Will chuckled and we turned the horses for home. 'Where did you learn?' he asked, entertained.

The sun was warm on my back and I was happy to be out on

the land. A cuckoo was calling loudly and contentedly away over to our right and some early gorse was making the air smell sweet. Will pulled his cob alongside Sea and we went along companionably side by side and I told him about Da and his cheating at wayside inns. I told him how I was taught, when I was just a little child, to go around the back of the card players and to see what cards they had and to signal it to my da. I told him how Da would tell me to fetch a fresh deck of cards from the landlord and how I learned to stack them in the right order to suit Da, whoever had the deal.

'And did they never spot you?' Will asked, amazed.

I laughed at him for being a gull. 'Of course they did, sometimes!' I said. 'I was only a little girl, my hands weren't big enough to hide the stack. Mostly they didn't. She was there too . . .'

I broke off. I had been about to say that she was there too and she would sing, or do a little dance with her skirts held out, and that the men who were fools enough to play with Da were also fool enough to take their eyes off him when a woman, even a little girl, was up on a table where they could see up her skirt.

I lost the thread of what I was saying and my face went bitter.

'I can't remember what I was saying . . .' I said.

'Never mind,' Will said. 'Perhaps you'll tell me another time.'

'Perhaps,' I said. I knew I never would.

Will glanced at the sky. 'About noon,' he said. 'I have to go up to the Downs later to check on the sheep. The lambs are with the ewes – would you like to ride up with me? They're a pretty sight.'

I was about to say yes, but then I remembered Lady Clara.

'I cannot,' I said. 'Lady Clara is coming to see us this afternoon and I should change into the riding habit.'

Will nodded equably. 'I'll take you home then,' he said turning his horse's head. 'Can't keep the Quality waiting.'

'I'll ride alone,' I said. 'I know the way.'

Will paused, looked at me. 'Pain bad?' he asked, knowing with his quick cleverness that it had not passed as I said it would. He did not know, as I did, that this was a pain that would never pass. It was not a share of bad meat which was tearing my belly, it was the loss of her which hit me afresh, every time I laughed, every time I saw something which would have given her joy.

'No,' I said, denying his insight, and denying the comfort he might have given me. 'I've no pain. But I can ride home alone and you can go to your work.'

He nodded and held his horse still as I rode away. I felt his eyes on my back and I straightened in the saddle and even sang a little song which the wind would blow back to him and tell him that I was light-hearted. It was the song Robert used to order when he could get a fiddler to play the ponies in. It was a song from the show. My life was still all show.

I rode home slowly, watching the high green horizon of the Downs and the little shapes of white which were Will's flock of sheep moving slowly across it. The Downs were like a wall around this little village, they held it like you might cup your hand on something rare and strange like a butterfly or a tiny bright beetle.

I passed some people on the Common, gathering brushwood and furze. They waved as I went past and called: 'Good day, Sarah!' and I smiled my empty smile back at them, and called back: 'Good day,' and thought that I had come a damned long way still to have no handle to my name.

The path led me down to the back of the house and there was a little drystone wall which Sea popped over, hardly breaking his stride. A track led me to the back of the stables and I put him in his loose-box myself, he still did not like Sam. I was surprised that he let Will touch him.

I was rubbing him down, hissing at him between my teeth, and he was turning his head and nibbling the top of my curls as I worked when I heard the noise of wheels on the gravel of the drive and peeped over the door to see a carriage turning in the gate.

'Damme, it's her la'ship,' I said to Sea. 'I hoped to be in a dress before she came.'

I came out of the stables and watched the carriage draw up. I noticed the horses first. A pair of matching bays, very fine animals, well fed and with glossy coats. Their harness could have been better cleaned but the brass bits were shiny and bright. I nodded. I thought they had been made ready for a woman who liked the look of things to be right. The straps would wear out quicker for not being properly oiled but maybe she didn't care for that.

On the box was a driver in a bright ornate uniform, and behind the open carriage, looking like a pair of pouter pigeons, were a couple of footmen in the same livery. The carriage stopped at the terrace steps and they flung themselves off the box, opened the door – showing the linings of the carriage of pale blue silk – let down the steps and put out a respectful hand for Lady Clara.

She took her time. I came out into the yard to watch her. It was as good as a play. First she snapped her blue parasol shut, the footmen waiting like statues all the time. Then she loosened the veil which had gone over her hat to protect her from dust and pushed it back a little, then she stood up in the carriage, gave her skirts a little shake, and put out her hand to the footman who had been standing waiting, as if he could be there all day if she had a mind to it.

At her first gesture towards him he leaped closer to the carriage and took her gloved hand on his arm as if he were honoured at the touch. Lady Clara took two tiny steps down the steps of the carriage and then paused at the foot of the terrace.

Both footmen fell in behind her as she walked, slowly, slowly, like a mountebank preparing some trickery, up to the front door. Then she stood before the door in absolute stillness.

The footmen waited. I waited. Sam, who had come out from the tack room, waited beside me. Then she slightly nodded her head and one of the footmen stepped forward and hammered at the front door as if he were going to beat it down for her ladyship to step over the ruins.

It swung open at once and Mr Fortescue stepped out.

'Lady Clara!' he said pleasantly. 'What a time it took you to manage the steps. Don't tell me you are troubled with rheumatism? Come in out of the draught, do!'

I gave a muffled shriek and ducked back into the loose-box to yell with laughter against Sea's side. I thought James was no match for her ladyship, but as an opening attack it couldn't be faulted.

Sam looked at me dourly over the half-door as I snorted for breath.

'Quality,' he said, and spat on the cobbles of the yard.

I made haste then and got indoors and up the back stairs and into the purple riding habit, then I went half-way down the stairs, thinking to join them. The parlour door was shut. I hovered, uneasy, on the stairs and then I heard Lady Clara's tinkling empty laugh. I did not think I could interrupt them, and I didn't know if they wished me there. In the end I waited in my room until I should be sent for.

Becky came up after a while and asked would I go down and take a dish of tea with Lady Clara and James.

I glanced at myself in the mirror. I had spent some time tying my hair back. The purple ribbon was twisted and looked like string, but at least my hair was not tumbling around my shoulders. I straightened my back and went down the stairs.

Lady Clara was sitting at her ease in one of the parlour chairs with her tea cup and a little cake on the table beside her. She smiled at me as I came in, the smile of a woman who has everything she wants. I looked across at James. He looked irritable.

'Ah Sarah!' she said. 'Your guardian and I have been discussing your education and prospects. Come and give me a kiss.'

I went carefully over and pressed my warm cheek against her cool powdery one.

She gestured to the chair beside her.

'Your guardian fears I am about to kidnap you!' she said smiling. 'I have assured him we just want your company.'

James nodded. 'Miss Lacey has a lot to learn on her estate,' he said. 'She has been riding with her manager and she needs to learn to read the estate books.'

'Certainly, certainly!' Lady Clara said easily. 'But she also needs dresses, hats, gloves, a hairdresser, a number of teachers, all manner of things so that she can be a Miss Lacey of Wideacre!'

James stirred his tea and made a little clatter with the teaspoon in his cup. Becky passed me a cup and went out, closing the door softly behind her. I wondered if she was listening in the hall. I knew I would have.

'Wideacre is not an ordinary estate,' he said gently. 'And Miss Lacey is not an ordinary young lady. She needs to learn and approve the plans for the land before anything else. There will be plenty of time for fashionable trifles later on.'

Lady Clara raised her arched eyebrows in surprise. 'Plenty of time?' she exclaimed. 'But the child is sixteen! When do you propose she should be presented at Court?'

James blinked. 'Court?' he asked, and his surprise was real. 'What should she want to go to Court for?'

Lady Clara put her cup down and flirted her fan open. 'For her London season, of course,' she said reasonably. 'She must have a London Season, and who is to present her?'

James ran his hand through his hair. 'I had not thought of a Season,' he said. 'It is hardly something which matters. The most important thing is to teach Sarah how to go along in the country, to learn her way around, to understand what is being done here on her land, and to prepare her for when she is twenty-one and comes into her own fortune.'

Lady Clara laughed a delicious tinkling laugh.

'The most important thing!' she exclaimed. 'Mucking about on a little farm!' She broke off. 'Oh! forgive me! I did not mean to be rude! But who spends all their life in the country except working people? You would hardly condemn Sarah to being stuck down here with some dreary little companion, I daresay, when she could be living the life of a young lady in London.'

'It is hardly incarceration!' James said heatedly. 'She will come to love living here.'

'You don't live here,' I observed. 'You live in London!'

Lady Clara flirted her fan to hide her face for a second and behind the shelter of it shot me a wink.

James got to his feet and took a turn about the room. 'Sarah!' he appealed to me. 'Surely you don't want a life with the Quality in London. It's not what you were bred to, you cannot wish it?'

I looked at him thoughtfully. He had run my estate to favour the workers and to profit them. He had not claimed my rents as he should have done. He had not sought for me, and he had not found me. By the time I came here she was gone; and all the benefits of the life here could not help her.

'I want the best,' I said, and there was no softness in my voice at all. 'I have not travelled this far and worked this hard to live a life which is second-best. I want the best there is. If that is London then that is what I want.'

There was silence in the pink elegant parlour. James was looking at me as if I had taken some long-beloved dream away from him.

'I thought that this would be the best for you,' he said gently. 'It would have been your mother's first choice.'

Lady Clara snapped her fan shut with a little click, got to her feet and shook out her skirts.

'Well then,' she said. 'I must go, and we are agreed. Sarah may come and visit me while she continues learning her way around her estate, and I will advise her as to clothes and behaviour and how to go on. When you are ready to go back to London, Mr Fortescue, then Sarah can stay with me until the start of the Season. My lawyers will contact you with details of how her allowance should be paid.'

She moved towards the door but James Fortescue made no move to open it for her.

'Is this your wish, Sarah?' he asked me again.

I flared up. 'For God's sake!' I exclaimed. 'Haven't I just said so?'

Lady Clara tapped her fan sticks on her hand with a little click and I turned to her. 'Don't swear,' she said. 'Don't raise your voice. Don't answer a question with a question. Now try again.'

I looked at her, my eyes blazing with temper at her, and at James Fortescue and at this whole world of choices and decisions where there was nothing and no one I could trust.

Lady Clara looked back at me, her blue eyes limpid. She reminded me of Robert Gower, and how he trained me to his trade. Then I saw how she had got her way with James without raising her voice. You could use Quality manners as sharp and as hard as a honed knife blade. She raised her eyebrows at me, reminding me she was waiting.

I turned to James and I smiled at him with no warmth in my face. 'It is my wish to go to London for a Season,' I said. 'It is where I belong, I want to be there.'

Lady Clara put her hand out to me and I walked with her to the carriage. 'Well done,' she said, when we were out in the hall. 'You're a quick learner. I'll send Perry around with the carriage and he can take you for a drive this evening, then you can ride over to the Hall tomorrow and I will have a dressmaker from Chichester come to fit you. Perry will come and fetch you.' She paused. 'I think you and Perry will enjoy each other's company,' she said. Then she got into her carriage, spread her blue parasol, and was gone.

24

She was right. In the days that followed, Perry and I found an easy, undemanding friendship together, and the instant liking I had felt for him when he had come weaving down the road at his lame horse's head grew almost without my knowing. He was the easiest man or boy I had ever known. He was never sour, he was never impatient. I never saw him anything but smiling and happy.

His mother encouraged our friendship. When she wanted me to come to Havering Hall she sent Perry over to fetch me, rather than one of the footmen. When it grew late and I had to go home she would let me go on horseback if Perry was with me, she did not make me take a carriage. When she wanted to show me how to curtsey when a man bowed it was Perry who stood opposite me with his hand on his heart.

He was seldom drunk as I had seen him on that first day. He was rarely unsteady on his feet, and if he had taken too much port after we had left him for dinner he was clever at concealing the fact that the floor was wavering at every step. If his mother was in the room he would lean nonchalantly against a chair, or sit at a stool at my feet. Only if he had to rise and walk would his look of owlish concentration betray him.

I was not sure if she noticed. She was an inscrutable combination of manners and frankness. Sometimes Perry would say something which would amuse her and she would throw back her head and laugh. Other times her eyes, as blue as his but never as warm, would be veiled and she would look at us under her lashes as if she were measuring me. I did not think she missed much, and yet she seldom checked Perry, and I never heard her caution him against drinking.

But they were Quality – a Quality family as I had never seen before. They lived by different rules entirely, in a world apart. Lady Clara would laugh till she wept over her letters from London and read aloud titbits of scandal about the royal dukes and the society ladies. The Quality behaved in ways which we would never have dared, even on a showground. There was no one to gainsay them. There was no one to watch them, order them. There were no parish authorities, or justices, or vicars or beadles watching them. No wonder they were lovely and feckless and wicked. The whole world belonged to them.

But Lady Clara was no fool. I could not take her measure because she had lived a life I could not imagine. She was born the daughter of an Irish peer, married young and beautiful to Lord Havering who had been rich and gouty and cross. I had a few glimpses into that marriage from Perry who spoke of long lonely years for his ma in the country, while his lordship drank and gambled in town. She knew she'd been bought and she did her duty, stony faced. While he was alive she gave him the sons he needed. When he allowed her up to town she spent as much of his fortune as she could. I guessed she must have waited, waited and longed, for his death. When she would still be young, and still be lovely, and rich and free. But when he was gone it was not as she had thought. There was money, but less than she had hoped. It must have been bitter for her then, to have waited all those years and find the old lord had cheated her at the end.

But it took a lot to beat Lady Clara. She got in a bailiff and told him she wanted profits off the land. She rack-rented the tenants – they had to pay a fee to keep their leases, they had to pay a fee to marry. They even had to pay a fee if they died. She planted wheat everywhere and she kept them on barley bread. She brought in pauper labour – and she even paid them less than she should. She was a sharp, hard master on the land, and she had made it pay its way until she had the sort of money she wanted. It was not enough – a king's ransom would not have been enough for Lady Clara, she had a life of resentment to repay – but she had a fully-staffed Hall in the country, a beautiful London town house, a wardrobe full of dresses and a stable full of horses.

I watched her, and I learned from her. I did not like her, and no one could have loved her. But I understood her. I knew hunger and that hardness for myself. And I liked the thought of how she had taken an estate and made it pay.

I could not have chosen a more vivid contrast to my quiet dutiful guardian James Fortescue if I had ransacked the whole of England. We both knew it. I think it hurt him.

At the end of the second week when I had spent nearly every day at Havering Hall he asked me to wait a few moments before I went upstairs to bed. I went with him into the parlour and smoothed one of my new silk gowns over my knees.

'It is time I prepared to return to Bristol and to my business, Sarah,' he started cautiously. 'I have given you this time to become acquainted with the Haverings and to take their measure. Lady Havering is a beautiful woman and Lord Peregrine an attractive young man; whatever their faults they are engaging people. I wanted you to see them for a little time before I asked you to decide whether or no you wanted to have Lady Havering as your sponsor in society.'

'You don't like her,' I said bluntly.

He hesitated, then he smiled. 'It's better if I am frank,' he said. 'You are right, I do not like her. Her reputation was not good either as a wife or a widow. More importantly, I do not like how she farms. The tenants on her land are rack-rented down to the level of utter poverty and live in great hardship. She plants field after field of wheat and allows them no grazing for their animals, and nowhere to grow their own crops. Every time the price of bread goes up there are people who starve to death on that estate, die of hunger in ditches that run alongside wheatfield after wheatfield. Some people blame it on her bailiff, but she has told me herself that he obeys her orders. She may be charming in the parlour, Sarah, but if you were to see her as her servants or her workers see her she would not look so pretty.'

I nodded. 'What do you think she wants with me?' I asked.

Mr Fortescue shrugged. 'She has done well for gowns and hats while she has been dressing you,' he said. 'She enjoys moving in the best society and it would be no hardship for her to take you around with her next Season. I had thought that you may be a diversion for her – she must find it dull in the country.' He hesitated. 'She may well enjoy thinking that I do not like her influence.'

'But you can do nothing,' I confirmed bluntly.

He nodded. 'I can do nothing,' he said. 'I am a trustee of the estate only; you are not my ward. I can control your finances until you are of age or until you are married. I can advise you, but I may not order you.'

'You could refuse to let me have any money,' I pointed out to him.

James Fortescue smiled. 'I would not so coerce you,' he said gently. 'I may seem very dull compared with the Haverings but I am not a little shopman tyrant, Sarah. I loved your mother very much and for her sake I wish only for your happiness. If a society lady like Lady Clara pleases you, then I am glad you have her company. Certainly she can do a better job of introducing you into Quality society than anyone I would have known.'

I was suddenly impatient. 'I want the best!' I exclaimed. 'The lady you spoke of, the one who would have come and lived with me, she was second-rate! I knew it as soon as I heard of her! She would have taught me how to live here, quietly in the country, and be grateful for a card party in Chichester! I don't want that! There's no point in me coming all this way from the gypsy wagon to here, if at the end of it I don't get the best, the very best there is!'

James Fortescue looked steadily at me and his smile was very weary. 'And do you think Lady Clara is the best?' he asked. 'And Lord Peregrine?'

I hesitated. One part of my mind knew full well that Lady Clara was an adventuress as tough and as wily as myself. That she was as hard and sharp and cunning as any old huckster selling short measure. And her son was a lovely child, nothing but a weak and lovely child, with nothing to recommend him but blond curls and blue eyes and a nature sweetened with drink.

But they made me laugh, and they had made me welcome, and they had promised to help me win my fortune back from the villagers and the land-shearers of Wideacre.

'Yes I do,' I said lying stubbornly. Lying to James Fortescue's disappointed face. Lying to myself. 'I think they are the best of the Quality, and I want to be part of their world.'

He nodded. 'Very well then,' he said. 'I have written you and Lady Clara a note to tell you how much you can spend a quarter, and the bank you can draw on for funds, and my London and Bristol offices. I shall like to see you every month or so wherever you are, whether London or here. And if you should change your mind about the Haverings you must write to me at once and I shall come and take you away.'

I nodded, ignoring the feeling that I was making a rather serious mistake. 'All right,' I said tightly.

'If you should change your mind, Sarah,' he said kindly, 'if you should change your mind after a little of that life and want to come back to Wideacre, your home is always here for you, remember. We can find someone you would enjoy living with here. You do not have to go to the Haverings.'

I shook my head. 'I like them,' I said defiantly. 'I am not your sort of person, Mr Fortescue. You would not understand. Their life, their society life, will suit me very well.'

'I am sorry for it,' he said gently, then he gave a little bow. He did not offer to kiss my hand as he had done once before, and he left the room.

I sat in silence for a while. I supposed I should feel triumphant for I had taken on a powerful man, and the manager of my fortune, and come out best, come out with my own way. But it did not feel like a victory. It felt instead as if I had been offered a little gold but had preferred to take false coin. I felt around my neck where I still wore, out of habit, the string with the gold clasps. And I wondered what Celia would have made of me, a vagrant granddaughter. And what my long-dead mama Julia would think if she could see me rejecting the man she had loved and turning my back on the land she called home.

*

I was silent and blue-devilled for that night only. The very next day, Lady Clara swept down on to Wideacre Hall, exchanged documents and addresses with Mr Fortescue, ordered my bags packed, and took me away. I only saw James Fortescue once more, when he rode over to bid me farewell the day before he went back to Bristol. He did not even cross the threshold but held his horse and stood on the terrace till I went out to join him.

'Will Tyacke will call on you tomorrow and take you out riding,' he said as we stood on the terrace. 'It is my wish, Sarah, that you ride with him and learn all you can about the estate. I know your heart is set on London and your Season but Lady Clara herself will tell you that you can be in the best of society and still know what is grown in your fields.'

I nodded. 'I want to learn,' I said. I did not say, 'So when I am of age I can make changes,' but that thought hung in the air between us.

'Maybe when you have seen how things are run on Wideacre and how things are run here, you will come to see things my way,' Mr Fortescue said gently.

'Maybe,' I said.

He put out his hand and I held out mine, in the way I had been taught. I had already learned not to pull away. Lady Clara had scolded me for being missish about another person's touch, and had forced me to stand still while she circled me and patted my cheeks, my shoulders, my arms, and messed my hair. 'There!' she had said at the end of the circuit. 'I don't expect you to drape yourself over your friends but you are a girl, and girls must be available for petting.'

So it was no hardship to step close to Mr Fortescue and wait for his kiss on my forehead, or even on my hand. But he did neither. He shook hands with me as if I were a young gentleman, and his grip was very firm and friendly.

'You have my address,' he said turning his back and getting on his horse. 'And whatever you think of my trusteeship you should remember that I am your friend and I have tried to do the best I can, for both you and the land. If you are in any need at all you should send for me and I will come at once.'

I smiled wryly at that, thinking of the years when I had gone hungry. Now I was being offered help when I lived in a house with twenty servants and had four meals a day.

'I think I can care for myself,' I said.

He settled his reins and looked down at me. 'We differ on that, too,' he said gently. 'I think you have tried to care for yourself for too long. I think that you have tried so hard to care for yourself that you have shut up all your pain inside you, so that no one can ease it for you, or comfort you. I should dearly have loved to see you settled here where you were cared for, where you could have had something of the childhood you missed.'

He tipped his hat to me, and to Lady Clara who waved a lace-trimmed handkerchief to him from the parlour window, and then he clicked to his horse and rode away down the drive.

I watched him go, his square shoulders and slightly bowed head. I watched him go and knew that if my real mama Julia had been able to choose, he would have been her husband. If she had lived, he would have been my papa. I watched him ride away and leave me with the Haverings and I refused to hear what he said about shutting my pain inside myself. I would not acknowledge any loss. I would not feel the loss of him. I refused to feel bereft.

'Now,' Lady Clara said as she joined me on the terrace and we watched his departing back. 'Now, my girl, you are going to start work.'

I laughed at that, for I had known work that Lady Clara could never have dreamed of. But I laughed a good deal less once the work started.

Of course it was never hard, not like trapeze work or horse-training. But it was wearying in a way that those skills had not been. I found I was as tired in the evenings as if I had been working hard each day, and I could not think what ailed me. Lady Clara never stopped watching me, she had me walk across the room a dozen times, she had me sit in a chair and get up again, over and over. She ordered the carriage out into the yard, and a phaeton and a curricle, and sent me up and down the steps into each of them time after time, until I could engage not to tread on the hem of my gown, or bang my bonnet on the carriage roof.

At mealtimes we dined quite alone. Not even Perry ate with us; the servants laid the table and were then dismissed. Then patiently, like a warder with an idiot, she taught me how to hold my knife and, at the same time, to hold my fork, how to put them down on the plate between mouthfuls, how to drink from my glass only when my mouth was empty so there was no greasy stain left on the rim. How to talk while I ate, and how to cope with chicken wings and chop bones without seizing them up and gnawing and sucking at them. She taught me to wipe the tips of my fingers on my napkin, she taught me to balance it on my knees so that it did not slide to the floor. How much wine to drink, and when it was polite to refuse or polite to accept.

All the time, every minute of the day, she corrected my speech. By just raising one of her arched eyebrows she warned me that I was talking Rom, talking rough, or talking bawdy. Over and over again I would try to tell her something and she would make me try the phrase, like a horse at a difficult jump, until I could get it out with the right words and the right inflexion.

'Fortunately, some of the best ladies in society talk like farmhands,' she said acidly. 'And a good few can read and write no more than you. But still you will learn, Sarah. You are coming along fast.'

I could not help but respect her. She never so much as flickered one of her long-lashed eyes, whatever I did. Whatever the mistakes I made – and I was too ignorant even to know how much she must be offended – she never even looked surprised. One evening, after an especially hard day when she had been trying to teach me to pick flowers in the garden and arrange them in a glass, I had burst out:

'Lady Clara, this is hopeless. It is driving me half mad, and you must be fashed to death of me. I'll never learn it. I've started too late. You are trying to school me in tricks I should've learned when I was learning to walk. I am too old for them now.'

I'll go back to my own place and I'll get Mr Fortescue's old lady to live with me. I'll never learn all I ought, and you must have had a bellyful of teaching me.'

'Don't say bellyful,' she said instantly. 'Or fashed.' Then she paused. 'No, my dear,' she said. 'I am not weary of it, and I think you are learning well. I am not disposed to give it all up. I think you will be a credit to me, to all of us. I want us to go on. I am pleased with your progress.'

'But Lady Clara,' I said. 'The Season starts in autumn. I shall never be ready in time.'

She leaned back her head on the parlour chair. We were in the Blue Parlour and the colour of the upholstery matched her eyes as if it had been chosen with her colouring in mind. It probably had.

'You must leave that decision to me,' she said. 'I am your sponsor into this new world, you have to trust my judgement. I shall tell you what is best for you, and I shall tell you when you are ready.'

'And then what?' I asked baldly. 'When I am ready, when I am introduced into your society? What happens then? What do you think happens then?'

She raised her eyebrows, her blue eyes were very distant, very cold. 'Why, you amuse yourself,' she said. 'You are the heiress to a considerable estate. You are sponsored by a woman of immaculate credentials (that's me) and you will be squired by the best-looking young man in London, a peer of the realm himself (that, God help us, is Perry). If you want to be in Society, you will have reached the pinnacle of your ambitions.'

'And then what?' I pressed her.

She gave me a weary cold smile. 'Then you decide, my dear,' she said. 'Most young women marry the best offer, the highest bidder. Their parents judge for them, their elders advise. But you have no parents to judge for you, and the circles where I will take you would never receive Mr Fortescue. You are your own mistress. If you fall head over heels in love I suppose you could marry your choice, whether he is footman or groom. No one would stop you.'

I looked back at her, and my green eyes were as hard as her blue ones. 'You know as well as I do, that will not happen,' I said blankly. 'I am not the sort for that kind of love affair. I don't like it.'

'Then I suggest a marriage of convenience,' she said. 'Once you are married you can take control of your own estates and you need no longer apply to Mr Fortescue for your allowance. You can run your land as you wish and send these land-sharers and profit-stealers packing. You can make Wideacre a highly profitable place again and live as you please. If you choose a husband who will not trouble you, you can pay him an income to stay away from you and you can live the life you wish.'

I looked at her, and suddenly I understood. 'Peregrine,' I said flatly.

She did not even flinch. 'Peregrine if you wish,' she conceded. 'Or any other. The choice is yours, my dear. I should never coerce you.'

I nodded. I had been waiting a long time to discover what Lady Clara was after. I knew a pitch for a gull when I saw one, she had been patient with me, she had played me on a long line. But I understood now what she was after. And I admired her for not denying it.

'I am sorry,' I said flatly. 'I should never want to marry. Not Peregrine, not anyone. I am ready to go home at once. Mr Fortescue will arrange a companion for me. I am grateful to you for your kindness. But you need teach me no more.'

The languid movement of her fan waved me back into my chair.

'I said it should be as you wish,' she said gently. 'If you do not wish to marry Perry then you need not. I would have thought you would have liked to get your hands on your own land and on your own wealth; and if you do not marry Perry it will be a long and wearisome wait for you – five long years, Sarah! – but the choice is yours. Wideacre is yours, whatever happens. And I am happy to teach you and present you at Court – whatever happens.'

I dipped my head. Once again, as happened nearly every day,

she had shown me the elegance and generosity which came so easy to those that had never been hungry, who had never been short of space, who were never pressed for time. She had the generosity of a woman who had never known hunger. It came easily to her. I longed to learn that same casual, easy nonchalance.

'Thank you,' I said gruffly.

'Voice,' she said, without a change in her tone.

I lifted my head and spoke more clearly. 'Thank you,' I said.

She smiled at me, her eyes an impenetrable blue. 'Don't mention it,' she said charmingly.

25

I did not like Mr Fortescue being gone. I did not like it that Wideacre Hall was lived in only by Becky and Sam. I did not like it that there was no smoke coming out of the front chimneys when I rode along the Common behind the house and looked down on it. I did not like it that the front door was always shut.

It had been comforting, in some way, to know that though I had defied him and left him for the Haverings, James Fortescue was still there if I had wanted to go back. But now the furniture in the parlour and the dining rooms, and all the front part of the house was under dust sheets and James was gone.

It made me glad to see Will. Only he knew about Wideacre, only he loved the place as my mother had done. And he came to ride with me every day – as James had asked him to do – and he took me over every field, explaining what was being ploughed and planted and what was being left fallow.

Lady Clara raised no objection at all. 'Of course,' she said. 'You have to know every inch of it if you are ever to argue against your trustee and his manager. You will have some difficult battles ahead of you over the next five years. Your only chance of winning some of them is if you know the land as well as Will Tyacke.'

So, included in my schooling as a conventional young lady was an afternoon ride every day with Will. I never wore my breeches now. Instead I had a choice of two new riding habits – a pale green one to show off the colour of my eyes, and a slate-coloured grey one. I always waited to be called, as a young lady should, in the parlour. So it was he who waited in the stable yard while I pinned on my hat and took up my gloves and whip.

'No need to rush, Sarah,' Lady Clara said looking at me over the top of a journal she was reading. 'Move more slowly and you will move more smoothly.'

I nodded and went as smoothly as I could over to the mirror and adjusted my hat a careful half-inch.

'Better,' she said approvingly.

I looked at myself. I could not see a fraction of difference. But it was not my trade. She no doubt thought she saw an improvement.

'It's a hot day,' she said languidly. 'Do try and keep your face shaded, Sarah, you are already far too brown.'

'Yes, Lady Clara,' I said.

'When you come back from your ride you can offer Will Tyacke a glass of small beer in the kitchen,' she said.

I hesitated. 'I don't think he'd like that,' I said.

She raised her arched eyebrows. 'Why not?' she asked. 'Don't tell me he's a water drinker as well! That would be too too ridiculous!'

'No,' I said. 'I've seen him drink beer and wine. But he's a proud man. I don't think he'd like being offered beer in the kitchen when I go into the parlour.'

Lady Clara put the journal face down on the little table beside her and took up her fan. I knew her well enough now to note the little signs which showed that she was thinking carefully about what I was saying. I was on my guard at once.

'Would you regard him as someone suitable for my parlour?' she asked carefully.

'No,' I said. 'He does not even like the parlour at Wideacre. We always talked in the dining room.'

She nodded. 'Are you suitable for my parlour?' she asked.

I hesitated.

'Are you?' she asked me again.

'No,' I said blankly. 'I know you have taught me how to walk across the floor and how to sit on a chair without flinging myself into it. But in my heart I am still not Sarah Lacey a young lady. Inside me I am still . . .' I broke off. I had been about to say 'Meridon the bareback rider' but I never wanted that name spoken in this house. I never wanted Lady Clara to know how low my life had been before I found my way here.

She gave me a cool little smile. 'Sometimes in my heart I am a naughty little girl who would not wash her face until her father beat her, who liked to play with the peasant children outside the castle in Ireland,' she said. 'We are all other people in secret, Sarah. There is nothing unusual in that. But I learned to be a lady of the first Quality in London. You will learn that too. It is what you want, is it not?'

'Yes,' I said. It was. I wanted to leave the old life, and the old loves, far behind me. It was too great a pain in my heart even to think of them. I had to be far far away from them, and never go back again.

'Then you come into my parlour and Will does not,' she said. 'I instruct you to offer him a small beer in the kitchen at the end of your ride. It is correct to be thoughtful towards one's servants, Sarah. You should offer him a cool drink after he has escorted you in this heat.'

I nodded. 'Yes, Lady Clara,' I said, and then I left the room opening the door with my right hand and closing it carefully behind my back with my left.

Will was sitting, patient as a tree stump, in the afternoon sunlight in the stable yard. He was holding Sea's reins. Sea turned his head and whickered when he saw me, Will smiled too.

'Quite sure you're ready now?' he asked with his warm easy smile.

'Aye,' I said. 'I was delayed on my way out. I'm sorry I kept you.'

'I'm in no hurry,' he said pleasantly. 'Shall I get you up?'

There was no need. I could have vaulted up as easily as ever but there were two grooms and a stable lad who all appeared out of the shade to lift me up.

'He's fresh,' one of the older grooms warned me, pulling his forelock. 'Begging your pardon, Miss Lacey.'

'She'll handle him,' Will said with quiet confidence, and we turned away down the woodland track which led out to Wideacre land.

'Where today, Sarah? Up to the Downs to gallop the fidgets

out first? You've not seen the sheep for a few days, we're about
ready to start shearing.'

'Oh yes,' I said. 'And I'd like to come out when shearing
starts. Is it a lot of extra work?'

'We use travelling shearers, or extra men from Midhurst,'
Will said, his long-legged cob falling into stride beside Sea's
dancing steps. 'We usually get it over and done within a week.
We set up shearing pens beside the barns on the Downs, and
send the fleeces to London to be sold. This year we have a
contract with some woollen mills in Hampshire so we're selling
direct at an agreed price. Once the shearing is over there's a bit
of a party for the shepherds and their families and the shearers
in the barns.'

I nodded. We were trotting down the woodland track, the way
I had come the first time I had brought Perry to Havering Hall.
The sunlight was dappled on the track, the sound of the River
Fenny low and musical. The birds were singing in the upper
branches of the trees and the air smelled sweet and warm and
summery.

'Oh,' I said in longing. 'I'd love to sleep outdoors again.'

'Tired of Quality living already?' Will said with a wry little
smile. 'There's always a bed for you in Acre.'

'No,' I said. 'I don't go backwards. But this summer is so fine,
and I seem to spend all my days indoors.'

'Aye,' he said gently. 'You don't get out and about much, do
you? It'd irk me badly. We've not been bred to the indoors life,
you and me. I'd go half mad cooped up all day in a parlour like
that.'

'I am learning things,' I said defensively. 'Things I need to
know.'

Will nodded, tolerant. 'Good,' he said. 'If you are sure you
need them.'

'I do,' I said firmly, and he nodded and said no more.

We rode together as old friends, talking when we wanted,
silent most of the time. He rode well. His horse Beau could
never match the speed and stamina of Sea who was a full-bred
hunter. But he could give us a good race and if we gave them a

ten- or twenty-yard start we were sometimes hard-pressed to catch them before the winning post.

Will said little, but we never passed working people or a newly planted field without him ensuring that I knew exactly what they were doing. Whenever we passed anyone in the lane, or working on a hedgerow or digging a ditch, we would pull up and Will would introduce them by name, or remind me when I had met them before. Watching him with these people I could tell he was well liked and, despite his youth, respected. The older men deferred to his judgement and reported to him, the younger men were pleasant and easy with him. I guessed that they teased him about his rides with me; but when I was there they were respectful and easy. The young women stared at me, taking in every detail of my clothes and boots and gloves. I did not mind. I had stood in the centre of a show ring when coins and flowers were thrown in at my feet. I was hardly likely to blush because half a dozen girls could not take their eyes from the golden fringe on my jacket. I saw more than one of them glance at Will with an intimate special smile and I guessed he was popular with the young women too.

We passed two girls on the lane who called, 'Good day,' to me and flicked smiling eyes at Will.

'You're a favourite,' I said dryly.

'You know those two, remember?' he asked. 'They're the Smith girls. They live in the cottage opposite the forge. The Smith's daughters, they call him Littl'un.'

'Yes,' I said diverted. 'Why does everyone call him that? He's hardly little!'

Will smiled. 'His real name's Henry,' he said. 'His ma died while she was giving birth to him and he was real small and puny when he was a child, always ailing. No one thought he'd live, so no one took the trouble to give him a name of his own. They called him for his brother. Then, when Julia Lacey started setting the village to rights again, her Uncle John the doctor took special care of him and he grew strong. He survived but the nickname stuck.'

I nodded. Even in the names of people you could trace the

power that the owners of the land had over the people who worked it. There was the compliment that women of twenty and older were named Julia, after my mother, and there were several Richards in the village and a little crop of Johns. But the blacker side was the children who had not been named at all during the hungry years when my family had ruined the village with their greed. During those years children were given nicknames or the same names as their brothers and sisters. It was so unlikely that they would all survive. And the graveyard had many little mounds with blank headboards of wood, where there had been no money to have stone carved or, in the despair of hunger, nothing anyone wanted to say.

'Very few children die in Acre now,' Will said, accurately reading my thoughts. 'Very few. Of course they get ill, and of course there are accidents. But no one dies of hunger on your land, Sarah. The way we run the estate means that everyone has a share of the wealth, and that is enough to feed everyone.'

We turned the horses up the little lane which leads up to the top of the Downs. I could ride it now with confident familiarity.

'It will have to change,' I said evenly. 'When I am of age, I will change it.'

Will smiled at me, and reined back so that I could go ahead of him up the narrow track. 'Maybe you'll change first,' he said. 'Maybe you'll come to see that to live on a land where people are well fed and where they have responsibility for their own work is a greater pleasure than a little extra money. The land is farmed well, Sarah, don't forget that. But it is not farmed at the expense of the people who work it.'

'I've no time for passengers,' I said. I was glad Lady Clara could not hear my voice which was harsh and flat. 'In this new century it is a different world. There are great markets overseas, there are huge fortunes to be won or lost. Every farm in the country has to compete with every other one. If you give in to your workforce you are fighting with one hand tied behind your back.'

I drew up to let him come alongside and I saw the sudden heat of anger go across his face.

'I know you have been taught to speak how the landlords speak,' he said and his voice was very controlled. 'But all of you will have to learn that the wealth of a country is its people. You won't be able to produce much wealth with a half-starved workforce. You won't be able to make machines and tools with a workforce which cannot read or write. You will make a little profit for a short time by working everyone as hard as you can and paying them a little. But who will buy the goods if the working people have no money?'

'We'll sell abroad,' I said. We had reached the top of the Downs and I pointed to where the sea was a slab of clear blue, shading to violet at the horizon. 'We'll sell to native countries, all around the world.'

Will shook his head. 'You'll do the same things there as you do here,' he said. 'You and your new-found friends. You'll buy cheap and you'll sell dear. You'll overwork them and you'll underpay them. When they revolt you'll bring in the army and tell them it's for their own good. You'll refuse to educate them and then you'll say they can't be trusted because they're so ignorant. You'll keep them underfed and ignorant and dirty and then complain that they smell different or that they cannot talk properly. You'll do to them what you've done to working people in this country!'

He paused. I said nothing.

'It won't work,' he said quietly. 'You'll never be able to keep it up. The native countries will throw you out – oh yes, and your cheap whisky and bad cottons with you. The working people of this country will insist on their rights – a vote, a right to decide who governs them. Then it will be estates like Wideacre which will show people the way ahead. Places like this which have tried sharing the wealth.'

'It's my wealth,' I said stubbornly. 'It's not *the* wealth.'

'Your land?' he asked. I nodded.

'Your people?' he asked.

I hesitated, uncertain.

'Your skies? Your rain? Your birds? Your winds? Your sunshine?'

I turned my head away from him in sudden irritation.

'It doesn't work,' he said. 'Your idea of ownership makes no sense, Sarah. And you should know that. You have lived on the very edge of the society right on the borderlines of ownership. You know that out there the world is full of things which nobody owns.'

I shrugged. 'It's because I was out there that I'll call it my land,' I said sourly. 'You don't know because you've never been that poor. You've slept soft and ate well all your life, Will Tyacke. Don't tell me about hardship.'

He nodded at that. 'I forgot,' he said spitefully. 'We are all to be punished for your misfortune.'

Then he turned his horse and led the way across the top of the Downs in a day so sweet and sunny and fine that I was angry with myself for calling up the old feelings of being robbed and abused, even now; when I should be glad that I had won through.

He let it go, he was too kind to harangue me when I looked as I did then: hurt, and angry and confused. Instead he demanded an outrageous long start in a race, claiming, with no cause, that Beau was threatening to cast a shoe and would be slower. Instead he took off like a whirlwind and I had to bend low over Sea's neck and urge him on to his top gallop to catch Beau before he reached the thorn tree which acted as our winning post at the top of the Downs.

We reached there neck and neck and we pulled up with a shout – Sea just a nose ahead.

'I think he's getting faster!' I said, all breathless with my hair tumbling down and my hat askew.

'It's the practice he's getting,' he said, smiling at me. 'I never rode races before.'

'I wish you could have seen Snow,' I said, careless for a moment. 'I wish you could have seen Snow. He is an Arab stallion, an absolutely wonderful white colour and Robert can do anything with him. He can count, and choose coloured flags out of a jar. And he can rear and dance on his hind legs. Robert is teaching him to carry things in his mouth like a dog!'

'Robert?' Will said, his voice carefully neutral.

'A friend I once had,' I said flatly. Something in my voice told him I would say no more so he merely smiled.

'I wish I had seen him too,' he said. 'I love good horses. But I've never seen a grey to match this one. Where did you get him, Sarah? Did you have him from a foal?'

I hesitated then, wary. But the day was too warm, and the song of the larks was beguiling. Far below me I could see the little village of Acre as snug as a toy village on a green carpet. The patchwork of fields, green and yellow with their different crops told of the easy wealth of my estate. The thick clumps of darker green were the trees of the parkland around my home, my house, Wideacre.

I smiled. 'I won him!' I said, and as Will listened I told him how I had first seen Sea and how he had been called unridable. How I had persuaded my master to let me ride him (a horse-trader he was, I said), how he had started the book and made hundreds of guineas from the bet. Will laughed and laughed, a great openhearted bellow, at the thought of me hitching up my housemaid skirts and getting astride Sea. But he went quiet when I told him how Sea reared and plunged at the end and threw me down.

'You must have had many falls,' he said gently.

I nodded, smiling at the memory of that day in Salisbury, uncaring about past pains.

'Is that how you banged your face?' he asked. 'Falling off horses? Your nose is a little bit crooked.'

I stroked it, self-conscious. 'No,' I said. I was about to tell him of the fall from the trapeze but the thought of it called her, my sister, from the quiet silent place where I had buried her in my mind. I could feel my grief swelling up in my throat, as if I were about to choke on a sorrow too big to live inside my chest.

'No,' I said husky, and turned my face away so that he should not see that my mouth was turning downwards in an ugly grimace of pain, and my eyes were going red and hot. I dared not start crying. I knew that if I started I would never stop. A lifetime would not be long enough to have my cry out for the loss of her and the loneliness I was left with.

'No,' I said again.

'We'll go back over the Common,' he said suddenly, as if he had forgotten what we had been talking about. 'There's some land there which could take trees. I want you to tell me what you think about it. They're mining a lot of coal quite deep in Kent these days and there's a good market for small straight timber to prop up the ceilings of the galleries where they dig for coal. We could plant pine trees and they would be ready for cutting in as little as ten years' time.'

'Oh,' I said. My throat was still tight.

'And you can have a look at the north side of the Common and the Havering estate,' he went on. He was talking faster, louder than usual, giving me time to pack my heartbreak away again, where no one could see it. 'You've never been around that side, I don't think, unless you've been with Lord Peregrine. D'you ride much with him?'

'Hardly at all,' I said huskily, but I had myself back in hand.

Will glanced at me, gave me one of his fleeting sweet smiles. 'He'll be off to town soon, I daresay. Or wherever else they go in summer.'

'No,' I replied. 'He's staying with us for a while longer.'

We were riding side by side in an easy walk, eastwards along the crest of the Downs, following an old drovers' road which goes all the way into Kent. Will looked sideways at me, his brown eyes questioning.

'He's never stayed in the country so long before,' he said. 'Why's he stopping now?'

I gave him a clear look back. I would never trouble to mince words for Will Tyacke. 'He likes me,' I said blankly.

'His ma'd have something to say about that,' he said.

'She likes me,' I said with a little smile.

He saw my smile and scowled at me. 'Is that what you're after?' he asked. 'With all you could have? Is that what you want?'

I grinned at him, it was funny to see him so vexed. 'I'm not wedding,' I said. 'I'm not the type. I'll never marry, I don't burn for a husband, I never have.'

Will nodded, as if what I had said confirmed a thought of his. His satisfied expression rubbed me wrong. 'But if I were husband-hunting, I can't think of a better-looking man,' I said, my deceitful voice clear. 'He's as lovely as an angel, and never out of temper. He's fun to be with, he makes me laugh. And he's gentle with me, as sweet as a lover.'

Will lost the smile from his face as if I had slapped him. 'Don't bring him here as squire,' he warned me with sudden impatience. 'We'd none of us stand for Havering ways on this land.'

'Oh, leave be,' I said, suddenly irritable myself. 'I get sick of hearing what you will and won't have on Wideacre. I spoke so to vex you, I don't expect to hear threats for something that'll never happen.'

I dug my heel into Sea's side and let him have his head along the smooth track so that we raced ahead of Will and Beau and increased our lead until they were just a toy-sized horse and rider far away down a grassy track. I pulled up then and waited for him to come alongside me, my temper blown away with the gallop. And when he thundered up, Beau blowing hard, his grin was rueful. He leaned across and slapped me on the shoulder, like he would another lad to mend a quarrel.

'I'm done,' he said with his open, friendly grin. 'I know you don't want him. He sets my teeth on edge with his ways, but I'm glad he's good company for you. I'd begrudge you nothing, Sarah, you know that. I'm sorry I spoke hard to you.'

I smiled back, and then we rode together over the Common, and looked at the place where we might plant pine trees, and then checked the blossom in the apple orchard where the petals were falling like snow, before we rode side by side homeward.

That was the last cross word between us that afternoon, and it was a typical afternoon with laughter and temper. We never bored each other, we never rode in a sullen silence. We might ride quietly through fields, looking all around us, or through hushed woodlands, or stand motionless looking up at the sky where a rare buzzard circled; but we never stayed silent for lack of things to say.

We often flared up; Will had a knack of igniting my temper, and as I knew him better I grew more and more able to fire up at him and then make friends. He was like a traveller, a wagon dweller. You could flare up in utter and absolute anger and ten minutes later it was forgotten. There was nothing to remember. Everyone had said all they wanted to say, the scene was closed. Only in houses, where people have to keep their voices down and to keep smiles pinned on their faces did quarrels rumble on and on in sweet voices and range over every thing.

When we clattered in to the stable yard I remembered my instruction and turned to Will with a considering look on my face.

'Would you like a drink of ale, Will? It's a hot day,' I said.

He was about to accept but he checked and looked more closely at me. 'You have a voice,' he said pleasantly, 'and a look in your green eyes which always warns me when something comes from these new-found airs and graces of yours. I suppose if I say "yes" then you tell me I may go to the kitchen?'

I felt myself flush up.

'Gracious of you,' he said with irony. 'I'll go to the kitchen for a drink of small beer gladly. You'll come with me?'

I hesitated, and his face suddenly cleared and he smiled at me with all his heart in his eyes.

'Oh Sarah!' he said, and he jumped off his horse and came around to me and lifted me down from the side-saddle. 'Come and have an ale, Sarah!' he said his voice warm with the invitation. 'Come with me into the kitchen and have an ale and stop pretending to be what you're not.'

I let him hold me, his arms were warm and safe around me, and I suddenly wanted to go with him to the clean kitchen and sit at the scrubbed table and drink a great deep draught of cold ale and watch the cook peeling the vegetables for my dinner.

His hands on my waist were firm, and he kept one hand around my waist as we turned for the kitchen door. I did not pull away from his touch.

'Sarah!' the voice was Lady Clara's, she was standing on the end of the terrace which overlooks the stable yard. I flushed and pulled away from Will. I knew very well she had been watching me.

'Come in out of the sun, Sarah!' she said. Her voice was low but it carried clearly to me in the stable yard, the Quality voice which does not have to be raised to give orders and be obeyed. 'You will get as tanned as a field labourer standing there!'

I moved in unthinking obedience towards her, then I turned back to Will.

'I'm sorry,' I said. 'You can see I have to go, I'll ride with you tomorrow.'

His face was as black as thunder. He turned back to his horse and swung himself up high on his back.

'No,' he said curtly. 'Tomorrow I am busy. You may go up to the Downs barn on Thursday if you want to see some shearing. They will start at seven.'

'Will?' I called him, but he rode past me without another word. He went so close that Beau's flicking tail stung me in the face.

'Will?' I said again, hardly crediting that the warm smile had gone from his face as quickly as a summer storm blows up, just because I had turned to do Lady Clara's bidding.

He did not hear me or he chose not to hear me. He hunched low over Beau's neck and he set him to a canter as soon as he was past the terrace. He went past Lady Clara without a nod or salute. As soon as Beau's hooves touched the earth of the track towards Wideacre he gave him his head and they went as if all the fiends in hell were after them.

I turned slowly, and went up the terrace steps to Lady Clara. She smiled at me as if she had seen something which had amused her very much and then she drew me into the parlour where there was a jug of iced lemonade waiting with two chilled sugar-rimmed glasses.

26

I saw Will Tyacke hardly at all for the rest of the summer. He held to his promise to James to teach me about the land, but that was the last ride we took when he teased me and harangued me and quarrelled with me and let me ride away and then caught up with me so that we were the best of friends after all.

From that day onwards it was much more like work. He would make me known to the leaders of the hay-making gang or tell me the name of the shepherd and leave me with them, riding off as if always there was something more important to be done elsewhere. I thought the people changed towards me too. They no longer smiled slyly when they saw Will and me riding close. Somehow they knew we were no longer easy friends, and they were more businesslike with me. They would tell me what they were doing clear enough, well enough, but they did not smile and wave at me when I rode past a field.

I went down to the haymaking and watched them scything the crop under a pale warm sky, and tossing the sweet-smelling green grass to dry in the summer wind. The girls with the rakes smiled and called, 'Good day,' to Will with a note of affection, but to me they nodded and said nothing.

I knew what was happening and I did not blame Will for blabbing about our breach. I did not think he was the tattling sort and I did not think he would take every village slut into his confidence. But they knew that I was staying with the Haverings to learn to become a young lady. They knew that I was riding with Will to learn all I could about my land to strengthen my hand against them when the time came for me to make changes. They knew that although I had come home I was not at ease on the land, I was still rootless, hopeless in my heart. And so they wasted neither love nor words on me. They knew I did not belong. They knew I did not want to belong. I wanted to own the land. I did not care about loving it.

Every day that I rode with Will he became more like a clerk, or a bailiff or some middling sort of servant. He stopped calling me Sarah and speaking directly to me. Then one day he called me Miss Lacey and I knew myself to be set at a distance indeed. I could have summoned him back. I could have recalled the affection which had been growing between us. But . . . but I was damned if I would. When I saw his stiff back and his proudly held head trotting away from me I could have sworn and slung a flint under his horse's hooves for being a stubborn fool. But I was learning to be a lady; and ladies do not swear and throw things.

I thought he was foolish and proud and I decided to ignore him. So I made no effort either to challenge or reconcile with him. Instead I was as haughty and as ill-tempered as he through all the hot summer days when the birds called for their mates and the swallows dipped and dived in the lingering lonely twilights. When I was alone at the top of the Downs, with Sea cropping the grass around me, I knew that I was missing my friends – not just her, but James Fortescue whom I had sent away, Will whom I had put at a distance, and all the people of Acre who had welcomed me with smiles and bright curious faces, and who had then learned that I would not live at Wideacre Hall, that I would not stay with them, that I was hard set on changing things, on changing everything.

I knew myself then to be bereft, but I had been so lonely and so hungry for so long that I did not jump up on Sea and ride down to Acre to seek Will out and make things clear with him. Instead I hunched up my shoulders and hugged my knees and watched the sun set redly in the sky, and huddled my feelings of loneliness and sadness within me, as a familiar longing.

In Will's absence I rode with Perry, and sometimes Lady Clara took me around her own fields, or ordered her bailiff to drive out with me in her pale-blue lined-landau. He was a sharp hard-faced man; I could not like him. But I could recognize his ability to price a crop while it showed just inches above the soil, or to adjust a rent in his mind during the walk from the gate to the back door.

Will was right about the hardship on the Havering land. I saw it on every drive. Havering village was more like a campsite than a village. The houses were ready to tumble down and half were down already with their tenants sheltering in the lee of a wall with a half-thatched roof over their heads. The slops were thrown out in the village street, the stink under the hot summer sun was enough to turn your stomach. The people worked from dawn to dusk for wages which were as low as Lady Clara and Mr Briggs could keep them. More and more work was being done by the wretches brought in by a jolting wagon daily from Midhurst poorhouse. 'It's a service to the community to save them from idleness,' Mr Briggs explained to me, smiling.

They planned to clear the village of Havering altogether. Lady Clara was sick of the dirt of it and the continual complaints which not all of Mr Briggs's smiling threats could keep from her ears. The villagers who lived in the dirt and the squalor believed that if she really knew of their poverty she would pity them, she would do something.

'All I'm likely to do is to set the soldiers on them and burn them out,' she said grimly. 'It's disgusting how they live! They must lack all sense of shame!'

I said nothing. Will's angry denunciations of the Quality were echoing in my head: 'You leave them ignorant and then you complain they know nothing,' he had said. I kept my eyes blank and I said nothing when Lady Clara threatened to clear the village.

I had thought she was threatening idly something that would never take place. But one day I came down to the parlour in my riding habit pulling on my gloves and she looked at me very hard and bright, and said: 'Don't go to Havering village today, Sarah, it's being cleared.'

'Cleared?' I asked.

She nodded grimly. 'I've had enough of them,' she said. 'Their complaints, their needs, their dirt and their diseases. There's a case of the typhus fever been reported down there as well. I won't have sickly people on my land.'

'What will they do?' I asked.

She shrugged. She was wearing a peach silk morning gown and that elegant movement of her shoulders made the pattern of the gown shimmer.

'They'll go to the Midhurst poorhouse I suppose,' she said. 'Any of them who can claim rights in other parishes will go to where they can, if they have money for the fare. I don't care, it's none of my concern. I won't have them on my land any more.'

I hesitated. This blank ruthlessness was not new to me. I had been sold from a stepfather who despised me, to a master who loved me only when I earned him money. I saw no reason why I should worry over the fate of a dozen dirty villagers who were not even my tenants. And yet, in some part of my mind, I did worry. I did not feel comfortable to be sitting here in the sunny parlour looking at the sheen of Lady Clara's peach silk while three miles away there were people arguing with bailiffs and begging them not to evict. I knew what it was to have nothing. I knew what it was to be homeless. I wondered what the people would do, those with young children who would be separated from them in the poorhouse. Those young women with husbands who would lose their homes and have to sleep apart.

'I'll ride the other way,' I said uncertainly. 'Towards Wide-acre.'

She put both hands up and carefully smoothed her cheeks as if she would stroke away the faint fretwork of lines from under her eyes.

'Certainly my dear,' she said pleasantly. 'If you see any of the evicted tenants don't go too near. They may be carrying the fever and they will certainly be ill natured. They did have fair warning of my intentions, you know. Mr Briggs told them a day ago.'

I nodded, thinking that a day's warning was perhaps not enough if you had been born and bred in a cottage and lived all your life there.

'Perry can ride with you,' she said. 'Pull the bell.'

I did. At Havering we all did what Lady Clara wished. Within the hour Perry and I were obediently riding together up towards the Common at the back of the Havering estate.

The path wound through a little coppice of silver birches, their heart-shaped leaves shivering in the summer air. It was another hot day, the scent of the thick bracken heavy and sweet. When the path came out on a little hill Perry drew rein and we looked back.

There was little trouble in the village. We could see from where we watched a couple of soldiers standing with Mr Briggs at the end of the village street while half a dozen men went workmanlike down one side, pulling off rotting doors and knocking axes through old dusty thatch. Drawn up in the street, ahead of the wreckers, was a large cart with a handsome shire horse between the shafts. The Havering people were loading their few goods on to the cart, a man standing on the cart helping them. I screwed my eyes against the glare of the sunlight but I hardly needed to see him to know it was Will Tyacke.

'Who's that?' Perry asked me.

'I don't know,' I said. I lied before I had even considered the lie. 'Perhaps someone from the poorhouse.'

'Oh,' Perry said innocently, and we stood for a little while, watching in silence.

The wreckers reached another house and there was a moment's hesitation. We were too far to hear or see anything clearly but I guessed that someone inside had refused to leave. I shrugged. It was not my land and anyway Lady Clara was probably in the right. Since she was not going to spend money on making the cottages habitable they were better pulled down. The tenants would have to make lives for themselves elsewhere. There was no reason why Lady Clara should be responsible for each and every one of them.

'What d'you think is happening?' Perry asked. 'The sun is so bright I can hardly see.'

I shaded my eyes with my hand. Sea stirred restlessly as he felt my weight move on the saddle.

'Someone, I think a woman,' I said. I could just make out a little figure standing in the dark doorway of one of the hovels. As I watched, the wreckers made a rush for her and she grabbed the post which propped the thatched porch. In a ludicrous pose, like a comical print, one of the men got hold of her legs while she clung to the post of her house.

I sniggered, and Perry laughed beside me. 'She'll pull it down herself if she doesn't watch out,' he observed.

We watched together smiling, but there was no sport. Will Tyacke went quickly to her and made the man put her on her feet. He bent over her and I saw she was quite a small woman. He put his arm around her and he led her to the cart. Out of the cottage behind her came three little children, the smallest a baby, lugged by the others.

Will lifted all of them one by one, into the cart and then went back into the cottage for their goods: a cooking pot, one stool, a clutter of plates and bedding. Not much. Even less than we had in the old days in the wagon.

'Poor sport,' Perry said in sudden distaste.

'Aye,' I said. I had a bad taste in my mouth and I went to spit but then I remembered that ladies do not spit. 'Let's ride!' I said and touched Sea with my heels and turned his head.

We cantered along the crest of a hill until we came to the stone post which marked the start of my land. At once the path was wider, it had been cut back as a firebreak and there was a wide track as good as a race-course of the pure white sand bordered with the black peat of the Common.

'Race?' Perry called, and I nodded and held Sea back so that we drew level and then let him have his head.

We thundered along the track together, Sea going faster than I had ever known him go at the challenge from another high-bred horse. Perry's horse was probably the better, but Sea was fitter from my daily rides. He was carrying a lighter rider too and we managed to pull ahead before the firebreak crested up a hill and I pulled up at the top.

Perry and his hunter were half a length behind us and Perry came up smiling and jumped from the saddle.

'Lost my hat,' he said with a grin. 'We'll have to go back that way.'

Without his hat his golden curls had tumbled into a blond mop. His blue eyes were clear and shining, his colour bright.

Any girl in the world would have fallen in love with him at first sight.

I put my hand down and touched the top of his head. He looked up at me, and reached up to lift me down from Sea's back, his hands on my waist for a brief moment. Then he released me as soon as my feet touched the ground.

'I didn't like seeing that at the village,' he said.

I shook my head. 'Me neither,' I replied.

Perry turned from me and swung his jacket down on the heather. We sat side by side looking down into the Fenny valley. Havering Hall woodland was a dark mass to our right, Acre was over to our left. My home, the home I had longed for but seldom even visited was below us, hidden in the trees at the back of the house.

'It's Mr Briggs's doing,' he said. 'I have no say in how the place is run until I am married, or reach my majority.'

'Twenty-one?' I asked.

He nodded. 'Four years,' he said.

'It's even longer for me,' I said. 'I'm only sixteen now. I'll have to wait five years.'

Perry looked sideways at me. 'I know it is what my mama wants,' he said carefully. 'And to be honest, Sarah, she told me to ask you. In fact,' he said with scrupulous honesty, 'she said she'd pay my gambling debts if I asked you.'

'Asked me what?' I said. But I knew.

'Asked you to marry me,' he said without any heat at all. 'I tell you why I said I would.' He lay on his back, as idle and as lovely as a fallen angel, and counted his white fingers up at the clear sky.

'One, I would get hold of my land and capital. Two, you would get hold of your land and capital. Three, we could run them together and we could make sure that Wideacre is run sensibly but that people are not treated so badly as they have been on Havering. Four, we would not have to marry anyone else, or court, or go to London parties unless we wanted.'

I stretched alongside him and leaned my head on one hand so that I could watch his face.

'Why don't you want to court girls?' I asked. 'I've lived with you for months now and I've never even seen you sneak out late at night except to get drunk. Don't you like girls, Perry?'

He turned his head to face me and his eyes were clear and untroubled.

'That's point five,' he said. 'We neither of us like being touched like that. I don't mind my sisters, and I don't mind you. But I cannot stand being pulled about by girls. I don't like how they look at me. I don't like how they stroke my sleeve or find ways of touching my shoulder or standing close to me. I just don't like it. And I know I'll never get married if I have to court someone and kiss them and pull them about.'

I nodded. I understood well enough. It was my own prickly independence but perhaps a little worse for a young man who would be expected to fondle and fumble and get his face slapped for his pains.

'If we married we'd have to get an heir,' he said bluntly. 'But once we had a son we could live as friends. I thought you'd like that, Sarah.'

I drew my knees up to the ache in my chest and hugged myself for comfort.

'I don't know,' I said softly.

Perry closed his eyes and turned his face up to the sunshine. 'I thought it would be a way out for both of us,' he said. 'I know you're afraid of going into Society, even with Mama there. This way, you'd be known as my affianced bride. You'd not have to go around so much. Men wouldn't trouble you. My mama or my sisters could always be with you. And you could always have me there.'

I nodded. Deep inside myself I had been dreading the London Season, and cursing the obstinacy in myself which had insisted on moving in the best of circles when I was no more fitted for it than any bareback dancer.

'I'd like that,' I conceded.

'And you could run your own estate,' Perry pointed out. 'As you wanted, without having to wait all that time.'

I nodded. Five years was an unimaginable lifetime from my

sixteen-year-old viewpoint. I could not imagine waiting until I was twenty-one. And the shrewd business streak in me warned me that five years was a long time to leave Will Tyacke and James Fortescue in charge of my fortune.

'And we're neighbours,' Perry said. 'If you marry anyone else they'll take you away to live in their house. They could live anywhere. You'd only be able to get back to see Wideacre when they let you.'

'Oh no!' I said suddenly. 'I hadn't thought of that!'

'You'd have to,' he said. 'And your husband would put his manager in and he might do it even worse than it's being done already.'

I put my hand out and turned his face towards me. He opened his eyes.

'Kiss me,' I said.

The kiss was as gentle and as cool as the brush of his mother's fingertips on my cheek. His lips barely touched mine, and then he pulled back and looked at me.

'I do like you,' he said. 'I do want us to be friends. Mama wants us to marry and I think she is right. But I do want us to be friends anyway.'

The loneliness and sadness I carried with me always suddenly swelled and choked me as he offered his friendship. The kiss had been as light and as cool as Dandy's good-night pecks and I suddenly thought how long it had been since I had been touched by someone who liked me. I gave a little moan and buried my face in my hands and lay face down on the heather.

I did not cry. I had promised myself that day that I would never cry again. I just lay, stiff as a board and heard myself give three or four little moans as if my heart were breaking with loneliness.

Perry did nothing. He sat there like a beautiful flower, waiting for me to have done. When I ceased and lay still he put out a hand and rested it on the nape of my neck. His hand was as cool and as soft-skinned as a woman's.

'I'm unhappy, too,' he said quietly. 'That's why I keep drinking. I'm not the son Mama wants. That was George. She'll never love me like she loved him. I thought that if you and I could marry we could both be less lonely. We could be friends.'

I turned around. My eyes were sore with unshed tears, as sore as if I had grit from the road blown into them. I rubbed them with the back of my gloved hand.

'Yes,' I said. I spoke from the depths of my loneliness and from my despair in knowing that I would never love anyone again. 'Yes, it might work. I'll think about it,' I said.

Nothing could be worse than this arid waiting for the pain to pass. Perry and I were children who had been left behind. My sister had gone, his talented, brilliant brother George had gone. We two were left to inherit all the wealth and the land and the houses. We might be able to help each other feel more at home with them all. 'Yes,' I said.

'All right then,' Perry said. We got to our feet and he shook his jacket carefully and put it back on, pulling down the coat-tail and smoothing the sleeves down. 'Mama will pay my gambling debts now,' he said pleased. 'Shall we tell her at dinner?'

'Yes,' I said. It seemed like years since someone had shared a decision with me and asked for my help. It was good to be part of an 'us' again, even if it were only poor silly Perry and me.

'We can marry when the contracts have been drawn up,' Perry said. 'In London if you like, or here.'

'I don't mind,' I said. 'It doesn't matter to me.'

Perry nodded, and cupped his hand to throw me up into the saddle.

'Mama will be really pleased with me,' he said and smiled up at me. He feared his mama at least as much as he loved her, probably more.

'She'll be pleased with both of us,' I said, and I felt glad to be part of a family, even a cold-blooded Quality family like the Haverings. I smiled for a moment, thinking of her and her hopes of a Quality marriage, of netting some flash young squire. Who'd have thought in those days that plain dirty little Meridon would be saying 'yes' to marriage with a lord! My smile turned into a little rueful grimace, and then I clicked to Sea to follow Perry's horse back down the slope. And who'd have thought that

I'd say yes to a marriage not for need, nor for desire, nor in any hope. But because need and desire and hope were gone and I was instead looking for power and wealth and control over my land.

Love I did not think of at all.

We told Lady Clara that night at dinner. I think if she had shown the least gleam of satisfaction I would have been on my guard. As it was she looked at me steadily across the table and said:

'You are very young, Sarah, this is a big step. Do you think you had not better wait until you see what London society has to offer you?'

I hesitated. 'I thought this was your wish, Lady Clara?' I said.

The door behind me opened and the butler came to clear the table. Lady Clara made one of her graceful gestures and he bowed at once and withdrew. I knew I would never in a million years learn how to do that.

'Certainly it is my wish that the estates be run together, and I can think of no two more suitable young people,' she said. 'Your upbringing has been unusual, Sarah, but Perry is the only young man of Quality that I know who is entirely free from any snobbery. He is informal to a fault, and you two are clearly very fond of each other.' She paused and smiled slightly at Perry who was sitting on her right, between us. 'And you two are well suited in temperament,' she said delicately.

Perry looked glumly down at his plate and I nearly snorted with suppressed laughter at the thought of Lady Clara recommending him to me because he was cold and I was unwomanly.

'But I do not know what Mr Fortescue will say,' she said. 'It will mean that you can take the running of the estate away from him at once.'

'There is nothing he can say,' I said brusquely. 'The matter will be out of his hands. He cannot control my choice of husband, and in any case, no one could object to me marrying Perry who is a lord, and a neighbour, and a cousin.'

'Voice,' said Lady Clara.

'Sorry,' I said.

She raised her eyebrow at me.

'I mean, I beg your pardon,' I amended.

She smiled.

Perry kept his head down and poured himself another glass of port.

'If you are so determined then there is nothing I can say,' Lady Clara said with a fair show of helplessness. 'The engagement can be announced at once. Then Perry can be with you at all the balls and parties of the Season and when the Season is over we can come back here and perhaps have a wedding next spring at Chichester cathedral.'

I nodded and Perry said nothing.

'You should write to Mr Fortescue at once to tell him of your decision,' Lady Clara said. 'And inform him that I will be notifying my solicitors to draw up a marriage contract. They will contact his solicitors for sight of the deeds of Wideacre, of course.'

'Wideacre will still be mine,' I said. 'It is entailed upon the oldest child, whether male or female.'

Lady Clara smiled. 'Of course, Sarah,' she said. 'It will be entailed upon your first-born. Havering is entailed upon the first-born son. There should be enough meat in that to keep the lawyers occupied all summer and autumn.'

'But Wideacre will still be mine,' I repeated.

Lady Clara paused. 'Married women cannot own property, Sarah,' she said gently. 'You know that. Wideacre will become Peregrine's when you marry. Any husband of yours would own Wideacre.'

I frowned. 'Even though it is me that inherited it?' I asked.

'Even though it is I who . . .' Lady Clara amended.

'There's nothing I can do about that?' I queried.

'It is the law of the land,' she said dryly. 'Wealthier women than you have had to hand over bigger fortunes. But you could consult your lawyer or Mr Fortescue if you wish. You'll still be better off with the estate properly run under Peregrine's name, than held for you by Mr Fortescue and his band of Jacobins.'

I nodded. 'I know that,' I said certainly.

'Anyway, Sarah can run it herself,' Peregrine said. He had taken another glass of port and his cheeks were pink. He smiled at me very sweetly. 'No reason why not,' he said. 'She's been riding all around learning about the fields. If she doesn't want a bailiff she could run it herself.'

Lady Clara nodded and picked up her fan. 'Certainly,' she said. 'That is for the two of you to decide. How nice to have another wedding in the family!'

Peregrine rose steadily enough and took his mother's arm as she went towards the door. He opened it and held it wide for her and me to pass through. As I went by he gave me a grin as brotherly and warm as an urchin who has scraped out of an adventure.

'Pretty fair,' he said under his breath, and went back to the table.

27

I went to bed early that night, and drew back my heavy curtains from the window. After years of sleeping in a wagon I should have rejoiced in the space and the comfort of having a whole room to myself, of being able to see the moon through clear clean glass. But I was a silly, ungrateful drab. After all my pining for the gentry life I was low that night and missed the wagon and the noise of other people snoring, breathing, dreaming all around me. I missed the warm dirty smell of the place. I missed the sight of Da's rumpled head and Zima's dirty locks. I missed the little snorting breaths of the baby. I made sure I did not think about the bunk opposite from where I used to see her dark head and her slow lazy waking smile.

Robert Gower had been good to me, by his lights. He had paid me my ten guineas and he had cared for Sea without charge. When I came off the trapeze he had me nursed in his own house and I never paid him a penny out of my wages for the doctor's bill. I thought of the little house off Warminster High Street, I thought of the wagon with the painting and the curly writing on the side and how, somewhere, it would be parked up for the night, the fire burned down to embers outside the steps, a pan of water nearby for Robert to wash in the morning. On the side of the wagon there was my likeness and my name. My old name. The one I would never use again from the life I had left.

It seemed that all my life there were departures. The one I had only seen in my dream, when the little baby was held to a strange breast and did not hear her mother call after her. The crude sale when Da handed us over and drove out of town too quick for us to change our minds. And the evening when I took my horse and my gold and my string and gold clasps and went away from Robert Gower as if he had been my enemy. I thought now that perhaps he had been a good friend and I could have stayed there, and that he would have helped me with my grief. Here I could not speak of it, could not be seen to be grieving. Here I had to lock it up in some cold part of my heart and never let anyone know, never let anyone see, that I was cold and aged and as dead as a smashed doll inside.

I leaned my head against the cold glass of the window and looked out. The sky was cloudy tonight, the moon three-quarters full, misty and shaded by ribbons and lumps of clouds over its face. My room faced east, over the paddock at the back of the house, towards the Common. I looked towards the skyline where a little clump of firs showed black against the sky. I had wanted to sleep and wake with this view all my life. I was home. It was foolish to find that it gave me no joy at all.

I turned from the window and drew the curtains. The room seemed too big, too full of echoes and ghosts and longing without the cold light of the moon showing a bed far too big for me, in a room far too big for me. With a little sigh I slipped off my costly dress and laid it carefully over a chair. I kept on my chemise and petticoat and wrapped myself in the coverlet from the bed and lay down on the hard carpet without a pillow. I knew tonight would be one of the nights when I would get no rest unless I slept hard and woke cold. Sometimes the life was too soft for me, I could not bear that it should be so easy for me when the one who would have loved it, who would have been extravagant and playful and laughing and spendthrift, she – and I still could not say her name – she had gone.

If I had been the crying sort I would have wept that night. But I was not. I lay wrapped tight in the coverlet on my back. When I woke in the night my face was wet and the carpet under my head was damp as if all the tears from the day, and from all the days, had crept out from under my eyelids when I was asleep. I got up then, stiff and chilled, and slid between the sheets. It was about three o'clock in the morning. I wished very much that it had been me who had died and not her.

I woke early, and I looked at the cool light on the white ceiling, and then I said it. I said the words that had gone with me all my life, which I had hoped to escape here: 'I don't belong here,' I said.

I lay still then for a few moments, listening to the desolation of that voice inside me which told me that I was alone, that I was lonely, that I belonged nowhere now, that I had never belonged anywhere, that I never would belong anywhere. I knew it was true.

I was keeping travellers' hours and I was as restless as a stable cat shut indoors. There was no noise from the kitchen nor the sound of the maid cleaning the fires, it was too early even for her.. I trod softly over to the wardrobe and looked for my riding habits. One was being washed and the other was not there. I had torn a seam the day before and Lady Clara's maid had taken it away to mend it. She would bring it back at breakfast time, but I needed to be out now. At the bottom of the wardrobe, pushed well back, were my old clothes. Jack's old breeches, his boots, Robert's thick jacket. I pulled them out and dressed myself quickly. I pulled my good riding boots on and they fitted me a deal more comfortably than ever had Jack's hand-me-downs. I went soft-footed to the door and opened it a crack to listen.

I had been right, it was too early for anyone to be stirring. As I crept down the wooden stairs I heard the clock in the hall strike the quarter-hour. I looked at it in the pale light. It was only a quarter past five. I stepped as delicately as a mare on an icy road over the black and white tiles of the hall and through the baize door to the kitchen. All was clean and tidied away and quiet. A red eye of embers glowed inside the kitchen stove, a black cat asleep on the flat top.

I shot the bolts on the kitchen door and let myself out into the cold dawn air. Robert's jacket was warm and rough against my cheek. It smelled of the earlier life: of his pipe tobacco, of fried bacon, of horse sweat, of oats. The smells of my childhood, which was no childhood at all.

Sea was turned out in the paddock wearing just a headcollar. There was a spare rope by the water pump, I needed nothing else to ride him. I went to the gate and whistled for him (a lady never whistles) and he raised his head and pricked his ears and came blithely towards me as if he were glad to see me in my old familiar clothes. As if I were about to take him back to the old life. I clipped the rope on his headcollar and led him through the little white gate. I had forgotten how high he was. I had been lifted into the saddle as if I were a child or an old lady for months. I had nearly forgotten how to vault.

I said, 'Stand,' to him and found I had lost none of my skill. I was on his back in one clear leap and his ears went forward as he felt me astride him as I had always ridden him before we came here. I touched him gently with a soft squeeze of both legs on his warm flanks, and he stepped out gently down the drive towards the old woodland track through the parkland to Wideacre.

A blackbird had started singing, his voice sounded surprised to be awake this early, but all the other birds were still silent. The sun was not yet up, the morning was cool and grey. Sea and I were like ghosts of ourselves, leaving in dawnlight as we had come in moonlight. I put my hand in my pocket and felt the golden guineas were still there safe. We could go as we had come and disappear into the world of the common people. The world of wagons and travellers and shows, and no one would ever be able to find us again. Wideacre could stay as it was – fair, fruitful, generous. Nothing need change if I was not there, demanding my rights like a late-hatched greedy cuckoo chick. Perry could drink and play, annoy his mother and seek her forgiveness without me. He would come to his fortune at the end. It would make no difference to Lady Clara.

I could sink from the sight of this new life and no one would grieve for me. Within three months they would have forgotten all about me again.

Sea's hooves rang as he came out of the woods on to the stones of the lane towards Acre and I turned his head east towards my land. I had half a will to look at it once more and then to go, to leave it for ever. I belonged neither there on the land, nor in my old life without her. I belonged nowhere and I had nowhere to go and no idea what I should do. I rode as I had ridden that night, without direction and Sea stopped at the little stream, as he had stopped that night and dipped his head to drink while I smelled the cold mist off the water.

'Sarah,' a voice said, and I looked up. My eyes were blurred – they had been watering as I rode – and I blinked to clear them. It was Will Tyacke standing under the trees on the other side of the stream.

'You,' I said.

Sea put his ears forward and went out of the stream towards Will and put his great head down for a pat. He liked Will; he was the only man he did like.

'Sarah, in your old clothes,' Will said.

'My riding habit's being mended,' I said. 'I wanted to ride early.'

'Sleepless?' he asked.

I nodded and he gave me a little smile. 'Too soft for you at Havering?' he asked.

The months of our quarrel slid away from us both. 'Too soft, too big, too grand,' I said in a little voice. 'It's not my place.'

'Where is your place?' he asked. He patted Sea's neck and came close to stand at his shoulder so that he could look up into my face.

'Nowhere, as far as I know,' I said. 'I've come too late for this life, and I don't care to go back to the old one. I'll never learn to be a lady as Lady Clara. I suppose now I couldn't be happy with the work I used to do. I'm betwixt and between. I don't know where I should be.'

He reached up to me and rested his hand on my leg. I stayed still, I did not mind his touch. 'Could you be here?' he asked very low. 'Could you be with us in Acre? Not up at the Hall as gentry, but in the village with the ordinary people? Living with us and working with us, making the land grow and feeding the people, selling in the market and working and planning?'

I looked down at his face and saw his brown eyes were full of love. He wanted me to say yes. He wanted me to say yes more than he wanted anything else in the world. Despite our quarrel, despite my turning from him to go to Lady Clara's parlour, he wanted me to say yes and to go to Acre with him, as his equal.

'No,' I said. 'Don't waste your hopes on me, Will Tyacke. I am dead inside. There is no place for me to be happy, not in the Hall, not in the village, not at Havering nor Wideacre. Don't look like that and don't talk like that. You are wasting your time. I have nothing for you and nothing for the village either.'

He dropped his hand and he turned away. I thought he was going to walk from me in a rage but he took only a few steps and then he turned to face the stream and dropped down to his haunches and watched the flow of it go past us. Sea had stirred up the mud of the river bed and as we watched it grew clearer and then flowed clean again.

'I've just walked back from Havering village,' he said. 'Some of them have moved into Acre, sharing cottages. One lass wanted me to see if I could find something she had left behind, but they have burned it out.'

I said nothing.

'They even carted the stones away,' he said wonderingly. 'In a few months' time you won't be able to tell there ever was a village there. They have wiped the land clean of the people who lived there for hundreds of years.'

'Were you there with the cart?' I asked.

Will looked quickly up at me. 'Aye,' he said. 'I didn't see you.'

'I was riding, up on the Common behind,' I said. I suddenly remembered that I had been with Perry and that we had laughed at the woman who clung to the doorpost. 'I wasn't allowed to come near,' I said. It was a weak excuse. 'They had the typhus fever.'

Will shook his head. 'Nay,' he said. He was angry but his voice was so low and soft no one but me could have guessed it. 'There was a woman there who was feverish and delirious through hunger. She didn't have typhus, she was dying in a fever. She had been giving her smallest child the breast to try and keep her alive and so when there was no food to be begged or bought it hit her the hardest.'

'Did she cling to the doorpost?' I asked.

'You saw that, did you?' Will asked. His voice was thick with condemnation of someone who could see that naked need of a woman and leave her to the mercies of paid wreckers. 'Aye, she clung to the doorpost. She had nowhere to go. She was afraid of going to the poorhouse and the babbies being taken off her. I've taken her into my cottage and her three children. It'll do for them for a while.'

'Will you play nursemaid to three little babies?' I said laughing. I wanted to hurt him, I wanted him to flare up at me since he thought I was so much in the wrong. I was angry with him for taking the woman and her children in. I did not like the thought of him living there, like a husband and a father with a sickly wife and three babies.

'I'd rather live with three babbies than up at the Hall with one great baby and his ma,' Will said, scowling at me.

'You mean Lord Peregrine?' I said in a tone as near to Lady Clara's disdainful drawl as I could manage.

Will got to his feet and met my eye squarely. 'Don't speak to me like that, you silly slut,' he said. 'I've heard you learn to talk like that and I'm damned if I know why you want to turn yourself into something you're not. I've heard Ted Tyacke talk about your ma, Lady Lacey she was, and she once rolled in the mud cat-fighting with one of the Dench girls. Her best friend was a village girl and she was in love with James Fortescue. She'd never have talked like that! And your grandma Beatrice swore like a ploughboy and would have tanned your backside for talking to a working man like that.'

I dug my heels in Sea and turned him so sharply that he nearly reared. He plunged down the bank into mid-stream again and from there I turned and yelled at Will: 'You're sacked, Will Tyacke!' I shouted. 'Sacked and you can get off my land and go to hell! You'll pack up today, you and your cottage-full of drabs. Get off my land all of you, and don't you dare come back.'

He put his fists on his waist and shouted back at me. 'You don't own this place or run it, Sarah Lacey. You're a minor still, you can sign nothing, you can appoint no one, you can sack no one. I takes my orders from James Fortescue and I will do for another five years. So take that back to Lord Perry with the compliments of his neighbour.'

'I'll have you off the land in a twelvemonth,' I shrieked back at him, all my grief and anger and frustration boiling over at once like a pot with a lid forced on too tight. 'I'm marrying Lord Peregrine as soon as the deeds are drawn and the Season over! Then he and I will own all the land from Midhurst to Cocking and we'll see then who gives orders and who takes them, and whether you can ever find work in west Sussex again.'

He leaped down the bank in one fluid movement, faster than I would have thought he could move. He was in the water and at my side in an instant and Sea shied sideways with a snort of fright. He laid hold of my knee and my waist and then my arm and pulled me off Sea's back and down so that I tumbled into the stream beside him and my best new riding boots were knee-high in water. He grabbed me by the shoulders and shook me so that my head rocked on my neck.

'What?' he shouted. 'What are you saying? What are you saying?'

I blazed back at him, angry and unafraid of his violence. 'That I'm marrying Lord Peregrine,' I said. 'His mother knows. It's to be announced. It's true.'

His brown eyes burned at me for one moment longer then he flung me away from him so that I stumbled backwards against Sea. He waded downstream to the shallow part of the bank and stumbled up it, his boots heavy with water. I turned and vaulted on to Sea's back as easy as if I were in the ring and I wheeled him around like a triumphant cavalryman.

The look on Will's face wiped the smile off my face with the shock. He looked as if I had stabbed him in the heart. I gasped when his eyes met mine, his gaze was so intent.

'You will marry him?' he asked.

'Yes,' I said low. All the anger had gone, there was nothing in the world except his brown eyes, dark and narrowed as if he was hurting inside.

'You've told James Fortescue?'

'I will write today.'

'This is your wish, Sarah?'

'Yes,' I said. I wanted so much to tell him that it was my wish because I did not know who I was nor where I should go. Because I had to have some family, some place where I belonged. Because Perry and I were two of a kind: both lost, both unloved, both unlovable.

'I'll leave on your wedding day,' he said coldly. 'And I'll warn the village that everything – all our hopes and plans for the future, all the promises made by the Laceys – everything is all over for us.'

He turned and walked away from the stream. Sea and I looked after him. His waterlogged boots squelched at every step. His shoulders were bowed. I tried to laugh at the picture he presented, but I could not laugh. I sat very still on Sea's back and watched him walk away from me. I let him go. Then I turned Sea's head and rode back to Havering Hall.

I did as I had said I would, and everything followed on from that almost without my choosing. I wrote and told Mr Fortescue of my decision and I waited and read his reply without emotion. He was concerned and unhappy but there was nothing that he could do. His honest, anxious, stumbling reply made me feel that I was running very fast in the wrong direction, but Lady Clara insisted on seeing it, and read passages aloud, and rocked with laughter.

She composed for me a cold-hearted rejoinder which thanked him for his advice but said that my mind was made up. It referred him to the Havering lawyers if he had any queries.

'You had best remind him that he is a little late in the day breaking his heart over your happiness. He never made much effort to find you in all the sixteen years when you were lost, by all accounts. Too busy re-creating Eden at Wideacre, I daresay.'

That made me angry and resentful, and the letter I sent to Mr Fortescue was cold and ungenerous. I did not hear from him again.

I heard no more from Will, either. I often seemed to see his face looking at me with that especial sharp anger. Once I dreamed of him trudging away from me, heavy-footed with wet boots. In my dream I called out to him and when he turned around he was smiling in a way I had never seen him look. But when I woke I knew that I had not called out to him, that I never would call out to him. That a gulf had opened between us which was too deep for mere liking and sympathy to bridge.

Perry and I grew closer, he was my only comfort in the late summer days while Lady Clara taught me how to pour tea and how to deal cards like a lady and not like a card-sharper. Perry would sit with me now during my lessons and when his mama praised me for doing well he would beam at me like a generous incapable student watching some bright friend do better.

'You will be the toast of the Season,' he said to me idly, as he watched his mama and me take a hand of picquet.

'I don't know about that, but she will be the gambler of the Season,' Lady Clara said, discarding cards and finally conceding the game to me. 'Sarah, whatever hell you learned to play in must sorely miss you.'

I smiled and said nothing, thinking for a moment of Da and his seductive pack of greasy cards on an upturned beer-keg outside a country inn.

'Anyone fancy a game?' he would offer. 'Playing for beer only, I don't want to be taken for a ride, I just want a fair game, a bit of sport.' One after another they would come. Plump farmers with rents in their pocket. Middling tenants with their wives' butter money burning a hole in their jackets. One after another Da would pluck them. Drunk or sober it was one of the things, perhaps the only thing, that he did quite well.

'Sarah will restore the family fortunes in cash as well as in land,' Peregrine said lazily with a smile at me. He did not see the sharp look his mama shot at him. I did. It warned him to be silent about the Havering debts.

She was wrong to fear me knowing, I was no fool. I would tell my lawyers to ascertain how much the Haverings owed before I honoured my promise to marry. Mr Fortescue was a careful man and would make sure that the capital of the land was entailed upon my children in such a way that no husband, however spendthrift, could waste it on gambling. Perry and I smiled at each other with easy knowledge. We needed each other, we liked each other, we trusted each other. We neither of us wanted very much more.

We walked that evening in the garden. It was getting colder at nightfall and he put his silk embroidered evening jacket around my shoulders and offered me his arm. I took it. We must have made a pretty sight, the two of us, my auburn ringlets brushing his shoulder and my head held high. My green gown hushing the grass and Perry as golden and as lovely as an angel. We walked together in the twilit garden and we talked of money and friendship. We did not talk of love. It never entered our heads. When Perry saw me to my bedroom door at night he stooped and kissed me on the lips and his touch was as cool as his mama's social pecks.

I stopped him as he turned to leave. 'Will you never feel desire, Perry?' I asked.

He looked frankly alarmed. 'I doubt it, Sarah,' he said uncomfortably. 'Would you ever want me to?'

I paused. It was as if there were two people inside me: one the girl who could not bear to be touched except by one other person, the girl who had seen too much and heard too much at too young an age to ever think that love could have anything to do with a heaving bunk and a rocking wagon. The other was a girl growing into womanhood who had seen a man look at her as if she had murdered him by leaving him. A man who looked at her with passion and love and then turned and walked away.

'No Perry,' I said honestly. 'I would never want desire from you.'

He smiled at that, his blue eyes a little blurred for he was a little drunk as usual. 'That's fine,' he said encouragingly. 'For I do like you awfully, you know.'

I smiled wryly. 'I know,' I said. 'It is all I want from you.'

I opened the heavy panelled door and slipped inside. I paused and heard his footsteps go waveringly down the long corridor. There was a sudden clash and clatter as he stumbled into the suit of armour which stood at the corner and his owlish, 'I beg your pardon,' to it. Then I heard his feet scrabble on the stairs and step one after another, until he reached the top and was gone to his room.

28

I went over to the window to draw back the curtains. It was still early and the moon was coming up. As I stood, looking out towards the moonlit Common, I saw a horseman come riding down the silvery track towards the back garden of Havering Hall. I saw him ride under the lee of the wall and then I lost sight of him. He must have left his horse tied up, because in a few moments the figure appeared on the top of the wall, swung a leg over and dropped down into the informal garden at the back of the house. I watched in silence. I would have known Will Tyacke from fifty miles away.

He walked across the lawn as if he did not care who saw him trespassing in darkness, and then he stopped before the house, scanning the windows as if he owned the place. A low laugh escaped me and I leaned forward and pulled up the sash window and stuck my head out. He raised a hand in greeting and came unhurriedly to the flower bed beneath my window and for a moment I thought of some other Lacey girl, and some other young man, who had whispered together on the night air and known they were talking of love.

'What is it?' I said peremptorily.

Will's face was in shadow. 'It's this,' he said. He had something white in his hand. I could not see what it was. He stooped to the path at his feet, and straightened up, wrapping the paper around a stone.

'I thought you would want to know,' he said. He was almost apologetic. 'From something you once said, earlier this summer, when we were friends.'

He made as if to throw it, and I stepped back before I could ask if we might still be friends. His aim was sure, the stone came sailing through the window wrapped in the white paper. By the time I picked it up and was at the window again he was walking across the lawn and scaling the wall. I watched him go. I did not call him back.

Instead I unwrapped the stone he had thrown for me and smoothed out the paper. The white was the wrong side, the blank side. On the inside, very creased as if half a dozen people had pored over it, spelling out the words, was a bright scarlet picture with a white horse in the middle and two trapeze flyers going over the top: a man and two girls. In curly letters of gold it said: Robert Gower's Amazing Equestrian and Aerial Show.

It was them. Their tour had brought them here. I should have expected them earlier if I'd had my wits about me. Selsey to Wideacre was just a little way, they must have gone on down the coast, or perhaps they stopped for a while after burying her. Somewhere they must have found another fool for the trapeze. They were going on as if nothing had happened.

For a moment there was a rage so hot and so burning that I could see nothing, not even the garish poster, for the red mist which was in my head and behind my eyes. It had made no difference to them . . . the thing which had happened. Robert was still working and planning, Jack was still standing on the catcher frame, still smiling his lazy nervous smile. Katie was as vapid and as pretty as ever. They were still touring, they were still taking good gates. It had made no difference to them. It had killed her, it had killed me. It had made no difference to them at all.

I dropped the handbill and walked to the window and threw it open again to breathe in the cold night air to try to slow the rapid thudding of my heart. I was so angry. If I could have killed every one of them I would. I wanted to punish them. They were feeling nothing; although her life was over, and mine was an empty shell. I stood there for a long time in the cold but then I steadied and I turned back to the room, picked up the paper, smoothed it out again and looked to see where they were working.

They were playing outside Midhurst. They were doing three shows, the last one a late, lantern-lit show in an empty barn just a little way down the road. If I had wanted I could have gone and seen them tonight.

I gave a deep shuddering sigh. I could let them go. I could let them work my neighbouring village. I could let Rea poach the odd rabbit from my Common. I could let them pass within four miles of me. They did not know I was here. I had no need to tell them. They could go on into the high roads and byways of travellers, of gypsies. These people were my people no longer. Their ways were not my ways. We would never meet. I would never have to see them. They were a life I had left behind. I could cut myself in two and say, 'That was the old life, the old life with her; it is gone now, all gone.'

I smoothed out the handbill and put my finger under the words, spelling them out, looking at the pictures again. There were the clues which had made Will bring it to me. 'Robert Gower' it said in curly letters. I had told him I worked for a man called 'Robert' and beside the picture of the white stallion it said 'Snow the Amazing Arithmetical Horse'. I had told him of a horse called Snow which could do tricks. I knew that he remembered things I said to him, even light, silly things. He perhaps thought that these friends, these old friends from another life might help me look at the Haverings and at Perry with new eyes. He knew that he had lost me, that Wideacre had lost me, that I belonged nowhere now. Perhaps he had thought that the old life might call me back, might help me to find myself again.

He did not know that to think of the old life made me more careless about myself, more feckless about my future than anything else could have done. For they, and I, were still alive. But she was dead.

I sat in the window-seat and watched the moon for a while, but I was uneasy and could not settle. I looked at the little ormolu clock on the mantelpiece, there was still time. If I wished, I could ride and see the show, see how it was for them without her, without me. I could go and be concealed by the crowd, watch them in silence and secrecy, satisfy my curiosity. I could watch them and learn how it was for them, now we two were gone. Then leave among the crowd, and come slowly home.

Or I could go and be among them like an avenging fury, my eyes black with unsatisfied anger. This was my land here, I was the squire. I could name Jack as a killer, call Rea as a witness and no one could gainsay me. With my word against his, I could get Jack hanged. Not even Robert could stand against the squire of Wideacre on Wideacre land. I could confiscate the horses, send Katie back to the Warminster poorhouse, Rea back to the Winchester Guardians, send Robert to Warminster to die of shame. I was gentry now, I could settle my scores as gentry do – with the law and the power of the law. I could break them all with my squire's law.

Or I could run now, from the power and from the boredom of the Quality life. I could put on my old clothes – their clothes, which they had given me – and tuck up my hair under my cap and go back to them. I knew how they would receive me, they would welcome me as a long-lost daughter, the ponies would whinny to see me. They would hug me and weep with me – easy, feckless tears. Then they would teach me how the acts had changed now she was gone, and where I could fit in the new work. I could walk away from my life here and leave the special loneliness and emptiness of Quality life. I could leave here with pockets as light as when I had arrived; and the man who hated gin traps and Mr Fortescue could run the land as they wished, and need never trouble themselves about me again.

I did not know what I wanted to see, what I wanted to feel. It seemed like a lifetime since I had walked away from them and said to myself that I was never going back. But I had not known then what it was to be lost.

After half an hour I could stand it no longer. I trod softly over to the wardrobe and pulled out my riding habit. Perry would be drinking alone in his room, perhaps humming quietly to himself, deaf to the rest of the house. Lady Clara would be writing letters in the parlour or perhaps reading in the library. Neither of them would hear my steps on the servants' stairs. No housemaid that I might chance to meet would have the courage to interrupt Lady

Clara to tell her that Miss Lacey had ridden out into the twilight. I could come and go as I wished in secret.

I dressed quickly, familiar now with the intricate buttons at the back, with the way to quickly smooth my gloves and pin the grey hat. It had a veil of net which I had never used but now I pulled it down. I glanced at myself in the mirror. My eyes glowed green behind the veil, but my betraying copper hair was hidden by the hat. I had eaten well all summer and my face was plumper. I was no longer a half-starved gypsy brat with a bruised face. If someone did not know who I really was, if someone thought I was gentry, they would have called me beautiful. My mouth pulled down at the thought. In my head I saw her dark glossy hair and her rosy smiling face, I thought how she would have looked in these clothes and there was no pleasure for me in them. I turned from the mirror and crept down the servants' stairs which led straight down to the stable yard.

Sea had been brought in now that nights were getting colder and I went first to the tack room and then to his loose-box. Both were unlocked, they would water-up at twilight and lock up then. The light was only fading now. I humped his saddle myself and he lowered his head so that I could put on his bridle. As I tightened his girth and led him out, a stable lad came out of the hay loft and looked warily at me.

'I'm going for a ride,' I said, and my voice was no longer the muted tones of the young lady. I was Meridon again, Meridon who had ordered Rea, who could shout down a drunken father. 'I'm going alone and I don't want them told. Them, up at the house. D'you understand me?'

He nodded, his eyes round, saying nothing.

'When they come to feed and water the horses and they find Sea gone you can tell them that it is all right. That I have taken him out and that I will bring him back later,' I said.

He nodded again, boggle-eyed.

'All right?' I asked, and I smiled at him.

As if my smile had made the sun come out he beamed at me.

'All right, Miss Sarah!' he said, suddenly finding his tongue. 'Aye! All right! And I won't tell nobody where you've gone an' all.

Aye! an' they won't even know you've gone for they all went off to the 'orses show and left me here on my own. They went this afternoon and they'll have stopped at the Bull on the way back. Only I know you're out, Miss Sarah. An' I won't tell nobody.'

'Thank you,' I said, a little surprised. Then I led Sea to the mounting block, got myself into the side-saddle and walked out of the yard.

I took the main drive to Midhurst, I thought Gower's show would be on the south side of the town, quite near, and I was right. I could see the lamplight glinting from the half-open barn door from a while away. In the road, tethered, were a handful of horses belonging to farmers and their wives who had ridden over to see the show. There were even a few gigs with the horses tied to the fence to wait.

I checked Sea and looked at the barn. There was no one on the door so they were all working around the back. I thought my fine clothes and my hat with the veil would serve to disguise me, especially if they were all in the ring and I kept to the back of the crowd. I took Sea over to the side of the road and tied him alongside the farmers' nags in the hedgerow. Then I picked up the swooping extra length of my riding habit skirt and strode up the path to the barn door.

I heard a great 'oooh!' as I entered and I slid in along the wall, steadying myself with the wall against my back. I feared I was going to be sick.

Jack was there. Jack the devil, Jack the child, Jack the smiling killer. Jack was standing on the catcher frame where he had been before. And it was as I had feared and as I had dreamed and as I had sworn it could not be. It was the same. It was the same. It was the same as it had always been. As if she had never been there, as slight as an angel on the pedestal board, as trusting as a child flying towards him with her arms out. Smiling her naughty triumphant smile because she had been so certain that she had won a great wager and earned herself safety and happiness for the rest of her life. It was the same as if he had not done it. It was just as if she, and I, had never been.

I shut my eyes. I heard him call, 'Pret!' as I had heard him call it a thousand times, a hundred thousand times. I heard him call, 'Hup!' and I heard the horrid nauseous 'oooh!' of the crowd and then the slap of firm grip on moving flesh as he caught the flyer, and then the ecstatic explosion of applause.

I should not have come. I turned and pushed my way past a man, heading back towards the door, the back of my hand tight against my mouth, vomit wet against it. As soon as I was outside, I clung to the wall and retched. I was sick as a wet puppy. And between each bout of sickness I heard again, Jack's gay call of, 'Pret!' and then, 'Hup!' as if he had never called a girl off the pedestal bar to fling her . . . to fling her . . .

'And so my lords, ladies and gentlemen, that concludes the show tonight. We are here until Tuesday! Please come again and tell your friends that you will always command a warm welcome from Robert Gower's Amazing Aerial and Equestrian Show!'

The voice from inside the barn was Robert's. Confident show-ground bawl. I would have known it anywhere. The braggish joy in his tone hit my belly like neat gin. I wiped my gloved hand around my mouth and went to the doorway and looked in.

People were coming out, well pleased with the show. One woman jostled me and then saw the cut and cloth of my riding habit and bobbed a curtsey and begged my pardon. I did not even see her. My eyes were fixed on the ring, a small circle of white wood shavings inside a circle of hay bales. In the plumb centre was Robert Gower, arms outstretched after his bow, dressed as I had seen him at that first show, in his smart red jacket and his brilliant white breeches, his linen fine, his boots polished. His face red and beaming in the lantern light, as if he had never ordered a girl to be taught to go to her death with a smile on her face and her hair in ribbons.

I pushed through the outgoing crowd and went, blind to their looks, towards the ring fence. I stepped over the bales and went on, right to the centre of the ring where in my own right I had stood and taken a call. Robert turned as I came towards him, his professional smile fading, his face beginning to look wary. He did not recognize me, in my fine riding habit with my long hair piled up under my hat. But he saw the quality of my clothes, and he gave a half-smile wondering what this lady might want of him. I stopped directly before him, and without warning raised my riding crop and slashed him – right cheek, left cheek – and stepped back. His hands were in fists at once, he was coming for me when he suddenly hesitated and looked more closely.

'Meridon!' he said. 'It is Meridon, isn't it?'

'Yes,' I said through my teeth. I could feel the anger and the grief rising like bile in my throat. 'That blow was for Dandy.'

He blinked. I could see the weals from the whip growing red on his cheek. The people in the crowd behind me were murmuring, those at the doorway had turned back, trying to hear our low-voiced exchange.

Robert looked quickly around, fearing scandal. 'What the devil is with you?' he demanded, angry at the blow, his hand to his cheek. 'And where the hell have you been? Whose clothes are they? And how dare you strike me?'

'Dare?' I spat out at him. 'I *dare* strike you. When you killed her, when you let your whoreson murdering son kill her? And then you go on as if nothing had happened at all?'

Robert's hand went from his red cheek to his forehead. 'Dandy?' he said wonderingly.

At her name something broke inside me. The tears tumbled out of my eyes and my voice choked as the words spilled out. 'She did as she was told!' I shouted. 'David told her. "Let the catcher to his job," he said. "You trust him to catch you. You throw the trick, let the catcher do the catching."'

Robert nodded, his hand on the long ponies' whip was shaking. 'Aye, Meridon,' he said. 'Aye, I know. But what's this to anything? An accident can happen. He caught her on that trick, we both saw him catch her. Then she slipped out of his hands.'

'He threw her,' I shouted.

He gasped and the blood drained from his face until the marks of the riding crop were livid streaks on his yellowish cheeks.

'He threw her against the wall,' I said, sparing him nothing. 'He caught her perfectly and then as they swung back he threw her. He threw her out, beyond the safety net, against the back wall and broke her neck. She smashed into that wall, and was dead before I could hold her. She was dead while I still heard her scream. She was dead like a broken doll. He broke her.'

Robert looked like a man struck dumb of apoplexy, his eyes started, his mouth was blue.

'My Jack . . .' he whispered to himself. Then he looked at me again. 'Why?' he asked, and his voice was like a little whipped child.

'She was pregnant,' I said wearily. 'She hoped to catch him, carrying his baby, your grandson. He did no worse than you, when you left your wife on the road. He's your son right enough.'

Robert blinked rapidly, several times. I saw him choke a little and swallow down the sour taste in his mouth.

'He killed her,' he said softly. 'She was carrying his child, and she's dead.'

I looked at him and felt no pity for him as his plans and his pride tumbled around him. I looked at him with hot hatred, staring out of eyes which were dry again. 'Oh aye,' I said. 'She is dead. And I'm dead too.'

I turned on my heel and left him, left him alone in the ring under the gently swinging trapeze, with the two marks of a whip cut on his pale face and his mouth trembling. I walked through the crowd which had gathered at the doorway, craning their necks to see the scene. They were pointing like that crowd had pointed in Selsey, all those lifetimes ago. I found Sea where he was tethered and looked around for a gate to use as a mounting block.

'Here,' a voice said and I blinked the haze from my eyes and saw two calloused hands clasped ready for my boot. It was Will Tyacke, standing beside Sea, waiting for my return.

I nodded and let him throw me up into the saddle. I turned Sea's head for home and rode off without waiting for him. In a few seconds I heard his horse trotting and he came alongside me, without a word. I glanced at him. His face was impassive, I did not know if he had seen me in the ring – but I could be sure he would hear all about it next market-day. I did not know if he had been in earshot of my anguished shout at Robert, if he had heard her name, if he had heard my name of Meridon.

But no one ever knew anything by looking at Will. The glance he gave me back was as discrete as stone. But his brown eyes were filled with pity.

'Back to Havering?' he asked.

'Yes,' I said. I was as desolate as a chrysallis after the butterfly has flown. A little dry dessicated thing which has outlived its time and can tumble over and over and crumble to dust. 'Nowhere else for me to go,' I said quietly.

He did not drop behind me, like a groom guarding his mistress as he might have done, given that he was as angry with me as he had ever been with anybody in his life; but he rode beside me as if we were equals. And in the empty heartbroken hollows of myself I was glad of his company and felt less alone as we rode up the drive to Havering Hall and the stars came out unseen above the dark canopy of the trees.

'Thank you,' I said as we reached the stables and the lad came out to take Sea. My throat was sore. I must have screamed at Robert, back there in the ring.

He turned his gaze on me as dark as a magician. 'Wait,' he said. 'Don't marry him. It won't hurt to wait a little.'

The yard was very quiet, the lad at my horse's head stood still, stroking Sea's white nose.

Will nodded. 'The pain will fade,' he said. 'You will be less desolate in time.'

I shook my head, I even found a slight unconvincing smile. 'No,' I said huskily. 'I never was very happy, even before I lost her. I don't expect much joy now.'

He leaned forward and with his hardened dirty hand he touched my cheek, and my forehead, smoothing the tense hot skin, rubbing at my temples with roughened gentle fingers. Then, before I knew what he was doing he took my face in both his hands and kissed me, one soft kiss, full on the lips as confident as an acknowledged lover.

'Good luck then, Sarah,' he said. 'You can always walk away from them all, you know.'

I didn't pull away from his touch. I closed my eyes and let him do as he would with me. It made no difference at all. I put my hands up and closed my fingers around his wrists and held him, held his hands against my cheeks and looked into his eyes. ˙

'I wish to God I was dead,'˙ I said to him.

We stood there for a moment, in silence. Then Sea shifted restlessly and our grip broke. The lad at Sea's head reached up for me and jumped me down from the saddle. Will stayed unmoving on his horse, watched me walk across the yard, the water trough shining like ice in the moonlight, watched the yellow lamplight from the house spill out in a square on the cobbles as I opened the back door, and then watched me close the door behind me and heard me shoot the bolts.

The next day we left for London, so Lady Clara's spies had not time to tell her of the show, and of the young lady who looked like me, but who answered to another name.

We travelled heavy. I thought of the old days, of one wagon carrying everything a family of five would need. Of the first season when we travelled with bedding for four, costume changes, saddlery and a scenery backdrop all loaded in two wagons. Lady Clara and I travelled in the Havering carriage, Lord Peregrine rode alongside for his own amusement. Behind us came the baggage coach with all our clothes and with Lord Peregrine's valet and two maids. Behind that came a wagon with various essentials necessary to Lady Clara's comfort: everything from sheets to the door-knocker, and either side of this little cavalcade ranged outriders – stable lads and footmen, armed for this journey with blunderbuss and bludgeon in case highwaymen might stop us and rob us. By the end of the first hour, bored and restless, I heartily hoped they would.

I was a bad travelling companion for Lady Clara. She had a book to read but I was still unable to read anything but the simplest of stories and the jogging of the chaise meant I could not put my finger under a line and follow it. I had with me some of the accounts of Wideacre in the days of my mama Julia, but I could not read her copperplate script and Lady Clara would not trouble herself to help me. And to my surprise, and then increasing discomfort, I found I was sickly with the movement of the carriage.

I did not believe it when I started to feel headachy and dizzy. Me, who had spent all my life on the driver's seat of a wagon, or eating or dozing behind! But it was true. The chaise was slung on thick leather straps and it bounced like a landlady's bubbies, and it swayed from side to side too. A great lolloping pig of a chaise, lined with sickly blue. I would have blessed the highwayman who stopped us. I would have been out of the chaise in a moment and begged him a ride on his horse.

'You're pale,' Lady Clara commented, looking up from her book.

'I'm sickly,' I said. 'The chaise makes me feel ill.'

She nodded. 'Don't say "sickly", say "unwell",' she said, and reached for her reticule. She pulled out a little bottle of smelling salts and handed it over to me. I had never seen such a thing before.

'Is it drink?' I asked, holding it to the light and trying to see.

'No!' said Lady Clara with her rippling laugh. 'It's smelling salts. You hold it under your nose and smell it.'

I took the stopper off and held the little bottle under my nose. I gave a hearty sniff and then gasped with the shock of it. My head reeled, my nostrils stung.

Lady Clara rocked on her seat. 'Oh, Sarah!' she said. 'You are a little savage! You wave it under your nose and breathe normally. I thought it might help.'

I stoppered the bottle again and handed it back to her. I fumbled in my pocket for my handkerchief and rubbed my sore nose and mopped my eyes.

'I should feel better if I could ride,' I said.

'Out of the question,' Lady Clara said, and that was the end of the conversation.

I shut my eyes against the swaying dizziness of the movement, and after a little while I must have slept, for the next thing I knew the wheels of the coach were squeaking and banging on cobblestones. I woke with a jump of shock and all round me was the bustle of the city and the shouts of the porters. The smell was appalling and the noise was as bad as Salisbury on market day, and it went on for mile after mile. I could not believe there were so many people in the world, so many carriages, so many paupers, beggars, hucksters, tradesmen.

'London!' Lady Clara said with a sigh of relief which showed how hard her stay in the country had been for her.

I nodded but instead of excitement I felt only dread. I would rather have done anything in the world than be where I was, Miss Sarah Lacey, come to town for my first Season as a young lady, driving up to the Haverings' town house with little Miss Juliet in the nursery and the newly wedded Lady Maria de Montrey coming to see her mama in the morning.

'You will not dislike my daughters,' Lady Clara said to me, her blue eyes veiled as if she could guess my thoughts as I grew paler and quieter.

'No,' I said without conviction.

'You will not dislike them, because they will mean nothing to you,' she said equably. 'Juliet is an ignorant schoolgirl, a little forward for her age, quite pretty. Maria is a little vixen. I married her well before her husband discovered the sharpness of her tongue. She ought to thank me for that but she will not.' Lady Clara gleamed over the top of her fan. 'She will hate you,' she said candidly, with a smile.

I hesitated. Sarah Lacey the young lady was in conflict with Meridon the gypsy. Meridon won. 'I hate cat fights,' I said bluntly. 'I don't want her scratching at me. It will be bad enough without that.'

Lady Clara smiled mischievously. 'Don't say "cat fights", Sarah,' she said. 'And don't be dull. It will not be bad. It is your coming-out into your rightful society. And you may rely on me to curb the worst excesses of my daughter's malice.'

I hesitated. 'You won't always be there,' I said. 'And Perry . . .'

Lady Clara's fan flicked the dusty air. 'Perry is as afraid of Maria as he is of me,' she said. 'He'll be no help to you, my dear. So I will always be there. Maria is selfish enough and conceited enough to try to make a fool of you in public. I shan't permit that. You will do well enough with me.'

'I'm grateful,' I said. There was a world of irony in my voice but Lady Clara chose not to hear it.

Instead she leaned forward. 'We're nearly here,' she said. 'This is Grosvenor Street, and here is our street, Brook Street, and here, on the corner, is our house.'

She spoke with pride, I stared in surprise at it. It was a handsome white house with a flight of four shallow steps down to the pavement, a great army of black iron railings around it, and a heavy triangular carving of stone over the doorway. They must have been waiting for us, for as the carriage drew up the double doors were flung open and two footmen in livery and half a dozen maids in black dresses and white aprons came out and stood in a row up the steps. Lady Clara put her hand to her bonnet and cast a swift look over me.

'Straighten your cape, Sarah,' she said abruptly. 'And don't smile at them.'

I nodded and tried to look as haughty and as disdainful as she did. Then they opened the carriage door and let down the steps and Lady Clara glided into the house nodding as the maids rippled down in a curtsey on either side of her, and I followed her in.

I was not awkward then. I was not gawkish. I had stood in a show ring before now and been stared at till the crowds had their full pennyworth. A row of housemaids would not discomfort me. I nodded impartially at their bowed capped heads, and followed Lady Clara indoors.

It was a grand lovely hall. If Lady Clara had not shot me a quick frown I should have gasped. The stairs came curling down the wall on our right, broad and shallow with a fancy curved banister. The wall behind it was crusty with plasterwork making picture frames and niches for white statues – indecent, I thought they were, but I barely had time for more than a glimpse. Inside the square gilt plaster frames were painted pictures of people wrapped up in coloured sheets and rolling in waves or lying about in woods. There was a door on our left to a room which would overlook the street but Lady Clara walked past it and followed the butler up the stairs to a parlour immediately above it, facing the street.

He threw open the door. 'We lit a fire in the parlour, my lady, thinking you might be chilled or tired from your drive,' he said. 'Would you like some tea m'lady? Or mulled wine?'

I stepped into the room behind her. It was the most extraordinary room I had ever seen in my life. Every wall was done up fancy with great mouldings and painted so that every wall was like a frame for a picture, or for the four tall windows. The fireplace was so covered with swags and curls and ribbons that you wondered they could ever find where to light it in the mornings. It was very grand. It was very imposing. I missed the simple comfort of Wideacre the moment I was over the threshold.

'Dust,' Lady Clara said walking into the parlour stripping off her gloves and handing them to the waiting maid.

The butler, the Havering man who had set off early yesterday night from Sussex to be here to greet us, shot a furious glance at the housekeeper, a London woman I had not seen before.

Lady Clara sat down before the fire and put her feet up on the brass fender. She held out her hands to the blaze and looked at them all, parlourmaid, housekeeper, butler, without a smile.

'Dust on the outside windowsills,' she said. 'Get them scrubbed. And bring me my post and a cup of mulled wine at once. And bring a cup for Miss Lacey and Lord Perry as well.'

The butler murmured an apology and backed from the room. The housekeeper and the maid flicked out shutting the door behind them. Lady Clara gleamed her malicious smile at me.

'There's never any call to be pleasant to servants, Sarah,' she said. 'There are thousands who would give their right arms for a good place in a London household. Treat them firmly and sack them when you need to. There's no profit in doing more.'

'Yes, Lady Clara,' I said, and I pulled out a chair from the fireside and sat down beside her.

The door opened and Perry came in with the parlourmaid behind him carrying a tray.

''Llo, Mama,' he said pleasantly. 'Sarah!' He waved the maid to the table and flapped her from the room and handed us our cups himself.

'Load of letters,' he said thoughtfully. 'Mostly for you, Mama. Half a dozen for me. Bills, I suppose.'

He handed the tray of Lady Clara's letters over to her and watched her as she sipped her drink and started to slit them open with an ivory paper knife. While her attention was distracted he reached deep into an inside pocket of his jacket and brought out a dark little flask and slopped a measure of some clear liquid into his drink. He winked at me, as roguish as a lad, and then sipped at his mulled wine with greater appetite.

'Invitations,' Lady Clara said with pleasure. 'Look, Sarah, your name on a gilt engraved card!'

She handed me a stiff white card and I put my fingers under the words and spelled out slowly: 'The Hon. Mrs Thaverley requests the pleasure of the Dowager Lady Clara Havering and Miss Sarah Lacey to a ball . . .'

'Lord! She mustn't do that in public, Mama!' Perry said, suddenly alarmed.

Lady Clara looked up from her letters and saw me, tortuously spelling out words.

'Good God no!' she said. 'Sarah, you must never try to read in public until you can do so without putting your finger under the words and moving your lips.'

I looked from one to the other of them. I had been so proud that I had been able to make out at all what the invitation said. But it was not a skill I had learned, it was a social embarrassment. Whatever I did it was never good enough for high society.

'I won't,' I promised tightly. 'Lady Clara, may I go to my room and take my hat off?'

She looked sharply at me and then her gaze softened. 'Yes, of course,' she said. 'I had forgotten you felt ill. Go and lie down and I will send your maid to call you in time for you to dress for dinner.'

She nodded me to pull the bell rope by the mantelpiece, and I looked at the clock. It said three o'clock.

'We will not dine for hours yet!' Lady Clara said airily. 'We keep town hours now! We will dine at six today, even later when we start entertaining. Mrs Gilroy can bring a slice of bread and cake up to you in your room.'

'Thank you,' I said. Peregrine held the door for me and then followed me out. The parlourmaid appeared from the back of the long corridor where I guessed the servants' stairs were, dipped a curtsey to both of us and waited. Perry's gaze was blurred, he had been drinking as he rode and the gin in the mulled wine had added to his haziness.

'I'll fetch the cake,' he offered. 'We'll have a little picnic. It can be like it was in the woods that first day when I thought you were a stable lad, and we said we'd be friends.'

'All right,' I said desolately.

I followed the maid down the corridor trailing my new bonnet by the ribbons so that the flowers on the side brushed on the thick pile of the carpet. The maid threw open a panelled door and stood to one side. It was a spacious pretty bedroom which I guessed had belonged to the vixen Maria before her marriage. There was a white and gold bed and matching dressing-table with a mirror atop and a stool before it. There was a hanging cupboard for dresses and cloaks. There was a window which was painted tight shut and looked out over the street where carriages went to and fro and errand boys and footmen sauntered. It smelled of indoors as if clean winds never blew in London. I wrinkled my nose at the stale scent of perfume and hair-powder. I could not imagine how I would ever manage to sleep there. It would be like living in a prison.

There was a great crash outside my door as Perry stumbled against it, tray in hands. I crossed the room and opened it and he weaved unsteadily in. The open bottle of wine had tipped over and was rolling on the tray, wine streaming out over plum cake, fairy cakes, little biscuits and slices of bread and butter. The little dish of jam had skidded to the back of the tray and was sticking, unnoticed, to his waistcoat. The tray was awash with red wine, the food sodden.

Perry dumped the lot on the hearthrug before the fire, quite unaware.

'Now we can be comfortable,' he said with satisfaction.

I giggled. 'Yes we can,' I said. And we toasted each other in the remainder of the wine and we ate soggy plum cake and red-stained biscuits, and then we curled up together like drunken puppies and dozed before the fire until the maid tapped on the door and told me it was time to dress for dinner.

29

Lady Clara had told me that I was fit for London society and I had doubted her when every move I made in Sussex was somehow subtly wrong. But once we were in London she criticized me very little, and I remembered with a wry smile how Robert Gower would never criticize a performance in the ring. It was the rehearsals where he was an inveterate taskmaster. In the ring he smiled encouragement.

Lady Clara was like that, and my life in London was like one long performance where I showed the tricks she had taught me and relied on her to skim over the errors I made. She covered for me wonderfully. When a young lady went to the piano to play and turned to me and said, 'Do you sing, Miss Lacey?' it was Lady Clara who said that I was training with one of the best masters and he insisted that I rest my voice between lessons.

They all nodded with a great deal of respect at that, and only the young lady at the piano looked at all put out.

Dancing I was excused until we had been to Almacks, some sort of club where I should dance my first dance with Perry.

Sketches were loaned to me from the schoolroom and Lady Clara insisted that I squiggle my initials at the foot of them, and had them framed. They attracted much praise and I thought my modesty was particularly becoming. The embroidery which was cobbled together by the governess in the schoolroom as an extra unpaid duty I left scattered around the drawing room, and Lady Clara would sweetly scold me in front of visitors for not putting it away. My flower arrangements were done by one of the parlourmaids who had once been apprenticed to a flower-seller. Only my horse riding and my card-playing were entirely my own and they were skills from my old life.

'Far too good for a young lady,' Lady Clara said. She wanted me to ride a quiet lady's mount and offered me a bay from her stables. But I held true to Sea and she sent down to Sussex for him. The stables were around the back of the house, down a cobbled street. Some afternoons, when Lady Clara was resting, I would wear a hat with a veil pulled down and sneak round to the stables to see him. I was not supposed to walk out without a footman, the horses should be brought to the door. But I did not trust the London stable lads to keep his tack properly clean. I was not sure they were reliable about his feeds and his water. To tell the truth, I simply longed to be with him and to smell him and to touch the living warmth of him.

Lady Clara would have known within a few days what I was doing. She said nothing. I think she knew, with her cunning common sense, that there was only so much I could bear to be without. If I had to live without the land, without travelling, and without the girl who had been my constant companion since the day I was born, I had to find things which would make me feel as if I touched earth somewhere. Sea, and sometimes Perry, were the only things in London which seemed real at all.

I was allowed out riding early every morning, provided I took a groom as a chaperone and did not gallop. When the clocks were striking seven we would trot through the streets which were busy even then. Down Davies Street, across Grosvenor Square which was dusty from the building work, and along Upper Brook Street to the park where the green leaves were looking dry and tired, and some of the bushes were yellowing at their edges. Sometimes the gate-keeper at the Grosvenor Gate lodge would be up, and tip his hat to me, more often only the groom and I were the only people in the park. There were ducks silent beside the still pond, there were great flocks of pigeons which wheeled around us. One morning I heard a low rushing creaky noise and looked up to see a pair of white swans circling the water and landing with a great green bow-wave of stagnant water cresting against their broad white breasts.

On Wideacre at this time of year I thought the berries would be very bright and ripe in the bushes. The nuts would be in thick clusters on the trees. In the London park there was fruiting and nutting going on, but it seemed more like a diversion. It hardly seemed a matter of hunger, of life or death. The squirrels in the trees and the ducks by the reservoir seemed like stuffed pets, not like live hungry animals.

The groom rode behind me at half a dozen paces, but I was as aware of him watching me as if he had been a gaol keeper. Sea longed for a gallop but I had to keep him on a tight rein. The noises of the city puzzled and fretted him, his ears went back all the time as we rode home through the crowded streets. When I rode him down the cobbled mews and left him in his stables I thought he looked at me reproachfully with his great dark eyes as if to say that the place he had found for us, that night when we had been quite lost, had been better than this. I would shrug as I walked home, as if I were trying to explain in my head that we had to be here. He had to live in a street filled with other stables where rich carriages and beautiful horses awaited their owners' commands. Among all that wealth and elegance I could not understand why I did not feel triumphant. I had wanted the best, the very best. And now I had it.

Perry would never ride with me in the early mornings. He was out too late every night of the week. Sometimes he went to gambling hells, sometimes he went to cock pits or boxing rings. Once he went to a riding show and offered to take me. I said I did not want to go, that his mama would not approve of me going, and he went alone. I did not even ask him who were the riders and what tricks they did.

He did not rise until midday and would sometimes take breakfast with us dressed in a brilliant-coloured dressing gown. When his head was aching badly he would take strong black coffee cut with brandy. When he was well he would drink strong ale or wine and water. Whether he ate well, or whether his hands were shaking and his face white, his mama never seemed to notice. She read her letters, she chatted to me. One time he was swaying in his chair and I thought he might faint, but Lady Clara never said one word. She never tried to check his drinking. She seldom asked him where he had been the night before. He grew paler and paler every week of the Season, but Lady Clara seemed to see nothing but her own pretty reflection in the mirror over the mantelpiece; she watched no one but me.

I met Juliet and her governess that first evening. She came downstairs to be introduced before dinner, but she did not stay to dine with her mama. She made her curtsey to me without raising her eyes, and when she was told that Perry and I were to marry and that she and I would be sisters she gave me a cold kiss on the cheek and wished me very happy.

I made no effort to get on closer terms with her. I did not want a sister.

Lady Maria arrived in a flurry of ostrich plumes the first morning after our arrival.

'Expensive,' her mama said coolly as she fluttered into the room. Maria kissed her and then stood back and twirled around so that Lady Clara might see the full effect of a blue velvet walking gown, blue jacket, blue hat and blue feathers with a dark fur cape thrown over the shoulders.

'Vulgar,' Lady Clara said simply.

Maria laughed, not at all abashed. 'Where's the pauper-heiress?' she demanded.

Lady Clara frowned and affected deafness. 'Sarah, may I present to you my daughter, Lady de Monterey. Maria this is Miss Sarah Lacey.'

Maria gave me a gloved hand and a look as cold as ice. 'I hear you and Perry are to be married,' she said coolly. 'I hope you will be very happy I am sure.'

I smiled, as cold as her. 'I am sure we will,' I said. 'I believe you are newly wed aren't you? I'm sure I wish you very happy.'

We stood smiling at each other as if we had lemon slices in our mouths. Lady Clara stood back as if enjoying the spectacle.

'How is Basil?' she asked briskly, pulling the bell pull for morning coffee.

Maria unpinned her hat before the mirror and patted the tightly crimped blonde curls into place. She turned and made a face at her mother.

'Just the same,' she said. 'Still working, working, all the time; just like a tradesman.'

'A rather successful tradesman,' Lady Clara said wryly. 'He did not quibble about the price of that ball gown which you wrote to me about?'

Maria beamed. 'I slipped it in along with a whole lot of bills from his estate,' she said. 'Compared to a forest of trees which he is planting I am positively paltry.'

Lady Clara smiled. 'It would be as well not to play that trick too often,' she warned. 'You've only been married a quarter.'

The maid set the coffee tray before me and then waited to pass the cups around when I had poured them. My hand was as steady as a rock and I did not spill a drop. Lady Clara was watching me from the corner of her eyes. Maria had forgotten I was there.

'I'm flush now,' she said airily. 'I had this quarter's dress allowance and I doubled it last night playing *vingt-et-un* at Lady Barmain's. I had such a run of luck, Mama, I vow you would not have believed it! Four hundred pounds I won clear! You should have seen her ladyship's face! She was nearly sick when I rose from the tables a winner. They say she rents her house on her winnings at the table, you know. I must have cost her a month at least!'

Lady Clara laughed her sharp London laugh, and Maria told her some more gossip about people whose names I did not know, but whose vices and sorrows, drink or gambling or un-fulfilled desire, were the same in high society as in a show-ground.

I was surprised at that. In my first month in London my greatest lesson was that there was less difference than I had seen when I had been at the bottom, the very bottom of the heap of society looking up. I had been dazzled then by the cleanli-ness and the food they ate, at the fineness of the gowns and the way the ladies were so dainty, and dressed so bright. But now I too was washed and fed, and could talk in a high light voice as they did. I could curtsey to the right depth, I could spread a fan and smile behind it. I could mince across a room, not stride. They were all signals, secret code-words, as impen-etrable as the signs of the road which tell you where it is safe to camp and where you can poach. Once I had learned them, I had the key to a society which was the same as that of a fairground: nothing more and nothing less. They were drunkards and gamblers, wife-beaters and lovers, friends, parents and children; just the same. The greatest difference between the world of the gentry and those of the landless was just that: land. When I had been on the bottom of the heap I owned nothing and they had taught me to think the worse of myself for that. The only thing which had brought me to the top of the world was land and money, they would forgive me everything if I remained rich. I would never have got beyond the area railings if I had stayed poor.

And while I rode Sea on my lonely way in the park in the mornings, or watched dancers swirl around on the floor while the clock struck midnight and footmen yawned behind gloved hands, I recognized more and more that the wealth of the ballroom and the poverty of the farmyard were alike unjust. There was no logic to it. There was no reason. The wealthy were rich because they had won their money by fair means and foul. The poor were poor because they were too stupid, too weak, or too kindly to struggle to have more and to hold it against all challenges. Of the people I met every day, only a few had been rich for many years, the vast majority were quick-witted merchants, slavers, soldiers, sailors, farmers or traders only a generation ago. They had succeeded in the very enterprises where Da had failed. And so Da had grown poorer and more miserable, while they had grown rich.

I did not become a Jacobin with these observations! Oh no! If anything it hardened my heart to Da and those like him. It strengthened me. I was never going to fall out of the charmed circle of the rich. I was never going to be poor again. But I saw the rich clearly, as once I had not. I saw them at last as lucky adventurers in a world with few prizes.

And, by the way, for all the extravagant profits they made, the wealth they earned, not one of them worked half as hard as we had done for Robert's show. Indeed few of them worked as hard as feckless, idle Da.

It took me only a month to see through the Quality life and thereafter I was not afraid of them. I had seen Lady Clara condemn a woman for hopeless vulgarity and cite her bad connections, and yet include her on the guest list for a party. I learned that a great many mistakes would be forgiven me if I could keep my wealth. And all the little obstacles which they liked to invent: the vouchers for Almacks, the proper costume for presentation, the sponsor at court – all these things were just pretend-obstacles to weed out those with insufficient capital or land, to challenge those who did not have enough money for three tall ostrich-plumes to be worn once, for half an hour of an evening only, to complete the formal court gown.

But I had enough money. I had enough land. And if I forgot how to hold my knife once or twice when I came across a new dish at dinner, or if I spoke a word out of place, it was quickly forgotten and forgiven to the beautiful rich Miss Lacey of Wideacre.

They thought I was beautiful, it was not just the money. It was the fine clothes, and how I rode Sea in the park. The young men liked how I walked with them, long easy strides and not the hobbled minces of usual young ladies. They called me a 'Diana' after some old Greek lady. They sent me housefuls of flowers and asked me to dance. One of them, actually a baronet, asked me to break my engagement with Perry and become engaged to him. He took me into a private room as he led me back from the ballroom and flung himself at my feet swearing eternal love.

I said, 'No,' brusquely enough and turned to leave but he jumped to his feet and grabbed me and would have kissed me. I brought my knee up sharply and I heard the hem of my gown rip before I had time to stop and think what a young lady should do. Lady Clara came spinning into the little lobby room in time to see him gasping and heaving on a sofa.

'Sir Rupert! what is this?' she demanded. Sir Rupert was white as a sheet and could only gasp and clutch his breeches.

Lady Clara turned on me. 'Sarah?' she said. 'I saw Sir Rupert take you from the supper room, he should have brought you back to the ballroom. What are you doing here?'

'Nothing, Lady Clara,' I said. I was scarlet up to the eyebrows. 'Nothing happened.'

She took me by the elbow and dragged me over to the window. 'Sarah! Quick! Tell me what took place,' she hissed.

'He grabbed me and tried to kiss me,' I said. I hesitated. I did not know how to tell her what had happened in genteel language.

'And then?' Lady Clara prompted urgently. 'Sarah! The man is one of the richest gentlemen in England and he is rolling on the sofa in his mama's house! What the devil has happened?' She clutched my arm hard and her eyes suddenly widened. 'Don't say you hit him!' she moaned.

'No,' I said. 'I kneed him in the balls. He'll recover.'

Lady Clara let out a shriek of laughter and clapped her gloved hand over her mouth at once. 'Never say that again,' she said through her fingers. 'We are leaving at once.'

She tucked my hand under her arm and swept me from the room without pausing to say a word to Sir Rupert. She nodded regally to his mama from the other side of the ballroom but did not deign to bid her farewell. A surprised link boy was sent flying for our carriage. Lady Clara would not let me speak until we were in our own house with the door closed behind us, then she sank down into a chair in the hallway and laughed until she gasped for breath. When she lifted her head I saw her eyes were streaming.

'Oh Sarah!' she said. 'I would not have missed tonight for the world! Never do that again Sarah! Scream or faint or have the vapours. But don't do that,' she paused. 'Unless it's a common man of course. But never attack anyone over the level of a squire.'

'No, Lady Clara,' I said obediently.

She looked at me keenly and stripped off her evening gloves and smoothed the skin under her eyes. 'Did he offer to marry you?' she asked acutely.

'Before he grabbed me,' I said. 'Yes, he did.'

'But you are betrothed,' she said.

'I didn't forget it,' I said. 'He asked me to break my promise to Perry and I said I would not.'

'You prefer Perry,' her ladyship stated.

'Yes,' I said truthfully. 'I do.'

'Even though Sir Rupert is good-looking and pleasant,' she said.

I paused. 'He is,' I agreed. 'But I think Perry suits me better.'

I would have said nothing more, but Lady Clara was curious.

'Why?' she asked. 'Why Perry rather than Sir Rupert?'

'Sir Rupert is passionate,' I said. 'He thinks he is in love with me. He would want his passionate love returned. I cannot do that.'

'And Perry is content with nothing,' Lady Clara said, her lip curled slightly.

'Perry and I are friends,' I said defensively.

'You have never kissed, he has never touched you?' Lady Clara asked.

I felt myself blush slightly. 'We neither of us want that,' I said. 'It is our decision.'

She nodded. 'Does he have a woman?' she asked. She rose from the chair and slung her fur wrap down and went to the stairs.

'No!' I said, surprised. I had thought of Perry for so long as a man quite without desire that I was almost shocked that his mother – whose view of him was so acute – should have thought him capable of having a mistress.

She paused, one delicate satin-shod foot on the lower step. 'I suppose he can get an heir?' she asked crudely. 'He's not impotent, d'you think, Sarah?'

My face was as hard as hers. 'He knows his duty,' I said. 'He knows he has to.'

Her face softened and she smiled. 'That's all right then,' she said, as if the inheritance were all that mattered. 'Good-night, my dear.'

I said good-night and watched her as she went lightly up the stairs to her room and shut her door.

I thought of the show and of the women I had seen with Da. Of Zima and of Katie the whore. And I thought that never in my life had I seen a woman as beautiful and as cold-hearted as the women who was to be my new mama, when I married her son.

The late nights did not make me weary. I woke every morning when the clatter of the street outside my bedroom started, and the day after the ball was sunny and I was glad to be up early and take Sea out to the park.

The weather was getting colder. I shivered as Sea trotted down the cobbled road towards the park. The groom beside me had a blue muffler around a blue chin and looked as if he would have preferred another hour in his bed.

Sea's ears were back, as they always were when we were riding in town, but they suddenly went forward and he gave a ringing neigh of welcome as a square figure on a heavy bay horse pulled up as if waiting for us at the end of the road.

'Will Tyacke!' I declared, and my heart lifted with delight.

He was beaming, his face bright with joy at seeing me, and I reached out my hand to shake his. If we had not been on horseback I would have flung my arms around his neck and hugged him.

'How are you?' he said at once. 'How are they treating you here? You look pale, are you happy here?'

I laughed and put my hand on his shoulder. 'Stop!' I said. 'I am quite well. I was out late last night so perhaps I do look tired, but I am happy enough. Is everything all right on Wideacre?'

'Aye,' he said. 'Well enough. We've ploughed and planted winter crops. The apples did well, and the plums. We've enough feed and wheat to get through the winter. Things are well at home.'

I swallowed a lump in my throat. Will seemed like a messenger from another world, I could almost smell the cold autumn air of Wideacre on him. I thought of the house nestling in the parkland and the trees turning yellow and gold. I thought of the beech trees going purple and dark and the animals coming down from the higher fields.

'Does the land look nice?' I asked. It was a foolish question but I did not have the right words.

Will's smile was understanding. 'Aye,' he said. 'The roses at the Hall are still flowering though it's getting late in the year. The Fenny is high, you'd hardly recognize it. The trees are turning colour and all the swallows are gone. The owls call very loud at nights. The moon has been very bright and yellow. I miss you.'

I drew my breath in with a little hiss and froze. Will's gaze dropped from my face to his horse's mane. 'I've come to town on business of my own,' he said. 'But I promised myself I could come and find you and tell you this. I understand that you wanted your Season, that you wanted to see what the Quality life was like.'

He paused and then went on softly, persuasively. 'You've seen it now, you've seen it all. You've been to balls and danced with lords. Now you should come home. I'm come to tell you that, and I'll escort you home if you've had enough of being here. Your bedroom is ready at the Hall. You could be home by nightfall. We'd all be glad to see you back.'

A cart loaded with milk churns came noisily down the street and Sea flinched and I had to steady him. 'Come to the park with me,' I said. 'Sea needs exercise.'

Will nodded at the groom. 'I'll take her,' he said. 'Away and get yourself something to eat. You look half clemmed.'

'I am that,' the man said gratefully and pulled his dirty cap in my direction. 'Shall I come round to the house for the horse when you've finished your ride, Miss Lacey?'

'No,' I said. 'I'll bring him back.'

He wheeled his horse and trotted down the street back to the stables, and Will and I turned towards the park, riding abreast.

Will told me other news of Wideacre, a baby had been born and was to be called 'Sarah', the vicar had been away for a week and was greatly put out on his return to find no one had attended church for the curate he had installed in his absence. A vagrant had come through the village begging and had stolen all the linen off the washing lines. The gypsies were back on the Common where they always camped. They were early which was the sign of a hard winter.

'Everything the same as ever,' Will said with a smile.

We rode side by side in a sedate canter. Sea remembered the races on Downland and Common and threw up his head and wanted to gallop but I held him back.

'And you?' Will asked. 'Is it how you expected?'

I shrugged. 'It passes the time,' I said. I shot a sideways look at him and then I told him how it was in truth. I told him about the pleasures of the new life: the dresses, the hats, the morning rides. I told him about the extraordinary people who were accepted as normal in this odd new world. I told him about the young men, and I made him laugh until he had to cling to his horse's mane when I told him about Sir Rupert left gasping on the sofa clutching his balls.

'And Lady Havering? And Lord Peregrine?' Will asked. 'Are they good to you?'

I hesitated. 'As much as they can be,' I said. 'Lady Clara is as cold as ice. I've met kindlier women laying-out paupers. She cares for nothing but the Havering estate and the succession.'

Will nodded. 'I heard she cared for her oldest son well enough,' he said. 'The one that died.'

'Aye,' I said crudely. 'Men are always more lovable when they're dead!'

Will laughed at that. 'But Lord Peregrine,' he said and his voice was carefully bright. 'Do you see much of him now? Is the engagement still on?'

I nodded. I did not look at him. 'The contracts are with the lawyers,' I said. 'I will marry him, you know.'

Will was looking straight ahead, down a little avenue where the pale yellow fronds of the chestnut trees made an archway over our heads. We were quite alone and the clatter of the town in the early morning seemed far away.

'I thought you might meet someone you fancied better,' he said. 'I thought you were using him to get yourself comfortable in London – that you'd throw him over when you were settled.'

I smiled a little wry smile. 'You think highly of me, don't you?' I asked.

He shrugged. 'It won't be the first time a girl's jilted a

milksop,' he said. 'I thought when you had a chance to look around you'd see someone you fancied more.'

'No,' I said. 'I don't think I'll ever have a fancy for a man.'

'Hard luck on the man who loves you,' Will offered neutrally.

'Very,' I said. I shot a sideways look at him. 'A disaster for the man who loves me,' I repeated. 'If he married me he would find me always cold. If he did not he could waste his life in loving me and I would never return it.'

'Because you loved her, and now she is dead?' he asked very quietly.

I flinched as soon as he even neared the pain that was as sharp and fresh inside me as the evening she died.

'Yes,' I said. 'Perhaps because of that. But even before, long before that, I think it was already spoiled for me.'

'Lord Peregrine gets short measure then,' Will said.

I smiled. 'He gets what he wants,' I said. 'He's cold. He doesn't like women much. He's mortal feared of his ma, he likes me because I don't fuss him and want petting.'

'He's an odd one,' Will suggested.

I frowned. 'He's a drunkard, I think,' I said. 'And I think he's a gambler. He was well enough in the country, but now he is out every night and I think gambling has a hold on him.'

I paused, thinking of men I had seen at fairgrounds losing everything they owned on the turn of a card. 'I am afraid it might get to him,' I said. 'I should like to take him away.'

There was an open stretch of grass before us. We let the horses' stride lengthen and then Sea threw his head up. I caught his wildness in a moment and in my mind, my gypsy-brat voice said, 'Damn the rules,' and I let Sea go. The ground seemed to leap from under us, and I heard Will yell with pleasure behind us as his horse gave chase. We were in the lead, and Sea was going as if he wanted to gallop all the way to Sussex. I had to steady him, I had to pull him up. We were nearly by the road which intersects the park. It would have caused talk if I had been seen galloping, and that with a working man.

Sea blew out softly, but he was not winded. He could have

gone on for hours. I could tell by the feel of him that he was puzzled that we had stopped so soon.

Will's big bay thundered up to us and spattered us with mud as Will pulled him up.

'That's better!' Will said. 'That's the first real smile I've seen on your face since I've been here! You should gallop more often, Sarah.'

I shook my head, still smiling. 'I'm not allowed,' I said.

Will said something under his breath which sounded like an oath. 'Not allowed!' he said. 'You're the squire of Wideacre. Why take these damned rules? Why take this hopeless man? You say yourself he's a drunkard and a gambler. Haven't you had enough sorrow and trouble without taking on a fool as well?'

I turned Sea's head homeward, and I bit back a quick and angry reply.

'I need to run my own land,' I said carefully. 'I need a husband so I can live as I please without Mr Fortescue's old chaperone, or anyone bothering me.'

Will nodded, but looked like he wanted to interrupt.

'I can't marry an ordinary man,' I said. 'You know why. I'd drive an ordinary man mad within a week. I've no love to give, and I want none. I can manage Perry. I can keep him from gambling and from the drink when we live in the country. It doesn't matter that he is a weak fool. He's kind-hearted enough, he's gentle with me. I can manage him. He is the only husband I could deal with.'

Will looked at me carefully. 'He might like lads,' he said bluntly. 'Had you thought of that?'

'What?' I asked. I pulled Sea up and stared blankly at Will. 'Lads?'

Will cleared his throat in embarrassment. 'Don't be so daft, Sarah, for the Lord's sake,' he begged me. 'I just thought you should think about it. He might like lads. You know. He might be a gentleman of the back door. You know!'

I exploded in a shout of laughter. 'A what? A gentleman of the what?'

Will was scarlet with embarrassment. 'Now have done, Sarah,' he said. 'You should think about this. You're going to marry him and you won't always have his ma there to keep him in order. If he gets drunk he might ill-treat you. If he likes lads he could fill the house with them and there's no one to say him nay. He could get the pox and give it to you. Think about it, for God's sake!'

I sobered then, and nodded. 'Thank you,' I said frankly. 'Thank you for thinking of me. I had not thought that Perry might like lads. I will consider it. But for me it is no great disadvantage. I don't want a normal husband, I want one that will leave me alone. He's told me we have to get an heir and then we will not bed together again. That's a bargain for me in return for a gentry husband and an estate next door to Wideacre.'

'And you'll use the Havering power and knowledge to break the Wideacre corporation,' Will said frankly.

I sighed. I looked into his honest brown eyes. 'Yes,' I said.

He nodded. 'Thought so,' he said. We turned the horses and walked on.

'What have you come to London for?' I asked. 'You said you had business here.'

'I have,' he said. 'Though I couldn't have left the town without seeing you. I've come for a meeting of a society of corporations. There's a few other places trying to farm the land together, and we all meet together every six months or so to see how things are going. There's talk of a newspaper as well. Wideacre is one of the more successful corporations. There's lots who want to know how we do it. I'm to give a speech to a public meeting tonight.'

I nodded, rather impressed. 'What will you say?' I asked.

Will smiled. 'You'd not like it,' he said. 'I'll tell them how Wideacre suffered most harshly from enclosures – that was your grandmother, Beatrice Lacey. Then the estate went into ruin after the riot. Then I'll tell them about the rebuilding of the estate and running it as a sharing scheme with the landlord during your ma's lifetime, when Ralph Megson was manager. And then I'll tell them that when the estate was run by the Trust we set up the corporation.'

'And what will you tell them about me?' I asked.

Will's face was grim. 'I'll tell them that we don't know what the future will hold for us,' he said. 'That if the new squire chooses to go against us we will see the corporation ruined and we will have to leave and start again elsewhere or accept that we will become again an ordinary poor village.'

'Leave?' I said blankly. I had never thought that anyone might one day leave Wideacre. I had never thought of any greater change than that I should have more of a share of the profits, that it should be my decision how the land was to be used.

'Oh aye,' Will said. 'There's a few who will be there tonight who are thinking of setting up corporations: gentlemen farmers and owners of big factories in the north who want to try their hand at co-operative farming. They'd be glad to have a manager who had done something of the sort before – and made it pay,' he added with a smile. 'There's a few from Acre who'd rather move than be ruled by a landlord again.' He looked at me sideways with a half-smile. 'Once you start changes Sarah, you may find they take you further than you meant to go.'

'Who would stay in Acre if you went?' I asked.

Will shrugged as if it were not his problem. With a sudden jolt of apprehension I realized that it would indeed not be his problem.

'Those that didn't mind working for a landlord again,' he said. 'Those who had not saved money over the last few years and could not afford to leave. Those who had saved enough to pay the new expensive rents you would bring in.' He thought for a moment. 'Each family would feel differently,' he said. 'Some would not bear to go. Some have been there so long, and love the countryside so well.'

'I had not thought anyone would leave,' I said.

'Most would,' Will said bluntly. 'I'd not stay one day after your marriage. I've no time to waste.'

'You'd go to one of these experimental farms?' I asked.

'Or America,' he said.

I gasped, involuntarily. 'America!' I said.

Will looked at me and his brown eyes were smiling. 'I could be persuaded to stay,' he said.

I smiled back, but my eyes were steady. 'I have to have the money and the land,' I said.

He shrugged. 'Then you could not keep me,' he said gently. We turned the horses and headed for home.

'When's this wedding to be, then?' he asked, as we turned down the little lane towards the stables.

'At the end of the Season,' I said. 'Spring, next year.'

'Aye,' he said. 'Plenty of time for you to see his paces. Time for you to change your mind if you wish. No one can constrain you, Sarah.'

We had reached the stable yard and the groom came out to take Sea. I slid from his back and patted his neck. He turned his great wise face around and lipped at my pocket, seeking a sugar-lump stolen from my breakfast tray.

'Will you come to London again?' I asked. My voice sounded desolate. I had not meant to sound like that.

I turned and walked out to the street outside the stable yard, Will swung down from his horse's back and led him, following me.

'Do you want me to?' he asked.

I turned and faced him. 'Yes,' I said honestly. 'If you're coming up to town I should like you to come and see me and bring me news of Wideacre.'

He nodded. 'If you needed me, I should find a room and be here for you, to ride with you every morning, to see you every day,' he said. He spoke in the same level tones as if he were asking me if the plough horses should be shod.

'No,' I said sadly. 'I should not ask that of you. You should be at Wideacre.'

He swung into the saddle and looked down at me, where I stood on the pavement. 'So should you,' he observed.

I raised a hand to him. 'When shall I see you again?' I asked.

He smiled. 'You tell me when, and I will come,' he promised.

'Next week?' I hazarded.

Will smiled, a warm generous smile. 'It just so happens that I need to come to London next Wednesday. You have just put me in mind of it. I'll stay overnight and ride with you in the morning.'

'Yes,' I said, and I reached up my hand to him. Will took it and bent down low and pulled back my glove so that my wrist was bared. He pressed a kiss on to the delicate skin of the inside of my wrist and then buttoned the glove again. It was as if the touch of his lips was kept safe inside.

'Send for me if you need me,' he said.

I nodded, and stepped back. His horse trotted forwards and I watched them go.

30

Even if Will had not warned me of Perry I should have been watching him anyway. His drinking was getting worse, his nights were getting later. One morning, when I came out for my ride I found him retching hopelessly, clinging to the railings in broad daylight.

I took his collar in a hard grip and hauled him to his feet, and then slung his arm over my shoulder and half dragged, half walked him up the steps to the front door. The tweeny, who was up to light the fires before anyone else, let us in, horror-struck at having to open the door, which should be done by the butler, and aghast that it was his lordship.

'Help me,' I said sharply. 'I'll never get him up the stairs on my own.'

She bobbed a scared curtsey and dived under his other arm. 'Yes'm,' she said. 'But if you please 'm, I'm not allowed up the front stairs.'

'Doesn't matter,' I said through my teeth. Perry had got a grip on one of the railings and would not let go. 'Come on, Perry!' I said. 'Stay here much longer and your ma will see you!'

I thought that would shift him, but it did not. He turned his face towards me and I saw his blue eyes were suddenly filled with tears. 'She wouldn't care,' he said. 'She never did care for me, and she doesn't care for me now.'

'Nonsense,' I said briskly. I unclasped his hand from the railing and nodded at the maid. We both made a little rush at the step and got him over it. I heard a clatter of hooves behind me and there was Gerry, the groom from the stables riding his horse and leading Sea. 'Wait for me!' I called, and then grabbed Peregrine as his knees buckled underneath him as we made it into the hall.

Peregrine collapsed on to the bottom step of the stairs and looked up at the maid and me. 'That's funny,' he said. 'Sarah? Now there are two of you.'

'Oh come on! Perry!' I said. 'We've got to get you to your room. People will be getting up soon, we don't want them to see you like this.'

Perry's perfect mouth turned down again. 'I don't care,' he said. 'They don't care. Everyone knows I'm not as good as George. No one expects me to be as good as George. No one likes me as much as they liked him.'

I nodded to the maid and we grabbed hold of an arm each and turned him around to face the stairs.

'Everyone loved George,' Perry said glumly.

The maid and I went up two steps and then, borne back by the dead weight of Perry, we went back one.

'He was the image of my papa,' Perry said. 'And my papa loved him like his own son.'

We made a bit of ground while Perry considered this, nearly as far as the first landing. But Perry grabbed at the banister and turned to explain to me. 'He was his son, you see,' he said.

I nodded. 'I know, Perry,' I said soothingly. We got hold of him again and started the ascent up to the next landing.

'I am too,' Perry said sadly. 'It just didn't seem so important.'

I was watching his feet in the expensive boots. He was half-walking, half-dragged by us.

'Papa always said I looked like Mama. Not like him,' he said. 'He said I looked like a girl. He used to call me little Miss Peregrine.'

This time it was me who stopped, it cost us a few steps downwards.

'What?' I said.

'He called me Pretty Miss Peregrine,' Perry said. 'I never got the feeling he really liked me. Sent me away to school when I was six. Never had me home for the holidays when he was there. All over the place I was. Scotland, London, even France one holiday. Never home with him and George.' The tears had overflowed and his face was wet. 'Once George and Papa were dead I thought it would be different,' he said. 'But I suppose I just don't look like a lord.'

'You do!' I said fiercely. 'You do look like a lord. You look like an angel, Perry. You are the best-looking man I know. And if you could stay sober you would be a really good man.'

'You think so?' Perry looked a little brighter. 'Well, I think I might be.' He thought for a moment. 'But I'd rather be a drunk,' he said.

We were at his bedroom door now and the maid and I pushed him through.

'Should we take his boots off?' I asked her.

She dipped me a curtsey. 'Please'm, I'm not allowed in the bedrooms,' she said.

'That's all right,' I said. I was weary with the conventions of this house, of this life where a six-year-old boy could be sent away to school and never allowed home again. 'You can go now.'

I put my hand in my pocket and found a sixpenny piece. 'Here,' I said. 'Thank you for helping.'

Her eyes widened, and I suddenly remembered how far sixpence could go if you were just a young girl like this one. Like the two of us had been.

She went out and closed the door behind her, and I set to work on Perry's boots. By the time I had them off he was lying on his back and tears were seeping out from under his closed eyelids. When I sat on the bed beside him he turned his head to me and buried it in my lap.

'I'll never love anyone like I love George,' he said sorrowfully. 'I wish he was still here, and then I wouldn't have to be a lord any more. I wouldn't have to get married or have an heir, or anything.'

I stroked his blond curls and twisted one perfect circle around my index finger.

'I know,' I said gently. 'I miss someone too.'

His grip around my waist tightened, and I could feel his shoulders shaking as he sobbed.

'Sarah,' he said, his voice muffled. 'Oh God, Sarah, get me

out of this mess. I seem to be more and more unhappy every day and nothing helps.'

'There,' I said helplessly. I patted his shoulder and stroked his back as if he were a little boy crying from some secret hurt.

'I've got to take Papa's place and everyone knows I'm not good enough,' he said. He lifted his head and looked at me. His eyes were red from weeping and from the drink. 'I've got to take George's place and no one will ever love me like they loved George,' he said.

I put my hand up to cup his cheek. 'I will,' I said. I hardly knew what I was saying. My grief for her, and my sorrow and my loneliness at the emptiness of the life we were all living seemed to well up inside me and call that there should be love between us. That at least Perry and I could be kind to one another. That here was a man suffering like a little child, and that he was brought so low that even I, with my own pain and failure, could help him.

'Don't grieve, Perry,' I said gently. 'I can care for you. We'll not be here much longer and then we can go home and live near Wideacre together. People will forget George, they will forget your papa. We'll run the estate well together and people will see what a good man you can be. Even your mama will be pleased when she sees how well you can run the estate.'

'She will?' he asked, as trusting as a child.

'Oh yes,' I said. 'We will both learn together. You'll see. We'll be happy in the end.'

He let me press him back gently to the pillow, and pull the coverlet over him. He closed his eyes but he held on tight to my hand.

'Don't leave me,' he said.

I held his hand firmly. 'I won't,' I said.

'Don't ever leave me, Sarah,' he said pitifully, then his grip on my hand loosened and in minutes he was asleep and snoring. I remembered a friend of Da's, who had choked on his vomit and I turned Perry's young face to one side on the fine linen pillow so that he was not lying on his back. Then I tiptoed to the door and went softly downstairs and out of the front door where Sea's ears went forward at seeing me.

The groom lifted me into the saddle and we headed for the park, riding in silence. As I moved instinctively with Sea, and checked him when a top-heavy wagon swayed past us, too close, I thought of Perry. I thought of him with such a great tenderness and pity. I thought of him with love, and sympathy. And a tiny little part of me spoke with the voice of the hard-faced gypsy who was always there, in the back of my mind. That voice said, 'This is a weakling and a fool.'

He was still asleep when I got back, but Lady Clara's maid was walking up the stairs with her ladyship's pot of hot chocolate.

'I'll take that,' I said impulsively, and carried it in.

Lady Clara was awake, she smiled when she saw me.

'Why Sarah! Good morning! How nice to see you so early! How very strong you do smell of horse! My dear, do go over to the window and air yourself a little!'

'I am sorry,' I said, immediately confused. 'It may be my boots.'

'Of course it may,' she said agreeably. 'But don't mention it. I am sure the rugs will wash.'

I flushed scarlet. 'Don't tease me, Lady Clara,' I said. 'Are you telling me I should not have come?'

She smiled. 'No,' she said. 'You are welcome, even smelling of hunter. Ring for another cup and tell me why you have come to see me so early.'

I waited until the maid had brought up another cup, and poured the chocolate, and brought Lady Clara the morning's post, and taken herself off, and then I took a deep breath and started.

'It's about Perry,' I said.

Lady Clara's blue gaze at me was clear and guileless.

'Did he not come home last night?' she asked coolly. 'Is he drunk? Or gambling?'

'No!' I exclaimed. 'I found him on the doorstep this morning. He got himself home but he is dead drunk.'

She nodded and gestured to me to pour her another cup.

'His drinking is getting worse and worse,' I said. 'And he

seems to be very unhappy. I can't help thinking that this town life is very bad for him. He should have some occupation. All he does every day is ride with me in the afternoon and then go out every night. He does nothing else.'

'There is nothing else,' Lady Clara pointed out. 'He is leading the life of a young gentleman of pleasure. What do you want him to do, Sarah? Steer a plough? Take up silk weaving?'

I shrugged. 'I don't know,' I said. 'But he drank less when he was down at Havering. It is making him ill, Lady Clara. He is paler and thinner all the time. I have seen men very bad with drink. I would not like that to happen to Perry.'

She looked suddenly alert. 'Not before there was an heir, certainly,' she said.

I scrutinized her face. She was not speaking in jest. She meant it.

'What?' I said blankly.

'Not "what",' she said instantly.

'I am sorry,' I said. 'I meant to say: I beg your pardon?'

She nodded. 'If Perry died without an heir then the whole estate would go to my late husband's brother, a commander in the Navy,' she said. 'I would have only the Havering Dower House, which is in all but ruins, and you would have to look about yourself for another husband who would let you run your land as you please.'

I gaped at her. 'You talk as if you don't care for Perry at all,' I said.

Lady Clara lowered her gaze to the embroidered coverlet on her bed.

'That hardly matters,' she said coldly.

'He's your son!' I exclaimed.

She looked up at me and her face was smiling but the smile was not in her eyes. 'That means little or nothing,' she said. 'When he comes of age he will command my fortune. Of course I want him settled in a way that suits me, of course I want him alive and well married. Of course I do not love him. He is a feckless selfish child; but in four years' time he will be my master. Of course I cannot love him.'

'He says you loved George,' I accused. 'He thinks you never loved him, he thinks you loved George.'

She shrugged her broad white shoulders. 'Not especially,' she said. Then she looked at my aghast face and she smiled. 'You and I are not unalike, Sarah,' she said. 'We both came to a life of wealth having known another life, a less comfortable one. We are both cold women. I think neither of us could afford the luxury of passion for a man, nor loving any other living thing. I quite like all my children, I see their faults but I do quite like them. I am quite fond of you. I respected and obeyed my husband. But I never forgot that I lived in a world where women are bought and sold. I swore that when my husband died – and I chose an old man for my husband in the hope that he would die before me – I would never marry again. I would be free. I wanted to be free of the control of men.'

She paused and looked at me. 'It was for that reason that I wanted to help you be free of Mr Fortescue,' she said. 'Your way out is marriage, Sarah. Marriage to a weakling like Perry! If you want to keep him sober and industrious in the country I think you will be able to do that. If you want to buy him off and send him away, you can: he is very biddable. He won't trouble you. And as long as my allowance is paid you will have no trouble from me.'

She broke off and smiled at me, her eyes were like ice. 'Why do you look at me as if I were some kind of a monster, Sarah? Did you think I was a loving mama? Did you think I doted on him? Is this a great shock to you?'

'I don't know,' I said feebly. 'I thought that people were hard to each other when they were needy. When I was with working people I thought they were hard then because there was never enough money. Never any time to love each other, to think about what would make people happy, to share. I thought it would be different for the Quality.'

Lady Clara laughed, her pretty musical laugh. 'No,' she said frankly. 'There is not enough money for the Quality either. We live in a world where money is the measure of everything. There is never enough money. However much you have, you always want more.'

'I want to take Perry back to Havering,' I said.

Lady Clara nodded. 'You'll have to marry him then,' she said. 'I shan't leave town in the Season to chaperone the two of you playing at milkmaids.'

I took a deep breath. 'Very well,' I said. 'I'd like to bring the marriage plans forward. We can marry as soon as the contracts are ready, and live in the country.'

She smiled at me, kindly. 'If that's your wish, Sarah,' she said. 'But it's a cruel world in the countryside too.'

'Not on Wideacre,' I said with sudden pride, thinking of Will and the way the profits were shared.

'No,' she agreed. 'At Wideacre it is hard only for the owner! And you are determined to end all that.'

'Yes,' I said, uncertainly. 'I am.'

She smiled and beckoned me over to her bedside. I went to stand before her and she reached up and patted my cheek.

'Don't fret,' she said. 'Talk to Perry. If he wants to go back to the country with you and he wants to bring the marriage forward then I am agreeable. But leave your thoughts about Wideacre alone until you know a little more about running the estate, Sarah. They are not sharing with you, remember. They are taking from you. It is you who are giving there.'

'Yes,' I said. I dropped her a curtsey and went towards the door.

'They are thieves wrapped up pretty,' she said softly. 'All their ideas, all their sharing is being paid for by you. They are playing Mr Fortescue, they are playing you. You are being gulled, Sarah.'

My shoulders slumped. My moment's certainty, my moment's faith in a world which was not harsh and uncaring was eroded at once. 'Yes,' I said again. 'I shall stop it when Wideacre is my own.'

'Good,' she said. 'And I shall get up. We are going to a breakfast at Lady Gilroy's house, remember? I shall wear my white gown with the twilled white bonnet I think. And you, you must wear your dark green. Her daughter is miserably fair, you will quite drown her with that colour. And wear your hair long.'

'Yes,' I said. I went to the door and paused. Lady Clara raised her eyebrows to see what more I wanted of her.

'You have planned a future for us all, have you not?' I asked. 'You had this in your mind for some time?'

She slid from the covers and went to her dressing-table. She gazed at herself in the mirror and patted the skin under her eyes where the fretwork of lines told of her age.

'Yes,' she said. 'When little George was alive I worked on him to ensure that when his father died and he had my fortune he would be utterly under my control. Then when he died, I knew it would have to be Perry instead.'

She sighed and sat before the mirror and pulled off the lace nightcap and tossed it on the floor.

'Perry is easier in some ways,' she said. 'He always was a weak little boy, easily frightened. I can manage him. My only worry was that he would fall for some high-mettled slut who would set him against me.'

Her eyes met mine in the mirror and she smiled. 'I trust you,' she said. 'You are cold as ice, like me. I recognized you the moment I saw you.' She smiled. 'When he brought you in to me, I said to myself, "Here she is, this is the one that is going to keep Perry steady and me safe."'

I nodded. 'You planned our marriage from the start,' I said levelly.

'Yes,' she said. 'It was good for all of us. Perry could never cope with a high-spirited well-bred wife. She'd cuckold him in days, and then put her by-blow in the Hall. I needed a daughter-in-law I could trust, not some silly child with parents who would watch over the two of them. And you need someone to help you against the Wideacre trust and against Mr Fortescue before you are ruined. You need a family.'

'It all sounds very convenient,' I said.

She smiled. 'Don't think I'll rule you,' she said. 'I've told you my feelings and I've hidden nothing. If you want to marry early and take Perry back to the country you can do so. I won't stand in your way. You can marry him and order him as you please. All you must do for me is make sure my funds are safe, and that there is an heir to the estate. The rest is your own affair.'

'I'll go and see the lawyers today then,' I said.

She smiled, as beautiful as a woman half her age. 'As you wish,' she said. 'Send a footman round with a note to them. But get ready for the breakfast now, and try and do something about the smell of horse.'

I curtseyed, and left her to the contemplation of her lovely face in the mirror.

The lawyers could see me in the early afternoon so I left a message with Perry's valet that his lordship must be up and dressed by three. When Lady Clara and I came back from the breakfast Perry was downstairs in the library, glancing at a newspaper, a mug of ale untasted on the table beside him. His mama glanced in at him and gave him a slight smile, and then went to sit in her parlour. Perry rose from his seat when he saw her, and remained standing, smiling and blinking at me.

'I'm at your service,' he said. 'But I have a devilish head. Did you want us to do something special? I'm damned if I can ride, Sarah.'

I crossed the room and put my hand against his forehead. He was as hot as if he had a fever.

'Are you ill?' I asked.

'No,' he said. 'It was drinking too much brandy, I suppose. It always makes me hot.'

His face was flushed, his curly blond hair a riot.

'Go and wash your face, and brush your hair,' I said. 'We have an appointment to see the lawyers. I want us to bring the date of our wedding early.'

He was instantly wary. 'What does mama say?' he asked.

I shrugged. 'She says we may do as we wish,' I said. 'I want to go back to Havering, back to Wideacre. Your mama is determined to have her Season. This town life is no good for you, Perry. You are drunk every night and ill every morning. We should go back to the country where we were happier.'

'I'm happy here!' he protested. 'Dammit, Sarah! The whole

point of our getting married was so that I could get my hands on my money and kick up some larks. There's not much point being well breeched and stuck in the country in the middle of the Season.'

'You were crying,' I said flatly. 'You were clinging to the railings this morning crying like a baby. You think you are having a good time but you were weeping this morning. You were never sad like that at Havering. We should go back home, Perry.'

He hesitated. His mouth downturned. 'I had a bad night,' he conceded. 'It was some damned awful brandy which Miles had. It made us all maudlin.'

'No,' I said firmly.

Perry swayed slightly, put his head on one side and tried a charming smile.

'No,' I said.

'We'll bring the marriage forward but we'll stay in town,' he suggested.

'No,' I said again.

Perry made a face at me like a naughty child.

'We'll marry at once and we'll go to the country,' I offered. 'We'll stay there until you've stopped drinking every night. Then we'll come back to town. But you might find you prefer the country, once you're there.'

He brightened. 'I might,' he said agreeably. 'And once it's my own house we can always have some fellows down to stay. And there will be parties and hunting.'

He made up his mind. As fickle as a child with a new toy. 'All right,' he said, suddenly agreeable. 'As long as Mama approves.'

'She does,' I said, steering him towards the stairs. 'Go and wash your face, the carriage is waiting.'

He did as he was bid, and we were only a half an hour late for the lawyers. I had made the appointment in Perry's name and when Mr Fursely came forward bowing low, he looked surprised that we had got there at all.

I told him that we wanted the marriage brought forward, and the contracts written quickly and he retreated behind his desk and rang for the right papers to be brought to him. His servant brought us glasses of madeira and little biscuits. Perry had three glasses to my one, and his face lost its hectic flush and he looked better for it.

'We are nearly ready,' Mr Fursely said. 'The trustee's lawyers have been most helpful. There is still some problem about the Wideacre estate if you should die without heirs.'

Perry poured himself another glass of madeira and strolled over to the window and looked out.

Mr Fursely looked up and saw that at least I was listening.

'The entail,' he said. 'It specifies that Wideacre is inherited by the next of kin, whether male or female.'

I nodded.

'Normally, it would pass to your husband's family, as your dowry which you bring with you to marriage,' he said. He put his fingers together one by one, placing them like a pyramid over the papers. 'But here' he said, 'I think one could argue that the situation is quite different.'

I waited. He was slow. Perry turned back and poured himself another of the little glasses. I looked at him, but he was careful not to catch my eye.

'The intention of the entail is quite clear,' he said. He looked at the papers. 'Harold Lacey set it up,' he said. 'Your grandfather, Miss Lacey.'

I nodded.

'A solid document,' Mr Fursely said, complimenting the long-dead lawyers who had drawn up the entail. 'The wishes are clear. The estate goes to the next of kin of the Laceys whether male or female. I don't think it can revert to the Havering family in the event of your death.'

Perry turned back from the window and seemed to waken to the discussion.

'That's all right,' he said, dismissing a fortune in good agricultural land with a wave of his glass. 'We can agree to that. Mama said we could. If we have a male heir first, then he gets both estates. If we have a girl first she gets Wideacre. If we die without children then Havering goes to Havering kin, and Wideacre goes to the Lacey next-of-kin.'

Mr Fursely blinked at this sudden explosion of information from Perry. 'I should prefer Wideacre to come to the Haverings,' he said. 'It is Miss Lacey's dowry so Wideacre is really part of the Havering estate once you two are married.'

There was a high cool singing noise in my head, the sound I had heard when I first came to Wideacre, that lonely night in the dark. It was as if Wideacre was calling me, calling me home to the house which waited for me in the burnished woodland of the autumn trees where the lawns were white in the morning with frost and where the sun was bright red when it set at early evening. As if Wideacre should belong to me, and to no one else.

'It's fair enough as it stands,' Perry said expansively. 'Mama said we could take it as it is. Don't you think, Sarah? Wideacre comes to the Havering estate as Sarah's dowry, but it's entailed on our first-born child. If we have no children it goes back to the Laceys.'

I shook my head to clear my ears of the calling noise. It was too late to think that I was signing the land over to Perry and to Perry's family. I wanted us to be away from London, I wanted to take Perry away from the clubs and the gambling hells. I wanted to be back on the land with the money and the authority to run it as I pleased.

'I agree to that,' I said.

Perry went to the table and brought the decanter towards me. 'We'll drink to that!' he said happily and poured us all another glass. I noticed his hands were quite steady.

'And will Mr Fortes . . . Fortescue's lawyers agree?' he asked, slurring his speech a little.

Mr Fursely put his fingertips against each other once more. 'I think so,' he said. 'It is a reasonable proposition. They cannot have wished to face the problem of breaking the entail if we had been stubborn.'

'Good,' said Perry. 'We'll be off then. How soon can the papers be drawn up?'

Mr Fursely nodded. 'As soon as Mr Fortescue's advisers are ready,' he said.

'And the deeds?' Perry asked. 'I should like to take them with us.' He put one finger owlishly to his nose. 'I could raise some cash using them as security,' he said. 'Absolutely safe, of course. But if I had them in my hand they could tide me over some little difficulties.'

Mr Fursely looked as if he had suggested something improper. 'I could not possibly ask Mr Fortescue for such a thing until the contracts are signed and the marriage has taken place,' he said shocked. 'And I would warn you, with respect, Lord Peregrine, against using your lands as security against debts. If the deeds fall into the wrong hands . . .'

'Oh gad no!' Perry said with a smile. 'This was an arrangement between gentlemen. But no matter. It's nothing urgent. We'll have a crust to eat tonight.'

Mr Fursely permitted himself a thin smile. 'Of course, my lord,' he said.

Perry held the door for me as we left the office and then Mr Fursely escorted us to the carriage and stood on the street bowing as we drove away.

'Y'know what?' Perry said pleasantly. 'If they can sport some canvas on these contracts, there's no reason why we should not be married at once.'

I nodded.

'I'll go and see the vicar,' Perry said, suddenly confident. 'You can drop me off on your way home and I'll go and see the rector or the vicar or whatever he is. You wanted a quiet wedding anyway, Sarah. I'll ask him when we could be married.'

I paused. High over the noise of the cart and carriage wheels, I could hear that warning singing noise again. It sounded loud in my head. I shook my head to clear it, but I could not be rid of it.

'You all right?' Perry asked.

'It's nothing,' I said. 'Yes, we could be married this month. Do go and see the parish priest, Perry. I want to be home at Wideacre. I want us to go home as soon as we can.'

'You'll miss all the Christmas parties,' he warned me.

I smiled. 'I don't care that much for them, Perry,' I said honestly. 'I'd rather be at Wideacre for Christmas.'

Perry smiled. 'Well, I'll see what the vicar says then,' he said pleasantly and pulled the cord to warn the coachman to stop. 'You don't have some money on you, do you, Sarah?' he asked. 'I have to pay a fellow some money I lost at cards. It'd suit me to settle at once.'

I opened my reticule. My purse was inside with a couple of gold sovereigns I was carrying for a dressmaker bill.

'Here,' I said, handing it over.

I remembered for a moment times in my life when money was hard earned and slowly spent. I remembered begging Da for money, and the bargain we would strike that I had to stay on an unbroke horse for a penny. I remembered her dancing with her skirts lifted high, and picking pockets, and pretending to be lost on street corners when fat old ladies came by. But that was a long long time ago. Now I gave away gold sovereigns lightly, as if I had forgotten how hard they were to earn.

'You're a darling,' Perry said pleased. The coach stopped and he jumped out without waiting for the steps to be let down.

'Tell Mama I'll not be back for dinner,' he said. 'I'll go and see this vicar and then I'll go on out.'

I nodded and waved as the carriage moved off. It was the first time I had given him money.

31

It was not the last. He was late home that night, even later than us, and we were in yawning after a dull ball and supper party at half-past one. So I did not see him that night. But at noon the next day he tapped on the door of my room and came in while I was sitting before my mirror to set my bonnet straight.

He nodded casually to the maid and she swept him a curtsey and went from the room without another word. I watched him in the glass. I did not think I would ever learn that knack, that Quality knack, of getting what you wanted without even having to ask for it.

'Sarah, d'you have much money by you?' he asked abruptly. 'I'm short, and I lost again last night.'

I reached for my gloves and smoothed them out.

'I have most of my quarter's allowance left,' I said. 'But I will need that for my bills. Your mama and I have been buying dresses ever since we arrived in London.'

Perry nodded. His eyes were red-rimmed again, his hands were shaking slightly.

'Be a darling and lend it to me,' he said. 'I need it this morning, I'll pay you back tomorrow.'

I hesitated. 'I don't think I should, Perry,' I said. 'If you have overspent your allowance on gambling, I suppose you should settle your debts before you have more.'

He chuckled at once, and his grin was rueful. 'Dammit Sarah, don't talk like Mama!' he begged. 'I've never pretended for a moment that I could stay inside my allowance. Just because you're a little goody with your money, doesn't mean I can save mine.'

I laughed outright. 'I'm not a goody,' I said. 'I just don't think I'll ever see it again once it gets inside your pocket.'

Perry smiled. 'So what?' he said carelessly. 'When we are married we'll have all the money we need, I'll repay you then.'

I turned to face him and laid my gloves aside. 'Easy talking,' I said shrewdly. 'If you're a gamester you'll get through your fortune and mine. There's never enough money for a gambler.'

He was instantly penitent. 'I know,' he said gravely. 'Don't preach, Sarah. It's the life we lead in London. I gamble and I drink. I owe so much money I can't even add up how much it is. One of my friends has sold my vowels to a money-changer and so he is charging me interest on my debts. I'm in a mess, Sarah. I wish we were well out of it.'

'D'you like gambling?' I asked. I had seen enough men half-ruined when all they had to bet were pennies, it made me sick with nerves when I was in the great houses of London and saw people staking hundreds of pounds.

'No,' he said frankly. 'I like winning well enough, but I hate losing. And I hate losing when it goes badly. Trust me this once, Sarah and I'll clear as many of my debts as I can, and I won't gamble any more.'

'It's exciting though, isn't it?' I asked him. I was wondering if Will was right, and Perry had gaming in his blood.

'Not when I lose,' he said ruefully. 'I only really do it to pass the time, and everyone gambles, you know that, Sarah!'

I nodded. It was true. People bet on the turn of a card, on the fall of a die. I had been in a group which had a thousand pounds on the table as to whether Lady Fanshawe would wear her awful green dress in public again. My belief was that Perry played because it was part of his London life. He was not a gambler at heart. And I could take him away from London, I could take him away from gambling and drink.

Besides; I had promised I would not leave him. He had asked me to stay with him for ever. We were betrothed. I did not want to sour it by haggling over a handful of guineas.

I opened the right-hand drawer in my dressing-table. 'Here,' I said.

I had my quarter's allowance of gold coins in a purse, locked in the little jewel-box. It opened with a key. The purse clinked, it was heavy with the coins. There were fifty gold sovereigns in it; Mr Fortescue had been generous in his estimates of my needs.

'You can have forty,' I said. 'I must pay the dressmakers something on account or they will be charging me for loans too.'

Perry caught at my hand and went to kiss it before he took the purse. I pulled my hand away and he did not try to hold me.

'Thank you,' he said. 'That will clear the worst of it, and I've another quarter's allowance due next month and I know my luck will change soon. I can feel it. Anyway, soon we will be married and I shall be able to get at my money without waiting for an allowance.'

'Why don't you ask your mama to give you more?' I suggested.

Perry was heading for the door but he turned back towards me with a little half-smile. 'She likes me in debt,' he said as if it were obvious. 'She can make me do whatever she likes when I am in debt to her.'

I nodded. It was all of a piece.

'Well, keep it safe then,' I said. 'Or I shall make you do what I like when you are in debt to me.'

He hesitated, with the door half open. 'But all you want me to do is to go home with you, and away from London, isn't it?' he said. He gave me one of his endearing half-smiles. 'You can order me, Sarah,' he said.

I was going to reply but there was a clatter at the front door.

'There's the carriage!' I said, grabbing at my gloves. 'I must go, Perry, I am driving in the park with Lady Jane Whitley.'

Perry swept an ironic bow in a jest at my enviable company, and I pulled on my gloves and ran down the stairs past him and out to the wintry sunshine.

Lady Jane and I had the nearest thing to a friendship which I had found in London, and it was not very like a friendship at all. She had pale brown hair and light hazel eyes and she believed that beside my unruly ripple of red curls she looked pale and beguiling.

She was given over to invalidism and she had fainting fits and vapours and she had to keep out of draughts and not dance after midnight and not touch food and drink which was either too hot or too cold. I think her mama thought that suitors who found me too boisterous for their taste might turn to her with relief. Lady Jane herself was frank to me about her absolute urgency to find a man and marry before her bedridden and mean papa worked out how much her Season was costing him and ordered her home.

She was an only child so she had no sister to go about with, and I was convenient as a companion. I liked her as well as any other young lady because she had no curiosity about me and did not trouble me with questions about my family and childhood. The only thing about her I could not stomach was the way she leaned on me as we walked, or took my hand when we rode in the carriage together. I had schooled myself not to shake her off but when I stepped into her carriage and sat beside her I had to grit my teeth not to pull away as she slid her hand under my elbow. I could even feel the back of her hand against my body. The intimacy of that touch set my teeth on edge.

We were riding in her papa's landau and we both unfurled our parasols to protect our complexions. Lady Jane was as pale as a skinned mushroom, beside her I knew I looked wind-burnt, sun-burnt. It could not be helped. Lady Clara had loaded me with one cream and lotion after another, but nothing could bleach the warm colours of my skin. I had slept in the open air with my face up to a midday sky too often. However, I kept my parasol over my bonnet as I had been taught and I listened to Lady Jane's prattle in my right ear as we set off down the road towards the park.

She was telling me about some gloves she had bought, and I could hear my voice saying 'No!' and 'Fancy!' when she paused for breath. I was watching the coachman guide the horses through the traffic and watching the streets slide past us. It seemed a long time since I had driven a wagon myself. These long weary weeks in London had come to seem like a lifetime. I felt I knew this way to the park and back as if I had ridden or walked it every single day of my life. I knew it better than I had known any other street, any other landscape. I thought with sudden regret that if I had stayed anywhere, and learned anywhere so very very well, it would have been better for me if that place had been Wideacre.

My throat was suddenly tight thinking of my home. Winter was making London cold and damp, the street vendors had set up braziers at street corners to sell baked potatoes, hot gingerbread, and roasted chestnuts. They were the lucky ones with hot wares – the girls carrying pails of milk were pinched and wan with the chill; the flower sellers and the watercress sellers shivered in the damp winds.

I knew it would be cold at Wideacre – I was not one of Jane's poets sighing for pretty landscapes and forgetting the hard ache of bare feet on frozen earth. But I thought that the trees would grow stark and lovely as they shed their leaves. I thought the woods would smell nutty and strong if I had been there to kick my way through the piles of leaves. I thought the chestnut tree at the curve of the drive would show its shape, as rounded as a humming top now the great fans of yellow leaves were carpeting the drive beneath it. I wanted to be at Wideacre while autumn turned into winter. I felt as if the land needed me there.

'. . . and I don't even like white,' Jane finished triumphantly.

'I do,' I said contributing my two words.

'It's all right for you . . .' she started again. The coachman turned left when we reached the park and started the slow trot around the perimeter road. We were following Lady Daventry's coach, I could just see her famous matched bays. Jane continued to talk but she was keeping a sharp eye out for anyone who might see us and wave. Every time the bright colours of a guardsman's uniform came into sight she lost the thread of her thought until she had taken a good look at him and made sure she could not stop the carriage to beckon him over.

'It's so old-fashioned to be presented in white . . .' she said.

It was the presentation at Court which was on her mind. Her mama was making her wear a satin which had been ripped back from her own wedding gown, Jane had told me and sworn me to secrecy. She could not have borne the humiliation if it had been widely known.

'It must be lovely for you to be rich . . .' she said longingly.

All at once she brightened. She had seen a young man, I knew it without turning my head.

'Coachman, wait!' she shouted and he obediently pulled up the horses while Jane leaned forward and waved frantically at two distant figures strolling on the grass. It was Sir Robert Handley and Mr Giles Devenish.

'How d'you do, Sir Robert, Mr Devenish!' I said as they came closer. Jane nearly fell out of the carriage.

'Oh, Sir Robert!' she cried, and laughed at once as if he had said something extraordinarily amusing other than a simple 'Good day'. He smiled and went around to her side of the carriage. Mr Devenish lounged towards me as if I ought to be grateful for his attention.

'Shall I see you at Lady Clark's tonight?' he asked me.

I nodded. 'Yes,' I said. 'Well, at any rate, I shall be there. I doubt if you will see me. She told us she had invited two thousand people.'

'Oh yes,' said Giles. 'But then so few of them will come!'

I could not help a malicious chuckle. 'I'm surprised you have accepted if people are priding themselves on staying away,' I said.

'I have to go,' he said. 'Her mama and mine were bosom bows, I shall be there, at my post, from first to last.'

I nodded. 'We are going there early, and then on to Lady Meeching's card party,' I said.

Giles raised his eyebrows. 'Practically out of town,' he said.

I let it pass. 'Then we are going to Lady Maria's supper party,' I said.

Giles raised his eyebrows even higher. 'The fair Maria,' he said. 'Your sister-in-law to be. I should have thought that Lady Meeching's was not far enough. If I was going to marry poor Perry and dine with the fair Maria I should flee to Brighton at the very least.'

I gave him a level glance. 'Who do you like in London society, Mr Devenish?'

He smiled to conceal his irritation. 'I'm quite fond of George

Wallace,' he said judiciously. 'And my papa commands my filial respect. But apart from them . . .' he paused. 'But what about you, Miss Lacey? I take it that I am reproved for failing to love my fellow man. So do tell me, whom have you met in London that you especially like?' His gaze drifted past me to Jane who was leaning forward, twirling her parasol, laughing with her mouth wide open at one of Sir Robert's frigid quips. He looked beyond her, across the park, where one fashionable Quality person after another walked, rode or drove in diminishing circles, trying to waste the time until it was afternoon, then wasting some more time until dinner.

I shrugged my shoulders and shook my head. Suddenly I lost all desire to be a proper young lady. The little Rom chavvy called Meridon spoke through my lips though I was seated in a landau talking to a beau at the pinnacle of fashion. 'I've met no one,' I said. 'I don't reprove you or anyone else. I've seen no one to admire and I've made no friends. I am lonelier now than when I was a little gypsy chavvy. I've slept better on the floor, and ate better off wooden platters. I've no time for this life at all, to tell you the truth. And you –' I paused and looked at him speculatively. 'I've met better-mannered polecats,' I said.

His eyes went purple with rage, the smile wiped away. 'You are an original indeed,' he said. It was the worst thing he could think of saying to a young woman, not yet presented at court. He stepped back from the side of the carriage as if he were pulling the skirts of his coat away from contamination. Sir Robert saw his movement away and was swift to say farewell to Jane and tip his hat to me. Jane tried to detain him, but he was too polite and skilled.

'How could you let him go!' she said crossly to me as the carriage moved on again. 'You must have seen that I was talking to Sir Robert. I am certain he was about to ask me for a dance at Lady Clark's ball, and now I have no supper partner at all!'

I was suddenly weary of the whole thing. 'I am sorry,' I said. My throat was as tight as if I were choking on the London air. 'I'm sorry,' I said. 'That poisonous Devenish was being spiteful and I wanted to be rid of him.'

Jane gasped. 'You never upset him!' she said, appalled. 'If you said something he didn't like it'll be all over London by tomorrow! Oh, Sarah! How could you!'

I sighed. 'I didn't say anything that wasn't the truth,' I said miserably. 'And anyway, I don't care.' I hesitated. 'Jane, would you mind very much dropping me off when we get around to Grosvenor Gate again? I have a sore throat.'

'Oh no!' she said. For a moment I thought her anxiety was on my account. 'Sarah, can't you stay with me for just one more circuit? We might meet someone, and I really don't want to go home yet.'

I nodded. Jane wanted to arrange a partner for tonight's ball and she was not allowed to drive around the park alone. I tightened the collar of my jacket around my throat and sat back in the carriage. The autumn sunshine was warm enough, I had gloves; only months ago I should have thought myself in paradise to have owned such a warm jacket.

'All right,' I said. 'But only one circuit, mind.'

She nodded. 'And if there is anyone you know, then you introduce me,' she said.

'All right,' I said disagreeably, and I settled back in the carriage seat to scan the people walking past to see if there was anyone I knew who would be likely to take Jane in to supper at the ball that night. For if I knew Jane, we would be circling the park until nightfall if she could not find a partner.

I was nearly right. We did three circuits before I saw Captain Sullivan with Captain Riley and introduced them both to Jane. They were both penniless fortune-hunters but they knew how to dance and how to take a girl in and out of a supper room. Jane was flushed with triumph at having her dance card finally filled, and I was aching all over as if I had the ague.

'Thank you, my dearest dear!' she said, heartfelt, as she dropped me at the front door. 'You saved my life! You really did, you know! Which do you think is more attractive, Captain Sullivan or Captain Riley?'

'Sullivan,' I said at random, and turned to go up the steps.

Jane was rapt. 'Shall I wear my yellow or my pink?' she called to me as the door opened.

'The yellow,' I said. 'See you tonight!'

The Havering butler closed the door as I heard her call, 'And how should I wear my hair . . .'

I went wearily to the foot of the stairs, planning to go to my room. But the butler was ahead of me.

'Mr Fortescue is with Lady Havering and Lady Maria,' he said. 'Lady Havering asked for you to be shown to the parlour when you returned from your drive.'

I nodded. I paused only before a mirror on the stairs to take off my bonnet and gloves and as the butler opened the door for me I pushed them into his hands.

'James!' I said. He was the first friendly face I had seen in a parlour in all the long stay in London.

He jumped to his feet as I came in the room and beamed at me. I glanced from him to Lady Maria and Lady Havering. I imagined he had been thoroughly uncomfortable with the two of them and I wished I had been home earlier.

'How good to see you!' I said, and then I curtseyed to Lady Havering and did an awkward sort of bob at Maria before I sat down. The parlourmaid came in and poured me a dish of tea.

James said how well I looked, and Lady Havering said something about town polish. I saw Maria look very much as if she would have liked to say something cat-witted.

'And have you made many friends? Is London as fine as you expected?' James asked, making heavy weather of it all.

'Yes,' I said, not very helpfully.

'Such sweet friends as you have,' Maria chimed in. 'You were driving with Lady Jane Whitley, were you not?'

I nodded in silence. James looked glad that Maria had volunteered something.

'Is she one of your especial friends?' he asked. 'I am glad you have found someone you agree with.'

'Oh she's quite the toast of the Season!' Maria enthused, her eyes sharp with malice watching me. 'She and Miss Lacey together are quite the beauties of the Season this year. Miss Lacey has been claimed by our Peregrine of course, but I'm certain Lady Jane will be snapped up in a moment.'

I thought of Jane and me driving round and round the park trying to find her a partner and I smiled grimly at Maria.

'Thank you,' I said. 'We cannot all hope to have your good fortune in finding a husband who is so peculiarly appropriate.'

Since Maria's Basil was fat and fifty-five I thought that would do. Lady Clara thought so too, for she interrupted before Maria could reply.

'Mr Fortescue has some business to discuss with you, Sarah,' she said. 'Perhaps you would like to talk with him in the dining room?'

James rose to his feet with uncivil haste.

'Thank you,' he said, and I led him downstairs to the ornate room with the heavy round table and the high-backed chairs.

He pulled one out and sat down, clasping his hands before him. 'Are you happy, Sarah?' he asked. 'Is it the life you wanted?'

The tightness in my throat had not eased despite coming in from the cold. 'It's well enough,' I said. 'It's a style I'd have had to learn.'

He waited for a moment in case I should say something more. 'I'd not discourage you from anything you set your heart on,' he said hesitantly. 'But I'd not be doing my duty by you, nor showing the love I still bear your mother, if I let you go on into this without speaking once more with you.'

I put the back of my hand against my forehead. It was hot though I felt cold inside. 'Go on then,' I said unhelpfully.

He pushed back his chair and looked at me as if he did not know how to start. 'I keep thinking what I should say and then it all comes out wrong!' he said with sudden irritation. 'I have been planning and planning how I would speak with you and then you look at me as if it does not matter at all how you live or whether you are happy or sad. I won't tell you things. I will ask you instead. Sarah . . . how would you like to live?'

I paused for a moment and thought of her, sprawled under the fine silk of her flyer's cape, her dark eyelashes sweeping her pink cheeks. I thought of the smell of her – part cheap toilet-water, part sweat. I thought of her smile as she slept and her certainty that the world would keep her well, and how for all the years of our childhood she had poached and thieved and stolen and never been caught. Not once. And how the very same night that I had come to the life which she would have loved was the night she was gone.

'I want nothing,' I said. My voice was husky because of my throat.

'D'you think Lord Peregrine will make you happy?' James asked.

I shrugged. 'He will not make me unhappy,' I said. 'He has no power for that.' As I saw James scowl, I added: 'There are not many women that could say that. It's not a bad start. He will never make me unhappy. I will have Wideacre and I will put my child in the squire's chair at Havering and Wideacre. It's a sensible arrangement. I'm content with it.'

James' brown eyes stared into mine as if he were looking for some warmth that he could grasp and beg me to care for love and passion like an ordinary girl. I knew my look was as opaque as green glass.

'You want the marriage put forward,' he said, and I knew by his voice that he had accepted it.

'Yes,' I agreed. 'We want to be married before Christmas. I want to be home then.'

James raised an eyebrow. 'Why the sudden hurry?' he asked. 'It was to be spring, I thought.'

I nodded. 'The town life does not suit Perry,' I said honestly. 'And I don't like it. I'm glad to have come, and I have learned a good deal. But I should not care if I was never in London again as long as I live. I hate the streets, and the life is too confining!' I turned and went over to the window and drew back the heavy drapes and looked out. 'It's bad enough sleeping in a house with all the windows shut, without forever looking out on to streets,' I said.

James nodded. He could not feel as I did, but he was always trying to understand me.

'I'll tell my lawyers to go ahead, then,' he said. 'If you are sure.'

'I am sure,' I said.

He nodded and turned to the door. 'I will wish you happiness,' he said. 'I am not likely to see you until after the wedding.'

I put out my hand and we shook, like old friends. 'You can wish me a little peace,' I said. 'I don't look for happiness, but I should like to be at a place of my own where I don't have to watch what I wear and what I say all the time.'

He nodded. 'Once you are Lady Havering you will be above criticism,' he said. 'And I believe that you knew all the essentials of being a good person when you rode up the drive in your cap and dirty jacket.'

I smiled. 'Thank you,' I said.

'I have something for you,' he said. 'It is the interest on your share of the profits of Wideacre over the past sixteen years. I have a note of the exact profits each year, and I had it placed out with a bank. They have just declared a dividend and I thought it prudent to take the money in notes in case you had any strong feelings about what you wanted done with it. The capital remains with the bank, but I have the notes of interest for you.'

I nodded. James pulled a bulky package out of his pocket.

'They do not pay very high rates,' he said apologetically. 'But they are a safe bank. I thought it best.'

I nodded and opened the envelope. There were eleven large pieces of parchment inside, they all promised to pay the bearer £3,000 each.

'I've never seen so much money in my life before,' I said. I was awed into a whisper. 'I don't know how you dared carry them on you!'

James smiled. 'I was travelling with guards,' he said. 'I had to bring some gold to London so I took the opportunity to bring it all together. Then I walked around here. Perhaps I had better leave them with you for safe-keeping tonight and collect them tomorrow. I can pay them into your bank account then.'

'Yes,' I said.

We went out into the hall together and he shrugged himself

into his coat. The butler held the door for him and I watched him down the front-door steps. I went back into the dining room and folded the bills very carefully together, then I took them upstairs to my bedroom and locked them into the right-hand drawer of my dressing-table, where I kept my purse and the jewels Lady Clara had picked out for me, and my piece of string with the gold clasps.

32

I cried off from the ball that night, from the visit and from
Maria's supper party. I pleaded sick and offered as evidence my
sore throat and my hot forehead. Lady Clara put her cool hand
against my head and said that I might be excused tonight but
tomorrow I must be well because the Princess Caterina was
giving a luncheon party and we had managed to get an invitation.
I nodded and I submitted to being dressed in my nightdress and
wrapper and confined to the stuffy little bedroom with a bowl of
soup and a pastry and some fruit.

I tried to read one of Lady Clara's novels but I found it heavy
going. It was by a man called Fielding and I was angry with him
because the chapter headings at the top of the pages did not tell
me what was happening in the story. They were no use for me,
who only wanted to appear as if I had read the book.

For some reason I thought of the bills from the bank and took
the fancy to look at them again. The key to the drawer was in the
top drawer, where I always kept it. The drawer unlocked easily
and slid open. It moved smoothly as if it were lightly laden.

It was lightly laden. I had given Perry most of my gold in the
morning, and the eleven folded bills of £3,000 each were missing.

I said, 'Oh,' very softly, and I stood still for a little while, then
I pulled up the pretty white and gold chair and sat before the
table and looked at the empty drawer.

I thought of the maid – but she had been with the Haverings
for years and Lady Clara's jewels alone were worth far more. I
thought of the kitchenmaid who had helped me to get Perry to
bed, but she was not allowed upstairs. I thought of the footmen,
but they were rarely upstairs and never in my bedroom.

No one entered my bedroom except Lady Clara, my maid,
myself and Perry.

I had known it was Perry as soon as I saw the drawer was empty. I had been trying to avoid knowing that it was him.

I sat very still and quiet and thought for a little while.

He was a gambler. I had seen gamblers before. Not like my da who did it for a living, and not like men I had seen who did it for fun. For some men it is a lust worse than drink when it gets them. They cannot leave it alone. They believe themselves lucky and they bet on one game after another. They don't care what the game is – the bones or the cards, horses, cock-fighting, the dogs, badger-baiting – it is all alike to them. Their faces sweat and get red, their eyes get brighter when they are gaming. They look like men about to have a woman. They look like starving men excited by food. They were a blessing to Da for you can cheat them over and over again when they are mad to win.

I was afraid Perry was one of them.

I was not even angry.

I suppose I knew he could not help himself. I suppose that inside I was still a pauper and the thick wads of paper money never really felt as if they belonged to me. I think also that my heart was not in this marriage, nor in the life I was leading. Rich or poor, wed or single, she was not here. I could not see that it mattered. And I had very low expectations of Perry.

I had known he was a drinker. I had thought he might be a gambler. If I had been asked, I could have predicted that he would steal from me, or from his mama, or from anyone who was close to him and ready to trust him.

But something had to be done about it. I would have to see Perry, I would have to tell Mr Fortescue, I would have to tell Lady Clara.

I sighed. My sore throat was no better and my head was aching from weariness. I walked across the room to my bed and thought I would lie down and rest, wait for Perry to come in and then speak to him.

I must have dozed then, for I next stirred when the clocks struck three, and a little after that I heard a stumble and a bump on the carpeted stairs. I raised my head but I did not move. Then in the firelight I saw the handle of the door turn, very very slowly.

Peregrine staggered into the room.

I lay still and did not say a word. I half closed my eyes and watched him through my eyelashes. He took a half step inside the room and shut the door behind him.

'Sssshhh,' he said to himself; and giggled.

I lay in silence, waiting for what would come next. The drunken repentance, the blustering explanation, the tears, the promises to reform.

He stepped quietly over to my dressing-table and there was a sudden scuffle as he collided with the chair.

'Careful!' he cautioned himself loudly. 'Not too much noise now! Don't want to wake her up! She's going to have a surprise in the morning!'

I opened my eyes a little wider. I had not expected Perry to be joyful. I had thought he had come back for the last ten guineas, perhaps for my jewels.

In the flickering light from the dying fire I saw him pulling something out of his pocket, pieces of paper, and then I heard the chink of coins.

'Perry, what on earth are you doing?' I demanded and sat upright in bed.

He jumped like a deer.

'Damme, Sarah! Don't shout at me like that when I'm trying to give you a surprise!' he said.

'You've already given me one,' I said tightly. 'You've robbed me, Perry. There's £33,000 in bills made out to me missing from that drawer, and I know you took them.'

'These you mean?' Perry said joyfully. I reached over for my candle and lit it. He was waving a sheaf of papers at me. I squinted against the sudden light. They were the same ones.

'You brought them back?' I asked in surprise. 'You didn't gamble?'

'I won!' Perry declared.

He staggered over to the bed and caught at one of the bedposts. He pushed his hands deep into his pockets and shovelled out papers and coins. 'I won and won and won!' he said. He giggled delightedly and spilled coins and notes of hand over my bed.

'I have an unbeatable system,' he said. 'An unbreakable system. I have an unbreatable system an unbeakable system a beakless system, a breathless system!'

'How much?' I asked, a gambler's daughter again.

Perry put my notes to one side and shovelled out the rest of his pockets and we made piles on the counterpane of coins, and notes of hand, and paper money.

Altogether it came to something like £22,000.

'Perry,' I said, awed.

He nodded, beaming at me. 'Unbreatheable!' he said, with satisfaction.

We were silent for a moment.

'You shouldn't have taken my money,' I said.

He blinked at me. 'I had to, Sarah,' he said. 'I'd have asked you, but you weren't here. I had to. Mama was talking of wearing her diamonds to present you at Court – I had to have money.'

I frowned. 'What do your mama's diamonds have to do with . . .' then I broke off. 'Have you lost them at play?' I asked.

'Pawned,' he said gloomily. 'I had to get them back, Sarah, or I'd have been really sunk. She keeps me on such a short allowance I can never manage to stay out of debt. And a little while ago I found the key to her strongbox. It was before the Season started and I knew she wouldn't need them for months. So I prigged them, and pawned them.'

He paused gloomy for a moment, but then his face brightened. 'And now I'll be able to get them back!' he said delightedly.

He glanced at my face. 'You don't mind, do you?' he asked.

'You're a thief,' I said. 'A thief and a drunkard and a gambler.'

Perry looked contrite. 'I did win, though,' he offered.

'I'm no better,' I said. 'I was a thief and a card-sharper and a horse-trader. You are what you have to be, Perry. But don't ever steal from me again.'

His face brightened. 'I'll make a promise with you,' he offered. 'I will never steal from you again, I will never steal from Mama again, and I will never pawn anything of hers or yours again. It has been dreadful, Sarah, I thought I'd not be able to get them back and then she would have known!'

I nodded. I could imagine how afraid Perry must have been.

'All right,' I said. 'I hold you to your promise. You must never steal from me or your mama again. And I'll never steal from you or cheat you.'

He put out his long-fingered soft hand and we shook firmly.

'Done,' I said. 'Now get your winnings off my bed, I need to sleep, I have a throat like charcoal.'

Peregrine gathered up his papers and crammed them back into his pockets. My bank bills he counted out carefully on to my dressing-table and he added to them the guineas he had borrowed from me.

Then he came to the bedside again and leaned over me. I could feel his warm brandy-sweet breath on my face as he leaned over.

'Good-night Sarah,' he said softly and kissed me on the cheek. 'Good-night, my best of friends.'

I cat-napped after he left me; once, I turned and was wideawake and found I was chuckling, thinking of Perry coming into my room, his pockets bursting as if he had been sharping cards all night. Then I heard the clock strike seven and I got up, splashed cold water on my face, and slipped into my riding habit.

Only then did I remember that it was Thursday, and Will was coming to ride with me today.

I brushed my hair in a hurry and coiled it up on my head, then I pinned on my hat and went to the door. I ran down the stairs pulling on my gloves and the kitchenmaid met me at the front door, her face all grimy and her hands black with soot from the fires.

'Beg pardon, m'm,' she said, dipping a curtsey.

I nodded to her and opened the door myself and slipped out. There was a figure of a man, holding two horses waiting in the street opposite the front door. But it was not Gerry the groom there, waiting for me holding his horse and Sea. It was Will, standing with the reins of his bay horse in one hand, and Sea's reins in the other.

'Oh Will!' I said and I beamed at him.

'I'm freezing,' he said crossly. 'I've been waiting here for half an hour, Sarah, and that softy maid of yours wouldn't find you and tell you I was here.'

I chuckled and ran down the steps and took the reins. 'You're a weakling,' I said. 'This is just bracing.'

'Bracing!' Will said under his breath. He cupped his hands and threw me ungently up into the saddle. Sea sidled and I patted his neck.

'Yes,' I said provocatively. 'If you had lived in a wagon like I did you'd count this good weather. But you're a soft gorgio you are, Will Tyacke.'

Will scowled and swung into his own saddle and then his brown face crumpled and he laughed aloud. 'Why are you so damned full of chirp?' he asked. 'What have you got to be so glad about?'

'Precious little,' I said. The horses fell into step side by side and I turned and smiled at Will. 'I've had some trouble, I waked all night. But it's come all right now, and I'm glad to be out of that house, and with you. I'm so glad to see you.'

His glance at me was warm. 'I'd wait all night in a snowstorm to see you and count myself lucky,' he said. 'I rode up in darkness last night to make sure I'd be here in time. Sarah, you're the first thing worth seeing this week.'

I put my hand out to him in a swift instinctive gesture, and he did not kiss it like a lover but took it in a firm gentle clasp, as if we were shaking on a deal. Then his horse shifted and we let go.

'What's your trouble?' he asked.

'Tell me about Wideacre first,' I said. 'And how did your meeting of the corporations go?'

'All's well on Wideacre,' he said. 'The oats and barley is sown, we're setting to the hedging and ditching. The root crops are coming up. All's well. I'm bid send you people's love and to tell you that we all want you home.' He straightened a little in the saddle as we came down the road towards the park. 'They elected me chairman of the National Association of Corporations,' he said. 'I was proud. I'm honoured to be asked to serve.'

'Oh, well done!' I said. Then I paused. 'What does it mean?' I asked.

Will smiled. 'Oh, little enough,' he said. 'We will meet every two months or so for debate and discussion, but we have more than enough trouble with spies and the government to want to do more than that.'

'Spies?' I asked blankly.

Will nodded. 'They think they see traitors and Boney's agents in every bush,' he said. 'It's the way of this government – aye and others! They can't bear to think that they might be in the wrong. They can't bear to think that another Englishman might disagree with them. So they will only believe that if you disagree with them you have to be a paid spy, or a foreigner.' He paused for a moment. 'They think they own the world,' he said simply. 'The landlords and those in power. They think they own what it is to be an Englishman. If you think differently from them they make you feel like you don't belong in their country. It's not their country, but they won't hear a word of dissent.'

His face was dark. 'It's a nuisance,' he said. 'I have all my letters opened and read before I ever see them, and it makes them late. Since the last meeting there were two men prowling around Wideacre asking people in the village if I was a rick-burner!' Will snorted. 'Damn fools,' he said.

'I never knew,' I said. The enemies of my childhood had been the thief-takers and the gamekeepers. I did not know there were gamekeepers of ideas too.

'They make little difference,' Will said. 'They sit by the door and every single thing you say they scribble down in their little books and then they run off and copy it all out fair for their masters to read. Everyone makes sure they speak civil and say not a word against the government or the king. And I never write if I can send a message.'

'Oh,' I said blankly.

'But it was a good meeting,' Will said. 'There were some northern gentlemen there who are planning experimental farms in the north. One of them took me out to dine afterwards. We talked till late into the night. He wants to set up an experimental farm outside his potteries for the workers. I was telling him about the children's school on Wideacre, and about how we farm. He's coming down to see it when he's next in the south. He seemed a likely man.'

I nodded. I was dimly aware of a world outside my knowledge, outside my understanding, where neither a gypsy brat nor a pretty young lady would be of much account, and for a moment I envied Will his contact with a weightier world.

'That's enough of me,' Will said abruptly. 'What of you? You look a bit pale, Sarah. And what of this trouble of yours?'

'Not my trouble,' I said. 'It's Perry. You were right about his drinking, he does take too much. But the fool must needs think he can gamble, too. He stole some bank bills of mine, and as if that weren't bad enough he won handsomely with them. He was in my bedroom last night scattering gold on my bed as if I were a princess. It's all right now, he's brought my money back, and he's won enough to keep himself for months. But I'll never be able to teach him not to gamble if he's a lucky one!'

Will pulled his horse up so sharply that it gave a little half-rear. 'He did what?' he demanded, his face white with shock, his brown eyes blazing.

I lost my smile. 'Took some money of mine, and then won with it,' I said lightly.

We said nothing for a moment and then Will loosened his reins and let his horse go forward.

'Don't you mind?' he asked me. I could hear the anger behind his voice but he was keeping his tone steady until I told him more.

I chuckled. 'Oh for God's sake, Will, remember where I came from!' I said. 'I've lived among gamblers and thieves all my life. I'm angry that he should steal from me, but I had the money back within the day . . . and I can't help but find it funny that he should win so well! Thousands and thousands, Will! He was shovelling money out of his pocket all over my counterpane.'

'You were in bed?' Will asked sharply.

'Yes,' I said. 'This all happened last night when he came home from gambling.'

'And he just walked into your room?' he demanded.

I pulled Sea up and faced him. 'We are to be married,' I said reasonably. 'He didn't come in to see me, he came to put the money back. I happened to be awake.' I remembered Perry crashing into the chair and warning himself to be quiet and I smiled.

Will saw the smile and it fired his anger. 'Goddammit, Sarah, you must be mad!' he said loudly. 'You are still talking about this damned marriage as if you meant it! If you go on down this road you will find yourself married in very truth and unable to get out of it.

'For God's sake, Sarah, tell me that you see now the crew you're among. Lord Peregrine is a drunkard and a gamester and a thief into the bargain. His ma can do nothing more with him and so she lets him drink himself to death and damnation as quick as he can, and neither of those sluts his sisters are worthy to tie your laces. He's cheated you, and he's used your money to pay for his gambling, and you're not even wed yet!'

Will's voice had risen to a shout, and he shook his head, as if to clear his thoughts and then he said tightly, 'You'd be a damn fool to go further with this, Sarah, and you know it. Promise me now that you'll go back and tell Lady Clara that he's stolen from you and that you are withdrawing from the betrothal. Write to Mr Fortescue and tell him what's to do, and then order out the carriage and come home. I'll wait to escort you. Stay any longer in London and you'll be robbed blind.'

I shook my head. 'You don't understand,' I said. 'You've never understood me.'

'Don't understand!' Will was thunderingly angry now. 'Do you think I'm blind or as stupid as your pretty lordling? I've seen the quarterly accounts, I've seen the allowance you have! I've seen the bills come in! And while we're mending and making do on Wideacre with broken ploughshares spliced and used again, season after season, and while we have old carthorses pulling heavy loads and no new stock at all this year, you're preening before a glass to go out dancing with a gamester!'

'Nonsense!' I said heatedly. 'I've spent very little!'

But Will would not listen. 'You're a damned parasite!' he said roundly. 'And he's a worse one. He's not even bedded you and the pizzle has hold of your money while you sit up there, on your horse, and tell me you're not coming home! By God if I could pull you off the horse and make you walk home I would!'

'Don't you threaten me, Will Tyacke!' I said as angry as he. 'I'm not one of your alehouse drabs. I didn't come to you for help, I can manage my own affairs. I don't overspend and I don't listen to a bawling from any man, least of all you.'

'You don't listen to anything!' Will said. 'You don't listen to Mr Fortescue when he warned you off them, you don't listen to me. You don't even listen to your own common sense when the man has robbed you before marriage and you know his whole family will rob you later. Any woman with anything in her head but vanity and wind would call off the wedding and run for her life away from such a band.'

'The wedding's to be brought forward!' I said, as angry as he and picking on the one piece of news which would make him angrier. 'We're to wed and be home on Wideacre by Christmas! So there, Will Tyacke, and don't you dare try to tell me what to do!'

'Brought the wedding forward?' Will looked at me open-mouthed. Then he leaned forward and put his hand on Sea's reins and drew the horse closer to his own.

'Sarah, by God, I don't know what game you're playing,' he said low-voiced. 'I thought you'd taken up with them so they would take you into society, then I thought you were tied to him because you'd given up on yourself and you didn't care what happened to you. Now you tell me he's creeping into your bedroom and you've brought the wedding forward . . .' he broke off. Then he suddenly dropped Sea's reins as if they had burned him. 'You whore!' he suddenly yelled. 'You stupid little whore! He's bedded you, and you're handing over your money and your land to the first man who's ever looked twice at you!'

I gasped. 'How dare you!' I started but Will interrupted me.

'Thank God I'll not be there to see it,' he said. 'I promised myself I'd stay and see you safe in your home even if you went through with this whore's deal. I thought you'd need a manager, I thought you'd need advice. I thought you might need help against him, if he raised a hand to you or started robbing you.' Will scowled. 'The more fool me!' he said bitterly. 'I've met your sort before. They like a fool in the bedchamber, and they don't care what he does to them. They've no pride and no sense. I'll leave you to your flirting and your ruin. I'll be gone, and I'll never see Wideacre again.

'There've been Tyackes on Wideacre since it had that name. A damn sight longer than the cursed Laceys, but you've won now. I give you joy of it. Little Lord Perry will have it mortgaged and lost within a year, mark my words. And then you'll be Lady Sarah of No-Acre, and see how he looks to you then!'

'Where would you go?' I demanded. 'Who'd have you manage them into bankruptcy, to teach their workers your sort of manners? Don't come to me for a character for I'll give you none!'

Will snorted with rage. 'You know so little!' he said witheringly. 'And you think yourself so clever! I'll go where I'm wanted, to Mr Norris's estate in the north. And I'll take a woman with me. I'll take Becky, Becky and the children with me, I'll wed her, and we'll settle there. And if I don't see you till you rot in hell it'll be too soon for me.'

'Becky?'

Will turned and his smile was mean. 'Aye,' he said. 'Becky. The woman your mama-in-law flung out of her cottage half-starved with three bairns. She's my lover, didn't you know? She lives with me with her bairns. I'll marry her and take her with me. I was a fool not to do so at the first. She's a lovely girl, warm and full of love to give.' His cold eyes raked over me, over my rich green riding habit, my white face under the hat. 'She's a proud girl,' he said. 'She deserves the best and she knows it. She loves me, she adores my touch. She wants to give me a son. I'll be happy with her in a way I would never be with anyone else. And she is the most beautiful girl I've ever had in my bed, or ever seen.'

I raised my riding crop and brought it down with one wicked

slash across his face. He snatched it off me and he broke it across his knee and threw the two pieces towards me. Sea shied and reared high, frightened by the noise and the anger, and I had to cling to his mane to stay on.

'I hate you,' I shouted. I was choked with abuse which would not come.

'I hate you,' Will replied instantly. 'I've been a fool for months over you, but every time I have been with you I went home to Becky and she took me into her arms and loved me, and I knew that was where I belonged.'

'You go back to her then,' I said. My voice was choked with anger, and my cheeks were wet though I was not crying. 'You go back to her and tell her that she is welcome to have you. I don't want you, I never have wanted you. You're a dirty common working man and I've seen thousands like you everywhere I have ever lived. You're all the same. You're all boastful and braggart, randy as dogs and weepy as chavvies. I'd rather have Perry than you any day. So go back to your slut, Will Tyacke, and her dirty little bastards. Go to your stupid farm in the north and rob and ruin another landowner. I don't want to see you ever again!'

I wheeled Sea around and thundered away, forgetting all about the rule of not galloping in the park. I raged against Will, shouting abuse and swearing out loud, all the way back to the gate, and then as we trotted through the streets I swore under my breath, the rich filthy language of my childhood. I stormed up the steps to the front door and hammered on it loud as a bailiff. The footman gaped at me and I ordered him to take Sea around to the stables for me in a voice which made him leap to do my bidding. Then I raced up the stairs, two at a time, to my room and slammed the door behind me. I was so angry I could not think what to do or what to say.

I leaned back against the door, my hat squashed against the wooden panels and I shut my eyes. They felt hot in my hot face. Then I remembered what he had said about Becky, and I found I had clenched my hands into fists and I was cramming them both against my lips to stop me screaming in rage. He had told me that he loved her, that he loved her body, that he loved to hold her in his arms, that he was going to marry her.

That last took the rage from me as if I had had the breath knocked out of me with a fall. I thought of him smiling and kissing my wrist and then going back to his cottage where she waited for him. I thought of her three little children around his table, pleased to see him home. I thought of her sitting on his lap in the firelight after the chavvies had gone to bed, then I thought of him holding her in his arms all night long. He had said that she adored his touch.

I stood with my back against my bedroom door staring into the room, silently, for a long time.

I went over to the writing table and I drew a sheet of the expensive notepaper towards me. It was embossed with the Havering crest in gold, and on the right-hand side I spelled out the London address. At Havering Hall they had notepaper with the Sussex address. One day soon I would be the new Lady Havering and all this, two sorts of notepaper and everything, would be mine.

It took me a while, for I could not write swiftly. I had to print the words and many of them were spelled wrong for all I knew. So it did not look as proud and angry as I wished. I wanted to hurt him, to cut him to the heart.

> *To Will Tyacke,*
>
> *Your behaviour and language in the park today were not what I expect of one of my farm workers. I would be grateful if you would terminate your work on Wideacre forthwith and leave my land.*
>
> > *Yours faithfully,*
> > *Sarah Lacey.*

Then I wrote another:

> *Dear Mr Tyacke,*
>
> *You have no right to speak to me as you did today, and you know it. I pledged my word months ago to marry Peregrine*

*Havering and of course I intend to hold to that promise. Your
own affairs are your own concern. I have no interest in them.
If you wish to leave Wideacre I am sure I am very sorry to see
you go. If you wish to stay I will accept your apology for
speaking in an improper fashion.*

> *Yours faithfully,*
> *Sarah Lacey.*

I slid that version to one side and went to look out of the
window. Then I turned and went back to the little writing table.
I was in an anger hotter than anything I had felt in years,
perhaps ever. I could not let it go with formal words.

Dear Will,

How dare you talk to me like you did today!

*You must be mad to even dream of speaking to me as you
did!*

*Let me tell you two things. One is that I am your employer,
the squire of Wideacre and shortly to be Lady Havering. One
word from me, one word and you don't work in Sussex any
more. And don't think that you could get work elsewhere.
There isn't an employer in the country who would take you on
after I tell them that you abused me to my face, and in the
coarsest of terms.*

*I have no interest whatsoever in your messy little intrigues
with your woman, nor in your opinions. I want you gone from
Wideacre at once, but before you leave I insist that you come to
London and see me at once. At once, Will.*

> *Sarah Lacey.*

I sat with that version before me for a long time. Then I
sighed and pulled forward another sheet of paper. The anger
was seeping away from me.

Dear Will,

*I am angry with you, and I am sad. You are right and I am
a fool. I have lived my life here in London, and also with them*

*at the Hall as if I were blind, as if I had forgotten where I was
raised and what mattered most to me.*

*You don't understand how it is with me and Peregrine, and
I let you misunderstand me. He comes to my room because he is
like my brother, like a little brother to me. I can't withdraw
from the marriage – he needs me, and I like how I am when I
am with him. I like to give him the care and courage he needs.
I have never given anyone anything, except one person once.
And I failed her at the last. Now there is someone who needs
the things I can do, who looks to me for help. I want to be good
to him Will. That cannot be wrong. Forgive me, it is truly
what I want. I am afraid it is all I am fit for.*

> *Your friend,*
> *Sarah.*

The clocks chimed softly; it was eleven already. I should be
changing for breakfast at noon, and then I should change again
to go out to the princess's luncheon. I swallowed experimentally.
My throat was sore. It was not sore enough to let Lady Clara
excuse me from lunching with the princess. I put my hand to
my forehead. It was hot, but not hot enough. I would have to go. I
would write a letter and put it in the post for Will before I went.

I thought of him riding back to Sussex, in a rage; alone. And I
wanted to speak with him, to take back the things I had said
which I had not meant. I thought of the weal of the riding whip
which had come up on his cheek and though I had known blows
and bruises a-plenty, I felt that this single blow was the worst I
had ever known. And it had been from my hand.

I was too rough, I was too wild. I was wrong for Perry, I was
a foul-mouthed little pauper, no match for Perry's delicacy. But
I was too hard for Will. It was all wrong. I belonged where I
had been raised, down among the fighters and the swearers,
where you lived by your wits and your fists, and you never loved
anybody.

Dear Will,
You are right, they have trapped me. I thought I was so

*clever and I thought I was winning my way through to the life
I wanted to lead. But I was wrong and they caught me while I
thought I was catching them. They have caught me – all of
them. The Haverings and the Quality and the lords and ladies
and the life we live in London. I have been a fool Will and I
have to pay for it.*

*Not Perry. I know you hate him because he is what he is – a
drunkard and a gamester and a fool. But he is also like a
child, he is not a cheat. He loves me Will, and he needs me.
And his love for me and his trust in me will make me a better
person, a kinder woman. If I stay with Perry I may learn to
love him as a woman ought to be able to love a man. If I stay
with Perry I think I can rescue him from his folly, and myself
from my coldness. I think I can get him away, away to the
country, and we will find some way of treating each other with
tenderness and love. He will do as I wish. He will run Havering
as I order, and I shall run Wideacre. And then we can do the
things which you have wanted all along. I know I was wrong
to suspect you, and James Fortescue. I have met Quality
rogues now, and I understand how they work. I know you are
not liars and cheats, not you, not James, not all the people at
Acre. I shall come home to you, with Perry, and everything
can be different. We can run the whole Havering–Wideacre
estate as you would wish, as a corporation, and you will see
that Perry is a good man. You will come to like him Will.*

*I am sorry that I have been so foolish about you, and about
Becky. I will try to be glad about that, glad that you love her.
I have been selfish I think. I did not know that there was that
between you, I should have guessed – I lived in a wagon long
enough! I just did not think. I am sorry. I feel foolish that I
did not think, but I am glad that she loves you, and that you
love her. I am sorry that I was selfish in asking you to come to
London to see me as I did. I was lonely here, in this big city,
and I wanted to hear your voice and see your face. But I
should have realized that you loved her. I think I have never
understood love like that. I warned you quick enough not to
love me didn't I? I was a fool not to know that you would find*

someone else. I am glad she loves you, and that you are happy.
I hope she will let me come and see her children and you when
I am married and come to Wideacre.
                              Your friend,
                              Sarah.

I paused then, and put my head in my hands for a long time. I
was a slow writer and that muddle of thoughts had taken me an
hour to spell out. I flushed with shame at the thought that Will
might write very well for all I knew and he might think me
ignorant and stupid not to be able to loop my letters and scrawl
all over the page.

But then I heard noon strike and my maid tapped on the door
and I called for her to go away, that I would be down for
breakfast in the instant. And then I laid my head on the paper
on the writing table and groaned as if I was injured, knifed to
the heart. I felt as sick as a horse and I could not think why.
When I thought of the red weal on his cheek and him telling me
of his Becky I wanted to throw up my accounts.

. I pulled a sheet of notepaper towards me and I knew I was
down below the lies, well below the level of anger and pride.
Below even the level of trying to be pleasant about his woman. I
was down to where I belonged. Where I had always belonged.
And down below that. For I was no longer Mamselle Meridon
dancing on horseback who was cold as ice. Now I was no longer
Meridon the slut horse-tamer who could make her da spit with
rage. I was now someone whose name I did not know who was
longing, longing, longing for someone to love. Longing for him.

Dear Will,
    This is all wrong.
    Please do not promise any more to her. Please come back to
London. I do not want to marry Perry. I want to be with you.
I have loved you and wanted you from the moment I first saw
you, that night at Wideacre. Please come for me at once. I beg
your pardon for having struck you. You were right, it is no
good here. It is hopeless with Perry.

I am sure she is lovely, but I cannot believe you do not love me, and if you do not come for me now, I do not know what I will do. Please come to me. I love you with all my heart.
Sarah.

I took the six pages of notepaper and I screwed them up into a fat ball. I cast them in the fire and I held the poker and watched them burn. I mashed down the clot of embers so that there was nothing left. I turned my back on the fire, I turned my back on the writing desk.

I could not be betrothed to one man and write like that to another. I could not break faith with Perry, I could not abandon Lady Clara without a word. They had treated me well, by their lights, I could not walk away from them as easily as I had walked in.

I would have to wait, wait and plan. I would have to get free, honourably free, before I wrote to Will, before I thought of him again.

I leaned my forehead against the cold thick glass of my window and looked at the grey sky and thought of Will riding home with the scarlet weal from my whip on his cheek. I had no right to strike him, I had no right to make a claim on him. The letters were burned, I would not write another. I would never write to Will. Not in anger, not in love. Our ways lay by different roads. Perhaps one day he would forgive me for the blow. Perhaps one day he would understand.

I rang my bell for my maid to come and dress me in my morning dress.

I could think of nothing else I could do.

33

I was ill, and it was that which made my eyes seem red and made me so dull at the luncheon.

'You are cruel!' lisped Sir Richard Fuller.

I looked at him blankly.

'Cruel to one who adores you!' he said smiling. His lips were painted a delicate pink, he had a black patch in the shape of a heart at the corner of his mouth.

'Yes,' I said stupidly. 'I suppose I am.'

He gave his ringing peal of laughter and a couple of old dowagers looked around at us, saw Sir Richard and smiled indulgently.

'A Diana! A very Diana!' he cried out.

I shrugged. Half the time in this mannered social world I could not understand a word of what people said to me. The other half I understood well enough but I could not think why they troubled.

'Do you think I have not seen the newspaper this morning?' he asked teasingly. 'I knew it was coming but oh! the blow to my hopes!'

I stared at him again. We were seated in the window seat of the princess's parlour, looking out towards the park. Will had been right about it being cold. The hoar frost was still white in the sheltered corners, a yellow sun was harsh in the sky.

'What are you talking about?' I asked.

Sir Richard's pale eyes danced with malice. 'About my heartbreak, about my heartbreak!' he said.

I was no good at this kind of flirting. I sighed and went to get up and walk away from him.

'I knew you were half promised, but I had no idea he would be so speedy,' Sir Richard twinkled, putting out a hand to detain me. 'Have his losses really been so bad?'

'Perry?' I said, coming through the maze of innuendo.

'Of course!' Sir Richard said limpidly. 'Who else are you engaged to marry?'

I looked at him blankly and said nothing.

'Don't look so surprised, Miss Lacey!' he begged. 'You are charming, charming. But I cannot believe that even Perry would post your engagement in the newspaper without consulting you!'

I nodded. Perry was quite capable of it.

'Which is why I ask!' Sir Richard cried triumphantly. 'What freak has Perry taken up now that he must run through your fortune as well as his own? We knew his losses at faro were staggering, but I hear now he is playing piquet like a fiend! And why, heartbreaking Miss Lacey, do you hand your fortune over so readily? Is it love? Do you tell me to abandon all hope?'

I gritted my teeth and got to my feet. 'You must excuse me, Sir Richard,' I said politely. I held my embroidered silk morning gown to one side and dipped him a polite curtsey. 'I see Lady Clara wants me, I must go.'

I crossed over to the other side of the room and stood at Lady Clara's elbow. She was playing whist with the princess and I waited until she had taken a trick before I interrupted her. I wished her son had half her skill at cards.

'Perry's put our engagement in the *Morning Post*,' I said in her ear.

Her face never changed. She should have worked as a gull sharper in the taverns. She was wasting her talents on rooking Quality spendthrifts like the princess.

'I did not see,' she said softly. 'You don't object, do you?'

'He might have told me,' I said. 'I have had Sir Richard Fuller raking me over. I looked a fool.'

Lady Clara nodded. 'He should have told you indeed,' she said. 'I'm glad you warned me. There he is, speak to him your-self.'

I glanced up. Perry was coming through the crowd of people who were standing near the door by the buffet table. As he came through with a smile and a word for many of them, he caught my eye and he beamed at me and came to my side.

'Sarah!' he said. 'I thought I'd find you here. Have you seen the newspaper this morning? We are in! Isn't that nice! I gave them an extra guinea to get it in at once!'

He kissed my hand, and then, at his mother's nod, drew me closer and kissed my cheek gently. His touch was cool, my cheek was hot.

'Why the hurry?' I asked.

He grinned roguishly. 'Come now,' he said. 'You know that yourself. I was all out of credit at the start of this week and now they are falling over themselves to lend to me.' He beamed. 'And the cream of the jest is thatI don't need the money now!'

I kept the false smile pinned on my face and I nodded as if he were telling me excellent news.

'I'm finished with gaming anyway,' he said. 'We'll marry as soon as the banns are called – in a fortnight – and then we'll go down to the country and live like fat old squires. As you wish, Sarah. Just as you wish.'

If half a dozen curious people had not been watching us I think I would have wept. I was so tired from my sleepless night and my throat was so tight. And the memory of Will riding from me in a rage, riding back to Becky and that safe little cottage made my head throb.

'Good,' I said. I would never live in a cottage with Will Tyacke. I would never love him as his Becky did. I would never lie in his arms at night. But I had learned how to love a man and some of that love I could give to Perry. We were young, we would find many good things to do together. And if we could farm the land well, and make Wideacre and Havering good places to live and work, we would have done something more than any squires or lords before us had ever done.

'Don't play piquet,' I said.

Perry shook his head. 'Not a card,' he replied. 'You look tired, Sarah, and you are all hot. Why don't I take you home?'

I shook my head. 'I can't,' I said. 'Your mama . . .'

Perry smiled at me. 'I am your engaged husband-to-be,' he said with a joking little play at dignity. 'I think you should come home and rest. You are to be out tonight, are you not? And you hardly slept at all last night! Come on. I shall tell Mama that you must rest.'

I was about to tell him 'no' but the truth indeed was that I was tired, and I longed to be away from that bright room with the tinkling chandelier above the hard laughing faces. I thought I would see Perry try his paces. It was the first time I had ever seen him go against his mama's wishes. I wanted to see if he could do it.

He walked up to the table and leaned over her shoulder. Lady Clara's look was impatient but the dowagers who were playing cards with her all leaned forward to hear the exchange between her and her son and I saw her glacial social smile smooth away her irritation. She nodded sweetly enough, and then she waved her hand to me. Perry threaded his way back towards me and offered me his arm with a cheeky grin.

'Tally ho!' he said. 'We're away!'

I smiled back at him though my eyelids felt heavy. 'You stood up to your mama,' I said.

Perry smoothed both lapels with a braggart's gesture. 'I'm the fiancé of one of the richest women in London!' he said with a flourish. 'I'd like to see anyone get in my way.'

I laughed at that, despite my throbbing head. And I took his arm and we went to bid our farewells to the princess. Sir Richard was bending over her chair as we came up and he smiled at me under his arched eyebrows.

'Rushing off to snatch a few moments together alone?' he asked acidly.

The princess laughed and tapped him over the knuckles with her fan. Her jowls wobbled, her little eyes sparkled. 'Now, Sir Richard!' she said in her deep fruity voice. 'Don't tease the young people. Shall I see you at Court tomorrow night my dear?' she asked me.

I curtseyed to what I thought was the right depth. 'No, your highness,' I said. 'We don't go. I am going at the end of this month.'

'As the new Lady Havering!' Sir Richard said. 'How ravishing you will look in the Havering diamonds!'

My stomach lurched as guiltily as if it had been me who had taken them and my face fell, but Perry let us down altogether. He exploded into giggles and had to whip out his monogrammed handkerchief and turn it into a cough. We shuffled away from the princess in disarray and got ourselves out of the door to where we could collapse in the hall out of earshot.

'How did he know?' I demanded.

Perry leaned against the blue silk-lined wall until he could catch his breath. 'Oh, Lord knows!' he said carelessly. 'It's the sort of thing that gets around. Just as well I got them back though, Sarah!'

'Just as well,' I said faintly.

Our coach was ready at the door and Perry helped me in. I dug my hands deep inside my fur muff and lifted it up to my face to sniff the warm smell of the pelt.

'Have a nip of this,' Perry offered, pulling his hip-flask out of his pocket.

I sipped it cautiously. It hit the back of my throat and burned like fire.

'What is it?' I said, my eyes watering.

'Hollands gin and brandy,' Perry said, swigging at the flask. 'All the rage. We call it Dutch and French. Takes your head off, don't it?'

'Yes,' I said.

The carriage swayed forward, the wheels sliding without gripping on the ice between the cobbles.

I nodded and laid my head back against the cushions of the coach. I shut my eyes and dozed. When the carriage pulled up I had to lean on Perry's arm to get up the stairs into the house and then Sewell, my maid, was waiting to help me change into an afternoon gown.

'I'm not driving,' I said. My throat had tightened even more and I was hoarse.

She looked at me. 'You look unwell, Miss Sarah,' she said. 'Shall I fetch you a posset? Should you like a rest?'

I paused for a moment, looking at the bed with the clean white sheets. The girl I had been could walk all day behind a wagon and then ride horses for a living all evening. Now I was tired in my body and weary deep into my very soul.

'Yes,' I said. 'Undo the buttons at the back here, and I'll take a nap, I'm not promised anywhere until this evening.'

I climbed between the cool sheets and sat up and sipped the posset she brought me. I slept at once but jerked awake when she came to stoke my fire.

'It's five o'clock, Miss Sarah,' she said. 'Her ladyship has come in and changed and gone out again. She said you and Lord Peregrine could follow her in the second carriage. I told her you were lying down.'

I nodded. I pushed back the sheets but they seemed heavy, my arms were weak. I put my feet down to the floorboards and the very wood seemed to sway beneath me.

'I have a fever, Sewell,' I said stupidly. 'I'm not well enough to go. Ask Lord Peregrine to take my apologies. I shall stay in bed tonight and be well tomorrow.'

My eyelids were hot. I fell back against the pillows.

'Will you dine up here?' she asked indifferently.

'No,' I said. Poor little hungry wretch that I had been. I felt now that I never wanted to eat again. 'No. Bring me some lemonade and then leave me to sleep please.'

I heard her rattle the fire irons in the grate and then I heard the floorboard creak as she crossed the room for the door. I dimly heard her voice speaking to Perry and then the sound came and went in my ears like the sound of the sea, like the sounds of the waves that last day at Selsey.

Then I fell asleep again and I dreamed that I was not in London at all. It was a dream of the fever all fractured and short with strange frightening ideas lost in the darkness as I struggled awake and was rid of them, then they came back when I was drowsy again. I thought I was back in the wagon and I was calling and calling for her to bring me a mug of water. My throat was parched and I was so afraid it was the typhus and I was going to die. In the dream I could see her humped back and hear my thin child's voice begging her to wake and fetch me a mug.

I was disturbed because I was feverish. I did not know myself.

In the fever dream I thought that I was angry that she had not wakened for me, and I called out to her: 'I've waked for you often enough, you lazy slut!' And I thought of all the times I had waked for her and served her, and how she had repaid me with a smile and perhaps a touch, but often with nothing at all. And, though it was like the tines of a rake over my heart, I thought that there were many and many times when she had taken much from me and given nothing in return. That she was a selfish young silly tart, and if she had listened to me she would not have gone up the ladder that day. If she had listened to me she would not have tried to trap a lad who was not fit to wed. If she had had anything in her head but vanity and wind she would have seen that she was sailing gaily down the wrong road, the worst road of all. And if she had listened she would not be dead now, and I would not be ill now, ill and lonely and so out of joint with myself that I was all wrong.

All wrong too.

And so wrong that I could not tell who I was nor what I should be doing.

I struggled awake with that, and reached out in the darkness for the lemonade. It was night then, night and going on for dawn. Someone had brought me a drink while I slept. Someone had made up the fire again. Some time in the night I had reached out for the glass and drained it for it was empty and the jug half full. In the cold grey light of the early morning before sun-up I was able to see enough to sit up in my bed and pour the drink.

It was icy. It made me shiver as if a finger of snow had passed down my throat into my very belly. I gulped it down to sate my thirst and then I huddled back down under the covers again. I was cold, chilled and cold. But when I put my hand to my forehead I found I was burning hot.

I knew I was ill then, and I knew that the dream of her, of seeing her as a fool and a cruel fool at that, was part of my illness. I had to hold to the things I knew. I had to remember her as she had been, my beloved. I had to hold on to Perry as I knew he could be, a careless youth who would grow into a good man. I had to remember that Will Tyacke was an angry, vindictive working man who had done very well out of my land and was now taking himself off in a rage, and good riddance to him.

I shivered in the grey coldness of the early morning. I had to hold on to those things or I did not know what would happen. If I opened my mind just a little crack, to the doubts and uncertainties, I would lose my memory of her and my love for her, I would lose my certain future.

'I want to be Lady Havering,' I croaked into the still cold air of the room. 'I want to farm Havering and Wideacre together. I want to be the greatest landowner in the county. I want everyone to know who I am.'

The thought of being known by name to everyone for hundreds of miles around was a comforting one. I slid down on the pillows a little deeper. And I slept again.

I woke in the morning hot and blinded with my eyelids so red and swollen I could hardly open them. I was wakened by a squawk when my maid, coming to my bedside, caught sight of me and dashed for the door. I opened my eyes slightly and shut them again quickly. Even with the window curtains closed the room seemed far too bright and the flicker of the newly lit fire was so loud it made my head ache. I was burning up with fever and my throat was so sore that I could not have spoken even if I had wanted to.

The bedroom door opened again and there was Lady Havering's maid Rimmings herself looking very tall and regal despite the curl papers sticking out from under her nightcap. She ignored my maid, who was twittering behind her and approached my bed and looked down at me. When I saw her face change I knew that I was very ill indeed.

'Miss Sarah . . .' she said.

I blinked. I tried to say 'Yes?' but my voice was burned away in the hotness of my throat. I nodded. Even that slight movement made all the swollen muscles in my neck shriek with a pain which clanged inside my head like an echoing belfry.

'You look very ill, do you feel unwell?' Rimmings voice was so sharp it cut into the tender places behind my eyes and inside my ears.

'Yes,' a little whisper of sound managed to creep out. She heard it, but she did not bend closer to hear me better. She was keeping her distance from my breath.

'It's the typhus for sure!' said Sewell, my maid. I turned my head stiffly on the sweaty pillow and looked at her. If it was the typhus I was done for. I had seen my Rom ma die of it and I knew how hard the illness was, like a harsh master who breaks your spirit before throwing you aside. If I had been on Wideacre I think I might have stood against it, I might have fought it. But not in London where I was always tired, always ill at ease, and with so little joy in my days.

'That'll do!' Rimmings said abruptly. 'And not a word of this in the servants' hall if you want to keep your place.'

'I don't know I do want my place with typhus in the house,' the girl said defiantly, backing towards the door, her eyes still on me. ''Sides, if it's typhus she won't need a dresser will she? She won't need a maid at all. Her la'ship had best get a nurse for as long as Miss lasts.'

Rimmings nodded. 'I don't doubt she'll have a nurse,' she said. I watched her through half-closed eyelids. I did not think I could bear to have a stranger pushing me around the bed, pulling me around, stripping me and washing me. I knew the London nurses. They worked as layers-out and midwives too; dirty-handed, foul-mouthed, hard-drinking women who treated their patients – quick and dead – the same: as corpses already.

Rimmings remembered me. 'Some of them are very good,' she lied. Then she turned to Sewell. 'Get some fresh lemonade, and a bowl of water. You can sponge her face.'

'I'm not touching her!' The girl stood firm.

'You'll do as you're ordered, miss!' Rimmings burst out.

She didn't care. I closed my eyes and the squabble came to me dimly in great heaving waves of noise.

'I won't touch her! I've seen typhus before,' she hissed defiantly. 'It'll be a blessed miracle if we don't all of us get it. Besides, you just look at her face! She's not long for this world, she's grey already. Sponging ain't going to bring down that fever. She's a goner, Miss Rimmings, and I ain't going to nurse a dying woman.'

'Her la'ship will hear of this Sewell – and you'll be out on the streets without a character!' Rimmings boomed, her voice seemed to echo again and again in my head.

'I don't care, it ain't right! I'm a lady's maid, hired for a lady's maid! No one can say I don't keep her clothes right and it ain't my fault that she wears riding habits all the time. It ain't my fault she's been so peaky ever since she came to London. I've dressed her right and I ain't ever said one word about her coming up out of the hedgerow. But I won't nurse her. It'd be up and down those stairs twenty times a day and certain to take it and die too. I won't do it!'

My cracked lips parted in a little smile as I heard them wrangling, though my head was thudding like an enlisting drum. It had all gone wrong then. Sewell was right with her sharp servant's eyes and her quick wits. I was worm's meat already, she had seen the look in my face which I remembered from my ma. When the typhus fever puts its hot sweaty finger on you, you are gone. Perry would not clear his gambling debts with my dowry, I would never be Lady Havering. Her ladyship would never have an heir from me.

All our work and lies and lessons would be for nothing. I had always thought they were good for nothing, and now nothing would come of them, except that I should have a fashionable funeral instead of being tossed into a common grave. But I would die in this beautiful London town house as surely as I would have died in that dirty little wagon if we had taken the infection when we were chavvies. The disease which had taken my weary travel-worn ma in her poverty and her hunger could slip past the butler and take me too.

I was not even sorry. Not even sorry that I would die and not see my seventeenth year. I could not find it in my hot shivering body to care a ha'pence either way. Ever since she had died I had been marking my time out, waiting. Now I was going too and if there was such a thing as the gorgio God, and a gorgio heaven, then I would see her there. I thought of her with her hair tumbled down, dressed in shining white with pink fluffy wings rising up behind her. She would be lovely. I wanted to be with her.

'The kitchenmaid can do it,' Rimmings said decisively.

'Em'ly?' my maid asked. 'Of course! The kitchenmaid should do it. Will you wake her la'ship and tell her about this?'

'This' was me on my deathbed, not a fit subject to broach to Lady Havering before she had woken in her own good time and rung the bell for her morning chocolate.

Rimmings hesitated. 'I suppose so,' she said slowly. 'She'll have to send for the doctor for her, I can't take the authority. But I doubt he'll be able to make much difference, she's that far gone.'

She looked at the clock on my mantelpiece. 'I daren't wake my lady before eight,' she said. 'Not even if she was breathing her last already! It won't make much difference to her whether she waits till nine or later. I'll give Emily some laudanum to give her.'

She came back to my bedside and stood a judicious three feet away. 'Can you hear me, Miss Lacey?' she asked. I gave a painful nod.

'I shall send Emily to nurse you, she shall give you some laudanum. That will make you feel better.'

I nodded again. Emily or Sewell, it made little odds. Sewell was right. The fever had me in its grip like a hard rider forcing a horse at a gallop towards a cliff. I did not expect to leap across.

They took themselves off then, still fretting, and I lay in the throbbing hot pain of the stuffy little room and let my red eyelids close on my hot eyes, and I dozed.

At once I dreamed of a girl who looked like me and rode like me, but dressed in bulky uncomfortable clothes. She had a riding habit of grey velvet, but thicker and heavier cut than my smart outfit. She had eyes even greener than mine, as green as mine are when I am happy. She looked happy enough. She looked as if she had never shed a tear in her life.

I heard her laugh, I saw someone lift her into the saddle and I saw her smile down at him with love. But though her face was warm I knew that all the time she was teaching herself to be cold and hard, that she would throw him away, she would throw away anyone who stood in her way. I knew she was my grand-dame.

The great Beatrice Lacey who made the land grow and made it eat up the people who worked it. Beatrice whom they had stopped with fire and anger. Nothing else would have made her even pause. I knew then, that I was a Lacey indeed, for that bright hard smile was my smile when I stood in the ring and knew I had an audience in the palm of my dirty little hand. And that coldness which she swung around her, like an icy cloak, was the coldness which I had been born and bred to. The coldness which says: 'Me! Me! Who is going to care for me?' It seemed odd, that this moment when I was galloping like an arrow towards my death should be the time when I saw her, when I knew at last that I was a Lacey through and through.

My bedroom door opened and I stirred in my sleep and saw poor little Emily the kitchenmaid with her hands swiftly washed and her cap pulled straight and her dirty pinny swapped for a clean one.

'Please'm,' she said. 'They said I had to give you this.' She held a bottle of laudanum in one hand and glass of water in another. 'They said I should be your maid while you're ill, until her la'ship gets a nurse,' she said. 'But please'm I ain't never done it and I don't know nohow what's to do.'

I tried to smile and nod her to the bedside, but I could not move my neck at all now. I must be getting worse very quick for I had been able to speak earlier in the morning and now it had gone altogether.

She was made bold by my stillness and silence. 'Are you very bad, miss?' she asked. I blinked my eyes and she came a little closer.

'Bloody hell,' she said.

I gave a little croak of laughter and she jumped back as if I could bite.

'Beg pardon, miss,' she said hopelessly. Then when I made no more sound she held out the bottle at me. 'They said I was to give you this,' she said.

I could imagine how a strong dose would take the pain away. I forced my head to nod, the movement made my senses swim and I closed my eyes while the room swirled and the bed heaved like a ship in a rough sea.

'I'll put it 'ere then,' she said helplessly, and moved my pitcher of lemonade and put the phial and the water on the bedside table. 'You helps yourself when you wants it.'

She looked around the room for something that came within her experience. 'I'll make your fire up again!' she said brightly, and went to the hearth.

The little part of me which had clung to life like an obstinate succubus in the wagon through beatings, even through the deadly pain in my heart on that night when she died, held me tight now; and ordered my throat to cry out. I strained and strained to speak, looking desperately from her turned back as she worked on the fire, to the little glass of water and the laudanum alongside it. If the laudanum took the pain away I would sleep. If I slept I would not be weary when the crisis of the fever came and then I might fight it. I might win.

I tried to cry out, but all I could make were little choking noises which she could not even hear above the rattle of the fire irons and the poker knocking ashes in the grate. She got a blaze going and straightened up. The room which had been hot and stuffy was now a furnace, the firelight stabbed my eyes with its fierce heat.

'That's better!' she said. She approached the bed a little closer. ''Ave you got everythink you want then?' she looked around. The lemonade was out of reach, I could not raise myself up to get the laudanum. 'Got everythink? Good.'

'Emily,' I croaked.

She was instantly alarmed. 'Don't you try to talk now,' she said. She came a little closer but she did not dare to touch me. She had been ordered too often out of the good rooms, told to use the back stairs, to avoid the Quality and to curtsey low when they went past. She was too well schooled to dare to lay a finger on me. 'Don't you try to talk,' she said again.

She scuttered towards the door and dipped a little curtsey, and was gone. I tried to call her back but my throat was swollen so badly I could make no sound. I stared at the painted ceiling, at the pretty frieze at the top of the walls showing cupids and love-birds in white and gold. I remembered Meridon the gypsy and her sly toughness and I heaved myself upwards in my bed.

It was no good, I was Meridon no longer. I was little Miss Sarah Lacey with my throat closing so tight that I could not breathe and the smell of stale sweat and death all around me, and the pain behind my eyes and in the very bones of my face so bad that I could have cried except my tears had dried in the heat of the fever.

I dropped back on the pillow again and tried not to be afraid. I knew why Sewell had refused to nurse me, I knew why Rimmings would not touch me. I knew why Emily had said 'bloody hell' when she had seen my face. I had caught a brief glimpse of myself in my mirror when I was sitting upright for that moment. My face was so white I looked like a corpse already, my eyes were rimmed orange, my lips were so dark and so cracked that they looked black with dried blood. The typhus fever had me.

34

I lay for more long hours. No one came to see me. The house was silent around me in the early morning quietness which Lady Clara demanded. Outside in the street a ballad-seller started singing a snatch of song, and I heard our front door open and close and one of the footmen tell him briskly to be off. The church clock at St George's struck the hour. I started trying to count it but there were so many echoes in my head from each chime that I lost count and could not make it out. I thought it was about ten.

I could feel my throat closing tighter and I could feel panic rising in me as I thought that soon I would not be able to breathe at all. Then I supposed that I would die. I could no longer feel resigned and ready for death. When I thought of dying, clutching for my breath in this stuffy little room, I knew that I was most terribly afraid. It was as bad as it had been up on the trapeze when I had hung in utter terror of falling. Now as I sucked each gasp of air down into my body I felt the same shameful terror. Soon I should not be able to breathe at all.

I shut my eyes and tried to drift into sleep so that my dying would not be a terror-driven scrabble for breath; but it was no good. I was awake and alert now, my throat dry as paper, my tongue swollen in my mouth. I felt as if I were dying of thirst – never mind typhus. The jug of lemonade hovered like a mirage, well out of my reach. The phial of laudanum, which would have eased my pain, was beside it.

I could hear a horrid rasping noise in the room, like a saw on dry wood. It came irregularly, with a growing gap between the sound. It was my breath, it was the noise of my breath as I struggled to get air into my lungs. I opened my eyes again and listened in fear to the noise, and felt the pain of each laboured

459

heave at air. I remembered then my ma in the wagon and how she had kept us awake with that regular gasp. I was sorry then that I had cursed her in my hard little childish heart for being so noisy and interrupting a dream I had been having. A dream of a place called Wide.

The bedroom door opened as the clock started chiming the half past the hour. I tried to open my eyes and found they were stuck together. I was blinded and for a moment I thought I was stone-blind with the illness.

'Sarah, I hear you are unwell,' Lady Clara's voice was clear, confident. I shuddered at the noise of her footsteps which echoed and banged in my head. Then I heard her quick indrawn breath. I heard the noise of her skirts whisk as she crossed to the bell-pull by the fireplace, and then the running feet of Rimmings, Sewell and Emily.

She ordered a bowl of warm water and in a few moments I felt someone gently sponging my eyes until they fluttered and I could open them and see Rimmings holding me as far from her body as possible and sponging my face at arms' length. Sewell was weeping quietly in the corner with her apron up to her eyes and I guessed that the low-voiced exchange I had heard had been her refusing to touch me and Lady Clara's instantaneous dismissal.

'You may go, Sewell,' she said. 'Pack your bags and be out by noon.'

Sewell scurried from the room.

'She needs a nurse, your ladyship,' Rimmings offered, turning my pillow so that the cool side was under my hot neck. 'She needs a nurse.'

'Of course she needs a nurse, you fool,' her ladyship said from my writing table. 'And a doctor. I can't think why I wasn't called.'

'I feared to disturb your ladyship, and she was sleeping well after Emily gave her some laudanum.'

'Did you?' Lady Clara shot a look at Emily who bobbed a curtsey with melting knees.

'Yes'm,' she said faintly.

'How many drops?' Lady Clara demanded.

Emily shot an anguished look at Rimmings who cut in smoothly: 'I thought three, your ladyship, for Miss Sarah had lost her voice this morning but she was not overheated.'

Lady Clara nodded. 'None the less she is seriously unwell now,' she said firmly. 'Rimmings, take this note to a footman and tell him to take it round to Doctor Player at once.'

Rimmings stepped back from my bedside gladly enough and whisked out of the room.

'You,' Lady Clara said to Emily. 'You clear up in here, understand?'

Emily dipped a curtsey.

Lady Clara came and stood at the foot of my bed. 'Sarah, can you understand me?' she asked.

I managed a small nod.

'I have sent for the doctor, and he will be here soon,' she said. 'He will make you well again.'

I was so weak with fear and so hopeful of being able to breathe again I could have wept. Besides, I remembered my ma's weak terror as she died alone, fighting for her breath. I didn't want to be alone like her, I wanted someone to smooth my forehead and tell me that I would be well.

'Sarah, have you made a will?' Lady Clara demanded.

I choked with shock.

'Have you made a will?' she asked again, thinking I had not heard.

I shook my head.

'I'll send for your lawyers then, as well,' she said brusquely. 'Don't be alarmed my dear, but if it is typhus then I know you would want to be on the safe side. I'll have the footman go for him as soon as he gets back.' She paused. 'Is there anything you would like?'

I forced myself to speak, to force a word through the sandpaper of my throat. 'Drink,' I said.

Lady Clara came no closer but she nodded Emily to the bed. 'Pour Miss Sarah a drink,' she said sharply. 'Not like that. Up to the brim. Now lift her up. Yes, hold her around the shoulders and lift her. Now take the glass and hold it for her.'

The cold glass touched my lips and the sweet clear liquid slid into my mouth. The first few mouthfuls choked me and Emily nearly drowned me before Lady Clara snapped at her to stop and let me breathe. But then the sweet clear ease of it opened my throat and I drank three glasses before Emily lowered me to the pillow again and said softly:

'Beg pardon, m'm.'

Lady Clara ordered her to sit by my bedside and give me more lemonade if I asked for it. Emily hesitated, but then sank into a chair when her ladyship scowled.

'Beg pardon, m'm,' she said.

Lady Clara gave a swift comprehensive look around the room, and at me. I was breathing a little easier now I was higher on the pillows but that eerie rasping noise came every time I drew a breath. I saw a shadow cross her face and I knew she thought I would die and she would have to find another biddable heiress to marry her son, and she would have to find her quickly before his gambling debts ruined them all.

'I'll see you in a moment,' she said shortly and left the room.

Emily and I sat in silence, listening to the awful hoarseness of my breath. Then I was too weary to do anything more but doze again.

That was my last lucid moment for days.

A lot of the time was very hot, but there were also long times when I shivered with cold. There was a man who came from time to time whose touch was gentle, and I mistook him for Robert Gower and thought I was back in the parlour hurt from falling from the trapeze. There was a woman, a nurse I suppose, who smelled of spirits and who rolled me from side to side when she had to change the sheets on the bed. My skin flinched when she touched me with her hard dirty hands and she used to laugh in a loud beery voice when I winced.

Sometimes Lady Clara was there, always asking me if I felt well enough to sign something. Once she actually put a pen in my hand and held a paper on the bed before me. I remember I thought she was going to take Sea from me – an odd fancy from my fever – and I let the pen fall on the white sheets and closed my eyes to shut her out. I remember my hair became matted with sweat and tangled and the nurse had her way and hacked it off. I wandered a little in my mind after that; with the short ragged bob I thought I was Meridon again.

Often, very often, Perry was there. Sometimes drunk, sometimes sober. Always gentle and kind to me. He brought me little posies of flowers, he paid a ballad singer to sing songs under my window one afternoon. He brought hot-house grapes and pineapples and sliced them up small so that I could eat them. When I was rambling in fever I always knew Perry, his hand was always cool against my cheek and the smell of gin and his favourite soap was distinctive. One time when the nurse was out of the room he leaned over me and asked if he could take some guineas out of my purse.

'I'm desperate short, Sarah,' he said.

I knew I should not allow it. I knew he had promised me, in what seemed another lifetime, hundreds of years ago, that he would never never gamble again. But I had no will to match against his imploring blue eyes.

'Please Sarah,' he said.

I blinked, and he took that for assent and I heard the chink of gold coins and then the soft closing of the door behind him as he left me.

The doctor came again and again. Then one day, when I felt so weary and so sick that I half wished they would all leave me, leave me and let me die in peace, I saw him nod to Lady Clara and tell her there was nothing he could do. They would have to wait and see. I realized, only dimly, that they were talking about my death.

'Her mother died of childbed fever,' Lady Clara said.

The doctor nodded. 'But it's strong stock,' he said. 'Squires, the backbone of the country.'

Lady Clara nodded. I knew she would be thinking that I had not been reared as a squire's child, with nothing but the best to eat and drink.

'She is very strong,' she said hopefully. 'Wiry.'

The doctor inclined an inquisitive eyebrow. 'What of the estate if she goes?'

Lady Clara looked bleak. 'Back to the Laceys,' she said. 'All the contracts depend on marriage between Perry and her. Betrothal is not enough.'

The doctor nodded 'You must be worried,' he offered.

Lady Clara gave a little moan and turned towards the window where the winter sky was greying into darkness. 'Perry will be ruined if he cannot get his hands on his capital soon,' she said. 'And I was counting on the revenues of the Wideacre estate. It is a gold mine, that place. My income depends on the Havering estate remaining strong. And if Perry does not marry at all . . .' she trailed off but the desolation in her voice echoed in my head. She was thinking of the tumbled Dower House, and the Havering kin who would take her place.

Doctor Player glanced towards the bed and his look at me gleamed. I had my eyes shut and they thought I was sleeping. Indeed, I was only half conscious. I drifted in and out of awareness as they spoke. Sometimes I heard it all, sometimes I heard nothing.

'Special licence . . . marriage,' I heard him say, and I heard Lady Clara's swiftly indrawn breath.

'Would it be legal?' she demanded.

'Her guardian has already given his consent,' Doctor Player said judiciously. 'If she herself wished it . . .'

Lady Clara came swiftly to the bed and, forgetting her fear of the typhus, put her hand on my hot forehead.

'Would she agree? Is she fit to consent?' she asked. 'She can scarcely speak.'

Doctor Player's urbane voice held a gleam of amusement. 'I should be happy to testify that she was fit, if there should be any dispute,' he said softly. 'Especially to oblige you, my dear Lady Havering. I have always thought so highly of you . . . and always loved your part of the world. How I have longed to be a neighbour of yours, perhaps a little house . . .'

'There's a pretty Dower House on the Wideacre estate,' Lady Clara said. 'If you would do me the honour . . . rent free, of course . . . a lease of say, thirty years . . .?'

I heard his stays creak as he bowed, and I heard the smile in

Lady Clara's voice. The special smile, when she obtained what she wanted.

'Doctor Player, you have been most helpful,' she said. 'May I offer you a glass of ratafia? In the parlour?'

He took a little bottle of medicine from his bag, I heard it clink against the brass fastening.

'I shall leave this for her, she should take it when she wakes,' he said. 'I can tell Nurse on my way out. And as for her marriage with your son, I should risk no delay, Lady Clara. She is very ill indeed.'

They went out together, I heard them talking in low voices as they went down the stairs and then I was alone in the silence of my room with only the soft ticking of the clock and the hushed flickering of the flames in the fireplace.

I slid into a hot daze, and then I woke again seconds later, chilled to the bone. If I had any voice other than a rasping breath I should have laughed. I had thought my da a big enough villain but even he would have balked at marrying his child off to a dying girl. He was a rogue but he had given me the string and the clasp of gold because his dying wife had asked it of him. In our world we took the wishes of the dying seriously. In this Quality world where everything looked so fair and spoke so soft, it was those with land who gave the orders, who had the world as they wished. Nothing was sacred except fortune.

Lady Clara did not dislike me, I knew her well enough and I knew that had I been her daughter-in-law she would have liked me as well as she liked her own Maria – probably better. She neither liked nor disliked anyone very strongly, her main concern was with herself. In her eyes it was her duty to preserve her personal wealth, her family's wealth and name, and to increase it wherever possible. Every great family on the land had made itself rich at the expense of hundreds of little ones. I knew that. But I never knew it so clearly as that evening when I watched the ceiling billow like a muslin cloth as my hot eyes played tricks on me, and I knew that I was in the care of a woman who cared more for my signature than for me.

What happened next was like a nightmare in a fever. I woke

one time to find Emily washing my face with some cool scented water. I pulled away from her touch. My skin was so sore and so burning that it stung when she touched me. She said, 'Beg pardon, m'm,' in an undertone and made a few more ineffectual dabs at me.

I was sweating still – burning up with fever. My bedroom door beyond Emily opened, the white paintwork seemed to shimmer as I looked at it, and Lady Clara came in. Something about her face struck me, even in my heat-tranced muddle. She looked determined, her mouth was set, her eyes, as she glanced to the bed, were as hard as stones I think I shrank back a little and looked to Perry.

He was ill from one of his drinking bouts, his face was pale, his hair curly and damp from a wash with cold water in an effort to sober in a hurry. But most of all I noticed his clothes. He usually wore riding dress in the mornings, or one of his silk dressing gowns over white linen and breeches. But this morning he was dressed immaculately in pale grey, with a new waistcoat of lavender and a pale grey jacket. In one hand he carried pale grey gloves.

I think it was the gloves which made something in my mind click like a clockwork mechanism. I heard my old voice, my worldly gypsy-child's voice say: 'Damn me, they're going to marry me as I lie here dying!' and a sense of absolute outrage made me sweat with temper and made my eyes go bright and dizzy.

Perry came to my bedside and looked down at me.

'Not too close, Perry,' his mother said.

'I'm sorry about this, Sarah,' he said. 'I did not mean it to be like this for us. I really wanted us to marry and make each other happy.'

His anxious face was wavering as he spoke. That burst of temper had tired me.

'You're dying,' he said bluntly. 'And if I'm not married to you I'll be ruined, Sarah. I have to have my fortune, please help me. It will mean nothing to you when you're dead, after all.'

I turned my face away and closed my eyes. I was black with rage. I should do nothing for him, nothing for them, nothing.

'She should have some laudanum to soothe her,' I heard the doctor say. They were all here then. Emily's nervous pulling at my shoulder raised me a little and I opened my mouth and let the draught slide down. At once I felt a golden glow inside me. It was far stronger than usual. It was strong enough to make me drunk with it. Clever Doctor Player was earning his fee – the Wideacre Dower House which belonged to me. My sense of anger and my panic-stricken scrabble for life eased away from me. My rasping breath grew quieter and steady. I was getting less air, but I minded less. I would have protested against nothing while the drug worked its magic on me. It all seemed a long way away and wonderfully unimportant. I felt easy; I liked Perry well enough, I did not like to see him look so afraid and so unhappy. He should have his fortune, it was only fair.

I smiled at him, and then I looked around the room, Maria's room which I had disliked on sight, and yet would be the last thing I saw before I closed my eyes for the last time. They had put flowers on my writing desk, white lilies and carnations and the little flap was down ready for the ledger which the rector would bring. There was fresh ink and mended pens and a blotter and sealing wax. They were all ready. There were more flowers on the mantelpiece by the clock. The stuffy room was heavy with their perfume, I looked around at them and I laughed inside. They would do nicely for my funeral too. I guessed Lady Clara would choose white flowers for the wreath. She would never waste hot-house flowers in mid-winter.

There was a tap at the door and I heard Rimmings' voice say: 'The Reverend Fawcett, ma'am,' and I heard a brisk tread into the room. Through half-closed eyelids I saw him go and make his bow to Lady Clara, and shake the doctor's hand. He bowed to Perry then he approached my bed, halting a careful distance from me, and his smile was less assured.

'Miss Lacey, I am sorry to see you so ill,' he said. 'Are you able to hear me? Do you know why I have come?'

Lady Clara came swiftly to my bedside, her silk morning dress rustling. She came to the other side of the bed and fearless for once, took my hand and put her other hand against my cheek as if she loved me dearly. I flinched. She knew I hated being touched, she was not a loving woman. All this was for show. I understood that. I had been a circus child.

'Dear Sarah understands us, when her fever is abated,' she said firmly. 'This marriage has been her dearest wish since she and my son met last spring.' She lowered her voice. 'We none of us could bear to disappoint her,' she said. 'They have been betrothed for months, I could not deny her the right to marry before . . .' she broke off as if her emotions were too much for her. My breath rasped in the silence. I had no voice to deny it, even if I had wished. Besides, the drug had robbed me of determination. I felt sleepy and lazy, idle and happy, as feckless as a child on a hot summer's day. I did not care what they did.

The rector nodded and his dark shiny head caught the grey winter light from the window. 'Is this your considered wish, Miss Lacey?' he asked me directly.

Lady Clara looked at me, her wide blue eyes had a look of desperate pleading. If I found my voice and said 'no' her son would be ruined. I could hardly see her, I could hardly see the rector, or Perry. I was thinking of the high clean woods of Wideacre and how, when he was teaching me my way around the estate, Will used to ride with me. How very loud the birdsong was, in those afternoons, under the trees.

I thought of Will, and smiled.

They took it as consent.

'Then I will begin,' said the rector.

He did Lady Clara's work for her. He began at the beginning and missed out nothing – as far as I knew, for it was the first wedding service I had ever heard all the way through in all my life. When we were chavvies she and I used to hang around the back of churches at wedding-time for sometimes kindly people would give us a penny, pitying our bare legs and thin clothes. More often they would give us a ha'pence to scout off and leave the church looking tidy. We never cared for their motive, we only wanted the coppers. I knew some parts of the service, I knew there were questions to be answered, and I puzzled my tired hot mind with whether I should say 'no' and stop this farce while I could. But I did not really care enough for anything, the drug came between me and the land.

When he came to the section where I should have said 'I do' he slipped through it, and my confused blinkings were consent enough. Lady Clara was at my side, reckless of infection, and when she said firmly, 'She nodded,' that was consent enough.

I was fair game. I seemed to be back in time on Wideacre and it was night. I was riding Sea wearily down the hill from the London road. At the ford at the foot of the hill he splashed in and then paused, bent his head and drank. I could smell the coldness of the water and the scent of the flowers on the air. In the banks along the river the primroses gleamed palely in the darkness. In the secret darkness of the wood an owl hooted twice.

'I now pronounce thee man and wife,' a voice said from somewhere. Sea lifted his head and water dripped from his chin, loud drops in the night-time stillness, then he waded through the swift water and heaved up the far bank and on to the road again.

Lady Clara was pushing something into my hands, a pen. I scrawled my name as she had taught me to do on the paper she held before me. In the darkness on the land Sea headed purposefully between two open wrought-iron gates and a shadow of a man came out from under the trees and looked up at me. It was a man who was out looking for poachers because he hated gin traps. It was Will Tyacke.

'She is smiling,' said the rector's voice from the foot of the bed.

'It was her dearest wish,' Lady Clara said quickly. 'Where do you wish me to sign? Here? And the doctor for the other witness? Here?'

They were going. Silently in the dream Will reached up for me on the horse and silently I slid from Sea's back into his arms.

'We will leave her to rest now,' Lady Clara said. 'Emily, you sit with her in case she wakes and needs something.'

'She will be mentioned in our prayers,' the rector said. 'It would be a tragedy . . .'

'Yes, yes,' Lady Clara said. The door closed behind them. In the world of the fever-dream Will Tyacke bent his head and I lifted up my face for his kiss. His arms came around me and gathered me to him, my hands went to his shoulders, tightened behind his neck to hold him close. He said. 'I love you.'

'Don't cry, Miss Sarah!' Emily said. She was patting my cheeks with a wad of damp muslin. There were hot tears running down my flushed cheeks, but my throat was too tight and I was too short of breath to weep. 'Don't cry,' she said helplessly. 'There's no need to cry. Beg pardon,' she added.

They were sure I would die, and they wrote to Mr Fortescue, telling him of my illness and of the wedding in the same letter. He was away in Ireland on business when the letter came, and it awaited his return to Bristol. With him away there was no one to tell them on Wideacre that they had a new master. That the London lord whom Will had warned them of had won their land indeed, and he and his hard-faced mama would run the land as they pleased. They carried on, using their own money to mend the ploughs, spending the common fund on seeds for the winter sowing, ploughing the land for the spring sowing, hedging, ditching, digging drains. They did not know they would have done better to save their money. No one in London troubled to tell them of the changes they would face, as soon as Perry and his mama arrived in the country in springtime.

No one expected me to arrive. They expected me to die.

It grieved Perry. He had moved his things to the room next door, to reinforce his claim to the marriage if anyone should dispute it in the future, after my death. He kept the adjoining door unlocked and he often came through to sit with me. Often he would stumble in to see me after a night of gambling and he would sit at my bedside and mumble through the hands he had played and the points he had lost. When I was feverish I thought he was Da – forever bewailing his ill luck, forever blaming others. Eternally gulled by those he had set out to cheat. Perry was not a cheat but he was a ripe fat pigeon. I could imagine how the card-sharpers and the gull gropers would beam when he rolled into a new gambling hell and smiled around with those innocent blue eyes.

When I was cool and the fever had given me a moment's respite I would ask him how it was with him, whether his creditors had given him time now that it was known he was married. He dropped his voice so low that it would not disturb the rough night nurse who sat, snoring, by the fire, and he told me that everyone had offered him extra credit, that he had gone through the figures with his lawyers and that he thought he could very well manage to live the life he liked on the profits from the joint Havering–Wideacre estates.

'It has to be ploughed back,' I said faintly. I could feel the beat of the fever starting deep inside my body again. Already the covers were feeling hot and heavy on the bed, soon I should start to shake and to shiver. Laudanum would stave off the pain, but nothing would hold back the waves of heat which drained my mind of thoughts and dried my mouth.

'I can't plough it back this year,' Perry started. 'Maybe next, if there is enough . . .' But then he saw how my face had changed and he broke off. 'Are you ill again, Sarah?' he asked. 'Shall I wake the nurse?'

I nodded. I was drowning in a wave of heat and pain, slowly, in the crimson darkness I could hear the rasp rasp of my breath coming slowly into me, and then I felt my throat thicken yet tighter and I knew I would not be able to get my breath for much longer.

Dimly I heard Perry shouting at the nurse and shaking her awake. She stamped across to the bed and her broad arm came under my shoulders and my head fell back against her sweaty gown. She tipped the laudanum down my throat in one smooth practised gesture and I retched and heaved for breath.

'Her throat's closing up,' she said to Perry in her hard voice. 'It's the end. Best get her la'ship if she wants to bid her g'bye.'

Her voice seemed to come from a long way away. I did not believe it possible that this could be the end for me. I felt as if I had hardly lived at all. I had been raised in such a rough poor way, and I had been less than a year in luxury with the Quality.

To die now, and of a disease which I could have taken at any time in a damp-clothed hungry childhood made no sense at all. The drug began taking hold and I felt the familiar sense of floating on a golden sea. If she was right and I died now I should have died without knowing a proper childhood, without knowing a proper mama, without knowing what it is to be loved honestly and truly by a good man. And worse of all, I would die without knowing what it was to feel passion. Any slut on a street corner might have her man; but I had been cold as ice all my life. I had only ever kissed the man I loved in my dreams. In real life I had whipped him around the face and told him I hated him.

I gave a little moan – unheard among the hoarse scraping noise as I breathed. Lady Clara came in and looked down at my face.

'Is there anything you want?' she asked.

I could not reply but I knew truly that there was nothing she could buy for me, or sell to me, or barter with me, which I could want. The only thing I wanted could not be bought. It was not the ownership of Wideacre, but the smell of the place, the taste of the water, the sight of that high broad skyline.

She looked at me as if she would have said far more. 'I hope I have not treated you badly,' she said. 'I meant well by you, Sarah. I meant Perry to marry you and to live with you. I thought you might have suited. I did need Wideacre, and I am glad to have it, but I wanted it to be your free choice.'

She looked at me as if she thought I could answer. I could barely hear her. Her face was wavering like water-weed under the Fenny. I felt as if I could taste the cool wetness of the Fenny on my tongue, as if it were flowing over my hands, over my face.

She stepped back from the bed and Perry was there, his eyes red from weeping, his curls awry. He said nothing. He just pressed his head on my coverlet until his mother's hand on his shoulder took him away.

Still I said nothing. I thought I could see the gates of Wideacre Hall as I had seen them on that first night, open, unguarded. Beyond them was the drive to the Hall edged with the tall beech trees and the rustling oaks. In the woods was Will, watching for the men who would set gin traps which injure and maim. It was dark through the gates. It was quiet. I was weary and hot to the very marrow of my bones. I wanted to be in that gentle darkness.

In my dream I waited beside the gates.

Then I stepped through into the blackness.

35

The blackness lasted for a long time. Then from far away there was the sound of a robin singing, so I knew it was winter. There was a smell of flowers, not the familiar clogged smell of sweat. There was no sound of the rasping breathing, I could breathe. I could feel the blessed air going in and out of my body without a struggle. I raised my chin, just slightly. The pillow was cool under my neck, the sheets were smooth. There was no pain, the rigid labouring muscles were at peace, my throat had eased. I was through the worst of it.

I knew it before anyone else. I had woken in the grey light of morning and I could see the nurse dozing before the embers of the fire. It was not until Emily came in to make up the fire and wake the nurse and send her away for the day that anyone looked at me. Emily's face was there when I opened my eyes after dozing and I saw her eyes widen.

'I'll be damned,' she said. Then she raced to the idle old woman at the fireside and pulled at her arm.

'Wake up! Wake up! You ole butter-tub!' she said. 'Wake and look at Miss Sairey! She's through ain't she! She's stopped sweatin' ain't she? She ain't hot! She's broke the fever and she's well, ain't she?'

The nurse lurched up from her chair and came to stare at me. I looked back. Her ugly strawberry face never wavered.

'Can you hear me, dearie?' she asked.

'Yes,' I said. My voice was thin, but it was clear at last.

She nodded. 'She's through,' she said to Emily. 'You'd best get her summat sustaining from the kitchen.' She nodded magisterially. 'I could do with some vittles too,' she said.

Emily scooted towards the door and I heard her feet scamper down the hall. The fat old woman looked at me calculatingly.

'D'you remember that they did marry you?' she asked bluntly. I nodded.

''E slept with your door open to 'is room, an' all,' she said. 'It's right and tight. Was it what you wanted?'

I nodded. She could be damned for her curiosity. And I did not want to think of Perry, or Lady Clara, of the doctor who had been promised the Dower House on my land, nor of the rector who had married me while I could not speak. All I wanted to do was to hear the robin singing and look at the clouds moving across the white winter sky, and to feel the joy of my hand which was no longer clenched and sticky with sweat and a breath which came smoothly to me, like gentle waves on a light sea. I had come through typhus. I was well.

I was weary enough though. In the weeks that followed it was as if I were a chavvy again, learning to walk. It was days before I could do more than sit up in my bed without aching with tiredness. Then one day I made it to the chair by the fireside on my own. A little later on and I bid Emily help me into a loose morning dress and I made myself walk out into the corridor and to the head of the stairs before I called her and said I was too faint and would have to go back to my room. But the next day I got downstairs, and the day after that I stayed downstairs and took tea.

It was not little Miss Sarah who had come through the fever. It was not that faint shadow of a lady of Quality who had fought through. It was not little Miss Sarah who ordered Emily through gritted teeth to damn well give her an arm and help her walk, even while her legs turned to jelly beneath her.

It was the old strength of Meridon, the fighting, swearing, tough little Rom chavvy. A lady of Quality would have died. You had to be as strong as whipcord to survive a fever like that, and nursing like that. A lady of Quality would have been an invalid for life if she had survived. But I would not rest, I would not have a day bed made for me in the parlour. Every day I went a little further, every day I stayed up for a little longer. And one day, only a week after I had first walked across my room, I had them bring Sea round from the stables, up to the very front door, and I walked down the steps without an arm to support me and laid my white face against his grey nose and smelled the good honest smell of him.

It was that smell, and the sight of him all restive in a London street which took me back in to the parlour, to rest again, and to ready myself for a talk with Peregrine.

I had hardly seen him, or Lady Clara, since my recovery. Lady Clara was out of the house at all hours. At first I could not understand why, and then Emily let slip some gossip from the servants' hall. Lady Clara was running all around town trying to keep the lid on scandal about her daughter Maria. Only months into marriage Maria was humping her piano tutor, and if Lady Clara did not buy the man off and silence Maria's complaints, and scotch the rumour fast, it would reach the ears of the hapless husband; and Basil was already weary of Maria's dress bills, and her temper, and her sulks.

I knew Lady Clara well enough to know that she was not doing this for love for her daughter, nor for her respect for the holy estate. She was in mortal terror that Basil would throw Maria out, and she would be back home with the piano tutor in tow, her reputation ruined: a costly disgrace to her family.

Lady Clara said as much to me when we passed on the stairs that afternoon.

'I am glad to see you up, dear,' she said. 'And glad to see you are well enough to dine downstairs. Perry is home from Newmarket tomorrow, is he not?'

'Yes,' I said. I hesitated, my hand on the cold metal banister. 'You look tired, Lady Clara.'

She made a little face. 'I am,' she said. 'But I have to go out at once to Maria. Basil is coming home to dine this evening and I dare not let the two of them be alone together. Maria has such a sharp tongue she'll goad him, I know it. There are enough people who would tell him what has been going on if he were willing to hear it. I shall have to be a peace-maker.'

I looked at her coolly. 'You specialize in profitable marriage-making,' I said. 'But making the marriage stick is more difficult, is it not?'

She met my eyes with a gaze as hard as my own. 'Not when it suits both parties,' she said bluntly. 'Maria is a fool and cannot see beyond her own passions. You are not. You have access to Perry's fortune and to your own. You are welcome to live in the country, in the town, or on the moon for all I care. You wanted to be launched into society and I did that for you. I will sponsor you at Court, your child will be the biggest landowner in Sussex. You consented to your marriage Sarah, and it will serve you well. I'll take no blame.'

I nodded. 'I'll learn to live with it,' I said and my voice was hard. 'But I did not consent.'

She shrugged. She was too wise and too clever to be drawn. 'It will serve you well,' she said again. 'And anyway, now you have no choice.'

I nodded, but I still had a gleam of hope that I might get free. It was one thing to consent to marriage to Perry when I pitied him, and pitied myself and respected – almost loved – Lady Clara. It was another damned thing altogether when I had seen Perry steal from my purse when I was ill, and seen Lady Clara rob me of my lands when she thought I was dying. If I could break free I would. And if I could break free there would be Wideacre, waiting for me. And Will might still be there.

I sent a footman flying with a note to James Fortescue's lawyer and took him privately into the dining room and told him bluntly what had happened. His jaw dropped and he strode around the room like a restive cat before placing himself before the hearth.

'I did not know!' he said. 'All I heard was a special licence because you were unwell. And I knew you had been living in this house as part of the family for months.'

I nodded. 'I'm not blaming you,' I said. I had little energy for this conversation and I wanted to hear if I was indeed, trapped tight. 'I'm not blaming you,' I said. 'It is no one's fault. But tell me if the marriage is valid. If I have any choice now?'

He turned to the fire and studied the logs. 'Has he slept in your bed?' he asked delicately.

I nodded. 'Yes,' I said. 'They took care of that. But we never did it.'

His whole body jumped as if I had stuck him with a pin at my indelicacy. But I was little Miss Sarah no more.

'I see,' he said slowly, to cover his nervousness. 'So a medical examination, if you could bear to allow such a thing would establish that you are indeed . . .' he hesitated.

'An examination by a doctor?' I asked.

He nodded. 'To prove non-consummation of the marriage, with a view to obtaining an annulment,' he said watching the hearthrug beneath his boots and blushing like a schoolboy.

I thought of the horses I had ridden and the tumbles I had taken. I thought of riding bareback and climbing trees. I made a grimace at his turned-away face.

'I've not had a man, but I doubt I could prove it,' I said. 'Where I come from there's few girls who stain their sheets on their wedding night. We all live too hard.'

He nodded as if he understood. I knew damn well he did not.

'Then we would be faced with the problem of obtaining a divorce,' he said carefully. 'And a divorce would not return your lands to you, even if it were possible.'

I leaned back against the padding of the chair. I was very weary indeed. 'Let me get this straight,' I said. 'I cannot get the marriage annulled.'

He nodded.

'I might be able to get divorced.'

'Only for flagrant abuse and cruelty,' he interjected softly.

I shot an inquiring look at him.

'Imprisonment, torture, beatings, that sort of thing,' he said quietly.

I nodded. Where I came from, if you were tired of your husband or he was tired of you, you could stand up in a public place and announce you were man and wife no more. That was the end of it and you went your ways. But the Quality had to think about land and heirs.

'I've had none of that,' I said. 'But even if I had, and I could make a divorce stick, are you telling me that I'd not get my land back?'

The lawyer turned from the fire and faced me, and his expression was kindly but distant.

'It is his land now,' he said. 'He is your husband and master. Everything you owned at marriage became his, at marriage. It is his to do with as he pleases. This is the law of the land, Lady Havering.' He paused. 'And you have been offered a most generous allowance and settlement,' he said. 'I have seen the contract and it is very generous indeed. But both religion, law and our traditions insist that it is better if the husband owns everything.'

'Everything?' I asked. I was thinking of the beech coppice on the way up to the Downs where the sun filters through the leaves and the shadows shift on the nutty brown leaf-mould at the foot of the treetrunks.

'Everything,' he said.

I nodded. 'I'm good and wed then,' I said. 'And I'd best make the most of it.'

He picked up his hat and his gloves. 'I am sorry for this confusion during your illness,' he said formally. 'But once you put your name to the marriage register the deed was done.'

I managed a smile, my hard-eyed beggar-girl smile. 'I understand,' I said. 'And I should have been on my guard. I'd lived among thieves all my life, Mr Penkiss. I should have known I was among them still.'

He dipped his head at that. He did not quite like the widow of a peer of the realm being lumped among a parcel of thieves, but he was paid by the estate which had been mine and he would not correct me to my face.

He went and I rang the bell for Emily. I wanted her strong young arm around me to help me upstairs to rest on my bed. I was as weak as a half-drowned kitten.

I did not see Perry during the long weeks of my convalescence because he was out of town, at Newmarket for the races. He came home the day after my conversation with the lawyer, on a bright crisp January day with the smell of snow in the air that not all the smog of the London streets could steal.

I had tried a drive out in Lady Clara's oversprung landau and was coming in, weary with overtaxing myself in my gritty struggle back to health. Perry was bright as a new guinea, golden-haired, blue-eyed, smiling like sunshine.

He was also drunk as a wheelbarrow. He fell out of the travelling chaise and giggled like a baby in sunshine. The footmen coming gracefully down the steps to fetch in his baggage suddenly put on a turn of speed and heaved him up out of the gutter. Perry's legs went from under him and tried to race off in opposite directions while he laughed aloud.

'Why Sarah!' he said catching sight of me. 'You up and about already! You look wonderful!'

I scowled at him. I knew I was as white as ice and my hair was a copper mop of curls again which looked ridiculous under a bonnet and half-bald under a cap.

'I've had such luck!' he said joyously. 'I've won and won, I am weighed down with guineas Sarah! I'll take you out to the theatre tonight to celebrate!'

'Bring him in,' I said abruptly to the footmen, and went ahead of them into the parlour.

Perry walked steadier when he was in the house. He dropped into a chair and beamed at me.

'I really have done well, you know,' he offered.

I managed a thin smile. 'I'm glad,' I said.

There was a tap on the door and the parlourmaid came in with tea. I took a seat by the fireside and my cup when she handed it to me. Perry drank his eagerly and refilled it several times. 'It's good to be home,' he said.

'I've seen my lawyer,' I said abruptly. 'The marriage is un-breakable and the contracts are going through. They'll send the deeds of Wideacre to you at once.'

Perry nodded, his face sobering. 'I was washed up, Sarah,' he said. 'I was quite under the hatches. It would have been the debtors prison for me if we had not married.'

I nodded, but my face was stony.

He shrugged. 'Mama said . . .' he started, then he broke off. 'I'm damned sorry if you are angry with me, Sarah,' he said. 'But I could think of nothing else. The doctor told us you would die, I was not even thinking of getting Wideacre. I was just thinking of getting my own money, and I thought you would not mind. It's not as if you wanted to marry anyone else, after all. And we are very well suited.'

I looked at him, I was too weary for anger. I looked at him and I saw him as he was. A weakling and a drunkard. A man too fearful to stand up to his own mother and too foolish to stay out of gambling and off the bottle. A man no woman could fall in love with, a man no woman could respect. And I thought about myself – a woman spoiled from the earliest childhood so she could not stand a man's touch, nor accept a man's love. A woman who had dreamed all her life of living in a certain way, of seeking a certain place. And when I had found it, it had meant very little.

I was no longer little Miss Sarah with her hopes of a brilliant London season and her eagerness to learn how society people lived, her belief in the best. I was Meridon who had been cheated until my heart was hard all my childhood, and had been robbed in adulthood by the people I had thought of as a refuge.

'We're well suited,' I said wearily. 'But I don't have a lot of hopes for us.'

Perry looked dashed. 'You wanted to go home . . .' he offered 'Home to the country. When you're well enough for the journey, we could go to Havering,' he glanced at me. 'Or Wideacre if you'd prefer.'

I nodded. 'I would like that,' I said. 'I would like to go to Wideacre as soon as possible. I should be well enough to travel in a few days. Let's go then.'

He gave me a little smile, as appealing as a child.

'You're not really angry are you Sarah?' he asked. 'I didn't mean to make you angry, or disappoint you. It was Mama who was sure. Everyone was certain that you would die, I didn't think you'd mind doing it. It would have made no difference to you, after all.'

I got to my feet, steadying myself with a hand on the mantelpiece.

'No,' I said. 'I don't really mind. There was no one else I wanted to marry. It is not what I planned, that's all.'

Perry stumbled as he went to hold the door open for me. 'You are Lady Havering now,' he said encouragingly. 'You must like that.'

I looked down the long years to my childhood to where the dirty-faced little girl lay in her bunk and dreamed of having a proper name, and a proper home, and belonging in a gracious and beautiful landscape. 'I should do,' I said thoughtfully. 'I've wanted it all my life.'

That reassured him and he took my hand and kissed it gently. I held still. Perry had inherited his mother's diffidence, he would never grab me, or overwhelm me with kisses, or brush against me for the pleasure of my touch. I was glad of that, I still liked a distance between me and any other person. He let me go and I went past him and up the shallow stone stairs to my bedroom to lie on the bed and look at the ceiling and keep myself from thinking.

For the next week I worked at becoming stronger. Lady Clara complained that I never went into society at all. 'Hardly worth your while to make me take the title of Dowager if you're going to be a hermit,' she said to me at dinner one day.

I gave her half a smile. 'I am too grand to mix with the common people,' I said.

That made her laugh and she did not tease me further. She was still too busy trying to keep Maria with her husband to waste much time on me. A notice of our private marriage had appeared in the paper but all of Lady Clara's friends knew that I had been seriously ill. They would hold parties for me later on. I told everyone I met in the park that I was not well enough to do more than ride a little and walk, at present.

Sea was very good. He had missed our daily rides and the grooms in the stables did not like to take him out because he was frisky and naughty. If a high-sided coach went past him he shied, if someone shouted out in the street he would be half-way across the road before they could steady him down, and if they so much as touched him with a whip he would be up on his hindlegs in a soaring rear and they could not hold him.

But with me he was as gentle as if he were a retired hack. The first outing I let the groom lift me into the saddle and I gathered up the reins and waited to see what would come. I would have felt a good deal safer astride, but we were in the stable courtyard and I was in my green riding habit, pale as skimmed milk in the rich colour.

I had a silly little cap perched on my head instead of my usual bonnet – but with only short curls no pins would hold. Lady Clara had been scandalized when I had threatened to ride bareheaded.

Sea snuffed the air, as if wondering whether to race for the park at once, but then he tensed his muscles as he felt my lightness.

'Sea,' I said, and at my voice his ears went forward and I felt him shift a little beneath me. I knew he remembered me, remembered the red-faced man who had been his owner before I had come to him. Remembered the little stable in Salisbury behind the inn, and how I had sat gently on him, half the weight of his usual rider, and spoken to him in a quiet voice. I thought he would remember the journey home, tied to the back of Robert Gower's whisky cart, with me dripping blood and drooping with tiredness, my head on Robert's shoulder. I thought he would remember the little stable at Warminster, and how I would go down to him in the morning, clattering down the little wooden staircase to greet him before going in to breakfast and bringing him back a crust of a warm roll. And I was sure he would remember that night when there had been no one on the land but him and me. No one in the whole world but the two of us going quietly through the sleeping Downland villages. Me, as lost as a child without its mother, and him quietly and certainly trotting along lanes where he had never been before, drawn like a compass point to our home.

I reached down and patted his neck. He straightened and obeyed the touch of my heels against his side. He moved with his smooth flowing stride out of the stable yard and into the mews lane, then down the busy roads towards the park. The groom fell into step behind us, watching me nervously, certain that I was not well enough to ride, that Sea would be sure to throw me at the first sight of a water cart, or a shrieking milk maid.

He did not. He went as steady as a hackney-horse with blinkers. Past open doors and shouting servants, past wagons, past delivery carts and street sellers. Past all the noise and bustle of a big city to the gates of the park. And even then, with the smooth green turf before him and the soft furze beneath his feet he did nothing more than arch his neck and put his ears forward as we trotted, and then slid into a smooth steady canter.

He would have gone faster, and I was finished with the conventions of polite society for ever: I would have let him. But I could tell by the light buzzing in my ears, and the strange swimmy feeling, that I was pushing my new strength too far, and I should go home.

We turned. Sea went willingly enough though I knew he longed for one of our wild gallops. He went back through the streets as gentle as he had come, and pulled up outside the front door as sweet as a carthorse on a familiar delivery round.

'He's a marvel with you,' the groom said. 'I wish he'd be as good with us. He was off with me last week and I thought I'd never get him turned around for home. I couldn't pull him up, the best I could do was bring him around in a circle. All the old ladies were staring at me an' all! I was ashamed!'

'I'm sorry, Gerry,' I said. I had one hand on the balustrade to support me and I patted Sea's cool flank with the other. 'He's never liked men very much, he was ill-treated before I got him. It spoiled his temper for a man rider.'

The groom pulled his cap and slid from his own horse. 'I'll lead them both,' he said. 'That way I won't get pulled off if he plays up as soon as you're gone.'

'All right,' I said. 'I'll come around to the stables tomorrow, same time.'

'Yes, miss,' he said politely. Then he corrected himself. 'I mean, yes, Lady Havering.'

I hesitated on hearing my title, 'Lady Sarah Havering'; then I shrugged my shoulders. It was a long way from the dirty little wagon and the two hungry children. She would laugh if she knew.

I grew stronger after that ride. I rode every day, I walked every day. Sometimes Perry was awake and sober and he came with me. Otherwise, in the middle of a dazzling London season I lived alone, in quietness and isolation. Sometimes they stopped in their carriages in the park to bid me good day and ask me if I would be coming to one party or another. I always explained I did not yet have my strength back, and they let me be excused. Sometimes I would be in the parlour when Lady Clara's guests came in and I would sit quietly in the window for some time before saying that I needed to go to my room for I was still a little tired. They let me go. They all let me go.

I did not need to stay. I was accepted, I was an heiress in my own right, I had a title, I was married to the largest landowner in Sussex and, apart from Perry's growing scandalous drunkenness, there was not a breath of rumour about me. I was odd and unsociable, certainly. But they could not complain of that. And I think the hard eyes of Meridon looked out from under the short-cropped hair, and they knew that I was strange and alien in their world. And they let me go.

36

Two days later I received a letter:

Dear Sarah,

I cannot tell you how sorry I am that I should have been away from home when you were ill and that in my absence your marriage took place. I understand from Penkiss and Penkiss that you have consulted them as to the legality of such a marriage and they have told you, and confirmed to me, that the marriage is legal. I feel deeply unhappy that I was not available to help you at that time. It is as if I had lost your mother all over again to serve you so badly.

I can offer you little consolation except to say that I do indeed believe that your husband may steady now that he is married, and that if he does not, he is well used to having his estate run by a woman. You may find yourself in the position of being responsible for the running of both Havering and Wideacre estates and you will find that work rewarding and enjoyable.

It would have been my wish that you had made a marriage of choice, for love. But I believe that you yourself had little wish for a 'love marriage'. If that were the case then no arranged marriage could have been more suitable, if you and Lord Peregrine can agree. I know you liked him when you first met him, it will be my most earnest prayer, Sarah, that you continue to enjoy his company and that he treats you well. If there is anything I can do to assist you in any way, I beg you will ask me. If you two should not agree, I hope you know that whatever the world may say, you may always make your home with me, and I would provide for you.

I hope you forgive me for not being able to protect you from this marriage. I would not have left the country if I had known how ill you were. I would have come to London to see if I could serve you. Regrets do nothing, but I hope you believe that mine are sincere; and when I think of your mother and the trust she placed in me, my regrets are bitter.

Yours sincerely,

James Fortescue

PS. I have just this day heard from Will Tyacke. He tells me that he gave you notice that he would not serve under Lord Peregrine and he writes to offer his formal resignation which will take place at once. This worry I can help with. I shall advertise at once for a new manager to take his place. He will be sadly missed by his friends on Wideacre but perhaps a new manager to start with the new squire is advisable. Will has only just seen the notice of your marriage, apparently he did not know you were unwell. He has taken a post in the north of England and is leaving at once.

I read the letter through several times, sitting at the mahogany table in the parlour, the noises from the street very loud in the room. I was sorry James was so grieved that he had not protected me against the Haverings' marriage plans. I could shrug that off. No one could have predicted that I would fall ill. No one could have foreseen that I would get well again. If I had died, as everyone had expected me to do, then there would have been little harm done. The Wideacre corporation, the great brave experiment of Wideacre would have been ended under a new squire, either way. It was bitter indeed that I should be persuaded of the rightness of running an estate as if the very poorest villager's life was of value at the very moment when I had put a new man in the squire's chair. But James was right, I would be the mistress in my house, the land would be run as I wished, and I would run Wideacre as Will had done. I made a sad little face. It would be a different place without him.

I opened the letter again and re-read the postscript. I nodded. He had said he would go when we had parted in anger, that day in the park. He had tried to warn me and I had refused to listen.

He had tried to keep Wideacre safe as one of the few places, one of the very few, where the wealth of the land could go to those who earned it. Where people could work and earn the full benefits of their work – not what was left after the squire had taken his cut, and the merchant, and the parson. I had been on the side of the squires and the merchants and the parsons then. I was not now. Since then I had been as close to death as most people ever get, and I had felt someone take my sweating hand and sign away my land for me. I would never again believe that some people deserved higher wages or finer lives than others. We all had needs. We all sought their satisfaction. Some people were clever rogues, they managed to get a little more – that was all the difference there ever was.

I would never be able to tell him that. He had gone, as he had sworn he would go, to a new corporation, a new attempt at creating some real justice in the way England was run. Not words on paper, not ideas in people's minds, not pleasant civilized chat across a dinner table. Real changes for real people. And I knew that after that experiment failed – as fail it surely would, for it was too little in a world too big and too implacable – after that he would go to another, and to another and another. And though Will might never win he would never stop, travelling from one place to another, doing whatever he could in small brave ways to set a wall against the greed and corruption of the world we of the Quality were building.

I folded the letter carefully and then I bent down and poked it into the fire. It would be of no help to me, nor to any of the Haverings if they knew that I would have gone against their wishes if I could. I had spoken once against Lady Clara, I had accepted Perry's awkward apology. They had won as the rich always win. They write the rules. They make the world. They win the battles.

I was sorry it had taken me this long to learn it. I had come from a poverty so grinding that I had seen the Quality as a race apart, and knew nothing more than a longing to be part of them. They made it look so easy! They made fine clothes and good food and polite chatter look like a God-given right. You never saw their struggle to keep their money earning more and more money. You never saw the ill-paid servants and clerks who serviced their needs, who earned the money for them. All you ever saw was the smooth surface of the finished work – the Quality world. I leaned against the mantelpiece and looked down at the fire. It was as if I were to say that marble like this of the mantelpiece came straight from the ground smooth and carved, and never needed working. They managed to pretend that their wealth came to them naturally – as if they deserved it. They hid altogether the poverty and the hardship and the sheer miserable drudgery which earned the money which they spent smiling.

I had been as bad as any of them – worse; for I had known what life was like down at the very bottom, and I had thought of nothing but that *I* should be free from that hardship, that *I* should win my way up to the top. And sour it was to me, to learn when I made it there, when I was little Miss Sarah Lacey, that I felt as mean and as dirty as when I had been a thieving chavvy in the streets.

It is a dirty world they've made – the people who have the power and the talents and who show no pity. I had had enough of it. I would be little Miss Sarah Lacey no more.

There was a knock on the parlour door. 'Lady Sarah, there is a parcel for you,' the parlourmaid said.

I turned with a scowl which made her step swiftly back. I had forgotten I was little Miss Sarah no more. Now I was Lady Sarah and damned nonsense it was to talk of being on the side of the poor while I sat in the parlour of the great Havering town house and was waited on by a dozen ill-paid people.

I took the parcel with a word of thanks and opened it.

It was from my lawyer, Mr Penkiss. It was the contracts for the marriage and the deeds of Wideacre for Perry. Wideacre was out of the hands of the Laceys. Wideacre was mine no more.

I spread the old paper out on the parlour table and looked at it. It meant nothing to me, the writing was all funny, and the language was not even English. But I liked the heavy seals on the bottom, dark red and cracked, and the thick glossy pink ribbon under them. I liked the curly brown lettering and the old thick manuscript. And now and then, in the text I could see the word 'Wideacre' and knew it was telling of my land.

The Laceys had earned it in a grant from the king. The Norman king who came over some time and beat the people in a war and won the country. That was how it was told in the gentry parlours. In the taproom at Acre they said that the Laceys had stolen it, robbed farmers like the Tyackes who had been there for years. In the wagons of the Rom they said that once they had held all the land, that they had been the old people who had lived alongside fairies and pixies and old magic until the coming of men with swords and ploughs. I smiled ruefully. All robbers: generation after generation of robbers. And the worst theft of all was to take someone's history from them. So the children who went to school from the Havering estate believed the Haverings had always been there. And they were taught that there was no choice but to doff their caps to the power of the rich. And no alternative but to work for them – and try to become rich yourself.

I rolled up the parchment carefully and put it back in its package along with the marriage contract. If Peregrine were not too drunk tonight he might be well enough to take it to the lawyers tomorrow.

I glanced towards the window. It was getting dark with that cold, damp, end-of-January darkness which made me glad of the warm fire and the quiet room. I rang the bell and ordered more logs for the fire, and I heard the front door bang as Perry came home.

He was unsteady on his feet, but I had seen him a lot worse. He beamed at me with his good-natured drunkard's smile.

'It's good to see you up,' he said. 'I'm glad you're well again. I missed you when you were ill.'

I smiled back. 'You'd have made a tragic widower,' I said.

Perry nodded, unabashed. 'I'd have missed you all the same,' he said. 'But oh! it's good to have as much money as I like!'

'Are you winning or losing these days?' I asked dryly.

'Still winning!' Perry said delightedly. 'I don't know what

devil is in the cards. I haven't lost a game since I came back from Newmarket. No one will play with me any more except Captain Thomas and Bob Redfern! I must have had a thousand guineas off them both!'

'Oh yes,' I said. 'Shall you mind leaving all this excitement to come home? I want to go back to Wideacre, and I'm well enough to travel now.'

Perry rang the bell and ordered punch made strong when the butler came.

'When you like,' he said. 'But the roads will be bad. Why not wait until it is warmer, and the roads less dirty? We'll get stuck for sure.'

The silver bowl came in and Perry poured himself a cup and handed me one. I sipped it and made a face.

'Ugh Perry! It's far too strong! It's solid brandy!'

Perry beamed. 'Keeps the cold out,' he said.

'Will you stop your drinking, once we are at Wideacre?' I asked a little wistfully. 'Will you really stop your drinking, and the gambling? Is it truly just being in London which makes you do it?'

Perry stretched out his legs to the fire. 'I'll tell you the truth,' he said. 'I started gambling because I was bored, and I started drinking because I was lonely and afraid. You know how it was for me before.' He paused. 'I am sure I could give it up like that,' he snapped his fingers. 'Any time I wanted to. I could just walk away from it and never touch it again.'

I looked at him curiously. 'I've seen men who said that who would kill someone for a drink,' I said. 'I've seen men who would shake and vomit if they couldn't get a drink when they needed it. I even heard of one man who went mad without it, and killed his little chavvy, and didn't even know he'd done it!'

'Don't talk like that!' Perry said with instant disdain. 'Don't talk about those horrid people you used to be with, Sarah. You're not among them any more. It's different for us. I'm not like that. I can take or leave it. And in London, in the Season, everyone drinks. Everyone gambles. You'd be gaming yourself if you weren't ill and staying at home, Sarah, you know you would.'

I nodded. I was not sure. 'Maybe,' I said. 'But remember you promised to never use Wideacre as security against a loan.'

Perry smiled, too sweet to be scolded. 'Of course,' he said. 'I'd never use your land, or my own. Mama explained it all to me, how it has to be handed on intact if we have a child. All I'm doing now is spending some of the interest and the extra rents. No one was able to touch it for years, it's just been mounting up in the bank. And anyway . . .' he said conclusively, 'I'm winning! I'm winning faster than I can spend it. D'you know what they call me down at Redfern's club? "Lucky Havering"! That's what they call me! Rather fine, isn't it?'

'Mmm,' I said dubiously. But then I decided to let be. I had seen Perry in London, and down at Havering. And I knew he did not gamble when he was away from the city, and from the boredom of the London season. I knew he did not drink so hard when he was in the country. And I thought it very likely that he might not drink at all when we were on our own in the country.

I was not such a fool as to believe that he did not need drink. But we were wed and inseparable. There was little gain for me to scold him. The only thing I could do was get him into the country as quick as I could where I could have the keys to the wine cellar and Perry would be away from the clubs and his drinking, gambling, dissolute friends.

'Are you out tonight?' I asked.

Perry made a face. 'You are too,' he said glumly. 'Don't blame me, Sarah, it's Mama. She says we've both got to go to Maria's, she's having a music party and Basil is to be there and we have to go too to look happy.'

'Me too?' I asked surprised. Since my illness I had done very well at escaping all the Quality parties. Lady Clara was content to let me rest and convalesce at home, she had done her duty and introduced me to her world as she had promised. She was working night and day to keep Maria and Basil shackled, and she did not care whether I took and returned calls or not.

'Your mama wants me to go?' I asked.

Perry ran a grimy hand through his hair and chuckled. 'Scandal,' he said briefly. 'They're saying Mama saddled Basil with a light-skirt, and that we've robbed you and got you locked up at home. Mama's had enough of it. You're to come out to Maria's party. Maria has to look happy and behave well, and you have to look happy and behave well.'

'And you?' I asked, amused.

'I shall be radiant,' Perry said glumly.

I laughed.

'Actually, I shall stay for the first half-hour and then I shall cut along to Redfern's club, I promised him a game of piquet. He wants to win his losses back,' Perry said.

'I don't want to stay long myself,' I warned.

Perry beamed at me. 'Well bless you!' he said. 'We'll say you need to be taken home, and I can escort you. That way we can both leave early.'

'Done!' I said, then I pointed to the punch bowl. 'But leave go that, Perry, it's too strong, and your mama won't want you there half-cut.'

Perry got to his feet. 'To please you,' he said and held the door for me.

I gathered up the parcel of our marriage contract and the deeds for Wideacre. 'The papers from my lawyers,' I said, as Perry held the door for me and we went up the stairs together. 'We'll have to take them to your lawyers tomorrow.'

'At last!' Perry said. 'They've taken long enough!' He held out his hand for them and I passed them over. He tucked them in his coat pocket and gave me his arm to help me up the stairs.

We parted at my bedroom door and I went in to dress for dinner. I did not mind going out this once, and I was spiteful enough to anticipate some pleasure from the sight of Maria, daggers drawn with her husband, having to smile and play foot-licker to him.

My new maid was waiting and I had her open my wardrobe so I could choose a gown grand enough for Maria's music evening. I had a shiny silk gown, as bright as emeralds with little white puff sleeves, cut quite low, and a white shawl to match.

'I'll wear that one,' I said to the girl, and she got it out while I splashed water on my face and slipped out of my afternoon dress. She fiddled with the buttons at the neck while I stood impatiently, and then I sat before my mirror and she took up the hairbrush.

Then I caught her eye and we both laughed.

'You're wasting your time,' I agreed. 'It's so short I can't even put a ribbon through it without looking odd. I shall just have to leave it all curly like this until it has grown a little.'

'Perhaps a cap, and maybe some false hair?' she asked tentatively, looking at my bright copper mob with her head on one side.

'Leave it,' I said. 'Everyone knows I had a fever and they cut my hair. I won't hide it as if it had all fallen out and I was bald.'

She dipped a curtsey and then I went down to dinner.

Lady Clara was there, looking very grand in a lovely gown of pale blue watered silk which matched the colour of her eyes. She was wearing fine diamond earrings and a diamond necklace.

'They might as well see we're not in utter poverty,' she said acidly when Perry made a nervous little bow and said how fine she looked. 'The gossip is that you were bankrupt and that I locked Sarah up until she agreed to marry you.' She made a little grimace of disdain. 'We'll scotch it tonight, but after tonight I expect you both to come out more into society until the end of the Season.'

'I want us to go back to Wideacre, as soon as the roads are fit to travel,' I said. 'I don't want to stay in London any longer.'

Lady Clara looked at me under veiled eyes, but said nothing while the butler served the soup. When he had stood back at the sideboard she looked from me to Perry and said: 'It would suit me very well at the moment to have you both in town for at least another month. I should like you to go out and around together. People expect it, and Sarah you have not yet been presented at Court. That should be done as soon as your hair is grown long again.

'I don't think you would either of you enjoy the country at this time of year. At any time it is dreary enough, but in February I should think you would both go mad with melancholy cooped up at Havering.' She paused. I waited but Perry said nothing.

'Besides,' she said. 'Many of the Havering staff are here, there is no butler nor chef in Sussex. You had better wait until the Season ends in the spring, Sarah.'

'We were planning to go to Wideacre,' I said. 'It does not matter that your staff are here, Lady Clara. Perry and I are going to stay at Wideacre.'

'Better not,' she said smoothly. 'There has been gossip enough, I should like you to be seen around town, Sarah. I don't want you down in the country, it looks too much as if we had something to hide.'

I looked back at her. Her blue eyes were limpid, the candles before her made her face glow with colour. She was sitting at the head of the dining-room table, Perry at the foot. I was placed in the middle, insignificant.

Perry cleared his throat. 'Sarah did want to go, Mama,' he said. 'She has not been well, she needs to rest in the country.'

His mother flicked him a look which was openly contemptuous. 'I have said that is not possible,' she said.

I could feel my temper building inside me but I was not a young lady to shriek or have the vapours, or throw down my napkin and run out of the room. I took a sip of water and looked at Lady Clara over my glass.

'We've lost our manager on Wideacre,' I said. 'I need to be down there to meet the new man. I don't want to be away so long. There will be talk down there too about this marriage. I'd like to go down. I had planned to go down within a couple of weeks.'

The footmen started to remove the plates, the butler brought a plate with slices of beef in a red wine sauce to the table and served Lady Clara, then me, then Peregrine. There were artichokes and potatoes, carrots and small green sprouts. Perry fell to and ate as if he was trying to deafen himself to any appeal I might make to him. But I was not such a fool as to think that Perry could help me.

'It's not possible, Sarah,' Lady Clara said pleasantly enough. 'I am sorry to disappoint you, but I need you both in London.'

'I am sorry,' I said mirroring her regret. 'But I do not want to stay in London.'

Lady Clara glanced at the footmen and at the butler. They stood against the wall as if they were deaf and blind. 'Not now,' she said.

'Yes. Now,' I said. I did not care what London society thought of me, I certainly did not care what Lady Clara's servants thought of me. 'I want to go to Wideacre at once, Lady Clara. Perry and I are going to go.'

Lady Clara looked down the table at Perry. She waited. He had his head bent low over his plate and he was trying not to meet her eye. The silence lengthened.

'Perry . . .' she said; it was all she needed to do.

Perry looked up. 'I am sorry, Sarah,' he said. 'Mama is right. We'll stay in London until the roads are a little drier, later in the year. We will do as Mama wishes.'

I felt myself flush red but I nodded. There was nothing more to say. I had not thought that Lady Clara and I might pull Perry in opposite directions, I had not thought that I would be under the cat's paw. But the laws of the land said that Perry was my master, and he was ruled by his mama.

I nodded at her, indeed I bore her little ill will. I had wanted my way and she had wanted hers, and she had won. I had learned about power in my hard little childhood. I had been a fool to think people lived in any other way just because they ate well and slept soft.

'I thought it was agreed that I might live as I please?' I asked levelly.

She looked around uncomfortably at the footmen again, but she answered me.

'I did agree that,' she said. 'But that was before this nonsense with Maria blew up. I need you, Sarah, I need Perry too. I cannot afford any scandal talked about this family if we are to hold Basil. Once this Season is over it can be as you wish.'

I nodded. I did not doubt she meant it, but I had learned in that brief exchange that I was as tied to her as I had been sold to Robert Gower, and owned by Da. I was not a free woman. I was apprenticed for a lifetime. All I could ever hope to do was to change the masters.

They cleared the dinner plates and served the puddings. There were three different sorts. Perry got his head down and ate as if he never expected to see food again. He was on to his second bottle. Both his mama and I saw his flight into drunkenness, and she shook her head at the butler when Perry's wine glass was empty again.

All in all, it was not a happy meal. Elegant; but not happy.

Nor a happy evening. Maria was dressed in scarlet as if to shame the devil and she greeted us at the head of her stairs with her head held high and Basil looking hang-dog at her side.

'Why, here is your mama-in-law!' she exclaimed as Lady Clara came up the stairs. 'And Perry, and the gypsy heiress!' she said in a lower voice.

'My dear . . .' Basil complained. He took Lady Clara's hand and bowed low. Maria stepped forward and kissed her mama, Perry, and then me. Her cheek was cold and dry with powder, she was white under her rouge.

'Everyone's here!' she said brightly. 'I don't think there's been such a squeeze since Lady Taragon ran off!'

Lady Clara's face was stony at the reference. 'Keep your voice down, Maria,' she said in a biting undertone. 'And behave yourself.'

Maria shot a bright defiant look at her, but she greeted her next guests more soberly, and nodded to the servants to pass around chilled champagne among the crowd.

Basil came over and drew Lady Clara into the window-seat. I could see his bald head nodding and his thin voice droning on. Lady Clara spread her fan to shield them and looked compassionately at him, over the top. Perry and I were alone. He took another glass off a passing waiter and downed it.

'I am sorry, Sarah,' he said. 'I couldn't tell her "no".'

'Why not?' I asked. 'All you had to do was to tell her that you agreed with me, I'd have done the rest.'

He shrugged. One of Maria's footmen came and took the empty glass and exchanged it for a full one. 'I don't know,' he said miserably. 'I don't know why. I've never been able to stand up to her. I suppose I can't start now.'

'Now's the time you should start,' I said. 'I'm there to help you, we both know what we want to do, and you have control of your fortune. What can she do if she doesn't like it? She can get angry, but she can't do anything.'

'You don't know what she's like . . .' he said.

'What who's like?' Maria asked from behind me.

Perry made a face at her. 'We wanted to go down to Havering, but Mama is keeping us in town,' he said dolefully. 'She wouldn't have minded if you hadn't been kicking up a dust, Maria.'

He turned away from Maria's reply, looking for another glass of wine. Maria looked hard at me. 'I suppose you think it's awful,' she said harshly.

'Not at all,' I said steadily. I was not afraid of Maria.

'I'd have thought a young bride like you, and married for love, would think it was awful . . .' she said again.

'I'm not married for love and you know it,' I said. I kept my voice low and the hum of conversation around us and the distant ripple of a harp and a violin were enough to drown out my words for anyone but Maria. 'But I'd not be fool enough to marry a man old enough to be my father for his money and then hope to get away with playing fast and loose.'

Maria's eyes were very bright. 'Is that what you think it is?' she asked her voice hard. 'I fell in love with Rudolph, I didn't hope to get away with it. I wanted us to run away altogether. I didn't even care about the money.'

I said nothing. Maria looked around and saw her mama side by side with her husband, their heads together.

'She's got me where she wants me,' she said resentfully. 'And he has. The two of them together. They bought Rudolph off – I know! I know that shows he wasn't much good! – I never said he was much good. But he made me feel alive, he made me feel as if I had never been young before!' She looked at me and her eyes which had been bright went hard again. 'You wouldn't even begin to understand,' she said bitterly.

I shook my head. 'No,' I said sadly. 'I've never been like that with a man.'

She held out her hands before her and looked at the heavy rings. 'He used to take my rings off and kiss each one of my fingers,' she said. Her voice was heavy with longing. 'And every time the tip of his tongue touched that little place between each finger I used to tremble all over.' She glanced at me. 'All over,' she said.

I was thinking of Will Tyacke and how I had warned him that I had no love to give a man. I was thinking of the time he had peeled down my glove and kissed me on the wrist and pulled the glove up again as if to keep the kiss warm. I was thinking of how he had followed me to Gower's show that night and seen me wrecked with grief for her. I was thinking that even though he had Becky and her love, he had come to London whenever I asked him. It was me who named our meeting days. He never failed me. He never promised me one thing he did not do. And at the end he said that if I married Perry I would not see him again.

He had kept that promise too.

'I shall never forgive them,' Maria said. She suddenly smiled, a hard bright smile. 'I shall never forgive those two,' she said, nodding towards her husband and her mama. 'That fat old bawd and that cheap lecher. She sold me and he bought me, and he is making her keep to her side of the bargain.'

Lady Clara and Basil had risen from their seats and were coming towards us.

'You should have run when you had the chance,' Maria said to me. 'When I first met you, when you were just up from the country. I thought then that if you'd had any wit you'd have got out of Mama's clutches. But you wanted to be a lady, didn't you? I hope it brings you much joy!' she laughed, a hard bitter laugh which made a few people turn around and look at us, and made Lady Clara come to her side.

'It's time to hear La Palacha sing,' she prompted. 'I'm longing to hear her, Maria, Basil has been telling me how charming she is.'

Maria nodded obediently and turned to summon one of the footmen.

'I have to go,' I said firmly. Lady Clara turned to me with a frown.

'Don't you start,' I said warningly and she heard the old toughness in my voice and hesitated. 'It's my first time out and I can't abide standing around,' I said. 'Perry said he'd take me home. I've come as you bid me, and I'll be staying in London as you wish. But don't push me, Lady Clara, I won't have it.'

She gave me a tight little smile at that. 'Very well,' she said. 'Make your curtsey to the princess as you go out. You are going to her luncheon tomorrow.'

'Yes 'm,' I said in imitation of Emily's servitude. 'Thank'ee 'm.'

Lady Clara's eyes narrowed, but she leaned forward and kissed me on the cheek. I smiled at her, my clear showground smile and then made for the door. Perry was swaying slightly on his feet, his eyes glazed, a glass in his hand.

'Time to go,' I said tightly. Perry nodded. We paused for a moment by the princess to bid her good evening. She exclaimed over my cropped head and my paleness and said I must promise to come to her luncheon tomorrow and eat some good Russian food. And now I was a wife too! How had that been?

'Private,' Perry said owlishly. ''Stremely private.'

The princess's sharp little eyes were bright with curiosity. 'So I had heard!' she said. 'Was only your family there?'

''Stremely private!' Perry said again.

The princess looked to me, she was waiting for an answer.

'It was during my illness, your highness,' I said. 'A quiet ceremony, at home. We were anxious to be married and we foresaw a long illness.'

Perry made his bow. ''Stremely private indeed,' he said helpfully.

The footman mercifully opened the door and I put my hand on Perry's arm and pinched him hard to get him out.

'You drunken doddypoll, Perry!' I said irritably. 'I wish to God you'd stay sober!'

'Oh, don't scold, Sarah!' he said, feckless as a child. 'I had enough of that with you and Mama at dinner. Don't scold me, I can't bear it. Be nice, and I'll see you home.'

I took his arm and we went downstairs, he was steady enough on his feet.

'You need not,' I said. 'You can go straight to your club if you will promise me that you'll come away if you start losing.'

'Yes, I promise,' Perry said carelessly. 'I'll come away if I lose and I'll only drink another glass or two. And tomorrow Sarah, if you're well, we can go riding in the park together.'

'I'd like that,' I said. The link boy outside the house waved for our carriage and it came up. Perry helped me in and kissed me on the hand. His lips were wet. Unseen, I wiped my hand on the cushions of the chaise.

'Call me tomorrow morning,' he said, ''bout ten.'

'All right,' I said. 'Good-night.'

I watched him as the carriage drew away from the brightly lit doorway. The petulant rosebud mouth, the mass of golden curls, his downcast blue eyes. He was exactly the same young man as he had been on the London road that day, who was too drunk to find his home.

The same, and yet not the same. For when I had met him then he had worn his joy in life about him, like a cloak from his shoulders. But the young man outside the wealthy house stood as if, in reality, he had nowhere to go, and would find no pleasure in anything he did.

37

I tumbled out of the carriage and up the broad stairs without a word to the butler or the footmen. I could have wept with my tiredness, there were some times when I thought I would never get my strength back. At those times, if I had been little Miss Sarah, a lady born and bred, I should have wept and taken the next day in bed, and the next, and the next after that.

But I was not one of the Quality, I was a hard little Rom chavvy and I would not rest. I let my new maid undress me, and tuck me into bed; but then I told her to call me at eight for I was going riding, and I ignored her murmured advice. I would get well by fighting through. All my tough work-hardened life I had got sick and got well again by fighting through. I knew of no other way. I did not even know when I was sick and tired deep into my very soul, and that fighting and struggling and trying would not make that any better.

I slept at once, as soon as the door closed behind her, and in my deepest early sleep I dreamed of a day of sunshine, when I rode by the sea and someone loved me. Suddenly, I started awake. I had heard something which did not fit with the usual night-time sounds. Soft footsteps past my bedroom door, a slight noise from the stairs and then I heard the well-oiled click of the front-door latch and a carriage drive away down the street. I guessed then that Peregrine had come back for something.

Some instinct, some old hungry Rom instinct made me raise myself half up on one elbow and stare in the flickering firelit darkness across my bedroom. Something was not right.

I pushed back the covers and stepped out of my bed, walked unsteadily across the room, opened my bedroom door and looked into the hall. It was all quiet down there. A footman dozing on a chair, the butler back in his own private room. I shrugged, and turned back for my room, irritated with myself for losing the rest I needed for some nervous fancy.

Then I heard a carriage draw up outside the house and saw the footman unfold himself out of the chair in a hurry and rush to the butler's room. I turned, silent in my bare feet, and scurried back to my room, shut my door in a hurry and slipped back into my bed and shut my eyes to feign sleep. I heard the front door open and Lady Clara's high-heeled slippers tapping loudly on the marble floor as she crossed the hall. I heard her ask the butler if I was well and his quieter reply. I lay still and listened for her footsteps to go past my bedroom to her own.

I waited until I heard her door close for the last time and I heard her maid sigh as she carried the soiled clothes down the corridor towards the back stairs where they would have to be washed and perhaps ironed overnight if Lady Clara wanted them in the morning.

They would all be in bed now, except for the kitchenmaid. Perry did not order his valet to wait up for him, a candle was left for him in the hall, and his fire was banked in to burn all the night and most of the morning in his empty bedroom. The last person working was the kitchenmaid – watching the copper in the kitchen and washing Lady Clara's linen. She would wring them out and then leave them drying before she crept up the stairs to her little bed. Everyone else was quiet.

I slipped from my bed and threw my wrapper around my shoulders and stepped, quiet as a cat, barefoot to my bedroom door, opened it, listened. There were no lights shining, the house was in silence. I stepped delicately on to the carpet in the corridor and stole softly down towards Perry's room. His door opened with the quietest click. I froze and listened. There was nothing. I opened the door a little way and slid inside and closed it carefully behind me. I stood in silence and waited. Nothing.

The flames flickered in the grate, a candelabra was by Perry's bedside with three of the five candles lit. I lifted it and stood it on his washstand so I could have the best light, then I turned and opened his wardrobe doors.

He had been wearing his mulberry-coloured coat with the green waistcoat this afternoon, when I had told him our marriage contract had arrived, and the deeds with it. I opened his wardrobe door and the coat was hanging, along with twenty others on hangers. I put my hand in the right-hand pocket, and then in the left-hand one. I took the coat out of the wardrobe and felt in every pocket and I even shook the coat in case I could feel the weight of the bulky papers in some pocket which was concealed.

There was nothing there.

The deeds of Wideacre were gone. I laid the coat on the floor and smoothed my hands all over it, alert for the rustle of thick paper, waiting for the feel of bulky documents under my finger-tips. The deeds were not there. I had known they would not be, but I still had held to a little flicker of hope. That was foolish of me. In the hard, hungry corner of my mind I knew the deeds were not mislaid. I knew I had been robbed.

I tossed the mulberry coat into the corner and took down another from the wardrobe. This was a fine ball coat of peach silk, wonderfully embroidered with green and gold thread, stiff with peach velvet at the collars and cuffs and the pocket flaps. I thrust my cold little hands into every pocket and felt thoroughly inside. I shook it hard in case I could feel the weight of the deeds. Then I spread it on the floor, careless of creases and smoothed it all over, feeling for the weight of the packet of papers which would give the owner title to my land, my land of Wideacre.

Nothing.

I bundled the fine coat into a ball and tossed it into the corner with the other. I took down a third . . . and a fourth . . . a fifth. I took down every coat in the wardrobe and searched each one as if I thought I might find the deeds to Wideacre carelessly stuffed in a pocket. I searched as though I had any hope left. I had none. But I felt as if I owed it to Perry, to Lady Clara, to my own Quality self, to little Miss Sarah Lacey, that I should believe that the life of the Quality was not the life of the midden. I wanted to believe that Perry was not a drunkard and a liar, a gambler and a thief. So I gave every coat a thorough searching, as if I thought I might find something more than disappointment and disillusion in every fine-stitched empty pocket.

Nothing.

I started on the drawers next. In the top were his fine linen shirts. I lifted each one out, shook it out of the carefully pressed folds and waited in case the deeds fell free. I dropped each shirt behind me on a chair, one after another until the drawer was empty and there was a snowdrift of creased fine white linen on the chair and on the floor. I took the drawer out then and threw aside the little muslin purse of dried lavender seeds, lifted the sweet-smelling paper lining of the drawer, and rapped with my fingers on the drawer base, in case Perry had taken care with the title deeds to my land. In case he had prized them so well that he had wanted to keep them safe, concealed where no one could steal them.

I knew they had been stolen. And I knew the name of the thief. But still I searched each drawer of the wardrobe, and then I went to the washstand and cast out his shaving tackle and his sweet-smelling soaps. His toilet water and the soft muslin cloth which he used to sponge his face. Everything I cast on the floor so that I could pull out the drawer and see if the deeds were safely hidden there.

Nothing.

I went to his writing desk, in the corner by the window. It was packed with papers, writing of every kind. I carried one drawer after another and heaped them on the centre of the bed. Small pasteboard calling cards, snippets of paper torn from dinner menus, sheets from notebooks, hot-pressed letter paper, a little mountain of papers and every one of them a note of gambling debts, written in Perry's careless drunken scrawl. A score of them, a hundred of them, a thousand of them.

I moved the candelabra to the bedside table and lit the two new candles so that I might see better, then I smoothed the paper into a pile and sat amongst them, at the head of the bed. I drew the candles closer and lifted the first piece of paper, smoothed it out, and lifted it close to my eyes so that I could read. I spelled out the word carefully, whispering under my breath: 'Ten guineas George Caterham'. Then I laid it on a pile and reached for the next.

Minutes I sat there, taking one paper after another, smoothing it, struggling with the words, placing it with the others. All the time my brain was working, calculating, adding and adding until all the little pieces were in a pile and I knew Perry owed two and a half thousand pounds in gambling debts to his friends.

There was a bigger pile, of proper paper, not crumpled scraps. Now I started on this. They were receipts from moneylenders against security and charging usorious rates of interest. They took me a long time to struggle through, I did not understand the words they used, nor some of the terms. I pulled my wrap around me and settled back with my back against the chair in the wreckage of the room. The deeds might be among them. They might be hidden among them. The bed was piled with papers, the chair heaped with Perry's shirts, the floor covered with his coats. It looked as if someone had wrecked his room in anger. But I was not angry. I had been looking for the deeds of Wideacre. I cared for nothing in the world but my land. And as the clocks struck two all over the house in sweet muted tones I sat again in silence and knew what I should have known all along. That I loved Wideacre, that it was my home. And the man who tried to take it from me was my enemy. That whatever I had lost in the past, whatever I might cling to in the future, Wideacre was my source and my roots. I needed it like I needed air on my face and water in my cup. I had loved my sister and lost her. Wideacre I would keep.

I sat very still and gazed into the fire as if I could see my future there. I thought, for the first time ever, about my mother, my real mother, and thought how she had planned for me to be found and brought to Wideacre to be raised there as a country child. I thought of what James Fortescue had told me, that she had loved the land and loved the people. I thought that one of her friends had been a Tyacke, kin to the first man I met when Sea took me to my home. And for the first time my hardened roughened heart reached out to her memory and forgave her for letting me go, for throwing me out into that dangerous world. I forgave her for failing me then, when I was new-born. And I gave her credit for trying to do the best for me by putting me in the care of the man who loved her, and bidding him teach me that the land belonged to no one.

I felt that now . . . I smiled at myself. The moment the deeds were held by someone else I felt that no one should hold them. But I thought it was not my simple quick selfishness which made me feel thus, I thought it was something more. A sense of rightness, of fairness.

You should not be able to buy and sell the land people walk on, the houses they call homes. You should not be able to gamble it away, or throw it away. The only people who can be trusted with the land are those who live on it, who need it. Land, and air, and sunshine and sweet water can belong to no single person. Everyone needs them, everyone should be able to claim them.

I sat there in silence, in silence and weariness. And I wondered where in all of the gambling dens and hells of London Perry had gone with the deeds to Wideacre in his pocket and the desire to gamble making him mad in his head. I had known at once what Perry was staking tonight. He had gone out gambling with our marriage deeds and the deeds of Wideacre in his pocket. The imp of mischief which had made him slip them into his jacket had been born in the parlour when I stopped him drinking, had grown strong at dinner when his mama and I pulled him and worried at him like a pair of hungry curs over a strip of cowskin. Perry would never stand up to her. Perry would never stand up to me. He was a coward. He would lie and steal and betray us all as he sought to prove himself to us, in his hundreds of little vengeances.

And I knew where he was playing, too. I knew that his new-found friends, Redfern and Thomas, were bilkers. I had seen all the signs – Perry's amazing luck which started when he met them, just as he came into his fortune. They called him 'Lucky Havering' he had told me and I had not thought quick enough with my clever cheating mind. They were gulling him and tonight, when he was drunk and peevish, they would spring the trap.

I gnawed on my knuckle and pulled one of Perry's expensive coats around me in the darkness. I was racking my brains to think of a way to find him, to trace him before it was too late.

There was a sudden rattle against the glass. A tapping like hailstones. It was someone in the street outside, throwing stones up at the bedroom windows. My heart leaped for a moment, perhaps it was Perry locked out and afraid to wake the house by knocking. Another shower of stones came, and I jumped out of bed and crossed to the window, afraid for the glass.

The windows had been sealed shut, thick with white paint. I could not open them. I pressed my face up to the glass and squinted down into the street below. Whoever was throwing stones was hidden by the angle of the house, but then a figure stepped back into the road to look up at my window and I recognized him at once.

It was Will Tyacke, standing in the dark street like an assassin come to murder me.

I ran to the bedroom door and wrenched it open. I flew down the hall, my bare feet making no noise on the thick carpet, and pattered down the icy stairs. The front door was bolted and chained, but I had often let myself out for my morning rides, and I pushed the bolts back and unchained the door and threw it open.

I tumbled out on the stone step, wearing only my nightdress, my arms outstretched. 'Will!' I said. 'I need you!'

He fended me off roughly, pushed me away from him, and with a sudden shock I saw his face was dark with anger. I fell back.

'I've no time for that now!' I said suddenly. 'You may be angry with me, but there is something that matters more. It's Wideacre. You have to help me save it!'

Will's face was as hard as chalk. 'I have come to ask you one question,' his voice was thick with rage. 'One question only and then I will go.'

I shivered. It was freezing, the pavements glistened with hoar frost. I stood barefoot on the stone step.

'Do you know what stake your husband is using to gamble with tonight?' he asked.

'What . . .?' I stammered.

'Do you know what stake your husband is using, for his gambling tonight?' Will repeated. His voice was very harsh, the whisper was charged with anger.

'Yes,' I said. 'He came home to get the deeds. I have just found them missing.' I put my hand behind me and gripped the knocker of the big black door so hard that it hurt. 'D'you know where he is?' I asked.

Will nodded. 'I wanted to see you,' he said. 'I went to that woman's party, where you were this evening. They said you'd gone home to bed. I thought I'd see his lordship instead, if I could find him.' He paused. 'I found him,' he said. 'He was in a new gambling club, in a mews behind Curzon Street, he was dead drunk, trying to play piquet. The gossip in the club was that he had won all evening but was starting to lose. The stake on the table were the deeds to Wideacre. Whoever wins them, wins Wideacre.'

We neither of us spoke. The wind blew icy down the street and I shivered but I did not step back into the hall.

'It was not lost when you left?' I asked.

'No.'

'Did you see him?' I demanded. 'Did they let you in?'

Will's hard mouth twisted in a smile. 'It's not a gentleman's club,' he said with the precise discrimination of a radical. 'They let in anyone who is rich enough or fool enough. It's a mews turned into a club with a porter down at the bottom of the stairs, and where the grooms would sleep is where they play. It's only been open a few weeks.'

My mind was spinning as fast as if I still had a fever. 'Wait here,' I said. 'I'm getting my cloak.'

Before he had time to answer I turned and raced back upstairs. I pulled my cloak from the wardrobe and I pushed my icy feet into my riding boots. I was not tired now, my head was thudding with anxiety and I was shuddering with the cold, but I was in a mad rush to get downstairs again in case Will should leave, without waiting for me.

I snatched a purse full of guineas from the drawer in my desk and clattered down the stairs, hardly caring how much noise I made.

Will was still on the doorstep.

'Come on!' I said, pulling the door shut behind me and starting down the street at a run. 'Is that your horse?'

Will's big bay was tied to the railings. Will nodded and unhitched him. At my nod he threw me up to the saddle and then swung up behind me.

'Where to?' he asked.

'The stables,' I said.

We trotted around to the mews, the horse's hooves clattering loudly on the frozen cobbles. A dog yapped inside, and we saw a light go on. I banged on the stable door and I heard the horses inside stir, then I heard someone coming down the stairs from the sleeping quarters above the stable and a voice, gruff with sleep, shout: 'Who is it?'

'Lady Havering!' I yelled back. I could feel Will behind me stiffen with anger at the title, but the groom pulled back the bolts of the door and poked his head and his lantern out through the gap.

'Lady Havering?' he asked incredulously. Then, as he saw me, he tumbled out into the street. 'What d'you want, your ladyship?'

'I want to borrow your best suit, your Sunday suit,' I said briskly. 'I have need of it, Gerry, please.'

He blinked, owlish in the lamplight.

'Quickly!' I said. 'I'll change in your room. Give me the clothes first.'

Will dropped down to the ground and lifted me down.

'You heard her,' he said to the man. 'Do as she says.'

The groom stammered, but turned inside and led the way up the rickety stairs.

'There's the suit I had for my brother's wedding,' he said. 'He's a tailor, he made it up for me special.'

'Excellent,' I said. The smarter I looked the more likely we were to pull this off.

He went to a chest in the corner of the room and lifted it out reverently. We were in luck so far, he had kept the linen with it, and a white cravat. It was a suit almost as good as a gentleman's; in smooth cloth, not homespun. A dark grey colour. You'd expect a city clerk to wear such a suit, or even a small merchant. If Perry's club would admit Will dressed in his brown homespun, they'd certainly admit me in this suit, if I could pass for a young man.

There was a tricorne hat with it, in matching grey, and I could swing my own cloak over the whole. My boots would have to serve. I did not want to borrow the groom's shoes with shiny buckles, they would be obviously too big for me whereas the jacket and trousers just looked wide-cut.

I dressed as quick as if I were changing costume between acts and clattered down the stairs as Will and the groom were leading his bay horse into the stables. Will stared at me and the groom gaped.

'My God, Lady Havering, what are you about?' the groom exclaimed.

I brushed past him and swung my cloak around myself.

'What d'you think?' I demanded. 'Would I pass as a young man, a young gentleman?'

'Aye . . .' Gerry stammered, 'But why, your ladyship? What are you about?'

I gave a low laugh, I felt as mad as I had been with my fever.

'Thank you for the loan of your suit . . .' I said. 'You shall have it back safe. Tell no one about this and you shall have a guinea. Have Sea and the bay ready for us at daybreak. Wait up for me.'

He would have answered, but I turned on my heel, Will at my side. His smile gleamed at me in the moonlight. I grinned back. It was good to be out of the house, and dressed easily again. It was like an enchantment to be with Will in the dark deserted streets of London. I laughed aloud.

'Lead the way,' I said. 'To Perry's club, as fast as we can.'

Will did not wait to ask me what I planned. I had known months before that moment that I loved him, but when he nodded with a smile, I loved him even more. For the way he turned and started down the street at a steady loping run, even though he did not know what the devil I was planning.

I was only half sure myself.

The new club was only minutes from home; Perry had taken a cab to it, and would have planned to reel home later. As we turned around the corner from the broad parade of Curzon Street we went arm in arm and strolled to the dark doorway, as leisurely as lords.

'This is the place, Michael,' Will said loudly. His voice was as clear and as commanding as a squire in the saddle. I had to bite back a smile.

'Bang on the door, then!' I said. I made my voice as deep as I could, and I slurred as if I were drunk. 'Bang on the whoreson door!'

It swung open before Will raised his hand. The porter inside, dressed in a shabby livery which looked as if it had been bought off a barrow cheap, smiled at us. He had a tooth missing. He looked an utter rogue.

'This is a private club, gentlemen,' he said. 'Private to the gentry and their friends.'

Thank the lord they were saving money on the lighting and the hall was illuminated only by a single candelabra, and two of the candlesticks were guttering. My face under the hat was in shadow anyway; he was looking mainly at the cut of my coat which was good, and assuring himself that, although we might look like rustics, we were neither of us the watch come to check on this new gambling hell.

'I'm an acquaintance of Sir Henry Peters,' I said, braggishly, like a young man. 'Is he here tonight?'

'Not tonight,' said the porter. 'But please to come in, there is a small, a very small membership fee.'

I put my hand in my pocket and at his mumble of two guineas each I tipped the gold coins into his hand. His eyes gleamed at the weight of the purse as I tucked it back inside my cape.

'Certainly,' he said. 'Most certainly, this way.'

He led the way up the rickety stairs to the upper floor. I could hear the sound of voices and the chink of bottle against glass. I could hear Perry's own voice say, 'Gad! Against me again! My luck's sick as a dog tonight!'

I hesitated, wondering how drunk Perry was, whether he would see my face under the heavy tricorne hat and cry out in surprise. But then the porter pushed open the door and I saw how dark and smoky it was inside, and I went on, fearless.

The smoke hung like a pall in the room, cigar smoke in thick wreaths. The stench of it made my eyes water as soon as I stepped inside, but I saw how it darkened the room so that the gamblers were squinting at their cards. No one even noticed us.

'Waiter!' Will said behind me.

The man appeared and Will ordered a bottle of burgundy and signed for it with a flourish. He did not once glance at me for approval. You would have thought we had been bottle companions, gambling and wenching together for years.

The porter had gone across the room to whisper in the ear of a man who was sitting sideways to the door. He glanced up towards us and rose to his feet, came across the room twirling his glossy red mustachios. 'Captain' Thomas, I bet silently with myself. And as like a captain in the cavalry as any fool and coward can reasonably appear. His partner at the table stayed seated. I guessed that would be Bob Redfern.

'Morning gentlemen,' he said. He even had the voice to perfection, the cavalry officer's confident drawl. 'Good of you to come to my little place here. Can I interest you in a game?'

I hesitated. I had not thought further ahead than to get to Perry before he gambled Wideacre away for ever. But he was deeper in than I had dreamed. Captain Thomas was not running a cheap little fleecing here. This was a well-staffed club with three servants at least within call and a dozen wealthy patrons, most of whom wore swords.

I looked around quickly. With his back to the entrance, slumped in his chair, was Perry. His golden curls looked dark and dirty in the flickering candlelight, his head was bowed as he stared at his hand of cards. The empty place opposite him, which had been the captain's, was surrounded with a pile of papers and gold coins. They were unmistakably IOUs from

Perry. Any one of them might be the Wideacre deeds, and Will and I were too late.

'You certainly can,' I said. My mouth was very dry, and my throat too tight. My voice came out a little higher than I meant, too girlish. But it did not tremble. Beside me I saw Will shift a little, like a wrestler places his feet when he is ready for a fight. I reached back to the table where our wine was poured and took a gulp.

'What's your game?' I asked. I nodded towards Perry's table with assumed confidence. 'What are you playing?'

'Lord Havering and I were playing piquet while waiting for a partner for whist. Perhaps you and your companion . . .?'

He glanced at Will who swayed on his feet. 'I'll sit this one out!' he said hastily.

'Well, let me introduce you then to Mr Redfern who will take a hand with us,' Captain Thomas said smoothly. 'I'm Captain Thomas, this is Lord Peregrine Havering.' Perry glanced up, his blue eyes hooded. He blinked owlishly and slumped back down again. 'And this is Mr Redfern. Play whist, Bob?'

Perry straightened, he looked bemusedly at me, blinking like a daylight owl. I tensed. He had seen me dressed as a lad before, that spring morning in the Havering woods when he had thought we might be friends. He stared at me.

'Do I know you?' he asked confused.

I nodded confidently. 'Aye, but I doubt you remember, my lord. We met at Brighton races, at the start of last summer. I was with Charles Prenderly, staying at his house.'

'Oh,' Perry said blankly. 'Beg pardon. Of course.'

'Will you play whist, my lord?' Captain Thomas asked.

Perry blinked. 'No,' he said firmly. 'Got to keep the same stakes. Got to have a go at winning them back. Daren't go home without them. That's a fact.'

Captain Thomas shot me a rueful look. 'His lordship's dipped deep tonight,' he said. 'He wants his revenge from me.'

I pushed my hat back carelessly on my red curls. Building inside me was a mad recklessness I had never known before. The hard-working, tough little child seemed to be melting, in this most unlikely moment. I felt as if I could have laughed aloud. My whole life was on the table of a common gambling house, my legal-wedded husband dead drunk and defeated before me, the only man I loved tense as a twitched horse behind me. I tipped back my head and laughed aloud.

'Maybe I'll bring him luck!' I said. 'Will you play whist with me, m'lord?'

Perry blinked, his rosebud mouth down-turned as if he felt like crying. 'Shouldn't change the game,' he said. 'How can I win it back if we change the game?'

Captain Thomas hesitated. Perry could turn nasty if he was not humoured, but the porter would have whispered in his ear about the heavy purse in my pocket and how it chinked with gold. Perry's friend Charles Prenderly was a wealthy young man. Any bilker would keep a friend of his at the gambling table if he possibly could.

'Well, keep the stakes,' I said cheerfully. The insane temptation to laugh aloud kept rising up in me. I was Meridon the gypsy tonight indeed. No land, no husband, no lover, and no chance of getting out of here without a thorough beating if I set a foot wrong. 'Keep the stakes as they are, I'll buy into the game. Then m'lord can win his fortune back if the cards fall his way.'

Captain Thomas gleamed.

'I'll buy in, too,' said Bob Redfern quickly. 'Say a hundred guineas, captain?'

I reached into my purse and counted out the coins. I held the purse still this time so that they should not see that it was near empty now. This was my stake for Wideacre. I would only have one chance.

Will lounged over to the doorway with his glass of wine to watch the play. His mouth was set hard and I saw him swallow. He had no gambling instinct, my solid Will Tyacke. I slid a wink at him and he scowled a warning at me. He had no idea what I planned to do.

Captain Thomas slid some counters across to me and to Bob Redfern. Perry had a handful in his pocket. He brought them out and turned them over and over as if he had hoped they had bred into more in the darkness of his pocket. Even in my fear for Wideacre I had a second's pity for him. He had lost everything tonight, and he still only half knew it.

Captain Thomas dealt. I watched him as he did so. It was a straight deal as far as I could tell. Clean cards, new pack, dealt from the top. He pushed the pack to Perry who cut the cards to choose suit. Diamonds.

I had a moderate hand and I won a couple of tricks and lost a couple. I did not care much during this game. I wanted to see how they worked. The deal passed to Perry and he fumbled with the cards but got them out. Bob Redfern called the suit. He called clubs. I had a wonderful hand. I won four of the six tricks and the deal and the calling of the suit came to me. I called clubs again for a mixed hand and took two tricks. Bob Redfern took three, and took the call for the next deal.

So far I had seen nothing. At the end of the game I was eight guineas down to Captain Redfern. Perry had lost ten. I could not see how they did it. As far as I could tell Perry had lost by simple incompetence. He was not able to remember what cards had been played and who had called the suit. The tricks he had won had come from luck – a high card in the right suit.

In the second game I saw it. I should have spotted it at once. I had watched card-sharpers at work all my life. These two had, no doubt, a repertoire of all the tricks: dealing off the bottom, marked cards, hidden cards, stacked decks of cards. But with Perry and me in the game they worked as a simple team. I remembered my da at the steps of the wagon sitting me opposite him and holding his mug of tea up to his ear, 'Ear means ace,' he had said. 'Ear: Ace. Mouth: King. Shoulder: Queen. Easiest trick in the world, Merry. And don't you forget it. Right hand red. Left hand black. Hands clenched looks like a club, see? Third finger on thumb looks like a heart, see? Hand out fingers together looks like a spade. Fingers open looks like diamonds. Easy.'

I never thought I should thank that man for anything in the world. I never thought he had given me aught worth having. But in that dirty smoky little club I bent my head to hide my smile.

I had them. The two damned cheats who were robbing me of

my land. I knew what they were doing. Whichever of them had the best cards of any suit signalled to the other. One or other of them could keep ahead of the game to win the deal most times. They could let me and Perry win from time to time to keep our interest in the game and our hopes up. The first trumps were called by cutting the pack and they could cheat on that by stacking the pack if they needed. Most times they would not need. It was a simple game and a simple cheat.

And all it needed was a simple opposition.

They were using the code my da had taught me. I watched them under my lowered eyelashes and smiled inwardly. I could read it as well as they. I could see that Bob Redfern had high diamonds, and that was why the captain called diamonds when he had only one or two in his hand. I knew then to use my low couple of diamonds to trump tricks to keep myself in the game.

They were going for me. For my little pile of guineas. Perry's miserable bewailings of his luck meant nothing to them. He would scrawl some more IOUs as he staked more to try and win back Wideacre. But they had sucked Perry dry for tonight. The IOUs were well and good but they preferred gold – like mine; or deeds to property – like Perry's.

I held them off. I lost a guinea at a time, slowly, slowly, until I took their measure. I watched them. I did not have the time, nor did I think to watch Perry.

The table suddenly jolted as he pushed it back.

'I won't play any more!' he announced. He rocked his chair back and then dropped it foursquare on its legs. He scowled around at us, I saw his lower lip trembling and I knew he was sobering fast. I knew he was realizing what he had done.

'Jolyon,' he said piteously to the captain. 'Jolyon, for God's sake take my IOU for the deeds. I should never have put it on the table. You should never have accepted it.'

The captain smiled but his eyes were cold. 'Oh come now,' he said. 'You won a fortune off me at Newmarket. A fortune in gold too! Not some damned place miles away in the countryside entailed to the hilt. It's the luck of the game lad! And my God! What a gamester you are!'

'Never seen a finer one,' Bob Redfern corroborated at once. 'Never seen a finer.'

Perry blinked rapidly. I knew there were tears in his eyes. 'I broke a promise,' he said. 'I promised . . . a lady . . . that I'd not gamble with those deeds. It was only owing you so much, Jolyon, and thinking it would be a fine thing to stake Wideacre to clear all the debts in one gamble that led me on. I shouldn't have done it. I hope you'll accept a draft on my account instead.'

Captain Thomas rose to his feet and clapped Perry on the shoulders.

'Surely,' he said pleasantly. 'Surely. I'll attend you tomorrow, shall I, old fellow? I'll come around to your house at noon, shall I? I want you to see a new hunter I have, I fancy you'll like him.'

'And I can clear my debt with you then, can I?' Perry demanded urgently. 'You won't let a day go? And you'll keep the deeds safe?'

'As safe as a babe new-born!' the Captain said. He guided Perry to the door carefully and the porter swathed him in his silk-lined evening cloak. 'Mind your step as you go home, Perry, I want you in one piece for tomorrow!'

Perry paused at the top of the stair, his mouth working. 'You won't fail me, Jolyon, will you?' he asked. 'I promised her, I promised this lady most especially . . .'

'Of course,' Jolyon assured him. He waved his cigar and we heard Perry clatter down the stairs and then the bang of the outer door as he went out into the streets.

The captain and Bob Redfern exchanged a slight inoffensive smile. They'd let Perry redeem the deeds for Wideacre only when they had priced the estate and checked its value.

I laughed aloud, like a reckless boy: 'Gambling for land, are we?' I demanded. 'Well, I've a fancy to win some land! What d'you say I put my place against this place of yours?'

The captain laughed as careless as me, but I saw him shoot a quick, calculating look across the table at me, and also at Will.

'And you, Will!' I exclaimed. 'Come on! It's not often we

come to London, and to be in a gentleman's club and with a chance to win a fortune and all!'

Will straightened up reluctantly. 'I'd not put Home Farm on the table, not for all the money in the world,' he said. 'And you'd be mad to put your estate up, Michael. Why, you don't even have the deeds yet, your pa's shoes are still warm.'

I thought that was pretty fast lying for an honest farm manager but I kept my eyes down and I laughed defiantly. 'So what?' I challenged. 'It's mine right enough, isn't it? And why should I want to be buried in the country for the rest of my days?'

I turned to the captain. 'It's the sweetest little estate you ever did see, just outside Salisbury,' I said. 'Not one good thing have I had out of it in my life. My father scrimped and saved and bought one little parcel of land after another until he had it all together. Not one penny would he spend on me. It's only since his death I've been able to go to a half-decent tailor even! Now I'm in London I'm damned if I'll sell myself short. I'll put Gateley Estate on the table, up against your – whatever it's called – and let the winner take both!'

'Not so fast,' the captain said. 'Lord Perry was anxious that I keep the deeds safe.'

I shrugged. 'I'll sell them back to him, or gamble 'em back to him, never fear,' I said. 'You talk as if I'm certain to win. I surely feel lucky!'

Will came forward softly. 'This is madness,' he said aloud. 'You'll never gamble your inheritance. The rents alone are worth four thousand pounds a year, Michael!' In an undertone, for my ears alone he leaned forward and hissed: 'What the devil are you playing at, Sarah?'

I leaned back in my seat and beamed at him. I had that wonderful infallible feeling I had known when I saw Sea for the first time and knew that he would not throw me.

I winked at the captain. 'I don't live like a rustic!' I said. 'I've come into my own at last, I'm ready to play like a gentleman, aye and live like one too.'

'Well, good luck to you!' said Bob Redfern. 'Damme that calls for a bottle. Are you drinking burgundy, Mr . . . Mr . . .'

'Tewkes,' I said at random. 'Michael Tewkes, Esquire, of Gateley, near Salisbury. Glad to meet you indeed.'

I let him take my hand, it was still as rough and as calloused as any working squire. They had cut my nails short in the fever, my grip was hard.

A fresh bottle was bought, and a new pack of cards.

'What'll it be?' asked the captain. His eyes were bright, he had been drinking all evening but it was not that which made him pass his tongue across his lips as if for the taste of something sweet. He could smell a pigeon ripe for the plucking.

'Michael, I promised your mother . . .' Will said urgently.

'Oh, sit down and take a hand,' I said carelessly. 'This is a jest between gentlemen, Will, not serious play. I'll put my IOU for Gateley on the table against this other estate. If I come home with a house and land in my pocket d'you think anyone will complain? Sit down and play or sheer off!'

The captain smiled sympathetically at Will. 'It's a hard row, keeping a young man out of trouble,' he said. 'But we're all friends here. We'll put the deeds on the table if that's your wish. But we'll have a gentleman's agreement to buy them back at a nominal sum. No one is here to be ruined. All anyone seeks is a little sport.'

Will unbent slightly. 'I don't mind games of skill,' he said stiffly. 'Games of skill between gentlemen for a nominal sum.'

'Slow coach!' I said easily. 'Captain, get me a sheet of your paper and I'll write out the deeds of my land fair. We'll put them on the table with Lord Perry's farm and they can be the stake.'

'I'll put my hundred guineas in,' Will said, warming to the game.

'Dammit so will I!' said Bob Redfern as if he had suddenly decided. 'I could do with a little place in the country!'

Will checked at once. 'The properties to be re-sold at once to their rightful owners,' he said.

Bob Redfern smiled. 'Of course,' he said. 'For a nominal sum. This is but a jest. It adds zest.'

'For God's sake, Will, we're in polite society now,' I hissed at him. 'Don't count the change so!'

Will nodded abashed, and watched as I wrote out a brief description with a line-drawing of what was, in fact, Robert Gower's farm. I chose it on purpose. It looked real. My da always used to say, when you're getting a gull, tell him a story as straight as you can. I thought of him as I drew in the river which flowed near the bottom field.

'Pretty place,' the captain said approvingly.

'A fair stake, for a jest,' I said.

Bob Redfern leaned forward and dealt the cards with his swift white hands. I dropped my eyelashes and watched him like a hawk.

I was not a card-sharper, I was a horse-trainer, a petty thief, a poacher. I could call up a show or ride a horse for money. I could take bets, make up a book, drug a bad horse into steadiness, or ride a wild pony into the ground for a quick sale. Here, in this London club, with a man's hat pushed back on my forehead, sprawled in my chair like a flushed youth, I was in the grip of men who cheated at cards for a living, and for a handsome living. I was the pigeon here. The little skills I had learned at Da's knee would not preserve me from a thorough plucking if I stayed too long. Whatever I was going to do I had best do quick.

News of the bet had spread to other parts of the room and several gentlemen had quit their own games to come and watch ours. I didn't know whether any of them would signal to Bob or Jolyon what cards we held. I didn't dare wait to find out. There was no time, and I did not have enough skill. For the first time in my life I wished with all my heart that my da was at my side. He was no artist, but he could spot a cheat. And I did not know if they would use the same signals with others watching.

They did. The first tricks I saw them do it. They moved like gentlemen, that was what made it alluring. When you saw Da pinch his ear or scratch his shoulder it looked foolish, as if he had nits. But when Captain Thomas brushed his collar with the tips of his fingers he looked merely debonair. I risked a quick glance at Will, he was scowling over his cards. He would know they were cheating but he would not have a clue how it was done. I could not hope that he would have wits quick enough to follow me. He had not had the training, he was no easy liar, no quick cheat. He did not know how to do it. I should have to do it alone. I should have to do it quickly. I should have to do it now.

38

They were going for me, for the convincingly pretty little farm I
had drawn for them. All good card-sharping is a war of imagination in which the card-sharp convinces the pigeons of two
things at once: that he is honest, and that they are skilled. I
watched them under my eyelashes and saw that they thought
Will too staunch, too unwilling, possibly too poor for their skills.
But I was a flash young fool. They looked from the little rough-
drawn map to my open eager face and licked their lips like
hungry men before sweet pudding.

I tapped my cards on the table and shot a look at Will. 'Seems
you were right, Will,' I said. 'I'm well out of my depth here.'

Will kept his eyes down and his face still, but he must have
been reeling at my sudden change of tack.

'Let's finish this game and be off then,' he said. He glanced at
Captain Thomas and Bob Redfern. 'Begging your pardons, sirs,
and thanking you for your hospitality. But I promised this
young man's mother I'd bring him safe home. Aye, and with his
inheritance safe in his pocket.'

Captain Thomas cracked a laugh that made the dusty chandelier tinkle. 'You're a bear leader, sir!' he cried. 'I think Mr
Tewkes here is a very sharp player indeed!'

He switched the card he was about to play for one further
away from the cleft of his thumb. It was a low trump. He
probably knew I had higher. I took the trick as he had intended.

'Look at that now!' he said. 'I missed that you had a trump
that high, Mr Tewkes.'

'Let's have another bottle,' Bob Redfern said genially. 'Up
from the country you should enjoy yourselves gentlemen! A
shame to go home with no tales to tell! They'll open their eyes
when you tell them you played here, I warrant!'

Hearts were trumps and I had two or three low cards. I led instead with a King of diamonds and everyone followed my lead with lower cards except Captain Thomas who discarded a low club card, giving me the trick. After that I drew out their low trump cards with one heart after another until all I had left in my hand was the Jack of spades and I gambled on no one having higher. But Captain Thomas had the Queen and at the end of the game we were neck and neck for tricks.

'I think we should go now,' Will said. 'It's a fair ending to a good jest.'

I laughed excitedly and hoped my colour was up. 'Leave when I've hit a winning streak?' I demanded. 'Damme no, we won't! I won't leave this table until I've had a crack at winning that little farm in Sussex. It's only a jest! And the night's young! And the cards are going my way now! I can feel it!'

'Oh, you've a cardman's instincts,' Redfern said wisely. 'Sometimes I feel that too. You just know that you cannot lose. I've had that feeling once or twice in my life and I've left tables with a fortune in my pockets! It's a rare gift that one, Mr Tewkes . . . may I call you Michael?'

'Oh aye, Bob,' I said carelessly. 'You believe in luck, do you?'

'What true-bred gambler does not?' he asked smoothly. He shuffled the cards and I picked up my glass and drank, watching him around the rim.

Then I saw it. He had picked up the discarded cards and flicked out of them a selection of cards into his right hand, palmed them in his broad white hand. The backs looked plain enough to me but they might have been marked so he could tell the picture cards from the rest. Or they might have been shaved thinner – I couldn't tell from looking, I would only be able to tell from touch when the deal was mine. And I would have to wait for that. He shuffled the pack with vigour, the ruffles from his shirt falling over his working hands. He was not too dexterous, he was not suspiciously clever. It was an experienced player's honest shuffle. He passed the pack to me for me to cut. My fingers sought for clues around the cards in vain. There was no natural point to cut to, he had not shifted the deck or made a bridge to encourage me to cut where he wished. Nothing.

I cut where I wished and passed it back to him. Then he dealt. What he did then was so obvious and so crass that I nearly laughed aloud and stopped longing for my da, for beside me was a man as greedy and as vulgar as my da ever had been. And I had his measure now.

He had not stacked the cards, he had not made that instant calculation of where the picture cards would have to be inserted into the stock of ordinary cards in his left hand. He just thrust the picture cards on top of the deck and dealt a selection of the cream of the pack off the top to me and Will, and off the bottom to him and Captain Thomas. It was a childish simple cheat, and my glance shot to Will to warn him to say nothing when he saw it.

I was safe enough there. Amazingly, he did not see it. Will was indeed the honest country yeoman and he watched Bob Redfern's quick-moving hands, and collected his cards as they were dealt, and never spotted the movement where Bob's long fingers drew from the top or the bottom of the stack as he pleased.

I glanced cautiously around. No one else seemed to have seen it either. It was late, they were all drunk, the room was thick with smoke and shadowy. Bob's shielding hand hid everything. Only I saw the quick movement of his smallest finger on his right hand as he hooked up a card from the bottom of the pack for him and his partner so that they could ensure that they would lose to us.

I had good hands during the game. Good cheating hands. Nothing too flash, nothing too stunning. I fidgeted a good deal, and by holding my breath once and squeezing out my belly I made my face flush when Bob dealth me the Ace of trumps. I won by three tricks ahead of Will and there was a ripple of applause and laughter when I crowed like a lad and swept the heap of IOUs and the tied roll of the Wideacre deeds towards me.

At once a waiter was at my side with a glass of champagne.

'A victory toast to a great card-player!' Bob said at once, and held out his glass to drink to me.

Will looked surly. 'We'd best be off now,' he said.

'Oh, drink to my victory!' I said. 'You shall come with me to Lord Perry in the morning for him to buy back his farm. How he will laugh! Drink to my victory, Will! It's early to go yet!'

'And gambling's in the air!' Captain Thomas shouted joyously. 'I feel my luck coming back! Damme if I don't'! Stay with your luck, Michael! Dare you put both your properties on the table . . . your new farm and your own place at Warminster?'

'Against what?' I demanded with a gleam.

Will said 'Michael!' in exactly the right mutter of anguish.

The waiter filled my glass again, the voices seemed to be coming from a little further away. I cursed the wine silently. I was not used to it, and I was still weak from my illness. Much more of it and I would be in trouble. 'Damme! This place!' Captain Thomas yelled.

There was a roar of approval and laughter, and shouts to me: 'Go on, country squires! Take the bet! Let's hear it for the Old Roast Beef of England!'

'I'll do it!' I said. I slurred my words a little. In truth I was acting only slightly. Will's dark look at me was not feigned, either.

I piled the deeds back into the middle of the table again, and Captain Thomas scrawled something on a sheet of headed note-paper handed to him by the waiter. Bob and Will added their IOUs.

'Your deal,' Bob said to me. He gathered up the tricks loosely, and pushed them towards me. I took a deep breath and patted them into a pack. I slid my fingers along the sides. I shuffled them lightly. I was pouring my concentration down into my fingertips. It was possible that the pack was a clean one. With the partnership they had of cueing to each other's cards, it might be that the pack was unmarked. And the dealing from the top and the bottom ploy looked very much as if they used no sophisticated tricks.

Then my fingers had it. Just a touch of roughness on one side of the cards, as if a very fine needle had just pricked the veneer of the surface. They had only marked one side too, so sometimes the mark was on the left, sometimes on the right, and it was hard to tell.

'You're scowling,' Captain Thomas said. 'All well with you, Michael?'

'I feel a bit . . .' I said. I let my words slur slightly. 'I will have to leave you after this game gentlemen, whatever the outcome. I'll come back tomorrow.'

'Surely!' Bob said pleasantly. 'I get weary this time of night myself. I know what you want lad! Some claret! Claret's the thing for the early morning.'

They took my old glass of champagne away and brought a fresh one filled to the brim with the rich red wine. Will's face was frozen.

While they were fussing with the wine I was quietly stacking the deck. I thought of Da. I thought of him in a new way – with a sort of rueful pride. He had played on upturned barrels for pennies yet he would have scorned to deal off the bottom like these fine cheats had done. Not him! When my da was sober and cheating he counted the number of hands to be played, the number of players and stacked the deck so the cards would fall as he wished to the players he wished. While they tasted the wine, and quarrelled as to whether it was cool enough, I counted swiftly in my mind, seven cards to each player, the second hand as I dealt it to be the strong one. Strong cards must occur every four cards at the right time for me to get them to Will who was sitting opposite me. Thus in the first deal there had to be a strong card at number 2, number 6, number 10, number 14, number 18, number 22, and number 26. I felt for the marked cards. I thought they had only marked Aces, Kings Queens and Jacks . . . there didn't seem to be more than twenty-eight marked cards.

'Ready, Michael?' Bob said pleasantly. I shot him a quick look. He had not been watching me. He was smiling at Captain Thomas, an honest neutral smile, which passing between those two said, clear as a bell, 'We have them now.'

I riffled the pack. It was stacked as well as I could do, in the time I had, and I was not in practice as I had been when I was Meridon.

I went to deal.

'Cut,' Captain Thomas reminded me.

I flushed. 'Oh yes,' I said.

They cut before they dealt in this club. Captain Thomas was waiting for me to cut my carefully stacked deck towards him so that the cards I had prepared for Will would be cut to the bottom of the deck where they would go at regular and surprising intervals to any one of us.

'Agent shifting cut,' I heard Da's voice in my head. I saw his dirty hands squaring up a pack on the driving seat on the front of the wagon. 'See this Merry? D'ye see?'

It was a tricky move. Da used to bodge it, I learned it from watching him failing at it. I glanced around. It was growing light outside but it was still dark in here with the thick musty curtains at the window. Someone at one of the tables was disputing a bill and people were glancing that way. I looked at Captain Thomas.

'Trouble?' I asked, nodding towards the table. Captain Thomas looked over. A man had lurched to his feet and tipped the table sideways. I grasped the pack in two hands, my left holding the top half of the pack, and my right holding the bottom. With one swift movement I pulled the bottom half gripped in my right hand and put it towards Captain Thomas.

'Nothing really,' he said looking back. He completed the cut, moving the half-deck which was furthest from him on top of the one nearest to him. Without knowing it, he had put my stacked deck back together again. And no one had spotted it.

I heard my heart thudding loud in my ears, in my neck, in my throat. So loud that I thought they would all hear it over the jostle and confusion of the drunk man being thrust down the stairs and out into the street.

I dealt with a trace of awkwardness and the cards lay on the table. Will picked up his cards and I saw his eyes widen slightly, but his hand outstretched to the wine glass did not tremble.

He won, of course.

I saw Captain Thomas squinting at his cards, and at the backs of Will's. I kept my cards low, held in my cupped hands in case there were markings in the back he could see. I watched the two

of them warning each other to call spades for trumps, or diamonds. Hearts or clubs. It would make no odds. Will had a
King, a Queen or an Ace in every hand. The other good cards
which I had scattered around the table were just to dress the act.

They couldn't nail it. They were so sure of me as a pigeon.
They had seen me shuffle clean enough, and then they had seen
me cut. And they believed, as many fools before them have
believed, that you cannot stack a cut.

I slid the last card across the table. Captain Thomas took the
trick, it was his third. Will had five, Bob Redfern had three
tricks, I had two. Will was a truly awful card-player; with the
hands I had given him he should have wiped the floor with the
three of us.

'I've won!' he said incredulous.

Bob Redfern was white, the sweat on his forehead gleamed
dully in the candlelight. He slid the heavy document of the
deeds of Wideacre across the table to Will. I pushed the deeds of
my farm, and the paper for the club, and Redfern's IOUs.

'I'm done for tonight gentlemen!' I said. My voice came out a
little high and I took a breath and clenched my fingernails into
my palms under the table. I was not out of the ring yet. I rubbed
my hand across my chin as if I were feeling for morning beard
growth. 'I've won and lost a property, and lost my own as well!
A great night! We shall have to settle this very day, Will.'

Captain Thomas smiled thinly. 'I shall call on you,' he said.
'Where are you staying?'

'Half Moon Street,' I said glibly. 'Just around the corner,
with Captain Cairncross at number 14.'

He nodded. 'I'll call on you a little after noon,' he said. 'And
I'll bring Lord Perry. We will all need to settle up after tonight!'

There was a murmur from the men all around us.

I smiled around at them. 'It's been a hard gambling night for
me!' I said. 'Not often I get to play in such company as this. I
shall come back tomorrow evening if I may.'

'You'd be very welcome,' Captain Thomas said pleasantly.
His bright eyes above the curly mustachios were cold. 'Play
always starts around midnight.'

'Grand,' I said.

Will got to his feet, as wary as a prize-fighter in an all-comers ring.

'My cape,' I said to the waiter behind me.

Will tucked the precious deeds deep into his jacket, and shovelled the other papers and guineas on top of them.

'We'll settle up tomorrow,' the captain said, watching his every move.

'I'm in no hurry,' Will lied. He stepped towards the door, his eyes on me. The waiter came and draped my cape around my shoulders. I picked up my hat which I had tossed off during the game, ran my hands through my curls and crammed it on.

'A grand evening!' I said. 'I thank you both.'

I stepped towards the door. I was as loath to turn my back on those two as I would take my eyes off a snake. I felt utterly sure that once I could not see them they could spring on me.

I took two steps towards the doorway, Will was through the door, starting to descend the stair, I was in the doorway, I was through. I went down each stair one at a time, making myself go slow, forcing myself to walk cautiously, as a drunk walks.

'Thank you, good fellow,' Will said as the porter fumbled with the bolts of the door. He was hesitating as if they would hold us. Hold us at the bolted door while they rushed us. I risked a quick glance behind me. Redfern and Thomas were at the top of the stairs looking down at us. I felt my throat tighten in panic.

'Good-night!' Will called. His voice was assured. I did not trust myself to speak, I waved a casual hand and hoped to God that my face was not too white. The last bolt slid free, the porter swung open the door, the grey light of dawn and the clean cold smell of a spring morning flooded in upon us.

We stepped out, arm in arm, into the silent streets.

The sun was not yet up, it was that pearly pale time of the morning when it is half-way between dark and dawn. I glanced at Will; his face was lined as if he had aged ten years. I knew my own face was bleached with the strain, my eyes dark-shadowed.

'Are we clear?' he asked me, his voice very low.

'I think so,' I said.

It was a hopeful lie and we both knew it. We did not think so.

'Walk slowly,' he said softly. 'If they're going to get us it'll be before we get out into the main street.'

We strolled, five steady paces, away from the doorway of the club. Then there was a shout from behind us:

'Hey! Hey! Michael! You've forgotten your cane! Come back!'

'Run!' Will said and grabbed my hand.

As soon as we had taken our first strides I heard them shout behind us, confused instructions to head us off. We hurtled around the corner into Curzon Street. The road was absolutely deserted, the place empty and silent.

'Damn!' Will said.

'This way!' I said quickly and led him down the street, running close to the wall of the buildings, hoping to be hidden by the shadows.

From the mews behind us we heard their boots on the cobbles, the noise of them stopping and then a loud voice yell, 'They went that way! That way!' and I knew we had been spotted.

I led Will across the road at the run and dived up Queen Street. I glanced behind me. There were five of them, a little slower than us and we had a good lead. But Captain Thomas was gaining a little, he looked fit. Already my breath was coming in gasps and I could feel my knees starting to go weak.

We ran without speaking up the length of Queen Street, they were about a hundred yards behind us. I could not believe there were no lighted doorways, no carriages, no late parties, not even a neutral witness. There was no one. Will and I were on our own against five villains and the deeds to Wideacre in Will's pocket.

At the corner I did not hesitate even for a second. I was running without a thought in my head except to get away from them. Now I dived over the road and up John Street hoping to be into the shadows before they came to the crossroads and saw us.

We nearly made it, but we heard Thomas shout, 'Stop! Listen for them!' and then the triumph in his yell. 'They're going that way! After them!'

The road was narrow and the clatter of boots on cobbles

behind us seemed to get louder and louder. My cape was twisted around my legs, hampering me like hobbles on a horse, I could feel myself slowing. Only fear was moving me on now; and I was not going fast enough.

'Which way?' Will gasped.

My mind reeled. I had been heading for home, instinctively threading my way through the fashionable streets and the dark secret mews streets behind them. But I knew I could not keep up this pace. They would be upon us, and in any case I would lose my way in this warren of new gracious squares and back lanes.

'The park!' I said. I thought of the cool trees and the dark hollows where we might hide. I thought of the icy grass shining under the pale light of early morning. It was as like to country as we would get in London and I had a great longing for earth under my feet. Both Will and I were country children, we needed to be home.

We swung left down Farm Street and I could see the high trees of the park, it seemed like miles away at the end of the street.

'Down there,' I said. I was running even more slowly, my throat was tight and my chest heaving. 'You run, Will, you've got the deeds. Get them away. Get away with them.'

He shot me a swift sideways look, his teeth gleaming in the half-light. The idiot was smiling.

'We'll make it,' he said. 'Keep running.'

I was so angry with him not understanding that I could not keep running, I was finished, that my anger gave me a spurt of energy which bore me up. Also, I was afraid. That made me faster than our pursuers. Behind us were men, angry and greedy for my land, but they were not scared as I was. I had run from men too many times in my life not to feel my heart race when I heard boots on cobblestones behind me. My heart was thudding in my chest, and my breath was hoarse, like in my illness, but I could still run and run and run.

We burst across the road. There were one or two carriages in the distance, but no one close enough, and anyway, the hue and cry was after us. If we called for help we might find ourselves before a magistrate, and I had a law-breaker's terror of the justices.

'Those trees . . .' Will gasped. He was near the end of his strength too, he was wet with sweat, his face shiny in the pale light. He headed towards a little coppice of beeches and silver birches. They were stark in the pale shadows, their bare branches thin threads of blackness against the lighter sky. But they would give us some shelter.

I shot a look behind me. They were hard on our heels, crossing the road even now. They would see us go into the coppice, we would not have time to hide. They would cast about and catch us.

'You go on!' I said peremptorily. 'I'll hold them up! For God's sake, Will!'

He turned roughly on me as soon as we were hidden from sight.

'Drop your breeches,' he ordered. I gaped at him and he dragged my cloak from my neck and bundled it under a bush of blackberry.

'Drop your damned breeches!' he whispered harshly. 'You pass as my doxy!'

Then I understood. I ripped the boots off my feet and tore the breeches off. My cravat went the same way, and I stood before Will in my night-shirt. Without hesitation he took a handful of the material at the neckline and ripped it so that it dropped down to my bubbies, showing my milk-white neck and shoulder, the rounded curve of my breast and the rosy nipple.

Behind us, at the edge of the coppice we heard Thomas' voice, and Redfern shouting:

'Look up to the trees, check the boughs!'

Will flung himself upon me and bore me down to the ground.

'Open your legs for God's sake, Sarah,' he said impatiently, and rolled himself over so that he was lying on me. I felt him fumble at his breeches and I felt my white face burn red as he pulled them down so he was bare-arsed.

'Will!' I said in whispered protest.

He had a moment to rear up and look at me, his face was brimful with mischief. 'Stupid little cow,' he said lovingly, then he dipped his head into my naked neck and started thrusting at me with his hips.

'Holloa!' came the yell behind him, Captain Thomas skidded to a halt and his bully-boys craned over his shoulder. Will kept his head down, I risked a peep over his shoulder. They were staring at me and at my bare splayed legs. I ducked my head down into Will's warm jacket and inwardly cursed them and every damned man on the whoreson earth. I hated Will, and Captain Thomas, and Wideacre with every inch of my frigid angry body.

'Did ye see a couple of gentlemen, run through here?' Thomas rapped out.

Will let out a great bellow of rage, or it would have passed for frustrated lust. 'What the devil d'you think I'm doing, keeping watch?' he hollered. 'O'course I didn't. What does it look to you that I'm doing? Go your ways, damn you. I've paid for twenty minutes and twenty minutes I'll have!'

They hesitated, two of them fell back.

'They went that way . . .' I said. My voice was silky, slurred. I gestured with an outflung hand and they saw my naked shoulder and the line of my throat, gleaming in the pale light.

Captain Thomas bowed to me, ironically. 'I am much obliged to you ma'am,' he said. 'And I apologize for disturbing you, sir.' We heard him take two steps. 'It seems the lady is less attentive than the man,' he said and the men laughed. Then his voice changed. 'Is that them? Boarding that coach? Dammit! After them!'

We heard the noise of them crashing through the undergrowth and their yells to the coachman. We froze, as still as leverets in bracken, while we listened to the coach pull away, and them chasing after it, yelling to attract the guard's attention. Then it was quiet. They had gone.

Will Tyacke lay on top of me, his face buried in my neck, breathing in the smell of my sweat, his face rubbing against my skin, his hardness pushing insistently through my rumpled shift at the deep inner core of me where I could feel I was as soaking wet as any loving strumpet behind a hay stack.

'It's all right, Will,' I said, my voice warm with laughter. 'You can stop pretending. They're gone.'

He checked himself with a shudder but the face he raised to look at me was alive with love.

'My God, I love you,' he said simply. 'It would be well worth being hanged for card-sharping to rip your nightgown open and lie between your legs – even for a moment.'

I stretched in a movement as languorous and sensual as a cat. I felt as if blood had never flowed in my veins before this moment. I felt warm all over, I felt alive all over. My skin, the inside of my wrists, the soles of my feet, the warm palms of my hands, the tingling tip of my tongue, every tiny fraction of me glowed like gold. And deep deep between my legs I felt a pulse beating as if I had never been alive there before, as if Will was a plough to turn the earth and make it fertile, and that suddenly my body was no longer wasteland; but rich fertile ploughland, hungry for seed.

'Not now,' I said unwillingly. 'They'll be back when they've stopped the coach. They're not stupid.'

Will leaped up. 'No!' he said. 'Here! Your clothes!'

He reached into the blackberry bush, stamping his feet and cursing in a whisper when the briers scratched him. Then he turned his back in incongruous chivalry while I got dressed. I crammed my hat on my head, and wrapped my cloak around me.

'Home to Wideacre,' Will said decisively.

'I've got to fetch Sea,' I said.

Will checked, looked at me to see if I was jesting.

'We cannot!' he said. 'We cannot risk retracing our steps, going back the way we've come. We should strike across the park now, go west, double back later.'

'I want Sea,' I said stubbornly. 'Sea will get us home. And you'll want your horse.'

'They'd send them on . . .' Will started.

'Not they,' I said certainly. 'I'm finished with the Haverings for all time. They'll not send on as much as a pocket handkerchief of mine. I'm getting my horse out of their stables before they know their pigeon's flown the coop.'

Will hesitated, looked from my resolute face to the streets of the city which were getting noisy and busy as the sun rose.

'I'm not going without Sea,' I said.

'Oh very well,' he said sullenly, and we strode out of the coppice shoulder to shoulder without a spark of passion or even affection between us. Cross as cats.

39

We saw a hackney coach going down Park Lane and we hailed it and bundled in. Will counted his silver in the pale light through the window to see if he would have enough to meet the fare without flashing his gold guineas around. He was always as cautious as a yeoman, Will Tyacke.

I leaned back against the dirty squabs of the coach and sighed. 'How much have you got?' I asked.

Will pulled out his gold coin by coin and carefully counted. 'Ninety-eight guineas,' he said. 'You lost all your stake, didn't you?'

'Aye,' I said smiling at him under my half-closed eyelids. 'I like to play like a gentleman.'

'You play like a cheat,' he said instantly. Then he cocked his head. 'What was that?'

I dropped the window and we listened.

There were shouts from behind us, I heard a voice say: 'Hey coachman! Wait!'

Will's face was white. 'They turned,' he said. 'What now?'

'We outpace them!' I said.

Before he had a chance to protest I grabbed his handful of guineas and stuffed them in my pockets. I went head-first out of the coach window clutching the door frame and up on to the box beside the driver like a street urchin.

'What?' he said. He was already pulling up his horse in obedience to the shouts from behind.

'Go on!' I yelled.

He gawped at me.

I put a fistful of guineas in his hands. 'Card-sharpers,' I shouted over their noise. 'They don't like losing. And they're blown. Keep this old nag going and there are twenty guineas for you at the end of the ride!'

He glanced quickly behind. Only the captain and a couple of men had kept up. They would not catch us if the damned nag between the shafts could go faster than a knock-kneed stumble.

'Faster!' I said.

The man broke into a wide broken-toothed grin. 'Twenty guineas?' he asked.

'Thirty!' I said.

He flashed his whip over the horse's back and the creature, startled, broke into a shambling canter. Will, sticking his head out of the window, could see we were drawing away from the gamblers.

'Howay!' he yelled.

I laughed aloud.

Then I looked to the front.

Some damned hay-wagon was blocking our way. It had turned on its side and there were half a dozen men scurrying around trying to right it, a couple of idle milkmaids pausing to watch, and four or five link boys.

The hackney could edge around the wagon if the people would give us space but they were all over the road. I looked back. Captain Thomas was red in the face but he saw we were stuck. I saw him smile.

'Stop thief!' he yelled, damn his strong lungs.

I thrust my hand deep in my pocket.

'Let me pass, lads!' I yelled. 'Look here!'

With a great broadcast sweep I flung the coins in my pocket – guineas, silver, coppers – wide into the sky. The urchins and the milkmaids dived to the ground out of our path. The men righting the hay cart looked blankly at me and then chased after the rolling coins.

'Drive on!' I ordered. Another handful of coins as we got through and, as from nowhere, beggars and street-walkers and urchins and thieves were all out of their doorways and lodgings falling over each other in their haste to chase the money.

'Sarah!' Will exclaimed, anguished.

I laughed. 'Look!' I said pointing back.

Captain Thomas had pushed someone in his haste to get

through the crowd and the man had pushed back. What had been a little scramble was now a promising street-fight. The man had punched Thomas roughly in the shoulder and had hold of his coat collar and would not let him pass. I danced up and down on the box waving farewell and holloaing.

'Goodbye, pigeon-plucker!' I yelled in triumph. 'Goodbye, curtal! Goodbye, you glim-glibber! You poxy tatsman! You hog in armour!'

The hackney whirled around the corner and threw me off balance. I fell down to the seat and grinned at the driver.

'Drop us at the corner of the mews behind Davies Street,' I said, and he nodded and drove where I ordered.

'A fine night you've been having,' he observed.

I stretched luxuriously, thinking of the deeds safe, and Will safe, and me safe away from the Haverings and the Quality life at last.

'A fine night,' I agreed.

The coach drew up at the corner and Will tumbled out. He shook his head at me. 'Good God, Sarah!' he said. 'That was near all the money I had!'

'I promised the driver thirty guineas if he got us away,' I said. 'Turn out your pockets, Will.'

The driver came down from the box as Will and I went through every pocket in our coats and breeches. We mustered seventeen guineas and some coppers.

'I won't hold you to it,' he said. 'Seventeen is fair, I'll have that off you.'

He helped himself to the coins out of Will's reluctant palm and drove off, beaming.

Will's face could have modelled for an etching of a countryman fleeced in the big city.

'Sarah that was *all* our money!' he said. 'How d'you think we'll get home?'

'Ride,' I said cheerily.

'And go hungry?' Will demanded. 'We've little money for food.'

I gleamed at him. 'I'll steal it,' I said. 'Or you can call up a crowd and I'll ride on the street corners.'

Will's cross face collapsed into laughter. 'Oh you're a rogue,' he said. 'By rights I should never bring you to Wideacre, they're an honest crew there and you are a brigand!'

I laughed back, then we turned and walked side by side down the cobbled street to the stables.

It was early still, and quiet in these back streets. In the distance there was the noise of milkmaids and the water-carrier; at the end of the road the night-soil cart went past with a stench blowing behind it. The city was not yet awake. Only working people, with the hardest jobs, were up this early.

The groom was waiting for us, his eyes wide at the state of me, and the state of his best suit, and Will with his shirt hanging out the back.

'My lady . . .' he said helplessly.

'I'll have to keep your suit,' I said pleasantly. 'But I'll send you money for another and for the service you've done me this night, when I get to my home.'

'To the house?' he said hopefully.

'Sussex,' I said.

His face looked stunned. 'M'lady, you're never running off,' he said. 'I'll lose my place if they know I let you go, and you'll be ruined. Go home, m'lady, I'll say anything you want.' He turned to Will. 'You know she's not for you,' he said fiercely. 'I could see how you looked at her, but you know she's Lady Havering now. You'll ruin her if you take her away.'

Will gave a snort of laughter. 'I take her!' he said. 'I don't want her. She can go home if she likes, I can no more control her than I can order the wind to blow. I've got what I came for. I want nothing more.'

I had my hand on the stable door but at that I turned and smiled at Will with all my heart in my eyes. It was the smile of a woman who knows herself to be utterly and faithfully beloved. There would never be anyone for Will but me, we both knew it. There would never be anyone but him for me.

'I want Sea,' I said. 'And Mr Tyacke wants his horse. Put a man's saddle on Sea, I'm riding astride.'

He gave an audible moan at that, but he went into the

darkness of the stable and I heard him curse Sea as he blew out as the girth was being tightened. Then he led the two horses out into the street. Their hooves clattered loudly on the cobbles and he looked around nervously.

'What am I to say?' he demanded. 'They'll ask me where Sea is. What am I to say?'

'Tell them her ladyship ordered it,' Will said curtly. 'How could you argue with her?'

'They'll ask what she was wearing! And that's Lord Perry's saddle . . .' the man said despairingly.

'Oh dammit, you come too,' I said, suddenly impatient with the nonsense. 'Take a horse and come with us. We're going down to Wideacre. There's work you can do there. We can send the horse back later, and it will be better if there's no one here to gossip.'

Will looked at me. 'We take a groom with us?' he asked incredulously.

I grinned. 'Why not?' I demanded. 'I thought it would appeal to your radical conscience. We release him from his servitude, we break his chains. We stop him bellyaching on about what they will say to him.'

Will nodded, his eyes dancing. 'Get a horse,' he said to the man. 'What's your name?'

'Gerry,' he said from inside the stables. 'Could I have one of Lord Perry's hunters?'

'For God's sake, no!' Will exclaimed. 'A working horse, what d'you think this is, a picnic?'

'Seems a waste, if we're stealing a horse, to take a cheap one,' I muttered mutinously, but at Will's sharp look I fell mum.

Gerry led a handsome black hack out of the stables and swung into the saddle. He was beaming.

'Now we'd better move fast,' Will said. 'When will they notice you gone, Sarah?'

'Not till eight,' I said. 'And no one will disturb her ladyship before ten.'

Will squinted at the sky. 'Must be six now,' he said uneasily. 'I'd give a guinea to be safe home.'

He helped me up into the saddle and swung up into his own. Sea's ears went forward and he side-stepped and danced on the spot, impatient to be off.

'Knows he's going home,' Gerry said admiringly. 'He's a fine animal, I've never seen better.'

'You lead the way,' Will said to him. 'Get us on the Portsmouth road, but use as many back streets as you can. I'd rather we weren't seen.'

Gerry nodded importantly, and led the way down the mews street. The hooves echoed loudly and someone looked out from a high window. Will glanced at me.

'Pull your hat down,' he said, then he looked a little closer. 'Are you all right?' he asked. 'You look awful pale.'

'I'm fine,' I lied promptly.

We paused at the corner of David Street and I looked down the road to where the Havering House stood on the corner. I could see smoke coming from the chimneys as Emily went around lighting fires, back to her usual back-breaking work now the dirty work of nursing me was done.

'Emily,' I said.

She had cared for me when no one else would do so. She had let me out to see Will and told no one about it. She had helped me get Perry up to bed and kept mum. And she had held me and bathed the sweat off my forehead and sat with me night after night with no thanks, and no tip, and no rest. She would go on lighting the fires and cleaning the grates and sweeping the stairs and sleeping in a cramped bare attic until she grew too old to work. Then Lady Havering would throw her out and if someone had said to her, 'But the old woman will have to end her days in the poorhouse,' her ladyship would widen her blue eyes and ask why Emily had never saved her wages since she had worked from childhood? and exclaim, 'How improvident are the poor!'

'Emily,' I said.

'What?' Will asked. They were hesitating, ready to turn down the street, waiting for me. Sea champed at his bit, reined-in too tight.

'I'm taking Emily,' I said, deciding suddenly. 'She shouldn't be left there. She shouldn't be left with Lady Havering, in that house. She should come with us to Wideacre.'

Will's face was a picture of rising rage. 'You are taking your maid?' he demanded. 'You, a jumped-up gypsy brat, need to take a maid with you?'

'No, you idiot,' I replied briskly. 'She was the only one in that whole household who ever showed me a ha'penny of love. I'm not leaving her behind. She'd be happy on Wideacre. She can ride pillion behind Gerry.'

I slid down from Sea and tossed the reins to Will. He caught them, and before he could protest I had run up the street and tapped on the big front door. I heard Emily's little feet pattering down the hall and her nervous: 'I ain't allowed to open the door . . .' tail off as she opened the door and saw first a slim young man in grey, and then my face under the grey tricorne hat.

'Sarah! I beg pardon m'm, I means your ladyship!'

'Hush,' I said peremptorily. Not all the escapes in the world could make me unstintingly pleasant. 'Don't chatter, Emily. Fetch your bonnet and all the money you have. You can come away with me if you want. I'm running away to my home in Sussex and you can come too. There's work you can do there, farm work – but fairly paid and not too hard. You might like it. D'you want to come? I'm leaving now.'

She flushed scarlet. 'I'll come,' she said defiantly. 'Dammit! I will!' and she turned on her heel and bounded up the main staircase where she was not allowed to go, and then scuttered along the passageway to the attic stairs.

I glanced back down the street. The daylight was getting brighter, the sun was up in a sky the colour of primroses, it would be a fine day. A cool clear day. A good day for travelling. Will made an impatient beckoning motion at me. I smiled and waved back.

I was not afraid of being seen, I was not afraid of being caught. Since I had lain beneath Will in the darkness of the park, I had lost every scrap of fear I had ever known. There was a warmth and a lightness about me as if I would never fail or fear anything ever again. I did not fear Lady Havering, nor poor

Perry. I knew at last who I was and where I was going. A lifetime of travelling had not taught me half so much.

There was a rush along the hall and Emily came out, wrapped in a tatty shawl and with a bonnet on her head. She carried a shawl roughly knotted in one hand, and a little withy birdcage in the other with a starling in it.

'Can I bring 'im?' she asked me anxiously. 'I've 'ad 'im for a year, and 'e sings marvellous.'

I glanced down the street to Will who was now rigid with anger. 'Of course,' I said and my voice shook with laughter. 'Why not?'

Emily pulled the door gently to close and came down the steps. We walked back towards the horses.

'Your young man,' she said with quiet satisfaction as she saw Will. She did not seem in the least surprised.

I held her bag and the cage as Gerry jumped down from his horse and lifted her up and then mounted behind her. I passed the bundle up and then the cage. The starling, annoyed by the jolting, began to sing loudly. I shot a sly look at Will.

He was not fuming at all, he was not seething with irritation. He sat on his horse as easily and as calmly as if he were taking the air on Wideacre.

'Quite ready, my darling?' he asked me, and I started to hear an endearment from him and then smiled and coloured up like a silly wench.

'Quite ready? Nothing and no one you have forgotten? No one else you would like to bring with us? No chimney sweeps, or lap-dogs, or crossing boys?'

'No,' I said. I took back my reins and swung myself up into the saddle and then burst into laughter.

'Do tell me you're glad I brought the starling,' I begged as Gerry led the way south, towards the river.

Will laughed joyously, his brown eyes filled with love. 'I am delighted,' he said.

40

Gerry led us southwards, across the Green Park and then down
the Vauxhall road, a part of the city I did not know. It was odd,
sometimes like countryside, sometimes a town. There were little
fields and byres where they kept dairy cattle, and carts with
young women riding on them came down the road towards
London and waved to us. There were a few grand houses too,
and many many tumbledown cottages with barefoot children
peeping out of unglazed windows. We crossed the river by the
Vauxhall Bridge. Sea threw his head up at the sound of his
hooves ringing hollow, and I held him still for a moment and
looked downriver.

The early morning mist was slowly lifting, the river was all
silver and pearl. There were river-trading ships with sails,
ghostly in the mist, and wherry boats and fishing smacks fading
in and out of sight as the mist curled around them. The city
eastwards gleamed like a new Jerusalem in the morning sunlight.

'It could be a wonderful place,' Will said softly beside me.
'Even now, if they used the new machines they are inventing,
and the new ideas they have, for the benefit of the poor. If they
thought of the land and how to keep it sound, if they thought of
the river and how to keep it clean. This could be the most
wonderful city in the world, and the most wonderful country.'

'People always say that,' I said. 'People always say it could
have been good. But then they say it's too late to go back.'

Will shook his head. 'If we go on as we are going, with people
thinking of nothing but making fortunes and caring nothing for
their workers and caring nothing for the land then they will
regret it,' he said certainly. 'They think they can count the cost
of living like that – a high rate of accidents perhaps, or no fish in
a river where fish once used to spawn. But the cost is even

higher. They teach themselves, and they teach their children a sort of callousness, and once people have learned that lesson it is indeed too late. There is nothing then to hold back rich people from getting richer at the expense of the poor, nothing to protect the children, to protect the land. The rich people make the laws, the rich people enforce them. Time after time we have a chance to decide what matters most – wealth, or whether people are happy. If they could only stop now, and think of the happiness for the greatest number of people.'

I smiled at him. 'They'd tell you that the way to make people happy is to make them rich,' I said.

Will shrugged and the horses moved forward. 'I don't think people can be happy unless they are well fed and well housed and have a chance at learning,' he said. 'And you'll never do that by opening the market place and saying it's all free to those with money to buy it. Some things are too important to be traded in a free market. Some things people should have as a right.'

I thought of the Havering land and the clearing of the Havering village. I thought of some of the people I had met in London who had no more skill nor wit than Da, but lived in great houses and dined off gold plate. And I thought of her, and of me, dirty-faced little children with never a farthing of a chance to get out of that miserable life and think of something other than getting and keeping money.

'I got from the bottom to the very top,' I said. I thought of Robert Gower's long struggle from the failed cartering business, to the horse-riding act, and then his own show. And I thought of what it had cost him. It had made him a man with stone where his heart should be, and it had made his son a murderer.

'It's not the rising or falling which matters,' he said. 'There shouldn't be a bottom where children are cold and hungry and beaten. Not in a rich world.'

I nodded, and we rode in silence for a little while.

'You're pale,' he said. 'Are you well?'

'I'm all right,' I said, lying again. I was deathly tired, but I wanted to ride to my home, to Wideacre. I wanted to ride without stopping until midday when we might have enough money between the four of us to buy bread and cheese and a flask of ale. 'I'm all right,' I said.

Emily looked back. 'She does look poorly,' she confirmed. She scanned my face. 'You're still too weak to be up all night, Miss Sarah,' she said. She looked at Will. 'She didn't ought to be riding,' she said.

Will glanced at me in surprise. 'Are you still weak?' he asked. 'I heard you were ill, but then I heard you were married and I thought you must have recovered.'

I gave a wry smile. 'I'm well enough,' I said.

'Don't 'e know?' demanded Emily of me. 'Don't 'e know what happened?'

'Apparently not,' Will said tightly. 'What is this?'

I looked down. Sea's neck and mane were rippling under my gaze as if we were swimming through water. The sun was growing brighter, its glare hurt my eyes and I was hot, wrapped up in my cape.

'It's nothing,' I said softly. 'I'll tell you later, Will.'

'She's awful white,' Emily said. Gerry pulled his horse up and looked anxiously back. 'She shouldn't be riding,' Emily said. 'Not after being out all night.'

'What the devil is wrong?' Will said in sudden impatience. 'Sarah! What's the matter.'

'Nothing,' I said irritably. 'I was ill for a long time, and now I am better. I get a little tired that's all.'

'Are you well enough to ride?' he asked.

My tough little Rom spirit rose up in me. 'Of course,' I said. The road was shimmery and bright, I half closed my eyes.

'Ride all the way home?' Will demanded.

'Of course,' I said again, my voice was softer, my throat seemed to be tightening like it had done when I had the fever. 'How else can we get there?'

'Are you sure?' he asked again, and now his voice was tender.

'Oh Will,' I said wearily, accepting my weariness and my weakness at last, just as I had accepted the joy in my body earlier in this long night. 'Oh Will, my love, please help me. I'm as sick as a dog,' I said.

Then I pitched forward on to Sea's neck and the darkness of the road came up to meet me.

When I came to, it was broad daylight and I was being jolted, rhythmically like a rocking cradle. I was lying on straw, wrapped warm in my heavy cloak, bedded as snug as a winter fieldmouse. I blinked up at the winter sky, bright and blue above me, and I looked to my right and there was Will Tyacke unstoppering a flask of ale and looking smug.

'Drink,' he said and held it to my lips. It slid down in a cool malty swallow.

'Whaa?' I asked.

'More,' he said firmly, and I gulped again and my parched throat was eased at once.

'Emily and Gerry are coming along behind us, leading Sea, riding the Havering horse and my bay,' Will said. 'You and I have bought a ride with this carter who is taking a load of Irish linen bales to Chichester. He will ride straight past your very doorstep, m'lady.'

'Money?' I asked succinctly.

'Gerry had a handsome sum saved against his wedding day,' Will said happily. 'I promised I would repay him when we got to Wideacre, and he split the hoard. I'm so glad you decided to rescue him from his servitude. We'd have been stuck penniless without him.'

I chuckled. 'Where are they now?' I asked.

Will nodded behind. 'Dropped back to rest the horses. The carter has an order to meet in Chichester, he'll be changing his team as we go. We'll be home by nightfall.'

I snuggled a little deeper and put my hands behind my head to gaze up at the sky.

'Then we have nothing to do . . .' I said.

'Nothing,' Will said sweetly. 'Except rest, and eat, and drink ale, and talk.'

He shifted round so his arm was behind my head and I was leaning against his shoulder, comfortable and warm. He held the flask of ale to my mouth and I took a gulp, then he stoppered it up and leaned back and sighed.

'Now,' he said invitingly. 'Tell me all about it. I want to hear everything, all the secrets, and all the things you thought about when you were alone. I want to know all about you, and it's time you told me.'

I hesitated.

'It's time I knew,' he said decisively. 'You must start from the very beginning. We've got a long ride and I'm not at all sleepy. Start from the very beginning and tell me. What's the very first thing you remember?'

I paused and let my mind seek backwards, down the years, a long way back to the dirty-faced little girl in the top bunk who never heard a kind word from anyone except her sister.

'Her name was Dandy,' I said, naming her for the first time in the long sorrowful year since her death. 'Her name was Dandy, and my name was Meridon.'

I talked as the carter drove. I broke off when we went into inns, and we climbed down from the back and bought the man an ale. He took up another passenger one time, a pretty country girl who sat in the front with him and giggled at the things he said. We sat still and quiet during that time, around noon. But we did not court as they were courting. Will did not kiss me, and I did not box his ears and blush. I rested my head on his shoulder and I felt the tears roll down my cheeks for the two little children in the dirty wagon, and even for Zima's little babby we had left behind.

When the girl had gone, climbing down at her home, a dark-shuttered cottage, leaving with a wave, Will had said softly, 'You asleep?' and I had said 'No.'

'Tell me then,' he said. 'After that first season with Gower, where he took you for winter quarters, tell me about that.'

I thought of the cottage at Warminster, of Mrs Greaves and the skirt which I stained so badly, falling from Sea, that I never had to wear it again. I told him about Dandy and her pink stomacher top and her flying cape, and of David who trained us so kindly and so well.

Then I buried my face in his jacket and told him about the

owl which flew into the ring, and about David warning us about the colour green. And how I had forgotten.

I wept then, and Will petted me as if I were a little well-loved child, and wiped my face with his own cotton handkerchief, and made me blow my nose and take a gulp of ale. He took some bread rolls and some cheese from his pocket and we ate them as the sky was growing darker again with the quick cold twilight of winter.

'And then . . .' he prompted, as I finished eating.

I sprawled back against the softness of the straw and turned my face to the sky where the pale stars were starting to show. The evening star hung like a jewel above the dark latticework of the twigs of the passing woods.

My voice was as steady as a ballad singer, but the tears seeped out from my eyelids and rolled down my cheeks in an easy unstoppable flood as if I had waited for a year to cry them away. I told him of Dandy's plan, and how she trapped Jack. How she teased him and courted him until she had him, and how she got a belly on her which she thought would bring us to a safe haven with the Gowers. That she thought Jack would cleave to her, and that Gower would be glad of a grandson to inherit the show. That she was always a vain silly wench and she never troubled herself to wonder what others might want. She was so anxious to seek and find her own pleasures, she never thought of anyone else.

I should have known.

I should have watched for her.

And I confessed to Will that I had known in some secret shadowy way, I had known all along. I had been haunted. I had seen the owl, I had seen the green ribbons in her hair. But I did not put out my hand to stop her and she went laughing past me, and Jack threw her against the flint wall, and she died.

We were quiet for a long time then. Will said nothing and I was glad of that. It was silent but for the creak, creak noise of the wheels and the steady jolting of the cart, the clip, clop, of the dray horses and the carter's tuneless whistle. A wood pigeon called for a few drowsy last notes, and then hushed.

'And then you came to Wideacre,' Will said.

I turned in his arm and smiled at him. 'And I met you,' I said.

He dipped his head down to me and kissed my red swollen eyelids, and my wet cheeks. He kissed my lips which tasted of salt from my tears. He buried his face in my neck and kissed my collar-bone. He reached into my little nest of straw and hidden by my cape his hands stroked me as gentle as a potter moulding clay, as if he were shaping my waist, my breasts, my arms, my throat, my cheekbones. Then his hands slid down over my breasts to the baggy waistband of Gerry's breeches, and his flat hand stroked down my belly to between my legs.

'Not now,' I said. My voice was very low. 'Not yet.'

He leaned back with a sigh of longing, and pulled my head on to his shoulder. 'Not long now,' he said in reply. 'You'll come to my cottage tonight.'

I hesitated. 'I can't,' I said. 'What would Becky say?'

Will looked puzzled for a moment.

'Becky,' I said. 'You told me . . . that day in the park . . . you said you were promised to wed her. You said that she loved you. I can't come to your cottage . . . I don't want to spoil things for you . . .' I tailed off. I lost my words at the thought of having to share him with another woman. 'Oh Will . . .' I said miserably.

Will Tyacke let out a great guffaw of laughter, so loud that the carter craned around one of the bales to beam at the two of us with his toothless smile.

'Oh you poor silly darling!' he exclaimed, and gathered me up into his arms and kissed me hard. 'You poor silly girl! I told you that in a rage, you simpleton! When you were so full of Lord Perry in your bedroom and his luck at cards! I was angry, I wanted to hurt you back. I've not seen hide nor hair of Becky in months! She lived with me while she was ill, and she bedded me then once or twice. Then she worked her way through half the village and when she'd taken her fill of all of us she was up and off to Brighton! We've not seen her since.'

'But her children . . .?' I exclaimed. I was stammering with anger. I had pictured her so clearly, and the little faces at the fireside, I had tortured myself to tears thinking of Will beloved in that little family. 'Will! You lied to me! I broke my heart imagining you and her children all in your cottage together. I have been dreading and dreading the moment you would tell me that you had to stay with her and the children.'

'Oh I have the children,' Will said carelessly, and at my astounded look he said: 'Well, of course I have! She was running around with every man in the village, someone had to look after them! Besides,' he said reasonably. 'I love them. When she left, they said they'd like to stay with me. They asked me if I would marry someone so that they might have a new mother.' He grinned at me sideways. 'I take it you've no objection?' he asked.

I gaped. 'Three children?' I asked.

'Aye.'

'And all very small?'

'It's easier if they're small,' he said reasonably. 'They get accustomed more quickly. It's like training puppies.'

'But I know nothing about children,' I said. 'I couldn't possibly care for them.' I thought of Zima's whimpering babby, and my own bitter-hearted indifference to it. 'I don't know how to look after children, Will. I don't know how to run a house, I don't know what to cook for them. I couldn't do it!'

He gathered me close to him again and silenced me with soft quick kisses.

'My silly love,' he said softly. 'I didn't chase around the country after you, and bring you here to apprentice you as a housekeeper. I don't want you to feed them and keep them for me. I do all that already. I want you to live with me so that I can enjoy the sight of you morning noon and night. I don't want you to skivvy for me.

'As for them – I want you to love them. Think of them as little foals and love them. I'll do all the rest.'

I would have protested, but he held me close and when I raised my face to say: 'But Will!' he kissed me with warm dry kisses so that although I knew it wouldn't do; though I knew he was wrong, and that I would not be able to love them; I gave myself up to the easy warm pleasure, and stayed silent.

He reached over me and piled some more straw over us for warmth.

'Cold night,' he said. 'Not long now.'

The carter in the front lit his pipe and the sweetmeat smell of the smoke blew back over us, I could see the embers glow in the darkness. He hitched the reins over the post and took down and lit the lantern in the front.

'Can 'ee light the one at the back?' he called to Will, and Will wriggled out of our burrow of straw and went to the back of the cart to light and hang the lantern out. Then he came back to me, treading carefully over the big bales of cloth, and banked more straw around me, and slid in beside my warmth. He put his hand behind my shoulders and drew me to him again.

'And in all that time,' he said. 'All that time of your travelling childhood and girlhood, in all those villages and towns and out-of-the-way places, I suppose there were many men, many men, who saw you and wanted you, and loved you. Maybe you had them, did you? And maybe a child you had to be rid of? Or leave?'

'No,' I said, half offended. 'No, not one. I told you Will, I was cold; cold as ice, all through. You know how I was when I came to Wideacre first. I didn't like to be touched by anyone, not even Dandy. I'd never have taken a lover.'

'What of Perry?' Will asked.

I made a face which he could barely see in the gathering darkness. 'I don't think Perry quite counts,' I said.

Will snorted with male conceit.

I thought for a moment about Lady Havering and poor Maria, and the sacred importance of a woman's chastity. I thought of the way men prize virginity in their women, as if we were brood mares who need to be kept away from bad-bred mates. And my face hardened a little in the darkness, that Will, my Will, should be a man like all the rest, and care that I had slept with no one, even though he had lain with Becky and with a score more, I daresay.

'If it matters at all, I've never properly laid with a man,' I said ungraciously. 'You can call me a virgin if it pleases you.'

He could not see my face clearly in the half-darkness, but my tone of voice should have been enough to warn him.

'A virgin!' he exclaimed in simple delight. 'A virgin? Really?' He paused.

I said nothing, I was seething in silence.

'A virgin!' Will said again. 'How extraordinary! To think you can see unicorns and everything! I've never had a virgin before. I don't think I've ever met a virgin before! I hope it won't hurt me very much!'

'Why . . .!' I had no words. I clenched a fist to punch him but he caught it by instinct, and hugged me tight. 'You silly little cow,' he said lovingly. 'As though I care whether you've had half of Salisbury or not. You're with me now, aren't you? And you love me now, don't you? I only wanted to know if you'd left your heart somewhere on the road behind you. But if there's no jealous lover battering down my door then I can sleep quiet in my bed with you.'

We did sleep quiet enough. The carter dropped us at the Acre corner and we bid him farewell and watched the tail-light of his wagon jogging away down the dark lane. The sight of the little lantern going away into the darkness reminded me of something, something sad, though I did not know why. Then I remembered the woman who had run behind a wagon calling, 'Her name is Sarah' – my mother, who had wanted to send me away from Wideacre because she could not believe that it was possible to be a landlord and not to be cruel. I put my hand out and drew Will's comforting bulk close to me. It would be different for me.

'Boots all right?' Will asked.

'Yes,' I answered. 'They're my own, my riding boots.'

'Come on then,' he said and took my hand and led me down the lane.

The woods on the left of the road were dark and secret, there were quiet rustles and far away an owl hooted. Will sniffed at the air like a hungry dog.

'Good to be home,' he said.

On our right the fields were pale under the moonlight where the winter grass was light coloured. A ploughed field, ready for wheat, breathed out a smell of dark earth, wet loam. As we walked past, very quiet on the pale-coloured road a deer raised its head and looked at us, and then melted away across the field into the trees.

I could hear a very faint whispering in my ears, like the high light singing noise which had drawn Sea and me to Wideacre all those long months ago. Then I heard the rippling of the river, as clear as a carol.

'High,' Will said. 'Stepping stones will be covered.'

We paused at the ford.

'There used to be a bridge here,' Will said. 'Years ago. It came down twice and no one troubled to rebuild it the second time. We should maybe do that.'

'Yes,' I said. In the deepest part of the river, in the middle, the reflected moon bobbed like a floating porcelain plate. The river sucked and gurgled at the bank's edge, a cool breeze blew down the valley bringing the smells of the Downs, the frozen grass and the winter thyme.

'Carry you?' Will offered. 'Carry you like a bride over the threshold?'

'Nay,' I said and smiled at him. 'We'll both paddle. You don't want to be seen carrying lads over rivers at midnight, Will, people'll begin to talk.'

He chuckled at that and took my hand and we both went cautiously into the dark current.

I gave a little gasp as it flowed over the top of my boots. It was icy and my boots were filled with water in an instant, my stockings and breeches soaked. Will held my hand steadily until we reached the cobbled bank on the far side of the ford. He looked down at my expensive leather riding boots and smiled.

'You'll be glad enough to be carried another time,' he said.

'Not I,' I said stoutly. 'You'd be better off with your Becky, if you want a woman to pet and carry, Will!'

He chuckled again and took my hand and we squelched along the road together.

The Wideacre gatehouse was a dark mound on our left, there were no lights showing, the gates stood open as always. Will nodded.

'Come up tomorrow, set the house to rights,' he said. 'Will you live here?'

I hesitated, searching his face which was shadowed in the half light of the moon.

'It's not mine,' I said. 'You won it, it belongs to you.'

'Now . . .' Will started, then he paused. 'You wanted me to win it?' he asked. 'I thought you lost it to me so that we had a better chance of getting out of that place in one piece. But did you want me to win it in truth? Win it and keep it for Acre?'

'Yes,' I said. 'I think the Laceys have had it long enough. I want the village to have it now. I lost it to you to make it safe. If I had won it, Perry or Lady Havering would have been after it, or after me, at once. As Perry's wife it would be his as soon as I claimed it. But you won it, it is yours now. I want the village to own it.'

Will nodded slowly. 'You are sure?' he asked. 'I don't want this to go sour between us in a few years' time.'

I took a deep breath. Behind me were generations of owners of land, it was a wrench to turn my back on them, on their striving and hunger and give the land away. But I was the last of the Laceys, the old gypsy woman in Salisbury had said I would be the best of them all.

'Yes,' I said. 'All I want is a little cottage in the village. I want to live here and breed and train horses.' I stole a look at his intent face. 'I want to live with you,' I said bluntly.

He put his arms around me and drew me close to him. I lifted my face to his kiss and I breathed in the warm country smell of him, and tasted the warmth of his mouth as it came down on mine.

'I love you,' I said, and it suddenly struck me that I had never said those words before, not to anyone. 'I loved you from the moment I first saw you, when you came out of the woods, out of the Wideacre woods, and found me at my home.'

Will nodded. 'I was looking for gin traps,' he said softly, remembering. 'I hate gin traps.'

I nodded. 'I know,' I said.

A cold wind blew down the lane, icy as if it had come from the very heart of the moon. I shivered.

'You'll catch your death!' he said, and caught me to his side and marched me down the road to Acre, to his cottage, to my home.

41

Will tapped on the door and called: 'It's me,' and I heard someone stir inside. 'It's Sally Miles,' he said to me. 'She watches the bairns for me when I'm away.'

The door opened and Will pushed me into the firelit room. A woman in her thirties smiled at me, and then gaped when she recognized me. 'Miss Sarah?' she exclaimed. 'I mean, Lady Havering?'

Her eyes widened even further when Will took my riding cape and she saw my jacket and breeches.

'Your ladyship?' she gasped.

Will chuckled at her face. 'Sarah's left Lord Peregrine,' he said simply. 'She's come home to us. She's come home to me. She'll live here now.'

Sally Miles blinked, then she dipped a curtsey and smiled at me.

'Well!' she said.

I put out my hand and shook with her. 'Don't curtsey to me,' I said. 'There's no need. I never was a proper lady in the manor. Now I'm where I belong, and right glad to be here. I'll need you to teach me how to go on with the children and the house.'

She nodded, still bemused. 'Aye,' she said. 'Of course.' Then she looked at Will. 'How's all this then?' she asked. 'I thought you were moving up north, just going to London to say your farewells?'

Will kneeled at my feet and pulled off my wet boots. 'It's as you see,' he said. 'I'll tell you all about it in the morning, Sally. We want to get to bed now, we've been travelling all day, and we were up all last night too.'

She nodded. 'Of course,' she said blankly. 'Well, there's porridge in the pot and ale in the jar. I could make you some tea?'

Will glanced at me and I shook my head.

'No,' he said. 'Babbies all well?'

'Yes,' she said. 'Sleeping sound.' She paused, she was longing to stay. 'I'll be off then,' she said hesitantly.

'Good-night, many thanks,' Will said briskly.

She paused in the doorway to look at me. 'I knew your ma Miss Julia,' she said softly. 'I think she'd be glad to know you've come to live among us. It's an odd thing to do, but I think she'd have done it herself if she could.'

I nodded. 'I think so,' I said.

Then she opened the door and a cold gust of air blew in and made the flames leap in the little hearth, and she was gone.

'Be all around the village by daybreak,' Will said philosophically. 'Saves telling people. Hungry, are you?'

'No,' I said.

'Bed then,' he said softly.

Now we were so close to being lovers I was suddenly cold with nerves.

'Yes,' I said uncertain.

He drew me towards him and he took me in his arms, lifted me gently, and carried me up the creaking wooden staircase to the upstairs room at the back of the cottage where the window looked out on a dark field and beyond it, the Fenny, with the stars in the night-time sky above and the black downs of Wideacre all around us. He took off my wet stockings and breeches, as gentle as a lady's maid, took off my linen shift, and laid me down on the soft hay mattress. Then he loved me until the sky paled with dawn and I heard the spring birds singing.

I woke so slowly and so silently that it seemed hours before I even knew I had woken. The first thing that caught my attention was the silence. There was no rumbling of carts, no shouting of London street-traders, it was so quiet that you could hear your own breath, and against the silence, sharpening it, was the twittering of birds.

I turned my head. The man who hated gin traps was still asleep, as warm as a fox cub in a burrow. His face tucked into my shoulder, his nose pressed against my skin. I smiled as I remembered him saying last night, 'Dear God, I love the smell of you!'

I moved away from him cautiously, so as not to wake him. The sunshine was bright on the lime-washed wall. The bedroom faced east and the shadow of the lattice window made a fretwork of patterns above the bed. I raised myself on one elbow and looked out of the window.

There had been a light frost overnight and the grass was soaked and sparkling. Each blade of grass held a drop of water which shone in the sunlight. Our window was half open and the air that breathed in was sweet and cold as spring water.

I moved to sit up and at once Will's arm came around me in a demanding, irresistible grip. He held me like a child might hold a favourite moppet – quite unconscious in sleep, quite unyielding. I waited till his grip loosened slightly then I stroked his arm and whispered: 'Let me go, Will. I'm coming back.'

He did not wake even then, but he released me and buried his face deeper into the pillow so that his face was where my head had laid. I crossed barefoot to the window and swung it wide, I was home at last.

The hills of the Downs were on my left, higher and more lovely than I had remembered. Soaring up, streaked with white, reaching to the clouds, massively solid. On the lower slope there was a scar where timber had been felled, and then further down, the plough line where the horses could not drag a plough so our fields ended on a continuous curving line which girdled the high slopes.

I could see the pale dried fields of stubble and the rich dark fields where the earth was new-turned. The fields which were resting looked green and lush. Even the hedges looked dark and fresh where they were still clinging to their leaves. They had burned the stubble in one field and there were little black tracks where the flames had been. The ash would make the land grow. The burning had come and gone, and the land would grow the better for it.

Immediately below the window was the cottage garden – a

little chequerboard of hard labour. One main path, and then a score of others like a grid so that the garden was divided into square, easily reached beds. I could see clumps of lavender, and mint, and thyme and a great pale-leaved sage bush. There was some rue and fennel and whole beds of other plants I did not know. I would have to learn them. Someone in the village would teach me. I knew I would learn the country remedies as if I had known them all my life. I was no longer little Miss Lacey who could be drugged and tricked by a London charlatan.

A wood-pigeon called softly, as sweetly as a cuckoo. Beyond the garden was a rich paddock of good grass and as I looked I saw Sea walk from one end to another, ears pricked, moving like a waterfall. They must have brought him in late last night, he had taken no hurt from the journey. I called softly to him: 'Coo-ee, Sea!' and he looked towards the window with his grey ears pricked up towards me, and then nodded his head as if in greeting before turning back to crop the grass. He looked pleased to be in the little field. He looked at home.

A floorboard behind me creaked and a broad arm came around me and the man who hated gin traps lifted my thick mop of curls and kissed the nape of my neck.

'Mmmm,' he said by way of greeting, and then his other arm came around me and I leaned back against him and closed my eyes, and let the sunlight and the cool morning, and the greenness of the fields and the warmth of his body against my cool skin wash over me in a great wave of delight.

He slid his hand down my flank and cupped one rounded buttock gently in his hand, then without hesitation his hand went between my legs from behind and his fingers, skilled and knowledgeable, parted my gentle flesh and found the core of the little maze of my body, and stroked me so that I sighed again and again until, still holding me with my back pressed against his warm chest, he entered me and I clung to the window-sill and rested my head against the cool of the window frame and thought for one moment, 'I have never never felt such delight.'

Then we tumbled down together on the hard floorboards, giving and taking pleasure, moving and seeking, demanding and contented in a great frenzy of happiness until I sighed out loud – and then there was a silence and nothing but the birdsong and the wood-pigeons calling in the silence and the sun was very warm on my shoulder and on my rapt face.

We lay very still, and then Will reached up to the bed and drew me up too. I sat naked on his bare thighs and felt the pleasure of being close and naked like innocent animals. He looked more like a fox cub than ever, his eyes brown and smiling and sleepy. He was radiant with love, I could feel the glow of it on his skin, all over.

'I hope you're not going to expect that every morning,' he said plaintively. 'I'm a working man, you know.'

I laughed delightedly. 'And I'm a working woman,' I said. 'I must go into Chichester this very day and see about leasing the Hall. It would produce a good income for the corporation, and a nice couple, a London merchant, or a retired admiral or someone like that, would be good neighbours to have.'

'It'll be odd: them coming to a cottage to pay rent,' Will offered. He stood up and stretched so that his head brushed the low ceiling. 'Odd for them to see you living here.'

'I have low tastes,' I said lightly and I kissed his warm chest and rubbed my face against the soft hairs.

I pulled on my breeches and Gerry's best shirt. 'I'll need some more clothes, too,' I said.

'I knew it,' Will said gloomily. 'Can't you make do with hand-me-downs?'

'I'll work in breeches,' I said thoughtfully. 'But I'll have one – no, two! – dresses for best!'

There was a clatter from the room next door.

'Is that the chavvies?' I asked. I was alert at once. I could not help but fear them, Becky's daughters, the children Will had chosen to raise.

Will nodded, and the next thing the door burst open and all three of them were upon him swarming all over him like puppies.

'And look who's here!' Will exclaimed as he got clear.

They all three turned to look at me, six unwinking eyes surveyed me from head to bare feet.

'Is this Miss Sarah?' the oldest one asked uncertainly, taking in my rumpled hair and my breeches.

'She was Miss Sarah,' Will said. 'But now she has come to live with us. She's finished with living in London, and with grand folks. She's my true love and she's come home to me.'

The middle one, very ready to believe in princesses coming to cottages, came forward and put her hand out to me. 'And will you be my ma and comb my hair without pulling?' she asked.

I took a deep breath. 'Yes I will,' I said bravely, and took her hand. Will beamed at me across their heads.

'Will can be your da, and I'll be your ma,' I said plunging in. 'But you'll have to help me go on, I was never anyone's ma before.'

'She's a circus girl,' Will said impressively. 'She can dance on horseback and she can swing on a trapeze. There's not many little girls who have a ma who can do that. You come on downstairs and she can tell you all about it while I make the porridge!'

They tumbled downstairs in a rush at that offer and while they spooned porridge into their mouths and Will made strong hot tea for them I told them a little about Robert and Jack and learning to ride bareback and the falls. Then I told them about winning Sea and they all rushed upstairs to pull on their woollen stockings and their clogs under their nightshirts so that they could go out at once and meet Sea.

'Will you do circus tricks for us here?' the oldest one pressed me. 'Will you teach us how to dance on horseback, and we can all be in a circus?'

Will laughed aloud at my aghast face.

'Nay,' he said. 'Her travelling days are over. She may teach you some tricks for fun, but her main work should be training horses for people to buy.'

'To dance with?' asked the littlest one, eyes and mouth round.

'No,' I said smiling. 'To ride. But I will show you how I used to dance bareback if we ever have a horse who will let me do it. Sea would not stand for it for one moment!'

Will sent them upstairs then to get dressed in earnest and

wash their faces in time for school. Then he and I walked together to take them to school and went hand in hand down the village street to bid good-day to other people of Acre and to tell them that I had come home at last.

It was a busy couple of days. There was Gerry and Emily to settle in with two familes down the village street. Emily bloomed like a rose in the countryside but Gerry was surly and cross until he went into Midhurst and got himself a job at the Spread Eagle, then he was very full of bragging to the other ostlers about London ways. He brought home a good wage, and he paid a share of it into the common fund for the corporation. He seemed settled, and Will and I repaid him our debt.

I went, as I had promised, to Chichester and the Hall was offered for rent. We would get a handsome sum for it, the agents thought. I spoke to them before I went to the dressmakers for new clothes so they had to deal with me in my breeches. It was to their credit that they never so much as glanced at me. They called me Lady Havering throughout and I did not know how to stop them. They never so much as mentioned Perry, nor the fact that the name on the deeds of the Hall was now 'The corporation of Acre, manager Will Tyacke'. But I knew that once I had set so much as a step out of the office, the tale would be all around Sussex – aye and Hampshire too, by tea-time.

I had to go and see the vicar and tell him how everything was changed, and the world upside down for him. He could not comprehend why a rich woman could choose to be poor. He could not understand why I should wish to live in a cottage and rent out the Hall. Finally I told him bluntly that though I was married to Lord Havering I would never live with him, and that Will was my lover. He had been trying to maintain a pretence that I was living in Will's cottage as a rich woman's whim. But when I said outright that Will and I loved each other, and loved the land, and would live here together for the rest of our lives, he went white with shock, and rang the bell for me to be shown the door.

'I'll never be able to go to church,' I said to Will that evening. I was sitting on the settle, skinning a rabbit with my sleeves rolled up, as he cooked the supper. 'I'm a scarlet woman. I'll never be able to take the chavvies in to say their prayers, not even sat at the back. Vicar'll look badly at you too.'

Will turned, a wooden spoon in his hand and licked it with relish before he smiled and answered me. 'Small lack,' he said. 'But he'd best remember which side his bread is buttered.'

When I looked blank he beamed at me. 'You've made the village into a squire!' he said grinning. 'We own the living. If he's impertinent I think we can refuse him his wages, certainly don't need to pay the Wideacre Hall's share of his tithe. If you don't fancy having a vicar we can leave the post empty after he is gone. You can persuade the whole village to turn pagan if you wish.'

I laughed in return. 'I had forgotten!' I said delightedly. 'But I wouldn't do it! The whole place is pagan enough already! But I had forgotten we own the living, the vicarage and all!'

'Aye,' Will said, and turned himself to the important task of game stew.

The only thing which fretted me at all in those busy spring days was the thought of Mr Fortescue. I spoke of him one morning, when the letters for the estate came in and there was no reply from him. Will took a handful of my curls and gently shook my head. 'He's a good man,' he said softly. 'He only ever wanted your happiness. He'll be shocked, but I reckon he'll take it. He was deep in the dismals when he knew you were set on marriage to Lord Peregrine. And I never heard a word from him that you'd been forced to it. It shook him to the marrow, he was too pained even for speech. He'd think that anything was better for you than that. I wager he'll be glad enough that you've run away from that Havering crowd. And we have Wideacre safe. Safe for ever, safe for the corporation. He'll be glad enough of that.'

I nodded. And Will was right. Only a couple of days later, when I was turning over the earth in the front garden with Lizzie helping and getting in the way with a spoon in her grimy hands, and mud on her face, the post-boy came down the street with a letter addressed to Lady Sarah Havering, care of Will

Tyacke, which I thought a masterly compromise between postal accuracy and scandal.

James Fortescue was brief and to the point: 'I am more happy than I can say to know that you two have found happiness together. Please do not think of the opinions of Society. You are building a new world on Wideacre, you cannot expect to be welcomed by all those who live in the old. You have my blessings on your brave attempt to break free.'

I tucked the letter into the pocket of my breeches to show Will when I met him in the fields at midday.

It was good to know that I had not disappointed James Fortescue. He was the only contact with the mother I had never known, Julia Lacey. If he could see that we were trying to build a new world, to be new people, maybe she would have understood too.

It was only Mr Fortescue who had worried me. I did not think of Perry at all. All of the Haverings, all of their bright talkative social world, had fallen away from me as if it had never been. They had gone, I could barely remember the meaningless lessons I had learned from them and the empty life I had lived with them.

Lizzie and I returned our attention to the flowerbed. Will had promised me a rose bush in the middle of the patch of earth and Lizzie and I were turning over the soil and digging in muck. My thoughts were running so much on James Fortescue and his letter, that when I heard hooves coming up the lane and the noise of carriage wheels, I straightened and scooped Lizzie up and set her on my hip to go down to the little garden gate, thinking I would see a hired post-chaise, and James smiling out of the window.

It was a bright morning and I put up my hand to shield my eyes, the other hand clasped around Lizzie's little body, her chubby arms around my neck. With a shock of sudden surprise I saw that it was not James's carriage pulling up outside my little gate. It was the Havering crest, and as the footman lowered the steps I saw it was Perry on his own.

'Sarah?' he asked in bewilderment. He came down the steps, blinking in the bright sunlight. 'Sarah?'

I saw he was so bad with drink, that he could hardly recognize me. He was shaking, and his eyes were clogged with sleep and screwed up against the light. The footman was standing like a block, eyes straight forward. A man trained so well that he could appear deaf and dumb, especially when dragged into scandal such as this. Perry put a hand out on the footman's shoulder and leaned on him like one might lean on a gate.

'Is that a baby?' he asked, bewildered.

'No I ain't!' said Lizzie, immediately argumentative.

I tightened my grip to hush her and I said, 'It's a little girl, Perry, Will Tyacke is her da. I look after her with him.'

He looked past me and Lizzie to the little cottage. There were a few late-blooming roses still in frozen buds around the front door. A bush of forsythia was yellow as brass at the garden wall.

'Charming!' he said uncertainly. Then he paused. It was as if he did not know what more to say.

'I've come to fetch you home,' he said. His mama's lesson had suddenly returned to his wandering mind. 'If you come at once there'll be no scandal and I'll say no more about it. I will forgive you,' he said pompously. 'We can live in the country all the time if you wish. I'll give up gambling, and I'll give up drinking.'

He paused for a moment and screwed up his eyes as if he were trying to recapture some thought. 'No!' he said. 'I've given up already. Shock of your leaving us like that. I've given it all up already. So you should come back.'

'Oh Perry!' I said gently. 'What is in your pocket?'

Blinking owlishly he put his hand into his right pocket and then flinched as he closed his hand on the hip flask which I knew he would have there. From his other pocket he pulled out a handful of papers. They were gambling vowels: IOUs from other gamblers. The wintry wind caught a few of them and blew them down the street. It was small loss. I guessed they were useless.

'No, Perry,' I said softly. 'I am not coming home. Tell your mama I thank her for her kindness and that I will not contest a divorce action. Tell her I have a criminal connection and she can have me put aside so that you can marry again. Tell her I am sorry, but I shall be living here on Wideacre with the man I love.'

Perry blinked again. He took out his flask and unstoppered it and took a swift swig. On the clean cold Wideacre air the smell of warm gin was sickly-sweet. He turned and stepped unsteadily back into the carriage. The footman, as impassive as a statue, folded the steps in and shut the door and swung on to the back of the carriage. His hands were blue with cold. He did not look at me.

Perry dropped the window holding the leather strap. 'I don't know *what* people will say about you,' he said with the sudden spitefulness of a thwarted child. 'They will say the most dreadful things, you know. You will never be able to go anywhere again. No one will blame me. No one will blame me at all. They will say you are at fault, and no one will call you Lady Havering ever again.'

I shifted Lizzie's warm weight and I smiled at him with compassion. I was far from his world now. I was far from the world of the landed, of the squires, of the owners. I was the last of the Laceys and I had turned my back on ownership, I was trying a new way. I wanted to build a new world.

'I don't need your name,' I said. 'I don't want your title. I am Will Tyacke's whore, that's good enough for me.'

'Sarah . . .' he said.

I stepped back a pace and the coachman flicked the horses.

'My name is not Sarah,' I said. And I smiled at him in my sudden certainty. 'My name is not Sarah. My name is Meridon. Meridon; and this is where I belong.'